BRIGHTBLADE

- UnderVerse -

2nd Edition

JEZ CAJIAO

TABLE OF CONTENTS

Thanks…and an explanation...5

Prologue 7

Chapter One 17

Dream 1 24

Chapter Two...32

Chapter Three...36

Chapter Four 40

Chapter Five...54

Dream 2 68

Chapter Six...73

Chapter Seven 89

Chapter Eight 111

Chapter Nine 124

Chapter Ten...132

Chapter Eleven 143

Chapter Twelve 152

Chapter Thirteen 158

Chapter Fourteen...169

Chapter Fifteen..179

Chapter Sixteen 188

Chapter Seventeen...196

Chapter Eighteen...205

Chapter Nineteen...215

Chapter Twenty..225

Chapter Twenty-One..233

Chapter Twenty-Two 247

Chapter Twenty-Three 255

Chapter Twenty-Four...272

Chapter Twenty-Five 283

Chapter Twenty-Six 290

Chapter Twenty-Seven...303

Chapter Twenty-Eight..312

Chapter Twenty-Nine 331

Chapter Thirty 342

Chapter Thirty-One 356

Agamemnon's Wrath... 368

Chapter Thirty-Two... 371

Chapter Thirty-Three... 378

Epilogue... 388

The End of Book One... 390

UnderVerse Omnibus Two.. 392

UnderVerse Omnibus Three... 393

UnderVerse 7.. 394

Reviews 395

Facebook and Social Media... 396

Patreon!.. 397

Recommendations 398

LITRPG!... 399

Facebook.. 400

THANKS...AND AN EXPLANATION

Hi everyone! Okay, so for those of you that actually read these bits, thank you! For those who don't...well. We can all pretend I called them names, they'll never know after all!

So, first of all, the thanks! When I first released 'Brightblade', currently just a little over two years ago, I did it with the absolute expectation it'd tank. It'd never go anywhere, and 'being an author' would join the list of jobs I'd love to have been able to do, but never managed. (Interviewing strippers was always high on that list, but that's life!)

Instead, after two years, and thanks to all of your support, I'm now a full-time author! I get to sit here, and write, all day every day. I can pay my bills, put my kids through school and have a good life with my family. THANK YOU.

I couldn't have done it without your support. *Literally*. You buy these books, you give your time up, escaping into the worlds of madness I spin out, and you spread the word about them to others. Its massively appreciated and I wanted to thank you all first of all.

Next, I need to thank my wife, Chrissy. She looks after our hellspawn—I mean *children*—I totally mean that. She picks them up, runs around after them, wipes their tears and bandages their scuffed knees. She feeds them, and keeps them more or less sane, while I sit here, wondering if that joke is a step too far, and if anyone will spot that 'Easter Egg'.

Thank you Chrissy, you make the sun shine, and the flowers bloom. I love you Glitterbum.

To Max and Xander, my little madmen, you'll probably never read this, but if you do? Know that even now, when I'm at work, I'm thinking of you both, I love you, and I'm proud of you every day.

To my family, especially my mother, who spent so much time encouraging me to read, and never giving up on me, despite my abysmal school reports and results. I love you all, and who I am today, is thanks to you all.

To my second family, those here, and those who have gone ahead across the bridge already, thank you. You always support me, and always believe I can do it, even when I'm damn well sure I can't!

I love you all.

Lastly, I need to thank my team!

Firstly, Geneva and Kristen, my assistant and her assistant, who keep me more or less rolling, pick up the discarded madness and pat me on the head, straighten the wheels and push me back on the road. Thank you ladies, you're wonderful!

To my editing team, Jenny, Jack, Evan, Michelle, and now Sean! We're getting there, and thank you all for your help!

To my Beta and ARC readers, You have the most thankless job, you read the 'finished' article, you find all the typos and ask me if I really meant 'that'. I massively appreciate you all!

Lastly, lastly; an explanation!

The omnibus editions came about because I've always felt that as my 'first' Brightblade deserved a polish, a second pass and more to 'fix' little issues, and when I'd finished the first season? Well it seemed the perfect time to do it, especially as I'm now slightly more experienced.

I didn't want to change the story, not at all, but I wanted to tighten up the prose, cut the repeated notifications and more, and basically just improve on it.

Then it occurred to me, why stop there?

So, the Omnibus edition—or 2nd Edition, if you're reading the books individually—was born. The entire first season, lightly polished, tweaked, and with new art included!

Hope you enjoy it!

-Jez

29/07/2022

PROLOGUE

"**F**ucking get ready! Incoming!" Came a frantic scream from somewhere farther into the rats' nest of corridors up ahead.

"Heads up!" Thomas bellowed to the others, all hope of stealth lost as Rin, the party's scout, appeared from around the corner. He jumped off the wall and doubled down, head low as he pumped his arms, racing as fast as he could.

Before the echo of his scream had finished dying away, a new sound rose. The experienced adventurers shifted, getting room to work as they listened to the low susurration.

It was almost gentle at first, building from the distance. But as the seconds passed, the sound of hundreds of claws, teeth, and masses of flesh rubbing and bouncing off each other grew stronger and louder.

Overlaying that and building quickly was a garbled repeat of Rin's cry, rising from a thousand throats in awful mimicry, even as one of the party behind Thomas identified the sound. "Oh shit, Feenals…that's all we need!"

Thomas grimaced and fell in with Dirik, the party's tank, and prepared to receive the charge while agreeing wholeheartedly with the muttered sentiment. He quickly cast Identify, the details popping up in his augmented vision.

> **Feenals:**
>
> Feenals are a hivemind-controlled ambush predator. They have six limbs consisting of four legs and two forward-facing flexible tentacles ending in barbed spines. The danger comes not from the individual, as they are usually easily dispatched, but from the sure knowledge that a nest can number from dozens up to tens of thousands, if enough food is available.
>
> Feenals can mimic the cries of other creatures, often attracting the unwary to their doom. Feenal bites frequently bring additional infection, due to their propensity to feed on carrion, and they generally attack in swarms.
>
> **Best defense**: Feenals are afraid of fire, and their bodies are naturally flammable.
> **Resistances to**: Earth, Water, and Air magics.

"Well, that's just fucking peachy!" Thomas swore, checking through his available spells, trying to guess at the number of incoming vermin, and the best strategy. "Fireball, maybe?" he muttered, chewing on his lip as he adjusted his shield. Ratcheting the strap tight, he stepped forwards to stand side-by-side with Dirik.

He'd worked hard on Fireball, deepening his understanding of the School of Fire as both a magical element and the science behind it, as much as he could. The combination meant that, after leveling the spell a handful of times, it was now pretty devastating...but also seriously expensive.

Like, 'three, maybe four spells were all he'd get off before he was completely dry' expensive.

"Yulin!" Get ready to slow them down!" he called to the party's mage. "Helios, Hinko! Pick off any you can. Dirik, get ready to pass Rin through to the rear. Wena! Save the damn heals until we need them, 'cause we're *really* gonna need them this time!" With the party orders given, Thomas readied his shield and shortsword and waited.

Rin covered the last dozen feet to the group almost at the same time as the Feenals finally appeared. The revolting creatures rounded the corner in a collapsing wave of bodies, rolling over one another and bouncing off the walls. Thomas and Dirik closed ranks and set their shields as the oncoming swarm surged forward.

It was deceptively slow appearing, but all too soon they'd be knee deep in them. Feenals didn't give up; once they'd sighted prey, they'd keep going until they killed it.

If they had to literally run their target until it collapsed into unconsciousness from exhaustion, that was fine with them. The little creatures that made up the swarm died easily and fell for practically every trick in the book, but their strength lay in dogged persistence. Thomas *hated* the damn things, just like every other sentient creature he'd encountered in the UnderVerse.

"Yulin!" he bellowed, breath coming faster as adrenaline flooded his body. "Now!"

The mage had been listening, thankfully, and let loose with something that seemed to shred the very air as it screeched overhead. Thomas blinked at a small, black blur flashing into the middle of the oncoming mass instead of the expected 'Slow' or 'Tarpit' spell. The spell increased drastically in size just before it impacted the leading edge of the Feenal horde.

"You crazy bastard!" he screamed in horror, recognizing the spell from conversations he'd had with the mage.

He desperately hunched down behind his shield further and shouted a warning to the rest of the group. "He's used 'Althair's Breach'!"

Yulin had been one of the only mages available when he'd gone recruiting for this party; most wouldn't work with him, due to his history, so he'd been forced to take what he could get. In Yulin's case, that meant a dangerously powerful yet unstable mage who also held a fascination for other realms.

'Althair's Breach,' Yulin had explained on one of the rare occasions he'd talked about himself instead of pressing for information on the others' abilities, was an extra-dimensional rift, one that was self-sustaining and perpetuating, once the initial spell cost was paid.

It was also one of only a very few banned spells, on the grounds that, when you opened a rift in space and time, shit tended to go real bad, real fast.

Yulin had explained that he was working on an addition to the spell, one that let him close it again when the mana ran out, rather than needing a full circle of twelve. Thomas had exchanged one look with Dirik, and the pair of them had banned Yulin from ever, *ever* using that fucking spell around them.

The spellform had grown from a marble to a basketball in size in a split second, then it hit the first flying, desperately howling Feenal and converted its mass into mana, powering itself farther and faster. It changed from a tiny gravitational anomaly into a breach between the realms of existence in the blink of an eye. Air was sucked into the rapidly growing hole in reality as it formed in the corridor. By the time it approached its full size, even light began to bend into the vortex, and this was only the beginning.

Dozens, then hundreds were absorbed into the spell as it tore through the rolling mass, bodies leaping madly back and forth, biting and savaging each other in their manic bloodlust.

The Feenals flooded forwards, but in the next moment, they were suddenly vanishing, sucked from the hallway and gobbled up by the miniature black hole that flew onwards. As more and more vermin were absorbed into it, it hurtled down the hallway to impact the far wall, eating into the stone and ignoring the bend that led away.

For three seconds, the spell raged, Thomas and his group starting to feel the gravitational pull of the spell—a spell that was never designed for use in a confined area. Gravity shifted, slowly at first, flowing through ninety degrees and before anyone could do more than stare in horror and scream Yulin's name in disbelieving fury. They were falling, dragged through the air as *forwards* became *down.*

Then, fortunately, Yulin's mana ran out—over a thousand mana in three seconds—and the additional aspects to the spell went active, forcing the rift shut with a snap as wild energies flared and tore at the stonework around the edges of the hole.

Thomas and the rest of the party crashed to the floor, rolling and bouncing through the remaining Feenals that had escaped the spell.

For a second, all was confusion as everyone tried to make sense of what had happened. Then the sound of maniacal laughter filled the hallway, echoing off the walls. Thomas blinked the world back into focus. He was lying atop a Feenal that began to struggle as the hivemind overcame its shock. Thomas lashed out, crushing its head into the ground with the pommel of his sword before shoving himself to his knees and striking it with the blade, slicing it from end to end.

As the creature died, the growling from his left resolved into words...

"I'll kill him! You hear me, Yulin...you're a dead man! I'm gonna kill these things, then I'm gonna fucking murder you!" Dirik roared in rage as he laid about himself with his six-bladed mace, crushing disoriented creatures as they tried to regain their feet.

The entire party shifted from a position of partial control over the battle into being surrounded by their enemies, even if there were only a few dozen left alive rather than hundreds.

"Heheheheh! It worked! It actually...worked! And you're all still alive as well!" Yulin giggled, hugging himself and making no effort to help. The insane mage instead began staring down the corridor at the destruction he'd unleashed.

Thomas growled as he lashed out again, shield bashing one creature as it leaped off the wall toward him while stabbing his blade into a second creature's back. He'd seen Rin at the back of the group, face dark with anger as he drew a bead on Yulin's back with his hunting bow.

"Rin! I need support here; we'll deal with that later!" Thomas bellowed, unable to take the time to check whether Rin had heard him. When an arrow flashed past to embed itself in a crouching Feenal, he breathed a quick sigh of relief. His scout hadn't taken down his mage…yet. Now, just to hold the rest of the team together until he could gut Yulin personally.

The battle rolled around the party, dissolving into a frantic blur of gnashing teeth, scrabbling claws, and jabbing tentacles being met with flashing metal.

Screams filled the air behind Thomas as one of his team went down, but he had no time to react before Helios's health bar went black on his HUD. The entire team's health was dropping, several showing the mottled green and brown of poisoned status. Finally, Thomas stamped down on an arrow-pierced creature that writhed and coughed blood. Silence fell, broken only by gasps for air, groans of pain, and the occasional titter from Yulin.

Thomas stood there; his HUD flooded with notifications as the fight ended and he turned. Frantically trying to catch his breath, he checked on his team, heart hammering wildly. Notifications surged up, and he swiped them away with a thought. He straightened up and winced at an unexpected twinge of pain in his left leg.

Blinking, he looked down at the Feenal head still attached to his thigh. Its teeth were sunk deep into the muscle, though a line of bloody flesh dangled from the head towards a headless corpse on the ground nearby. He had no clue when that had happened. He shook his head as he pried the dead jaws apart and tossed it, then he spotted the body of Helios.

"Shit, Helios…sorry, mate," he muttered, shaking his head sadly. His throat had been torn out, and he lay slumped against the wall, pooling blood surrounding him. With a sigh, Thomas checked whether the rest of the group needed healing and began triage. He had enough for six healing spells, but one badly injured member could take all of that and more.

Some in the team were already reluctantly using expensive antidote and healing potions.

Others who couldn't afford those or weren't as badly injured, used cheap cloth bandages and washed the wounds down with their canteens, even as they glowered at Yulin.

The mage picked his way gingerly through the mess of bodies, lifting his robes in both hands to keep them from dragging through the already-cooling puddle of Helios's blood. He ignored everything in sight as he swished his way to the end of the corridor, reaching out with one manicured hand to feel the edges of the stonework cut by his spell.

"Fascinating! It's cut through cleanly; it's so smooth…" he muttered. The rest of the group silently watched him. Thomas exchanged a look with Dirik, then both looked back to find that Rin and Hinko, and even Wena, kind-hearted and slightly soft in the head, were all staring daggers at Yulin.

Rin stepped forward into the middle of the group and raised his bow again. This time, Thomas made no move to stop him. Helios's death could have been avoided; the mad mage's actions had killed him as surely as if he'd fired the spell directly at him, and the rest of the team had nearly followed him into the darkness.

Rin muttered a quick cantrip, activating the enchanted arrowhead as he drew a bead on the giggling mage. He half-released his breath as the arrowhead flared to life, red and black markings suddenly visible, and he fired, sending the mage-killer arrow at its target.

The arrow flashed down the corridor faster than Thomas could follow it, the zipping noise as it pierced the air clearly audible.

BOOM!

The air shook a second time as one of Yulin's amulets exploded. The shield spell it had contained was barely enough to slow the arrow, let alone stop it.

Yulin screamed, twisting in shock as he was alerted to the attack. The arrow should have killed him outright, but instead was deflected to pierce his chest on the right side and erupt from the front in a spray of blood.

The severely injured mage spun around fully, lifting his right hand in reflex to touch the glowing point of the arrow, even as his left grabbed at a second amulet and broke it in half.

A new shield spell flared to life, reinforcing itself over and over. Yulin snapped the end off the arrow and forced the shaft back out with a disgusting *shlurp*, followed by the wheeze of his lung sucking in air.

He scowled at the group, pulling a healing potion from his belt, followed by a mana potion. He quickly downed them both, ignoring Rin's normal arrows as one after another was fired, and watched each projectile bounce off and fall to the floor.

"Hinko…help Rin," Thomas ordered, knowing he had no choice now. He exchanged a look with Dirik, and they both turned and raised their shields, even as Wena flooded them both with healing magic. Yulin's shield spell darkened in color as the scout and ranger fired arrow after arrow, each strike draining the shield of more mana.

"It's like that, is it…fine! I'd hoped to get more loot in the pot first, but still, you'll all make useful test subjects either way!" Yulin broke off with a cough, then spat congealed blood onto the floor. Sorting through the mass of charms and more on his necklace, he found the one he wanted and grinned as he snapped it, shivering as the changes immediately took hold.

The man shifted, his red robes darkening to black even as his skin lost the healthy pink glow he had possessed before. As his cheeks grew sallow and his skin turned grey, his face lengthened and a small beard appeared. His ears grew pointed, each pierced with three golden rings.

"Drow!" Dirik growled, receiving an evil smile in response from the tall, stick-thin dark elf that had replaced the irritating human they had put up with for weeks of travel.

"Yes, that's right, Dirik! You have had the honor of escorting one of the chosen for these long weeks. Unfortunately, you'll never be able to brag about it…because my servants have no need of their tongues!" Yulin called back, both hands weaving another spell as his shield began to fail.

Seeing that Yulin was unconcerned by the group's reaction, Thomas went cold.

"Rin, stealth the fucker! Hinko, use your special arrows. Wena, keep us alive! Dirik, let's go fuck up his day!" Even as he shouted orders and set off running forward into battle, he knew it wasn't going to end well. Yulin had been with them for weeks. The questions he'd asked around the fire each night, the "friendly" competitions over ale to see who had spells and who didn't...their sneaky tricks, all of it had been to prepare for something like this.

"Ah, ah!" caroled Yulin, gesturing with both hands and slamming his palms down toward the ground. The rocks above Dirik and Thomas shifted ominously before dozens fell, smashing into both men. They raised their shields hastily, bracing themselves as the ceiling collapsed.

Thomas blacked out for several seconds before blinking and finding himself on the floor. Something heavy lay on his back, and screams sounded out nearby. He coughed, feeling a tearing pain in his chest. Blood spattered from his mouth into the dust before him as his vision swam. Cursing, he levered himself upright, forcing the stone chunk from his back with an almighty crash.

Glancing around the corridor, Thomas blinked again to clear his vision. Dirik was only a few feet ahead of him, but he was in bad shape. Dirik's once-gleaming plate mail was heavily dented and covered in blood. His shield lay on the floor to one side, his limply hanging forearm testament to why he no longer wielded it.

Dirik laid about with his mace, beating back blurred shadows that dodged and lashed out with claws, then another of the images in Thomas's HUD went black. Wena.

Thomas staggered, the world floating in and out of clarity as his concussion flared and pulsed, warring with a migraine and the steadily seeping blood that was trying to seal his right eye. The collective confusion was enough that, when he slipped and fell on a blood covered, cloth-wrapped bundle on the floor, he almost missed recognising it.

He hit the floor, forcing himself to finish casting the healing spell he'd begun instinctively, lips fumbling over the words he'd sub-vocalized a thousand times over the last few years. Finally, the world came into focus suddenly, sharply.

He'd tripped on Wena's body. The slight elven girl had been savaged by something with tremendous strength, her corpse practically shredded, but her face had been left intact. The horror in her eyes sent him stumbling to his feet, only for something to smash into his side, hurling him into the wall. Thomas brought up his sword instinctively, blocking a second strike as the creature lunged forward again, uncaring of the injury.

The black skin and deep red eyes of a Greater Imp made him flinch back again, slashing at it with his sword, even though the blade barely scratched its thick hide. The Greater Imp grabbed the blade directly, yanking it out of his hands and throwing it aside. It grabbed him by the throat and lifted him, slamming him against the wall. It licked the blood from his cheek with its long, prehensile tongue, then bared its teeth and was about to bite when a voice called out from further down the corridor.

"No! Bad kitty! That's mine!" Thomas was twisted to one side, then lowered and dragged along the floor through the blood of his friends until he looked up into the crazed eyes of Yulin.

KillThemAllTheyAreComingKillItKillThemAllKillIt...

Thomas suppressed the maddening voice at the back of his head, gritting his teeth and stamping it down firmly into a corner of his brain and glaring up at Yulin. Dirik's symbol suddenly turned black. Hinko's health bar was bleeding out steadily, the yellow color an indication that he was unconscious.

"Now, how about you tell me all about your world, hmmmm? You never wanted to talk about it before, but maybe if you do, I'll let you live, yes?" Yulin purred, stroking the side of Thomas's face, his fingers coming away bloody. He raised them to his mouth, his tongue flicking out to taste Thomas's blood. A sadistic smile tilted the corners of his mouth before a new sound became audible.

It was a sound Thomas had only heard recently; a scrabbling, babbling sound made of hundreds of tiny bodies with tiny mouths repeating the last sound they had heard…

"Yulllliiiiin…yuuuulin…yuliiin…yuuulliiinn…"

Thomas was unceremoniously dropped to the ground, discarded as unimportant, as the Greater Imp bounded forward to put itself between its master and the oncoming tide.

First a handful, then dozens, then hundreds of Feenals appeared around the bend, claws rasping on stone and carving furrows in each other in their desperate attempt to reach flesh.

A second, third, and fourth Greater Imp joined the first one that Thomas had fought. All four took up positions in the corridor, conjuring small Firebolts and hurling them into the oncoming mass.

They barely had any effect on the majority. A few caught fire, setting light to others nearby, but this horde numbered in the hundreds, not dozens. The Greater Imps were absorbed into a rolling tide of death and hunger mere seconds after they began their defense. A few short screams marked their deaths, followed by the inevitable explosions as their corpses went critical.

The corridor almost collapsed, momentarily holding back the cascade of death. The pressure wave from the quadruple explosions buffeted Thomas into the corpses of his friends. He gazed around the devastation, shell-shocked, the work of the healing magic he'd used so recently all undone.

Yulin stepped back into view, standing between him and the onrushing wave. The dusky mage began gulping down mana potions like they were going out of fashion and casting shields, flamewalls, and a series of spells Thomas didn't recognize in his stunned state.

The shields began to darken, faltering at the edges as first one, then a handful, then finally all the Feenals began to power forward again. Yulin began breaking charms and spell scrolls frantically to hold the vermin back.

He ripped chunks out of the Feenals. Waves of darkness cut them to shreds. Rents in space opened, claw-tipped hands reaching through to tear into anything within reach. Still, he was slowly forced backwards.

Thomas closed his eyes as the tide grew nearer and played dead. Surprisingly, the creatures piled over him, ignoring him and everything else in their mad rush to come to grips with Yulin.

Screams sounded from somewhere in the distance, and then more explosions. A scuttling multitude of chitinous legs carrying something heavy approached, then ran over him, one stabbing through his exposed hand before carrying on.

His mouth filled with blood from biting down on his cheek so hard. He dared to crack open an eyelid. The back of something being carried on the carapaces of dozens of small scarab beetles disappeared around the corner. Its grey-green hide, riddled with faintly luminescent veins, pulsed. The sight made him sick as he tried not to imagine what the rest of the damn thing looked like.

The explosions went on and on, as did the screams, until the corridor Thomas was in fell far enough behind the frantic battle to grow quiet. As the sounds faded, Thomas furtively slid a cautious hand down to his belt, feeling for the potion pouch there…and cursed inwardly as his fingers encountered sodden leather and tinkling broken glass vials.

He opened his eyes a crack, glancing around the room as he slowly began to sit up. A movement to one side caused him to flinch violently and reach for his spare dagger. One more thing that wasn't as he expected it. This time, he did curse aloud, his fingers scrabbling frantically in the bloody funk of battle that surrounded him. It seemed like forever before he finally found the pommel of the blade, and at the same time, a nearby voice whispered to him.

"It's okay, boss…it's me," said Rin, slowly moving into clear view from where he'd been crouching by Wena's corpse.

"I'm…I'm sorry, Thomas. I saw what he was, how easily he outclassed us all, and I stealthed. Then, when you all began to fall, I tried to get behind him, but his barrier already surrounded him. I barely managed to get past him without being noticed, so I did the only thing I could think of…I found the hive and shot the center with a flame arrow."

"You made them crazy," Thomas whispered, slumping backwards in pain. "You made them crazy and gave them a target…Yulin."

"Yeah, boss. I cast a rough illusion of him and sent it winging its way down the hall, while I stayed hidden. Let them come for him. I figured either they'd kill him or at least distract him long enough for me to stick a knife in his back." Rin shifted uncomfortably and sighed, looking around at the bodies surrounding them.

"Bastards nearly killed me, too, but I played dead." Thomas winced as he unwrapped his potion pouch and looked inside. It was full of broken glass and a slurry of liquid that was slowly seeping out of the bottom.

"Here…", Rin said, passing him a full health potion with a grimace. "It was Dirik's; don't think he needs it now."

Thomas caught it and winced again, both at the pain the motion caused and the implied reason behind their friend's condition.

"Ah, crap. I'm sorry, Rin. I…I hired Yulin. He was all I could find…all that'd work with me, anyway. I should have disbanded the party, released you all from the oath, and gone on alone. You'd have found another team easily, and they'd all still be alive. This is all my fault!" Thomas blinked away hot tears of shame.

He bit into the cork on the healing potion, pulling it out and spitting it aside before chugging its contents in one go.

Pain spread through his body in a rush as wounds flash-healed, his fingers popping back into place from where they'd been twisted by the Imp. As the high-grade potion spread through the rest of his body, he was left panting and weak. He felt like he'd just ran a marathon, but at least he was alive.

Unlike the rest of their team, anyway…Thomas forced that thought aside. Taking a deep breath, looked over at Rin to find him shaking a tear-streaked face.

"No, boss…I was…sloppy, prideful. I thought I could kill one of the Feenals and bring it back as a trophy. I wanted to show you all that's how good I was, even able to steal a part of the hive away, and nobody would know. Well, they knew…they fucking knew straight away! I caused this. I awoke the hive and dragged it down on us, giving that dick the chance to slaughter our friends." He knelt back down next to Wena, stroking her hair back from her face and gently closing her eyes. "I'm so…so sorry, Wena!" Great tearing sobs of grief shook him as he whispered to her, the words too low for Thomas to make out.

Thomas got to his feet and shuffled over to Rin, drawing him up to his feet with a hand on the rogue's shoulder. Half-supporting the man, he drew him into a bear hug and held him tight. At first, Rin stiffened, weakly trying to push free. Then, all of a sudden, something broke in him. He grabbed onto Thomas desperately, weeping his heart out on his friend's armored shoulder. Thomas couldn't help but be grateful Rin couldn't see the tears tracking down his own cheeks.

Again, he'd led another team to their deaths, *again!* Perhaps he really was cursed, like the witch had said.

They stood like that for several minutes until a loud explosion in the distance reminded them both of where they were.

They broke apart awkwardly, both men used to bottling up their emotions tightly around others, and grabbed their weapons.

"Right, how about we go cut Yulin a new arsehole, then loot the shit out of this place?" Thomas suggested, his voice rough as he swiped at the tears. He hefted his sword in his right hand and Dirik's mace in his left.

"Yeah…let's remind him why we've got such a bad reputation," Rin muttered, drawing a dagger and flipping it end over end before catching it and brandishing it.

"Too fucking right, mate!" Thomas grinned at him, all discomfort gone as they focused on the task at hand. If the Feenals hadn't killed Yulin, he'd wish they had.

SPOREMOTHER

CHAPTER ONE

"**J**ack!"

"..."

"Oi, Jack!" The shout came again.

I swore, dragging my head out of the fridge I was restocking and sat back on my heels, glaring over the counter at Jordan.

"Aye? Whadda ya want, ya bandit? I'm busy!" I called back, grinning despite the aching back and general exhaustion. It'd been a damn long shift tonight; Saturdays always were.

"Your turn to kick out, mate! Tenner says you get into a fight!" Jordan grinned back at me, lifting the note in one hand and waving it, even as he gestured over his shoulder to the now well-lit nightclub behind him.

I straightened, twisting and grunting as a pop and a crack sounded from my lower back, making me groan, then grin at him. Glancing around the club, I sent a long look at the drunken idiots that had been exposed in the corners when the lights had come on, then back at the stacked bottles wrapped in packaging plastic.

"Bottling up," as it was called, was one of my least favorite jobs. I hated being down on my knees and moving from fridge to fridge. Kicking people out? Yeah, that was more my style, though I couldn't get a door license with my record.

"Hey, I'm a good boy these days, ya know?" I blatantly lied, getting a low round of chuckles from the others as I pulled out a ten and stuck it onto the back counter. Grinning at the comments the others were making, I returned the slightly confused but suggestive smile I was getting from Grace, the new girl.

The other employees working the bar, cleaning down, or going over the tills and card machines laughed and started their own bets, mostly to trade away the shit detail jobs. By the time I'd cleared the bar and started to walk towards my first target, I'd been offered everything from cleaning the lines to a blow job, if I was good or bad, depending on the person.

I liked these assholes, I decided. I'd been working in the club for about six months now, starting as a barman, before gradually filling in the gaps to do all the jobs—a bit of sound work here, restocking there, cleaning when it needed to be done, and just occasionally, kicking out—I didn't mind it, really. I might be a Jack of all trades, as they called me, and I might never be great at any of them, but I always had work. Plus, working here is how I'd met Lou, and that was worth it in itself.

"Here, mate. Come on, wakey, wakey!" I tapped a drunk on the shoulder, then gave him a rougher shake as he mumbled something at me. "You don't have to go home, but you can't stay here!"

He pushed himself up from the table he'd been slouched against and nodded at me blearily before yawning and hauling himself to his feet.

"Wha'…what time ish it?" he slurred at me, weaving a little unsteadily as he tried to focus.

"It's after three, mate, leaving time," I said, shaking my head in amusement as he blinked, looking around in confusion.

"Ma…my mates…they…" he stammered, pointing off deeper into the club. I took his arm firmly, turning him towards the door.

"If they're here, they'll be kicked out now as well. If not, they're probably waiting for you outside. Go on, up the stairs there, good lad," I finished, giving him a gentle push towards the stairs to get him started. He stumbled a little, but started moving under his own steam, so I went to the next one, moving from small groups to singletons to passed-out drunks. A few words here and there, and people were moving along.

I finally reached the back of the club, a section we called Shagger's Alley. Sure enough, a couple occupied the narrow space between a pillar and the wall at the very back. I set off towards them, making a little extra noise and giving them plenty of time to hear me and stop.

Absolutely nothing changed. *The lights are all on full, for fuck's sake!* I thought as I called out again.

"Come on, guys, closing time!" The guy finally seemed to notice that the music had stopped, the lights were on, and there was nobody else around, then he turned around to look at me and sneered. Typical rich kid: nice shirt, expensive jeans and shoes, and one who obviously spent a lot of time at the gym, judging from his muscles. I groaned mentally. It was always the last ones I came across, the troublemakers I'd learned to spot a mile away.

"Fuck off!" he slurred, turning back to the girl he had pressed up against the back wall. She was short, dark-haired, and pretty, judging from the few seconds' glimpse I got, but her choices left a lot to be desired. Especially considering the dickhead trying to make a finger puppet out of her in the back of a nightclub.

"Come on, mate, no need to be a dick; it's just chucking out time," I said firmly, coming to a halt a few feet from him. "You need to leave…now."

What the hell the guy was thinking was beyond me. There was always one, and they even did this with Barry, the massive doorman. The fucker was as wide as the door itself, yet people thought they could tell you to get fucked and there'd be no consequences…madness.

"I said…fuck *off*!" He turned around fully, taking his hand out of the girl's jeans and held up his middle finger. "Go on! Get lost!"

I took a deep breath and tried to control my irritation.

There's always one. Why couldn't tonight be the night I get propositioned by a drunken group of girls? I don't mind when I get those nights, but noooo, I have to put up with this…Right. Just behave and get him out, easy money. I took a calming breath before starting again.

"Look, pal, the bar's closed, so grab your gear and fuck off." *Yeah, Jack, really subtle. Well done on the "well-behaved"…*

He stared at me as though he just didn't get it. He was maybe six-three, six-four, and about the same across the shoulders. A fair bit bigger than me, to be honest, but they never did understand. Gym-bought muscles weren't worth shit in the real world. He ran the conversation through his head again, clearly having an issue with the fact I'd not run away, and came to the obvious conclusion.

"You want a fight? Is that it? I'll kick your fucking..."

"Jesus, man, no...just get your coat and go home. Take her home, if she wants to go, just get out of here. We're closed!" I said, exasperated, and gestured to the door. He followed my hand, then looked back at me, then the girl. She had tried to make herself decent again and was pushing past him to stagger towards the door, looking mortified. Judging from her bright red cheeks, this was the first time she'd been caught like this...in fact...

"Excuse me, darlin'," I said, holding my hand up as she tried to walk around me. "Can I see some ID?"

She grinned weakly and clutched her handbag closer before shaking her head.

"I...don't...have...me..." she mumbled, and I frowned. I could already see the rich meathead behind her getting worked up again, but something was very wrong. She looked far too young to be in a club, couldn't string two words together, and could barely walk, not to mention the glazed eyes...that wasn't just a drink.

"Stop for a minute, please. I do need to see some ID." I wasn't sure if I had the right to ask for that, considering she wasn't trying to buy alcohol, but...

Meathead shoved me from the side as I turned to keep facing her, making me stagger and fall over, my foot shooting out from under me as I slipped on a discarded beer bottle.

"Fuck off, you prick!" he snarled before grabbing her roughly by the elbow and half-dragging her towards the door.

I landed hard, banging the back of my head off the floor and seeing stars for a second before blinking them away. I gave a growl of disgust as I braced my hands on the floor and shoved hard, coming to my feet faster than the guy had obviously expected. His eyes widened as he turned, and he shoved his partner towards the door with one hand, swinging a punch at me with the other.

The staff on the back bar, who could see everything, called out to the others; the thud of running feet grew as I stepped into the punch.

I swept my right hand across to divert his punch in a variant of a Tan Sau Kung Fu block, redirecting the blow to my right and sending him off balance, before twisting his wrist and locking his elbow at full extension.

Once he was immobilized, I dealt rapid-fire jabs with my left fist—one to the kidney, one to the ribs, one to the side of his head—before yanking his right arm up and shoving him backwards.

"Last chance, asshole!" I growled, my blood thundering in my ears and my instincts roaring to life at the threat. He staggered back, shaking his head and trying to figure out what had happened. Growling in anger, he rushed toward me and cocked his fist back for another strike.

I caught his arm when he swung, twisting it away as I punched out with my right fist.

19

His head rocked back, and I grabbed the collar of his expensive shirt and dragged him towards me even as I lunged in with a headbutt. He crashed to the floor, blood spurting from his broken nose.

Before he could get to his feet, I stepped in close, catching his flailing right arm and twisting it cruelly to immobilize him while setting my foot against his throat and taking a deep breath. He'd never back down, after all. Guys like him needed to be taught a lesson; they *deserved* to be taught respect…

"Jack! Fuck, man, let him go!" Jordan shouted.

I blinked, coming back to myself in time to see everyone come running. Most of them hadn't seen anything, so the first they saw was me basically kicking the shit out of someone. *Fuck…not again.*

I let the guy go, stepping back as he began screaming. I felt a momentary stab of amusement that his voice was higher-pitched than the young girl he had brought with him, who had started to scream as well.

In a flash, I was hurried back from the fight, Jordan pushing me with one hand as he gestured to the girl and the meathead on the floor, speaking quickly to the others. He quickly instructed the assistant bar manager, the boss's idiot son, to get a first aider and call both the police and an ambulance.

I took it and let him push me along, feeling sick as I realized what I'd been about to do…*I'd planned to crush his windpipe, to kill him, not stop him…oh, god…the dreams…*

"You fucking sit there, and get your story straight before the police arrive, all right? Seriously, man, this'll be all over social media tomorrow! The boss is gonna lose his fucking mind!"

"Shit…sorry, man," I muttered, realizing how much I'd let the fight get out of hand. They'd all been expecting me to get into trouble, maybe throw a punch or two, but probably just a bit of shoving before the bouncers would be called down to take them outside and "explain" things to them. Not this.

I walked over to a booth off to one side and sat down, watching the drama unfold. It wasn't long before the police were there, the paramedics and police checking the meathead over, while the girl made excuses and tried to leave.

One officer approached me and snorted in disgust before taking a seat opposite me and getting out his notebook.

"You're a fucking idiot, you know that, lad?" he said. I looked at him for the first time, tearing my eyes away from the guy I'd attacked.

"Jonno…" I faltered, seeing his face, rather than just the outfit. "I didn't mean…he swung for me, and I just—"

"Stop, lad," he said, holding up one hand. "I'm going to find a pen…then I'll take a statement. Maybe you should think hard about what happened…hmmm?" He waved his pen in his hand, and I took the hint. I drew in a deep breath, closing my eyes and thinking before I spoke.

"Okay…*Officer*…thank you. I asked him to leave, and he became aggressive. Then, when the young lady started to leave, I asked to see her ID. She seemed far too young to be in here, and he attacked me. I reacted in self-defense, then somehow tripped him when I slipped on the mess on the floor and nearly fell on him."

"At that point, the other staff arrived, having heard me shout for help, and I was told to back away, leaving them to give first aid."

It was a slightly bullshit answer, and judging from Jonno's look, he knew it. But I also knew where the cameras were here and what they were likely to show. I could get away with that, especially as an "innocent staff member" who'd been attacked.

He asked me a handful of questions and made sure they had my correct address. The ambulance staff took Meathead away before we both turned to look at the young girl. We sat watching her for a long minute; she was doing her best to be left alone in the corner, other than asking people if she could go home yet.

"What made you ask about her?" Jonno finally asked me quietly.

"I don't know, man, she just seemed…wrong. *Way* too young, but more than that, as well…I don't know. Her eyes looked wrong, stoned to fuck maybe. But her age, the look, and the way he was so aggressive, it just all screamed 'wrong,' you know?" I said, sitting back and huffing out a breath. "Honestly, man, it's been a long time since I saw you last, but I've been good, ya know? Since Tommy disappeared, I've been behaving myself, but seeing her…something just seemed off."

"I know, lad. I've not seen you in, what? Three, four years? You must have been behaving, or gotten a lot better at hiding the shit you've been up to…"

"Hah! Yeah, like this proves it!" I said bitterly.

"Bah. I know you, Jack. I saw what happened to the dealers down at Jesmond Dene. You've a dark gift. You don't like it, you try and keep it under control, and that's why I give you the benefit of the doubt." He shifted in his seat and got up, nodding to me before he set off to talk to the girl. "I'll look into her and see what I can find out. Go on, you get yourself home, and hopefully, we won't see each other again for a while."

"Thanks, man," I said, pulling myself out of the booth and walking in the opposite direction toward the bar and Jordan. The assistant bar manager looked pissed and more than a little scared of me.

"I…uh, guess you won that tenner?" I said with a weak grin, getting a snort from Jordan in reply.

"Yeah, I think that tenner is well and truly mine, mate, well done. Jesus, man, never seen anything like the way you did that! Fluid…like a snake. You're a scary bastard, Jack."

"Ah…yeah. I did a lot of martial arts when I was younger?" I said, lying through my teeth. I'd done some training, but most of my skills had been far harder won than in "training."

"Right, well…" Jordan ran his hand through his hair and took a deep breath. "Lucas wants me to tell you you're suspended while they investigate you 'attacking a customer.' He's giving a copy of the CCTV to the police now, so I guess it's a case of 'wait until the old man is in and have a chat with him about things.' Sorry, man."

I winced and shook my head in response.

"I guess I can't blame him for that, but making you tell me? Shitty move, man."

"Tell me about it. He's probably trying to figure out how to explain to Daddy that he was banging Maria in his office when it all kicked off." Jordan gave me a lopsided grin, and we both looked over at Maria, who was complaining fiercely about the damage to her nails as she did the jobs that were normally "beneath her" as Lucas's favorite. She saw us looking and went white, ducking her head and getting on with it in silence.

I grimaced as Jordan looked back at me, both of us realizing that she was afraid of me. If she was…I looked around at the rest of the staff and discovered only a handful would meet my eye. *Fuck, looks like it's time to move on, anyway…*

Jordan had grabbed my gear from the lockers and placed it on the back bar, so I collected it and thanked him, getting a sad smile and a fist bump as I headed for the door. Jonno had called a female PC over to sit with him and the girl, and he nodded at me as I headed out. I didn't need verbal confirmation that he could see what I had, something was very wrong with the girl.

I jogged up the stairs and past the bouncers at the door. Both of them seemed a little sheepish that it had turned into a brawl and they—the people who were supposed to deal with that, and make sure it didn't happen—had been absent. I understood, though; they were called doormen for a reason, after all. Couldn't expect them to deal with everything.

One opened the door for me, and I thanked them both as I left, shivering as I stepped out into the crisp snow. The club was in the bottom of an old building with three flights of stairs before you hit ground level. I was surprised to discover the heavy snowfall that had fallen in the last few hours.

It'd not felt cold or anything downstairs, and on my way in, I'd barely seen a few flakes, but now? It was all winter wonderland everywhere I looked.

Well, winter wonderland with staggering drunks, taxis blaring horns at anything and everything, flashing lights on a squad car, and a half-dozen girls pleading with a taxi driver to let them in.

Every time the driver said he was booked, they just hiked the skirts a little higher or the top a little lower.

He'd cave in soon; either that, or they'd freeze to death, as all the material that was left was barely more than a large belt at this point. I grinned despite myself and looked the girls over, having a momentary fantasy about grabbing my car, offering them a lift and seeing what I'd get in response. The tall blonde especially was…*no! Dammit, man, you've got Lou. Behave yourself!*

I shook my head again as I zipped up my jacket, crunching across the snow to the curb then jogging across the road, getting a few honks from taxi drivers as I went. It was barely a five-minute walk to the parking lot, but I was frozen solid by the time I squeezed past the barriers at the entrance, and oh so tired. The adrenaline that had flooded my system earlier had worn off and left me with a level of exhaustion that could fell an ox.

When I finally made it up the steep slope to my car, I ducked inside and fired up the heaters on full blast, deciding I'd rather let the snow melt off than trying to scrape it off, and pulled out my phone. I hadn't had it while I had been working due to a standard bar rule, and I hadn't wanted to get it out with the snow, just in case it got wet, even though modern phones had so many protective features these days. *Just a little holdover from older times,* I thought.

I read through a few messages and checked Find My Friends. Sure enough, Lou was back at her place now. I was tempted to drop by, even though she'd been clear she was having a night out with the girls. She wouldn't really mind if I came over now, would she?

Maybe stop off and grab a bottle of wine on the way, have a little drink, kick her friends out of her bed, and maybe get a little loving? Or ask if they wanted to play, too? *In your dreams...*

I sent her a message, quickly telling her good night and that I'd see her tomorrow. We'd been together about six months now, going from sex to more. I kind of thought it was love, but neither of us had said it yet, and I wasn't going to be the first. *Idiot...*

I drove home and had a quick shower, washing off the funk of the club before pouring myself a glass of rum and heading to bed, exhausted. *I'll deal with everything tomorrow,* I decided. *Fuck it all.*

DREAM 1

"It came over me slowly, like the feeling of falling that jerks you awake just as you fall asleep. But for me, it didn't end with a jerk and sitting up; instead, my soul was pulled by a thousand infinitesimal threads, and I fell faster and faster, leaving my world behind. I plummeted, summoned *elsewhere*...

I fell forwards, my mind flailing as I awoke properly from my dream state and hit the ground hard on all fours, inhaling sharply with the shock of the impact and the damn cold. I burst out coughing as my lungs filled with smoke and dust. Adrenaline slammed into me, sharpening the world as my heart blazed to wild hammering.

Looking around in the darkness, I shivered violently. The air was freezing, and my head was still reeling, trying to make sense of everything as I straightened up slowly. As my weight shifted on the scree scattered across the floor, I staggered, catching myself with one hand and leaned against the nearest wall.

I immediately pulled away as the icy stone numbed my skin, making me shiver even harder. My naked flesh covered in goosebumps, I coughed and choked. More smoke rolled through, and I blinked my way through the haze while I tried to work out what had happened. I stumbled away from the sarcophagus I'd been born again in, remnants of amniotic fluid dripping from me as I tried to make sense of my surroundings.

I was in a small room, or what was left of one, anyway. The sarcophagus behind me canted at a weird angle, and instead of the amniotic fluid being drawn away—it usually drained away slowly, waking me gradually—it'd released all over the floor, sweeping the snow back in weird patterns.

The lid of the sarcophagus was still swinging weirdly, hanging on by a single hinge, the other having given way. Rather than being recessed into the wall, it listed forwards at a weird angle, barely upright at all.

I looked around in bemusement; usually when I'd had one of these dreams, I had woken into a warm room that was well-lit and filled with supplicants who held equipment ready for me. Instead, this time the room was a mess of collapsed walls, shattered stone, and smoke. The roof was half-torn apart, letting snow swirl in.

The light of reflected flames flickered somewhere ahead through the smoke. The stands to either side, ones that should have held weapons and equipment ready for me were missing or shattered, their contents seemingly long since looted.

Half of the room looked like it had been buried by a landslide. I coughed again and staggered forward, awkwardly heaving myself over the stones and dirt of the collapsed wall as I tried to determine what had happened.

A dark shape appeared in the smoke, and I lurched toward it, coughing and raising a hand to get their attention.

"Hey! Dude, what the fuck?" I called out, and the figure turned and began to approach me. I shook my head, forcing myself to focus as I moved forward. A tingle of warning started in the back of my mind.

As I stepped outside, my feet crunching into the deep snow and disappearing up to mid-calf, the wind blew the smoke aside to reveal the man standing before me. He was tall, nearly as tall as I was, his face painted with blue and green designs.

He was dressed in heavy skins and carried an axe. An axe that dripped bright red blood onto the snow. He grinned at me, shouted something unintelligible over his shoulder at presumably another man, and hefted his axe. He strode forward, beckoning me eagerly as he sank into a fighting stance.

Ah, shit...not again, I thought to myself, my brain finally catching up and adrenaline banishing the last of the fog that had been filling my mind. *I haven't been pulled here in years. Why now, of all the fucking times?* I shook my head, discarding those thoughts as my mind went into overdrive.

Another glance revealed bodies in the snow, but the only living people were dressed as the first man, and all of them were covered in blood. Houses around the building I'd come from were burning, and a sudden scream filled the air from my left. The only house that wasn't alight resonated with high-pitched screams; all women, I realized grimly. I knew what those screams meant. I took a deep breath and screwed up my courage, even as I stepped back into the smoke.

My confusion had vanished entirely, driven away by the anger that filled me. I knew what I had to do, why I'd been summoned. Either I died, and those in the house continued to suffer, or these men did.

The first man I'd seen shouted something at me and hurried forwards, but quickly lost me in the smoke and darkness. Years of similar experiences came back to me as I hid. I crouched by the rockslide, lifting a stone the size of my fist in each hand, and waited.

The first man appeared quickly enough, a shadow at first, indistinct in the smoke. Then he grew clearer as he stumbled inside, wafting one hand to clear away the smoke as he glared around, missing me kneeling in the darkness. I grinned coldly as he turned, moving to my right. I came to my feet, slipping around behind him silently as he peered about in the dim haze. I followed his steps, stalking him in the night.

As he searched, he occasionally shouted into the darkness. Other voices answered him; they were hunting me, too, thinking I was one of the faceless villagers they'd faced already. That was a mistake on their side, a fatal one if I had my way.

One more step, and I was within reach, raising the rock high overhead. As if alerted by some sixth sense, he glanced back, but much too late.

His eyes widened in the split second before the rock landed, the bridge of his nose meeting cold, hard stone and breaking. Blood spraying, he wildly swung his axe, staggering backwards and blindly trying to defend himself.

I'd expected that and had quickly stepped back as soon as I hit him, slipping around to the side. Ducking beneath his blindly swinging blade, I swept up a new, slightly larger and pointed rock, dumping the smaller one, then smashed the pair of them into either side of his right knee, tearing downwards. The kneecap shattered with the blow, and I took two quick steps to my left, fading back into the smoke and darkness as he screamed and collapsed to the ground.

25

I shrank back against the wall to hide in a darker patch of shadow and waited, shivering but gripping the rocks tightly. Another figure appeared, running to the first man's side and skidding to a halt, staring down in shock at the bloody ruin of his face and the mess that had replaced his knee. I crept up behind the second man, bringing both stones together on either side of his head as hard as I could.

The noise was like a hammer hitting a coconut, and the garbled shriek that burst free as I crushed the sides of his skull in was unlike anything I ever wanted to hear again. Blood ran in bright rivulets from his nose, ears and eyes as he collapsed to the floor. His body started twitching spasmodically, his questioning last words never to be answered.

I chucked the rocks aside and grabbed his sword. Drawing it as quietly as I could, I hefted it to get an idea of its weight. It was bigger than I generally liked, a hand and a half affair, but it was better than a pair of rocks any day.

I melted back into the shadows again, leaving the injured man to wail in pain and fear, half-blinded and unable to stand, let alone fight. All he'd seen of me so far, after the first eye contact, was a shape in the smoke, maybe a clear glimpse of me for a second.

I'd been careful to stay out of sight since I'd briefly appeared like a deadly phantom to kill his friend then vanished again, adding to his terror. The remains of his face grew white with fear and blood loss as his one remaining eye rolled around in panic, screaming into the darkness for his companions.

I moved quickly, slipping inside and crouching in the burning remnants of another building a handful of steps further to the left. I had to force myself to ignore the pained screams coming from other houses nearby, and the pleading. Sightless eyes that stared at me from a handful of feet away, the body of an old man, half-dressed and gutted, his bedding smoldering and filling the low room with stinking smoke.

This time, there were three of them. Two appeared on the far side of the screaming man with another one coming from my right. His back faced me as he ran past, sliding to a halt in the deep snow. Before the man on the ground could warn them, I was out of the house and thundering forwards.

With the sound of my running feet covered by the screams and roar of flames climbing all around us, the closest man had no warning before my stolen sword punched into his lower back, the blade angled upwards to puncture the bottom of a lung.

I yanked the blade out, tearing it sideways as I pulled it back, spraying blood across the snow and drawing a surprised cry that ended in a wet gurgle and wheeze. He grabbed futilely at his chest, and I shoved him aside, sending him falling to the ground as he slowly suffocated on his own blood.

I leaped across the blinded one on the floor, whipping my blade around to build momentum and swinging hard for the heads of the remaining two. One managed to throw himself backwards into the snow, screaming a warning into the night and bringing his sword up. He deflected my blow enough to save himself, but the other couldn't back away fast enough.

The tip of my sword dug into his jaw, cutting deeply. The force of the blow tore the lower half of his face apart and sent him sprawling to the floor, thrashing and screaming, his jaw shattered with a spray of blood that appeared black on the firelit snow.

I twisted to face the one that had dodged, barely deflecting his sword as he stabbed at my gut. I grunted and backed up but he still managed to slice into the thin layer of fat covering my stomach. I hissed in pain as I backed up farther, swinging my sword warningly.

Two more figures emerged from the darkness towards me, illuminated by the flames. I didn't have the time to engage in a sword fight. I flicked my blade left, then right, testing him. I saw the way his eyes followed the sword, not me, and I acted as quick as a thought.

"Catch!" I yelled, throwing my sword up in the air in front of him.

He instinctively tried to grab it, and being the gentleman that I was, I kicked him as hard as I could in the balls. As the air went out of him, I grabbed his head with my left hand, using my right forearm to deflect the flat of his blade to the side. Then I pulled down hard, bringing his nose into my quickly rising right knee and sending him flying.

As he fell over backwards, stunned and blinded by the pain from his broken nose, I swept my sword back up and leaped forwards, swinging it overhead in a wild blow that he barely managed to deflect. I rolled my wrist, whipping the blade around again and again, battering him down hard as he raised his sword and attempted to get to his feet. The third time I hammered his sword aside, I finally saw an opening.

Instead of hitting his upraised sword squarely, I hit it at an angle, driving it aside to slam my own blade down into his gut. The point of my weapon pierced him through and pinned him to the ground as he began screaming.

I tried to pull the sword free, but it was stuck fast. The mixture of the frozen earth, snow, and my opponent's writhing body and spurting blood kept me from freeing it, so I abandoned the weapon and jumped over him, racing away from the incoming pair.

I landed awkwardly and tripped in the snow, staggering before I caught myself, blood slowly seeping down my own belly from my earlier wound. I stifled a groan of pain, my adrenaline keeping me moving as I gritted my teeth and kept going.

Mobility and surprise were my best weapons in this fight. Let them know there was only one of me? Let them corner me, unarmed and naked, and it was all over. They needed to be looking in all directions, unsure what was out here, if I was human or a monster.

The edge of another burning house lay ahead so I altered course, planning on looping around behind it. A man came running from behind it, spear raised. I cursed, having picked dead wrong, clearly, and dug deeper, screaming wildly in a hope of distracting him.

He panicked, having not expected a naked, screaming madman, and tried to stop, skidding in the snow. I plowed into him, taking us both to the ground. I punched wildly as he tried to bring the spear around, its length great for a normal fight, but a lethally poor choice in close.

I made the most of my strength—the bodies that I always had "here" being stronger than my own—as I pressed the spear down and punched him as hard as I could in the face, once, twice, then grabbed his jaw one-handed. I shoved it hard to my left, twisting his neck, and opening up the fullest range of movement then ripped it to the right as hard as I could, the branch-like snapping proclaiming to all the world that he was out of the fight.

I heard it then, the frenzied breathing, the crunch of snow. I rolled sideways, coming to my feet, as the dead man did me a last favor, catching the spear tip that had been aimed at the small of my back.

I backed up, the wall of the smoldering cabin behind me suddenly hard against my back, and I swore, moving to the left as the other man yanked his spear free and followed.

His first thrust was aimed at my guts as he came at me, and I barely deflected the spear with my left hand, smacking the haft just below the head. I managed to push the blow off course, but I still received a thin cut across the outside of my hip. It stung, but I would take the scratch instead of a fatal injury any day.

I brought my right fist across in an attempt to strike his jaw, but the punch was too fast and badly aimed, robbing it of any real force. We backed away from each other, circling as we went. I quickly scanned my surroundings again, jumping back to dodge another thrust, but I still couldn't see the other man. He was around, but I had lost track of him in the confusion. I couldn't help but feel a creeping sensation between my shoulder blades as I imagined him sneaking up behind me...

In between his strikes, I noticed that the screams from the building had stopped, and sobbing was all that remained of the cries, aside from the screams from my own victims. I desperately hoped that it meant there were only a few of them left, and they had abandoned their sport in favor of the fight. Or better yet, to flee.

The spearman rushed forward again, thrusting three times in short succession. They were fast, brutal attacks that would have gutted me if they'd landed, but he left me plenty of room to back up each time.

My eyes widened as I realized the pattern, and I dove aside, far faster than I normally could thanks to the body I was wearing. His spear grazed my back as I hit the snow and rolled over. A solid *thunk* came less than a second later from above.

I glanced up at the spearman, watching him raise a hand to the arrow suddenly protruding from his chest.

The fletching quivered just below his neck with each beat of his heart. He tapped it as if unsure where it came from. Suddenly, blood gushed from his mouth, and he fell to his knees before finally collapsing face down in the snow just to the side of me.

I grabbed the spear and tried to roll aside again, barely flopping out of the way of a second arrow. The cold and minor blood loss were making me sluggish, and god knew my balls were trying to find room to hide internally.

I struggled to my feet, hefting the spear in one hand as I backed up toward the nearest building. I had to get out of the archer's line of sight, but as I slogged through the deep snow, my left leg went out from under me suddenly, and I fell. Something in my leg snapped, and the pain suddenly roared through me as I frantically dragged myself around the corner.

As I looked down at my leg, my breath whistled through my clenched teeth. The arrow had embedded in the meat of my thigh. The shaft looked to have broken when I rolled over, leaving a wicked, barbed head protruding an inch from the front of my leg, with a short, broken bit still jammed out of the back.

I was lucky it'd missed the bone and gone straight through, but it still hurt like hell. My new spear rested peacefully in the snow, right out in the open a few feet out from where I laid shivering. I actually contemplated going for it, but the archer would be waiting for me to try.

Instead, I began to crawl along the side of the building, hearing sobbing from inside, and realized at least some victims of this assault were still alive.

I have to get to them; I have to defend them. It repeated over and over in my mind like a mantra. It was all that I could do to keep from passing out from the pain, but I couldn't turn my back on them. If I did, who would they have left? "No," I hissed to myself through gritted teeth. "I can do this. I can make it..."

I dragged myself as fast as I could, and I almost reached the corner of the building when a second arrow hit me from behind. The sharp, metal head punched through my back to tear the skin on my chest, completely piercing through my lung, and the majority wedged between my ribs. I coughed blood and fell forward onto my face, going into shock.

Time seemed to stretch out, my heart thudding in my ears, my breath coming in shorter and shorter pants. I tried to make sense of what had happened as I sprawled with my face turned to the side in the snow. Dancing flames illuminated the area and cast shadows. I almost lost myself to the beauty of the patterns, but a rough hand grabbed me and turned me over, throwing me onto my back and causing pain to roar through me.

"Yessik! Vatuch qe morra!" Someone screamed the words at me, the language harsh and guttural as they backed a few feet away.

I blinked in confusion, focusing in on the man's lips as he continued to shout, but the words made no sense to me. His lips were strange, I decided, one side dragging as he snarled at me. I focused on a thin scar running across the side of his head as I blinked, trying to bring the world back into focus. I stared up at the rage-contorted face of a boy barely out of his teens. He was big. Huge, by most people's standards, but the terror in his eyes told me that he was most likely the last of them.

I saw movement behind him and frantically tried to stop myself from looking in that direction. I coughed and spat blood onto my chin before gesturing to him to come closer. He drew back on his bow and fired another arrow at me, which slammed into my right leg and pinned it to the ground with the impact.

I gritted my teeth and grunted, the pain ratcheting higher and higher as I forced myself to grin up at him, gesturing again. He edged closer, sighting down his arrow and shouting something at me. He probably wanted to know what I wanted, who I was, and why I attacked them—or hell, maybe it was just what had been happening on "Lovely Island," for all I knew.

I grinned wider at him, then lifted my shaking left hand to point out into the darkness-shrouded forest to my side, beyond the remains of the village, diverting his attention for another few precious seconds.

When he looked back down at me, I reached down and shook my manhood at him with deliberate slowness while simultaneously giving him the finger with my other hand, wheezing and sputtering out a laugh.

His face went red with rage, as such a blatant act of disrespect and contempt crossed the barriers of space and time to make itself clear. He drew the arrow back farther, opening his mouth to shout something...then finally, the girl that had been creeping up on him slammed a wooden club down on his head, knocking him senseless. He staggered sideways, slumping to one knee and catching himself against the side of the cabin, his other hand rising to touch the back of his head in confusion as she stepped in closer and swung for the fences.

The blow hit him in the head, just above the temple, and smashed him into the cabin wall, a heavy construction of log and mud. He slid sideways, stunned.

Before he could recover, I grabbed the arrowhead protruding from my left leg and ripped it free. With a ragged scream, I drove it into his throat, a wash of hot blood spurting out as I cut deep into an artery before puncturing his windpipe.

Pain flared as the girl tried to drag me out from under him. With every pull, my injuries left me screaming in fresh agony. She managed to drag me slowly across the snow, up a handful of bumpy steps that left bloody splinters in my back, and into a thick-walled log cabin. The blood flowing from my wounds left a trail a blind man could follow.

I blinked open my eyes again, and I realized I must have passed out at some point.

Looking up at the shadow hovering above me, I found a pretty, blonde woman. Her clothes were torn and bloody, hair hanging from a half-unraveled braid, her face already swelling and bruised. She gazed into my eyes with tears running down her cheeks and begged me not to give up. She needed me; they all did, she whispered through her tears.

I blinked, realizing that she was speaking a language that I could understand. Suddenly, there were three of them, all fussing over my injuries. Voices argued in the background, letting me know that others had survived as well, and a rush of warmth filled me.

I had saved some of them, after all. I had not failed them, not like so many other times. I coughed again, weakly. Blood spattered across my chin and upper chest and brought a welcome warmth to my increasingly cold body.

The room began to dim, the edges of my vision growing fuzzy, and two faces came into focus as they rushed to my side. The young blonde woman was joined by an older one. She was an elf, my tired mind noted, and judging from the many wrinkles, an old one indeed. She lifted her hands over me, raising them to touch my face, my chest, and my collection of injuries. She turned her head and frantically spoke to the others, telling them to get bandages, and to look for survivors.

Before she could say more, a scream came from the youngest girl as the first man I'd fought hobbled into the room. He had to use his axe as a crutch, but he was upright and screaming something back at the women as he staggered in. When he saw me, he stopped. A cruel smile spread across the bloody ruin of his face as he looked down at me.

He was missing most of his teeth, an eye, and at least one of his cheekbones was broken. Obviously, so was his knee, but the bugger was upright again, and he was coming for me.

I forced myself to grin up at him and wave cheekily, even as I knew what would happen.

He went berserk, screaming at me and bringing his axe up overhead to hammer it down into my right leg, just above the knee. I felt it hit, a sensation like a sudden pressure and the cracking of a thick branch, then the pain came. It was horrific, made even worse as he yanked his axe back and forth to free it of both my leg and the divot it had dug into the wooden floor.

I screamed out in agony, without even trying to hold it in, and he raised the axe over his shoulder while hopping on his one good leg. He brought it down even harder on my left leg, higher up, cutting deep into my thigh as he collapsed over me, having lost his balance.

I howled aloud in abject agony, the pain ripping through me like nothing else. Then a moment of terrible clarity struck, the pain washed away by murderous rage, and my mind enjoyed a brief second of icy cold precision. I was dead; there was no helping that. That was nothing new. But I realized the pleasure he was getting from this, and I knew he would do worse to the people here, the ones that had summoned me, if he survived.

I lashed out, slamming both palms hard over his ears and rupturing his eardrums. He reared back in pain, still gripping his axe with one hand as the other flew to his head. I felt the movement of the axe, still firmly embedded in my leg, as he moved. Pain flared again, but it had become a distant thing, a candle next to the inferno that was my rage. I grabbed onto his face, digging my hands into the bloody mess. I gripped the bones, flexing my muscles and yanking my hands as far apart as possible.

He screamed, his hands grasping to stop my burrowing fingers. But as I heaved, his screams became far more terrible. His cries changed from rage and pain into a wet mewling.

I twisted my body and slammed his head down on the spike on the back of his axe. The impact tore another scream from me, although the cry was a mix of pain and triumph.

The women cowered away from me in the back of the room as I blinked and tried to focus again.

I tried to speak to them, but the pain was horrific. I managed a single question before blacking out in relief at the answer.

"Are there more?"

"No, my Lord."

"Thank fuck…for that…"

You have died.

Chapter Two

I woke up with a gasp, my hands grabbing at my legs. Reflexively reaching for the injuries, I found deep, thin cuts, and a lot of hot, wet blood. I moaned in pain as my fingers pressed into the tears. I felt them then, all the other wounds. Every single cut I had received in the dream was replicated faithfully.

They would heal, as they always did, with an almost inhuman speed. The majority would be sealed over in an hour, scabs looking like a week's healing by lunchtime, and fully healed, leaving only another scar by the time I awoke the following day. Years of these dreams had given me a pretty good idea of what to expect, and it was highly unlikely that any of the injuries were fatal.

The scars were another problem, though. My body was freely covered in them; dozens crisscrossed my chest alone.

I was lucky that the few on my face over the years were minor and helped to make me look "mysterious and dangerous," as an ex had said. Between long-sleeved tops and jeans, most people had no idea. The ones that saw more of my body tended to think one of two things, however: badass motherfucker, or serious self-harmer.

I tried to give people the impression of the former rather than the latter, but as people got to know me better, they realized I was a bit of a soft touch, and it tended to make people wonder.

I'd been kicked out of the army with a "psychiatric medical discharge," and I'd used the opportunity to search for Tommy. He'd gone down the rabbit hole, beating me on my escape by a few months but I'd lost contact with him after he sent me an odd message. Unfortunately, I'd been out in the sandbox at the time, and even when they'd shipped me back I'd not been able to find him.

I'd grown more and more frantic about Tommy as the days turned into months, making me seem even more unbalanced. In the end, I was marked down as regular crazy and released from service early, rather than extra special crazy and given an "I love me" jacket.

The only reason I managed to stay free was the fact that these dreams were intermittent. They'd come every night straight for a month, then nothing. This time had been the first one since three months after Tommy vanished; I'd had nothing for nearly five years. Somehow, the stress of trying to find him hadn't triggered any dreams, which had buggered that old theory as well.

Tomorrow would mark the fifth anniversary of the day he'd sent me the message. Five years of searching with no leads, no signs, not even a fucking body.

I shook myself free of memories and peeled the bedsheets back, hissing in pain as they pulled free of the congealing blood. As they came away, the wounds reopened but I forced myself to my feet and staggered over to the mirror, staring at the mess before me.

Blood covered half my body, the wounds looking far worse than they were, but I still recognized that I needed some help. I'd gotten out of the habit of keeping supplies on hand and had nothing to bind them with. I checked the time; it was close to six in the morning. Lou likely wouldn't be awake for hours yet, especially after being out on the drink all night. But at least she'd understand me coming to her in this state as a good reason to disturb her. Hell, maybe it was time to test the relationship properly, and tell her the truth?

I made a plan to hit the twenty-four-hour corner shop at the bottom of the road, get some bandages and so on, then head over to her place. She could put the bandages on and seal anything up I needed her to; she was a student nurse, after all, and we'd be able to keep this quiet. Plus, I'd kinda tried to explain to her about the dreams before, anyway. She'd either not believed me or hadn't understood, and I'd dropped it, wondering a little if they'd stopped anyway, it having been so long since the last incident.

Now, though? Now she'd have to believe me, that or she'd try to get me locked away for my own good. Hell, it might strengthen the relationship yet, and I might even get some sympathy affection out of it. Maybe today wouldn't be a total write-off after all, I decided, my optimism coming to the fore as a wave of exhaustion ran through me.

I used a ratty T-shirt to wipe the majority of the blood away, tore up another old shirt to make rudimentary bandages, and pulled on some clean dark clothes. I winced as the jeans pulled against the leg wounds, then bundled myself up against the cold, deliberately wearing clothes that I didn't care about getting ruined.

I limped down the stairs of the apartment, mentally cursing at how damn many of them there were and out into the parking lot behind the property, wincing with each step.

My beat-up Ford Focus sat in the corner, buried several inches deep under the snow. I made it over to the car carefully; a slip now would be horrifically painful. Once I had managed to dig one door out, I hunched myself down inside as I started the engine and got the heater on. Turning the heated windshield and rear window both on full, I rubbed my hands together and tried to blow some life back into them before forcing myself out to brush as much of the snow off the car as I could reach.

Leaning back against the wall and trying to catch my breath, I realized I was shaking like a shitting dog, and there were blood trails around the car.

My constant movement was just making things worse. I limped back into the car and took a few minutes to gather myself before setting off, wheels spinning and the car swaying from side to side as I powered out of the frozen lot and onto the nearby main road.

A handful of minutes later, I was at the shop, and I left the car running outside as I staggered through the main door. The security guard appeared by my side and began talking at me, frantically pointing at my leg and chest. I glanced down to see blood starting to darken my clothes in a handful of different places, and that I was leaving bloody footprints as I went.

"Don't worry about it, mate. Bandages and shit, I just need some bandages, okay?" I mumbled at him, head reeling, and I gave up on trying to understand his words. I pushed him aside and limped down the aisle, quickly finding what I needed, along with a first aid kit. Chucking them into a basket, I headed for the checkout with the security guard following me at a distance and talking desperately into his radio.

Somehow, I made it out of the shop and back into my car, which, even more surprisingly, hadn't been stolen. I slowly drove down the street, crossing over two more, then spent a few minutes on the highway before pulling off and reaching the bottom of Lou's street.

I managed to get the car into a space near her front door—well, it was *nearly* in a space—and half fell out of the door before grabbing my supplies and staggering up the path to her door. I rang the doorbell, then banged on the door weakly. Nothing.

Fumbling with my jeans pocket, I managed to find the key she'd given me. I clumsily unlocked the door on the second attempt, pushed the door open and fell into the house, stumbling over the shoes left in the hallway.

I staggered and fell against the wall, bracing myself and taking a deep breath as I tried to focus, the blood loss making things hard. The room swam before I focused in on the clothes strewn about. There were a pair of wine glasses, half-eaten pizza, and even clothes all over, but Lou was always so adamant she wanted the house spotless before her mates came around. Why would she leave her clothes down here?

I dismissed it; it wasn't important, and I forced myself upright, wincing at the bloody handprint I'd left on the god-awful patterned wallpaper as I staggered upwards. I forced myself to focus on her bedroom door. It was just ahead at the top of the stairs, and as I stared up, it opened.

My relief turned to white-hot fury, as it wasn't Lou that stepped out, but Martin. Big, goofy, "my 'work husband,' that's all, honest." He was Lou's best friend…and he was naked. Then she appeared, peering around him to look down at me in confusion. Confusion that turned to horror as my rage boiled over, and I started up the stairs, roaring in fury. The pain from my wounds only fueled my rage as I powered toward them.

The steps blurred as I hauled myself up, clearing them faster than I'd ever have believed possible. In no time, I had closed in on Martin as he tried to explain himself. His raised hands in supplication didn't slow me; neither did the way he was patting the air, as though trying to calm an enraged dog. I hit him with a right cross first, throwing off his balance, then pounding an uppercut into his chin, lifting him from his feet and sending him flying back. Lou screamed in terror and dived aside, landing on the floor next to the bed.

I looked down at her, seeing the red lacy outfit crumpled by her side on the floor. I recognized it as the one I'd bought her only a few days before, the one I'd not even seen her in yet. But she'd worn it for *him*?!

Everything became a blur then. Martin was trying to get back from me, attempting to hide on the far side of the bed.

I grabbed the bedpost and launched myself at him, an energy flooding my body like nothing I'd ever felt before. I grabbed him by the throat with my left hand, lifting him easily from the ground, and went to work. Pummeling his ribs, I felt them break, one with each punch. I could almost see them outlined in a glowing red light. I swore I could feel where to strike to make them break every time.

KillHimKillHimKillHimHeTookHerFromUsKillHimHeStoleHer

ThiefThiefTHIEF!

The normally tiny voice in the back of my mind was suddenly all I could hear. Even Lou's screams were muted by the sound as it filled the universe, the hammering of my own blood in my ears drowned out by the voice. It was one of the few times I'd ever agreed with anything it had said, but this time, my entire soul reverberated with its words…with its screams, its insanity and hatred.

"Plu—pl…ease!" he whimpered, looking up at me, his broken nose spread across his too-handsome face. Blood covered his mouth, along with snot and tears, as he begged for forgiveness. Sneering, I smashed a right hook across his face, blood spraying from his mouth to coat the bedside table; the goddamn bedside table I'D GODDAMN CARRIED FROM IKEA FOR HER! I'D BUILT THAT SHITTY TABLE!

My heart thundered even louder in my ears at the sight while the voice screamed its approval and rage…

WeWantMORE!

My lips drew back from my teeth in an animalistic snarl of fury, when something hit me in the small of my back and made me stagger. I whirled around, throwing him sideways into a mirror, sending it crashing to the floor in a shower of broken glass. A blur in the air flashed towards my face before the room tilted and spun away. I blinked my eyes and saw blood dripping from my face onto the floor between my outstretched hands. I realized I was on all fours at the top of the stairs; how the hell…?

I heard a sound and looked up, finding Lou's beautiful legs before me. As I lifted my gaze, my eyes lingered almost of their own accord on her perfect features, until I finally noticed the most important detail as she lifted it again. The baseball bat. I'd laughed when she'd first showed it to me and told me that she kept it "just in case." She drew it back, swinging it with surprising force to hit me in the temple. The blow sent me falling down the stairs and plummeting into darkness. The last thing I saw before it claimed me was the look on her tear-streaked face. It was the same as the one on everyone's faces earlier at the bar.

Horror and disgust at the animal in their midst.

35

CHAPTER THREE

The world was slow to return, sounds coming first. Low mutterings of conversations around me filtered in, electrical beeps and a speaker coming from one side. The rest of the world edged in slowly, in that way it often did while waking from a deep sleep: local sounds first, then further and further out. Light came next, rudely shining in one eye as a finger and thumb forced my eye open.

I blinked and recoiled from the sudden brightness at the same time a female voice cursed in surprise. Hurried footsteps pounded as people came running in response.

"He's awake!" someone called.

I lifted my hand in reflex, trying to push the intruding light away. My hand barely moved a few inches before a tug and a rattle of metal stopped its motion. I blinked again and tried to sit up, both eyes open now as I attempted to figure out where I was.

Blurry shapes resolved into police, one either side of the bed, and a nervous nurse stood behind them. The nearest cop put his hand on my chest and pushed me back down. Firmly.

As I complied, I realized what the feeling on my arms was. I was handcuffed to the gurney. My body ached like a sore tooth, but surprisingly hurt little more than that. I tried to speak but managed only a croak before coughing and whispering in a pained voice.

"Water...please."

The nurse hurried forward, reassured by me being secured. Her bout of nerves vanished beneath a professional exterior as she brought a plastic cup up to my lips letting a little trickle in, then a bit more. It felt like I hadn't eaten or drank anything in weeks. My stomach loudly spoke up, wanting to know when it was going to be sharing the tiny bit of water my throat had already absorbed.

I tried to lift my hands unthinkingly to the cup, but the handcuffs stopped me, and a gruff voice from one side told me to stay still. The nurse stepped away to get more water, and I glanced over at the man who stepped up in her place. Looking down into my eyes was a face I'd gotten used to over the years. Jonno. For the second time in less than a day, I was under his steely gaze.

He was "Beat Sergeant Ross, 4872," but after being arrested by him as many times as I had, well, I got to know names. I groaned and shook my head as I looked up at him.

"Really?" I croaked out, staring at him. "All the pretty nurses in the world I could wake up to, and it's your ugly mug I get?"

"You're getting the better end of the deal, kid. You look like shit, and that's before you did...whatever you did to yourself," he retorted, gesturing to my face.

I grinned weakly at him, and he shook his head in disgust at my antics.

"You feel up to talking, *sir*? Telling us what happened?" The second cop started to speak, but Jonno waved him off.

"Go get a coffee, Mick; I need a quiet word here." He grunted, and the second cop broke off, looking annoyed. But he released the pressure on my chest and walked out of the room, leaving us to talk, unofficially.

"New kid?" I whispered croakily, getting an affirmative grunt in return.

"He's smart enough, but too 'by the book' for the real world. We can have a quiet chat, and you can tell me why you fucked your life up and did *that*. Then we'll have an official chat, and you'll be fucking honest, and I'll do what I can. That's the deal, right?

"And believe me, kid, after what you did in the club and then at that house, that's more than I should be giving you." He gestured at my chest, and I realized I was bare from the waist up. He could see the scars crisscrossing my body, but all the new ones were almost healed, and angry red lines were all I had to show for the last dream.

"Thank god, they've healed," I muttered, looking down. I attempted to lift my right hand to my temple, where I could feel some residual pain, but the handcuffs jangled again. "Ah, shit. How bad is it?" I asked quietly.

"You mean your head, or the kid in ICU?" he asked, one eyebrow raised in question.

The memories of last night felt...wrong. I vaguely remembered the trip to Lou's, and Martin, but it was like I was watching someone else's actions. They ran through my mind almost like a movie, but with a red tint to everything and a roaring voice screaming for blood in my ears. That, and the sense of strength and power...and the fact that even still, I knew I wanted to feel it again.

"What happened?" I asked weakly.

"That's what I'm trying to figure out, kid. I've seen the CCTV from the shop. You were fucked up pretty bad, bleeding all over the shop, then you disappeared before either we or the paramedics managed to find you.

"Next thing I know, we're getting a call saying a lunatic has broken in, aggravated burglary, we think. We turn up to find you on the floor, blood everywhere, and your skull cracked, another kid beaten half to death, and a wee lass with a baseball bat broken in half. Now, start talking, before that dumb shit comes back."

"Ah, crap. I don't know, man..." I whispered, letting my head fall back on the shitty hospital pillow, the blanket resting around my waist and the bandages crisscrossing my chest were barely enough to make me decent. I shivered at the memory of everything that had happened, and I tried to ignore the beeping of the machines all around me and swallowed against the lump in my throat.

"Don't give me that 'no comment' bullshit. Not from you, and not after all these years!" he snapped at me.

"Ha, no. No, man, I mean I don't know what happened. It feels like months ago; it's all hazy. How long have I been here?"

"About six hours, and you better believe the doctors have some questions for you about that. I saw your wounds."

I blinked and looked at him, trying to make sense of the fact I wasn't dead. I'd always healed fast, insanely fast, but this was a new level, if I was healing from a fractured skull here, in the real world, like I did from the dreams. Jonno snapped his fingers in my face, and I flinched, looking back at him.

"Focus, Jack! What happened!"

"I…I…they fucked me over. I loved her, and…" I told him the whole story, not holding anything back, even the dream. It took a while, but he sent the rookie away when he came back and told the nurses to wait outside. Eventually it was over, and I lay back, exhausted and sad to my soul. Tears had long since covered my cheeks, and he nodded as I finished my story.

"…and I still don't know where he is, man. Five fucking years I've been alone, five years! She was the only one I cared about beyond him, and she did *that*."

"That everything, Jack?" he asked.

I nodded. "Aye, Jonno, honest truth. What state am I in? Fucked gently, or sideways with a chainsaw up my arse?"

He snorted at me and shook his head, gesturing for his partner to come back from the end of the corridor.

"It's not good, kid, but I understand some of it at least. You be honest and don't try to hide shit—it'll go better for you. I'll have a word with the CPS. See if they won't lower the charges, or at least spread them around. The other two were both found with a fuck ton of drugs in the house as well. Looks like one of them is a small-time dealer, so none of you were innocent, but you had cause, and the blood loss that you had to be suffering on your way there…the best you can hope for is a few years, I think."

"Well, that's me fucked, isn't it?" I muttered, finding it hard to get worked up about it. My head felt like it was packed in cotton wool, even as my heart sank into my boots. "Wait…where the fuck are my boots? And my top?"

"Really, Jack? After all this shit, that's what you want to ask?" Jonno looked at me with another of his signature raised eyebrows and a frown that said, "I've seen it all before, and you're barely higher in my eyes than a turd sandwich; don't make me downgrade you…"

"Oh, fuck off, man. It's been a shitty day, okay?" I snapped at him and tried to fold my arms over my chest to ward off the cold and rattling the handcuffs again. "And seriously, can we get these off?"

"Nope, but good try." Jonno turned to the nurse, who had returned to check the bag connected to an IV in my left arm. "Excuse me, miss, can I get an ETA of when we can move him to the cells?"

"He's certainly not well enough to go anywhere, officer, not right now and not for a good while, thank you!" an unfamiliar male voice interrupted, and I twisted my head around, trying to see the speaker. A tall, dark-skinned man walked in, pulling the curtain back and then half closed again behind him, separating my section of the room from the rest of the hall. "Six hours ago, this man had a cracked skull, needed nearly a hundred and sixty stitches, and had lost a tremendous amount of blood. Now he's severely dehydrated, malnourished, and appears to be in a state of shock on top of it all. Add to this, you, an experienced law enforcement officer, have been questioning him when he is in no fit state to defend himself. You can post a guard outside the door, but beyond that, you won't be interacting with my patient again until I judge that he is fit for an interview. Even then, I'll be making a formal complaint to the station about you taking advantage of him!"

Jonno straightened up to his full height and looked like he was about to blast the doctor, when his fellow officer chimed in.

"Leave it, Jonno; you know he's right," he snapped before turning as he stepped closer to the doctor and nodded to him amiably. "We can post someone at the door, sir. No need for any hard feelings here. We're all on the same team, after all, yeah?"

Jonno looked pissed, but he sighed and nodded his understanding. "Fair enough, doctor. Jack? I'll do what I can, son. Rest and recover, but...don't get your hopes too high, all right?"

With that, he was giving me a squeeze on the shoulder as he passed, heading past the doctor and out into the corridor.

I sat upright, or at least as near as I could, and the doctor gave a disgusted snort, turning back to the police.

"Are those really necessary, officers? He can barely stay awake, let alone assault someone or escape."

"They stay on, doctor. Both for the safety of your staff and to prevent him doing anything stupid," Jonno called back over his shoulder as he walked off, his partner taking the guard post outside my room after a muttered consultation with Jonno.

The doctor grunted and stepped inside, pulling the door closed and proceeding to adjust the drip. It took a few minutes, but by that time, even I could tell he was just trying to look busy.

"You're a bit clumsy, mate," I mumbled.

He flinched before raising a finger to his lips in a silencing gesture, then spoke quietly.

"The Baron has sent for his lawyers; I've been told just to delay things until they arrive. They know what to do, so don't worry!"

"The Baron? What fucking Baron? Listen, pal..." I mumbled, coughing and clearing my throat, before starting to sit up, catching myself on the handcuffs again, and swearing loudly. The doctor began frantically shushing me and gesturing wildly.

"The *Baron*! Look, I don't know what game you're playing, and I don't want to know, but you need to stop talking to them, or you'll get us both in even more trouble!"

"Fuck you! Listen, you prick, I don't give a shit about...hey, what's that?" He'd started swearing more and was visibly sweating, then pulled something from his pocket and grabbed my arm, stabbing it into my shoulder.

"I'm sorry, but you've got to be quiet!" he hissed.

My anger rose as he called back to the police that everything was fine in response to the question that was called in, then turned back to me.

"Look, it's just a sedative, that's all. It's one the Baron's man gave me, said it'd knock even one of you out for a while, so just relax; there's no need for stress," he muttered urgently in low tones, pulling the syringe out of my shoulder and patting my arm.

I glared at him and started to tell him where to go, and to call for the cops, but all that came out of my mouth was "Ergu, basip...meh...h."

Then the room spun, and the lights went out again.

CHAPTER FOUR

I came to with a start, the noise of a siren starting up loud in my ear as I was unceremoniously bounced so hard I nearly came off the stretcher. "Wha—" I cried, trying to grab something to stabilize myself, only to find that I was securely tied in place. Thick leather restraints on my wrists and ankles and chest bound me tightly to the jouncing gurney in what looked like an ambulance. One that was tearing through traffic with the sirens blaring like mad.

"You can relax, Jack. I am Mr. Johannes, and I was sent by the Baron to examine you and make you an offer, should you prove suitable."

I twisted around as far as I could, glimpsing a small figure sat almost behind me. He didn't bother to move. As I strained, I managed to see that he was holding a briefcase on his lap, a newspaper upraised in one hand as he looked at it. The fucker wasn't even looking at me.

"Wha...who?" I gasped out, my mind wrapped in a blanket of fog from the anesthetic.

"Humph. Not off to a good start, now are we?" he muttered to himself, folding the paper and putting it away. He shifted over to sit on the seat nearest to me and fixed me with a glare that was obviously supposed to be intimidating. "Very well; let's make this quick, shall we?"

"I...uh..."

"Please be quiet, Jack. This will go a lot more quickly if you do. Right, then. You've come to the Baron's—he's my employer—attention. He has instructed me to make you an offer, one that is exceedingly generous, in my opinion.

"You will be retained to work in his acquisitions team. This will involve a great deal of expensive training. Then, you will be sent to acquire certain objects that he desires and to complete a small mission. In return, you will be well-paid, and your current legal...difficulties...will be taken care of. As a gesture of good faith, we've already removed you from the hospital. See how generous we are?" He smiled perfunctorily at me, and I stared back at him, trying to figure out what was going on. This little bastard had broken me out of jail for a job offer?

"Look...I think you've gotten me mixed up with someone else. I'm not..."

"No, Jack, you have yourself mixed up, not us. A wolf wearing sheep's clothing to fit in is still a wolf, just a surprisingly stupid-looking one."

"I'm not a wolf; I'm a gamer, and I was a barman, but..."

"You *are* a wolf, Jack, or you have the correct genes to be one, at least. We confirmed that in the hospital, and your healing certainly dismissed any doubts I had personally."

"Huh?" I muttered, confused. I was starting to get annoyed with the weird way the little bastard talked. I looked him over. He was maybe five-foot-one, with oily skin, greasy hair, an expensive suit, and a generally weaselly yet still arrogant attitude. He was a lawyer, all right.

"Look, pal, I dinna know who ye are, but ya can either talk straight or let me out o' here and fuck off, all right? I've had a shitty enough night already." My accent came through, as it always did, whenever I was stressed or angry. Years of shitty call center jobs and speech training dismissed in an instant.

"Yes, well, I think I made myself clear, Jack, even to one of your ilk. I'll try to make it simpler. Baron offers you money, you be good and do as told, all good, yes?" He spoke in a sweet, sugary voice, like some people do when talking to animals and small children.

"And if I don't?" I asked, a low growl seeping into my voice at his words.

"If you don't? Well, then, you get to learn to fly! Won't that be wonderful?"

"Fly?"

"Yes, Jack, from the plane door, out over the channel. Look. You're obviously not bright; I had some hopes you would be at least smarter than your brother. But clearly, I was wrong. If you do what we tell you, the Baron will give you a great deal of money and some fabulous opportunities. If you refuse, then you're a problem. The Baron dislikes problems, and he tends to use them as examples to others. Very messy examples. Hence learning to fly would be a much better idea than disappointing him later on."

"Wait a minute. You're offering me a job and threatening to kill me if I don't take it and be a good little boy?" I growled.

"Ah! Yes, you can be taught; what a relief. After we had a similar discussion with Thomas, he became violent and had to be...disciplined."

"Wait, what? Hold the fuck up; you know Tommy?" I quickly replayed the conversation in my mind, realizing that he'd mentioned Tommy before.

"I see we're back to simplistic again. Okay. Yes, Jack, me know Tommy. Tommy was a naughty boy and got punished. Now you get a chance. Understand?"

"Punished! What the hell?!" I roared, my rage coming totally unhinged at the implications. I threw my full weight against the restraints, yanking them repeatedly as I rocked the stretcher from side to side, screaming obscenities at him all the while.

His face went red with anger, but when the restraints on my right arm slipped, giving me a few scant inches of space, he went white with fear. His hand dove into the pocket of his tailored suit to retrieve a small stone. He pressed it against my chest and frantically started reading off a small sheet in his other hand as I tried to get to him.

The words were gibberish to me, but as he cried out the final syllable, the stone flashed with a bright white light, followed swiftly by darkness as I collapsed back onto the bed.

This time, when I awoke, I did so gradually, and I kept my eyes closed, listening to the sounds around me as my mind tried to kick into gear. I was sitting upright, so I must have been transferred to a chair while I was unconscious. I heard an engine nearby...no, two engines...and a steady *thrummm* filled the air. A sudden shift made my stomach drop. Then it was back like I was riding a rollercoaster, and a voice nearby complained about the turbulence.

I was on a plane, then; that much was obvious. The conversation with the greasy little lawyer came back next, and the only thing that stopped me leaping to my feet was the memory of the threat to kick me out of the plane. I had to find out what had happened to Tommy first, then I could kick that prick's head in. I cracked my eyes and glanced around.

The cabin was dimly lit with almost all of the window blinds drawn low. A sound nearby made me close my eyes again and feign sleep.

"How much longer will he be out, sir?" a feminine voice asked from somewhere nearby. The air moved in time with a faint rustle of fabric and scent of expensive perfume, before a hand caressed my cheek.

"Who knows? Hopefully not too much longer. I had to use the stone to put him under. Damn fool tried to attack me!" Mr. Johannes whined as the fingers slowly stroked my cheek, several days of bristles rasping against their tips.

"He's certainly handsome enough, just like his brother," the voice said, and I opened my eyes involuntarily. I found myself staring up into bright blue eyes that looked back in shock before a smile covered her face. "Hello, sir, welcome back to the land of the living! How do you feel? Can I get you anything?"

I blinked at her, ignoring the indrawn breath behind me and the sounds of several people moving around nearby. She was a vision: tall, blonde, high cheekbones, and eyes that a man could fall into and get lost in. Her lips were cherry red with a perfectly even white-toothed smile.

I gazed up at her, trying to find a flaw, anything. As her mouth moved, I noticed she didn't even have a single filling. She wore a tight white blouse, unbuttoned low enough to show generous cleavage, a black miniskirt, and golden jewelry to finish the outfit off. All I could do was stare.

"Sir? Are you okay?" she asked again. I realized with a start that she'd been talking before, but I'd totally zoned out and simply been looking her up and down. *Get a grip, dude!* I cursed mentally, smiling an apology...even as Johannes sneered something behind me.

Instantly, the woman before me ceased to matter. Instead, the rage started to rise again as I tried to twist around. Finding myself tightly strapped to the chair by wrist, ankle, and throat, I nearly choked myself.

"Johannes? That you, ya wee prick?" I gasped out, shifting so that I could breathe properly again.

"It's *Mister* Johannes to you, Jack," a voice called out from behind me, and the beauty was gently but firmly pushed back by a pair of guards who had decided now was the best time to make their presence known.

I looked up at them. Both were at least a foot taller than me and probably weighed twice what I did, belly and all.

"All right, lads, I've no shit with you; so how about you loosen these restraints and fuck off for a bit? I just need a wee word with Johannes..." I growled at them, and I caught one of them covering a twitch of a grin with an impassive mask.

"Sorry, Jack. You'll continue to be restrained until the Baron decides otherwise," he said, looking down at me while his companion checked to make sure the straps were all tight enough. "Settle back and enjoy the ride. We've less than an hour to go before we land, and then we see what's what."

I opened my mouth to speak again, but the woman spoke before I could.

"Surely, he can have a drink and some food, Captain? He needn't be fully released, just a hand?"

"No chance. If you knew what his brother could do with just one hand; you wouldn't want to risk it either. Sorry, Melanie. If you want him to be fed, you'll have to do it yourself."

"Very well, captain," she said, disappearing for a few seconds before hurrying back to my side, taking the seat next to me and holding a tray of food that steamed as she removed a lid. She saw that I was trying to speak and, with a nod from the captain, she loosened the strap over my throat.

I coughed and whispered to her, "If he thinks Tommy was good with one hand, you've seen nothing yet..." and gave her a dirty wink, my cock speaking up before my brain could get back in gear.

To my surprise, she burst out laughing and winked back at me. "I *like* this one!"

I glanced at the guards, but the captain just rolled his eyes, muttering something about "great, another one," while the second one glared at me. Before I could say anything else, a spoonful of mashed potato was lifted to my mouth. I ate it quickly, my stomach crying out that it thought my throat'd been cut.

The mash was followed by buttered carrots, bacon, cabbage, and spiced sausage with a hint of chili and garlic, all doused with a light, flavorful gravy. By the time I'd finished and was able to speak again, I was amazed. The inflight food was the best I'd ever eaten, and the flight attendant, if that was what she was, was by far the hottest I'd ever seen.

"Okay, I give up. What airline is this?" I managed to get out, forcing a smile as I spoke. Yes, she was stunning and the food was great, but also if they all thought I was just a swinging dick without a brain, they'd underestimated me. "Seriously, if you're the inflight entertainment, I'm totally sold." I held her gaze. When she grinned at me, I looked past her to the second guard and spoke to him next.

"But you're a bit behind now; totally forgot to point out the exits and wish me a happy flight. Your makeup's good, though. Almost makes you pretty!" My natural stupidity spoke up while my brain ran in circles, trying to figure out what was happening while I hid behind a mask of bravado.

He glowered at me and started to speak, but I continued right over the top of him.

"Now, now, it's all right. Look, I'm flattered, I really am, but despite the way you keep looking at me, I'm just not interested. I don't swing that way, mate. No hard feelings and all that, though. Tell you what; you can hold the camera, just no sticking anything in my ass, all right?"

He went scarlet with anger, both Melanie and the captain trying to conceal grins.

I looked back to her and winked again. "You don't mind him holding the camera, do ya?"

"Well, that depends, doesn't it?" she said with a cheeky grin, playing the game as I'd hoped. "I don't mind him watching at all, as long as he holds it steady. None of that shaking around. After all, professional is as professional does."

"Glad to hear it! So, what's your name? As we're going to be co-starring together?"

"It's Melanie, and you're Jack, right? Jack Smith?"

"Aye, I'm Jack. Soooo, you met my brother, Tommy, then?" I asked, finally able to get her into the conversation in a way that wasn't too obvious.

I mean, I knew it was still somewhat obvious, but I'd lost my job, had the crap beaten out of me, been kidnapped, and then knocked out with a magic stone. My mind was mush. The only two things I could concentrate on right now were that these assholes knew something about Tommy, and Melanie…well, she was definitely out of my league, but that didn't mean I wasn't going to try.

It wasn't like I had a girlfriend anymore, after all. With that thought, my mood dropped like a stone. I forced myself to smile, bottling up the emotions that flared and demanded to be recognized.

Memories filled my mind. Only a few nights ago, sitting with her, a good Chinese takeout. She'd had a bottle of wine, I'd drunk my rum, and we'd laughed and joked. We'd talked about a house, one of the new builds at the end of the estate next to hers, how it'd have room for us to have a nice garden.

I'd joked about how she'd get complaints from the neighbors, walking around naked. She'd laughed, asking if I was complaining.

I'd picked her up in my arms and kissed her, the kiss turning savage as I swept food aside, making room on the table for her to lie back, and…

"Don't answer that!" I heard Johannes call out from behind me, even as Melanie opened her mouth to speak. She huffed in annoyance and slowly shook her head.

"I'm sorry, Jack, I can't say," she said quietly, turning away as Johannes said something else to her. I didn't catch it, but she looked angry, and she disappeared off to the back of the plane.

"You're a right cockgoblin, ya know that, Jo-jo?" I called out to him.

"IT'S MR. JOHANNES!" he shouted back. I grinned at the guard captain who sat across from me.

"Nah, it's not anymore. From now on, I'm gonna call you Daphne! You don't mind, do you, *Daphne?*"

There was silence from behind me for a second, until I felt hands roughly grab my seat and Daphne's face was suddenly inches from mine.

"You *dare* speak to me like that one more time, and I'll—"

"What? Threaten to chuck me off a plane? I'm not totally fucking thick, you prick. You don't do all this to recruit someone, then let your little errand boy chuck them outta the door! Your boss wants to see me, remember! Now fuck off…Daphne!"

I headbutted him. It didn't have much force behind it, especially with the restraint on my neck, but it had enough. He staggered backward and cried out in pain, a bit of blood leaking from his hands where they were tightly locked over his nose.

I'd had time to think by now, and I realized two things. First, these assholes knew something about Tommy, so I needed to find out what it was. Second, my life was already circling the drain like a turd with too much fiber in it. Going back was pointless. The best way forward was through whatever was in my way. The knowledge that my past was well and truly behind me now was freeing in a sense.

After all, I seriously doubted that the police would have just dropped the charges against me, no matter what this arsehole said, so if I went back? I'd be in jail in no time. No, whatever happened now, my old life was over, and that meant that it was down to me finding Tommy and starting again. I had nothing else to lose, not anymore.

He swore and punched me in the gut, once, twice, then the guards were there, separating us. I, being the responsible and sensible man that I was, immediately blew Daphne a kiss.

He went berserk, screaming and shouting, trying to get at me while both guards held him back.

It took a few minutes more to get things calmed down, with Daphne and the second guard—*I think I'll name him Grumpy*—both at one end of the plane, and myself and the guard captain at the other, with poor Melanie going from one group to the other.

Nobody spoke for a while, but I was sure I heard the guard captain whisper "daft bastard" once we were all settled. His face gave nothing away, though, so I just winked, on the off-chance I wasn't crazy, and settled back.

It wasn't that long before the plane began descending, and a short while later, as we taxied to a halt and the second guard reappeared, I was treated to a remarkably simple set of instructions by the captain.

"If you try to run away, we stun you. Speak to anyone, we stun you. Try to attack anyone, we stun you until you're drooling ten thousand volts. Understand?" the guard captain said, holding up a taser and making it crackle for emphasis.

I grinned and lifted one hand as far as I could. He sighed and nodded at me. "Go on, get it over with."

"Coolio. So, what if I fart really loud? If that gets someone's attention, that's not my fault, right? I don't get tasered then, right?" I asked.

He just shook his head in exasperation and just went ahead and tasered me anyway. I glowered at him once I'd stopped twitching. His friend, "Grumpy," helped to free me before putting my wrists and ankles in chains and holding the taser up to my face to make sure I understood that he would use it again happily.

"You seem like a bright kid, Jack, but you're far too much like Tommy. Both fucking stupid and having to push just to see how far you can get. I'll make it plain here. You piss the Baron off, he won't give you a beating or throw you out. He'll kill you, or more to the point, he'll make us do it. I don't need that shit on my conscience, so do me a favor and behave around him at least. Once he decides what happens to you, I'll fill you in on as much as I can, all right?"

I gritted my teeth and took a deep breath, forcing the anger down as I tried to get a rein on my mouth for a change.

"One condition," I said.

"Go on."

"You both call Daphne by his real name, too."

Johannes started swearing from the back of the plane before the guard captain let loose a little grin and called out to him.

"Shut the hell up. We don't need you making this worse...Daphne."

I grinned at him over the incoherent sounds Daphne was making and swore faithfully to be a good boy...for a bit. They released the choker on my neck and undid my seatbelt, but the wrist and ankle restraints stayed, making it difficult to walk.

When an additional chain was attached from my wrists to the ankles, I had to walk half hunched over. It was uncomfortable, but it wasn't like I had a choice.

I was quickly escorted from the plane, down a wide set of steps, and into a big black Mercedes parked on the runway. Daphne, Melanie, and someone else were getting into a second car. Wherever we were, we were clearly high in the mountains. The houses in the distance, beyond the edge of the little runway, were the kind of ones you saw in travel shows about the lucky rich bastards who got to go skiing and so on.

Snow covered everything besides the runways and a small row of cheerily glowing windows in a heavily constructed concrete building. It was night now and the snow was coming down steadily. As soon as we were all inside, the cars took off in convoy, and I watched out the windows at the falling snow. The side of the road was illuminated by the car's lights, which was lined with occasional trees and a lot of snow. That was it. At first, it was beautiful, but after a few minutes of the same damn thing over and over, it quickly grew damn boring.

I tried to mess with the guards, and even question them a bit, but a long look from the captain put an end to that. I'd agreed to be good, I reminded myself. I didn't want to be—hell, whenever I got nervous or hopped up on adrenaline, I'd always had a smart mouth, and this situation was only making that worse. My life was over, I was almost certainly a wanted man, and some dickhead had kidnapped me…my instinctual reaction to all of this was to act the idiot, then try to get loose. But Tommy…they knew about Tommy!

I stared out at the falling snow again and tried to make sense of everything that was happening. I was in their hands, but every time I opened my mouth, I was making things worse. I recognized what I was doing: putting a "big man" front on for everyone, acting like I wasn't scared. Inside, I was completely terrified, but if I let them know that, they'd use it against me.

The only weapons I had at the minute were the facts that they wanted me alive for some kind of job, and I was unpredictable.

Well, I'd make damn sure to keep that up.

After twenty minutes or so in the car, we finally began to slow. My ears finally popped from the altitude and speed we'd been going, and then a building came into view. It was a bit weird, part alpine ski resort, part gothic castle, and all evil overlord's secret lair.

I grimaced when we came to a stop, and I was half-dragged, half-led out of the back by Grumpy. There were armed guards all over the place. I saw maybe a dozen in a few minutes, all standing at attention as we walked in, watching me, rifles at the ready.

They led me through carpeted hallways, past enormous paintings and marble busts, all of which seemed to show the same man. He was huge and somehow wrong-looking, heavily built, with either really freaky hair or a terrible wig.

Every portrait looked different; here, there was a hint of scales on his skin, there, his eyes were different, the next he had claws…even his hair made me think of the governor from the "Pirates" series of movies, all rolling curls and powder. The only constant beyond the face was the expression on it. Every painting, without exception, made it clear that he looked down on anyone that saw him. Prick.

After three sets of stairs and a dozen rooms later, I was finally told to take a seat in an ornate chair near to the fire. I sat quietly, the events of the last day or so catching up to me. As much as I wanted to keep up the cocky bravado, I was just too tired.

Gold frames on the paintings, deep carpets, and marble seemed to make up the majority of the room. It fairly reeked of wealth and power.

"So, you said…" I started to ask the captain when he snapped at me to be quiet, and a sound from next door drew my attention. The room had two doors, the one we'd entered through from the hallway, and the second, which opened suddenly.

A tall guy wearing a full penguin suit stepped through and nodded to the guard first, then looked at me.

"The Baron Sanguis will see you now. Come quickly." With that, he turned around and marched back into the previous room. The guards grabbed my arm and hauled me to my feet before I could come up with a sarcastic response.

"Remember what I said, kid. Keep it buttoned," the guard captain muttered as they set me on my feet and gave me a rough shove to get me started. I walked through into the next room. It was larger than I'd have thought at first, maybe twenty meters long and ten across. A huge dining table took up most of the room, with a fireplace on one wall filling the space with flickering light and moving shadows.

Once the door behind me closed, the room returned to an eerie gloom, lit only by the firelight and a few flickering candles. I looked around, seeing nobody, but by the fire were two chairs, one regular and the other massive. They were turned away from me, but a hand appeared and gestured lazily toward the smaller chair.

I hobbled forward cautiously, circling the smaller chair and taking my time to look the Baron over as I sat down, before promptly being chained to locking points on the damn chair.

Even sitting, he towered over me, easily over seven feet tall, heavily muscled, with a beer gut that his tailored clothes struggled to contain.

His hair was thick and white, curls falling down to surround the face, and his eyes...his eyes were *wrong.* The hair was obviously a wig, and the size was weird, but his eyes didn't belong on anything human. The pupils were vertical slits, like a crocodile's, golden with streaks of silver through them. The whites of his eyes were a dark, blood-red hue that reflected the firelight.

Even as I hunched back from him in the chair, my eyes roamed over him, spotting the other differences. His skin was scaled like a lizard's, his fingers were longer than normal and tipped with black talons, and his teeth were pointed and sharp like a predator's. Combined with his eyes and size, I knew straight away he wasn't human. It wasn't just a costume or something; no, this was some kind of alien. That was the only possibility. I just hoped he wasn't going to kill me and eat me. Scratch that, I hoped he wasn't going to shag me first, then kill and eat me. Or shag me at all. *Please, god, don't let him want to shag me.*

"So. You're Jack," he said, sitting back and holding his hand out to the side. Before I could do more than wonder about the mannerism, a short, pretty Latino girl darted in and slipped a crystal glass into his hand. Amber liquid swirled, and ice clinked as he took a swig.

I had flinched, hearing a surprisingly human voice come from the creature, and a little of the terror faded, replaced with growing curiosity.

"Aye, I'm Jack. Who're you, then?" I asked, despite myself. I felt a little fear worm itself into my heart, and ruthlessly squashed it down. The man looked like a nightmare given form and sounded like Boris bloody Johnson.

Despite that, he held the power here, and I didn't doubt I'd regret crossing him. *Keep it cool, dude. Just see what he wants, find out about Tommy, and get the fuck outta Dodge...*

We stared at each other for a long second before someone moved between us. Before I could do anything, a fist slammed into my stomach, doubling me over in pain. I groaned and looked at the captain as he bowed to the Baron and stepped back.

"Prick!" I wheezed out, even as he glared at me.

"Humph! Right then, we will start this again. Johannes has told you of my offer?" the Baron asked, sitting back and staring at me. I took a deep breath and forced myself to straighten up and reply.

"You mean Daphne?" I asked, forcing out a breath and glaring at him. "All I got was that you had a job offer for me and you knew something about Tommy."

"Daphne?" he asked, looking to the captain, who cleared his throat and responded quickly.

"Mr. Johannes, sir. Jack and he didn't get on well, and Jack decided to rename him Daphne."

The Baron looked back at me and snickered, a cruel smile lifting the corners of his mouth as he gestured at me.

"I'd imagine that went down well. I like it. It can be his new name; should teach him some humility. Now, hit the boy again."

The second punch to my gut nearly knocked the chair over backwards, and my host called out, "Again."

I got another punch, this time to my face, breaking my nose, then another, and another, in response to called-out orders.

When he finally stepped back, I was on the floor, the chair tipped over long since. I was curled into a ball with what felt like a lot of broken ribs. The skin around my hand and ankle restraints were bleeding and raw from yanking at them.

Hands grabbed me and set my chair back upright before the Baron again. He gave me a few seconds to catch my breath and then spoke.

"I like your choice of name. It suits him. However, know your place. He, like you, is my property, and property doesn't name itself or others." The voice was light this time as he played with his glass, uncaring about my response and pain.

"I have chosen you to carry out a series of tasks for me, Jack. Your brother was employed to do the same and seems to have failed. As such, I require you to take on his contract. You will be paid handsomely for it and will have a great deal of expensive training before you represent me at the arena.

"Should you survive, you will be sent to do a small job, including recovering and claiming some few artifacts and carrying out a small task. If you do this well, you'll be rewarded. Fail, and you die. Fail me embarrassingly, and I'll make sure everyone you ever so much as smiled at is slaughtered and their corpses defiled. Are we clear?"

I glared at him, but before I could get a response out, I saw the captain's face. He'd moved to stand behind and to one side of the Baron. He shook his head slightly, his face white and strained. My immediate reaction was to tell them all to fuck right off, but I knew where that'd get me.

I needed to find Tommy, and they'd promised me that at least. I huffed out a breath and forced down my anger and the little worm of fear.

I grunted. "Aye, we're clear. I'll do it."

"Excellent. Now then, a little bit more to tell you, and I can finally get on with more important matters. You've already taken up more time than I wanted to devote to this. You will be spending the next few months training. You will learn the truth about your bloodline and your abilities, then we will see if you have what it takes to take your place in society.

"You are descended from me and my kind, Jack. As such, you have certain…gifts…that make you useful to me. Not least is the fact that your genetic code will be able to survive crossing through the Great Portal." He looked at me again and snorted in disgust. "It's obvious that this is beyond you. We will discuss things when you have had a chance to settle certain realities into your simian brain."

He threw back his drink and got to his feet, stomping back through the doors into the room beyond and casually called back to the guard captain that had brought me in.

"Take him to his room and give him some background so he understands his place, then beat him senseless so he knows just how valuable that makes him to me."

With that, his personal guards followed him, and the door closed, leaving the two of us in the room looking at each other.

"You're a right fucking idiot, Jack, you know that?" the captain said, walking over unchaining me and offering me his hand to help me up.

I slapped it aside and forced myself to my feet unsteadily, weaving a little with the pain.

"Suit yourself. Come on. I'll take you to your room and tell you what I can. Then, well, you earned it yourself."

I limped out into the hallway behind him, fantasizing about beating him to death, until I saw the two guards that waited outside. They followed us down the halls to a separate wing of the building in silence.

When I was finally led into a room, I was halfway between fury and tears of frustration and pain, due largely to what felt like broken ribs grating against each other with every step. I was used to a little pain, and my dreams produced significantly more than I'd received back there, but not being able to do anything except take it…well, that sat badly with me. I slumped into a chair, hissing in pain and the captain walked over to me, offering me a glass of water before pouring himself a drink.

The room he'd taken me to was small, but well-furnished, with a table, chairs, and refreshments. Another door on the far side presumably led into the suite, and faint voices and splashing sounded out as someone ran a tap.

"Jack! Focus, man. Jesus. You're just like fucking Tommy," he said, dropping into a chair opposite me and sipping. I raised my glass hesitantly to my lips and drew back in pain as the cool liquid poured over a split in my lip that I didn't even remember getting. I tasted it then took a large gulp, feeling the burn as it went down my throat, then looked at the man who'd just poured us both a highball full of vodka, straight.

"Who are you, who and what the fuck is the Baron, what the fuck just happened, and where's Tommy?" I growled at him.

"Right. Okay, let's start at the beginning, I guess. Some of this you'll believe, some you won't. Hell, maybe you will. I'm getting too old for this shit," he muttered, wiping a hand across his eyes tiredly before sitting up straighter. "I'm a captain in the Baron's Guard. The name's Adrian West, but you can just call me West. I've worked for him for the last twenty years, and you're the fourth I've seen recruited. Tommy was before you—that's how I know him. I'm gonna tell you a load of stuff now, so do us both a favor and hold your questions 'til the end, okay?"

I nodded at him, taking another swig, and he gave a tired grin.

He gave a tired grin. "Good lad. Okay, first things first. The Baron doesn't take any shit; when he says you're a dead man, he means it. If he offers to have everyone you know murdered and their corpses defiled, he means that too. As one of the men who'd have to do the actual deed, please keep your mouth shut around him from now on. I've got enough nightmares waking my wife up already. Secondly, the Baron is old and…sort of human. And I mean *old*. As near as we can tell—that's the other guards and I—he's over a thousand years old, easily, and he's not the only one. You ever hear of the Illuminati?"

"Aye, some conspiracy shit," I muttered.

"Yeah, well, some of it's made up, and some of it's real. Turns out, there's a whole gang of them. Nobles from the UnderVerse that ended up stuck here, some Cataclysm in their home realm that they all fled. Now they want to go back; issue is, it takes a fuck-load of mana to open a portal to there. Our world is shit for magic, and they all have to work together to send just one person through." He sighed and shook his head in irritation before going on.

"Seriously, Jack, this shit never gets any easier to explain. Once someone is on the other side, they can go to the 'Great Portal' on that side. It can make a connection to this realm easily, powered from there, and then it'll be stable enough for the nobility to return through. None of them want another to be the one to open the portal, as whoever has control of it has control of them, so they fight it out before they open it each time. Twelve champions get put forward, and all of them have to be 'blooded.' That means you must have both killed *and* you have to have an extremely specific genome. You, my boy, are related to the Baron somehow."

"Nah, man. Look, we didn't know our Da, but he's not gonna be a prick like the Baron. No way."

"Jack, sorry, man, but it's true. They took some blood at the hospital, and again on the flight over to make sure. You're definitely related. More importantly, it means that both you and Tommy are capable of being trained using their methods, and of using the portal.

"Tommy went through four and a half years ago, and now that it's getting close to the tournament again, you'll be trained and given a chance to do the same. That's the best I can tell you."

"Trained to do what? What the fuck is the tournament?" I asked, noting the way he'd skated around it.

"Ah, well, there's no easy way to put this, so…fuck it, I'll just say it. It's a deathmatch. Twelve people go in, one-on-one, and kill each other. The final round is three of you, all in a free-for-all. No rules beyond the weapons, no holds barred."

"Fuck off."

"Jack…"

"No, seriously, fuck right off. Nobody does that kinda shit anymore, not since the Romans!"

"I wish. Unfortunately, Jack, it's very much alive and kicking in this arena. Only difference is, it's not a colosseum anymore. The rich don't like the poor watching nobles bleed; gives them the wrong idea. It is very much a private affair, with the nobles all feasting and placing bets. Gives you a good idea of the kind of assholes they are, doesn't it?"

"Yeah, almost as bad as the kind of assholes that'd murder on another's orders and 'defile' their bodies!" I shot back, seeing him flinch.

"Yeah, well, it's not a choice. It's a geas."

"What, like in Canada? A fucking cobra chicken?"

"No, you idiot, not a Canadian goose, a geas. It's an old word. When you work for the Baron, you swear the geas. It's a magically enforced oath. We get paid well, but once you take the oath, you have zero choice. He says 'kill,' you kill; 'dance,' you dance. You understand?"

"Bullshit."

"Believe what you want, Jack. Just understand this: if he tells us to kill you, or anyone else, we will. We won't like it, but that's the way it is. Anyway, come six months' time, you're going into the tournament.

"How you do is up to you. You'll be given training, weapons, and, if you've got the aptitude, magic. It's up to you what you do with that training. You can toss it off, and we'll drag you to each session. You'll be beaten for not behaving, and maybe others will, too, or they'll be executed as examples.

"Then you'll go into the arena and get slaughtered like the little bitch you are. Or you can embrace it. Learn from some of the best in the world, survive the tournament, and get sent to Tommy. You pick, mate, 'cause I guarantee you the people you'll face in the arena won't hesitate to gut you."

I looked at him, and he stared back as I tried to make my way through all this bullshit mentally. What I came up with at the end was that I had two choices. People who were heavily armed and not averse to giving beatings had kidnapped me, and I could either go along with it for now or try to escape. They knew something about Tommy, though, so escape was out.

"All right, color me fucking interested, then!" I said with a wide, obviously fake smile. "I can't wait to get to fuckin' Narnia!"

"It's not Narnia, you prick, it's the UnderVerse. It's a realm that exists alongside our own, as it was explained to me. Think about all the mental shit people come up with: magic, vampires, goblins, and the weird nightmares that came out of Lovecraft's mind. All of it, and I mean *all*, is influenced by that place. There, the worst of your nightmares are real, not just in your head."

"And they want to fucking go there? And you're calling me crazy!" I huffed, leaning back and shaking my head in disbelief.

"Aye, well, it's also the home of all magic. All the good shit from the fantasy books is real there, too. Elves, dragons, flying cities, the fucking lot. Look, I know you don't believe me, and I can't say I blame you, but next week, you get to learn the same way Tom did. You get your Pearl."

"You're nice enough, and all that, but I ain't letting you give me a pearl necklace, if you know what I mean…"

"Shut the fuck up, Jack. Seriously, you're worse than Tommy was, and he came close to being murdered weekly. The Pearl is a device, part-magic, part-nanotech type of shit. You'll be given yours soon, then the world will change. For you, at least."

"What's this Pearl thing, then?" I asked.

"Fucked if I know," he responded. "It's some blend of nanotech and magic; you not listening the first time around? As to how it works, it's not wasted on the

51

likes of me. From what Tommy said, it's fucking painful when it joins with you, but makes training easier.

"You heal faster, plus it allows access to your magic. Last of all, it gave him some kind of magic heads-up display. Said he could adjust it, make it show him things he missed, and tell him details. Best and weirdest thing is leveling, though. Somehow—again, don't ask me 'cause I don't fucking know how—it absorbs experience from all you do. Every fight, every skill, everything, and it converts it into an ability to level up. Tom was level five when he went through to the arena and fought in the tournament. Faced guys that moved like greased lightning, and he still won. When he came out, he was level six."

"I watched when he dumped all his points into Strength. His muscles doubled in size; the man would have made Schwarzenegger crap himself. I've seen nothing like it."

"Leveling up, like in a game, you mean?"

"Aye, like in some kind of game. I played D&D as a bairn–don't look at me like that, you prick–I played as a bairn, and it reminded me of that. I'd get one myself, if I could," he said, shaking his head and staring off into the distance.

"Why?" I asked, nonplussed.

"Why? *Why*? Fuck, man, have you not listened? Tom said you were the bright one. It makes you practically immortal, able to do magic, and level up? All that, in exchange for a little pain?"

"Huh, fair point," I conceded.

"Well, like it or lump it, you'll be getting yours soon. Up to you how this next bit goes, though. The Baron said I was to arrange for you to get it once I'd filled you in some. You want to be a big boy and get it by choice, maybe earn a little respect from your guards, or you want to be tasered and chained down so they can insert it while you're drooling? The Baron says it's happening, so it's happening. Your choice is how to face it."

"You're a right little ray of sunshine, aren't you?" I muttered, earning a grin in return.

"Aye, lad, medicine does you no good if it doesn't taste bad! What's it gonna be?"

"I'll take it standing up," I said, climbing to my feet again and grinning back at the guard as I did so, despite my own misgivings.

"Good man. Right, best to get this bit over with, and then I'll let the girls take care of you. Sorry, but you had this coming."

"Wha—" I started to say, only to find his fist hammering into my face. I staggered to the side, getting a knee to the guts that doubled me over before I could respond. An elbow to the back of the head dropped me hard. I managed a few swings and kicks, but he beat me with embarrassing ease, kicking me in the stomach before finally dropping down and punching me in the face again, and I blacked out.

I came to a few minutes later. West was standing over me, an empty jug in hand, as I spluttered and tried to make sense of what had just happened. I glanced around, seeing the water he'd poured over my head mingling with my blood on the marble floor where I lay.

"What'd you do that for, you dick?" I mumbled, checking my teeth with my tongue, slowly rolling onto my back as pain radiated through my body. I wanted to get up and kick his ass, but as he'd made clear, I had no chance.

"The Baron ordered it, remember? Be thankful he didn't think to rescind your privileges as well. Now that my job is done for today, I'll go and leave you to—"

"Wait! One more question!" I whispered, unable to just let it go, despite the fact I really didn't want to hear the answer. I closed my eyes and let it out.

"Go on, lad," he said, cracking his knuckles as he regarded me curiously.

"The Baron. You say he's human, sort of, and I'm related to him. Well, what the fuck is he? I've not got scales and all that!"

"Ah, well, yeah, that's a fair question, I suppose, but that's one the Baron will have to answer. I don't get it myself. That's down to the Pearl, and that's all I know. Sorry."

With that, he walked to the second door and knocked once before turning and walking back toward me. The second door opened, and two women came in. They exchanged a sad look upon sighting all the blood, but they bobbed polite curtseys to me as West pulled me to my feet. He told me to try to get some rest, then winked and walked off.

The pair moved closer. The door behind me clicked as it closed, the sound of locks sliding home, and the girls curtseyed again, as one.

They were both stunning, one tall and blonde, the other shorter and dark haired, dressed in simple but clearly expensive maids' uniforms. I opened my mouth to speak, mystified and unsure of what to say. The blonde beat me to it, leading me by the hand to the next room, which held the tub that I had heard them filling earlier.

They shook their heads when I tried to speak through thickening lips, explaining that they were there to help me relax, and there was no need for words, not yet.

I was dumbfounded, but in the whirl of everything, meeting a living monster like the Baron, losing my girl and my entire life back home, and finding out I was to be put in an arena to fight to the death...

Well.

Two stunning girls that stripped me off, tended to my wounds and bathed me, hinting that they were happy to do more? It was just one more bit of mad shit on top of the rest.

I ignored their offers, despite a slight twitch that suggested that I might as well enjoy myself. I just wasn't in the mood, really, and I had no idea why these girls would do this. The bathing and wounds I could understand, the hints about their clothes getting wet and maybe hanging them up somewhere to dry, and that the bed was big enough for three, or more even?

No. Something was going on, and I wasn't giving in to the little head until I understood what the hell it was.

CHAPTER FIVE

T he next morning, I was awakened by two new girls who were dressed in identical uniforms as the girls from last night, and they, too, were smiling and happy. They brought me breakfast, a thick porridge and fruit, and a set of workout clothes before offering to help me in any way I wished. I'd barely woken up, not really, and grinned at them without thinking, opening my mouth to make a comment, then snapping it shut as the pretty redhead smiled in return and spoke up quickly.

"My lord, you have training with the arms masters this morning. I suggest that you prepare quickly, in order to avoid any repercussions for tardiness. We will, of course, be here to meet your needs when you return."

I just stared at them. Again, the phrasing, the look in their eyes. I flirted automatically, but this was more than flirting unthinkingly. I nearly came out and asked them outright, but at the last minute, I shook my head, forcing myself to smile and thank them instead.

I wasn't sure, but I thought I saw a little unhappiness that I'd left it at that, and I forced that thought away.

"Get over yourself, Jack," I muttered to myself as they left the room. "They're got far better taste than to have anything to do with the likes of you, not to mention if they did? Something's wrong."

They seemed so happy and willing to do literally anything I asked, but their behavior was just…off. I ate breakfast and dressed quickly. When I opened the door, a new pair of guards stood waiting, and they led me along the corridors to a gym, pausing outside and taking up station. I shrugged and marched in.

It looked much like any gym I'd ever been in, a collection of shiny machines and mirrors mostly, but on one side was a door that led through to a second room. The walls in that space were covered in weapons, and three men stood inside, talking. Two looked more average, fit and lean, but nothing special. The third, however, was a mountain of a man. He stood easily seven feet tall, and maybe the same across the shoulders. He looked like the kind of guy that'd kick sand on a heavyweight world champion when he was sunbathing and get away with it. Deep black skin contrasted sharply with the whitest teeth I'd ever seen.

A total lack of any body hair on his upper half and quite possibly the smallest shorts I'd ever seen on a grown man somehow served to make him even more intimidating.

He strode over to me as I opened the door and stepped inside, unsure of where I should be, while the other two walked away to look at the weapons. He folded his arms and looked me up and down, grunting in disgust at what he saw. One thick finger shot out and prodded me in the belly, causing my fat to ripple.

"Ouch!" I said, slapping his hand away. Or at least, I tried to. It felt more like I had backhanded a brick wall. There had been no movement on the part of the offending digit, and plenty on the part of my hand.

"You are fat. Weak, lazy, and stupid. This will change, or you will die," he said, his voice a low rumble. His African accent was so heavy, I barely understood him.

"Okay, so I'm a little outta shape. Seriously, dude, it's not me we need to talk about. I hate to break it to you, but some fucker stole your pants and left his kid's shorts in their place." My response was instinctive, shit talking as I always did, but the look he gave me made me regret it.

"Little man with a big mouth. I have seen many of you. We will see what it takes to break you now, yes?" He gestured toward the open area, and we took up position in the center, about ten feet from each other, facing in.

We started off with a light warmup: stretches, lunges, and running on the spot. I was out of breath by the end of the five minutes, but that was all right. I was unfit and had expected nothing else. After the basics, however, rather than taking a break, it got faster.

One minute of burpees, thirty-second rest, a minute of sit-ups, thirty second rest. It went on that way through sets of weights, the rowing machine, the exercise bike, fast rope, squats…the list seemed endless. The worst part was that he did the exercises with me, while lifting weights I couldn't move, and telling me I was lifting the girls' weights. He wasn't even sweating, while I could barely stand. We did ten different exercises before he let me collapse to the ground for a one-minute break. My ass had barely hit the ground when he let me know that there were five more rounds of this, then the "warm-up" was over, and we would start to exercise properly. I couldn't spare the air to tell him to kill me now, but I damn well tried to convey it with my eyes.

"Pathetic!" He sneered, looking down at me. "You just lost an hour of your evening rest. I will set you a regime to follow, to try to cure you of your failures, and I will speak to the kitchens. From now on, you will be eating like a man should. Now, up, worm! Begin again!"

When I didn't move quickly enough, he kicked my arm out from under me, then kicked my stomach hard enough to make me lose my breakfast. His disgust as he made me clean up the mess only made me feel worse. I struggled through two more hours with him before I was finally allowed to leave.

I collapsed into the shower in my room; my guards had practically carried me there. I was given ten minutes to clean up, with no sign of the girls this time. I luxuriated in the feel of the powerful shower washing the sweat away. Next was a two-hour session of etiquette.

The tutor seemed to hold me in almost as much contempt as the Baron had, barely lowering himself to acknowledge my responses. By the time the lesson concluded, it was lunchtime. I was hurried off from the tutor, ignoring his glare as I left. I was already ready for bed, never mind food and an afternoon yet to come.

Lunch was served in the staff barracks canteen. Even here, the unmistakable signs of wealth were everywhere. The Baron didn't lower himself to come here, judging from the good cheer and occasional horseplay I observed. West joined me, taking the piss out of my crippled state. He told me to cheer up and that I was getting "eased into training gently."

I told him to go suck a bucket of cocks and looked down at the "drink" I'd been given alongside my water. It was thick, almost sludgy, full of gritty mush, and it honestly tasted like ass. At least, I decided it tasted like ass, or perhaps as though someone had already eaten it once.

The "meal" consisted of a liter of water, this ass-sludge, two plain chicken breasts, a ten-egg omelet, and a load of kale.

"What the hell is this rubbish?" I asked West, prodding at the leafy greens, and he laughed, tucking into his enchiladas.

"Training food, mate! Builds muscles and all that; plus, all the protein makes your muscles heal faster. I heard you'd had a meal plan set. Seems they expect to get your belly gone and looking like a real man in no time!"

"I hate you all," I muttered, forcing myself to ignore the real food all around me as I chewed down the rough equivalent of half a tree in kale.

After lunch was swimming for an hour with a short German woman shouting at me to go faster, harder. Telling her she sounded like my ex didn't go down well and earned me an extra ten lengths after I'd already almost drowned from exhaustion.

Lastly, I was taken to a dojo and beaten soundly by one trainer after another for three hours more. In the end, the "training" was far worse than Army boot camp had been.

The only consolation was that the last hour of training was slowly moving through the forms they'd taught me, giving me an hour-long cooldown, which left me surprisingly refreshed.

When I finally dragged myself back to my room, I could barely stand. The pair of maids from the night before were waiting for me, and this time they made it clear that the hints last night weren't just flirting. I was stripped naked and manhandled into a massage bed.

I lay there facedown, staring at the floor, as hands skillfully worked my back, my shoulders, and more. I closed my eyes seconds after they started, enjoying it as they slowly working lower, until…

My eyes shot open as a hand slid up between my legs to grip and massage me, and I saw what I'd missed before. When the girls had started, they'd been dressed in their crisp outfits. Now said outfits were clearly and blatantly folded up and set on the floor under the table where I couldn't help but see them.

I lifted my head, rolling to the side, finding the pair of them were naked! I opened my mouth, confused, concerned and…the blonde put her hand over my lips, smiling and speaking in a low voice as her companion continued to "massage" me.

"We're here to see to your every need. No, we're not required to do this, and yes, we want to. I could explain further, but wouldn't you rather be doing something else right now?"

I opened my mouth again, about to complain, or something…I didn't know what. After all, these girls, yes, I wanted them. Of course I did; I was male, straight, and alive. I desperately wanted them both. The stunning brunette worked me, smiling up at me and making it seriously hard to concentrate on anything except how good that felt, but…

"Life is all about choices. You've had some of yours taken away, but not all. You can still enjoy your time here," the blonde said, before leaning in and kissing me, her hot lips on mine as the brunette's hot lips closed on me as well.

I stopped complaining or even thinking at that point.

This became the way of my life. The morning and evening massages from the girls were painful, but starting and ending the day with them made a hell of a difference. The diet, while awful-tasting, made a visible difference in just a few days. After the first week, I hated the world and wanted to die, despite the ladies that came to me.

In the second week, my etiquette and behavior lessons were replaced with woodland survival skills and first aid. The insane workouts stayed the same, though. The third week was filled with stranger studies: tracking, hunting, and stealth. These lessons, I took to with gusto, as I discovered that I loved this kind of training.

When the fourth week came, and I began to be trained in weapons, I was in my element. I took to the sword, mace, spear, and axe training with a joy I'd never known before. Even the basics of archery were covered, as I tried to forget the realities of my new life. I imagined it was like the army, where once you signed up, you were stuck obeying until your time was up. I forced myself to think of the trainers and guards as fellow soldiers and the maids as regular girls.

I got to know them better, the four girls who "worked" in my rooms. Talking sometimes long into the night with them, finding that they, like West, were forced to serve here in the citadel by a geas. That well and truly freaked me out at first, but the sex? It *wasn't* part of the job.

Well, it sort of was; they were all high-end hookers originally, hired for their skills, then retrained to be perfect maids. They were assured that sex was most definitely not part of the deal, but that if they wanted to, well, go for it.

The reasons they were so enthusiastic about it, and so wanton and willing, were simple.

First, this whole "trip to the UnderVerse" thing was real, or at least they believed it was. They also knew that there were others like the Baron, massively powerful immortals, and some few of them had "favorites" among the girls. Much like the way Hef had lived with his battalion of playmates, these immortals did. The thing the girls were working towards was basically "catching" an immortal's eye. Apparently, they were insanely rich, powerful, and were known to give gifts like Fabergé eggs when they were pleased.

They damn well knew I was going to be "upgraded" then banished through the portal. If I managed to do the job, though? I'd be massively rich, powerful, and practically worshiped, then I'd be coming back. They were looking for a part of that, as a wife, concubine, mistress, whatever.

It was cold-blooded, but they were happy with it. In their defense, they only had to occasionally clean a room, instead of the way they used to have to work round the clock.

Secondly, and this made me feel a whole lot better about things; they all loved sex. It was perfectly natural and healthy, after all. Or so Marie assured me, making me groan as she reached down and took me in her hand before asking if I wanted her to stop and go away.

Now that I'd been assured that they were fucking me for the most mercenary of reasons, both because they wanted to and were hoping one day I'd be rich, I was totally fine with it. Admittedly, if it'd been all about the possible future money, hell, I'd probably have been fine with it as well—I was a shallow bastard—and when a beautiful woman offered a deal like that? Yeah.

As soon as I knew that they weren't forced into it, and that they actively wanted to fool around, I threw myself into it with reckless abandon, even more so than my weapons training, truth be known.

In my training, I'd used dozens of weapons, and while swords and maces and so on were all good, the weapon I truly grew to love was the naginata. It was essentially a polearm variant with a sword blade, it could be used as a staff, a spear, a lance, and most of all, it was an insanely dangerous sword with a really long handle. I didn't care about the winces my arms masters gave me. I just loved that it was a giant murder stick.

After another week, an hour a day of swimming was changed to two hours of riding and animal care. I rode across wide fields, through snowy forests teeming with game and explored valleys near the Baron's citadel. Guards encircled me at all times, keeping me firmly in sight.

But as time passed, I cared less and less about them. I asked constantly about Tommy, always receiving the same answers: that he went through this same training, won his fights, and went through the portal. That was all they could—or would—tell me.

Soon my training was expanded to include "magical theory," and when I looked obviously unimpressed at the nature of the lesson, my trainer, an ancient Chinese woman, proceeded to summon a flame to her hand with only a few muttered words and a gesture. I sat there, stunned, as I watched the flame in her hand.

"Still, you do not believe?" she said, clearly displeased. "You think this a mere illusion?"

Before I could move, the flames spread across her hand like a glove, and she grabbed my hand in hers. I screamed in agony, my skin melting, the fat beneath crisping and popping in the unnatural heat. I tried to yank my hand free, only to find that the guards on either side of me had stepped forward, and they restrained me as she burned my hand to the bone.

I almost passed out from the pain, screaming in agony and feeling the world swimming out of focus, before a cooling sensation flowed through me. It concentrated in my injured hand and began to itch like crazy, the pain rapidly disappearing as new skin, muscles, and tendons regrew themselves.

I snatched my hand from her grasp, staring at it in wonder. Even the scar from where I'd crashed my first stolen bike as a kid was gone.

"What the hell!" I whispered, gawking at my hand. The guards released me and backed away, even as Xiao sat down heavily behind her desk, panting with the exertion of two spells cast so close together.

"You believe…me now?" she asked, trying to catch her breath.

"Yes, fuck yes! How the hell did you do that?" I demanded.

"Three things, boy. The Will, the Word, and the Motion. If your Will is strong enough, you can force the ambient mana to assume the form you wish. Then, you give it life through the Word, directing the formation. Finally, you give it the Motion. The more complex the spell, the greater the Motion required, although all three obviously increase in effort and complexity as you cast more and more advanced spells."

"Will and Word are reasonably clear, but the Motion?"

"Like this, fool!" She started to gesture with one hand, but when nothing happened after a few seconds, I smirked at her with one raised eyebrow.

"Look, there's nothing to be ashamed of. I hear performance anxiety takes a toll as you get older. Maybe you should see a therapist, get some Viagra…"

"Fool! I am not casting! I am demonstrating the gestures for a simple Firebolt spell! I will not cast again until my mana recovers."

"Sure, sure, you weren't even trying. I totally believe you. And so do they. Right, guys?" I said, looking over my shoulder at the guards.

"Mana is extremely limited here, *laowai*! It will take me days to recover the mana for a simple spell and months for a more complex one. Why do you think the Baron and his fellow nobles only cast the great spells once every five years? The amount of mana required to cast it is truly awe-inspiring. Even then, with all the Great Houses contributing, only a single person can slip through to the other side. The power needed to breach the walls of reality is far beyond anything your feeble mind can comprehend!"

"Okay, so color me impressed," I said, trying to downplay just how impressed I actually was. "If magic is real, and I'm gonna be chucked through a portal to the other side soon, how about you tell me a little more about what I'm expected to do once I'm there? I'm getting training in all sorts, but swords and shields, as much fun as they are, won't last long against guns. Why not send me through with an assault rifle and a fuck ton of ammo?"

"The Great Portal is extremely delicate. Explosives could be set off by the mana density near it alone, and what is ammunition but tiny explosives? You want that strapped to you as you jump between worlds?"

"Okay, point taken. What about when I'm there, then? Is there no way to, I don't know, put them in a lead box so that they survive the jump?" I asked cautiously.

"No! Think about it! The amount of lead shielding needed to surround all the ammunition would mean you would carry nothing but boxes, and you would be unarmed after a few short battles. No guns! The Baron has been most specific in the past."

"Yeah, but 'in the past' means that maybe he'll have changed his mind…"

"No! Now leave it. There is no point to this, and I grow weary of you. You will be delivered to a location that was previously used for portals in the UnderVerse. Your portal will latch onto the weakened area of spacetime that was left behind.

"Once there, you must travel to the capital, use the Baron's Glyph to open the Great Portal from that side, and the first step will be done. A portal opened from the UnderVerse will be self-powering and far more stable. The Baron will lead us across, and we will finally be able to live in the realm we were meant to, with the *power* we deserve!"

The more she spoke to me, the more I really didn't want these dicks getting back there. I nodded to her and listened as she ranted on about the life she deserved and the power that we would all wield. When the lesson finally ended, I was taken back to the training area where West waited for me.

"Hey, you ready for round two?" he asked, gesturing toward a clearly marked ring. I grinned savagely and climbed in, fully intending to teach the bastard a lesson.

There was a lesson taught, and it was violent. Unsurprisingly, it was West who walked out of the ring while I lay there in a puddle of blood. I had found during these weeks of training that whatever other genetics I had, one definite plus was that my healing was faster than anyone seemed to expect. Wounds and damage that they expected to take days to heal repaired themselves in hours. It was scant comfort as I crawled out of the ring, and the big Nigerian told me with disgust that we would be increasing our training regime tomorrow.

I made it back to my room with the help of my guards again and the girls took care of me, and my...needs...but oh so gently. I was incapable of anything more energetic.

The following morning, I was rescued from a particularly painful workout session by West.

"Well, lad, the Baron's decided it's time for your Pearl. You got your big boy pants on, or should we drag you kicking and screaming?" He winked at me as he said it, and I grinned despite myself. He was an asshole, a highly trained soldier that worked for the Baron, but I couldn't help but like the guy. He'd obviously gotten on well with Tommy and had transferred that good feeling to me.

"Aye, you old bastard, I'm ready," I said, putting the weights back on the rack and wiping myself down with a towel. The Nigerian refused to give me so much as his name, barely speaking at all beyond telling me "More!" whenever I collapsed in exhaustion, but I was starting to like him, despite my best efforts.

I'd noticed the way that he pushed and pushed, but only up to the limit. I was starting to realize that unlike anyone else I'd ever worked out with, he seriously knew his shit and was pushing me right up to the line of my capabilities but stopping before I injured myself beyond recovery. It was ridiculous, and his methods were horrifically painful, but...I was seeing gains like I'd never believed were possible before now, and leaving his training area a mess just smacked of disrespect to me.

Plus, if Xiao could summon fire like that, maybe the geas was real. As such, there was no need for me to be an asshole all the time.

With that, he gestured toward the door, and we both went out into the hall. West led me down a couple of corridors and into the medical section of the Baron's castle or citadel or whatever it was classed as. He waited until the corridor was clear at either end and paused, turning to shoot me a serious look.

"Listen, before we go in there, you need to know something, and we've got no time. The Baron seems to feel you still need to learn your place, and he's ordered me to report any slights towards him that you might show. No! Don't say anything!" He jabbed me in the chest with a finger and went on. "He's been asking which of the maids you prefer, if any. When I couldn't give him a favorite, he said that they can all be disciplined the next time you fail, and maybe that'll teach you respect."

I froze, thinking about the girls, feeling anger and fear rise in equal measure. "Wait...no, he wouldn't! They serve him, for fuck's sake—"

"He wouldn't think twice! He might decide to withhold their wages and give them a stern lecture; have them flogged; or hung, drawn, and quartered, depending on his mood. So, for their sake, bite your tongue around him, okay?"

With that, he spun around and started walking again. I stood for a second in shock, then hurried to catch up. My mind spun as I realized the Baron would do it all and probably worse, and he would make West do the dirty work, punishing me twice over. I had to make him believe I was loyal, for now at least. We passed down another corridor, this one decorated in black and red, with gold leaf practically dripping from the walls.

West informed me that we were approaching an area the Baron frequented, and I nodded, getting the unspoken warning. When we arrived, two doctors stood waiting, along with a handful of guards and Madame Xiao.

The crazy little magic teacher opened a vault at the back of the room while I stripped down at the doctor's insistence. They led me to a chair with restraints on the arms, legs, waist, and throat, and strapped me down, pulling each one as tight as it would go. As the last one across my throat was tightened, I found that I could barely breathe.

I lay there, repeating in my mind that it was the only way to see Tommy, I could do this, it was fine.... All the while, I had visions of the Baron coming in and starting to torture me for shits and giggles.

After what seemed like ages, Xiao finally stood over me, lifting a small, gleaming Pearl in her thickly gloved right hand. I heard a noise to my left and saw the Baron wander in, although he was mercifully quiet, keeping out of the way and seemingly content to just watch. I forced myself to not meet his eyes.

"You know what this is?" Xiao asked me in her usual clipped tones.

"Aye, I do," I whispered.

"Then you know you need it. When it begins, it will assess you, locating its primary station on your most advanced meridian. Then you will be given a choice to make.

"Depending on what it sees in you, you will be able to decide on the location of a secondary node. This will strengthen an area of your body in different ways. Each Pearl is unique, so only you can choose what is right for you. I have no doubt you will choose poorly, however, as you are a fool."

I grimaced and stared at her. When she said nothing else and realized I would not respond, she nodded.

"Once the Pearl has taken up its station, it will expand throughout your body, mapping your nerves and neural pathways, among other systems. This is where the weak usually fail and die. If you wish to live up to your potential, and indeed to live at all, then you will not surrender. You must remain conscious until the end. Are you ready?" she asked, one eyebrow raised in question.

I tried to speak. I wanted to know what the meridians were, what would happen if I passed out, and how long this would take. A hundred other questions filled my mind, but all I managed was a croak as the doctor by my head tightened my throat restraint.

"Excellent," she said, and she lowered the Pearl to my chest, releasing it and stepping away quickly. As soon as the Pearl came into contact with my skin, I felt a slight tickle. I twisted my head as far as I could, practically choking myself to see it, and saw a faint haze around it, which grew outward slowly. As the haze grew closer to my face, I saw that it was made up of thousands upon thousands of tiny strands.

So thin they made a hair seem huge in comparison, they spread out across my body, multiplying and growing thinner and thinner, until I was covered with a glistening, hazy blanket. It flowed over my tightly clamped lips, up and into my nose, over my eyes, and into my ears. I tried not to panic.

I barely managed a handful of seconds before I started to thrash. I could feel the damn things in my head!

My eyes felt gritty, as though moving them was encountering resistance, and I knew what that was. Those filaments were everywhere! They paused, suddenly drawing back, and I had a split second of relief mingled with panic. Had I failed, and was I about to be tortured to death, never to find Tommy, or was it over?

Then they struck. I thought they'd been bad before; now they were horrific. They branched down past microscopic levels, or so it seemed. They pierced me, driving into my body, cutting through cells and vessels, exploring my most intimate construction. Each strand of DNA seemed to be examined, evaluated, and found wanting.

While this was going on, I felt the Pearl moving, dragged up my chest to the hollow of my neck, upwards to my chin, and I felt my lips prized apart.

Teeth painfully locked in place, gritted against the further intrusion, were slowly broken, forced backwards until they gave way, joining the seeming rivers of blood pouring from my entire body. I felt the Pearl drag itself into the back of my throat then burrow upwards, digging its way into my brain.

It tore through cartilage and sections of bone, pushing aside and damaging sections of my brain. My mind filled with tastes and smells before losing all of them at once. I suddenly couldn't remember the taste of anything. I knew I loved food, but I had no clue what any of it tasted like anymore.

It was a stupid thing, considering what was happening to me, but it became a sign of everything that was being done, of the ultimate intrusion I was enduring. Regardless of the fact the filaments were mapping my entire structure, including my most delicate parts, the thing I screamed out loud was this:

"BACON?!"

After another indeterminate length of time, filled only with my screams and random sprays of blood, the Pearl finally stopped. My entire body had been mapped and examined minutely, small adjustments still occurring. The filaments had cut through my skin, leaving my entire body flensed. Countless tiny cuts covered my already heavily scarred body, and I couldn't understand how I was still alive. I should be dead; I'd felt bones crack, the filaments questing into every part, from exploring the marrow in my bones, to splitting cells, invading my eyeballs and altering the cones and rods found within. I'd even experienced the memorable feeling of my teeth shattering as they were explored while gritted tightly together. Now that the Pearl had finally come to rest, it seemed satisfied with what it had found. I saw only blackness before me. Then, out of nowhere, smoke seemed to appear, golden in color, and it flowed together to form words that shone in the darkness.

DO YOU ACCEPT THE BOND?

I tried to make sense of it, my mind traumatized by the agony and horror of my experience, until a snippet of memory came to me, as though from years ago. West, telling me that Tommy had endured this, and it had transformed him. It'd given him the strength to survive and to win at the tournament. I had to accept the bond. I *needed* the magic. I would *not* be beaten by something that Tommy could do.

*Yes...*I thought. As soon as I'd made that conscious decision, more text appeared.

BONDING ACCEPTED

...ASSESSING...

I felt heat flooding through my body, building up and fading, seemingly in waves that flowed outwards from the Pearl in my brain. With each pulse, I felt the damage diminishing, and sanity returned.

ASSESSMENT COMPLETE...

MULTIPLE COMPETING BLOODLINES DETECTED...

WARNING!

MULTIPLE STRENGTHS AND WEAKNESSES DETECTED.

DO YOU WISH TO PURGE AND REALIGN YOUR GENETIC CODE?

I had no clue what this thing had found, but as the words appeared and I focused on them, the desire to know more was highest in my mind, which caused the Pearl to move on without pause.

COMPETING BLOODLINES HAVE BEEN FOUND.

ANCESTRAL MATCHES ARE IDENTIFIED AS FOLLOWS:

- HOUSE SANGUIS 27%
- HOUSE GREY 19%
- HOUSE JORGU 15%
- HOUSE VERT LEK THUN 7%

REMAINING GENETIC CODE IS IDENTIFIED:

- LOCAL VARIANT HOMO SAPIENS 26%
- OTHER 6%

GREAT HOUSE GENETIC INTERMINGLING IS KNOWN TO GIVE RISE TO BOTH ENHANCED STRENGTHS AND INCREASED WEAKNESSES.

FULL POTENTIAL EFFECTS CANNOT BE CONFIRMED AT THIS STAGE.

DO YOU WISH ESTIMATES?

Fuck yes, I want to know what this shit is!

ESTIMATED STRENGTHS:

ENHANCED BONE DENSITY

Your bones are denser than average, resulting in a stronger, more damage-resistant skeleton. 5% Constitution increase.

ENHANCED MUSCLE DENSITY

Your muscles are denser than average, resulting in slightly higher strength. 5% Strength increase.

ENHANCED MUSCLE ELASTICITY

Your muscles have a greater degree of elasticity than average, resulting in slightly faster reflexes. 5% Dexterity increase.

ENHANCED HEALTH RECOVERY

You heal abnormally fast. This form of regeneration is exceedingly rare. 50% healing increase.

ESTIMATED WEAKNESSES:

GREATER BONE AND MUSCLE DENSITY

You have a particularly heavy frame, resulting in a body that is significantly slower when swimming and which requires higher levels of endurance to maintain activities. 10% Endurance decrease.

MENTAL INSTABILITY INCREASED

Anger becomes rage, attraction becomes infatuation. You are prone to bouts of rage that only a berserker would deem appropriate. 10% Self-Control decrease.

WARNING!!!

PRESENCE OF SECONDARY CONSCIOUSNESS DETECTED.

SECONDARY INHABITANT OF CORPOREAL FORM IS TENTATIVELY IDENTIFIED AS DECEASED NOBLE ANCESTOR.

BEWARE!!

SECONDARY INHABITANT CANNOT BE PURGED.

ADVISE CAUTION IN ALL DEALINGS WITH THIS BEING...

MENTAL COHESION ESTIMATED AT 23%.

THESE ARE ESTIMATES BASED ON CURRENT CAPABILITIES AND HAVE AFFECTED YOU UNTIL NOW.

PURGING THE GENETIC CODE TO INCLUDE ONLY ONE GREAT HOUSE MAY RESULT IN INCREASES OR DECREASES OF YOUR NATURAL GIFTS.

DO YOU WISH TO PROCEED?

I thought for a long moment. On one hand, I was who I'd always been. There was no telling what I'd become if I took the "purge" option. Could be stronger, could be weaker. But on the other hand, I could get something better, it was only a shame that there wasn't a way to be free of the voice.

I'd had it all my life, but I'd never known what it was or why it spoke to me. Tommy was a brawler naturally, quick to anger, quick to forgive, and never happier than when he was in the thick of it. I guess that came from our "mixed heritage" with the mercurial nature, but I'd always been slower than he was. Slower to anger, slower to trust, and more suspicious by nature. Once I grew angry, though, *he* would wake up. A little voice, a tiny murmur in the back of my mind; the voice of madness, I'd called it. I once made the mistake of speaking about it to the shrink. Said it was an aspect of my personality I'd suppressed.

It disagreed and told me in excruciating detail what we should do to the bastard who dared speak about it that way. Whenever I lost my temper, it was there, cheering me on. Looking back at it now, it'd been there a lot of late.

Ever since I'd caught Lou, and it'd come out again, I'd felt it watching, waiting, even if it didn't speak.

I considered life without it. I'd tried talking to it enough over the years, but it either didn't want to talk to me or couldn't, and the knowledge that it might be a genetic twist that perhaps might be silenced or quietened by a change, was tempting I had to admit. Even if Only to myself.

Thing was, though, it helped me sometimes. It egged me on, pushed me to be more violent and much more brutal, but it also saw things differently, showed me how to look at the world in a different light. Warned me when I was about to get into a fight. I knew when I heard it, and it was happy with what I was doing, I'd gone too far already. Mind you, other times, it could scream random words that made no sense or just sob mindlessly at the edge of my awareness.

No, I was who I was, and who knew what I could lose if I did that. Besides, the Baron was an asshole. Last thing I needed was to be more like him.

Anyway, there was no way I'd risk losing that fifty percent increase in my healing speed. I chose no after a lot of thought.

DECISION ACCEPTED

...BEGINNING PATTERN CREATION...

FIRST NODE IS ALIGNED...

CHOOSE POSITION OF SECONDARY NODE...

In my mind, an outline of my body appeared, with the pearl glowing like a star in the center of my forehead. I knew instantly, the knowledge filling my mind, that I would receive a point to distribute after every five levels, which could be used to improve a node, and five points to improve my body and mind with every level. The five points could be allocated to stats that corresponded to my characteristics: Strength to make me stronger, Wisdom to improve my memory and my mana regeneration, Perception to make me better with ranged weapons and more likely to spot things. They seemed obvious, yet a fantastic way to improve myself.

The nodes, however, were more complicated. Each meridian could hold up to ten points, and the body had meridians in the brain, heart, lungs, stomach, arms, legs, hands, and feet. I focused on my arm, curious, and the meridians appeared. They were dotted around, some close together, others further apart, but as I watched, they slowly brightened and dimmed.

Each pattern would change me in little ways. My first point was in the brain and allowed me access to my mana as well as some instinctive knowledge. If I added more there, I would gain a five percent reduction per additional point invested in the mana costs of my spells.

If I chose to increase my heart node, my health regeneration would increase. My lungs would increase my stamina, legs would increase speed, and hands would affect dexterity, but as I concentrated, I "knew" it wasn't only dexterity. Other options would be unlocked as I increased my abilities. As I grew in points, I would grow in abilities, and other greater abilities would unlock.

At a thought, the body in my mind's eye suddenly changed. Text options appeared, floating next to each Node, with the improvements listed out concisely.

Brain: PRIMARY: 1/10

    Spell Cost Reduction: 5% (Primary Bonus: 1 spell slot per point)

Eyes: 0/10 Vision Improvement

Ears: 0/10 Hearing Improvement

Mouth: 0/10 Vocal Improvement

Nose: 0/10 Tracking and Detection Improvement

Heart: 0/10 Health Regeneration

Lungs: 0/10 Stamina Regeneration

Stomach: 0/10 Required Sustenance Reduction

Legs: 0/10 Speed Increase

Feet: 0/10 Stability Increase

Arms: 0/10 Strength Increase

Hands: 0/10 Dexterity Increase

I looked them all over. The nodes were influenced both by primary and secondary placement first. My primary node was my brain. Choosing any additional secondary nodes would net me a five percent reduction in spell cost, but the fact that it was my primary node gave me a further bonus. Each point invested there would unlock another spell capacity.

For every two points I invested in my Intelligence, I would be able to memorize one spell. I wanted to go straight down the rabbit hole of my stats immediately, but I forced myself to stay on topic. I needed to understand this. If I made a mistake, my build would be ruined straight away, and I doubted there was a way to redo it.

Adding my secondary node gave me a new set of options. The meridians would be strengthened each time I invested a point into them. But as the secondary, it would be a stronger version of the usual bonus.

Head: Primary Node: Not possible to further augment.

Eyes: Visual Boost: Chance for valuable or important details will glow to your vision. This will level with the relevant skill.

Ears: Important sounds will become clearer with concentration

Nose: Scents will be stronger, aiding in tracking.

Mouth: Your voice will become 10% more likely to have a desired effect on a target, soothing, seducing, persuading as required.

Heart: You will gain an additional ten points of health for each point invested in your Constitution.

Lungs: You will gain an additional ten points of stamina for each point invested in your Endurance.

Stomach: You will gain the ability to resist poisons 25% of the time.

Legs: You will gain a boost of 10% to your speed.

Feet: You will gain a boost of 25% to your stability, reducing the chance of falling or being knocked down.

Arms: You will receive a boost of 25% to your carrying capacity.

Hands: You will develop crafting abilities at a 10% increased rate.

I stood there for a while, thinking about my usual play style, before forcing myself to accept that this wasn't a game; it was my life now. There were three choices that stood out to me: Eyes, Heart, and Hands. Extra health could be huge, literally a life-saver, and crafting was my favorite part of any game. I also loved to use my hands in my normal life. The basic crafting training I'd received at the Baron's citadel had been something I'd taken to with real pleasure. In the end, though, the real choice was easy. I needed to be able to see, and any improvement to that would be huge.

SECONDARY NODE CHOSEN...

PREPARING TO AUGMENT IN 5...4...3...2...1...

My world vanished into a sea of agony again. The pain was horrific, this time centered on my brain and eyes. As they were reconstructed to allow the Pearl better access, the needlelike writhing tentacles tore the structure of my eyes apart and rebuilt them. I lost consciousness when it finally ended, sinking into blessed oblivion. As I went, the last thing I saw was another set of smoky words appearing:

CONGRATULATIONS, ETERNAL

YOU HAVE REACHED LEVEL 1...

DREAM 2

I t happened again, the world flooding away from me as I fell, the feeling of terrible distances being covered in the blink of an eye. Then I was jerked to a stop like I'd fallen from orbit and hit the sidewalk.

I awoke suddenly, a phantom pain from the implantation still screaming through my mind as I thrashed wildly and hit something hard, inches from my face. I opened my eyes, seeing only pitch black everywhere, even as fluid raced down my throat and pulsed in my lungs in time to my frantic movements.

I panicked, all reason driven from my mind as this last change was too much to bear. I was alone in the dark, *drowning*. I pounded my fists, elbows, knees, and head off the inside of something, finding that it surrounded me on all sides. My mind screamed in panic, and all of this awoke *him*…

WhereWhatNooooNotAgainNotTheDarkAgainNoooo!

The voice inside my head roused suddenly, and a tiny, calm aspect of my mind noted that it seemed more aware, and more…*there* than normal, as though it was close by my side rather than barely at the edge of my awareness.

Between its screams and my own, I started to truly lose my mind. I thrashed around, feeling the surrounding liquid suddenly start to drain away as a faint light began to show around the edge of whatever was in front of me.

I grabbed at the suddenly visible seams and jammed my fingers in. I forced them through, feeling movement even as my index finger on my right hand lost its nail, the tip caught in a crack. I couldn't stop, jamming my fingers in further and whimpering as the nail tore loose.

I finally had enough space to get a good grip, and I desperately pushed, heaving at whatever stood between me and the light.

It held for a handful of seconds as my muscles strained and started to tear. Pain bloomed across my back, my upper arms, even my thighs as I dug deeper, forcing it to give way.

With a sudden sliding sensation and the grind of cracking stone, it finally moved, slightly at first, then with a rush. The slab was sent flying outward to impact the nearby wall with a resounding boom that echoed around the tiny chamber.

I fell forward from the box I'd been trapped in. My knees hit bare stone, and the rest of my body followed, even as the fluid I'd been suspended in washed across the floor.

I crouched there, shaking, dripping wet, and spasming as I vomited up the fluid, desperate for it all to end. As soon as the liquid was out, I sucked in a shuddering breath of warm, fetid air and cried out in pain, horror, and dismay.

I curled up into a fetal position, pulling my knees as close to my chest as they'd go, wrapping my arms around them and burying my face in the wet darkness. I lay trembling, un-manned by the experience in a way I hadn't felt since I was a small child, and I wept, unlike childhood when my twin brother had been here to share the pain and horror. Instead, I was all alone.

It seemed like seconds, but it was probably closer to half an hour before a sound drew me back from the brink. I raised my head shakily, my eyes burning from the tears.

My chest heaved as I panted. I tried to get ahold of myself, forcing my mind to examine the room I was in.

It was long and narrow. The thing I'd been trapped inside was a sarcophagus, and here and there in the room were the weapons racks I could remember from other dreams. Small spaces were set into the walls below bowls that had burst into flame with my arrival.

The spaces were usually filled with votive offerings, but these were all empty. I glanced around, finding no other people, but equally lacking, I saw no weapons, no armor.

I drew in another shuddering breath, visually searching the room while I tried to get my brain in gear. I was in a summoning hall, but every surface was coated in cobwebs or weird piles of dirt, and the carvings that normally adorned the room were...covered.

I forced myself to uncurl, coming to my feet with a little stagger. Looking closer, then wiping at the nearest wall, I realized that I remembered this section of carvings clearly. It stood above a weapons rack that normally held the daggers, and I had noticed it in every dream I could remember. It depicted a figure dressed in the armor that was usually set aside for me, saving people and killing creatures.

It didn't sound like much, but it had always spoken to me, the fear etched into the people's faces giving way to hope as a figure that looked like me helped them. It made me feel like a hero, and it gave me strength, gave me something to aspire to. In this place, though, it had been altered...defaced. Long scratches marred the stone, and something dark had been smeared across it. I sniffed as I moved closer, and the smell suddenly assaulted my brain.

It was as if my nose hadn't been switched on until now. Suddenly, I could smell it all around me, and as I spun, I could see more of it everywhere. Shit. Something, or a veritable *horde* of somethings, had smeared excrement across the walls, floor, and every surface in one of my halls, probably for years.

I gagged and heard a sound from behind. I twisted around. It must have come from the entrance to the hall. Where there had once been a stone doorframe leading out to a village or town, a packed dirt tunnel now led deeper into darkness.

I stalked forward hesitantly, ducking my head down to peer into the tunnel. It stood maybe four feet high and three feet wide, with a solid-packed earthen floor. Roots and rocks were intruding through the sides, and somewhere ahead, there was a faint light. I backed away as the sound came again from deeper inside the tunnel.

It was intermittent, a clicking as though something hard tapped on stone, followed by a low chittering. It was growing louder, and multiple sounds overlapped each other. I searched through the room frantically, trying to find a weapon. I ran to the racks on the far wall, but found that they were all empty, just like the ones closer to my sarcophagus, and I began hunting in desperation. Every single rack was empty, as were the slots below the firepits, and beyond that, there was nothing but the mounds of waste in the room.

Waste that, as I continued to look at it, began to have vaguely familiar shapes. I took two quick steps and, trying to contain my disgust, dug my fingers into one of the piles.

I felt a hard, flaky crust give way, my fingers digging in deeper until they felt something solid, and I drew it out. It was a bone, maybe six inches long, curved into a U shape and splintered at one end, with regular ridges sunken into it. One of the ridges crumbled and came loose under my questing fingers, and I dropped it in disgust as I realized what it was.

A jawbone with missing teeth and dozens of cracks and chew marks in it, pitted by the passage it'd taken through something's digestive tract before being deposited here.

I lost control when I realized how small many of the teeth were. It was a child's jaw. I vomited, turning aside as I heaved, my tiny amount of self-control fleeing me. I tried to vomit up everything I'd ever eaten, despite the only thing in my stomach being the amniotic fluid that my mana-wight body always seemed to be born in.

I shook and retched, continuing to dry heave as I gazed blearily around the room. Dozens upon dozens of shapes lay under the piles where something had fed on a huge number of bodies. Tiny, defenseless children had been devoured, even as this body had slumbered here, unaware.

The sound from the tunnel behind me became louder, arresting my attention as I spun around. I shook, my head spinning even as my stomach tried to rebel again. My mouth grew dry in fear, a fear that was burned aside by the heat of my swiftly rising rage.

TheySetThemFreeTheyLetThemFeedOnChildrenTheyKilledThemAllNoN oNotTheChildren...

The voice ranted away in the back of my mind, but as the first creature entered the room, it went silent. After a moment's pause, it exploded in screams so loud they echoed around my brain. I was nearly convinced the creature could hear it as well, by the way its steps faltered.

Its carapace was black and shiny with bright red streaks running down from the massive head, outlining the sharp mandibles that clicked and clacked on either side of the wide mouth. Those disappeared down the body that snaked out of view into the darkness. The creature had dozens of legs, each tipped with a hard, sharp point that clattered onto the occasional clear section of stone.

It reared up, half its body length seeming to lift until it stood nearly as tall as I was. I found myself facing a centipede, grown to monstrous size, that had developed a taste for human flesh. I met its eyes, its four red eyes, trying not to imagine the creature that rode this, with the straps and buckles of a saddle tied to its back.

It emitted a sharp, wet hiss as it began to weave sinuously from side to side, slowly moving closer to me.

Congratulations!

Drach's Mesmerize skill has failed!

Your anger and experience in past battles have allowed you to ignore the Drach's innate Mesmerize skill.

My lips drew back, exposing my teeth as a low growl forced its way up from the depths of my core. Before I could think better of it, or think at all, I lunged forward and grabbed the mandibles on either side of its mouth. It tried to dodge, surprised by the sudden attack. But I was faster, gripping the hard chitinous extensions tightly before forcing them backwards.

Resistance heaved against me, the muscles trying to close the mandibles, even as the rest of the body lunged forward.

Sharp claws dug into my legs and abdomen as it attacked. It was too slow, though, and the mandibles had been open too wide.

I flexed my arms, hunched forward, and ignored the burrowing pains across my body as I imagined the children this fucking thing had eaten. I heaved with all my strength and felt a slight give, followed by ominous cracking. I twisted both wrists, rolling them up and down, a spreading wave of cracks radiating out from the edges, before I tore the mandibles free of its face in a gush of blood and fluid.

It let loose a high-pitched squeal and thrashed about, trying to back away, but I followed it, anger and determination filling me like I'd rarely felt. I discarded the broken chitin from my left hand and grabbed onto the domed shell of its head, driving the pointed tip of the mandible in my right hand back into the hole in its face. The chitin cracked and fractured around the improvised weapon as I dug in deeper.

I screamed with pain and rage, yanking my makeshift weapon in and out, coring the inside of its face like an apple, even as it hissed, gurgled, and squealed back at me. Its madly twisting body took us both to the ground as it wrapped itself around me, legs digging into my flesh, tearing the wounds wider as it thrashed and dug in, trying to escape me. Something popped and crunched as the final bit of resistance gave way, and the tip of my makeshift weapon sank into its brain. The creature twitched and convulsed, tearing my wounds further, then stopped, its body relaxing into death.

I pulled the mandible back and then shoved it in harder, twisting it and dragging sections of the monster's brain out.

I yanked and dug, all reason gone as I unleashed my fury. After a few seconds, it dawned on me that it wasn't fighting back, and I slumped to the floor. The corpse slowly curled up as I rolled away from it to lie with my back against the wall.

I lay there, panting, bleeding heavily, and shaking as whatever passed for adrenaline seemed to wear down in this artificial body. I raised one trembling hand, pointing the ichor-coated mandible at the creature before muttering under my breath.

"Didn't...know who he...was fucking with...!"

As the final syllable passed my lips, another noise from the tunnel drew my attention. I watched in silent horror as a second, and then a third creature came creeping in, while a fourth clambered like a spider across the wall.

This last one had a small creature strapped to its back that glared at me with hatred clear in its tiny eyes. It was barely a foot tall, hunched over, with spindly arms and legs gripping the saddle tight as its mount climbed the wall farthest from me and came to rest in the top corner, well out of reach.

It freed one hand and pulled out a small collection of reeds bound together, which it began to play like a flute. With the eerie high-pitched notes filling the hall, the other two creatures separated to come at me from either side. More entered from the tunnel, climbing in along the walls, floor, and ceiling until I lost count of them.

The walls were alive with the clattering black mess of the creatures. Even though most were smaller than the one I'd already faced, there were so many…

I looked around wearily. Anger still filled my mind, but I was also well aware of my chances, even as I gingerly picked up the second mandible with my left hand. I struggled to my feet, rapidly cooling blood coating my body as I stared right back at the hateful little rider.

"Huuuuman?" it whispered, barely audible across the sound of claws on stone and dirt.

"Aye," I muttered, drawing a deep breath and spitting a wad of blood onto the floor between us.

"Diiiiie!" it rasped at me, blowing one last series of notes into the reed collection of pipes.

The creatures closed in, and I snarled, a mix of fear and dogged determination to take some of these fuckers with me. I leaped at the nearest, whipping the pair of "blades" down from on high into its face, the left one skittering uselessly across its carapace as the tip of the right caught, digging into its eyeball and making it squeal.

The fight vanished into a wild insanity of stabbing, kicking, and even biting as they tore into me from all sides. I fought frantically, but as first my left, then my right arms were severed, dragged free in great gouts of blood and screams, legs being chewed apart, I'd never stood a chance. One of my final sensations was from a small monster, only a foot or so long, digging its way into a wound in my stomach and tearing its way up through the inside of my chest.

You have died.

CHAPTER SIX

I bolted awake again, screaming and twisting around, my hands grabbing at my chest in an effort to stop the last creature, only to find quickly healing skin and leaking blood. I overbalanced, tipping off the medical gurney I'd been lying on.

Someone had released me at some point, and now two medical staff were trying to restrain me as I panicked...again.

I grabbed the man in front of me, yanking him forward and headbutting him before throwing him backwards. I bolted, hearing screams and shouts for help as doors nearby opened and the sound of running feet came closer.

"Jack, you mad bastard! Stop!" I heard West's voice, but I was too far gone. Too much had happened. Before I could make sense of my surroundings, I felt something stab into my back, then pain shot through me as a taser unleashed its charge into my poor, abused body.

I thrashed and bucked, my body no longer under my control as I flopped about on the floor. The wounds that had been closing burst back open, and blood sprayed around the corridor, coating the walls and more.

The next thing I knew, I was strapped down on a gurney in the medical room again, with dozens of people surrounding me. The Baron was there, looming over me and screaming with pure unbridled rage.

"...tell me now! Did *HE* plan this? Speak, fool, or die!" he spat at me, slapping me hard enough he must have dislodged a few of my teeth.

I managed a weak; "Wha—" before my abused body gave up, and I passed out again.

I had no way of knowing how long I was out for, but when I awoke again, it was a slower affair, the aches and pains of my body slowly blending together to raise my consciousness. I groaned, shifting on a bed, finding restraints tightly gripping me again.

I blinked slowly, muzzily as the world swam back into focus. The gurney I was strapped to had been placed in a raised position. I was propped up by pillows and chained down, but at least I had pants on, my brain muzzily noted, hoping that was a good sign.

I blinked and squinted around as best I could, my nerves screaming from all the abuse they'd suffered. I recognized the room I was in, my own bedroom, and that I was alone with the Baron. He sat in a chair, watching me with a cold light in his eyes.

"You're a Dreamer," he stated, watching me for a reaction. I frowned and looked down at my heavily scarred body and back at him before replying.

"Aye, I dream, sometimes. What of it?" I muttered weakly.

"Not *dream*, boy. You **DREAM**. You know the difference," he snapped.

I lay there looking at him, every instinct warring with my desire to know more.

I knew, I just *knew* it was a mistake to tell the prick anything, but I needed answers, and it wasn't as though I could deny it now. "I have Dreams, yeah, I guess. You know about them?" I asked. He met my eyes, and for the first time in our interactions, I saw something beyond scarcely contained anger or contempt. I saw a hint of fear, quickly covered up, but it was there. "I know of them. I should have realized, with the reports I had of your scars. Your brother, he had the same…affliction?" the Baron asked almost casually, quirking an eyebrow at me.

"Aye, Tommy had them, too. Why?"

"In these Dreams, is there a voice?" he asked, fixing me with an intense stare.

"I…" I could feel the other one, the voice or whatever it was—it was there now—watching the Baron through my eyes, and it *hated* him. My own hatred was like a candle beside an inferno in comparison, and without thinking about it, I lied.

"I don't hear a voice. There's sometimes people, and they talk to me, but that's it. One time…" I started to ramble before I managed to catch myself, and I frowned at the Baron. I didn't want to tell him anything, but I…I probably needed to tell him. He was important…wasn't he? I should do what he said. I should tell him about the voice, I decided. I started to open my mouth, and my tongue seemed to freeze.

PoisonHeLearnedOhYesHeLearnedButWeCantHaveThatNoNoNoCantH aveHimLearnWeStillLiveNotYetNot…

When I heard the voice mumbling away to itself, it was like a light switching on as a fog seemed to be banished from my brain.

I felt something prodding and pushing at the outside of my mind, fingers trying to dig inside, even as a strange taste in my mouth and a pain in my arm let me know that something was being slowly fed into my bloodstream to keep me compliant.

"No, there's no voice, just people I need to help…" I repeated.

"People? Describe them."

I began to talk, and he cut me off quickly.

"No, not peasants. People, nobles, places of power; tell me what they say, and everything you can remember."

I did, trying to appear drugged still, rambling on about the people I could remember, the fights, the deaths. The Baron interrupted me constantly, asking questions about the locations, the creatures, the wealth of the areas, always pushing for interactions with nobles or cities.

I told him all I could, keeping back any mention of the voice. Finally, he grunted, seeming satisfied.

"You've been luckier than you know, boy. I should have you killed, just in case, but with a Pearl in you now, you've risen in value. However, Daphne will be punished for this oversight…severely. I'll still allow you to fight in the arena, but just in case you haven't been honest with me, I've got a little gift for you." He hauled himself to his feet and strode over, extending one thick, claw-tipped finger.

He began to mutter under his breath before digging his claw into the skin over my heart. Slowly dragging it deeper, he drew copious amounts of blood as he carved a strange rune into my flesh. It took him several minutes. I swore and cried out, thrashing impotently, until he was finished. When he pulled his claw back, the rune began to glow a deep, dark green, pulsing until it settled down into a solid, bloody scar across my chest.

Containment rune activated!

Warning: you have been marked with a containment rune.

This magical construct will prevent any form of extraplanar communication, and will release a powerful, likely fatal attack on any who attempt to deactivate it.

"What the hell was that, you crazy old bastard?" I gasped out as the Baron examined his handiwork.

"Why, Jack, it's a gift, from father to son. With this, no creatures of the night will be able to whisper in your ear. See how well I care for you?" he replied sardonically.

So I hadn't been completely successful in hiding the voice's presence. He at least suspected, anyway.

"I suggest you don't attempt to remove it or ask anyone you don't want dead to remove it either. The effects could be…unfortunate." With that, he turned around and walked out of the room, leaving me to sag back on the gurney in exhaustion and pain.

I felt hands reaching around and releasing my bonds, and my anger flared with the realization that someone had been there all this time.

I leaped to my feet, spinning around to find Xiao backing away to sit on the far side of the room. She slowly clapped her hands as she enjoyed the view, and I clenched my fists in anger.

"Well, boy? Have you forgotten your first lesson in magic so easily? Hmm?" she asked, lifting one hand up and threateningly curling her fingers as though about to grab something.

"Oh, I remember; I remember just fine…" I growled, staring at her in challenge. It was a dumb thing to do, a small part of me screamed, but after all of that I'd just been through, hell no, I wasn't backing down from this crazy old bag.

"Good! Perhaps you do have some fire in you after all; you survived the bonding better than I expected. Now, before you are returned to your usual time wasting with pretty swords and so on, we will discuss your new abilities.

"Concentrate, and you will be able to summon descriptions of your status, screens that show you details, information, and even maps. You will be able to augment your vision, improve your pathetic abilities, and most important of all, you will be able to see how to improve yourself further at any time. You will be using this facility most of all, as you are so weak!"

"What? Seriously, you want to do this *now*?" I growled incredulously.

"The Baron ordered that I must prepare you as soon as possible, so sit and listen, or do I need to have you tasered and restrained again? Hmmm?"

I started to speak, only for her to snap at me to be quiet as she continued her tirade.

"First, we will discuss your status. Concentrate and think the word 'Status' at the Pearl."

I did so, the golden smoke flowing into existence once again. In under a second, it had shifted from a faint wisp to forming boxes and rectangles, words, and a page that floated before my eyes.

Name: Jack Sanguis				
Class: None		Renown: Unknown		
Level: 1		Progress: 0/300		
Patron: None		Points to Distribute: 0 Meridian Points to Invest: 0		
Stat	Current points	Description	Effect	Progress to next level
Agility	8	Governs dodge and movement.	-20% maximum movement speed and reflexes	0/100
Charisma	9	Governs likely success to charm seduce or threaten	-10% success in interactions with other beings	0/100
Constitution	13	Governs health and health regeneration	130 health, regen 4.5 points per 600 seconds	0/100
Dexterity	9	Governs ability with weapons and crafting	-10% to weapon proficiency, -10% to the chances of crafting success	0/100
Endurance	12	Governs stamina and stamina regeneration	120 stamina, regen 2 points per 30 seconds	0/100
Intelligence	9	Governs base mana and number of Spells able to be learned	90 mana, spell capacity: 5	0/100
Luck	8	Governs overall chance of bonuses	-20% chance of a favorable outcome	0/100
Perception	12	Governs ranged damage and chance to spot traps or hidden items	+20% ranged damage, +2% chance to spot traps or hidden items	0/100
Strength	12	Governs damage with melee weapons and carrying capacity	+2 damage with melee weapons, +20% maximum carrying capacity	0/100
Wisdom	8	Governs mana regeneration and memory	-20% mana recovery, 0.8 points per minute, 20% more likely to forget things	0/100

I stood there, gobsmacked. I'd never seen such an accurate or damning description of me. I read the stats out to her at her demand without much thought.

"Huh, as I feared! You barely have the capacity to understand the gift you have been given: immortality and the ability to improve yourself beyond the baseline breed of humanity. The Pearl is wasted on the likes of you!"

"What? Why is it wasted? Wait, why are you so pissed at me now?" I asked halfheartedly, most of my attention still on the screen before me.

"Why? Because *you* are a waste! Think what a true mage could do with this, instead of a boy who thinks with his dick and his muscles!"

"Yeah, well, shit happens, doesn't it, you old bag?" I snapped at her. The screen vanished according to my mental flexing, and I focused on her, seeing the anger and resentment there for the first time.

"You think you could have survived that? You want to feel your bones breaking and your teeth shattering? You want to know what it feels like to have something worm its way into your brain?!" I roared at her, making her step back in reflex at my sudden outburst.

"I...I could have survived..." she said, anger leaching from her as she glanced at the gurney behind me. I spun and contemplated the amount of blood staining the sheets, and then I remembered the state of the walls in the last room. There had been streaks and splatters all over the place: the walls, floor, ceiling. They had not registered before, but *now*...how the hell had I lived?

"You wouldn't, and we all know it." Another voice came from the door, and I turned around to see West walking in, a handful of beers in his arms. He casually cracked the top off a Corona, offering it to me. I snatched it from him and upended it, draining the entire bottle in one go. I wasn't sure if it was the moisture or the alcohol I craved more.

"God, you look a mess, lad. Go on, get dressed," he said, and I chucked the bottle at a bin in the corner. As I put my clothes back on, I found that I was covered in new scars. Thin lines crisscrossed my entire body, faint white ridges showing where the filaments had cut into me, adding to the new scars from my latest Dream.

"I...I am supposed to be teaching him how to use his Pearl, fool. How dare you interrupt!" Xiao snarled at West, only to have him shrug dismissively at her obvious dislike.

"So I noticed when I walked in. Looked like you were doing a fine job, complaining about the Baron's decision to gift his *son* with a Pearl. Perhaps I should tell him you disapprove of his actions?"

Xiao went white with fear, stammering that there was no need for that.

"Then teach him. I've been ordered to watch over all of his training from now on. I trust you won't dispute this. Perhaps we should go and interrupt the Baron so you can confirm his choices, and you can explain how he should do things instead?"

"Back the fuck up," I snapped, reaching out and pulling the bottle of beer from his hands and glaring at West. "You called him my father. He said it as well. Nah, mate, that's not right—"

"Sorry Jack, but it is. I suspected it with Tommy, but the Baron never confirmed it before. He's your father."

"No," I said flatly, shaking my head and glaring at him as I swallowed a long gulp from the bottle. "Our ma was no angel, right enough, and we never knew our da, but..."

"It's not what you think." West cracked the door open and spoke in a hushed voice to the guards I damn well knew were waiting out there. When he came back in, he took the seat the Baron had been sitting in and gestured to the bed. "You might as well sit, lad. I sent for some more beers, as we might as well get this out in the open now."

"I have to teach..." Xiao started to complain, only to have West cut her off with a glare.

"The Baron ordered me to see to it Jack knows all he needs to, so shut it, it's quicker this way."

Xiao grumbled to herself, but sat back, interlacing her fingers and glaring at us both as West went on.

"Look, the Baron and his kind, they need those with their genes to open the portal, right? Well, they like to spread themselves around, that's true, but..." He scratched his chin, thinking about how best to put it. "Look. The genes that show a member of the 'family' as a true blood, or close enough aren't well understood, not here. It's something to do with the 'mix' I guess, and well, you and Tommy have the right one. You're both natural fighters, excessive aggression, naturally compatible with the Pearls, you've got 'gifts' of your own, and you're a borderline psychopath."

"No, I'm fuckin' not!"

"Jack...you and your brother force-fed a dealer his own badly cut shit and choked him to death on it."

"A friend of ours died thanks to that shit..." I replied hotly.

"Yeah, Marie Warner, popular girl." He gave an amiable nod. "She was sixteen and had a bright future ahead of her until she started experimenting. Thing is, Jack, you and Tommy went after the dealer, you broke his legs with cricket bats, and you force-fed him a quarter of a kilo of his product."

"He deserved it."

"He did, not gonna disagree. The point that you and Tommy were thirteen though, and he was twenty-seven? That stands out. He'd served four years in the army and ruled his own little 'patch' through outright terror and violence. For two thirteen-year-olds to not only take him down, but to give hardened police officers nightmares over it? And the new dealer that moved in paid *you* protection money!"

"Damn straight. They'd better."

He snorted, shaking his head. "Still, some of the great houses haven't put a fighter forward for the arena in more than sixty years, simply because they haven't had a viable candidate. The Baron believes in playing the long game, so he set up several fertility clinics. Your mother was one of many who visited one of his, and in having certain checks done, was implanted with his sperm rather than that of your intended father."

"This is sick..." I muttered.

"Yeah, it's not nice. But the simple truth is: he is your father, he's powerful, and you mean less to him than the dirt under his fingernails, so remember that! The only reason you're alive right now is so you can go through the portal. If you win the fight in the arena, get to the Great Portal, and power it up with the Baron's sigil stone? It'll open a new portal from that side, all the way to the Baron's personal portal. All the nobles have one, but as it takes all of them to open a connection, they do it at the Great Portal on this side."

"And when you open the portal, we can go through!" Xiao interrupted.

"Yeah, the Baron and his lot, and probably most of us will end up going through," West agreed, taking the pair of bottles that a guard passed to him before closing the door quietly and leaving us to it.

West passed me one of the bottles and kept the other for himself. "I've got a family here. Given the choice, I'll stay, but most will go. You, on the other hand, will get the chance to find Tommy, and you can stay there as a high noble, ruling literally anywhere from cities to continents. Or, you can come back here and live as an immortal on this side.

"Now, some of the recruits come through as the Baron's 'pureblood' sons—that's a single generation from him, and a direct line, be that through 'donation' or personal...interactions with the mother. Others, the vast majority, are genetic throwbacks, where your great-great-grandmother might have been involved with a member of the nobility, and the genes have worked their way to the surface now. That's the more common occurrence."

"I don't need this shit," I muttered, taking a long drink. "I don't need it. The Baron can—"

"STOP!" West shouted, glaring at me. "Finish that sentence, and I'll have to report it. I don't want to, but I will. Might be you get punished, might be he shrugs it off, or might be he finds someone you care about and tortures them to death as a lesson! Stop your shit, Jack, and just think!" He glared at me for a few seconds.

I returned his hard stare, but he had a point, so I grudgingly nodded that I understood.

"Good. Xiao, your turn, and remember, I'll be required to give the Baron a report on your teaching methods later, if he fails to grasp the basics," West told her, sitting back. He waited until she was speaking again before winking slowly at me and making me feel at least a little better about things.

Xiao went even whiter, if that was possible, shaking her head emphatically before turning to address me again. "Your...'stats' are low...but can be improved. Each level you gain allows you to allocate five points to improve yourself. But, in addition to this, you can increase the stats by hard work. Your exercises, both physical and mental, will slowly count towards your potential. For example, if you practice running and swimming each day, this will increase your Endurance by a certain amount, depending on the effort you put in.

"An hour might gain you, say, ten points towards a stat increase. When it reaches one hundred, another point of Endurance will be added to your stats, and the counter will begin again. Each level will require more work than the one before." She paused and cocked her head to one side, taking a deep breath before going on. "You have a question?"

That was new. She'd made it clear in our previous training sessions that she hated answering my questions, so West had scared her more than I had realized.

"Yeah, any points I have below ten are marked as minuses, like minus ten percent chance to seduce in my Charisma. Does that mean the average is ten points in each?"

I ignored the snort of amusement from West as Xiao replied.

"Yes and no. The average for a human at your age is ten in each area. However, this is the average across the board. Some are far higher in one area than another, which is the result of their genetics and lifestyle choices. Those have been earned simply through their experiences.

"This is the standard in most realms without magic, but in those with access to magic, many people will assign their stats themselves. In those realms, the average is much higher. Consider the soldiers you knew, a man or woman that has fought for their lives? They will be stronger, not just physically, but mentally, able to dominate others perhaps, or more intelligent. This is from assigning their stats subconsciously.

"Where a normal human might be level ten, they might be level twenty, or in some rare circumstances, level thirty is reachable. These people become far more powerful than the average person.

"Then consider that a warrior in the UnderVerse might be even more powerful, as he would have both the points from his exercises and the points he has been able to allocate directly by choice. The average for a human in a realm without magic is ten. This is usually because they will have distributed points across all of their stats, with more from their life experiences. Imagine what a level thirty could do with possibly hundreds of points!"

I must have looked lost, because she cursed in Mandarin under her breath before continuing.

"You are a fool! A warrior might have put fifty total points into his Strength, Endurance, Dexterity, Constitution, and Agility, by concentrating ten points in each of these areas. Once their training is added in, they could have twenty or more in those stats. You understand, yes? A warrior that is twice as fast, strong, and skilled as you?"

"And a mage?" I asked, knowing I wouldn't like the answer.

"A mage here will never hold a candle to a mage there, as this realm has such a tiny amount of ambient mana available. If you were to concentrate on becoming a mage, it would be the first step towards enlightenment I'd seen from you. I would applaud it, but your mind is lacking anything special. There will no doubt be mages in the tournament, and they will be weak compared to what you will see on the other side, but regardless, they will be stronger than you can hope to become by then."

"In other words, lad, you can't become much of a mage, but you could become a mage killer!" West called out. I turned to him, and he continued. "There's nothing stopping you from learning spells now. But bear in mind, as low as the mana regeneration rate is here, you wouldn't get enough experience to make much difference. Add to that, while casting spells will improve your ability with that branch of magic, it doesn't seem to make any noticeable difference if you just cast it against a wall. It has to be a 'valid' use of magic, as Tommy explained it to me. Use it in a fight, and it'll level quickly; shoot it aimlessly into the air? Nada."

"Can you break it down further, please, mate?" I said, my head still reeling after the day I'd had.

"It is simple, Jack. Even you should be able to grasp the principles," said Xiao before going on. "A simple spell, such as Firebolt, will do ten points of damage and cost ten points of mana. Can you follow so far?" She looked at me askance.

"Yeah, I'm still here, you old bag," I muttered, earning myself a hard stare.

"Very well. With each cast *against a viable target*, you will grow more experienced with the spell. With each level up, you will increase its power by one point of damage, but the cost will remain the same. Once it reaches level ten, you can choose an evolution for it. It will then cost ten mana and do twenty points of base damage. Plus, you can alter the spell, like my FlameGlove."

"Okay, and how far can I take it? And why is it every ten levels? Why not six, or thirty?"

"Who knows? Ask the gods if you care that much, for I do not! There are known to be one hundred and fifty levels of magical advancement. Novice is level one to ten, Apprentice is eleven to twenty, Journeyman is twenty-one to thirty. Expert is thirty-one to fifty, Lord is fifty-one to seventy-five, with Master and Grandmaster at seventy-six to one hundred and one hundred and one to one hundred and fifty respectively.

"A Firebolt at level one hundred and fifty would do one hundred and fifty base damage for the same ten points of mana cost. If you choose the correct specializations, it could be far, far more. You understand still?" she asked, taking a deep breath and carrying on when I nodded.

"This is where it grows more complicated. For each ten levels of a spell, you gain one point in mastery of that school. So, ten levels of Firebolt would grant you one level of Fire magic mastery. The levels for mastery are calculated the same, one to one hundred and fifty. *However*...each corresponding level in mastery grants a one percent bonus, both a reduction in spell cost, and an increase in resistance to spells from that school used against you. A level one hundred and fifty Grandmaster would *gain* mana each time they cast a fire spell, and they would be actively healed by any enemy fire! It is said the Gods themselves were mortals that exceeded the Grandmaster level, but none know for sure. Do you see now, Jack? Magic is the path to *power!*"

"Okay, but you're saying I might as well not bother for now, as I'll never be able to get the experience with it? Surely starting now is better than later?"

"Any experience is good, lad, but we're saying make it a second string to your bow, not your primary focus, that's all. Learn the spells, get some practice, but leave it at that. Level it up on the other side...and don't call me Shirley," West said, walking around the room slowly, clearly uncomfortable with the conversation. Then he paused to see if I got the reference.

I blinked, then grinned weakly at him, responding with:

"'Looks like I picked the wrong week to quit drinking!'"

West grinned back and punched me lightly on the shoulder.

"You'll do well, don't worry. You've gone through a lot today, so we'll get this done as quickly as we can, and let you get some sleep, okay?"

I nodded, and Xiao took over again, sounding exasperated, but trying to be patient.

"Okay, now where were we...ah! As you grow to understand magic better, you can adjust your spells. The basic spells you learn can be...altered...to create many higher-level spells, aside from the traditional evolutions." She wagged a finger at me. "I should warn you, however, that adjusting spells is dangerous. It can make them highly unstable, so be warned!"

"I know this is a lot of crap to bombard you with in one go, kid, but seriously, it's important. Xiao, give us an example of a high-level spell, please," West said, watching me carefully.

"Hmm...GravityStorm is one the Baron has mentioned as a particularly fearsome weapon. It costs eight thousand mana to cast, and a further two thousand mana in maintenance for the ten minutes it lasts."

"It creates a storm over a target area that begins with heavy rain, then transitions to lightning that conducts through the standing water and ends with boulders the size of horses flying in all directions. Through all of this, gravity is made to shift to a random direction every few seconds without warning. Little could survive such a spell."

"Now just think, Jack. That's ten thousand mana to cast it, but if you could level it up? It'd increase significantly after only a few levels, while doing so much more damage? Tommy was convinced it was the route to real power. He was right, despite the fact that he was so shit at magic."

I thought for a while, and they watched me silently while I ran a bit of math in my head. "Okay, but what about the regeneration? You said there's hardly any mana here?" I asked Xiao.

"True, but there is some. What is your mana at?"

I frowned in concentration, and a translucent blue bar appeared in the bottom right of my vision. It was almost totally empty, with a faint blue flicker at the very bottom. As I focused on it, it displayed numbers that read "four out of ninety." I told Xiao, and she started to laugh, while West looked disappointed.

"Four? *Four*?! What is your Wisdom? Come, you fool, answer me!" She laughed mockingly, then clicked her fingers at me to be quick about it.

"It's eight," I said, feeling more and more irritated. It only grew worse when Xiao continued laughing, and West shook his head in disgust. Damn it. I'd told her those stats only a few minutes ago, yet still she had to taunt me.

"Okay, Jack. Maybe being a mage isn't the path for you at all, but what about a class? Has Xiao mentioned that yet?" West asked, clearly trying to move the conversation on. When I shook my head, he turned to her and growled about "discussing her work with the Baron," and she snapped her mouth shut with a sick look on her face.

"Your mana would normally regenerate at the amount of point eight mana per minute, giving you forty mana an hour or so. But in this realm, I've been told it's around one tenth of that, so don't be too downhearted about that for now," West added.

Xiao cut him off, glossing over his reassurances. "Very well. If you concentrate as you did for your stats, but think 'class' instead, your Pearl will give you a recommendation on your first class. It will be influenced due to your natural abilities and memories. This is no simple choice to make; however, it will determine how the Pearl grows with you.

"There is nothing to stop you from deciding you want to be a Thief or Assassin, but since you have chosen to focus on a Warrior build all of your life, you would waste a multitude of points. Every ten levels, you will be given choices to specialize or select classes that you have discovered, provided you have the aptitude. Check what is recommended for you, and I will explain further..."

I did so and a new screen appeared before me.

Class Recommendations

Primary:

Warrior: The path of a Warrior is a noble one; where others may flee the fight, you embrace it. Choosing this as your first class will grant you a one-off bonus of 5 points to Strength and 5 points to Constitution.

Ranger: A life as a man alone resonates well with you, exploring the wilderness and living in harmony with nature. Choosing this as your first class will grant you a one-off bonus of 5 points to Agility and 5 points to Perception.

Enforcer: Your lack of concern for the judgement of others, and a general lack of squeamishness make this a great choice for you. Choosing this as your first class will grant you a one-off bonus of 5 points to Strength and 5 points to Endurance.

Secondary:

Rogue: You have no issue separating the rich from their possessions; perhaps this path would suit you? Choosing this as your first class will grant you a one-off bonus of 5 points to Perception and 5 points to Dexterity.

Spellsword: This reflects your inner yearning. You wish to be more than you are, and improve on your weaknesses, a combination of mage and warrior, perhaps? Choosing this as your first class will grant you a one-off bonus of 5 points to Strength and 5 points to Intelligence.

Templar: This is a rare class, not often offered. Call down Holy Wrath with one hand and use cold steel to smite your enemies with the other. Choosing this as your first class will grant you a one-off bonus of 5 points to Endurance and 5 points to Wisdom.

Tertiary:

Mage: As a pure-blooded mage, you would wield the strength of the cosmos, but your memories and natural inclination suggest this may not be the one for you, despite your desires. Choosing this as your first class will grant you a one-off bonus of 5 points to Intelligence and 5 points to Wisdom.

Knight: You yearn to be the shield to the weak, but your temper is your downfall, as is your desire for easy money. Choosing this as your first class will grant you a one-off bonus of 5 points to Strength and 5 points to Wisdom.

Healer: You wish to help others and heal the sick, but your soul is not that of a healer. Choosing this as your first class will grant you a one-off bonus of 5 points to Intelligence and 5 points to Perception.

I read out the details to the others and observed their agreement, even as my own mind worked with the Pearl to betray me.

"Okay, Jack, the Pearl has worked through your memories and past, and has classified you into primary, secondary and tertiary probabilities of success. You can choose any area—it is a choice, after all—but when it comes to your future, I suggest you think carefully. This is a one-time bonus that the Pearl can give you, augmenting your natural abilities."

"Classes can be discovered at any time, provided you reach a set skill level or have an affinity for them. However, you are unlikely to ever gain another boost this large in the future," Xiao said, staring at me as she went on. "You have many weaknesses, but using your class to address those weaknesses could leave you at a serious disadvantage in the arena. Better to play to your strengths, yes?"

"Hold up!" West said, clapping his hands together loudly as I took in a deep breath, ready to give the old hag a piece of my mind. "We're getting sidetracked here. Jack, you can decide a class later. Take your time and pick what you want. It's your choice, and it's your future, so don't just toss it off in a moment of anger. Xiao, tell him what he needs to know, and quit with the shitty attitude. Remember, he *is* the Baron's son, so maybe fucking him over isn't a good idea, hmmm?"

"Very well," said Xiao, taking a deep breath before continuing. "You can make further adjustments to your vision; for example, choosing to make your stamina, health, and mana bars visible at all times, which I have heard is a common choice. Other alterations are adding the time, compass direction indicators, and notification alarms, to name a few. You will find that the possibilities are limited only by your mind."

"Tommy said he took the three bars, added a flashing light to show any notifications from the Pearl, and that was it," West chimed in.

"Okay, give me a minute," I said, concentrating. I'd already summoned a mana bar, but the health and stamina bars were even easier to summon into existence, colored red and green respectively. I added them and tucked them down to the right of my vision, along with the blue mana bar, opting to make them turn transparent when I didn't think about them. Then I added a small eye symbol in the bottom left, setting it to close when I wasn't being observed and open when I was.

I wasn't completely certain how it worked, aside from similar indicators I had seen in games, but it seemed to appear and settle easily enough. Finally, I added a small hash symbol in the very top right of my vision, where it wouldn't get in the way. I set it to pulse with light, and a Roman numeral appeared above it to indicate the notifications I had waiting. I scanned through current notifications, dismissing each as I finished with it.

Pearl integration is complete...

Current level: 1

0/300xp Toward level 2.

They were simple messages, but the fact that the Pearl could communicate with me like this freaked me out, making me think of a parasite in my brain. I took a moment to get ahold of myself before turning back to the others.

"Okay, I've done that. What else do I need to know?"

UnderVerse: Brightblade

"You can, as I've said, increase your level by exercising, but you can also increase your Wisdom and Intelligence through study and usage of your mana. I suggest you concentrate on doing this. With your Intelligence so low, you only have the capacity to learn five spells at this time. There are twenty that the Baron has ordered me to make available to you, so I suggest you study the list of possibilities and choose for yourself."

With that, Xiao passed a set of notes over. I read them carefully, growing more and more excited as I read.

Name	School	Description	Effect	Mana
Summon Water	Water	Summons clean, drinkable water	A magical spring erupts at the target location, lasts 10 seconds	10 mana
Icebolt	Water	Hurls a bolt of ice at a target	Icebolt does 10 damage per hit, plus 5% chance to freeze target: chance increases by 5% per hit	10 mana
Firebolt	Fire	Hurls a bolt of fire at enemies	Firebolt does 10 damage per hit, plus 5% chance to burn target: chance increases by 5% per hit	10 mana
Weak Flame	Fire	Summon weak flame in your hand, flame can be transferred and set fire to flammable objects	5 Damage per second. Lasts 10 seconds or until fuel is used up	10 mana
Cleansing Fire	Fire	Summon a ring of cleansing fire around the target. The fire damages enemies and heals allies.	Flames have a 10m radius and deal 10 damage per second to any hostile creatures within the AOE while dispelling any negative status effects and granting 2 healing per second to allies. The spell lasts 60 seconds.	50 mana
Earthen Armor	Earth	Summon armor made of earth to protect yourself from physical damage.	Allows you to ignore 10 damage per hit for 60 seconds.	25 mana
Earth Tremor	Earth	Summon a tremor in the earth around the caster.	1-6 damage per second in a 10ft radius around the caster, 5 second duration	25 mana
Oil Slick	Earth	Create a flammable oil that sticks to any surface it is cast upon	5m x 5m AOE, lasts 30 seconds	25 mana
AirBlade	Air	Create a blade of air that appears in an arc	15 damage to all targets across an area of up to 10m	25 mana

Weak Lightning Bolt	Air	Causes a weak bolt of lightning to hit the target, the bolt may arc to other targets	10 damage per hit, 5% chance to arc to other targets if within 5m: chance increases by 5% per hit	10 mana
Identify	Light	Shows the caster information on basic targets	Displays information on the target. Higher level or rarity targets may display less information.	10 mana
Chameleon	Light	Bend light around yourself, to blend into the background	You are 20% harder to detect while spell is active. The initial casting costs 15 mana, but the spell may be maintained for an additional 5 mana per 20 seconds	15 mana, plus 5 mana per 20 seconds to maintain
Simple Illusion	Light	Create a simple illusion that will distract those around it	The illusion lasts 30 seconds and will create a mimic of the target at the area chosen	50 mana
Darkbolt	Dark	Hurls a bolt of darkness at your target	Does 10 damage per hit, 5% chance to cause disorientation on hit; chance increases 5% with each hit	10 mana
Wall of Darkness	Dark	Creates a shield of darkness	Shield made of Darkness, can absorb 100 damage, lasts 45 seconds; enemies that touch this wall are struck blind for up to 15 seconds	50 mana
Minor Healing	Life	Heal a target over time.	Heals a target for 20 points of health over 60 seconds	25 mana
Sense Life	Life	Sense any nearby life forms	Sense any life forms within 30m of the caster	25 mana
Lifebolt	Life	Hurls a bolt of life energy at your target	Does 10 healing to living creatures and 20 damage to undead	10 mana
Sense Death	Death	Sense any nearby dead or undead	Sense dead bodies and undead within 30m of the caster	25 mana
Raise Weak Skeletal Minion	Death	Raise a skeletal minion to obey your commands	A Skeletal minion can be raised to obey your commands and will last until dismissed, destroyed, or the mana animating it has been withdrawn.	50 mana, plus 10 mana per hour to maintain

I read through the list several times, before realizing Xiao was talking to me. "What?" I asked distractedly. "Did you say something?"

"Yes, fool! These spells are tools, and all I've told you is advice, nothing more! A real master of magic would make the rules of reality bend to their will, not the other way around!" she snapped at me, then, catching West's disapproving look, she added, "It's like teaching a dog algebra! I waste my time! When I think of the potential of that Pearl wasted on him…bah!"

At this, she stormed off, leaving West and me alone.

"She's at least partially right, lad," he said. "The training that some of your opponents might have had 'quietly' over the years is far higher than the amount we're trying to hammer into you now, and we've only a few months left to go. So, as I said, don't waste too much time on the magic, at least not yet. Take the spells. Maybe you can learn to use them better on the other side, but between now and then, the most you will be able to do is hit them with one or two spells, then you'll be out. Better to focus on your fighting; at least then you stand a chance."

"Thanks, West. I'll think about it and let you know what I decide. One question, though: you say they'll have had years of training, but the Baron only picked me and Tommy up with, what, six months to go?"

"Aye, some of them will have. Some of the Great Houses are…well, they're a lot more sentimental and…nicer…than the Baron. They might send a son or daughter to fight in the arena, but they'll at least train them first. The Baron doesn't believe in 'wasting time with unproven meat,' as he puts it."

"Seems a bit stupid. After all, he wants me to win, right?" I asked.

"Aye, but remember, lad, he's sent probably hundreds to the arena, and will probably send a hundred more after you if you fail. He's immortal, so he's got plenty of time."

"Still seems shitty," I muttered before nodding as West opened his mouth. "I know, though, he doesn't give a shit. Fine. My life might mean nothing to him, but I'm attached to it, and Tommy's out there somewhere. I'll find him."

"Good lad. Look, I'll see you in the morning. Take the rest of the day to recover and think on what we've said. You'll need to choose, and then let me know, so I can tailor the rest of your training if I need to. One last thing to consider…you might not like it, but you're nobility now. Xiao isn't, despite her attitude. Just sayin'." With that, he turned and walked from the room, the click of the door loud in the silence that followed.

I sat for a while, thinking about the options I had. The classes would make a huge difference to me. I could be whatever I wanted in that world, it seemed. I just had to fight for it. I could have been anything here too, but I couldn't boost myself in the same way in "real" life.

I went and lay on my bed and thought about the future, about the characters I'd played over the years in games, about the books and movies I loved. I knew what I wanted to be, but I had not considered if it was really right to do it.

The *Dreams* had shown me a lot about myself. I'd jump in to help anyone, even dying to keep them safe, if need be. Yet here, I'd taken the easy route: the violence, the petty thefts, the threats and promises I'd made over the years. I got up, dragging a heavy chair across to the huge mirror on one wall, and sat there staring into my own eyes. Someone came in after a while, lighting the fire and turning on the lights. They talked to me, but seeing that I was absorbed in my reflections, they left quietly.

I'd been an asshole, I decided after a while. In the Dreams, in the games I'd played, and in all my favorite books, I'd played the hero. But here, where it really counted, I'd been lazy, a petty criminal, and an asshole. I'd helped people when I could, but I'd rarely gone out of my way to do so. Since losing Tommy, I'd been even worse.

This was an opportunity to change. I'd be damned if I wasn't going to take it.

CHAPTER SEVEN

I spent the rest of the day, as well as most of the night, in contemplation. I finally dropped off to sleep in the early hours as I came to terms with a decision I'd circled for hours. Namely, that I was going to be a Spellsword.

I'd forced myself to sleep on it, despite knowing in the first minute of reading the options that it was what I wanted. Giving myself the extra few hours to change my mind felt alternately like cowardice and common sense, but if this was a decision that would affect me for the rest of my life, I had to take it seriously. I'd been a waste of skin for enough of that time, and it was time to do something that mattered.

When I awoke the next morning, sandy-eyed and exhausted, it was to the smell of freshly cooked breakfast. Sausages, bacon, fried eggs, hash browns, and beans, all served with a mountain of toast dripping in butter waited for me. I rolled out of bed, coming to my feet in a rush as the girls arranged the food on the small table for me. I was across the room and sinking my teeth into a slice of toast so deep with butter that I left clear teeth marks before my brain kicked in fully.

"What happened to all the healthy crap?" I mumbled around a forkful of sausage dipped in fried egg, shoving food in around my words.

"Captain West gave special orders to the kitchen, my lord. He said you had 'suffered enough' and needed some real food," said Jenny.

She was the taller of the two girls who had first met me and had a smile that could melt a glacier in seconds.

She grinned at me as I wolfed down forkful after forkful. "Looks like the real way to your heart is through the belly!"

"Gods, yes. I don't care what's going on; if I get real food again, I'm ecstatic! West sent this?" I asked again, wanting to make sure it was him I owed.

"Yes, Lord Jack. Captain West, 'e said that you'd 'ad an 'ard day, and a bad decision to make. 'E said we 'ad to look after you!" Marie added, shorter, dark as Jenny was blonde and with curves that I usually fixated on like a hound on point. Now I barely paid her any attention beyond a groan of thanks as she poured me a drink.

The meal passed in a blur, over far too soon, yet my stomach was practically distended with all that I'd eaten. I sat back, wiping my mouth with a silk napkin, and belched long and loud before blushing and apologizing. If I'd been facing the Baron and his kind, I'd have ignored my manners. But with the girls, it just felt rude.

"So, my lord, can we 'elp you with anythin' else?" Marie asked flirtatiously. Jenny met my eyes and grinned at me, and I damn well knew what they wanted. Truthfully, what I wanted too, as the trouser snake stood to attention, but I'd put things off too long already.

"No, girls, thank you. I can't believe I'm saying this, but I need to get something handled, and it's not you two." As Marie pouted and Jenny sighed in disappointment, the words fell out of my traitorous mouth before I could stop them. "But tonight?"

With slightly happier expressions on their faces, the girls left, taking the dishes with them.

I sat forwards, summoning my status screen with a flex of a mental muscle, and lifted my tea to my lips. Blowing gently to cool it, I checked over the numbers and confirmed the changes I'd decided on last night.

A pop-up flashed in front of my eyes, overriding the character status screen and hovering there, pulsing with intent.

You have chosen Spellsword as your Primary Class. Are you sure?

Yes/No

(Please note: the changes this choice will cause are permanent and cannot be undone.)

I took a deep breath, a quick swig from my tea, and set it down before confirming yes. A momentary sensation of static building up all over my body reminded me of being too close to a lightning strike as a child. Then it began.

Pain! Pain ripped through my body and my brain, not as severe as the Pearl, but a mouse could have starved on the difference! The strands burrowed deep into my brain, widening and strengthening connections, speeding up the synapse relays and rebuilding pathways.

I writhed in agony, and blood filled my mouth as I bit my tongue. As they worked, time seemed to stretch out endlessly. The status page was long since gone, and I stared wildly around the room as my body went into convulsions. Muscles widened, growing bigger and thicker, even as the room changed yet stayed the same.

The room I'd been living in for weeks was full of tiny details I'd missed: gold leaf on the walls and ceiling, worn and obviously not as thick or well-maintained as the rest of the citadel, and every surface bore signs of consistent, heavy use by people who didn't matter. Scuffs on the side table, cracks in the wood—things I'd seen, but never understood—suddenly became glaringly obvious. This wasn't a bedroom. It was a gilded cell.

As my body slowly unlocked from its state of pain-induced rigidity, I struggled to my feet and looked around. Finding little dots in strategic places, I leaned in to inspect one, and sure enough, cameras. "So, the old prick is a voyeur as well, eh?" I muttered to myself before taking the time to give the camera the finger. It took only a few minutes' work to shift things until all the cameras I could find were covered, blocked, or—in one case—broken. I couldn't have caught them all, but I didn't care. I just wanted to piss off the Baron in a way that was too minor to cause a repercussion. Or so I hoped.

If this was the change that a boost of five points brought to my Intelligence, noticing all these details and understanding them, though? I was desperate to get more points in other areas! I looked down at my body, noting the larger muscles, the feeling of blatant power that I was suddenly filled with…and I loved it!

I sat back down in my chair, a faint smile on my face as I brought up my character sheet and looked over the changes.

Name: Jax				
Class: Spellsword		Renown: Unknown		
Level: 1		Progress: 0/300		
Patron: None		Points to Distribute: 0 Meridian Points to Invest: 0		

Stat	Current points	Description	Effect	Progress to next level
Agility	8	Governs dodge and movement.	-20% maximum movement speed and reflexes	0/100
Charisma	9	Governs likely success to charm, seduce, or threaten	-10% success in interactions with other beings	0/100
Constitution	13	Governs health and health regeneration	30 health, regen 4.5 points per 600 seconds	0/100
Dexterity	9	Governs ability with weapons and crafting	-10% to weapon proficiency, -10% to the chances of crafting success	0/100
Endurance	12	Governs stamina and stamina regeneration	20 stamina, regen 2 points per 30 seconds	0/100
Intelligence	14	Governs base mana and number of Spells able to be learned	140 mana, spell capacity: 8	0/100
Luck	8	Governs overall chance of bonuses	-20% chance of a favorable outcome	0/100
Perception	12	Governs ranged damage and chance to spot traps or hidden items	+20% ranged damage, +2% chance to spot traps or hidden items	0/100
Strength	17	Governs damage with melee weapons and carrying capacity	+7 damage with melee weapons, +70% maximum carrying capacity	0/100
Wisdom	8	Governs mana regeneration and memory	-20% mana recovery, 0.8 points per minute, 20% more likely to forget things	0/100

The first thing I saw was that my name had changed, no doubt in reaction to my feelings about the Baron. The Sanguis surname had been dropped, and my given name of Jack had been replaced with Jax, my preferred gamer handle.

I noticed the change to my Strength and Intelligence next. I could now hit harder, carry more, and perhaps I could figure things out better than ever before?

I'd also gained fifty points of mana to play with that was currently ticking up slowly toward a new limit of one hundred and forty points. Most importantly of all, I could now learn eight spells instead of the original five.

I dressed quickly, black pants and a grey top, and pulled the bell-pull next to my table. Jenny darted into the room a second later, and I grinned at the surprise in her eyes as she looked over my body. She apparently liked what she saw, if her grin was any indication. I grinned myself, but I had more pressing things to attend to, as she lifted her hand to the buttons of her top and raised an eyebrow suggestively.

"Ah! No, sorry, Jenny. I do need you, but not like that; not right now anyway. I need you to go to Madame Xiao. When you find her, I want you to tell her this, and make sure she understands it was my command to use these exact words, okay?

"I want you to tell her to get her wrinkled arse to the study in the training hall with whatever she needs to teach me the spells I've chosen to learn, and if she's not there waiting for me when I arrive, I'll kick her down the corridors to my…father…to explain her lack of understanding of her place. Also, find West, and *ask* him to come along too, when he's got the time."

Jenny gulped at having to say such things to the wizened old witch, but she bobbed a curtsy and headed for the door as I added a last request. "And I'll need some more—and bigger—clothes too, I guess!"

She laughed and nodded, then disappeared with a regretful last wink at me. I shook my head as I finished lacing up my shoes and set off out of my room and down the hall, rolling my shoulders and flexing in my top, loving the feeling of tightness I was getting in what had been a loose shirt yesterday.

Whether I liked it or not, the Baron had acknowledged me as his offspring, and it was high time I used that to my advantage, I'd decided. I still hated the monstrous prick, though.

I marched past marble busts and walls that practically dripped gold leaf and onyx inlays. All around me, the building was practically collapsing under the trappings of obvious wealth, and it annoyed me. All this opulence was rubbish. It made a person desensitized to the actual value of the pieces that stood in every crevice. If there had been a quarter of the lavishness, it'd still probably make any palace I'd ever seen in the movies look like a cheap, secondhand shop, but this amount was just overwhelming and boring.

I'd spent my entire life scrabbling for cash. I could literally reach out at random and touch something that was more valuable than every penny I'd ever earned put together, and it was just wasted. The Baron could have had legions of devoted men and women if he'd put a fraction of this wealth into helping them. Instead, it was here, making another corridor extra shiny. Wanker.

I crossed the training hall and opened the door to Xiao's study without knocking, striding past her as she spun around. Her face flushed with anger and hands trembled at being summoned to the room by me, and she'd clearly been pacing when I entered. I purposefully sat in the large, comfortable chair behind the desk, leaving the small stool she'd had placed before it as the only seat for her.

"How dare you—" she began, practically apoplectic with rage, when I cut her off with a raised hand. She stopped, more in shock than anything else, but she focused on my hand and gritted her teeth.

"That's enough, thank you, Xiao. I've spent most of the night in contemplation, and I realized a few things. First and foremost, I'm acknowledged as the son of the Baron...your Baron. And as such, our relationship has gotten off on the wrong foot." I fixed her with a steely gaze and read doubt in her eyes for the first time.

"You see, 'Madame' Xiao, either I die in the arena soon, in which case I have nothing to lose by deliberately sabotaging your career, or I win. In that case, I end up going through to the UnderVerse, and I'm your best chance of ever getting there yourself.

"If I get there, survive, and open the portal, you get to go through. Provided, of course, the Baron doesn't hear that you're sabotaging my chances, and decide to make an example of you." I smiled at her, showing my teeth in something closer to a Bond villain's sneer than anything else. I might be laying it on a bit thick, I reflected, but it needed to be clear.

"I'm listening..." she said, looking at me with narrowed eyes.

"From today, we will be working together regularly. You'll teach me the spells I've chosen, and you'll teach me how to increase my magical skills, Intelligence, and Wisdom. What will change is the attitude. We will work together as equals. Sound good?" I asked, sitting back and watching her face.

Fury filled her eyes, and she could barely get out her words as she replied to me. I tried to look bored and unconcerned, but this bluff could cost me the little help she currently was giving me. On the other side of it, though, actually having her wholehearted help could save me a *lot* of time and effort.

Thing was, it really *was* a bluff, as I had no idea what the Baron would do. He might support me or punish me or have her hanged. The seconds ticked away as we watched each other, but eventually, she replied.

"Equals..." She said the word like it tasted rotten.

"I don't think that's how two equals speak to each other, now is it?" I growled back, letting my anger rise enough to color my voice.

"I...I'm sorry, Jack.... I would like to work as *equals*," she ground out through clenched teeth.

"Good," I said, smiling coldly at her and relaxing. "You'll be glad to know I've chosen a few spells, so the first step is to learn them. How do I do this?"

"The spells are written in the Codex, a collection of spells the Baron has allowed for those of us with skill to study. Each time a spell is read, the parchment it is written on disintegrates as the magic binding it together is infused into the reader."

"And who replaces the spells?" I asked curiously.

"The librarian. He knows the spells and spends his time replacing spells or skillbooks as they are learned."

"Skillbooks?"

"Books that teach you the basics of certain skills, *obv*—Jack," she said, cutting herself off from the sarcastic answer. Closing her eyes, she took a deep breath and carried on. "Skillbooks teach you the barest basics, usually the simplest recipes and plans, but they take months or even many years to create and mere minutes to read."

"That translates as 'expensive,' then. I take it I don't have any of these books put aside for me?"

"Not that I am aware of. Just the spells, but these are boon enough! Can I ask which you have chosen? And the class you chose?"

"The class is Spellsword, with five points to my Intelligence and five points to my Strength," I said, shifting on the chair. My new size was taking some getting used to.

"The boost to your Intelligence is obvious," Xiao said slowly, reassessing me and gaining a hint of cautious respect in her voice. "Explain to me, if you would, why you chose it?"

"I needed to increase my mana pool, but I also needed to still be able to fight. It seemed the obvious choice, although now I wonder if a boost to my Wisdom for the mana regeneration might not have been more beneficial than the one to my Intelligence. Never mind. Besides, I haven't changed that much, have I?" I said, shifting again and flexing my chest and upper arms and feeling my clothes strain to contain me.

"The less obvious change is the greater. Well-chosen," she said, and I caught the implied insult to my previous Intelligence. I glanced at her sharply before deciding it wasn't worth it and moved onto the spells.

"I've chosen Summon Water, Firebolt, Cleansing Fire, Weak Healing, Weak Lightning Bolt, Identify, and Raise Weak Skeletal Minion. Do you have any comments?" I asked, noting her pensive expression.

After a minute she replied surprisingly positively.

"Water so you can survive, regardless of location, Firebolt and Lightning to fight with, Cleansing Fire to remove infections and diseases, Healing to heal yourself, and Identify to aid you, while Raise Minion can give you help. I am impressed, despite myself." She gave me a small nod of respect.

There was a knock at the door and West slowly opened it, clearly hesitant to enter in case of spells flying. When he found that we were seated, and that I was sitting in the "good" chair, he grinned and entered.

"So, lad, seems you've made your choice, then?" he asked.

"Aye, West. I've chosen Spellsword, with boosts to Intelligence and Strength. I'll need my training to reflect that from now on," I said, giving him a small smile in return. "Xiao is going to be teaching me the spells I need in a moment, then I'll be ready to start training…when, Xiao?"

"Tomorrow," she stated flatly. "You intend on learning all seven spells today?" I nodded in response, and she went on. "The pain of absorbing seven spells at once will be…memorable. You will be incapable of any rational thought afterwards. The stress of absorbing seven spells will be significant as well, and that kind of additional load added to your mind will have certain side effects."

"Go on," I said, a bad feeling rising in my gut.

"The human mind can only absorb so much. Although a single spell might not seem like much, there are hundreds of hours of arcane knowledge included, as well as imprinting the various words, gestures, and limits that you will need to know to properly cast the spell.

"Doing this with seven spells in such a short period could cause damage to your mind. The Baron has never allowed any of his servants to absorb more than one spell in an entire year, but your brother Tommy selected four, and others in your…situation…have taken more. Your brother was in excruciating pain afterwards. You don't have the luxury of time, but you must be aware of this. You are likely to be in some pain for a considerable amount of time."

"How long?"

"How long is a piece of string?" she replied with a wry smile. "It depends on you, Jack, on your mind and on your personal growth. I would say that even a failed absorption of a spell could be useful, however, provided you survive it."

"Well, just come out with it, Xiao. Don't blow sunshine up my arse!" I muttered, imagining my mind being snuffed out by a failed spell.

"If you partially absorb a spell, you will learn part of the knowledge by definition, yes?"

I nodded and gestured for her to go on.

"Well, a spell can be altered by one with the prerequisite knowledge. I altered my Flame spell to cover my hand, if you remember. Any knowledge could help you to unlock other spells. The seven you intend to learn will be the basis of hundreds of spells that you will have the capacity for once you progress your skill sufficiently.

"However, and this is important, Jack—I want your word that you won't attempt to alter any of your spells anywhere near me! The side effects can be spectacular." She glanced between West and me, registering the lack of understanding and letting out a frustrated sigh.

"Firebolt is one of the simplest spells, requiring only a few simple words and gestures, but behind those words and gestures are limits that you are placing on the spell both overtly and subconsciously. For example, you are allowing the spell a set amount of mana, ordering the growth of the Firebolt to cease at a certain size, directing it to fly at the target your mind specifies, then to detonate, mentioning just a few of the variables.

"Any one of these, if not formed correctly, could end badly for you. No limit on the mana? The spell drains your mana entirely, which would result either in releasing the entirety of your energy in an uncontrolled explosion in your hand or firing your entire capacity in one go.

"No limit on the size, perhaps it grows past the size of your hand and causes you injury? Maybe it seeks a friendly target or detonates in your hand, killing you. All these are possible and even likely results of incorrect or altered details in a spell. However! If you understand what you are doing, you can alter the spell positively. Imagine if you were to combine Firebolt with your water spell? You could summon a plume of boiling water at any location you desire. Under a heavily armored opponent, perhaps? Boil them inside their own armor?"

West and I exchanged glances, and I grinned at him.

"Oh no, you fuckin' don't, laddie! No experimenting in the training hall!" he cried out, leveling a finger at me in warning.

I turned to Xiao and found her shaking her head as well, one hand raised threateningly.

"Not anywhere near me, either! I have one life, and I will not lose it because a *laowai* like you makes a mistake!

"Wait until you reach the other side and experiment there, where your mana will replenish in minutes, not days! I want your word, Jack, or I'll take my chances with the Baron for refusing to teach you!"

I grimaced, thinking of the opportunities lost, but agreed to wait until I got to the other side, on the condition that Xiao would teach me all the theory she could on manipulating spells.

"I will teach you, Jack, as agreed," she said, starting to lean back in the stool without thinking, and fell off it. West burst into laughter, and she shot to her feet, running off a stream of Mandarin that made him give her the finger in response. "Cào nǐ zǔzōng shíbā dài!" She took a deep breath and held up her hands in surrender. "Can I please have a proper chair now?"

West left the room and returned in short order with a second chair, smaller than the one I now sat in, but undoubtedly more comfortable than the stool. Xiao directed him to put it to the side of her desk, then waited for him to settle before walking around me to the back wall of the room.

I got up and followed her over, watching as she shifted aside a large tapestry showing the human body in intricate detail. A large, modern walk-in safe sat recessed into the wall. She covered the pad as she input a series of digits, then placed her hand on a palm scanner, and finally rattled off a phrase in Mandarin so rapidly it sounded like a random collection of syllables, before the door unlocked.

As she stepped inside, I discovered that the safe was lined with shelves. One side held stacks of books, while the others held various items, small and large, from tiny rings to swords and breastplates. I looked around slowly, my mouth going dry as I tried to see everything at once. I started to follow her, and a ward flared to life before me, pushing me back hard enough that I staggered and fell to the floor.

"What the hell?!" I said, scrambling to my feet to see a glowing wall of sparks filling the space where I'd tried to walk.

Xiao spun at the flare of magic and quickly stifled a faint smile. "Apologies, Jack. I didn't expect you to try to follow me. Only the Baron and I can enter the vault." She walked through the glowing wall a second later, carrying a handful of books, and set them down on the desk before casually closing the vault again and shutting off my view of what must have been a hundred or more books left inside.

"Sooo…" I started, looking back at the vault, but Xiao cut me off quickly.

"No, Jack, there are no other spells you can choose from. Yes, there are magical items inside the vault, and no, as far as I know, you are not intended to have any. The Baron has said he believes you will be able to defeat the other houses' progeny without, as he put it, 'expensive baubles.' He was very clear; you will not have anything besides the weapons and armor you have been training with."

I started to curse him, and Xiao went on quickly.

"These spells are more than enough for you to win with, Jack, but even if they weren't, the Baron will not relent."

"Aye, because he's a fu…" I sneered, before being cut off abruptly by Xiao, who now sported a throbbing vein in her temple, suggesting she was seconds from death by high blood pressure.

"If you wish my help, Jack, you will not badmouth my liege lord in front of me again!"

I glared at her and she glared back, not backing down. Eventually, I managed to get control of my temper again. I'd had no idea that any of that stuff in the vault existed a little while ago, so I'd lost nothing. It didn't help much, but it did help.

I shrugged and turned away from her, taking my seat and drawing the first of the books to me. Examining the cover, I saw one word emblazoned across it…Firebolt!

I needed that one right at the beginning, as much as I'd tried to look at all the spells objectively. I'd always been a pyromaniac at heart, and that spell? Sure, it wasn't Fire*ball*, but it was as close as I was getting and hell to the yes.

As the old saying went, a bullet might have your name on it, but a Fireball was addressed "to whom it may concern." I was having that!

I cracked the book open, feeling the parchment it was written on. It was thicker than any paper I'd ever felt, and it seemed almost alive with energy. I glanced at the symbols and words that made it up, and seconds later I was lost, reading about the essence of fire and seeing strange circular symbols ringing the page from the center and radiating out. The first one, the very center, seemed almost familiar. I recognized parts of its symbolism from ancient texts that I'd seen on shows on the discovery channel, but these were slightly wrong.

With a slight change in perspective, I realized it wasn't wrong, the shows were wrong. If I linked this symbol with that one there...the resulting collection reminded me of a flame sparking to life. As I moved through the symbolism, I started to make more connections. This bit here meant fuel, so this must mean air, and maybe this was mana?

As I lost myself in the book, an hour passed in the blink of an eye. As I finished the final line, I *knew* why fire burned, the primal forces that it came from, the desire that was linked to it, and why people associated the element with moods like passion and rage; they were all linked!

Life flooded through my body as I moved, much like my blood pulsed as my heart beat. I stretched my right hand out and, staring at the far wall, I pushed the feeling of life in my body to run down into my palm, focusing it into as tight a ball as I could, and spoke the words.

I thrust my open hand forward and *willed* a Firebolt to hit the wall. A flicker of fire burst to life, growing in a second from a tiny spark to a ball the size of my closed fist.

It hurtled across the intervening few meters, the room filling with a whine as the air marked its passage, then a loud crack as the Firebolt hit the spot I'd targeted. A wash of flames burst out across the wall before guttering out and dying. Xiao yelped with surprise, and West reflexively shielded his eyes with an arm, shooting me a warning glare as he lowered it again.

"Hell fucking yes!" I gasped, looking down at my right hand in shock. "It worked, it actually worked!"

I realized that, even while casting, I'd been expecting something bad to happen, for the spell to fail somehow.

But I hadn't failed. I'd cast a Firebolt, for god's sake! I'd actually done magic, real freaking magic!

"Well, at least you show a modicum of talent, then, even if your Wisdom is so pathetic a child of ten could outthink you," Xiao muttered before swallowing hard as I shot her a withering stare.

I pulled out the second book, Cleansing Fire, and read that, too, followed rapidly by Summon Water, Weak Healing, Weak Lightning Bolt, Identify, and finally Raise Weak Skeleton.

By the time I was finished reading them all, I had a cracking migraine, and my head was spinning. I wanted to test each one, but my head let me know that it would be a mistake to cast any more magic yet. This wasn't something Weak Healing would help with, either. I'd overdone it, straining my brain, but some sleep would set me right.

I sat back in the chair, rubbing my eyes, and blearily tried to focus as I glanced around, before falling out of the chair. My sense of balance told me I sat upright, while the rest of the world disagreed. Then West was there, hauling me to my feet and staring into my eyes, before snorting and shaking his head. "Come on, lad, back to bed with you, I think!"

Xiao helped me to the door with West, then the guards who were stationed outside took an arm and my legs, and I was bodily hauled down the corridors and into my room.

The painted ceilings, the glittery paintings, tapestries, and more flowed past as symbols floated in my vision. The *life* flowed through me, drawn from the much, much weaker concentrations of it in the world all around me.

I drew in a deep breath, seeing the faint wisps of mana that floated smoke-like through the air. They shifted in response...then I lay atop my bed, one eye shut, unable to focus, as West lightly slapped my cheek, then peeled my eyelid back to peer inside. He spoke to someone elsewhere in the room, but the words were meaningless. I stared at him, seeing the weak collection of mana drawn to him naturally floating past.

He was gone, suddenly, and Jenny was there, smiling down at me, stripping me off, speaking as if from a great distance...then she was gone.

The night passed in a wild blur, like I was steaming drunk. But instead of the cheerfulness of drink, the world was pain. Pain that built and built. Jenny and Marie came to me again. I saw naked flesh and felt hands stroking me, but...it was all wrong, and I certainly wasn't capable.

I twisted my head sideways and vomited on the floor, a woman's voice nearby shouting and cursing in disgust. Then I was being cleaned up, rolled onto my side, and given cool water to drink, kind voices encouraging me as I sipped and tried not to shake.

I spent what seemed like eternity laid there, my head growing more and more painful, bloody tears slowly rolling down my cheeks, hot, wet blood seeping into the sheets under me as my ears, nose and mouth joined in...and that was the end of conscious thought.

The next morning, I awoke early again, with my head seemingly two sizes too small. I crawled from my bed, gulping down the water someone had left on the bedside table, and headed to the shower. After a long soak and some food, I felt vaguely human by the time Xiao came and found me.

"Learning new spells is always hard," she said, almost kindly, "but seven at once? I would not wish for your head right now! We shall practice meditation this morning. This afternoon, you are back with West and his musclebound fools. Meditation will help. Come." She helped me to my feet, and we went to her office. I caught a glimpse of a burn mark on one wall, and as I stared at it, it all came crashing back.

I'd done real magic! I could still feel the mana coursing through my body. I checked my mana bar, finding, to my surprise, that I'd recovered thirty-seven points of mana in total now, enough for three Firebolts! I almost cast another, just to be sure I could, when my head pulsed painfully, and I thought better of it.

Xiao sat me on a mat and sat opposite me. She folded her legs under herself like one of those meditating monks on TV, but when I tried to imitate her, I quickly gave up. I did *not* bend easily!

She ignored it and directed me to focus on my breathing, guiding me, raising her hand and lowering it, speaking calmly and patiently about the benefits of meditation, of the enhanced regeneration that came from having a body that was ready for mana and more. We spent the next few hours focusing on getting my breathing right and relaxing my muscles, working from the top of my head down to my toes and everywhere in between. All too soon, it came to a halt as an alarm on the desk went off, reminding me that I was due to meet West in the training area.

I was surprised as I got to my feet. My body didn't ache as much as it had when we'd started, my headache was gone, and my mana bar had jumped more than I had expected. When I asked her about it, she said it was normal, and that the relaxation eased blocks and allowed me to regain my mana at almost double the speed I would normally.

I spent the afternoon in the training rooms being beaten soundly by my instructors. They each had an opinion on the best choice for my extra points, it seemed, and all were intent on showing me why I should have picked anything else but Intelligence. I soundly cursed West for sharing that information around.

I settled back into a routine as the days and weeks passed. I would rise each morning at six, eat, then study with Xiao until noon. I couldn't cast spell after spell, as I'd run out of mana after only a few casts, and it took days to recover the mana. But I followed the method Tommy had used, according to West.

I would summon the spellform again, feel the mana build, and say the words, but just before the spell was ready to release, I would instead pull it back into myself, reabsorbing the mana. I spent the first half of each lesson using this practice casting method and devoted the other half to meditation.

The afternoons were spent on physical training, mostly in martial arts now, but eventually weapons were introduced again. It seemed that West had a very definite idea for my training, but all he would tell me was to work hard. Eventually, I gave up asking. I was told that all the exercises, the training, and the practice would enable me to level up, but West made me promise not to do so yet.

I was to learn how to do everything with my body at its lowest level. In the final few days before the arena, I would be allowed to activate the level up, allocate my points however I chose, and improve myself. He swore it would give me a better chance in the actual tournament, so eventually I agreed and gave my word. To remove temptation, I dismissed the notifications marker from my vision as well, knowing if I saw it, I'd want to break my promise and level early.

After two weeks of further study, I had learned all of the basics of magic that Xiao could teach me in the allotted time, and that lesson time was reallocated to more weapons training.

Xiao almost seemed sad as she delivered her final lesson, as we had at least a grudging respect for each other by now.

"You'll have the chance to pick your profession as well, Jack," she'd said in response to my questions about the UnderVerse and its differences. "You may not wish to, but you must consider them carefully!"

"I consider things!" I lied, blushing at the long look she gave me.

"Yes, Jack, I have heard. Trying to trick the guards out of hard-earned wages by playing dice when you could be practicing. That is your choice, though. More importantly, we need to discuss modifiers."

"Ah, okay?" I replied, settling back in my chair for another long-winded explanation.

"What profession will you follow?" she asked, causing me to frown as I sat up straighter.

"Well, I don't know. I was going to find Tommy and get back here; that's all I've been thinking about, really," I said, the words sounding foolish as they came out of my mouth.

"Really? You will survive a totally alien world, filled with monsters by just fighting, then? No trading, no repairing your armor, no earning funds of any kind?" The flat stare she gave me let me know what she thought of that idea.

"Well, no. I'll do something, obviously…wait, when am I going to be trained in a profession? I thought we were stopping these lessons now?"

"We are, Jack, and it is not my responsibility, nor that of any other member of the Baron's staff, to give you a profession. We are teaching you to survive!

"A profession may make that easier, and as such, you will be given some small basic training, but that is all. I'm trying to help you to understand the difference it can make to you."

"But—"

"No!" Xiao slapped her hand down on the table hard, making me jump. "It is not our place to do this. I am giving you free advice, Jack. You can waste it with complaints or listen!"

"I…I'll listen. Sorry, Madame Xiao," I said, forcing respect into my voice and swallowing my annoyance that I wasn't being handed everything on a silver platter. *Time to man up, Jack. Just listen and learn. This shit could be important!*

"Very well. I cannot cover everything today, since it is our last lesson, and I have too little time. The basic concept is this: everything you do is subject to situational modifiers. I can explain it no better than that. Think about a surprise attack; think of the difference in damage it does, compared to a straightforward fight.

"While there is the potential for a quick kill in either, a knife striking when the target does not expect it is far more deadly. No knotted muscles to stop the blade, no heightened awareness or adrenaline-fueled response. This is true of all aspects of life.

"The humble blacksmith will learn as he grows in his craft. With each new level that he reaches, his creations will be greater. It is quantified as a one-percent increase in quality per level he possesses, but this is not the whole story. If he mined the ore himself, used his skill to make the iron, then used this above-average iron bar he is already familiar with, the improvement would be greater."

"Wait, he can be a miner and a blacksmith?" I asked, confused.

"Of course…wait, explain why you look confused." Xiao looked at me askance.

"Well, how many professions can you get? Most games I've played, it's like two, or four at most," I said, my voice trailing off as I heard the words.

"Most…games? I see. You think this is a game?" Xiao gave me a look that made me remember Morpheus and Neo fighting in the dojo. *You think this is air you're breathing…*

"Well, no, of course not. I just…look, people have levels and shit! I didn't know if this was real as well?"

"Indeed. Do you want to take a minute to think about what you just said, Jack, and why you continue to prove to me, every day, that you are an imbecile?"

"No," I snapped, my face red with embarrassment.

"I will make this very simple, as I grow weary of this conversation. If a blacksmith has a level of twenty-five in blacksmithing and a level of fifteen in mining, his creations will have an average situational modifier increase of forty percent. "This is not a guarantee, however! Sometimes, he may do everything just right, which might make it fifty or even sixty percent. Other times, he may make mistakes, creating something that is less. I say this so that you understand: the more areas you are skillful in, the more your chances of survival increase, and more importantly, the better the chance you will have to get us through the portal!"

"Okay, well in that case, what if I—"

"No, Jack." She cut me off with a raised hand. "You have proven yourself again to be a fool. I have given you the information you need. Meditate for the remainder of the lesson; think on what I have told you, and you may find a way to turn it to your advantage. What I tell you is what I have gleaned from the Baron and others. I cannot explain how and why the UnderVerse works like this any more than I can explain why a bee can fly. It just can."

That was the way of a lot of our conversations. Sometimes, she was good and patient with me. Other times, she swore repeatedly in Mandarin and refused to answer questions, but then I'd find a note slipped under my door, explaining as best as she could. She was a pain in the ass and hated being questioned, but she wasn't all bad.

My other trainers slowly began to treat me with grudging respect as well, pushing me harder and making me fight for their approval. One-by-one, a change came over all the people I interacted with. They began to smile, nod, and generally approve as I threw myself into my training wholeheartedly.

I spent most of the nights in the arms of my maids. There were two maids on days and two on nights, and both sets were equally willing. I occasionally tried to protest, pointing out that I wasn't offering anything, and that they didn't have to do this, but in all honesty, I didn't try that hard.

With each week, there was a new theme for my training. Weapons took up the majority, but other strange skills were introduced: cartography, tailoring, even alchemy and blacksmithing. I was taught to maintain my weapons and the armor I trained in, to fix the damage, and how to spot weaknesses in others.

I wondered at the reason behind training in these various skills, until finally, months after my arrival and imprisonment, I was summoned to see the Baron again. In all this time, I had occasionally caught glimpses of him, heard his voice from a room as I passed, or received orders that came from him via my trainers. I had not met with him again in what seemed like ages, yet it was still not long enough.

It had been almost six months since my arrival when I was taken from the training room, still clad in heavy leather armor and dripping with sweat as my chest heaved with exhaustion. I was taken straight to see him, but they took my weapons from me first, unfortunately.

As I entered the drawing room where we'd first met, I came to a stop in front of him. I noted that I wasn't being offered a drink or a seat. The Baron met my eyes casually, holding a snifter of brandy in one clawed hand and tapping his foot as I growled internally and bowed alongside his guards in deference, forcing myself to focus on the carpet pilling rather than the arrogant cocksucker in the chair before me. I just had to get through this, just survive, and then I could get to Tommy...

"Much better, Jack. Seems you can be house trained after all. I'll make this brief, as your stench turns my stomach. This weekend, your training is at an end, the Great Tournament is here. In four days' time, you will either be in the UnderVerse or dead. I recommend the former. You will be sent through to our home, and you will begin your first quest. We have no way to be sure of the point of arrival, although the spells on the portal ensure you will arrive at a point that has generated a portal previously. This is likely to be a place that was a seat of power in our time. As such, it may still be in use now."

"If it is, I want you to kill whoever is there and take control of the surrounding area." He paused to take a drink.

I seized my opportunity. "Kill them? What if they've got guards? Hell, what if it opens into a maternity ward? You said you have no way of knowing where it'll open!"

"No, Jack, I said it will open at a place that previous portals have opened in the past, not just anywhere. Portal structures are highly expensive to build, and as such, they were all built at secure locations, in my day. Wherever the portal opens, that area will serve you well as a base, but if you're too foolish to understand that, then it's no great surprise to me. Once you arrive, you will need to secure the area as a base to work from and level your skills as quickly as you can.

"I'll allow you to make the decision between setting off immediately or waiting a bit, but certainly not more than a few days after you arrive, you will head for Dai'Amaranth. It is the capital city of the empire, and the location of the Great Portal. Once there, all you need to do is to place this sigil stone"—he held up a small, two-inch-long rod of black stone covered in silver symbols—"in the repository. It will activate and use the stone's destination, creating a link to the portal here in my grounds.

"I will march through with my soldiers and assume my rightful place as emperor. Once I am through, I will allow you to make a choice. Either you will serve me as my right hand, swearing allegiance and becoming a prince of the empire, or you may return to this realm and live out your days as an extraordinarily rich man. Perhaps I will even deed this citadel and all my possessions here to you. I am, after all, a generous liege."

"And Tommy?" I asked, trying not to show my skepticism.

"He was given the same quest as you, so after nearly five years there, I would expect him to either be working on this quest or dead in the attempt. Either way, you have the chance to find him, as I promised." He smiled at me sardonically and took another drink as I tried to stop myself from glaring at him. "You have questions, I expect; you may ask them now."

I took a long breath. I already knew there was no chance I'd ever really be made a prince, and even if I was, this prick would be the emperor, so he'd probably kill me even then. I just needed to get through this and find Tommy, so I was going to have to suck it up, buttercup. I had nothing left here anyway, besides my maids, and that was a very…physical relationship. I'd not miss this place.

"Okay…*Baron*. I was told that you came here to flee a cataclysm or something; what happened? What if nobody has managed to open the portal yet because the capital is a crater in the ground?"

"First, if the capital were truly destroyed, we would know. We have made a form of contact with the Great Portal before, but it snapped closed before we could pass through, and has been sealed in some way, thus causing the randomness of the arrival point from this side. It does still exist, boy, I assure you of that. Secondly, the Cataclysm...that is a sore point for myself and my fellow nobles. Suffice to say, the old emperor, our sire, had grown intolerable." He paused, taking another sip before swirling the brandy around, admiring the deep amber color as he spoke. "He had ruled for eons already and intended that state of affairs to continue indefinitely. We decided he should be removed.

"We struck a bargain with one of the gods, Nimon, the God of Death and Destruction. He agreed to assist us, on the condition that we aided him against the rest of the gods. We set a plan in place, and one night, we struck.

"Our assassins and soldiers attacked the priests and high priests of the other gods, killing them and cutting the gods off from the primary source of power, their worshippers. At the same time, when they were at their weakest, Nimon cast a spell that banished them for a thousand years or more, removing their blessings from the emperor and allowing us to kill him." The Baron's face grew red as he spoke, anger filling him.

"Then the traitorous swine showed his true colors, pulling the moon Ishtic from its orbit and sending it down into the south of the empire. The devastation was horrific. Clouds of ash blocked out the sun and the land shook as earthquakes struck. Whole cities closest to the impact were obliterated, priceless treasures lost forever.

"My own summer palace at Yermont was destroyed! Hundreds of my concubines and servants, creatures I'd spent a fortune in time and gold to obtain, all gone! We used our magic to stabilize the local area, ensuring that the Great Portal and the center of Dai Amaranth was saved. But we soon got word that the creatures closest to the impact point had been driven mad.

"Dark creatures not seen in centuries had been freed to roam the land, and our armies were out of position, too far to protect us. We didn't know where to go, where was safe, and even our playthings were rebelling against their rightful masters. We opened the Great Portal to its farthest reach and fled through, taking our wealth and the choicest of our servants with us.

"We arrived here, in this drab and worthless realm, and released the portal, trapping ourselves as far from our home as it was possible to go. Every five years since, we have gathered enough collective mana to open a fresh portal back. We've managed to carve out at least something related to a suitable life at least. So we come to now and your place in this. As I've said, you are to return us to our home or die trying."

I stood there open-mouthed, staring at him. This monumental cock had murdered the old emperor, his own father or ancestor or whatever, done a deal with the God of Death and Destruction, banished the other gods, and had personally helped to bring down a cataclysm that had practically destroyed his own realm. Now he expected me to help him get back there.

I forced my words out, frantically throttling the declaration that I'd burn in fucking hell before I helped this shit-biscuit with *anything*, let alone going back there. Instead, I spoke with as much respect as I could, although I sounded like a strangled cat.

"I...uh...roughly how many people died, would you say...my lord?" I asked, struggling to get my head around the utter arrogance he displayed.

"People? Who knows? A few hundred thousand peasants at the impact, perhaps. A few hundred times more than in the time that followed." He shrugged as if it'd never crossed his mind. "Probably another few hundred thousand dwarves and elves as well. Oh, and the naga capital was somewhere around the impact point, so I'd imagine most of them died. Why?"

"Hundreds of thousands of people...probably millions...and they all died because you wanted to be the emperor?" I whispered as I stared at him.

"Pay attention, boy! There weren't that many people in the south lands. I already told you that; it was mostly just elves, dwarves, and naga, lesser races and scum like that."

I continued to stare at him in wonder. I'd never understood racists, hell, I hated *everyone* equally until they proved they were either okay or deserved a good kicking, as that was easier, but he was a new level of even that, a speciesist. I'd seen a few dark-skinned men and women around the citadel, but only in low positions, away from him. I didn't know if that was a coincidence, and he was a racist, too. I shook my head and added it to the things I'd be thrilled to kick his teeth in for later, not willing to lose this chance to ask questions.

"Okay...you and I are related, I get that, but how come I don't have any of your more...obvious differences? I mean you tower over me, claws, scales, the works. How does that happen?"

"Hah! A good question at last! This is the result of following the path of Augmentation. Your Pearl grants you many abilities, as well as awakening your latent magical abilities. But one that is possibly both the greatest and the least understood is the ability to augment *yourself*. When you fight a particularly strong opponent they can drop Essence Cores, and you may have the chance to absorb some of their life force or *essence*. It depends on your nodes, really.

"If your Pearl has leveled to the point that it is capable of granting you a further node, and you haven't picked it, you can attempt to absorb this essence, including the creature's genetic blueprints, instead. This happens roughly every five to ten levels you advance, depending on your innate capabilities. Once it has successfully absorbed what it can, it will offer you a choice.

"It can augment you physically, granting you an ability of the conquered creature, or it can be used as your first and second were, and improve your meridian nodes."

"Okay, but doesn't that make it hard to blend in, though? I'm gonna stand out as I go through the empire, right? Plus, how does it work that you look down on other species, but you use bits of different creatures to strengthen yourself?"

"I am becoming greater, Jack, closer to the ideal of the gods! Why should I not augment myself with the greatest abilities from those I conquer? Make my skin harder to pierce, make my fingernails into my personal weapons, even grant myself the power of flight, if I so desire? Why should lesser creatures have these advantages? Besides..."

He shifted himself in the seat as though trying to get comfortable, and he suddenly seemed to shrink, his massive form blurring as he grew smaller, his clothes suddenly seeming to dwarf him, until he finally stopped. He sat staring at me, as fully human as I was, or so he seemed.

He was around five feet tall now, with greasy skin, greasy hair, normal nails and teeth, and a chubby little pot belly. The immediate similarities between him and a particular loudmouthed lord that failed to defeat everyone's favorite ogre made me bite back a laugh as he continued.

"I was going to make the change later on, but you might as well see the ease with which I change my form, even here, with the miniscule amount of mana of your world. The changes can be made at will...if you have the skill, anyway. We of the Great Houses often wear our full forms, but at the Great Tournament, it is agreed that we all wear our human skin. Prevents confusion, and all that." He gestured languidly at West and went on.

"That's enough questioning of your betters. Now, Jack, get out. I suggest you train hard; after all, it's your last chance to improve your skills before the arena!"

With that, West grabbed my shoulder and half-dragged, half-led me from the room. When we reached the hallway, I stopped again, staring at him in shock over it all.

He sighed, pulling me to one side, gesturing to the guards to move back and give me some room as we talked.

"Seriously, laddie, this whole place is a mindfuck. But one thing is more important than anything else: you have very little time before the fight, so let's get to it, eh?" he suggested.

I nodded dumbly, unable to believe all the shit that I'd just learned.

I spent the rest of the day getting knocked down repeatedly by West and his cadre of trainers. Before turning in, I'd just gotten naked and was about to call for the maids to chase them around the room, when West popped his head back in without knocking.

"Christ, that's unlucky for you," he said with an evil grin. "I'll have to start calling you 'pencil dick' from now on, rather than Jack!"

"Sod off, you old cock-goblin!" I retorted. "What do you want, or did you just want to come in and see a real man naked?"

"Bah, you know you'd love a moustache ride!" He laughed, walking in and closing the door behind him. Then he took a seat, throwing a towel at me to cover up with. "Right, though; remember the leveling system I asked you to ignore? I want you to activate it again now, if you haven't looked it over yet. Tell me what you've gained, and I'll help you decide where to use the points."

I brought back the notifications symbol, seeing it immediately start pulsing for my attention. A small *XI* symbol showed in the upper right corner. Eleven notifications, I translated, and opened it with a smile.

Congratulations!

Through hard work and perseverance, you have increased your Intelligence by one point. Continue to train and learn to increase this further.

Congratulations!
You have reached level 2.
You have five points to invest in your stats.
You are now at 10/600xp towards level 3.

Congratulations!

Through hard work and perseverance, you have increased your Agility by three points. Continue to train and learn to increase this further.

Congratulations!
You have reached level 3.
You have ten points to invest in your stats.
You are now at 20/900xp towards level 4.

Congratulations!
Through hard work and perseverance, you have increased your Dexterity by three points. Continue to train and learn to increase this further.

Congratulations!
Through hard work and perseverance, you have increased your Charisma by one point. Continue to train and learn to increase this further.

Congratulations!
Through hard work and perseverance, you have increased your Endurance by four points. Continue to train and learn to increase this further.

Congratulations!
You have reached level 4.
You have fifteen points to invest in your stats.
You are now at 50/2700xp towards level 5.

Congratulations!
Through hard work and perseverance, you have increased your Perception by one point. Continue to train and learn to increase this further.

Congratulations!
Through hard work and perseverance, you have increased your Strength by one point. Continue to train and learn to increase this further.

Congratulations!
Through hard work and perseverance, you have increased your Constitution by two points. Continue to train and learn to increase this further.

Congratulations!
Through hard work and perseverance, you have increased your Wisdom by three points. Continue to train and learn to increase this further.

UnderVerse: Brightblade

Name: Jax				
Class: Spellsword		**Renown**: Unknown		
Level: 4		**Progress**: 435/2,700		
Patron: None		**Points to Distribute**: 15 **Meridian Points to Invest**: 0		
Stat	**Current points**	**Description**	**Effect**	**Progress to next level**
Agility	11	Governs dodge and movement.	+10% maximum movement speed and reflexes	47/100
Charisma	10	Governs likely success to charm seduce or threaten	Average success in interactions with other beings	12/100
Constitution	15	Governs health and health regeneration	150 health, regen 7.5 points per 600 seconds	31/100
Dexterity	12	Governs ability with weapons and crafting	+20% to weapon proficiency, +2% to the chances of crafting success	71/100
Endurance	16	Governs stamina and stamina regeneration	160 stamina, regen 6 points per 30 seconds	52/100
Intelligence	15	Governs base mana and number of spells able to be learned	150 mana, spell capacity: 8	11/100
Luck	8	Governs overall chance of bonuses	-20% chance of a favorable outcome	17/100
Perception	13	Governs ranged damage and chance to spot traps or hidden items	+30% ranged damage, +3% chance to spot traps or hidden items	20/100
Strength	18	Governs damage with melee weapons and carrying capacity	+8 damage with melee weapons, +80% maximum carrying capacity	89/100
Wisdom	11	Governs mana regeneration and memory	+10% mana recovery, 1.1 points per minute, 10% more likely to remember things	43/100

I sat in stunned silence, not hearing West when he spoke again. I only realized he was waiting for an answer when he kicked me.

"What?" I muttered distractedly.

"How many points have you got, and what level, you pillock!" he growled out, annoyed.

"I'm...I'm level four, with fifteen points to allocate, and except for my Luck, I'm out of the negatives already!" I told him, catching him up on my new stats. He pulled out his phone and noted them all down, looking the notes over a few times before turning back to me.

"Well, Tommy pumped everything into Strength and grew like some kinda Olympic weightlifter. Here's your chance to show me how much smarter you really are. What are you going to do with the points?" he asked.

"Well, I know you and Xiao were telling me to play to my strengths, but my biggest strength was always being a sneaky bastard, so I'm not gonna do the obvious. Besides, I'm already sodding huge. I don't need more Strength; I need to be faster, smarter!"

"True. Think about your weapons. Are you going to use heavy armor, magic? This is your best chance to survive the arena, Jack, so use it well."

I sat and thought for a while, then grinned and thought *fuck it*. I'd go with my instincts. Either it'd work out, or I'd die, so there was no need to stress over it. I put four points into Luck, taking my last negative stat into the positive realm, and four into Wisdom, giving me a fifty percent faster mana regeneration than average. Another four points went into Agility for speed, and lastly three points into Dexterity, giving me a nice boost to my weapon handling skills. I confirmed it and told West what I'd done.

I had wanted to go more "min-max" and dump all fifteen points into something, just to see what I could do with it, but that would have been madness. I briefly imagined being able to do bullet time with them all in Agility, but I needed to be more than a one-trick pony. Maybe next time.

Immediately, I could feel a difference as my body changed. It wasn't like the first allocation of my points, when I had chosen my class, and it'd felt like my brain and body nearly exploded. This was much more gradual, like a toothache as opposed to breaking bones, but it still really feckin' hurt, leaving me hissing in pain as the changes took place.

"Good all-rounder, eh? Well, hopefully it'll work out for you, mate. One thing we didn't tell you before: the tournament is limited to level ten. So, on one hand, it's a good thing. No level-thirty mages or warriors. On the other hand...there's no limiting the points gained through exercise or study."

"Why the hell didn't you tell me that before?" I asked, surprised.

"Because you might have gone easy on yourself! Means there likely won't be anyone too much higher than you, as the noble houses all tend to give their kids their Pearl at the turn of the year. Anyway, I'll leave you to relax with the girls. Meet me in the training hall nice and early tomorrow, though."

As he left and Jenny and Marie entered, I caught their admiring glances and chucked the towel aside, rising to my feet...and the occasion. Who said a willycopter wasn't the way to a girl's heart, after all?

Early the next morning, I was down at the training hall as West had asked. I'd woken earlier than normal anyway, and I was excited to see the changes in my body now that I'd allocated the points.

West and I started the normal training exercises, finding my body to be much more responsive, stronger, faster, all of it. I asked him about it between reps, and he grunted out that the changes were held back by the Pearl until I acknowledged them. He had no idea why or how, but they were.

I set to work with a passion, pounding the punchbag, then moving on to the Mu Ren Zhuang. West gave up and simply followed along, shouting good-natured abuse at me as I went.

I'd always hated this damn thing. More than half the bruises I had were from hitting it, but my trainers made me go at it again and again, and so I did. I hit it harder and harder, faster and faster, until I finally hit one arm hard enough that it shattered, breaking apart in a shower of splinters. I stepped back, shocked out of my training fugue. I realized my fists, knuckles, the outside of my forearms, my elbows, and my knees were all bleeding, and pain radiated from them in hot pulses. I jumped when I heard clapping from behind me, spinning around to find the Nigerian standing there. With him were my guards for the day, my wing chun kung fu instructor, and my edged weapons trainer. Others were filtering into the room as well. Everyone who had been in the room long enough to watch was clapping, smiles on each of their faces. West stood in the middle, grinning widely. The huge Nigerian man stepped forward and rested a hand on my shoulder.

"Now *I* am proud of you, boy. Soon, you face the rest of your clan, and we shall not be ashamed of you. In these short months, you have become a man. Respect to you, my brother."

It was easily the most he'd ever said to me, probably twice the total number of words he'd ever used around me in one go before, in fact, and pride radiated through me at his words. He may have been enthralled to the Baron, but his skills and his dedication were his own, and he'd beaten me down and remade me.

In a few short months, he and his assistants had literally rebuilt me from the ground up. I'd walked in here a boy in many ways, but looking at myself in the mirror, I was stunned. I'd seen the changes day-by-day, but seeing at the full extent of them now, I had to admit they'd done an amazing job.

I stood just over six feet two inches, but where I had been…well…a little overweight before, with a good layer of fat to keep me warm, now I looked like an Olympic athlete. Heavy muscles, lean waist, and the reactions of a snake, with blood dripping from my injuries and a steely glare in my eyes. *Yeah,* I thought, *I wouldn't want to fuck with me!*

I checked the time, finding it was lunchtime already. I must have spent hours beating that wood, so I stopped for the day. None of my trainers complained. They all had a word of wisdom or a cheery clap on the shoulder for me, and even my guards smiled and nodded to me. I ate a good meal and relaxed, forcing my body to wind down in preparation for the next day.

That complete, I spent the rest of the afternoon asking questions of the guards and my trainers. I arranged a meeting with both the arms master and armorer the next morning to choose my equipment, then decided to retire for the night. Jenny and her friends were waiting for me. This time, I didn't refuse them, and the night passed in a sea of bliss.

I'd spent the day working some muscles hard, and that night, the girls worked others. As I finally dropped off to sleep, I had one last thought.

I was as ready for the fight as I could be.

CHAPTER EIGHT

The next morning, all four of my maids woke me, all of whom were fully dressed, thankfully. Jenny opened the curtains as the others arranged a large full English breakfast on the sitting room table for me: tea, toast, fresh orange juice, the absolute works. It was the kind of food I adored, and I thanked them heartily before plowing into my meal. I barely surfaced for air as the girls talked, preparing my clothes, cleaning the room, and generally trying to distract me from what was to come…even as they smoothly removed any and all trace of my time in the room, while I sat there.

Once I was finished, they lined up and curtsied to me in unison, wished me luck, and then, with tears in their eyes and brief hugs and kisses, they ran out.

I dressed quickly and walked to the armory. I'd been here plenty of times by now, but the sheer size of the room never failed to amaze me. It was bigger than I had thought it needed to be when I had first seen it, but I'd quickly learned that the huge variety of weapons and armor meant it needed every inch of the space, and more besides.

I'd been allowed to choose whatever I wanted from the room and was assured that the others would be given similar equipment. I sorted through it quickly, ignoring the majority of the room. I'd spent hours considering it over the last few weeks, and I'd come to the opinion that, while I was strong enough to wear something like plate mail, I had not had more than a few sessions of using it. If others were wearing it, they'd probably have had years of training and would butcher me. Speed and surprise were my best choices. Well…that and my array of dirty tricks.

I picked thick leather body armor, bracers, and greaves with solid steel plates built in. They were a little bulkier than normal leather but offered far more protection without the debilitating weight issues of heavier armor. I also chose a few "toys" from the assassin's gear section. Throwing stars, thin dirks I secreted everywhere I could, and a loop of razor wire that came built into my belt. They'd be nasty surprises for someone. I tried a variety of helmets on, but in the end, I chose a black helm from the assassin's section again. It was a cross between a ninja's traditional movie headgear and a plain leather helm, and it only minimally restricted my vision while showing only my eyes.

When it came to weapons, I played to my strengths again. The naginata was easily my favorite, and it earned a place with me. Again, I looked it over, marveling at the fact that I'd never seen it in movies before, considering its utility and lethality. It was a cross between a sword and a spear, but not as unwieldy as a polearm and others of that ilk. It stood seven feet in length, three feet of sword tipping four feet of solid oak, with the last half foot sheathed in metal. This section came to a wicked pointed end. The polished wood was smooth to the touch, yet I'd never found it slippery or unwieldy.

The entire thing was made with a mix of old school and modern techniques. Everywhere I looked, I saw attention to detail, and it was beautiful to boot, from the patterned steel blade to the small metal bindings and leatherwork.

I paired it with two shortswords, both in back sheaths, the hilts showing above either shoulder. Despite the way all the movies made it look, it made them a bit unwieldy to draw, but I found that it worked better for me than having the swords banging off either hip. A mace hanging on a belt loop and a dagger on the outside of each shin completed my arsenal.

When my trainers saw me, they all started grinning...then laughing their asses off. I got a variety of comments from how pretty I looked, to suggestions to include a cannon, a missile launcher, and a trebuchet as well. I looked at myself in the mirror and, with a sigh, I found I had to agree.

With all the daggers, throwing stars in a bandolier across my chest, dirks, throwing knives, the mace, the swords, and the naginata, I was *slightly* overloaded. I could walk...but probably not run for long. My speed and ability to dodge would be crap, even with all the points I'd added in. I looked myself over in the mirror and realized I'd probably only managed to carry it all so far because of the Pearl's enhancements to my body.

I went back to the drawing board, and my trainers helped me, offering friendly advice and a few pointed reminders of the real-world limitations of certain weapons. I stripped out almost all of them, keeping the razor wire in the belt, the naginata, a pair of thin dirks that were hidden in my bracers, and both swords. I got a lot of mockery for the swords, but I liked them, and I was a lot better with two swords than a shield and sword combo.

Looking at the pile of weapons I had left behind, I kept thinking "Just one of those, and the two throwing daggers....and maybe..." *Nope! I have to be strong!*

As I made to leave the room, the trainers all lined up and saluted me, right fist to heart, as they did the Baron. I froze, unsure of what to do, then my training kicked in, and I returned the salute. As I walked past the last of them, I felt something pressed into my hand. Looking down, I saw it was my phone and earbuds.

After everything I'd been through, it was a tiny and unimportant thing to have them returned, but it meant a lot to me.

"They're locked down to prevent calls and outside access, but that doesn't mean you can't listen to music, lad," West said. I grinned at him, and he winked back at me before saluting as the others had. As I walked through the halls, everyone I passed did the same.

Even the guards at the Baron's door saluted before knocking and requesting entry. Once they had permission, they let me through, but they followed me in, and the guards already inside the room hefted their weapons. Obviously, trust only went so far.

That was fine, though. Considering what an asshole he was, I'd have no issues kicking his ass. Especially after finding out the depths of his evil nature? Yeah, I'd use the naginata on him happily.

"Humph. A flair for the dramatic, I see. Typical Earthborn. Anyway, I've summoned you this morning for a remarkably simple reason: your Dreams." I froze like a deer in the headlights. I'd meant to ask him so many times, but never had the chance.

"Yes?" I asked cautiously. "What about them?"

"The rune I gifted you with, show me...now," he said, gesturing at my chest. I drew a deep breath and bit down my instinctual response. I exposed my chest, looking down hesitantly. I'd tried to avoid looking at it since he "gifted" me with it, but he grinned at it so proudly, I couldn't help it.

It was maybe six inches across, and looked vaguely familiar, despite glowing faintly with an eerie green light.

"What the hell is this? It looks...weird, but..."

"Ha! Your Han dynasty recognized a symbol of power for what it is. They called it 'demon,' but in fact, it's a containment rune. It can *trap* a demon!"

"What the hell is it doing on my chest, then? I'm not possessed, for fuck's sake!" I snapped at him. "And what the hell *are* the Dreams?"

"Watch your tongue, boy!" he snarled back at me. "The Dreams first. They are a remarkably simple spell, designed by the emperor as a last-ditch effort to save people if they ever needed help, and the legion wasn't around. They were primarily for monster outbreaks, that kind of thing. He commanded that the summoning stones be built and stocked them with all the various weapons the rider would need."

"Rider?" I asked faintly, not wanting to interrupt.

"It's what we call the one controlling the construct. The common people began calling them a 'mana wight,' as it is essentially a form of condensed mana that is forced into a mortal body created by a spellform and gifted with faster reactions than a mortal, enhanced strength and more. Anyway, they are one of the reasons we rebelled against the emperor. Who wants to be made to travel to some village every time some peasant's brat gets eaten by something? He said we were the rulers of all, and so should be the servants of all. Preposterous!" He shook his head in disgust.

I stared at him, wondering how many times I'd been summoned as a 'mana wight' over the years.

"The thing is, we learned how to stop being called. At first, it was a way for us to retain contact with our realm, and that was a wonderful thing, but we were always summoned to some monster, demon, or war, which meant we never got to enjoy ourselves properly, plus any injury followed us back here! So, we finally discovered the rune needed to stop the summoning, and I've gifted you with it. It was a gift to make you safe. All you have to do is tell me the truth, and in return for my generosity, you can do something for me..."

"Go on, Baron, I'm listening," I said, even as my mind whirled.

"All you have to do is put on a little show for me when you're in the arena. You're an animal, so it shouldn't be hard for you. Falco has crossed a line recently, bought a shipping concern I'd intended on investing in. So, if you do end up fighting his representative, I want you to make sure he understands the *true* cost of it. I want you to cut him limb from limb, then heal his wounds, leaving his son, or nephew, or whatever, as a limbless freak as an example! Oh, and take his staff while you're at it!"

"His staff?" I asked, frowning at him.

"His cock, boy! I want you to cut it off!"

"Get fucked." It slipped out before I could stop it. I took a deep breath and hurried on to attempt to forestall the shock in his eyes. "I'm not torturing someone just because you don't like their relative! Besides, what's gonna to happen to the people I could have saved, now that you've cut me off from the Dreams?"

"Don't you snarl at me, whelp!" he snapped back. The guards around me stepped closer, raising their weapons to their shoulders and taking aim. "Who cares what happens to the sheep? There's always more of them, so stop your whining. Look at the state of you, scarred from head to foot! You put yourself in that situation. You took the wounds because you were too slow, too clumsy, or too weak!"

"I took them because I could save people!"

"Exactly! You *chose* to take the wounds. Don't try to deny it! There was always a choice!"

"Deny it? Tommy and I were discharged from the fucking army for them! We both lost our places because they thought we were self-harming! We spent years in therapy as bairns. I kept being told I was crazy because of my Dreams. They medicated me to all hell to try and stop me from doing it! Now you say it's *normal?!* That we all get them?"

I was furious. I didn't even know why, really, except that maybe if he'd found me as a child, I'd have known what was going on. However, I had to acknowledge that him finding me while young would have been worse than anything I could imagine. I didn't know what to think or what to do. I just wanted to punch someone really hard.

"And your question?" I ground out, trying my hardest to stay in my seat and prevent myself from attempting to beat his teeth down his throat.

"A voice, a change, a difference of some kind!" he snapped, sitting forward in his chair, hungry for the answer. "Any change you've felt since the rune activated...anything at all."

I realized that I'd not felt the voice's presence since then, not heard it, nothing. I wasn't going to give him the satisfaction of that knowledge, though.

"No, nothing. What voice?" I answered curtly.

"Bah! I should have known. They said he'd have given up by now; maybe they're right..." he muttered, sitting back in the chair and gnawing on a knuckle in thought.

"Who?" I asked, trying not to swear at him.

"The others, of course, you fool!" he replied distractedly as he stared off into the flames of the fireplace. "They said the spell had failed, that the old fool had tied his consciousness to the entire bloodline. They claimed it'd eventually drive him mad, and he'd seek dissolution rather than go on. We killed everyone that showed the signs. We must have gotten him...we *must* have."

"You killed who? Your bloodline...your *kids?*" I whispered. The horrified shock clear in my voice drew him back to reality as he straightened up.

We sat staring daggers at each other, both hating the other, but needing them as well. I was the first to break, taking a deep breath and looking away. I had to swallow my pride. I had to be good, and not try and beat the fucker's face in. I needed to reach Tommy. "What else do I need to know?" I muttered to him.

"Nothing! That was the only reason I had to summon you, and your last chance to show proper humility, possibly earning a real gift from me to aid you. Now? Hah! Why would I bother?"

"Then I'm free to leave?" I asked. When he snarled at me and gestured at the door, I did just that, jumping to my feet and stalking out.

I had some of the answers I'd needed. I knew what the Dreams were and why I got them at least. Now I knew that it'd be an easy way to spot any others like me, cursed with the Baron and ilk's bloodline. They'd all suffer the same way Tommy and I had.

I shook my head as I stalked around the citadel, ignoring people and fuming all the way.

I'd resolved to do it. I'd fight in this tournament, as it seemed either I'd win, or I wouldn't have to worry about it. Now that I knew about the Dreams being real, I found that I had fewer inhibitions about violence.

I'd killed hundreds in that world over the years, always in self-defense, or to defend another, but still, I just had to keep doing that. They'd attack me, after all, so my conscience would still be clean. More or less.

I even bumped into West as I wandered around. I was surprised when he passed me a book and told me to read it when I had the chance. It was a dog-eared copy of *Ascend Online* by Luke Chmilenko. I was touched, but I couldn't resist the chance to get a dig in.

"West, seriously? I didn't know you could *read?*" I said in mock amazement.

"Aye, well, laugh it up, you ugly bastard. Unlike you, I have good taste!" he replied.

"Seriously, man, who did you steal this from?" I said, shaking my head in mock sorrow. "I know you, West. Your 'reading' consists of books about a big dog called Spot and the pop-up catalog for ladies of negotiable affection—"

West cut me off with a well-timed clip across the back of my head, but we both grinned at each other.

"Just take it, lad. Put it in your bag or whatever and read it when you get bored. We both know you'll love me for it."

I grinned and clapped him on the shoulder as we went our separate ways, his obviously well-loved book tucked into my bag.

A few hours later, a guard jogged up to me where I sat in the gardens, looking out over the snow-covered mountains. He saluted before speaking, which was a nice touch, I thought. "My lord, the Baron orders you to head to the helicopter pad immediately. He said that if you are late, you will be left behind."

I snorted in contempt. We both knew the Baron wouldn't leave without me. The crazy old sod needed me to fight. *He just has to be a prick all the time; couldn't take a day off, could he?* I thought to myself.

I made a point of sauntering along the corridors, taking my time approaching the rear helipad. But the arrival of six more guards, with orders to drag me if they had to, finally forced my hand, and I set off jogging. I reached the helicopter just in time to hear the Baron's screaming fit about "lazy, disrespectful sons."

I grimaced at him as I climbed in and quipped, "Been waiting long? You should have said you were in a hurry."

The throbbing vein at his temple and the bright red of his skin convinced me to leave it at that, though. I wouldn't have put it past him to kick me out here and write off his losses.

It took less than an hour to get to the airport, but the flight to the meeting place took another six hours, time that I spent enjoying the book West had given me and flirting with Melanie, the flight attendant from the flight over, so long ago. We finally landed late evening in mountain territory in southeast Greenland.

According to the map, it was considered deserted. Now that I was here, I could see a good-sized airport, bigger than those on most of the Greek islands I'd visited. The surrounding hills had guard towers, if you looked hard enough. There were good roads, a small town, and a harbor full of ships, from private yachts to what looked like modern warships. I looked around in stunned silence for a while until I couldn't take anymore.

"I thought Greenland was empty, or at least hardly any people. It looks like one damn big piece of ice from satellite maps!"

"Huh, and you believe them, I suppose? Good. Shows our money and influence isn't entirely wasted, then. This is the portal base; it's neutral territory. The Great Houses agreed we would build it so that none would have to accept an enemy into their lands. Even an idiot like you can see the sense of this, surely?"

I glowered at him, and he went on, hissing at me quietly so no others could hear.

"All of the Houses will have sent a representative, even if they have not submitted a challenger. We will all bend our magic to open the gate tonight after the tournament, regardless of who wins, but I tell you now, you had better win! If you don't, and you survive somehow, I will have you tortured to death! No more failures!"

I just grunted at him, and we walked down the steps and across the tarmac over to a large, luxury Humvee.

I'd seen them before and never would have associated the word "luxury" with a Humvee, until now. The seats were deep leather, and the back had drinks cabinets, a TV, a satellite phone; it had everything, and it was long! Easily twice the size of any I'd seen before.

The Baron looked around disdainfully. He might be totally unimpressed, but I decided I liked it. The seats folded down into a double bed, after all! I'd never need a house if there was a bathroom installed. I could tour the world…or not, if I was leaving it, but hey, I still wanted one.

When we pulled up to a large driveway with an impressive citadel at its peak, I started to get out, until the Baron stopped me with a snarl to "remember my place."

I apparently would be taken to the arena next, he informed me, where I would be able to prepare, and I would be given further instructions. This entrance was for the nobility only, not "common scum."

If it were possible to kill with a look, I'd have managed it by now, but he just laughed and told me to "earn my place" again.

Being the absolute bastard that I was, however, I decided it was time to start getting a dig in here and there, considering how stuck up this lot was. I leaned over and propped the door open before the Baron could walk away, and immediately spotted a likely target.

He was the biggest and most heavily muscled man in sight, and he was another noble, judging from his attire. So I shouted at him before anyone could intervene.

"Oi, ya baldy bastard!" I quickly closed the door and leaned back out of sight.

As everyone turned around to look, they saw only the Baron standing there, getting redder and redder by the second. The muscled man started shouting at the Baron as I was driven away, and I began sniggering as I relaxed. *Childish, maybe, but still funny.*

I was driven around the back and into a covered garage, which was barely large enough to contain the hummer. I grunted in annoyance as they made sure the door to the outside world was closed before I was to be let out. The guard up front dropped the privacy shield between us and spoke up when he saw me looking around in irritation.

"Apologies, my lord. We were instructed that no challengers were to see each other before the beginning of combat. The interior doors will open in a minute, once the guards have ensured that the route to your dressing room is clear." He spoke with a clear American accent, without the nasal twang of New York. But beyond that, he could have been from anywhere, as far as I knew.

I shrugged and reclined back in the seat, enjoying the luxury and trying to distract myself from what was to come tonight as I waited my damn turn.

A short while later, I was led through the bowels of the citadel and brought to a pleasant dressing room. A deep pool lay in one corner, steam rising from the water's surface and steps leading down into its depths. Two servants stood waiting for me, a tall man with short blond hair, and a shorter red-headed woman. Both bowed as soon as I entered and called out in clear voices in unison.

"We exist to serve, my lord. Use us as you will." When they straightened up, the woman announced that they were both skilled courtesans and could give medical aid and advice and would do all they could to make my stay enjoyable.

I thought I recognized the eager look in their eyes straight away: another geas. Even here, the bastards were enslaving everyone. I'd hoped it was just the Baron, even though he had said they were all at it.

I had them leave with instructions to come for me ten minutes before my first fight, then I settled down to stew and worry. I'd decided on the course of action I would take, but I didn't know how to pull it off. It would be the luck of the draw if I managed it, but it was the best I could do.

The hours passed slowly, but all too soon, they returned, announcing that the first round would begin in ten minutes.

With them came a pair of officials who checked my blood to be sure I was who I was supposed to be. They also asked a series of questions, from my background to any wishes for my remains if I fell in battle. They finished by reiterating the few rules, making sure I knew them. No attacking the nobles' booths, no magic in the corridors, and no use of healing potions in the arena. I gathered my gear when we were done and followed them out into the corridor.

A detachment of guards in the black livery of the Baron waited for me. They formed up and led me through a series of short, bare walled corridors until we stopped at a large portcullis. West turned to me and gave me a quick grin.

"Don't disappoint me now, lad. I've got money on you winning this!" He winked at me, clapped me on the shoulder, and paused, clearly wanting to say more. Shaking his head and squeezing my shoulder again, he walked away. I nodded to him before turning back and taking a deep breath, then striding under the portcullis.

I exited the corridor into an arena similar to the Roman Colosseum, just smaller I guessed. It was circular with enclosed areas built into the walls one level up for our "betters" to watch from in comfort, climbing higher and higher overhead.

I peered from one to another of the alcoves and, sure enough, quickly found that prick of a Baron sat there glowering at me. I made finger guns with my hands and pointed them at him, winking, before turning my back on him.

I wanted to give him the finger. Hell, I wanted to stab the fucker in either eye and nail his dick to his forehead, but for now at least, I had no choice.

It was "shut up and put up" time. Soon enough, I'd be fighting for my life and heading to the UnderVerse if I won; wasting time on the Baron wasn't worth it right now.

I examined the arena more carefully, noting that the sand was shallow enough to soak up blood, but not deep enough to bog you down. There were various small walls dotted about the place. Finally, sections of the walls were flat, while others had spikes protruding from them in waves. They'd probably come in useful later.

The entire arena was maybe a hundred feet across and fifty feet high, with the onlookers enclosed in clear glass I just knew was bulletproof. They wouldn't want to risk being injured during the "festivities," after all. On either side of each booth were banners that hung in the air. I'd entered through the iron portcullis, which had closed after me, and there was another one on the far side of the arena that remained steadily closed. Hell, there were dozens around the perimeter, which made me wonder if there were occasional free-for-all's as well.

The Baron had a hunting cat as his sigil. It looked vaguely like a panther and was all black, outlined in red, with a black background. I shook my head at its crudity; any halfway decent graphic designer could have done better. I'd have a better one made once I killed him and took over. I paused at that idle thought, then shrugged. I'd kill him for a penny, never mind replacing him as a Baron. Fuck it.

I walked around a little, getting a good look at the inhabitants of the boxes. Several were empty, but most had a few people in them by now with servants providing drinks and food. At a sudden rattle, I turned back to the portcullis opposite the one I'd entered from.

It slowly rose, and a tall man entered. He was dressed in dark leather armor with a sword on one hip and a quiver of arrows on the other, with a bow in his hand. A green cloak covered him from head to ankle, and he kept his face hidden. A hint of a short blond beard peeked out as he pulled his hood further forward, twisting its sides until they met in the middle and wound tight. As the cloak sealed shut, he straightened and started circling me.

I'd frozen, wondering what he was doing, until a gong rang out. He whipped an arrow up, sliding it into place, drawing taut and releasing all in one motion. I barely had time to dive aside, and it missed me by literally inches. I rolled to my feet, then on instinct, I jumped to the right, feeling another arrow pass through the air I'd just occupied. The bastard could see through the fabric of the cloak!

His face was totally covered. It even looked like someone had stitched it closed, and I couldn't even see a seam, but he could see me just fine!

I set off running, left and right, zig-zagging towards him as fast as I could, trying to cover the distance and close in on him before he could hit me. I managed to dodge the next two arrows and cover three-quarters of the distance to him before he managed to hit me with the third. It hammered into my left shoulder, piercing the armor to cut into my skin, but luckily it only embedded an inch or so, the angle and a last-second twist on my part keeping it from doing serious damage.

The real issue was that it staggered me, giving him time to fire another arrow, this time aiming for my head. It struck a glancing blow, but the small steel strips woven into the helm protected me, turning what could have been a stunning or even fatal blow into a painful and annoying one.

He was backing away as he fired, but I'd still managed to approach close to a dozen feet from him, and I staggered back on track, sprinting the remaining distance.

In response, he tossed his bow aside and drew his sword.

While I was fixated on the sword he swung back and forth, his other hand had been hidden from view until he shoved it forward. Red light danced across his fingers and flashed over the intervening space to strike me as I closed with him.

My world erupted into madness as the spell took hold of me. My limbs spasmed and shook as every nerve from my brain to my toes seemed to fill with agony. The spell was over in a few seconds, but I was already falling forwards, plowing a furrow in the damn sand as my brain stuttered back to life.

His sword slashed across my prone form as I tried to roll aside. Thankfully, most of the damage was deflected by the leather armor and the thin bands of metal sewn into it. The tip of his sword dug in, slicing across my ear in a spray of blood as it struck the side of my helmet.

I had rolled away instinctively, lunging to my feet as my mind cleared from the pain and shock and bringing up the naginata. I'd only managed to keep ahold of it by luck and my convulsing muscles' inability to drop it. But now I was determined to make the most of it.

He followed me, trying to keep inside the range of my naginata. But he was in for a surprise, I decided, teeth bared in a low snarl as I yanked my right hand back and high, left hand holding the haft near the blade and guiding it.

I'd fallen in love with the weapon for a damn good reason, and that was because gripping it low with my right for power, and high with the left, but loosely for guidance, meant I could stab forward and send the blade darting about with lethal speed.

He closed in fast, too fast.

I yanked the naginata in close, twisting my body and presenting it straight on to him, giving him the choice of backing off or skewering himself on it.

He slashed sideways, clattering his one-handed sword against the blade of the naginata. I rolled it, slapping his blade aside, then shoved forward with the right hand, sending my blade spearing forwards, the gleaming tip flashing towards his face.

He twisted, barely managing to dodge at the last second, and flicked his left hand forwards, a slim dart of a blade flying at me and making me dodge aside as well.

I rushed in and feinted at his head with the blade of my naginata before spinning and striking his left hand with the butt, numbing his fingers and sending a second dagger flying. He lunged at me, his sword being deflected down by my blade, but it left me out of position, and he knew it. While our blades were entangled, he shoved forward, driving his shoulder into my chest and sending me staggering back. I fell hard, landing on my ass, losing my grip on my weapon. So I immediately kicked out and swept his feet out from under him.

He hit the ground next to me and struggled to hold onto his sword while I rolled over and grappled him. I grabbed his right wrist and banged his sword hand off the ground repeatedly until he lost his grip, and it went flying.

At that point, the fight broke down into a barrage of fists and jabs, almost too fast for thought. We rolled back and forth, sand flying everywhere, until I ended

119

up on my back. It was a risk, but I needed to end this fight fast, as the arrow in my shoulder was doing more damage by the minute. The arrowhead was sawing back and forth, and my arm was already numb and weakening. Soon, I wouldn't be able to use it at all.

He took the bait, lunging on top of me, only realizing how easy it was when it was too late. I grabbed both his wrists, twisting them inwards as I pulled his arms straight. Locking his elbows, I pulled my feet up and planted them hard on his hips. I straightened my legs, powering him backwards, leaving his arms fully extended. Before he could move, I wrapped my left leg around his neck, tucking my foot under his chin for leverage. I pushed him back again with my right leg, then wrapped my right foot around his neck from the opposite angle. With his arms locked and his neck trapped between my feet, I twisted and straightened my legs as hard as I could, pile-driving him into the floor, face-first.

I pulled him back and did it three more times, the sand blunting what should have been a horrific impact into a lesser one, but I was still choking him out at the same time.

He managed to get one leg under him, forcing himself to his feet and lifting me before slamming me down hard. My back impacted the sand and again, robbing an impact that could have broken bones of its force.

He was grunting, frantically twisting and trying to break my lock, out of air and out of time, as he fell sideways. I couldn't see his face, not with the hood covering it as it was, and I bit down, closing my eyes, and shifted, knowing that I had to do it now.

I pulled my right foot back, left still extended as far as I could and keeping him pinned in place, arms still held…

Then I lifted my toes, locked my heel, and stamped as hard as I could, aiming high on the right side of his head where his temple should be, once, twice.

I felt the snap when it came, and his struggles stopped abruptly. I paused for a second, then unraveled my legs and kicked him away from me weakly. The cloak came undone, and his face was exposed for the first time since the fight began. It was a bloody ruin, and the angle his head sat at meant his neck was broken.

I coughed and lay back, staring up at the ceiling and trying to calm my racing heart as a voice rang out across the arena.

I'd won my first fight.

"My lords and ladies! We have a winner! House Sanguis wins and is through to the next round. House Orbis is defeated. The next bout will begin in ten minutes!" The voice sounded cheerful, excited, and as if it was a great spectacle. Meanwhile, I lay there, blinking and looking up at the booths that surrounded the pit.

I lifted my head, glancing around, and after a few seconds found the booth where the Baron sat, and he raised his glass to me. The smug bastard actually looked proud. I let my head fall back onto the sand with a bump. I couldn't believe it; I'd just killed a man for their entertainment, and that fucker was acting like he…like I…I hated him even more.

I slowly got to my feet as four people entered and raced towards me. I grabbed my naginata but recognized the first two as my chamber attendants from earlier, and none of them were armed.

The other two ran to my opponent's corpse, sobbing, and fell to their knees in the sand to check him over for signs of life. They didn't find any, unsurprisingly.

"My lord, you were amazing!" The male attendant gushed at me, while the female one was already stalking towards the other two on the ground and saying something. I ignored their byplay and spoke to the man.

"Just get me back to my room and get this thing out of me." I grunted, lightly touching the arrow with one hand.

"Of course, my lord! This way. Helena will see to your spoils, never fear! I can have that wound taken care of in no time. You were amazing though, my lord, truly! The way you baited him in, ignoring every defense against the arrows; you must be the bravest of all the competitors!"

The defense against the arrows? I didn't have any def—I remembered the small walls, dotted about the floor. Looking at them as I passed, I realized I could have run from one to another and covered at least half the distance safely. *Damn, I'm a fucking idiot, aren't I?*

I staggered along to my room, feeling exhausted and depressed. Once the adrenaline wore off, the knowledge that I'd just killed another man, a real human from my own world, not in a Dream, came crashing down. I felt sick, I felt confused, I felt elated, and that made me feel sick all over again.

Once inside my room, I let the servant, Justin, help me. He stripped my armor off and gently eased the arrow from my shoulder. When we looked at the wound, it was a mess. All the fighting and movement had allowed the sharp tip of the arrow to carve me up.

"Shit, man, can you stitch them?" I asked, knowing that if I lost the use of that arm, I had no chance of surviving the night, let alone keeping my ear attached.

"I can, my lord, but surely it would be better to heal them instead?" he asked me confusedly.

"Heal it? How can you heal it?" I asked, latching onto any hope like a drowning man.

"With a healing potion or spell, my lord. I am experienced with several basic healing spells, but using them now could mean I don't have enough mana to heal you fully later tonight? We also have one potion, but it is a single use, so using it for minor injuries like these would be a waste?" He stood waiting expectantly as I considered the options.

"No, if I don't have the use of that arm, I'll die anyway. Fuck it. Heal me." I held my ear and tried not to think about how close the blade had come. There was no point saving the mana. If I was going to have to fight another round, I needed to be at peak condition.

Justin lifted both hands to my shoulder, and began to chant the words clearly, the accompanying gestures similar to those I had learned for my own Weak Healing spell.

"Healing spells, do they work on diseases? What about cancer?" I asked suddenly, a horrible suspicion in my mind.

"Of course, my lord. Cancer is a simple thing to rectify using specific healing spells. Provided it has not gone too far, it would be relatively cheap in terms of mana, as well." He announced this merrily, as though it was such a simple minor detail, only of note because it allowed him to show his knowledge. Justin moved his hands, glowing with energy, across my wounds, healing them as he went and filling the air with inane chatter about his pride in his skills.

So, not only could the Baron have saved my mother if he'd wanted to, but it would have been simple for him. That rat bastard. I seethed inwardly as Justin finished up his spell. I watched the wound fill with healthy muscle, pushing out impurities, sand, and debris as the skin knit together. Within a handful of seconds, it was healed, with only a faint white line left to mark out its location.

"Uh, my lord, is something…"

"Just drop it. Now," I growled at him. I sat there fuming, trying to tamp my anger down as Justin tried to work out how he'd angered me. When his partner Helena returned, she came in with an armful of gear, dumping it on the bench next to me and curtsying. I looked it over and recognized the cloak my opponent had been wearing, as well as the rest of his gear. I stared at the blood seeping out of it, staining the bench next to me and turned to her in shock to find her smiling widely.

"Seriously, what the actual fuck?" I asked her, gesturing at the gear. "What is this? What, you stripped his body, just in case I fancied a trophy? What's wrong with you people?!" The smile dropped from her face, and she spoke up quickly.

"But…my lord, these are your spoils. Some of it could serve you well. The bow is strong and grants an increase to your archery skill. The armor is unenchanted but strong, and his breastplate is intact, in case your own is damaged? Lastly, his cloak was an heirloom of his house, and so must be powerful?"

I stared at her in confusion before turning back to the pile of gear. She didn't see any issue with looting a guy I'd just killed. Logically, I supposed neither should I. He certainly hadn't paused before trying to kill me. I checked through the gear, not seeing anything besides the occasional carved symbol in the wood on the bow to suggest it was special in any way. I touched the cloak, but it was drenched with his blood, and I could see bits of flesh in the hood. I backed away from it, refusing to touch it.

"Clean it. Clean it all and put it aside for me, " I muttered, trying to keep myself from being sick.

I turned away and stripped off, walking down the steps and wading out into the small pool until I could submerge myself. I took a deep breath and sank to the bottom, sitting cross-legged and letting the world above recede from my mind. I concentrated on my heartbeats, surfacing only to catch my breath, breathe deeply again, then sink to the bottom once more.

When I eventually felt myself in control again, I slowly waded out, climbed the steps, and laid down on the table. Justin and Helena began to massage my skin, rubbing the aches and pains away until I fell asleep.

Helena awoke me two hours later to tell me that the first round was over, and the second would begin soon. That meant six people were dead, and I had to survive this round to get to the final. I felt…different…about things, for some reason. More at peace with it. The asshole I had faced had gone in there to kill me. I was a prisoner. I had decided to try to win this and go help my brother.

I could have refused, and I had no doubt the Baron would have locked me away then thrown me into this arena without the training and weapons. I had no choice, but the rest of them?

They wanted this. Fuck it; I'd take their heads, and I'd go through the portal, all right. But the joke would be on the Baron yet. I'd get him somehow, even if I just embarrassed him as thoroughly as possible before going through.

I'd seen my notifications window flashing earlier, but I'd ignored it. Now seemed like the best time to check it, so I flexed a mental muscle and brought up the page before me.

Congratulations!

You have killed a level 9 Ranger!

You receive 180xp.

Progress to level 5 stands at 615/2700xp.

I dismissed it, pleased to see that I was climbing steadily towards the next level. I'd hoped for more experience, maybe even a level, but hell, it was better than I would have gotten without the Pearl. I dressed slowly, settling my gear into place and checking my weapons.

Before I finished, I put my helmet on the table and told the servants to wait outside and not to disturb me until it was time.

I walked back and forth in the small room, my nerves getting the best of me as I paced. I couldn't help running the fight over and over in my mind, trying to see other ways it could have gone. The truth of it was that I'd been damn lucky, and I threw myself down in the chair in one corner of the room. Paper crinkled, and I looked down in confusion, pulling a folded note from the side of the seat.

It seems you are not well liked by the Baron Sanguis.

Perhaps another House would be a better benefactor?

If you wish to know more of Thomas's tale, then look to us.

I turned the paper over, finding a stylized bird in flight on the back. I'd seen the symbol on the banners that flanked one of the booths, I was sure, but there had been so many. On impulse, I tucked the paper into my pocket. I didn't know who they were, but the last thing I wanted was the Baron knowing I was looking around. I sat for a few minutes after searching for any other notes and finding none, until a knock on the door jolted me from my musings.

"It's time, my lord!" Helena called out as she opened the door. It was time for round two.

CHAPTER NINE

I moved down the corridor slowly, surrounded by both attendants and my guards. West was saying something, but I ignored him, my mind whirling as I tried to figure out what the hell was going on.

Someone wanted me to swap sides? I mean, fuck it, I'd betray the Baron for a used popsicle stick, so yeah, fine whatever. But they knew Tommy? And more to the point, they knew him as Thomas?

He only went by that when he was being serious, we were in deep shit, or…or maybe they'd not known him? Hell, maybe they just heard on the grapevine about me? No, that didn't make much sense, either…

I strode out into the arena, feeling West clap me on the shoulder and back away as I turned, nodding to him and forcing a smile.

"Sorry man, just…ah you know," I muttered.

He nodded, watching me as the portcullis lowered, locking him and his men out of the arena, and me in it.

I nodded again as he wished me good luck, winking at him and turning back to the arena. Taking a deep breath, I surveyed the area slowly, noting the burned patches on some of the barriers, the sections where sand had been kicked over fresh blood, and the sections of wall that still glistened with the wet remnants of the last fight.

This place was a mess, yet every single mark in here was one of desperation, one that told a story I didn't want to hear.

I forced myself to examine the room more carefully. After all, my opponent wasn't here yet, so I looked over each of the banners intently. There was a wide variety of different animals, symbols, and designs covering them, and two houses had birds on them.

Examining the two more closely, I almost pulled the note out to compare. But, at the last second, I thought better of it. One had an eagle with a golden crown floating above its head, while the other was a falcon flying on a field of green. My eyes flicked to the inhabitants of the second booth. Two guards stood at the back, flanking either side of the door. To one side, a young woman sat, tall and regal, but with smudged makeup that had been hastily refreshed. The tracks of tears were obvious on her cheeks, and the way that she clutched something in her lap told me she'd likely lost someone recently. Glancing at the bloody marks on the floor, I grimaced. She had likely lost someone more recently than I had originally thought.

Finally, I studied the man in the middle, who nodded as I made eye contact. He was of medium height, as best as I could judge from the floor below, with an average build and short blond hair. A goatee and a conservative business suit gave him an understated, distinguished air.

The feature that stood out beyond all the others, for me, was his eyes. They were an icy blue, clear even from this distance, as they practically glowed and bored into my own. I broke my gaze away, looking around the room to make sure nobody had entered while I was distracted, then checked on the Baron. He wasn't even in his booth yet. The bastard hadn't even made it to the fight on time!

I shook my head and returned my attention to the man who I assumed was Falco, judging from the baron's hatred of him, and trying not to be too obvious about it. As soon as he saw me looking at him again, he raised an eyebrow as though in question and waited. I had found the author of the note, I guessed, thinking of the stylized falcon, the name 'Falco' and the look on his face.

I tapped my pocket and raised an eyebrow in return, receiving a slow nod. With a rattle, the portcullis to my left started to rise, and I moved to the center of the arena again. It was time. I couldn't afford any further distractions, so I gave a slight bow to Falco, then banished him from my mind, concentrating fully on the fight to come.

I hefted my naginata and readied my stance. The guy who stalked out of the portcullis was a rogue, fully dressed in black leather armor. From his head to his toes, the only flesh I could see was a narrow band across his eyes. Everything else was covered. He carried a whip in his right hand and a dagger in his left, and he didn't even pause for the beginning of the fight to be announced.

He set off sprinting at me, pulling something from a holster on his chest. He threw it at the ground before me, and it exploded, smoke billowing out and obscuring everything.

I started backing up and spinning around, trying to spot him. The whip flashed out from my right, wrapping around the haft of my naginata and yanking hard. The shock made me almost drop it, but I recovered in time to twist it and yank hard in return.

A shadowy figure resolved out of the darkness just in time for me to catch sight of his dagger flying through the air to sink into my leg with a meaty *thunk*.

"Gah! Motherfucker!" I screamed, twisting the shaft of the naginata and bringing the blade down hard as he skipped back. His whip uncurled as my blade passed through the space it had occupied a second before. I staggered forward, trying to catch up with him before he could disappear, but he was gone.

I started twisting around again, trying to guess where he'd gone. When I staggered forwards, my leg didn't hurt that much, but…it was numb, and the numbness was growing. *Poison!* I realized.

A green symbol flashed above my health bar, and the bar began to slowly drop.

Cursing under my breath, I grabbed the blade and yanked it free with my left hand. Peering around, I still couldn't see anything, but I noticed that the mist was also deadening the sound of a fucking *party* going on above me.

I closed my eyes and lowered myself to my left knee, figuring I still had enough power in my right leg to get up, and it made me a smaller target.

I listened as hard as I could, trying to make anything out. Nothing. It was totally silent, until a voice whispered in my ear, close enough to feel his breath on my cheek.

"Boo!"

As I flinched away, bringing both the dagger and the naginata around to strike at the origin of the noise, I felt a piercing agony as another dagger sank into my lower back, ripping into a kidney and staying stuck there. The small blade grated on bone when I moved to catch a glimpse of him as he disappeared into the fog again.

"Argh! Goddamn crazy cocksucker! Gah!" I cried out, forcing myself to my feet and limping in a circle.

Trying to reach the dagger, I dropped the first one on the ground and clawed at the new one, feeling the numbness begin to spread. Touching it sent a wave of sickness through me. My stomach clenched and bile rose with the pain. I wasn't removing it; I'd die faster with it out.

A foot materialized from the darkness to my right and kicked the naginata from my hand, followed by a spin kick to my face that had me sprawling in the sand before I knew what had happened. My mind struggled to catch up with the last few seconds, but the pain!

When I looked down, I could see the tip of the dagger sticking from my stomach. I'd landed on it and driven it clean through. The bleeding was horrific, and the entire wound was numb already. Not a good sign. I had to hold on, to lure him in close, or it was all over for me. Hell, even if I won this, that dagger was in my kidney, and now it was sticking out of my stomach. That wasn't a minor fucking wound!

I struggled to pull my knives from the hidden sheaths on the outsides of my bracers. My swords were too long and unwieldy at this angle. Before I could draw the daggers, the whip lashed out from the dark. Wrapping around my arms, it yanked me forward as the blades went flying.

I ended up sprawling facedown, coughing bright red blood into the sand. Hands jerked the swords from the sheaths on my back and threw them aside. A smack registered across the back of my head, contemptuous in its power. It barely would have been enough to annoy me normally. Now, it left my head ringing.

I coughed more blood into the sand and called out to my opponent as I sensed him stalking me.

"What, you...afraid to"—*cough*—"fight like a man?" I spat more blood out and continued. "You're...a coward...using tricks, can't...fight me fair...had to cheat. You that afraid...of me?"

"Only a fool fights 'fair.' Don't think I don't know what you want—an easy death. You'll not get it here!" He grabbed me, dragging me over onto my back. My arms flopped weakly, with my right fist obviously clenched around something.

He stamped down on my wrist, grinding his boot until my hand opened, and I dropped a healing potion onto the floor. His eyes widened in response to it.

"And you dare accuse me of cowardice? You who thought to bring a healing potion into the fight?!" He flicked it aside with the toe of his boot and flung his arms wide, turning in a circle and speaking to the booths that were slowly emerging from the thinning smoke.

"My lords and ladies! Do you see? He brought a h—"

With his attention diverted by the potion I'd let him find, I pulled the razor wire from my belt and flicked it up and around his neck in one motion. I quickly kicked him in the back of the knee with my right foot.

As he fell, his hands going to the razor wire instinctively, I yanked hard on the wooden grips in my hands. The garrote tightened, the flexible length studded with tiny blades that sank into his throat effortlessly as he hit the floor next to me. I looped the wire around his neck as he scrabbled at it, then I braced my foot against his chest and met his gaze as his eyes bulged in pain and shock. With a furious scream, I pulled on the grip and pushed as hard as I could with my foot, sawing the wire deep into his neck.

There was a gasp, a hiss of air, and a vicious spurt of arterial blood as the edge sawed into his throat. I snarled at him, shifted my grip, and pulled again, harder. This time the serrated teeth slid deeper, lodging in the gaps in sections of his spine, severing the nerves as his head flopped uselessly to one side, eyes still staring at me in horror.

I had won again.

I coughed and spat blood out again as I forced myself to stand. I raised my face to the booths, seeing them all in a blur, before turning back to the body on the floor as I called out as loud as I could into the stunned silence.

"It's…against the rules to…*use* a potion or healing…spell, you prick! Not…to carry one!" I coughed and spat more blood onto the floor as the announcer called out in a shocked voice.

"Well…my lords and ladies! We have a winner! For the second time tonight, House Sanguis wins and is through to the next round! House Dagomar is defeated. The next bout will begin in ten minutes!"

I reached down, almost falling as I grabbed the nearest dagger, then I rammed it into his eye, cutting off the gurgling as he died.

I straightened and turned, almost falling as my pair of servants sprinted for me. The Dagomar servants were walking slowly towards the corpse, heads downcast and arms crossed on their chests in apparent sorrow. Justin grabbed me around the waist, helping me to stand, while Helena brought the healing potion over at a run. She grabbed the dagger and yanked it from my back in one smooth motion while pressing the rim of the small phial to my lips and muttering something as it poured into my mouth.

A strange heat spread out from my stomach, flowing into my wounds and beginning to heal me, even as my knees buckled and I started to fall.

Despite their help, I passed out from the pain and had to be carried from the arena with the guards' help. When I regained consciousness an hour or so later, I was naked, and the pair of them were pulling me to my feet and dragging me off my bed to carry me into the pool. They lowered me slowly into the warmth and let it soak some of the dried blood away. The amount of red staining the water made my stomach lurch.

"Wha…" I coughed and spat out a lump of congealed blood and cleared my throat, trying again. "What"—*cough*—"happened?"

"You won, my lord, again! We feared for you, I confess it, but the razor wire loop, it was inspired! Combatants will be discussing it for years! The way you'd allowed him to stab you, to draw him in, even allowing him to disarm you! Your bravery is legendary, my lord!" Justin was babbling, his eyes shining as he knelt next to me in the pool. Helena leaned on the other side and washed my face gently, taking over for him.

"It was incredible, my lord, the skill you showed. You made it look effortless, the way you just flicked it up and around his throat…magnificent!"

Ha, joke is on them, I thought, *I'd been aiming for his arm.* I was luckier than I had any right to be.

I shifted and struggled free, and they let me rise to my feet. As I stood up slowly, the water flowed from my body, and I scanned myself in wonder. The wounds were almost fully healed. Thin scars were all that remained, still red and livid, but healed enough that I could fight again. I surveyed my body, then the pair kneeling before me.

"How?" I asked. I knew that the one potion we had couldn't have healed all this damage, surely?

"Osun Dagomar's gift, my lord!" Helena replied with a twinkle in her eye. "When I retrieved his possessions, he had two potion vials tucked into the waistband of his trousers. A last resort, I assume, but he certainly has no use for them now. You didn't give him time to use them!"

"And to think he was acting so outraged about you taking the one from here out there with you!" Johan butted in. "But you do know they would have struck you down if you'd used it during the fight, don't you, my lord?"

"I do," I replied. "But only because one of my guards told me on the flight over. Otherwise, I'd have been killed out there tonight. I made sure to ask one of the officials when I was getting ready before the first round if they were illegal to possess in the arena, or just to use. Lucky me..."

"Well, you won again, my lord. Only the final round to go now! We had to use all three potions on you to heal you to this point, but we have faith in you, my lord. You can do it!" Johan said. His smile was huge, and when I shifted my attention to Helena, she wore the same. Both were convinced I'd triumph regardless. They also thought it'd all been a feint, losing my weapons. If people wanted to believe that...I'd let them. I brought up my flashing notification again and found that Osun had been clearly recognized as a rogue. Yeah, I could see that. *Stabby, stabby little prick that he was...*

Congratulations!

You have killed a level 8 Rogue!

You receive 160xp.

Progress to level 5 stands at 775/2700xp.

There was a noise outside, and the door opened suddenly. The Baron marched in, surrounded by his guards. "Get out," he ordered bluntly, and the dripping wet pair floundered out of the pool and ran for the exit. He appraised me, and I lowered myself back into the water, dismissing the screen and floating there as we watched each other.

"You've done well, so far..." he admitted grudgingly. "You have two left to fight now, Ora and Wilhelm. Ora is an archer, skilled at stealth, and has mastered basic fire magic. Expect her to put it to use, as she hasn't yet. Wilhelm is a solid fighter, pairing heavy plate armor with a sword and shield or mace. Expect him to work to wear you down. Both are serious threats. What will you do?" he asked, settling back into a chair.

"Well, I thought I'd kill them, unless you have a better idea, Daddy dearest?" I asked, blatantly mocking him. He stiffened and replied with a low growl.

"You will never call me that again. Do you understand? *NEVER!*"

"Or what? You'll have me killed?" I asked with a snort of derision. We glared at each other, not speaking for a few minutes. Then he shook his head in disgust and broke the silence.

"We will have to address your level of respect, boy. If I have to, I will teach you your place. In the meantime, however, you have a fight to win. Once you've won, you will be given a short time to prepare and gather any equipment you choose before the portal is opened, and you are sent through.

"This is a chance to ask me any questions or make use of my knowledge. Do you really want to pass this up?"

I grunted at him and stood up, focusing on him properly.

"Okay. First, the other two fighters; any advice?"

"Use Ora to take down Wilhelm quickly, then get in close to her. She will want to hold her spells back as long as possible, to ensure she can use them to the greatest advantage. But she's rash, undisciplined. If you give her a tempting target, she will take it without pause.

"Wilhelm is a much more patient man. He will try to wear you down over time and won't fall for the little act you used to draw Osun Dagomar in." He hunched forward and clasped his hands together in his lap, trying to look nonchalant but failing miserably. "So, do you have a plan? Something hidden to take advantage of them?"

"Maybe. I have a few ideas. Why?" I lied cautiously.

"I want to know so that I know what to wager on the fight, of course!"

"Are you for real?" I exploded at him. "You want to know if it's worth betting on me?"

"Of course! If I think you have no chance, then I don't want to lose something valuable."

"Wait," I said as I looked at him in disbelief. "You've been betting on me so far. What were you doing? Betting small 'til you knew what I was like?"

"Yes, exactly. Why risk when I have no idea of the return?" he said offhandedly, as though it was far more important that he didn't lose some trinket than I lose my life.

"You're a real piece of work, you know that? Tell me the truth; am I your son?"

"Of course you are. You wouldn't be permitted to fight if you'd failed the bloodline test," he said, looking offended. "What has that got to do with the risk I'd be taking if I gambled on you?" He went on as I stared at him in shock. "You forget, Jack, until you prove your worth, you are no more than another bastard to me. Perhaps some perspective is in order. How many children do you think I've fathered?"

"I don't know, seventy?" I asked, refusing to be surprised.

"No, Jack. We were exiled here in the year 1346. It took us nearly two hundred years to build the Great Portal and hundreds more to build our own personal receiving portals.

"In that time, I have had literally hundreds of children, if not thousands, and dozens of them were pureblooded. I have seen seven of my true-born noble children pass through the portal to reclaim our world and dozens upon dozens of other bastards like you, pureblood or no. Not one has returned yet, but eventually one of you will, and what do we have but time?

"Even with the pathetic mana of this realm, we are able to hold off entropy. If you open the portal and return us, then and only then will I view you as worthy of my respect. Until that day, you are a servant that may prove valuable. If you die, the only loss is your potential. If I lose a valuable vineyard gambling on you, however, that will be a real loss."

I stood there, contemplating him with disgust. The date seemed to ring a bell for some reason. 1346; it wasn't the great fire of London, it was before Columbus set sail, but after the battle of Hastings…what happened around then…

"The Black Death?" I asked suddenly, the date finally coming back to me. "You arrived during the Black Death?"

"Humph! Arrived *during* it? One of the other Houses set it loose, you idiot. Not that they'd own up to it, but it was useful. It gave us a chance to secure lands on our arrival, despite the loss of a few of our servants to it."

"You brought the Black Death, millions died, and it was merely an inconvenience to you," I whispered, seeing again and again what a monster he was. "How old were you when you came through?" I asked numbly.

"One thousand, six hundred and seventy-four." He said the number as though it was nothing.

"The others you sent through…have you tried to send any through with decent weapons yet? Explosives, or the latest alloys made into armor? Most of the stuff I've seen is pretty standard."

"Which part of 'why waste my investment' are you having difficulty with Jack? Are you really this stupid, or is it a ploy to annoy me?"

"What about magic weapons, then? Some of my opponents have had such things. The first one had an enhanced bow and cloak, and the second had poison daggers, while I got nothing like that from you."

He smirked at my observation. "Of course not. Again, you haven't proven yourself yet. Why would I waste an invaluable, and possibly irreplaceable, item on you?"

"The others did!" I roared at him.

"And still they died, and House Sanguis has made a profit in taking their weapons. Well done, by the way."

"You can keep your hands off them, 'by the way,' you prick! They're mine!" I shouted, jabbing a finger toward him. His guards responded by lifting their rifles and taking aim at my chest. I was too angry to care.

"You can all fuck right off as well!" I shouted at them. "Yes, I have a plan. Yes, I'm going to win, and yes, I'm keeping *my* spoils of battle, you ancient shitbag! Now sod off while I prepare, or we can see how many of your guards survive when I come after you instead!"

He sneered at me but raised his hands placatingly. "Very well. I will leave, but remember, you were the one that cut our chat short. There is much I could have told you about that world…"

"Aye, and how much would be true?" I snapped back at him.

"At least some of it, probably," he replied, "But you'll never know now, will you?" He laughed and walked away, gesturing for his guards to open the door. Once they were gone, the servants returned and asked me what they could do to help. I ignored them and fumed as I gathered my gear and got ready.

A sudden knock on the door made me turn around, ready to tell the Baron to fuck right off again, when West poked his head in.

"There's a woman here to see you, lad. Says you sent for her?" The question was clear in his voice.

He opened the door slightly so that I could see past him, and I recognized the woman who had been crying in Falco's booth. She glared at me over West's shoulder, and my mind went blank.

"Did you call for her, or do you want me to run her off?" he asked, and I shook myself out of my stupor.

"Ah...aye! Send her in, and er...you both leave us, please," I stammered out, gesturing for Justin and Helena to leave the room. As they left, West gave me a pointed disapproving look and tapped his watch, then took up position on the other side of the door, keeping others away and giving us some privacy for what he clearly thought was a quickie before my fight.

CHAPTER TEN

O nce the door closed, we looked at each other for several seconds before I spoke. "So…want to tell me why you're here and who you are?" I asked, trying not to stare at her. She was tall for a woman, six foot three maybe, slim and clearly toned. Her partially unbuttoned cream blouse gave me a generous eyeful of creamy white cleavage. The tightness of the pencil skirt she wore only served to accentuate her figure and make me half hope she *had* come for a quickie.

"I'm Sintara, and my father sent me. With my cousin killed, he thinks you are our best chance, although why, I don't know." She had a voice like honey, with a slight European accent, Nordic, maybe? A shiver ran up my spine at the sound of her voice.

"You…your father?" I asked, swallowing hard before forcing myself to look away. I grabbed a glass and gulped down some water.

Come on, Jack! She's just a pretty girl; not like you've not seen one before! I shouted at myself in the privacy of my mind.

"Falco. You seemed to pick us out of the booths easily enough before. Is your brain damaged now?" she asked waspishly.

"I…okay. Look, let's start again. I wasn't expecting a visitor, okay?" I said, taking a seat on the table and gesturing for her to sit on the chair.

She looked at it as though it was teeming with fleas and shook her head delicately.

"I'll stand. This won't take long, as neither of us has any time. We have…employees…in the Baron's citadel, which is how we know you have no loyalty to him and why you're here."

"For Tommy!" I stated, the distraction gone from my mind. "I'm here for Tommy. Your note said you know something about him?"

"Yes, we do know something. We know which continent he likely arrived on and can arrange for you to enter near the portal where he did, as well as provide a base of sorts for you to start with. In return, however, we want something."

"Name it," I snapped, all business.

"You give me the Baron's portal stone now. I'll give you one in return that looks similar, but that will instead open a portal to us, giving us access to our home, instead of him." She held out her hand, a sigil stone sitting in her palm that looked identical to the one the Baron had given me earlier. I took it, compared the two, and could see no difference.

"Tell me what you know of Tommy, and it's a deal. The fat fuck won't be getting a portal from me," I said, throwing the Baron's stone to her as I tucked hers into my belt pocket. It wasn't a hard decision, as I'd planned on throwing the Baron's stone at him and giving him the finger when I went through anyway.

"He didn't go willingly," she said. "No matter what you've been told, Tommy was taken the same way you were, and he fought it all the way. Our spy talked to him, and he agreed to help us. We discovered the portals in the first place, and we have certain tricks the others don't know about. Most of the portals are inactive, either destroyed, buried, or whatever. But we know Tommy made it through a portal that used to be in the city of Narkolt, on the continent of Dravith.

"We had a tower close to there, one of the Great Towers, but it was under attack when the Cataclysm forced us from our realm. Its portal is…intact. We can send you there."

"Okay, now cut the shit and tell me what's wrong with it," I grunted, knowing from her pause that there was definitely something wrong.

"We sent my cousin through that portal sixty years ago. It worked, but he was never heard from again, and the Great Tower could still be in enemy hands. It would be a great prize for whoever possessed it. It is a magical structure, capable of remodeling itself according to its master's wishes. It was intended as a garrison and the beginning of a new city to increase the empire."

"What enemy?" I asked, my mind racing.

"It was being constructed some hundred miles from the border of the Plague Lands, an area ruled over by necromancers and the Night King. The tower could be inside that border now, or it could be a thousand miles from it. We have no way of knowing."

"Okay, and where is Narkolt compared to the tower?" I asked, a sinking feeling in my stomach.

"It was further down the coast, maybe two hundred miles, but the portal he went through is no longer active. This is the closest confirmed active portal you could use by at least a thousand miles. Without our help, you might end up on the other side of the realm, ten thousand or more miles in any direction, if not a hundred thousand."

"The Great Towers, as magical buildings, were all created with defensive enchantments. They grow to a height of up to three miles and are generally up to a half mile wide at the base. They can provide housing and facilities for tens of thousands and are cloaked from unfriendly sight until within a mile of the base. As such, it may be there still. For all we know, you may arrive and find Tommy there waiting, but equally, you might find a lich lord sitting on the throne. There are some bonuses to a Great Tower, though, if you'll listen?"

I nodded for her to continue, and she smiled a little.

"The Great Towers, as well as being bastions in their own right, were created to be all we would need in a hostile area. They are built with room to house and equip a garrison, crafting facilities, even the Hall of Memories, a secure location filled with spellbooks and the preserved skills and knowledge of hundreds of individuals."

She sounded tired. "It was our intention to send Yeveth there, until he was killed in the first round. We had intended to have you surrender to him if you faced each other in the final. Now, you are our only hope."

"Until five years pass, and you try this shit again, you mean," I snapped at her.

"No. The others don't know, but the Great Portal is failing. We have maybe six more cycles to go before it fails completely. At that point, we won't have the parts we need to rebuild it; we barely had enough to build it the first time. When it fails, the portals will be available from the UnderVerse to here still, but we will be unable to go the other way."

"Six cycles? So, thirty years, yeah? You can have another couple kids and train them up, I'm sure..." I grunted at her, lashing out in anger, despite her having nothing to do with my situation.

"No. Twelve houses put forth a champion each time, but the pattern is set. We will not have another chance to put one forth until the eighth cycle, and we are...not popular. No other house would swap with us. My cousin was..." She dashed tears from her cheeks and took a deep breath. "He was the best of us. The Baron is far from the worst, so I'll let you decide who you want finding their way back there: one of my house, or..."

I grunted at her and sat deep in thought for a long minute. "Maybe I don't want any of you going. Have you thought about that?" I said.

"If they discover they can't return, then they'll have to face reality here. They'll start wars again to increase their power. Millions died last time."

"Fuck. Guilt trip much?" I muttered darkly. "Look, I'll think about it. The deal is you send me there, and I'll take your stone instead of the Baron's, yeah?"

"Yes, the stone is marked with our authority as well, the guardian wisps will recognize it and permit you access, but once you're there—" she started, but I raised a hand to cut her off.

"Once I'm there, I'll decide what I'm going to do. For now, the best you're going to get is that I'll take your stone, unless you have some spells?" I asked hopefully.

Before she could reply, I heard West's voice speaking to someone outside the door. We looked at each other, knowing we had run out of time. I grabbed her hand and spoke quickly.

"Do you trust me?"

"Not in a million years!" she replied, but she looked apprehensive.

"Then this isn't going to help your opinion!" I said, grabbing the top of her shirt. The white silk fabric was overlaid with lace patterned with tiny birds in flight. The top few buttons already being undone allowed me to get a good grip. Her cleavage was further revealed when I tore it open, buttons popping off and flying everywhere.

"What..." she gasped, covering herself indignantly. I could hear the voices outside the door more clearly now, and I spoke quickly.

"I agree; now slap me!"

She looked shocked and confused for a second, then it clicked into place for her. She slapped me hard just as the door opened then stormed out, stopping only to glare at the guards in passing and snap at them that I was *"an animal"*!

West watched her stalk down the hall then looked back at me. My reddening cheek indicated what I wanted him to think, and he frowned and shook his head.

I'd clearly lost some of his respect, but at the end of the day, he worked for the Baron. I couldn't risk him knowing the truth.

One of my guards called out and told me it was nearly time, and on impulse, I called Helena in and immediately sent her to get the Baron to meet us on the way.

I knew there was a chance he wouldn't come, but I'd had an idea, and I had to try it. I was escorted back to the arena by the squad of guards that had been posted outside the room. But before we reached it, I heard a voice call out from behind me, and I let out a relieved breath.

"Stop. I will have words with my son in private before he enters. Give us some space." The guards backed away, moving to either end of the corridor to make sure nobody was eavesdropping on us.

"Well, boy, what is it?" he asked haughtily, his anger still apparent from my earlier dismissal.

"What do the other houses know about me?" I asked quickly.

"How should I know? And who cares what they know," he replied.

"This is important. Do they know much about me? Would they know if I was a mage?" I asked urgently.

"A mage? You? You haven't even begun to unlock your gifts. It'd take years for you to learn, if you even could." He didn't even attempt to hide his contempt.

"Yeah, yeah, you said that before. I get that, but do they *know* I'm not one?"

"Well..." He paused, considering me before continuing. "What have you got in mind?"

"If they don't know I'm not a mage, and they don't have much magic themselves, they won't know if I'm casting a spell, will they?" I said quickly.

"Of course, they will. It's bloody obvious if you're a mage, and if you were, you'd have a much bigger mana pool, and...hmmm."

"But they don't know! What do you have that could increase my chances? Make me look more like a mage?" I asked, sensing his reluctance.

"Hmmm, well, I have one item that might do. It creates a haze shield, but it requires a large amount of mana to keep it active. Trick is, you can't tell its active until it's being used...but you're too weak to use it, both in levels and in Intelligence!"

"I don't have to use it. I just need them to think I am! Now gimme!"

The Baron snarled at the impudent demand, but after a second, grunted and reached up to unpin a brooch from his tunic. It was an orb, about three inches in diameter, and glowed a lustrous white.

"The charge that's in it now will dissipate over the next few minutes without me channeling mana into it, but it should last long enough for them to see it and draw the obvious conclusion. I'll be clear though, boy: I'd better get this back, or those close to you will pay the price!"

With that, he slammed it into my waiting hand and abruptly about-faced, hurrying off down the corridor away from me. I grunted and pinned it on my belt, making sure it was obvious, then continued down the corridor toward the arena with West and his men.

As I came to the entrance to the arena, West halted me, putting a hand on my shoulder. I turned to him, and he stared me in the eyes.

"Good luck, lad. You can do it. The entire squad have bet on you." He grinned at me. "We heard the Baron might not be betting on you, but we watched over you these last months and more. Just our way of saying that we believe in you. Even if you are an ugly arsehole."

I grinned back at him.

"Look who's talking...your mum teach you to bob for apples in the chip pan or something?" I joked, before taking a deep breath and smiling at him. "Seriously, though...thanks, mate. I'll try not to let you down."

135

He nodded, giving me one last shake, then backed up as I walked through the gate, the iron portcullis dropping behind me to lock me in to fight for my life for the third time tonight.

For the first time, I wasn't the first into the arena. This time, the other two were waiting for me. We all paused for a minute, eyeing each other warily.

"You better win this, Jack! Kick their arses!" West called from behind the gate. I shifted my helm nervously, making sure it was seated right.

I made a conscious effort to slow my breathing, the sound of it loud, even muffled by the leather of my helm. With a hard swallow, I tightened my grip on the naginata, the leather of my gauntlets creaking as we watched and waited for the violence to start.

I shifted nervously, feet digging into the sand, and I glanced to my right, finding Falco's booth. His daughter sat by his side again, though she'd taken the time to change her shirt. When I met his eyes, he waited, clearly unamused by the treatment I'd given his daughter. That raised him in my eyes a little beyond the rest at least. I paused, then gave a little nod, which he returned, before taking a drink from his glass and subtly tapping his right hand to his heart in salute.

I thought about the Baron and decided I would burn in hell before I let that asshole loose in another world. But if I ever wanted to come back, I'd need a safe place to portal to. Falco would at least give me a chance to talk if I opened it in his citadel instead of the Baron's.

I shifted my attention back to the upcoming fight. Both of my opponents had noticed the brooch and were shifting their attention between each other and me, trying to judge the greatest threat.

I hoped the Baron knew what he was talking about, as the announcer called out across the room.

"Honored nobles all, it is the final round! Three of our scions stand before you, ready to battle to the death for the right to regain our home! Jack Sanguis, Ora Oyuntal, and Wilhelm Granth, are you ready?"

I lifted my naginata in response, and the other two lifted their weapons as well.

Wilhelm was a huge man, clad in shining, silver-filigree steel from his helm to his boots. He bore a sword in one hand and a shield in the other. As we started, he hunched behind the shield, his blade held ready as he looked from myself to our other opponent.

Ora stood a few feet away in an archer's stance, gripping her bow sideways with an arrow already nocked. She looked every inch the stereotypical ranger, complete with woodland-hued clothing, until I noticed the pretty gleaming metal and rune-inlaid gauntlets on both hands. Her face was veiled, and between that and her hooded cloak, all I could see was the occasional glint of her eyes.

"Fight!" the announcer roared, and I reacted instantly, diving to the side. An arrow split the air above me, hammering into the grate of the portcullis and bouncing off. I rolled further, then dove and rolled again, coming to a halt behind a barrier as arrows peppered the ground nearby. At a sudden jingling clatter, I risked a quick look. Wilhelm had decided to take advantage of Ora's fixation on me and was lumbering towards her.

She backed away, shifting her aim to target him. As she began to circle him, she switched to another, much heavier arrow and fired, backing away almost as quickly as he was closing on her.

I grinned and set off running after them, knowing Wilhelm wouldn't be able to see me coming with that helmet. I sprinted up behind him. Ora glanced at me, but she kept on firing at Wilhelm, obviously deciding that he was the greater threat for now. Distracting him while I took him down was good for her as well. Her arrows targeted weak points in his armor, the joints and his visor. The edges grew chipped as arrow after arrow landed, but the majority were deflected by his shield. He lifted it higher and thundered toward her across the ground at a speed I could never match in his place, encumbered as he was.

He was closing rapidly, maybe ten feet from reaching her, when I reached him instead. I jumped up, putting one foot on one of the barriers that were dotted around the arena, using it to push off harder, higher. With a heave, I raised the naginata overhead in both hands, point down.

I twisted as I flew, using my momentum to bring the naginata down hard and punch through the joint between his pauldron and breastplate. He'd lifted his left arm to hold his shield higher and exposed a section of chainmail, and I didn't let the mistake go unpunished.

The blade of my naginata pierced deeply, cutting through the thin metal, the gambeson below it, and deep into his shoulder muscle before wedging into the flesh at the top of his chest. It lodged in his lung, sticking fast, as my weight and the unexpected attack from behind combined with the injury to bring him down.

As his shield went flying from limp fingers, he fell forward and hit the ground face-first, crying out in pain and shock. I hit the ground, too, the impact knocking the breath out of me, but I had the foresight to roll as I fell. I sprang to my feet as fast as I could, diving behind another barrier I'd picked out during my sprint. As I slid behind it, an arrow winged me, leaving a shallow cut across my right bicep.

I heard Wilhelm crying out in pain and fear as he tried to get to his feet, but nothing else.

I tried to slow my breathing, my panting loud in my ears, and waited. Either Ora would try and finish him off, or she would…

Another arrow slammed into me, somehow penetrating the wooden barrier deeply enough to cut into my armor and leave a bruise, but no more than that, thankfully. I got the picture, though; she was after me, and sure as shit, I wasn't safe here.

I crouched behind the wall then had a sudden stroke of inspiration. I shifted around until I was close to the edge, then took off my helmet. Lifting it in my right hand, I let the very tip of it show above the barrier and *wham*! An arrow pierced it, nearly hitting my hand.

I made it disappear out of sight as though I'd fallen and waited a second, then lunged to my feet, a throwing knife in each hand. Ora hadn't been fooled. She had her bow raised and an arrow nocked, but she'd been watching the far side of the barrier.

In the time it took her to draw a bead on me and release, I'd thrown both daggers and set off running. Her arrow struck another glancing blow, cutting a furrow out of the leather armor protecting the area between my left shoulder and throat. The gash bloomed with a stinging sensation and a burst of pain, but with the adrenaline, anger, and fear, I barely noticed.

Jez Cajiao

I ran at her as she dodged one of my daggers, the second being widely off-target. She lifted another arrow to her bow again, the movement smooth as silk. I drew my right shortsword from my shoulder and lifted my left hand. I contorted my fingers as I'd been taught, unleashing a Firebolt at her. She noticed the brooch and the gesture and bought into my deception fully.

She screamed and dove aside, dropping her bow and lifting both hands in a defensive gesture as she shouted a handful of syllables, and a sparkling barrier flashed into existence around her.

She knelt there, secure in her bubble, as I rained Firebolt after Firebolt into her shield. The blasts kept her occupied, draining her mana as fast as I drained my own.

Her shield was far more powerful than my Firebolt spells, and we both knew it. But between firing my third and fourth spells, I'd cast one she hadn't noticed. A few feet behind her, a small spring had appeared. Outside of her shield as it was, she had not been alerted when it appeared, and it began to spread across the floor, most sinking into the sand, but some running across the surface, and inching closer and closer to her.

I had started the fight with one hundred and fifty mana. With the lack of mana regeneration that was all I had, but I'd only used fifty mana so far, so I began to alternate Firebolts to obscure her vision and distract her, and more magical springs around her. As each spring ran out of mana and dissipated, it left another soaked area of sand behind.

I cast one more, thinking that she was making it easy for me, when she finished her own spell.

She stood up, screaming the last word in triumph as the earth before me shook violently. The sand began building into a small lump, then a mound and more, growing upwards until it was taller than me, its bulk spreading out into a recognizable form.

A humanoid golem of sand towered over me, seven feet tall. Its features were roughhewn and unfinished, with huge fists, legs ending in flat-toed pads resembling an elephant's feet. It clumped about, trying to figure out where it was.

It slowly turned to look at Ora, and she laughed at the horrified expression on my face as she shouted out to it.

"Kill them both!"

It twisted around again, faster than I expected. I backed up, and it set off after me, its footfalls making the ground shudder. It started picking up speed, pounding the sand as I backpedaled furiously. I twisted around and started to sprint away, feeling the ground shake with its approach. Laughter erupted from the booths overhead.

I attempted to kite the summoned creation around the outside of the arena, twisting to hit it with a Firebolt as I ran, but the golem simply shrugged it off. I turned again, following the curve of the room, and found Ora waiting for me. She had dismissed her shield, and both of her hands pushed in toward a Fireball at least three times bigger than any my own Firebolt spell could create. I barreled toward her, closing the distance as I tried to come up with a plan and hoped I could get close enough to attack her before she could unleash that blast.

I'd covered barely half the distance when she looked up at me and thrust her hands forward, sending the Fireball sizzling through the air. I jinked from side to side, but it swerved to track me, guided by her gestures. As I closed the last few feet to it, I saw one chance, thankful for the boost to both my Luck and Agility stats, I took it. Jinking to the left again, I jumped back to the right.

Putting my right foot on the edge of a small wall, I kicked off, using it to do a Fosbury flop over the Fireball. I moved too fast for Ora to adjust to hit me, and I threw my sword overhand at her.

A *boom* thundered behind me, and a wash of superheated air picked my already airborne body up and hurled me even further. I smashed into another small wall and rolled to a halt, coughing and trying to force myself to my feet.

I shook my head to rid it of the ringing in my ears and focused on the world around me. The summoned elemental golem was now a pile of rubble; it must have taken the Fireball head-on when I'd dodged it.

"Feck, that was lucky!" I muttered, trying to focus as I lurched to my feet. Turning around, I suddenly found the world spinning again, and felt myself smashing into the barrier, as pain blossomed through my body.

I spat blood on the floor, reaching up for my helmet only to remember it was long gone. Blood trickled down the side of my head from a scalp wound above my right eye. I ached everywhere, and a strong smell of burning hair filled my nostrils. I shook my head again, looking around the arena and caught sight of Ora as she sauntered towards me. Balanced above her hands were two slowly spinning balls, one that appeared to be rock, and the other fire. She'd clearly hit me with one of each already, judging by the burns on my armor and the ringing in my ears.

Behind her, Wilhelm was struggling to his feet, although how he stood at all with my naginata sticking out of his upper chest like a flagpole was beyond me. My options were rapidly becoming limited. I had to keep Ora's attention so Wilhelm could reach her.

Staggering to the side, I lifted my right hand and started to weave it around my left, making it look as mysterious and occult as possible while muttering phrases under my breath.

She frowned, obviously trying to work out what I was doing, until I pulled my right hand aside, lifting my left to show one upright finger raised in defiance.

She froze for a long second, confusion changing to rage as she realized she was being mocked, which I further confirmed with a big, shit-eating grin. She screamed and flung both spells at me, summoning more as I ducked behind the barrier. It shook and cracked as the spells impacted, the explosions repeating as more followed. I crawled to the side, gathering my feet under me then springing up. I ran as fast as I could, diving into cover behind another barrier barely in time. A wash of heat and pain chased me as something clipped my heel.

I counted ten more hits before setting off to another barrier, but this time, I didn't quite make it.

Something sent me flying, and I bounced past the end of the last barrier, out into the open center of the arena.

"You dare! You, a mere insignificant weasel, *dare* to mock me! I'll boil your blood, I'll melt your eyes, I'll...ahhhhh!" Her screamed tirade cut off abruptly as Wilhelm stabbed her from behind, the point of his sword erupting from her chest just below her right breast.

He didn't have the strength to keep her upright, and she fell forward, twisting around and casting a flame spell at him as he staggered. His armor caught fire with spectral blue flames, flickering along the edges and digging in at the joints and damaged sections. He screamed in pain and flailed helplessly as he staggered backwards.

She pushed herself backwards, holding her right hand over her chest and lifting her left toward him. Another ball of rock appeared and began to spin and grow. Unknowingly, she'd also pushed herself back into the same area she'd been standing in earlier, and now lay in the middle of the wet sand, her own blood connecting the surrounding pockets of moisture.

I saw my chance and took it. With both hands, I cast Weak Lightning Bolt and sent it flashing into her. As the spell drain began to cut off, I forced more mana into it, opening some kind of a channel. What had started as a pair of weak arcs of lightning became a single, much more powerful version that lashed into her, making her scream in agony.

She writhed uncontrollably as the wet sand conducted the power through her, the sand turning to puddles of molten glass that fused with her skin. Blood vessels burst, and her eyes started to smoke, yet still I forced the last of my mana into her. Her screams died away into a faint whistling croak that faded to a whisper. As I ran out of mana, I fell to my knees, completely spent.

I sagged with exhaustion, catching my breath and fighting with a fierce mana depletion headache. Forcing the pain and light sensitivity away, I staggered to my feet. It felt like the worst migraine I'd ever had, but I couldn't let it stop me, not now, so close to victory or death.

Once I was standing again, I staggered a bit but remained upright. I grabbed my remaining sword, yanking it free from its sheath and nearly falling over again. I held my head for a second, before stumbling to Ora, who twitched and shook on the floor before me in obvious agony.

The sounds she made were more like mewling than crying now. Her skin was blackened, her eyes shrunken and boiled away in their own juices. I didn't hesitate, the distress of killing a woman dismissed the pity I felt for this blackened remnant of a human being.

I stabbed down, my sword cleaving her heart in two as it cut through her burnt armor easily. She gave a faint gasp and a final twitch, her last breath sighing out as I pulled my sword free.

I turned to Wilhelm, determined to finish it, and watched as he forced himself back to his feet, smoke rising from his armor as he struggled upright. I stumbled toward him as he planted his sword into the sand, using it to finish forcing himself upright. Blood dripped from his visor as he coughed it up, and more seeped from the bottom of his armor. He turned, trying to determine where I was, but the narrow slit in the visor cost him valuable time as I threw my sword at him. He spotted me just as I slid past him and instinctively tried to block my flying sword.

It clattered off his bracer, and he stumbled around, trying to find me. I'd made good use of the distraction, planting my feet into the sand and leaping up as high as I could. I grabbed the naginata, which was still buried in the side of his chest, wrenching it to the side as my momentum and weight jerked him from his feet and caused him to scream in agony.

I landed hard in the sand next to him and rolled to my feet. Sweeping up his sword from the ground where it had dropped to the ground near me, I hefted it over my shoulder and turned back to him.

His voice rattled from the depths of his helm, barely understandable over the coughing and crying.

"Please"—*cough*—"please, no...I surrender...I"—*cough*—"surrender! Let...me live!"

I paused over him and thought frantically. Did I dare let him surrender? I'd been told it was a fight to the death, but...

"Can I accept his surrender?" I called out. "He can't fight me now." There was a pause before the announcer responded to me.

"What terms will you impose, young scion of House Sanguis?" I could hear curiosity in his voice.

"He swears to never fight me again, and in any dispute between his House and me, he stands aside. And I get any magical items he would have taken to the UnderVerse!" I added the last bit in hastily, suddenly realizing I might lose any loot if I let him live. "If he swears to those terms, I accept."

"I acc"—*cough*—"accept! I accept!" a weak voice cried out from the suit of armor that lay on the arena floor, its inhabitant bleeding out. With that, the announcer called out again.

"My honored nobles, we have a winner! Jack Sanguis has accepted the honorable surrender of Wilhelm Granth and is our new champion!" Polite cheers and a round of clapping echoed around the arena from the booths, and I looked around slowly while trying to catch my breath. The attendants ran out, Helena beginning to strip Ora's corpse as her attendants watched in shock. Justin came to me, offering a glass of water that I greedily gulped down.

"Are you ready, my lord?" he asked, raising one hand in readiness.

"God, yes. Heal me," I whispered, stiffening as he expended the last of his mana on healing me as far as he could. When I could breathe again, I clapped him on the shoulder and thanked him, with the pain much reduced at last.

I turned to Wilhelm and saw his attendants using a healing spell on him immediately, before two more came to join them and tried to move him. His screams rang out as they dragged him to his feet, and I told Justin to go with them to retrieve my naginata and whatever magical items he had.

I spotted the Baron in another booth, smiling widely at an unfamiliar noble who grimaced as he handed something over. The bastard wasn't even looking at me.

He'd just rushed off to get his winnings. I shook my head and looked around, seeing others doing the same until I found Falco. He watched me until he was sure I'd seen him then handed something to his daughter. She took it and left, glaring daggers at me as she went.

He tapped a fist to his heart in salute again then left the booth by the rear door, disappearing into darkness.

My attention was diverted a second later as my guards surrounded me, clapping me on the back and laughing. Two grabbed my legs, and the next thing I knew, I was being paraded around the arena on their shoulders. I couldn't help but laugh at their antics. Despite their magically enforced loyalty to the Baron, I knew the guards liked me.

"You beauty! You absolute beauty!" one shouted as we went. "You won me a house! An actual house, in Italy!" Others called up to me as well. "Ten grand!" "A car!" "I got a fuckin' yacht!"

As they reveled in their winnings, I saw West grinning at me from the exit. I clambered down, receiving more bruises from the round of hands smacking my back than I did in the fight. I eventually got them to let me through, and they formed up at a command from their captain, although they still all sported grins that threatened to take off the tops of their heads.

"How did you do then, West?" I asked him quietly as he fell in beside me, escorting me to my room.

"Let's just say that your other trainers and I did well, Jack. We pooled our money and bet with the lord of one of the noble houses, rather than the guards of others. There's an estate we can all retire to in Florida now. Our families will be remembering you in their prayers for years to come when they find out."

"You have a family?" I asked in mock surprise. "Someone actually liked your ugly mug enough to come back? Must be blind, surely."

"Cheeky bastard. At least my partners don't have to be paid!" he replied, grinning. His humor was quickly replaced with a frown, however, as he shook his head at me, clearly remembering the woman he thought I'd abused in my changing room.

"Two little girls and a wife who complains she don't see enough of me, and I told you that before. Knew you weren't listening! They'll love the surprise break, I tell you, long as she who must be obeyed don't find out it's from gambling! We all have families. The Baron looks after them well, says they can serve in their turn, after all. It's a great honor."

I didn't know how to respond to that, so I just told him I was happy for him, and hoped his family enjoyed it.

CHAPTER ELEVEN

W e reached my room, finding the door already open and the bastard Baron inside, looking over some of the junk I'd collected from the earlier fights. "So, how did you do? Manage to turn a profit?" I asked sourly. That bastard was out to loot anything he could.

"Indeed, I did! Several nice estates and a vineyard!" He rubbed his hands together, looking inordinately proud of himself. "Now, I'll have my brooch back. You needn't think I'd forgotten." He held out his right hand and gestured as I pulled it off and passed it over to him. In truth, I'd hoped to keep it, but I'd known there was little chance.

A knock came at the door, and as I called out permission, both Helena and Justin entered, along with several other servants, all loaded down with my opponent's gear.

I gestured for them to put it on the floor, as there was too much for the tables. They'd even taken Wilhelm's armor. The damn thing must have weighed a ton, as it took three people to carry it! I asked Justin and Helena to catalog it all and tell me what was magical or valuable, and I turned back to the Baron. He spoke up quickly as he eyed the loot greedily.

"I'll take care of our winnings, don't worry. After all, you can't carry it all with you. Maybe just take a few items from here, and I'll see to it that the rest is cleaned and put aside for safekeeping…"

I frowned at him. He was trying to get away with something, but I had no idea what, and I was too tired to care.

"I'll take whatever I want from *my* winnings and dispose of the rest however I decide." I saw him take a deep breath and went on before he could interrupt me. "But! Whatever I don't dispose of is yours to do with as you please."

I wanted to tell him to get fucked, but also, I didn't want him to have time to think and ask to see his sigil stone again before I left.

"Excellent! That's agreed. You can take what you choose, and the rest is mine. Now, why did Falco's little bitch come here? What did she want?"

I felt my stomach clench. He knew who she was. Fuck. I thought quickly and said the first thing that came to mind to make him think I was like him.

"They wanted to do a deal to get his gear back. I said I'd consider it, but she didn't want to pay the rest of the price. That's when she stormed off and West interrupted me. She never even knew I didn't have it. I didn't fight him!"

"Ha! She'd have slit your throat after you were done, boy. And if she hadn't, Falco would have! He might be quiet, with a tendency to watch rather than stepping up like a real man and taking what he wants, but he's powerful. You'd have no chance if he came hunting you!"

"Great." I winced. "Thanks for the warning, late as it is!"

"Well, you're welcome, boy. Now, we will be opening the portal in about two hours. You have an hour to prepare, then you'll be brought to the portal chamber and given your equipment. Any last words or requests before I go? Anyone you want me to look after?" He smiled at me, as though I couldn't see the obvious ploy. Anyone I asked him to "look after" would be kidnapped and brought to his dungeons as extra leverage before my feet hit the ground on the other side. Sneaky bastard.

"No, there's no one. What equipment?" I asked, my curiosity obvious.

"Don't be foolish, Jack. The equipment will be the survival gear you've trained with these last months, plus food, weapons, and whatever other gear you choose to take with you. You are limited only by your ability to carry, but bear in mind that you may need to travel many hundreds or thousands of miles.

"Your trainers have put together a survival pack that should allow you to support yourself in the wild, and I will provide you with a small amount of gold, silver, and copper coins to allow you to purchase anything you should need on the other side. There's no way of knowing where you'll arrive, as many of the portals seem to be blocked or broken. You could end up anywhere there is an intact and uncontested portal: in the deserts of Jimbaii, the mountains of Egret, or even one of the ancient city's Great Towers."

"Great Towers, what are they?" I asked quickly, thinking that Falco's daughter had offered it as my destination.

Most of his ensuing tirade was things I'd already learned, except when he got a greedy glint in his predator eyes.

"If you can locate one, it would have its own portal, and if you can capture it and bind the resident wisps to serve you, then you could bring in reinforcements from here. Depending on how well you do, I may accept that as an alternative to opening the Great Portal, but we will see. It'd need to be returned to full strength to generate a portal of that magnitude, after all, and that would be beyond most. Do you have any other questions?" he asked.

I shook my head and declined, stating that I needed some time to think, to absorb all the information and everything that had happened to me so far.

The Baron and his retinue left, leaving me with Justin and Helena, and I proceeded to look over the piles of gear strewn about the room.

"What items are magical in all of this?" I asked, and Helena directed me to a pile of gear off to one side. Stacked neatly were Wilhelm's shield, Ora's gloves, a pouch, a small dagger, and the bow and cloak from the first fight. I'd never actually heard his name, I realized. There were also a pair of boots, another cloak, a ring, and a bracelet.

"Okay, how do we find out what all this crap actually does? I've not got enough mana to identify it," I asked the pair, and Helena responded.

"My lord, I was taught the basic identification spell, by the grace of the Baron. I can tell you all you need to know." I looked at her askance as I tried to make sense of that.

"How did you all learn magic? I thought not many could do it, but you both can, and Xiao. How many others?"

"Not many, my lord. All humans have the potential to learn magic, but our world is very weak with mana, so any spells we cast can take a great time to recover from. My Identify spell is weak, but I have enough for three more castings. After that, it will take me several weeks to recover enough mana to be back to full strength again. I used it earlier on some of your other possessions. Ummmm…"

"Out with it," I said abruptly, trying to figure out what I needed to identify the most. Definitely the ring; I knew the gloves were to help with casting spells, so I could find out whether they did anything else later. Maybe the pouch and the other cloak? Or the boots...

"You do know there's more than this, right, my lord?" she whispered, looking embarrassed and as though she really didn't want to say it.

"What do you mean, 'more'?"

"The winners of the other rounds all won their opponents' equipment and possessions, but when they ended up being killed, their winnings became the victors' property. Then you killed them, and..."

"So where is it all?" I asked, a sudden suspicion coming to mind.

"The Baron..." She looked as though she didn't want to say anything but couldn't stop herself.

"That rat bastard!" I hissed in anger, "He's got it, hasn't he?"

"Yes, my lord, I...I would assume so."

"And he just got me to agree that whatever I didn't take with me or dispose of myself was his!"

I stood there for what seemed like ages, seething, as I realized why he'd accepted my lame reassurances with Falco's daughter. He hadn't wanted to see anything because he'd been too busy planning to rip me off! After a few minutes, I began to calm down. I couldn't let this distract me. I had too much to do.

"Hell with it. I need your help with these now; I can deal with the Baron later." I turned to Helena, all business again. "Identify the ring first, then the pouch, and finally...yeah, do the bracelet," I requested.

Helena crouched over the items one at a time, placing her right hand on each one as she repeated a short phrase and gestured with her left hand. As she finished each incantation, the item glowed briefly with a soft white light before returning to normal.

"These are valuable items, my lord," she said, straightening up and wincing as her mana bottomed out. "The ring is a ring of healing, which grants fifty points of healing to the wearer twice per day. It has a requirement of a high level of Intelligence to use, however; higher than I possess, at least. Secondly is the pouch. It is a bag of holding and will reduce the weight of any item stored inside by seventy-five percent.

"It will also hold up to one hundred pounds of weight and can hold up to twenty-four separate items. Certain items can be stored as multiples, and it appears to hold several items already: there are ten each of chamomile, feverfew, ginseng, and milk thistle. They each take up one space, as well as a mortar and pestle, several dozen small glass vials, and an alembic, as well as a large container of water.

"Lastly, there is the bracelet. This is a truly valuable item, my lord. It is called the Bracelet of Spell Memory, and it will increase your ability to memorize spells. Most people can only remember a handful of them, but with this augmenting you, you will be able to remember two more than you should! It is a treasure indeed, my Lord."

I looked at the pile of other items that were still unidentified and decided I'd take my chances with it all.

I couldn't fit the shield into the bag of holding, since the bag's mouth was just too small, but the dagger, boots, and gloves went in. I put the second cloak with my armor and bundled up the bow and cloak from the first fight. I told Helena to carry them, sliding Ora's bow and arrows into the bag of holding as well.

I had the Identify spell; it was one of my earlier choices, after all, but in a couple of hours, I'd be going through the portal, and I'd need as much mana as I could regenerate for when I was on the other side. I'd take what I could and Identify it when I was there.

I picked up the shield and weighed it in my hands. The damn thing weighed a ton, far too heavy for me to use with my naginata, but I didn't want to just leave it here, plus taking it had the added advantage of pissing the Baron off. While I'd been busy looking over my loot, Justin had been occupying himself well, replacing sections of my armor with bits scavenged from the sets I'd won. It looked a bit less uniform and intimidating than it had before, but it also looked undeniably cooler when I put it all on and looked in the mirror.

I now wore a pair of boots that came to mid-calf, and black trousers with thin, strong sheets of metal sewn inside thick leather over the knees, shins, and upper thighs. My belt with the razor wire was back in place, and a thick, padded long-sleeved top was covered by a metal cuirass, with overlapping links of metal running down the arms in three slim lines. This reduced the weight and allowed for flexibility while still providing protection.

My shoulders were covered by simple metal pauldrons that linked with my cuirass, and I wore my assassin's helm, which covered my face as much as possible, as Justin had stitched the hole from the arrow earlier.

The cloak draped over everything and hung to my knees, with the hood covering my head. My shortswords were strapped onto my back and covered by the cloak, but I could move it quickly enough that they were still easily accessible. My hidden daggers had been secreted back in my bracers, and I had my naginata back. It had needed some repairs after the last fight, but they were minor and quickly done, thanks to modern equipment.

Once I was ready, I turned to my servants and thanked them for looking after me so well, then took the shield in one hand and my naginata in the other and set off for the Great Portal.

Helena walked behind me, carrying some of the gear, while Justin enlisted some help from my guards and a few other servants to carry the remainder.

As we entered the portal room, I gaped, stunned by the size of the facility. The circular enclosure was easily a hundred feet across and another hundred high, with three dozen raised areas surrounding what I could only assume was the portal. It was tall and rectangular, rising from the floor in the middle of the room, but it seemed twisted somehow. As I walked closer, I found it more and more difficult to follow its edge. It *had* an edge, I could make that much out clearly, but as I tried to follow it upwards with my eye, it twisted, seeming to move inside the structure somehow. But when I blinked, it would be clearly on the outside. The more I tried to follow it, the more confused I grew, and a migraine started to beat away steadily behind my left eye. I shook my head and forced myself to look away.

I saw dozens of people wandering around and talking. Thankfully, the Baron was on the far side and seemed unaware of my arrival.

"Jack," I heard West mutter, and I turned to find him staring at a tall, muscular man approaching. He was huge, with well-defined muscles evident even through his clothing, but he walked as though in pain, and when he stopped in front of me, he was slightly out of breath. We stared at each other for a long moment before he gave me a grudging salute.

"Young Lord Sanguis, I am Wilhelm of House Granth. I…I thank you for granting me mercy, and I am here to uphold the terms of my surrender." He spoke in heavily accented English, a Germanic or Russian background, I'd guess, judging from the accent. But as I looked into his eyes, I found that he was another of the nobles that might not be all I had feared. He seemed genuine, as opposed to the Baron and many of his peers. I decided to act as though he was honorable until he proved differently. It was the best I could do.

"Call me Jack, Wilhelm," I said. I passed my naginata to West and held out my hand. He looked taken aback, but after a brief pause, he grinned and clasped my hand in return, pumping it up and down with vigor.

"It is good to meet you and see you are a gentleman after all. I had wondered, as unknown as you were, and being a Sanguis. Ach, I am forgetting myself." He released my hand and reached into his cloak, and my guards tensed in reaction. "Ah, no! I bear your lord no ill will. He won, fair and square, and I agreed to give him whatever I was going to take with me to the other side, yes?"

He pulled out three items. The first was a thin silver chain with medallion of Saint Christopher on it, the patron saint of travelers, second was a ring, and lastly, a leather-bound book, heavy and old, with gilded pages that made my skin tingle as he deposited it in my hand.

"I agreed, Jack. Now you have a better chance, yes? Stone-Sight is the spell. I never had much skill with magic, but this I would have used. It grants the caster knowledge of the stone around him and any metals and other elements inside it! The ring gives a boost to Wisdom, making your mana regenerate faster, I have heard. The Saint Christopher was a gift from my mother to protect me, and now he will protect you."

I shook my head and handed the chain back to him as I slipped the spellbook and the ring into the bag of holding.

"I'm not taking a gift that you were given by your mother, mate. Not happening. I also brought your armor." I gestured behind me at the servants burdened down with the items.

"I trained in using it, but I prefer medium armor over heavy. Slows me down too much. You might as well have it back; I'm sure you can get it repaired. I can't get away with your shield either. I know it's magical, but I have no idea what it does. Regardless, it's too heavy for me. Here." I passed the shield back to the stunned man and ordered the servants to give him the armor. As he stammered and tried to find the words to thank me, the Baron finally saw me and came over.

"What is this?" he asked, glowering as he saw the armor and shield being taken away by Wilhelm's hastily summoned servants.

"I'm giving Wilhelm his armor back," I said breezily. "You remember I told you I would dispose of *my* winnings as I saw fit, don't you?"

We locked eyes, and for a long heartbeat, stared at each other, the tell-tale red of the Baron's anger mottling his neck and cheeks.

"Very well, Jack, but perhaps we should discuss it before you give any more away?" he responded between gritted teeth. Wilhelm seemed to catch the tension, and he bowed respectfully to the Baron before making a hasty exit. I winked at him and turned to face the Baron fully.

"I have a lot of winnings to dispose of; in fact, I haven't even had time to see them all, just the little that was brought to my room. I wonder where the rest is?" The last was said in a flat tone that the Baron recognized. We both knew what had happened to it, and that he had tried to hide it from me.

I turned to West and took back the naginata before asking the Baron to show me my supplied equipment. He glared but led me over to a table set off to one side where a large rucksack awaited me. I looked it over, searching through it and finding the expected survival gear, tent, bedroll, dried food, two flasks, equipment for making snares, chemical lights, and fire starters. There was even a decent first aid kit. It was exactly what I would need in the field, and not a single bit of it was magical. Not even a healing potion.

I exchanged a long angry look with my "father" before emptying out the rucksack. I put it all into my bag of holding, even rolling the rucksack up and shoving it in. The bag was three-quarters full now, but far lighter than it would have been. I also noted the lack of the promised coinage. That was fine, though. I had time for another dig, and a chance to maybe get some gear, too.

I told the servants to lay out the equipment they carried on the tables, and I raised my voice to the room at large.

"My lords and ladies, can I have your attention, please?" Various people turned to me and began to drift over.

"What are you doing?!" the Baron hissed at me.

I grinned. "It's called karma, Daddy dearest. Haven't you heard of it?"

He went white with rage and raised his hands as if to grab me by the throat before a nearby voice shook him out of it.

"You have something to say to us, boy?" It was Falco, and beside him stood his daughter, eyeing me with, I hoped, feigned disgust. Everyone had approached at least close enough to hear me now.

"Yes, I do. I killed your sons and daughters in the arena. It wasn't my choice to fight, but that didn't mean I didn't respect them. Because of this, I'm making you an offer. I will need supplies on the other side, both magical and mundane. Give me what you think is fair for the equipment your children bore, and besides the few things I've claimed, I'll give you the rest back."

Muttering arose instantly, as the houses that had put children forward to fight saw an opportunity to get some of their gear back.

"Jack…" the Baron ground out through gritted teeth in warning. Here, at least, he'd never dare to lash out at me publicly. I grinned back at him and replied.

"Yes, Baron? Oh, sorry. I should have mentioned this earlier, shouldn't I? *Never mind.* Have your servants bring out all the equipment you put aside for me for 'safe-keeping,' please, and put it on the tables here."

Silence greeted my demand, and the Baron became almost apoplectic with rage, inflamed further by the snickers as the other houses figured out what was happening.

"Is there a problem, Baron Sanguis?" a man asked from one side, his poorly concealed smile serving to make the Baron so angry he couldn't get the words out.

"Ah, I think my 'father' is so overcome with pride at my generosity that he's unable to speak. Don't trouble yourself, Baron, I'll take care of it." I turned to his servants, along with the two that had been attending me, and instructed them to gather all of it and bring it out, including extra tables if necessary. I then turned back to the Baron and spoke to him again. "And you, of course, want to make sure my orders regarding *my property* are carried out correctly and fully, don't you, Baron? Nothing 'accidentally' forgotten; you do confirm that *everything* is to be brought out, correct?"

I prodded, getting only a sharp nod from him in response to his servants' gazes before he returned his attention to me.

"I'd like a word with you, *son*," he ground out.

"Oh no, *father*, I think we said all we needed to say already. I know you get too emotional at times like this, but rest assured, I know the feelings you bear towards me. I feel *exactly* the same about you." I smiled mercilessly as I held my hands wide, then turned to the assembled nobles and addressed them again.

"So, my lords and ladies, who is first? Who values their children's equipment and would like to bargain for it? You can also make an offer on someone else's children's equipment, should the original house not be interested."

Almost before I was finished speaking, Falco pushed to the front of the gathered throng and stated that he wanted his nephew's helm and cloak, and that he would trade me a spellbook for it, specifically Undead Servant. I pretended to think it over for several seconds before agreeing.

Helena, who had just returned with an armful of gear, dumped it on a newly placed table and scooped up the items requested. She handed them to Falco, and he held them reverently for a second before telling his daughter to give me the book, unshed tears in his voice as he turned and stalked away.

I slipped the book into my pouch and clapped my hands together loudly. I'd look at the spellbook later. "Righto, then; who's next?"

The Baron tried to interject several times, but I managed to shut him down each time and handled each trade as quickly as I could. I ended up giving up both Ora's fancy-looking gloves and boots as well. I actually wanted them, considering they were clearly magical, but they were also sized for a woman, and one who was half my size, dammit.

In exchange for the random assortment of loot that the servants brought out, I got several better pieces of gear than I'd had before. In addition to replacing some of the more standard equipment in my bag with higher quality gear, I got a magically updating map that I was assured I'd be able to link to my Pearl, three health and two mana potions, forty gold coins, seventy silver, and four copper.

There were two more spellbooks, Chameleon and Featherfall, an ability memory stone for Darkvision that, when linked to my Pearl, would grant me the ability stored within, improving my ability to see in the dark.

Last of all, three skillbooks, tomes that would teach me the basic levels of the included skills: alchemy, herbalism, and trap making. I knew I'd gotten nowhere near the full value of the items, even with houses bidding against one another halfheartedly.

The best part of it all, however, was watching the Baron's face. He'd gone from red to white to blue and then back to red. It was worth the months of pain, the fighting, all of it. I could barely contain myself, though baiting him further could be crossing the line. He wanted me dead, and the only reason he wasn't coming for me right now was that the other nobles in the room.

Once everything was gone, even the armor and weapons I'd termed as junk sold for copper pieces, the nobles were directed to their places by a man I hadn't seen before.

He was old, like really fucking old. He walked with a staff and wore long purple robes down to his ankles, with his bald scalp surrounded by receding hair that reached his shoulders.

He muttered at people, coughing up phlegmy bits which he spat onto the floor as he went, until he climbed the last few steps to the portal in the center of the room. As he stood by its side, the various bystanders and guards were made to leave. Soon, only the nobles remained, taking their places on the dozens of raised platforms around the outside of the room.

West paused by my side before leaving, clearly wanting to say something, but unable to with the Baron glaring over at us. After a few seconds, he opened his mouth, and I beat him to it.

"Thank you, man, you made the time more bearable," I told him, giving him a wry smile. "Now punch me. You know the Baron's gonna be pissed if you don't."

"You're a good one, Jack. Good luck," he whispered, while glaring at me for the Baron's sake. Then he punched me in the face, sending me staggering. I glared at his retreating back, not needing to fake the anger, as the fucker hadn't pulled the damn punch at all!

I spat a bit of blood on the floor and wiped my mouth, before pulling my helm on, and glaring at the Baron, seeing a satisfied grin on his face.

Well, at least it worked, I guess.

Once they were all in place, the old fart began to chant. His weak voice was barely audible at first, but as he finished each recitation, he banged the base of the staff into the ground at his feet. With each impact, the staff flared to life, transforming it from simple wood into a masterwork of interlinked symbols and glowing lines. Each time he drove the staff down, the light lasted longer, staying lit for longer and longer each time.

A movement from the corner of my eye drew my attention, and I saw the Baron raise his hands to shoulder level, a ball of glowing energy appearing in each palm. I flinched, thinking he was about to attack me, until I saw his action replicated dozens of times by the other nobles around me. His eyes were closed, and sweat ran down his face as he strained with whatever he was doing.

At first, I wasn't sure if it was my imagination, but after a moment, I was sure. Each ball of energy had wisps of multicolored light lifting from it, almost like colored smoke, but rather than heading to the ceiling, they were drawn inexorably to the old man at the center.

As the colors gathered around him, it began to swirl and twist, as though moved by unseen eddies in the still air. Slowly, it formed a circle, then a square. Thin lines snaked from the corners to meet in the middle, forming multiple triangles that split away from each other and gradually revolved faster in the air. As they picked up speed, the glow was drawn into patterns that in turn were drawn to circle the spinning triangles until the longest sides of the triangles spun together and locked together. The linked triangles created a square in the center with outward pointing triangles.

The outermost tips flared with light that began to pulse in unison, and the remaining faint traces of color seemed to be sucked into them, spinning and trailing as they went, until a circle had formed around the outside. Around that circle formed dozens of smaller points that glowed with brilliant magic.

As I stood there, stunned, the old man turned to the portal that stood in the center of the room. The outside ring of lights flared once more before their light began to stream away, linking to small points I hadn't noticed in the twisted door frame before. Slowly, ever so slowly, the portal began to form. Light seemingly made solid began to pool within the frame, reaching, stretching, and swirling to mix in the center.

It looked like water flowing from the edges to meet in the middle, but instead it was a pool of brilliance, beautiful patterns in a thousand and one colors, many I'd never seen before and had no words to describe.

As the doorway filled, the old man stepped forward one last time and slammed the rotating mesh of magic into the pool before him. It disappeared with a ripple, then the portal seemed to explode in intensity. I could barely make out the old man as he gestured to me frantically. I had a split second of hesitation, but I was dead if I made them waste this power. I sprinted forward as fast as I could, my naginata's base slamming down hard as I used it to propel me forward faster than I'd ever ran in my life.

I had just enough time, as I raced across the floor and up the final few steps to flip the Baron the bird, then I was there. I cleared the last few steps and leapt forwards into the warp, feeling it envelop me as I passed from the world I'd known all my life and into the UnderVerse.

CHAPTER TWELVE

I fell through the pool of light, arms and legs flailing as the world changed. Everything was suddenly made of beautiful, colorful swirls, and before I could react, my feet reached the floor then passed straight through it. I fell into the earth, as insubstantial as mist on a sunny day, and plummeted down, deeper and deeper.

I was picking up speed as I fell through a world of colors. Concentrations of reds and blues flashed past, greens and a dozen colors more, which I guessed to be nodes of minerals and gems. As I passed them, they began to blur together until I couldn't make anything out beyond a faint glow that grew brighter from below.

As I dropped closer, I realized I was rapidly approaching a giant sea of glowing dots. It spiraled up around me in smaller concentrations, fighting to reach the surface, but it was interlaced with reds and pulsing blacks that seemed to sap its brightness. The world once again erupted in light, until I could make out nothing else. Dozens of worlds appeared suddenly, all linked to our own, with the core of one leading to the core of others.

I slammed into something, a barrier of some kind, at speed. The air was driven out of my lungs with the force, but before I could think, I struck another and another. The force of the impacts sent me spinning, the world breaking down into a mash of flashes, pain, and impact as I was yanked sideways. Portals seemed to be everywhere, open, closed, half-there and not, some had a glowing mesh across them, clearly closed and sealed, while others…I felt it in my balls as one reached for me, pulling me towards it, an evil red and black mass that seemed to be hungering to devour me…

…then I was yanked sideways again as the barrier before me parted like it was made of silken strands. They fell back from me, trailing across my skin as I fell forward into a room that was illuminated by the bright glow of the portal.

Creatures fled from the light even as I hurtled forwards through the air, arms and legs flailing as I tried to catch myself. Then my foot caught one of the things across the spine as it skittered away on six legs. The thing was scrambling back, screaming in pain and anger at the brightness that filled the room. I tumbled end over end, striking another barrier and coming to rest on the edge of something hard.

I shifted, trying to catch my breath, only to find myself toppling backwards as I overbalanced, a gulf behind me making itself known as I fell again. I bounced and rolled down a flight of stairs, pain flaring hot in my face as it collided with a hard edge. I continued tumbling until I came to rest against the far wall, somehow still holding onto my weapon.

Next time, I need a fully hardened faceplate rather than a fucking cloth! I silently swore as I raised my free hand to my face instinctively, clutching at my bloody, broken nose, heat radiating outward along with the pain. I forced myself to see past it, trying to bring the room into focus as my eyes watered involuntarily, and the light began to die.

I found myself in a large circular room, against one flattened wall where I had come to a stop. A flight of steps wide enough for a dozen men to walk abreast climbed from the middle of the room upwards to a platform that stood suspended in the air with the portal embedded in it. All around me, the walls rose and tapered together to meet a hundred or more feet above in an arched ceiling.

Great windows lined the walls, but all of them were covered by something, preventing even the faintest light from filtering in.

Dozens of eyes stared at me from under the platform, hatred and hunger obvious in them as *things* watched me from the darkness.

As the rays bled away, they began to inch outward, spreading out to slowly surround me, snapping jaws filled with pointed teeth at each other in warning. They seemed to be creatures of darkness themselves, sections of their bodies appearing insubstantial as smoke, then solidifying a second later.

Dozens of eyes peered at me from each of the creatures of darkness, roughly organized in a V shape across their face. Six legs spread out from each body as they crawled low, beginning to stalk towards me. They moved like spiders, with slow, precise steps, placing each leg carefully, followed by a flash of scuttling movement. They began to move quicker and quicker, spreading out around me in an increasing half-circle. My breath caught as I began to panic.

All that was holding them back from attacking immediately was the light. They seemed afraid of it, but as it slowly died, they grew bolder.

I cast around frantically, spotting an archway a few feet to my left. It looked like a door but was made of solid crystal. I had no choice.

Aches and pains forgotten in my fear, I leaped to my feet and rushed to the crystal. I looked back at the creatures, only to find that they were scuttling towards me in response to my burst of speed. I grabbed at the door and frantically tried to find a latch, a handle, anything. Claw-tipped appendages scrabbled across the floor from behind and all around. It grew closer as I desperately pounded on the semitransparent crystal.

I dragged my nails across it, trying to find a latch, a hole, anything. My fear spiked, an internal voice screaming at me to run, to get away, at the door to open…

I fell forwards as the crystal suddenly dissolved into mist. One second, I had been shoving at it, then it was gone. I staggered a few steps forward before catching myself and spinning around in the small room. There was only one door: the one I'd just fallen through.

I gripped my naginata in both hands and set my stance. There was only blackness showing through the doorway as the last of the light vanished. I wished I'd taken the time to use the DarkVision stone before leaving. The only remaining source of light was coming from the slowly swirling mist that hovered within the entrance to the room in place of the door. I stabbed forward, slashing from side to side, trying to catch the things as they entered.

The blade cut into something, slicing through flesh and embedding between bones. The resistance shoved me back a step while sharp claws flailed at me. Suddenly, a pulse of light filled the room, making the creatures scream and costing me the little night vision I'd adjusted to.

The creature kebabbed on my blade began yanking and writhing around, so I shoved harder. Something gave, and one of the claw-tipped limbs scratching at me went limp. The blade sank in deeper, and a spurt of hot, wet, foul-smelling blood covered my left hand and forearm. The tip of the naginata pierced something that fluttered and beat. Once the blade shredded it, however, it stopped, and the fight went out of the creature. I braced my boot against it and yanked my weapon free, taking a quick couple of steps backwards and turning to my right.

Something thrashed around and growled nearby, but I couldn't see anything, both of us still blind from the pulse of light.

I took a chance and began stabbing out. The first blow hit nothing but stone, but the second glanced off something, making it screech in pain and rage. I immediately struck again, hearing its claws scraping stone as it tried to scuttle away. In the distance, I could hear faint screaming and thumping, but the room I was in had become silent, save the scrambling of the creature I chased. A last gurgle rose from the throat of the first one I'd killed as its body accepted its death.

I chased the sound around the small room, stabbing and slashing, occasionally landing a blow, but more often than not hitting air or stone. I finally got a good hit, feeling a bone break, and I was rewarded with another loud scream. The naginata's solid base was sheathed in metal, so I spun it around, aiming for the sound.

It impacted something that gave way with a crunch, all sounds stopping as the creature collapsed. I attacked it again, alternating stabbing and smacking it with the blunt end until I regained control. When I was satisfied that it wasn't getting up again, I leaned against the wall for support, panting and covered in foul-smelling blood.

"Okay, Jack—*Jax*—it's dead. Whatever the fuck it was, it's *definitely* dead now," I whispered to myself.

It felt right to call myself by my old gamer handle and make it my new name, since I was making a new life for myself here. I wanted to leave everything but Tommy behind. I shifted until my back was against the wall and clutched my weapon tightly, forcing myself to breathe properly as my heartbeat stopped thundering in my ears.

I could only hope that whatever that pulse had been, it had trapped the other creatures on the other side of the door as I took the time to put my bag down and free a torch.

Looking around as I lit it, I found myself in a small room with two dead straight walls on either side, joined by a gently curving wall that I'd been leaning against. I was a dozen feet from the single doorway, which was solid crystal again, although there were…bits…of the creatures I'd just fought on the floor around it.

Using the light to scan around the room, I ensured that the ones that had gotten in were definitely dead. It seemed that the crystal that had become mist and let me through had solidified a few seconds later, cutting the creatures passing through into bits.

The light glinting against the crystal illuminated movement on the other side. Faint screaming accompanied the creatures as they fled from the light. Pleased to have found another weapon that worked against the fucking things, I turned back to the two I'd killed, grunting as I saw the damage. The first looked as though my blade had gone into its chest between its collarbones or whatever the equivalent of collarbones were for these demon-spider things.

Its own attempts to get at me, combined with my shoving, had cut deeply into its chest until it died. The second one, well...I'd really gone to town on it in my blind fury and terror. The entire room was covered in splatters of blood from my blind attacks, slashing and stabbing. The body was a mess as well, with multiple bones shattered. The head was crushed in on one side, and dozens of other breaks and wounds were clearly visible.

As I slowly moved the torch over it, I noticed that the skin was starting to bubble and decay from its caress. Whatever these things were, they must really hate the light!

I searched the rest of the space again, and, once I was sure I was alone, I turned to examine the actual room itself. The walls were covered in beaten gold and silver, with patterns inscribed along every surface that depicted animals, humans, elves, dwarves, snake people, centaurs, and a dozen other creatures I couldn't identify.

They were all standing together in a forest glade, with each figure cast in precious gems and metals. Above the trees flew an enormous red dragon. Each scale shone brilliantly as I ran the light of the torch over it in awe. The entire mural was beautiful, and in the center stood a man and a woman.

They held their hands out in friendship to the other races around them, but they were also heavily armed. I knew immediately this was both an offer and a threat. "We can be friends," it said, but it also warned against fighting the people in the middle. I liked it.

The next mural was a map. It was covered in symbols I couldn't decipher, but there were a few words I could make out. About a third of the way down the tower there was a floor outlined in gold, with the word "*Memorias*" written across it. Thinking about it, that might be the Hall of Memories Sintara had mentioned, or it might just be a weirdly similar word. Fuck it. Only way was down, after all. I'd find out at some point, I guessed.

I took another look around the room, then pulled out some food and water and sated my immediate needs.

When I had finished, I settled down as far from the corpses as I could. I pulled out the spell and skillbooks, the skill memory stone, and the map.

As dark as it was, I decided to use the memory stone first. It was a small, creamy white stone, almost like marble, but heavier. It was an inch wide and tall by six inches long, and as I held it, it warmed gently in my palm. After a second or two, a new prompt filled my vision.

DO YOU WISH TO LEARN DARKVISION?

THIS WILL CONSUME THE STONE.

I mentally confirmed that I did, and the stone slowly began to dissolve, evaporating into the air and forming a small, hazy cloud that hovered around my hand. I sat there, watching it and wondering what to do next, when it began to dissipate. I panicked, realizing I was losing my chance to use it, and leaned forward to do the only thing I could think of. I breathed it in.

As the cloud flowed forward, I expected it to enter my lungs, but instead it flowed directly into my eyes. I blinked, and…and…I hissed in pain as my eyes *burned*! It was like I'd dunked my head underwater in a pool full of chlorine then started rubbing the fuckers after chopping chilies!

It only lasted a few seconds, thankfully, but damn, it hurt! When my vision cleared, the world was filled with greys and greens, but it was undeniably clearer. So much so, in fact, that I put the torch out and set it aside.

I dismissed the prompt telling me that I'd learned a new ability and moved on to the spellbooks. They were the real treasure here, and I needed as many as possible. I could learn three spells now, as the bracelet increased my usual potential by two along with the spare slot I'd had before.

I'd either have to free up another slot by investing more points in my Intelligence when I leveled next, or save a spell for later, just in case. I decided to learn Chameleon, as neither Stone-Sight, Undead Servant, nor Featherfall seemed like they'd help a great deal right now. Being a stealthy motherfucker, though, was always worthwhile.

As I lost myself in the book, an hour passed in the blink of an eye. As I finished the final page, I realized that I now understood how Osun Dagomar had been so hard to see. The bastard had probably been using this or some similar spell and bending the damn light around himself!

I stretched my right hand out and, looking at the far wall, I pushed the feeling of life in my body to run down into my palm, focusing it into as tight a ball as I could. Then I *pulled* it back across my body, coating myself in something that felt like a thin layer of oil.

It spread across my body in less than a second, leaving behind a slight blurriness. I waved my hand in front of my face, watching it, then held it close.

My hand was covered by the same colors as the wall behind it. The colors were smeared, and not very good, but this was just a basic, entry-level spell, so it was fucking amazing! I brought up the spell description and read through it quickly.

Chameleon:

This spell bends light around your body, making you 20% harder to detect for 20 seconds at a cost of 15 mana. This spell may be maintained for an additional 5 mana per 20 seconds.

The possibilities of this spell, especially when leveled up, were awe-inspiring. It was probably safe to assume that even true invisibility was possible. More importantly, some experience with this, and I could become seriously lethal with this kind of stealth attack capability. Definitely worth learning, even more so because, beyond the gestures required for the spell, the spoken component was sub-vocal. If it was acceptable for this, why not everything else?

Concentrating, I sub-vocalized the chant for my Firebolt spell, thrusting my open hand forward and *willing* a Firebolt to hit the wall. A flicker of fire burst to life, growing in a second from a tiny spark to a ball the size of my closed fist before hurtling across the intervening few meters. The room filled with a whine as the air marked its passage, then a loud crack as the Firebolt hit the spot I'd aimed at. A wash of flames burst out across the wall before guttering out and dying.

"Hell fucking yes!" I gasped, looking down at my right hand in shock. "It worked! I actually did it," I whispered to myself, realizing that, even still, I'd been expecting something bad to happen, to fail somehow, now that I was in the UnderVerse rather than on Earth.

I sat back against the wall, thinking, my mind reeling from the possibilities of this new world, even as my mana bar refilled at a hugely increased speed. After a minute, I caught myself stifling yet another yawn and realized how tired I was. I'd spent a significant portion of the last twenty-four hours battling for my life, and I was exhausted now.

I pulled out my sleeping bag and curled up in the corner, trying to ignore the foul stench from the corpses of the creatures I'd killed earlier, and resolved to get some sleep.

It was slow in coming, thanks to the occasional noise that carried through the crystal doorway, and several times overnight I awoke with a jerk, fingers scrabbling for the hilt of my naginata, as nightmares of the crystal vanishing were put to flight.

CHAPTER THIRTEEN

W hen I got up the next morning, sandy-eyed and tired, I used the sleeping bag to make a more comfortable seat and gathered up the skillbooks.

I amused myself with casting Summon Water a handful of feet away, then cursing as the water started to spread from the cold magical spring…right towards my bedroll and books. I cut the magic to it, not really understanding how I did it, but relieved when it worked. Then I moved a dozen feet farther over and recast it.

This time, I managed a good drink, washing my face and hands, then cut the magic again and got some of the shitty rations out, munching on them as I looked the books over.

I read trapmaking first, as it was the one that called out to me the most. I'd always been terrible at biology and chemistry, and those were the basics of herbalism and alchemy, but I vowed I would get to them as well.

As I turned the pages of the book, examining diagrams and pictures, I slipped into a half-doze. Memories of the author slowly filtering through my mind, I watched through her eyes as she made simple snares, pitfalls, spring-loaded traps, and even experiments with contact poisons. Dozens of men died from her traps, and I started to notice common details in her memories.

The walls, floors, and clothing of the people that fell for her tricks were all familiar. They were from my world! Whoever had created this book had done so there and had amused herself by murdering people in their own simple labyrinth.

I came out of the trance soon enough and realized that I now knew how to create a few simple traps, as well as how to spot them. I quickly moved onto alchemy and herbalism. Each taught me the basics of the crafts, such as how to create basic potions from simple ingredients, to use my identify spell on herbs which I might suspect had alchemical properties, and how to improve my skills as I went.

It seemed that normal usage of the skills, like making potions, would increase the skill's level and allow me to make stronger and more useful items. I loved it.

A serious side effect was making itself known now, though, as a migraine the size of Canada seemed determined to move in behind my right eye…

Lastly, I activated the map I'd been given. It was blank when I unrolled it, but as soon as I looked at it, I received a prompt from the Pearl.

ENCHANTED MAP DETECTED.

DO YOU WISH TO SYNCHRONIZE?

UnderVerse: Brightblade

I approved it, and a tiny area near the middle of the map grew more detailed. At first, it was just a spot of color. But, as I focused, it grew larger, zooming in until I saw the outline of the room I was in as well as the cavernous one next door. I sat back against the wall and contemplated the room, noticing a small, faintly pulsing notification in the bottom of my vision.

I activated it and found that I now had both a magic page and a skill page added to my options, as well as a map section. I chose to examine the magic first, of course, seeing that I now had Chameleon added to the list of spells I knew.

My skills page had been populated with the skills that had transferred over to this world. A quick flexing of mental muscles was all it took to remove ones that were inappropriate, such as driving. All were set to level one, so for some reason practicing them before arriving in the UnderVerse clearly didn't count. They were broken up into sections, such as Melee, Ranged, and Survival. These skills were further broken down by sub-skill, such as archery or axes. I discovered a space for bonuses, but they were mostly blank, likely in anticipation for me to learn some skills. Lastly, there was a section on specialty knowledge, such as the knowledge I'd gained of common herbs, their likely locations and uses, and how to use some of these herbs to make a few simple potions and reagents.

Skill	Sub-Skill	Level	Bonus	Specialty knowledge
Ranged	Archery	1		Bowman (0/100)
	Throwing Knives	1		Small Blades (17/100)
	Throwing Axes	1		Axes (0/100)
Melee	Axes	1		(0/100)
	Dual Wielding	1		(0/100)
	Daggers	1		Daggers (17/100)
	Maces	1		(0/100)
	Swords	1		Swordsman (23/100)
	Staffs	1		Naginata (32/100)
	Unarmed	1		Unarmed (11/100)
Survival	Camp Making	1		(0/100)
	Cooking	1		(0/100)
	Tracking	1		(0/100)
Crafting	Alchemy	1		Minor Antidote (0/100), Minor Health Potion (0/100), Minor Mana Potion (0/100), Minor Stamina Potion (0/100), Weak Acid (0/100), Weak Poison (0/100)
	Trap Making	1		Tripwires (0/100), Pitfalls (0/100), Spike traps (0/100), Snares (0/100)
Gathering	Herbalism	1		Common Herbs

I then sorted through the contents of the bag further. I'd been given several items that I hadn't been able to identify before, so I took the time and cast Identify on all of the magical items that I'd gained, loving the speed of the mana regeneration in this realm.

Ring of Healing		Further Description *Yes/No*	
Details:		This ring provides a 50-point healing twice per day. Minimum Intelligence to equip this item is 11.	
Rarity:	**Magical:**	**Durability:**	**Charge:**
Uncommon	Yes	76/100	2/2

Ring of Wisdom		Further Description *Yes/No*	
Details:		This ring grants +5 to Wisdom for the wearer.	
Rarity:	**Magical:**	**Durability:**	**Charge:**
Rare	Yes	82/100	N/A

Bracelet of Spell Memories		Further Description *Yes/No*	
Details:		This bracelet allows the wearer to retain two spells more than their current Intelligence stat will support.	
Rarity:	**Magical:**	**Durability:**	**Charge:**
Rare	Yes	82/100	N/A

Cloak of Improved Stealth		Further Description *Yes/No*	
Details:		This cloak grants an additional level to the wearer's Stealth ability.	
Rarity:	**Magical:**	**Durability:**	**Charge:**
Uncommon	Yes	88/100	N/A

Bow of Accuracy		Further Description *Yes/No*	
Damage:		8-10 DPS	
Details:		This bow grants the user a 10% increase in accuracy when used	
Rarity:	**Magical:**	**Durability:**	**Charge:**
Uncommon	Yes	74/100	N/A

Dagger of Darkness		Further Description *Yes/No*	
Damage:		5-7 DPS	
Details:		Injuries caused by this dagger have a 5% chance to inflict the Darkness debuff on its victims, blinding them for up to ten seconds.	
Rarity:	**Magical:**	**Durability:**	**Charge:**
Uncommon	Yes	74/100	N/A

I looked over the magical items I'd gained. Slipping the rings and bracelet on and summoning my status page, I immediately saw a five-point increase in my Wisdom, increasing my mana regeneration from 1.1 points per minute to 1.6 points. A quick calculation confirmed that, with my current mana pool of one hundred and forty, I'd be able to fully regain that in just under ninety minutes.

That seemed insanely fast at first, but as my spells grew in power, they'd grow in cost as well. Regenerating enough mana for another Firebolt every seven to eight minutes was great, but if the next spell up was fifty mana or more, I'd soon find the ceiling of my powers. I'd also gotten a notification while I'd been using my Identify spell.

Congratulations!

You have gained a level in Identify.

More information will be displayed when your skill in this spell reaches level ten.

Increase this or other Light spells nine more times to reach level 2 in Light Magic.

Congratulations!

You have raised your spell Identify to level 2.

Once this spell reaches level 10, you may choose its first evolution.

I had another two notifications waiting. I'd dismissed them when I was too busy earlier, but I had time now, so I brought them up one after the other.

Congratulations!

You have killed a level 8 Ranger!

You receive 160xp. Progress to level Five stands at 935/2700xp.

Congratulations!

You have defeated a level 9 Knight!

You receive 180xp. Progress to level Five stands at 1115/2700xp.

I proceeded to equip all the gear and leaned the bow against the wall next to the door, hanging the quiver of arrows on my hip. It looked like I'd gained twenty points towards the next level of the spell with each magical item I'd examined until I reached level two, at which point, I'd gained ten points for the next item examined. I could live with that, especially now that I knew how to level it.

Looking back at things, I suspected I knew why the door had opened and then closed so abruptly, cutting the creatures into bits. The tower was responding to my mental orders. If I was right, I could open the door, fire a few arrows or Firebolts into the room, then close it again, picking the creatures off with ease. If I was wrong, though, I wanted a fallback plan, so I began to prepare.

I propped my naginata by the door next to the bow and checked my swords in their sheaths. I couldn't decide if I wanted to go all out, casting Cleansing Fire and shooting Firebolts and arrows until I ran out of both mana and arrows or play it safe. After a bit of thought, I decided to go with the second option.

After all, this was my life I was risking, not just a respawn in a game. Now that I was in the UnderVerse in truth, I'd not get to wake up after I died and heal all over again.

I paused, the sudden truth of that coming crashing home all at once. I was *here*. I was where I'd always wanted to be. Well, I actually *wanted* to be in a whorehouse with an unlimited supply of rum and good food. I wanted to know that I could have all the fun I wanted, then go downstairs and meet my brother and go have a party somewhere, then maybe kill something and be greeted as a fucking hero.

That wasn't the point, though. I was really here, like seriously, in another realm. Hell, I'd almost certainly never see Earth again. No more TV, no more pollution, no more politicians being lying scumbags, or…scratch that. There was only so far the nature of reality could be bent. Those fuckers were *always* scum.

No, I was here.

I was where I was supposed to be, ready to start my life all over again, to find my brother, and to fucking live the life I was supposed to have. I just had to slaughter my way down a damn tower and kill everything that stood between me and Tommy. I could do that.

I took a deep breath and jogged on the spot as fast as possible to get my blood pumping, working myself up to it.

I cast Raise Weak Skeletal Minion on one of the corpses, my hands flowing through the peculiar gestures and words as the mana flowed through me. I used both hands to cast and found that it seemed right somehow, even though I knew it could be cast with just one.

Lines of purple and black began to leach into the corpse, sinking through its skin and into its bones, which began to shake. The skin sloughed off, collapsing with the organs into a pile of noxious slime on the floor, revealing gleaming bones that slowly stood up on all six legs. It straightened and reared up, standing on the rear four legs, while holding the front half of its body more upright, like the centaur on the mural behind me.

Its front legs had more pronounced claws, with what looked to be greater dexterity compared to the middle and back legs. It stood motionless, watching me. A glow of purple fire shone in the center of its eyes, and its long teeth glittered in the torchlight. I took a step back, then another, instinctively grabbing my naginata.

The damn thing looked terrifying! It took a minute to regain my control, but then I began to direct the skeleton. I discovered that it responded to my will, not just spoken commands. I spent the next few moments directing it to walk the length of the room, stand on its back legs, balance on the middle and then front legs, and dance the Hokey-Pokey. Yeah, I could see definite uses for this.

Well, not the dancing, although it was already more skilled at dancing than half the people on reality shows. But a totally loyal undead creation that could act as my tank? Yeah, that, I definitely could use.

I ordered my minion to the doorway and instructed it to move through as soon as the door opened, stopping on the other side, and to attack anything that came within range. As it moved to obey, I concentrated on the door. It took a few attempts, but eventually I figured it out. The crystal collapsed into mist that was sucked into the doorframe, leaving the next room exposed.

A single screech rose from the far side, quickly echoed by others, as the waiting creatures began scuttling toward me. As my minion raced forward to stand on the far side of the door, I cast Identify on the nearest creature, quickly reading the page that formed before me.

Sporeling

This creature is the larval stage of the SporeMother. While it does not have the ability to create possessed slaves at this stage, its claws, venomous bite, and innate cunning have still been the end of many travelers.

Level: 2
Health: 80
Mana: 0

I dismissed the page and focused on the sporelings as they raced toward me. My minion stood stoically between us, waiting. I grinned as I summoned a Firebolt, firing it at the nearest one.

The impact caused several eyes on one side of its head to flash boil in their own juices, blinding the majority of the rest as the flames spread across its face. It collapsed and rolled to a halt practically at my minion's feet as its system went into shock.

The skeleton lashed out with its claws, tearing deep into its former sibling's throat and sending a wash of ichor across the floor as the creature spasmed in death.

Behind it, the others closed the distance rapidly. I counted nine more converging from all sides of the room, and I immediately started firing again, launching a Firebolt at one as it led two others across the floor. I hit it in the right foreleg, causing it to stumble, which tripped the others and took them all to the floor in a pile of limbs and snapping teeth.

I fired again, loving being a magic-wielding badass…and I completely missed, as I tried to aim too specifically at a leg, not adjusting for the movement as the creature scuttled forwards.

I cursed, and turned back to check on my minion. I watched it lash out, concentrating on the nearest target. As it turned to face the sporeling, another leaped onto its back, using its back to push off and jump at me. I took a step back, raising my naginata and bracing it with one foot.

The sporeling tried to adjust its aim when it noticed a huge blade waiting, but failed, managing only to spit itself nicely for me. A screen began to appear but dissipated as I shook my head.

I twisted and threw the corpse aside, my naginata's blade now wedged deep inside its chest, and going with it as I fired another Firebolt. The blast hit the creature my minion was battling and snapped its leg out from under it. As it collapsed with a scream, the skeleton's teeth ripped its throat out. My minion turned to reclaim its spot in front of the door. Before it could move, another two sporelings blindsided it, taking it to the ground in a heap of breaking bones, screeches, and flashing claws. I had a second to register teeth flying at me as another sporeling raced for the doorway, and I jumped back to give myself room.

I whipped out my right sword, casting a Firebolt with my left hand and lashing the blade across its face, aiming for the eyes.

It ducked, my sword passing harmlessly over its head, then bit down, sinking its teeth into my right leg and digging its claws in hard. I screamed in pain as I was taken down by the impact, and frantically tried to get the sword around to stab it. My half-formed Firebolt dissipated in a wash of mana as I lost control of the spell form.

A second wave of agony washed over me as the mana backlash ripped into my mind, leaving me further dazed and weakened.

You have been poisoned.

You will lose five points of health per second for the next ten seconds.

I screamed again, this time in rage, and the screen disappeared. I drove the sword down into the sporeling's back, but the blade glanced off bone. With no other options, I punched it in the side of the head with my left hand, making it rock slightly and dig its teeth in deeper.

My health bar suddenly flashed red, then green, then red again. It was down to half its capacity, and a red drop of blood hovered above it, which dripped down and disappeared into the ether.

You are bleeding.

You will lose five points of health per second until this injury is dealt with.

"Fuck!" I screamed, dismissing the prompt and discarding the sword. It was useless in these close quarters, and my dagger was underneath the damn sporeling. I was on my back now, with its jaws wrapped around my right leg, claws digging in and teeth chewing deeper into the muscle by the second. Every bite injected me with more poison as it ate me alive.

"Not fucking today!" I screamed at it, both hands gesturing wildly as I forced my mana down my arms and into my hands. I grabbed onto its skull, channeling the Firebolt spell as hard as I could with both hands, forcing more and more mana into it.

Instead of the spark of flames I'd conjured before, a burst of light erupted between my hands, growing into existence right in the middle of the sporeling's head. Glowing light shone out from around its teeth and deep under its skin.

Heat rose as its jaws released reflexively, its brain consumed by the spellform building as I poured mana into it. I was finally free of the bite, and the claws had released as well. But I suddenly had an unstable Firebolt growing to massive proportions inside a skull that was rapidly becoming too hot to handle.

Another sporeling started to head towards the small room as the pile of creatures above my minion began to unravel and head for me as well.

I drew back and threw the skull at them, its neck having given way from the effects of the spell. As it flew over the creature's head into the other room, I begged the doorway to seal itself.

Crystal poured from the doorway, its misty form lasting less than a second before it began to spiral into matrices that grew stronger and stronger, spreading across the intervening space. It was nearly complete when an explosion of flame and debris tore the crystal apart with a solid *whump* I felt in my bones.

The force of the detonation sent me skidding across the floor as flames billowed into the room. Small bits of bone, teeth, and flesh flew around and pinged off the walls. As the crystal wavered, light seemed to flow back and forth inside the misty doorway. I heard screaming from the far side, bubbling cries that were cut off as the crystal finally solidified.

I let my head fall back to the stone floor as I let out a long breath before focusing on my health bar. The indicator continued flashing red and green and was down to a quarter of its capacity. I quickly cast Minor Healing, breathing a sigh of relief as my health bar began to tick upwards again slowly, but between the bleed effect and the poison, it wouldn't give me much time.

I pulled out the first aid kit, sitting up and frantically pouring water to clean the wounds, then wrapping bandages around them. After my basic medical aid, I'd managed to slow the bleeding to a trickle, and the poison debuff had vanished, but I was down to eleven health out of one hundred and thirty. I started casting healing again as soon as I had enough mana and repeated the spell over the course of an hour or so until I'd finally raised my health back to full.

I unwrapped the bandages and examined my leg, hesitant to trust the magic at first. But as the skin repaired itself, I poked and prodded at it, amazed by the healing spell's capabilities.

I got to my feet, gingerly putting my weight on my leg to make sure it was totally healed before grinning to myself. I could *so* get used to magic.

I staggered across the floor to the left side of the room, stumbling over broken bones and bits of sporeling until I reached the corpse draped over my naginata.

I carefully retrieved it, letting out a relieved breath as I saw it was undamaged beyond a few scratches.

I'd seen the notifications tab flashing for ages now, but I'd had more immediate things to do, so I'd ignored it. I checked the doorway and made sure there were no immediate threats in the room, then focused on the notifications.

Congratulations!

Your minion has killed a level 2 Sporeling.

You have gained 10xp for your part in the battle.

Congratulations!

You have killed a level 2 Sporeling.

You have gained 25xp.

I dismissed the notifications after the second kill prompt, seeing that there were too many left for me to be remotely interested in reading them one at a time. After fiddling around with my interface for a bit, I got the kill prompts to condense into one notification.

Congratulations!

You have killed the following:

- 7x Sporelings of various levels for a total of 170xp.

A minion under your command killed the following:

- 2x Sporelings of various levels for a total of 80xp.

Total minion xp earned: 140xp.

As the controller of this minion, you gain 25% of all experience earned.

Progress to level 5 stands at 1,355/2,700

Congratulations!

You have learned a new skill, Mana Infusion.

Using this skill, you can infuse your targets with additional mana, or even overcharge spells! Be warned, however; too much mana can have explosive consequences!

Your minion has been gravely wounded.

You must heal or repair it to prevent its death before time runs out...7...6...5...4...3...2...1

Your Minion has died. All experience it earned has been lost.

"Wait, my minions earn experience as well?" I muttered in surprise. While the skeleton was useful, if it could earn experience, then it didn't have to remain a weak creature. It could become a real powerhouse if I could level it, too. The thought of leveling made me check my own progress out of curiosity and a little hope as well. I had thirteen hundred and fifty-five out of twenty-seven hundred experience.

"Bloody typical," I grunted, dismissing the screen with a thought. I didn't think there were many sporelings left on the far side of the door. From what I could remember, maybe only one remained, and it'd sounded injured.

I waited for my mana to refill before summoning another skeleton minion to fight by my side. This time, though, aware that it could end up being with me for a while, I named it.

"Well, Bob," I said to the skeleton as it clambered to its feet, taking up position by the door at my direction, "It's time we went and cleared my new tower up. Get out there and kick some ass!"

With a thought, the crystal disappeared from the doorway, and Bob scuttled forward, looking for something to dismember for me.

I followed cautiously, scanning the devastation before us. Bodies were scattered everywhere, or more accurately, bits of bodies. It looked like my spell had gone off like a grenade, blowing the sporelings apart and killing most outright. Only one looked to have survived the explosion, and it'd left a trail of blood and ichor behind as it had dragged itself out of the room through a door in the far wall, which now stood ajar.

I took a moment to scan the room I'd first arrived in, able for the first time to actually see it without being chased by creatures. When I'd entered through the portal, I'd seen the windows, or window frames in the walls, but they seemed to be covered in something.

I'd missed the door leading out entirely, seeing only the door into the room that I'd taken first. Now I noticed several other details as well; the platform I'd arrived on was centered in the middle of the room, seemingly unsupported by anything other than the spiral staircase leading up to it. On the farthest side of the room was one huge window, plastered with something that kept even the faintest light from passing through.

The walls and floor felt...unstable. Hell, the entire tower felt like it was shifting constantly, ever so slightly. I told myself it was my imagination, banishing the thought, after all it'd been here for literally hundreds, if not thousands of years, but...

A normal house would have collapsed in a fraction of that time. Move it up two or three miles into the air? With all that weight on the structure? The wind, the rain? Storms?

Fuck. I banished the thoughts, forcing myself to go back to looking around and at the big window.

Standing before it was a throne-like chair, with smaller chairs flanking either side of a rounded, crescent-shaped table. Both points of the crescent supported a large metal bowl. I approached cautiously, looking at the bowl in curiosity even as Bob moved to guard the door out of the room.

As I stood over the bowl, I found that it was shallow, maybe two feet across and six or seven inches deep. Whatever had filled it had long since been drunk or evaporated, but it stood here, in pride of place directly opposite the throne. Whatever had been here had clearly been important.

I ran my fingers across the empty interior, feeling...*something* as I did. It was a tugging sensation, weakly pulling at my fingertips.

I held them there for a second, curious about the feeling, until I noticed my mana bar. It was steadily dropping, and the speed was accelerating! I yanked my fingers back with an oath, feeling the connection break. I took several steps back before warily peering back inside the bowl.

Where nothing but dust had been before, now a single gleaming droplet sat. It glowed gently, and as I reached out my hand again, I felt the connection and the pull resume. I maintained it until my mana had dropped to ten percent, then I broke off again, finding that the droplet had grown. I wanted to give it more mana, to see what would happen when the bowl was full. But as I realized what I was thinking, I shook myself and stepped back further.

I had no idea what this thing was.

It was a bowl that sucked my mana out, in a room in some tower, in another world that had until recently been full of monsters trying to kill me. For all I knew, it was the local equivalent of a self-destruct button, and I was merrily mashing on it.

I'd figure it out when I knew I was safe. I started walking toward the open doorway to explore the rest of the tower when something else caught my eye. One of the eviscerated corpses was emitting a faint glow.

I advanced cautiously, discovering that the glow came from a small oval of flesh that had been exposed when it had been killed. The sight suddenly reminded me of my selection for my secondary meridian. I'd gained an ability to see valuable or important things, which were highlighted with a glow!

CHAPTER FOURTEEN

I took a quick survey of the room to make sure nothing was sneaking up on me, reassured by Bob standing guard at the door, and crouched down to take a closer look. Pulling out my dagger, I cut the glowing section free, sawing at the flesh around it and pulling away the bits that didn't glow. After a minute or so, I had it in my hand, rapidly cooling. It was disgusting, but now it shone to my eyes. I used Identify and grinned as I read the text.

Sporeling Kidney		Further Description *Yes/No*	
Details:		This organ comes from an immature Sporeling and can be used in alchemy. Uses Discovered: 1) Cure Poison 2) ? 3) ? 4) ?	
Rarity:	**Magical:**	**Durability:**	**Charge:**
Uncommon	No	88/100	N/A

I quickly set to it with the dagger, ignoring the revolting stench and the fact that I was getting…bits…all over me, and started to strip the nearest full corpse, starting with the head. In the end, after much effort and a fuck load of wasted Identify spells, I found that there were three items I could harvest from a sporeling: the kidney I'd already found, the venom gland, hidden in the roof of the mouth, and the eyes, which were a bit more of a task to remove.

Thankfully, while each corpse only had one kidney, and one venom gland, they all had multiple eyes, so even between my ham-fisted and unskilled work, I managed to come away with eight venom glands, seven intact kidneys, and thirty-five eyes. I also gained another notification.

Sporeling Venom Gland		Further Description *Yes/No*	
Details:		This organ comes from an immature Sporeling and can be used in alchemy. **Uses Discovered:** 1) Poison 2) ? 3) ? 4) ?	
Rarity:	**Magical:**	**Durability:**	**Charge:**
Uncommon	No	92/100	N/A

Sporeling Eyes		Further Description *Yes/No*	
Details:		This organ comes from an immature Sporeling and can be used in alchemy. **Uses Discovered:** 1) DarkVision 2) ? 3) ? 4) ?	
Rarity:	**Magical:**	**Durability:**	**Charge:**
Uncommon	No	68/100	N/A

You have learned the Herbalism sub-skill Butchery:

Because you have taken the time to examine the bodies of your enemies, you have found items that have alchemical properties. Level this skill to increase your chance to spot further opportunities and ingredients!

You have improved the Herbalism sub-skill Butchery to level seven; next level 0/100

"Hell yes!" I crowed, then flinched as my voice echoed back to me from the open door where Bob stood guard. "Okay…I need to be quieter. I can do that."

I muttered to myself, walking over to him and clapping him on one skeletal shoulder. "C'mon, Bob, let's go slaughter that fucker who's trying to get away. It'll be fun, honest!"

I checked my weapons, then commanded him through the door, trying my best not to grin. Tommy and I had spent most of our lives dealing with the Dreams and being dragged here and back constantly. The worst part out of all of it, was that after we lost our Ma, we agreed, we'd rather stay in the Dreams any day. The bodies that we had were incredible, powerful, naturally skilled, and lethal in ways that our own mortal forms weren't.

That difference had only been more apparent when we were kids, nine years old, suddenly catapulted into the bodies of grown men that were worshiped by those that summoned us.

Instead of two basically feral kids who'd been abandoned to the foster care system and were confused, emotionally fucked, and basically unwanted, we were respected warriors who could make a real difference to people's lives.

Now I knew that Tommy had made it here, and I was gonna find him, then we were going to fuck some shit up, get some beers and some meaningless sex, and get our lives on track.

Sure, the Baron might have trapped me here, as he thought of it, but as far as I was concerned? I was free. My entire life was over before I came here, so fuck it.

I followed close behind Bob through a short hallway that led down a long flight of steps. We spiraled down what I thought must be several revolutions, finding more windows that had been caked in the same black substance that blocked all light. Eventually, I came to another floor, which opened out from the stairs into a single corridor lined with rooms. At the far end of the hallway, another doorway stood open, revealing another set of stairs. The blood trail led straight down the hall and into the next stairwell, so I followed it.

As I passed, I quickly tried a few doors but found that they were all locked. I resolved to search them when I had time, but first, I was going to make sure that sporeling died before it could bring any others back.

I set off jogging down the hall and into the stairwell, my bony companion clattering down the stairs ahead of me. There was just no way to make it stealthy, as far as I could see.

It was literally a pile of bones smacking off every step. As we reached the next floor, it didn't matter, as we were both too late and too loud to hide our presence.

When I emerged from the stairwell, a trio of hulking forms were already running toward us, with the sporeling descending the stairs on the far side. I used Identify and started to swear.

DarkSpore-Possessed Shir

This creature was once a living, breathing inhabitant of this realm, but no longer. It has been infected with a parasitic DarkSpore, turning the peaceful Shir into an undead slave to the SporeMother that puppets it.

Level: 6
Health: 140
Mana: 0

I had no idea what a *normal* shir was, but these looked like a cross between a man and an ox. As the largest one lumbered toward me, its enormous, curved horns caught my eye.

The bony protrusions lifted straight out to the sides of its head before jutting forward, ending in sharp tips. Its head hung low between huge, heavily muscled shoulders, and it carried a club in one massive hand. The other appeared to have been burned off at some point. Its two legs barely seemed able to support the weight as it continued to charge. The other two that followed it looked much the same; all three were rotting, with muck-encrusted clothing that had been stained with years of funk.

Whatever they were, they were big. Despite being slow, if they got in one good hit, it'd be good night. With a thought, I sent Bob to engage them. He rattled across the floor and leaped on the lead creature, taking it to the ground and driving his teeth into its neck. His jaws tore flesh free as his opponent began beating on him with its club. A bone gave way with a crack as I cast a Firebolt, hitting the second one in the face and snapping its head back with the impact.

The third one kept coming, the floor shaking with the impact of each massive hoof as it closed the distance. The second one recovered from my Firebolt and continued towards me. The flesh had burned off its face, and small secondary fires were still going across its head and shoulders, but it seemed not to care in the slightest. My mind flashed back to the notification I'd read. "Undead slave." Yeah, that summed up this creature nicely, and explained why it wouldn't care about pain.

I cursed, ducking under a blow from a massive club. I could feel the wind from its passage as I lashed out with the naginata, driving deep into the shir's leg as I slipped to the side in an attempt to keep its body between me and the last one. My blade had sliced deep into its thigh, then stuck fast in the knee joint, sending it staggering and flailing to the floor. I pulled hard at the shaft, but it was no good.

I'd managed to cripple one of them, but the one whose face I'd burned was circling its fallen partner as I abandoned my weapon. I still had sixty-three out of one hundred and forty points of mana, but that equated to only six Firebolts. I still had one spell that I hadn't used yet, which I'd been given specifically to heal me and to fuck shit up. I backed up a little to get some room. I didn't know if it'd kill Bob as well, and I preferred to not have to raise him again.

I began the gestures to cast Cleansing Fire, using both hands as I muttered and concentrated on not mispronouncing anything. Light erupted from my fingertips as the spell wore on, causing the first sounds I'd heard from the shir as they hissed in anger. As the ten-second casting time ticked down, I dodged back and forth, lunging in between them just as the spell activated.

It had begun as a bright white light that centered on me, building up in spirals and waves of light as I'd cast, but now the lines erupted out. When the waves had reached ten meters in every direction, they branched out, linking to create a pattern like a wagon wheel full of spokes.

The spokes then connected to each other, with smaller tendrils joining together and radiating out to touch the outer rim. Once each line was set, they suddenly burst into flames. I shielded my eyes reflexively as the flames reached waist-height, then died down to lick along the lines. They gave off no heat, appearing to simply shimmer and dance. But the shir both screamed in agony as the flames raced up their bodies, clinging to themselves as they tried to escape the circle. I stepped forwards reflexively as they backed away, wanting to retrieve my weapon and crossing the lines of fire before I thought about it.

Instantly, I felt a warm sensation, like a gentle breeze on a hot day. Several flames jumped onto me, spreading up my legs and over my body. Once they reached my head, they simply flowed back down, and I exhaled a sigh of relief.

I hadn't even considered the potential effect on me. The spell recognized its caster, however; before I'd taken another step, the flames had returned to patrolling the spellform. My health bar also started ticking over, for the lack of a better description. The line kept flickering until I realized I was at full health, and I remembered that the spell also gave a minor healing bonus. God, I loved this one; I just wished it was faster to cast!

I grinned as I caught up to the shir with my blade still stuck in its knee. It was huge, but as badly balanced as it was, I managed to pull it over.

It fell to the floor, thrashing as the flames continued to spread across its body. I decided it was time to go hard or go home. A quick check of my mana revealed that I'd recovered two mana since the battle had begun. *Wow, I am fucking over-powered!* I thought.

I had fifteen mana, enough for one normal Firebolt, or I could experiment a little...all I had to do was survive long enough for my mana to recover further. I waited until the Cleansing Fire had begun to die out then attacked the final shir that stood waiting. It had been deliberately staying out of range as I kited it around the room, ignoring the injured creature that lay on the floor. I spent the next eight minutes stalling until I'd finally managed to build up a decent amount of mana.

I cast Firebolt with both hands, but instead of releasing it, I continued to force mana into it. The spell swelled and pulsed, but I waited until I had reached thirty mana input. My bar bottomed out, and I fired it at the remaining shir who had managed to escape the Cleansing Fire's reach. It thumped toward me, its body blackened and smoking and hatred in its eyes, until my overcharged Firebolt took it in the face. Rather than simply burning some skin away and momentarily shocking the creature, it caused a spectacular death. The Firebolt seemed to smash into the bovine face with the force of a hammer.

But as soon as its outer form was disrupted, the spell detonated. It crushed the front of its skull in, then blasted out in a wave that left the shoulders and upper chest denuded of flesh. The rotten clothes erupted in flame, and a horn went flying off to shatter against a nearby wall.

The remainder of the skull was reduced to part of the jawbone hanging from some blackened flesh, and the top of the spine stuck out. The rest was blown into shards and spread across the room. The demolished shir stood there for a second before collapsing, hitting the floor with enough force that I felt it in the soles of my feet.

I gaped at my hands in shock before returning my gaze to the one creature that had managed to crawl its way out of the Cleansing Fire. It lay there, badly burned and trying to recover. I waited, allowing my mana to refill as I planned out the chance to use it again. Once I'd built up to twenty-two mana, I cast Identify on the charred and barely intact creature in the hope of getting more information, or possibly being able to spam the skill higher.

DarkSpore-Possessed Shir

This creature was once a living, breathing inhabitant of this realm, but no longer. It has been infected with a parasitic DarkSpore, turning the peaceful Shir into an undead slave to the SporeMother that puppets it.

Level: 5
Health: 37
Mana: 0

I grinned, observing its smoking, trembling form as the last of the flames died out. Satisfied with its current state, I turned my attention to the fight that was still going on in the background between Bob and the first shir, and grimaced as I realized he wasn't winning.

I wanted to Identify his opponent to see how much health he had left, but I couldn't risk it. Bob was being slowly smashed into pieces, while the shir appeared largely unaffected by the damage he'd done. Huge sections of flesh and hair had been torn free, but as the thing was dead already, all Bob had managed to do was make some holes in its body. Some kind of black cloud that was inside the creature had extended tendrils out to Bob in comparison, however. They were burrowing deeper into his limbs, turning his bones brittle and speeding his demise.

I backed up to the farthest side of the room from the shir as the remaining badly wounded creature clambered to its feet and advanced on Bob from behind. I ordered him to disengage and run, but it was too late. With a few heavy blows from the club, Bob collapsed into a pile of bones as he was killed. Again.

With a grunt, I turned and started running, a hiss following me as I disappeared into the stairwell. Sprinting up the twisting steps, I was starting to feel the strain as I erupted onto the next floor and sprinted to the end of the hallway. My stamina was rapidly dropping, I noticed, and grunted to myself at the clear correlation between my rising tiredness and that little bar, but I'd gained a bit of distance. I paused at the foot of the next flight of stairs and sat down.

The two remaining shir were clumping up the steps, but I made a conscious effort to slow my breathing and chill. By the time they'd arrived, I had a surprise waiting. I had run for nearly thirty minutes up the steps, which was more of a workout than I'd been expecting, in all honesty, but that wasn't the point.

In those thirty minutes, I'd also recovered sixty mana, and as soon as I had heard them coming, I'd started to channel my mana into a single Firebolt.

I waited until they had both cleared the stairwell and charged toward me before I released it. I had invested nearly the full sixty mana into it, and it had begun to buck and shake in my grip.

I held on longer than I thought I would be able to, and the spinning ball of fire had evolved. It had grown to three times its normal size before changing color and beginning to shrink.

By the time I released it, it was barely the size of my thumbnail, but it glowed a bright white and spun so fast, the air around it whined.

When I sent it flying, I paused only for a split second to watch before throwing myself into the shelter of the stairwell. In the time it took me to take cover I saw it impact just above the lead creature's right eye. I watched the hit, but not the effect. As I scrambled up the steps, a bright light flared from behind, filling the area like a warship's searchlight. It lasted only a second before the force of the explosion rolled over me. My eardrums vibrated painfully as the air channeled past me into the tower with a great roar.

As everything went silent, I shook my head, trying to get the ringing out of my ears. Then I slowly edged back down the steps and looked around the corner.

It was a scene of devastation. Not only were the shir both dead, again, but a nearby door was smashed open, swinging crazily on one hinge. The floor was littered with debris, clothing, rotten flesh, and bone fragments everywhere, and my notifications tab was flashing busily again. I stalked into the hallway, ready to cast at any time, picking my way toward the impact point.

I scanned the corpses. There was no way I could use either of the scattered remains as a new Bob, and if they had ever had anything I could have looted, it was long gone. Dismissing them, I stepped into the room, which was small, but well-appointed. A table, chairs, and a bed sat against the walls, but in pride of place was a huge map on one wall. Set in the other was an undamaged window.

I ignored the map momentarily, choosing instead to look out over the new world I found myself in.

The window was grimy and covered in hundreds of years of dirt and dust, streaked where rain had slowly run down it, but as I peered through it into the night, tiny pinpricks of light appeared far in the distance, glittering against the darkness.

I resolved to return to the room soon. Now that I knew it was night, it would be a simple matter for me to come back in a few hours and see this world in daylight.

As I gazed through the dingy glass, I kept telling myself it was time to go, and countering with staying for just one more second. I was rewarded for my stubbornness.

A flash of lightning tore through the night, many miles away, but in the split second it covered the sky, it touched the earth and caused what might have been a tree to erupt in flames.

I waited, staring at the fainter light of the flames until a second flash lit up the world. I was indeed in a tower, and a huge one at that. The world below was covered in darkness, but I'd seen enough to determine that there was a forest out there and possibly a lake or sea in the far distance. I turned to the map on the wall, my eyes aching as the bright lights had not been kind to my DarkVision-enhanced sight, even as the patter of rain on the glass started behind me.

An examination of the map started to reveal patterns I thought I had seen from the window.

In the top right of the map was a land bordered with mountains. A single tower, outlined in gold, stood at the foot of the mountains, deep in the curve of the range. The highlight made me assume that it must indicate the tower I was standing in. South from the tower was a valley that led away, opening as it went onto rolling forests to the south, and the sea to the east, both the north and west routes cut off by the snow-capped giants.

Following the forested lands to the south, I found several large towns and a city with another smaller tower in its center. This one wasn't detailed in the characteristic gold, and as I quickly skimmed the rest of the map, I couldn't see any other locations marked as clearly as the first tower had been. From there, I traced a path across to the east to find the other city I'd noticed. It appeared to sit squarely in the middle of a bay surrounded by high cliffs.

Judging by the wilderness covering the rest of the land on this continent, it seemed unexplored, while across the sea were dozens of progressively more heavily populated islands and continents. Finally, I reached a single great city in the middle, marked as Dai'Amaranth, that seemed to fill the entire center island.

I knew where Tommy should be headed now, and that he had probably arrived in one of those cities. It was likely the one with the small tower, if Sintara had told me the truth, anyway. Leaning closer, I squinted at the two cities, finding the furthest one to be the harbor city marked as Narkolt, the closest as Himnel.

"Of course, it'd be the farthest away!" I grumbled to myself.

I leaned in again and started measuring distances off with my fingers. Yeah, if this was accurate, it was going to be a fucking long walk.

I started to curse, then stopped myself and forced myself to think about the fact I was actually here and grinned instead. I would find Tommy, then to hell with Earth. We'd make a proper new life here. I was practically immortal now, after all.

"Hell yeah!" I muttered, taking a deep breath and feeling freer than I had at any time in my life. I had no debts, nobody relying on me, save Tommy. Knowing him, he'd be hip-deep in women, booze, and sketchy gear by now. I had a forest below me to explore.

I'd been trained to forage and hunt, so I wouldn't be going hungry anytime soon. I grinned and searched the room quickly, finding nothing of value, then I turned to my notifications, a faint recollection tugging at my memory.

Jez Cajiao

Congratulations!

You have killed the following:

- 3x DarkSpore of various levels for a total of 160xp.
- 3x DarkSpore-possessed Shir of various levels for a total of 80xp.

Progress to level 5 stands at 1,595/2,700

Name: Jax	
Class: Spellsword	Renown: Unknown
Level: 4	Progress: 1,595/2,700
Patron: None	Points to Distribute: 0 Meridian Points to Invest: 0

Stat	Current points	Description	Effect	Progress to next level
Agility	15	Governs dodge and movement.	+50% maximum movement speed and reflexes	58/100
Charisma	10	Governs likely success to charm seduce or threaten	Average success in interactions with other beings	32/100
Constitution	15	Governs health and health regeneration	150 health, regen 7.5 points per 600 seconds	45/100
Dexterity	15	Governs ability with weapons and crafting	+50% to weapon proficiency, +5% to the chances of crafting success	84/100
Endurance	16	Governs stamina and stamina regeneration	160 stamina, regen 6 points per 30 seconds	61/100
Intelligence	15	Governs base mana and number of spells able to be learnt	150 mana, spell capacity: 10 (8 + 2 from items)	23/100
Luck	12	Governs overall chance of bonuses	+20% chance of favorable outcome	26/100
Perception	13	Governs ranged damage and chance to spot hidden items or traps	+30% ranged damage, +3% chance to spot hidden items or traps	29/100
Strength	18	Governs damage with melee weapons and carrying capacity	+8 damage with melee weapons, +80% maximum carrying capacity	94/100
Wisdom	20 (15)	Governs mana regeneration and memory	+100% mana recovery, 2 points per minute, 100% more likely to remember things	56/100

I quickly moved to the door and listened. Confirming nothing was coming, I ducked back inside and dropped to the floor, hammering out a series of burpees that would have made my trainers proud. I checked my Endurance and Strength and found they'd both had the "progress to the next level" markers go up slightly.

I resigned myself to doing a round of exercises each night and morning. I couldn't do much with Charisma out here for the time being, but the rest were all fair game.

My Intelligence and Wisdom had gone up almost the same amount, which would be the spell's effect. Spotting the alchemy ingredients in the sporelings' corpses probably boosted my Perception. Agility would be fighting, running, and dodging, same with Dexterity, but adding in crafting. Constitution would be a slow one to level, as I'd need to let myself get injured for that.

"Yeah, that one I'll just build up from investing points, I think..." I mused aloud. Luck would be another difficult one. Maybe I could find a casino?

I moved out to the corridor again and peered down into the depths of the tower. "Hell with it," I said aloud. The sporeling couldn't have gotten far, but if the SporeMother could "puppet" the possessed creatures, it knew I was there now. I set off running down the stairs again, scooping up my naginata, which had fallen a few revolutions of the tower down when it had finally been ejected from the creature's wounded leg. I swept it up and continued down, crossing the next few floors until I reached the floor where I'd met the three shir.

Continuing down the hallway, I found more of the same: a single corridor with rooms on either side, the occasional blood or ichor smear letting me know it was still ahead.

The distance it'd managed to cover stunned me, but at least it was a hell of a lot easier going down rather than up.

After two more revolutions down into the tower, I finally found what I had been looking for. The floor had grown much wider, and rather than a small level, the stairwell opened onto a huge single room. The vaulted ceiling overhead was supported by dozens of carved stone pillars, and the borders of the circular room were punctuated by ten alcoves. Each alcove contained a single altar, and huge windows in the middle of the walls on either side led out into gardens.

The windows on my left had been broken at some point, and trees had grown inside, twisting away some of the supports for the glass as they grew larger. I slowed, amazed at the verdant garden that was slowly overtaking a space reminiscent of a cathedral nave, before a movement caught my eye.

Off to one side, hunched down as low as it could get, was the sporeling. It cowered from the fragments of light that leaked in. Whatever the creatures had done to block the light and cover the windows on higher floors had clearly failed here. I moved closer to the injured beast and cast Identify.

Sporeling

This creature is the larval stage of the SporeMother. While it does not have the ability to create possessed slaves at this stage, its claws, venomous bite, and innate cunning have still been the end of many travelers.

Level: 3
Health: 11
Mana: 0

I grinned and was about to end its life with a Firebolt when I realized it was trapped. It had known I would kill it and had been forced to try to cross this open floor to escape. The light of the dimly rising sun had cornered it, obviously due to its fear. I decided to wait and see what would happen. I settled back, watching as its beady eyes shifted from me to the windows.

After a few minutes, sunlight began filtering in, and a ray touched its skin. It howled in agony and tried to escape, pressing itself down behind the bench it was attempting to use as a shield. It must have decided I was the easier foe to face, as it suddenly bounded upright and scuttled toward me.

I'd been waiting for it and blasted it full in the face with a Firebolt before it had crossed a fraction of the distance. Half of its face had been missing already, and the impact of the spell finished it off, sending the corpse sliding across the floor to rest in a patch of sunlight.

Immediately, it began to smoke, the skin blackening and curling up as the sun burned the creature. I probably should have pulled the corpse out of the light, knowing that I could have harvested parts of it. But I just stood there, mesmerized by the sun as it ate away at the creature.

In a matter of seconds, all that remained were smoking bones, until they, too, blackened and collapsed to ash, blowing away on the light breeze.

I understood why the sporelings–and presumably the SporeMother–wanted the windows covered. The sun was anathema to them. I had a new weapon against them, a much more powerful one!

CHAPTER FIFTEEN

I stood there for a few seconds, catching my breath, before realizing I'd been caught in a daze considering the potential of using the sun as a weapon. Shaking the thoughts away, I abandoned the corpse dust and emerged into the sunshine. I had to clamber through the warped remains of the window frame, breaking sections free as I went. The remnants of doors had been half-hidden by trees, bushes, and mounds of earth that had grown in and around them.

Brushing myself off, I surveyed the tangled mess of what had once been an ornamental garden set atop a huge balcony.

It extended out from the tower, forming a half-circle that was easily two hundred feet across. Ornamental stone planters had gradually shattered as the trees outgrew them, while more than a thousand years of shed leaves and dead plants had turned this place into a primeval forest.

Pushing my way through the bushes and various trees that stood tall and proud, I found a pool in the center. The melodic sound of birdsong filled the air. Fish flicked around in the water's depths as tiny insects buzzed from flower to flower. It was a small piece of paradise, I thought with a smile.

I moved on, circling the edge of the pool and continuing out until I reached the farthest edge of the balcony. Here, the stonework was crumbling, worn away by wind, rain, and questing roots, but I stood transfixed.

I could see for miles in all directions. To my left were snow-capped mountains marching away from behind the tower to vanish far to the north and reemerging on the far side of the tower to disappear into the distance to the south as well. I marveled at the beauty of hundreds of miles of verdant valleys and hills before me, overgrown with trees.

Small streams and wide rivers ran into one another and led out to the sea seemingly hundreds of miles directly ahead. Everywhere I turned, the world was teeming with life, while the sun shone with a welcoming warmth.

In the distance, I thought I could make out signs of civilization. As high as I was, I could see a surprising distance, nearly a hundred miles, I guessed; but it could have been a thousand for all I knew. I'd never tried to estimate like this before.

Here and there were what I could only assume were small villages or towns, judging from the smoke rising from them, although there were none nearby. More smoke was barely visible to the south east, which might have been one of the cities in that direction, or maybe just a forest fire.

Looking down at the lands surrounding the tower, I remembered a comment I'd overheard from Xiao about the "wonders of the lost realm." She'd been talking with one of the Baron's servants and had said something about defensive enchantments. Some locations were built with incorporated spells, defending them from assault by making them invisible beyond a certain distance, or reinforcing the walls to make them harder than steel, or…I couldn't remember the rest. There'd been a number of things they had discussed, mostly about what they'd do to their own castles if they had them. Magical traps they could watch being activated seemed to make up most of the conversation, as I remembered. *Sick bastards.*

The tower I was standing atop was hidden deep in the forest, easily a hundred or more miles from the nearest settlement, maybe more. Judging from where it stood and its proximity to the enormous mountain range that ran behind me, I could only guess that its location would deter potential explorers, especially when the forests that surrounded the area were so extensive. And as Sintara had said, this place had some kinda spell that hid it until you were within a mile.

I stood lost in thought for what seemed like mere seconds but was probably closer to ten minutes. Eventually though, I pulled myself back together and savored the gentle breeze and the fresh air before turning back to the garden. I picked my way through it carefully, finding fruits I recognized, like apples and pears, and others I didn't.

Like a bright red thing that floated by the edge of the pool and resembled a melon, and a tree laden with small white bulbs reminiscent of heads of garlic. I cautiously bit into one of the bulbs and was relieved to discover that it tasted of honey. I checked my notifications, finding that, for each one I tasted, I gained an alchemical ingredient usage.

God, I loved this world! I quickly ran through the descriptions of the rest of the ingredients I'd gathered and found that many of them were immediately useful in one way or another.

Several gave a stamina boost, and I resolved to try making a potion or three as soon as I'd settled myself somewhere safe. Perusing their details, I memorized their uses.

Crab Apple		Further Description *Yes/No*	
Details:		This fruit is fresh and full-flavored. It also has alchemical properties if used in the correct manner. **Uses Discovered:** 1) Fortify Perception 2) ? 3) ? 4) ?	
Rarity:	**Magical:**	**Durability:**	**Charge:**
Common	No	100/100	N/A

Junit berries		Further Description *Yes/No*	
Details:		The tartness of these berries is similar to lemons and other citrus fruits. They also have alchemical properties if used in the correct manner. **Uses Discovered:** 1) Cure Poison 2) ? 3) ? 4) ?	
Rarity:	**Magical:**	**Durability:**	**Charge:**
Common	No	100/100	N/A

Beetroot	Further Description *Yes/No*

Details:		These common plants are easy to prepare and go with many dishes. **Uses Discovered:** 1) Restore Health 2) ? 3) ? 4) ?	
Rarity:	**Magical:**	**Durability:**	**Charge:**
Common	No	100/100	N/A

Sweet Thyme		**Further Description** *Yes/No*	
Details:		This herb gives off a relaxing aroma. It may also have alchemical properties if used in the correct manner. **Uses Discovered:** 1) Paralysis 2) ? 3) ? 4) ?	
Rarity:	**Magical:**	**Durability:**	**Charge:**
Common	No	100/100	N/A

H'vart		**Further Description** *Yes/No*	
Details:		This star-shaped fruit tastes like melon but gives you odd feelings. **Uses Discovered:** 1) Fortify Perception 2) ? 3) ? 4) ?	
Rarity:	**Magical:**	**Durability:**	**Charge:**
Common	No	100/100	N/A

Alairt		**Further Description** *Yes/No*	
Details:		This egg-like plant tastes like rubber. Perhaps it would be better cooked? **Uses Discovered:** 1) Restore Stamina 2) ? 3) ? 4) ?	
Rarity:	**Magical:**	**Durability:**	**Charge:**
Common	No	100/100	N/A

Jarrin Tuft	**Further Description** *Yes/No*

181

Details:		These thin, hair-like strips give off a pleasing aroma and are fought over by the birds, so they can't be that bad for you, surely? **Uses Discovered:** 1) Fortify Agility 2) ? 3) ? 4) ?	
Rarity:	**Magical:**	**Durability:**	**Charge:**
Common	No	100/100	N/A

Gotang		**Further Description** *Yes/No*	
Details:		This strange bulb leaks an orange fluid that fizzes pleasingly on your tongue. **Uses Discovered:** 1) Restore Health 2) ? 3) ? 4) ?	
Rarity:	**Magical:**	**Durability:**	**Charge:**
Common	No	100/100	N/A

Orut Fruit		**Further Description** *Yes/No*	
Details:		These low-hanging fruits are appetizing to many creatures due to the flavor, intense sweetness, and the supposed boosts received from consuming them. **Uses Discovered:** 1) Stamina Boost 2) ? 3) ? 4) ?	
Rarity:	**Magical:**	**Durability:**	**Charge:**
Common	No	100/100	N/A

White Grapes		**Further Description** *Yes/No*	
Details:		These grapes are sweet and remind you of summer days. They also have alchemical properties if used in the correct manner. **Uses Discovered:** 1) Fortify Charisma 2) ? 3) ? 4) ?	
Rarity:	**Magical:**	**Durability:**	**Charge:**
Common	No	100/100	N/A

Pergola	Further Description *Yes/No*
Details:	These long tubers have an earthy taste but are oddly satisfying. **Uses Discovered:** 1) Tranquilizer 2) ? 3) ? 4) ?

Rarity:	**Magical:**	**Durability:**	**Charge:**
Common	No	100/100	N/A

Blood Oranges	Further Description *Yes/No*
Details:	These sweet oranges remind you of your youth. **Uses Discovered:** 1) Restore Stamina 2) ? 3) ? 4) ?

Rarity:	**Magical:**	**Durability:**	**Charge:**
Common	No	100/100	N/A

Ginseng	Further Description *Yes/No*
Details:	This root has many uses and seems to be uniquely beneficial to your health. **Uses Discovered:** 1) Cure Disease 2) ? 3) ? 4) ?

Rarity:	**Magical:**	**Durability:**	**Charge:**
Common	No	100/100	N/A

Feverfew	Further Description *Yes/No*
Details:	You get the feeling that this plant may have many beneficial uses. **Uses Discovered:** 1) Tranquilizer 2) ? 3) ? 4) ?

Rarity:	**Magical:**	**Durability:**	**Charge:**
Common	No	100/100	N/A

Milk Thistle		Further Description *Yes/No*	
Details:		This plant seems to have many uses for healing... **Uses Discovered:** 1) Cure Disease 2) ? 3) ? 4) ?	
Rarity:	**Magical:**	**Durability:**	**Charge:**
Common	No	100/100	N/A

Chamomile		Further Description *Yes/No*	
Details:		You get the feeling that this plant can heal you and promote relaxation... **Uses Discovered:** 1) Tranquilizer 2) ? 3) ? 4) ?	
Rarity:	**Magical:**	**Durability:**	**Charge:**
Common	No	100/100	N/A

Finally, after working my way slowly through the notifications for the plants, I took a few handfuls of the ingredients, making sure I had ten of each, and stashed them in my bag of holding. I moved onto the next notification, reading the acknowledgement for killing the sporeling.

Congratulations!

You have killed the following:

- 1x Sporeling, level 3 for 40xp.

Progress to level 5 stands at 1,635/2,700

"Hell yes!" I muttered. I was getting slowly closer to the next level. I was determined to get there, and hopefully soon. I returned to the edge of the balcony with a much heavier bag and stared down at the base of the tower. I didn't know how it was possible, but the damn thing looked to be at least a mile high, maybe two. Sintara and the Baron had said they were up to three miles high, but it just didn't seem real.

From my vantage point, I could make out hundreds of windows and dozens of other gardens and balconies before the base disappeared into the trees. I decided to try to clear another few floors, then head back up to the safety of the small reflection room no later than early afternoon. I'd be exploring the tower by daylight whenever possible from now on, and I needed some decent sleep tonight.

Before I could explore the rest of the tower, however, I needed to finish exploring this level. I moved back inside cautiously, searching the alcoves to make sure there was nothing hiding in them, then I started to examine the items that filled each recess. My earlier assessment was right; they were altars, and each was different. As I moved to inspect the nearest one, a notification began to flash.

Scalable Quest discovered!

Bring back the Old Gods:

Choose a patron deity and reawaken the Gods of Old to begin this quest.

Mana tithed to chosen Deity: 0/1000

Reward: Unknown.

"Okay, that's not fucking freaky or anything," I said, backing away. "Why the hell would I bring back the gods? Didn't one of them fuck this world over once already?" I stopped myself, realizing that the only source I had on *anything* in this world so far was the Baron and his retainers. "Besides," I argued, "I've decided to be an optimist, remember? Also, stop talking to yourself, Jax, it's getting weird."

Shaking my head, I moved back to the small altar and examined the patterns engraved into it. Rays of sunlight shone down from a cloudy sky to rest on a woman walking across a field. A name carved below her feet read "Ashante."

You have discovered an Altar of Ashante, Goddess of Nature and Life.

Will you choose her as your patron Deity?

Yes/No

I examined the altar from every angle, rereading the notification a few times, but there were no further details, no indication of what the quest reward would be, or whether she was a goddess that would suit me at all, so I moved on. The next altar to the left of Ashante was covered in carvings of flames dancing, with the name Jenae carved below the image of a figure wreathed in fire. I continued circling the room until I'd gained prompts for each of the altars.

You have discovered an Altar of Jenae, Goddess of Fire, Exploration, and Hidden Knowledge.

Will you choose her as your patron Deity?

Yes/No

You have discovered an Altar of Cruit, God of Earth and Stability.

Will you choose him as your patron Deity?

Yes/No

Jez Cajiao

You have discovered an Altar of Nimon, God of Death and Destruction.

Will you choose him as your patron Deity?

Yes/No

You have discovered an Altar of Sint, God of Light and Order.

Will you choose him as your patron Deity?

Yes/No

You have discovered an Altar of Tamat, Goddess of Darkness, Assassination, and Larceny.

Will you choose her as your patron Deity?

Yes/No

You have discovered an Altar of Vanei, Goddess of Air and Change.

Will you choose her as your patron Deity?

Yes/No

You have discovered an Altar of Lagoush, Goddess of Water, Healing, and Alteration.

Will you choose her as your patron Deity?

Yes/No

You have discovered an Altar of Svetu, God of Invention and Creation.

Will you choose him as your patron Deity?

Yes/No

You have discovered an Altar of Tyosh, God of Time and Reflection.

Will you choose him as your patron Deity?

Yes/No

I moved back outside and sat on the grass to think. After all, a god could grant some awesome gifts, if they wanted to, and it was a quest, but I had nothing beyond a basic description for information. There were some that I liked the sound of, like Svetu, a god of invention and creation? A craftsman's god, clearly, so that could work out well for me. If this was a game, I'd have chosen his altar immediately. After all, once I'd survived the early game; the gear I could craft for myself was always the best out there, eventually.

Thing was, it wasn't a game. I needed something to help me survive *now*. I moved on, considering Nimon. A god of death and destruction would likely have some awesome spells, but a creature who basically lived to destroy was never going to be a great match for me.

Plus he'd probably have some really shitty quests later on. Sacrifice this, murder that, and so on, blah, blah, blah. Never going to happen. The dick had already basically destroyed the world, so he was out. Also, I sort of remembered that he'd banished the *other* gods. That meant he was probably still around. If I swore to serve him, and he was still here? He'd probably not even notice, but bring back one of the banished gods? Yeah, that fucker'd owe me.

I dismissed Tyosh, Lagoush, and Vanei quickly as well, since time, water, and air just didn't feel that interesting to me. Tamat was basically a thieves' and assassins' goddess, so nope, moving on. Stealth was cool and all, but frankly I was shit at it, believing more in "heavy stealth," as I'd heard it called. After all, no fucker rang alarms when they were dead.

Cruit for Earth did make me pause. Stability I could do with, but if you let yourself get too stable, you never changed, and change was life. Nope.

That left me with three: Ashante, Jenae, and Sint. Sint was God of Light and Order. I could see an immediate use for Light magic here, but Order was a bit boring. I kind of liked disorder and chaos, so I doubted we'd mesh well.

It was down to Ashante and Jenae, Life and Fire, respectively.

Life magic would be awesome. I had one healing spell, and that was literally saving my life whenever I got injured here, but Fire…

I didn't know why, but I liked it. Always had. The comfort of sitting in front of a fire at the end of the day or in winter was tremendous, as was watching things burn. I'd always been a pyromaniac at heart. Most of all, though, I had two spells that were fire based, so if it gave me a boost, that would help immediately.

I shrugged and walked over to Jenae's altar and chose "yes" when I was given the prompt. Besides another notification, nothing else seemed to happen.

You have selected Jenae, Goddess of Fire, Exploration, and Hidden Knowledge as your patron deity.

Tithe currently gifted: 0/1000.

I took a deep breath and looked around. After a minute of nothing happening, I grimaced and decided to move on. Clearly, Jenae wasn't about to give out any freebies right away. Dammit. I guessed I had to fulfill the minimum part of the quest before I got anything, even an acknowledgement from the goddess I'd pledged myself to.

187

CHAPTER SIXTEEN

The whole swearing, soul searching, and choosing a god had taken only a few hours, including all the thinking, so I took the time to return to the garden and eat and drink my fill. There was no need to waste my stored food, after all. I sat back on the grass that covered the ground, enjoying the breeze, the sunshine, and the sounds of the birds surrounding me as I finished my second apple.

As I relaxed, I let my mana refill, then channeled it to the goddess for a while until I was almost out, then allowed it to refill a bit again. I did this constantly for the better part of an hour, figuring I'd better get on Jenae's good side, until I grew too bored. I heaved myself to my feet and headed back inside, confident that at least this level would remain clear of the sporelings, thanks to the light. I still scanned the room carefully before I moved inside, but that was more common sense than a belief that I'd be attacked.

I set off across the hall and down the far stairwell with more confidence than I'd had before. Passing the blackened windows as I went, I stopped and took the time to try and clean one. I found that the muck that coated it was deeper than I'd thought at first. Poking and digging at it, I managed to get a few flakes free, but that was all. I leaned my naginata against the wall and drew a dagger, chipping at the substance until a solid chunk came free, letting sunlight stream in. I gawked at the bit of black muck in my hand and couldn't figure out what it was for the life of me.

It looked like a thick wedge of mud, dried and baked until it was nearly as hard as brick, but how it had ended up covering the window, I didn't know.

I put it down to the creatures of the tower's hatred of the sun and resolved to start clearing them as I went. Not all of them, and not properly; it'd take months for a start, but some now and then would create issues for the sporelings, at least.

I sheathed my dagger after clearing as much of the substance away as I could in a few minutes, then gathered up my naginata and set off.

The next floor flew past, containing a dozen or more rooms on either side, and the hall was big enough that there were seats and planters on each floor, though whatever had once filled them was long dead and had crumbled to dust in the oppressive eternal darkness.

As I jogged down the stairs to the next floor, I resolved to turn back in another two floors. I wasn't far from the Hall of Memories now, but I needed to find somewhere safe to rest and spend the night. If I didn't find anything soon, I'd need to turn back and return to the Pearl chamber. At least I knew that room was safe.

I reached the next floor, but just as I was about to step out onto it, I saw movement. I jerked back out of sight into the stairwell, readying my naginata and slowly returning to peek around the edge of the doorway.

There, in the middle of the hall, steadily plodding towards me, was a creature from a thousand horror films: a desiccated, armor-clad skeleton. Its left arm was missing from the elbow down, and its leather armor seemed to have rotted into place. Small flakes fell off it as it moved toward me, holding a spear in its remaining hand.

It wasn't a full skeleton, not as I'd seen in some movies, but that was the best name for it. Zombies, as I supposed this might be called, were all about feeding on brains and shit. This one, well, it had been a guard once, clearly. Probably for the tower, but now it was undead, with the skin shrunken back to a thin layer over bone, missing in many places. The eyes were gone, replaced with a grim, red glow. The armor and clothing looked to have rotted into place on it then fallen apart from long centuries of steady, relentless movement.

I looked around but couldn't see anything else on this floor, and after a few seconds of thought, I guessed that I'd have to come across the undead, remembering Tommy talking about fighting them once. I guessed I might as well do it when there was only one, so I took a deep breath and stepped out to meet it.

It saw me instantly and crouched, extending its spear and clacking its teeth menacingly. Tiny red balls of hatred winked at me from the bony eye sockets, and I grinned back at it. We might have had similar weapons, a spear against a naginata, but I had both hands, and magic!

I lunged at the thing, covering the distance quickly as it stabbed out with a spearhead so covered in rust, it was more dangerous from the risk of tetanus than anything else.

I batted it aside easily and whipped the bladed end of my weapon through the bone soldier's neck, severing its head and causing it to collapse. I froze for a second, waiting for something else, but besides the head continuing to clack its teeth at me, nothing else happened. I grinned to myself, damn pleased with how easy that was.

I straightened up and walked across the floor to the skull and put my naginata down, picking the skull up to rest on my left palm. I took a deep breath and, staring into its hate-filled eyes, I began to speak.

"Alas, poor Yorick, I knew him—WHAT THE FUCK!" I cut off from my ill-advised and poor attempt at Shakespeare as the skull began to bleed black smoke that tried to enter my hand. I dropped the skull to meet my upcoming foot and punted it across the room.

The bony projectile trailed smoke before smashing into the far wall with a crunch of breaking bone as I practically shit myself. I used Identify and found out how stupid I'd been, picking the skull up in the first place.

DarkSpore

This creature is a parasitic form of life, acting as an extension of the SporeMother that birthed it. Although weak individually, and incapable of survival for long without a host, a single DarkSpore has been the downfall of cities. The queen sees all that her drones do, and she hungers.

Level: 5
Health: 5
Mana: 0

I glanced at the smoky mess that gathered and bunched around the skull before inching its way back towards the rest of the corpse. Grimacing, I fired a Firebolt into it, sending the skull careening across the room. I hit it again, detonating it in a small cloud of flying teeth and bone fragments.

I saw a notification flashing. Thinking of the way I'd managed to alter the HUD to my tastes so far, I concentrated. A small, black skull appeared, outlined in red, which floated up from the corpse to disappear out of the top of my vision. Cool. I now had a death indicator.

Congratulations!

You have killed the following:

- 1x Decrepit Skeleton Warrior, level 5 for 25xp.
- 1x DarkSpore, level 5 for 50xp.

Progress to level 5 stands at 1,710/2,700

Dismissing the notifications, I grinned, hoping that essentially killing two creatures in one would help me level faster, what with the DarkSpore being inside the skeleton and everything. I realized I'd passed the halfway point to my next level. At this rate, it wouldn't be long…

As the thought crossed my mind, I began to turn around to search the corpse for any loot, when reality caught up with me.

It came in the form of a bony fist exploding into my jaw and hurling me from my feet, my weapon clattering away into the distance.

You have been critically struck by DarkSpore Wandering Guardian for 20 points of damage.

You are stunned.

As I rolled to a halt several feet away, I tried to work out what had happened, shaking my head to clear it and spitting blood onto the ground. The notifications obscured my vision, and I shook my head again, wanting to be rid of them while I tried to rise to my feet. As they disappeared, the second skeleton of the day jumped onto me, bearing me to the floor and sinking its teeth into my defensively raised forearm.

"Arghhhh! What the hell!" I screamed its chipped, sharp teeth bit into the muscle, chewing deep as it could while landing repeated blows. I tried to curl up and cover my head reflexively.

The bastard thing's teeth were sharp enough some of them had managed to make it through the leather of the bracers already, and while they hadn't all made it, it was still painful as all hell.

Thankfully, the notifications didn't appear this time, but my health bar was dropping at a considerable rate. Between the bites, the hit that had laid me out, and the punches coming in thick and fast, I was already at half my health, and it was shrinking faster by the second.

The creature tore a chunk of my arm free with a savage jerk. As blood and several teeth rained down on me, the world changed, and my animal side took over.

Screaming at my attacker, filled with the pain and fear of the last day and previous night, I grabbed its shoulder with my left hand and swung with my right, punching it in the jaw and knocking its head askew. Twisting underneath it, the realization of how light the creature was faintly permeated my panicked and rage-filled brain.

I grabbed both its arms, straightening them out and twisting the elbows inward to lock them, giving me the breathing room I needed. Shoving the creature back, I planted my left foot firmly on the floor, then swung up and hooked my right foot under its chin. Using the leverage I now had, I straightened my right leg as fast as I could, twisting the skeleton around and driving its face into the floor with a satisfying crunch of breaking bone.

Quickly releasing my grip, I rolled to my feet and began casting the Firebolt spell with both hands. Concentrating first on one hand, then the other, I roared out the spell again and again, pounding it into the ground with the force of each impact. Each hit smashed its skull back into the ground as soon as it rebounded. As the skeleton broke apart, I continued the barrage into the inky cloud as it tried to escape the exposed skull.

Two further spell impacts were all I managed as my mana ran out and a headache flared to life, but it proved to be enough as the death notifications appeared in my vision. I allowed myself a split second to confirm them before staggering fully upright to check the rest of the room.

Congratulations!

You have killed the following:

- 1x DarkSpore Wandering Guardian, level 3 for 25xp.
- 1x DarkSpore Parasite, level 3 for 25xp.

Progress to level 5 stands at 1,760/2,700

Scanning the room, I saw no other creatures nearby, but a third skeleton was emerging from the stairwell. Well, fuck *that*. They didn't know who the hell they were dealing with. I'd fought monsters that would have made Hollywood directors shit themselves, and I didn't mean lawyers.

I wasn't taking this shit from a goddamn bag of bones!

I lunged and swept up the first skeleton's spear from the floor in both hands, running at the latest arrival before it could make sense of the destruction in the room. It began to raise its spear, a copy of the one I held, but I closed in before it could complete the movement.

I lashed out with the base of the spear, knocking its weapon aside as I brought the weighted butt back around and up, hitting it in the cheek. As it stumbled, I took the opportunity to bring the spear around to hook its knee as I shoulder-charged it back into the stairwell.

As we tumbled down the stairs, I could hear bones breaking. I lost my grip on the spear, my head colliding with one wall and stars exploding across my vision for a second before I managed to catch myself. Shaking my head and seeing blood splatter from a gash, I tried to stand and staggered, reaching to brace myself on a recessed window sill to keep from falling farther down the stairs.

Hearing a hiss from below, I turned to find not one, but three skeletons charging around the twist of the tower.

The first two looked fresh, or at least as fresh as their kind could, while the third limped along at the back. Bones that were clearly broken hung from it, and it was unarmed. That little bastard had gotten to its feet quicker than I had, to be returning up the tower already.

I straightened up, the same determination that filled my Dreams and had gotten me this far coming to the fore. I wouldn't get far by running, especially on what was starting to feel like a twisted ankle, so it was time to teach these creatures to regret cornering me.

Looking over the weapons they brandished, a rusty mace and a crossbow without any quarrels, I grinned. The one at the back had lost its spear, and I had the high ground. I liked my odds against three bags of bones, even if the DarkSpore parasites were more of a challenge.

Remembering the sporeling's reaction to sunlight, I spun around and hit the window with both fists as hard as I could, using precious seconds to smash the coating away and open the stairwell to the light of the sun. As I spun back around, the skeletons cowered back, hands raised to block the light from their skulls.

I ignored the pain in my ankle, forcing it to hold me as I sprinted forwards and jumped, twisting to land with my feet connecting to the head of the foremost skeleton. Its mace went flying as its skull detached from its body and bounced away down the stairs.

I tumbled down the spiral stairs with the two other animated skeletons and the rest of the headless one in a mixture of bones, fists, and feet, weapons forgotten as we all pounded into each other until we erupted onto the floor below.

Head spinning, I noticed my health bar flashing, with a sliver of red all that remained. I rolled away from the nearest movement, focusing blearily on a faint light off to one side and stumbled to my feet. Trying to run into the safety of the sunshine, I teetered dizzily and fell over.

I was probably concussed, so I gave up on standing and frantically crawled towards it. The only thought in my mind was that I needed to reach the rectangular patch of sunlight several feet away. At some point, the window on one side of the room had shattered, and that was my savior now.

As I neared the light, a sudden pain stabbed my left leg. A skeleton had grabbed it and was clawing its way towards me. Glancing back, I frantically kicked once, twice, and a third time at its head before it released me, and I scrabbled into the light.

As my head and my vision cleared, I checked frantically to find that, out of the three skeletons I'd collapsed down the stairs with, two were now dead–again. The remaining one had only one leg and was slowly dragging itself toward me until its grasping fingertips hit the light. It pulled back as if burned by it.

I turned my attention back to the other two corpses, watching the swarming clouds rise from the shattered bone piles. The parasitic vapors slowly mingled, hisses and flashes of chittering sounding across the room as they melded together. The hairs on the back of my neck rose as I looked down at the patch of sunlight I sat in and realized that it was getting smaller as the sun continued its journey. I had to kill these things and fall back to somewhere safe!

Desperate for options, I pulled up my status bars; my health was slowly climbing. With a thought, I added percentages to the HUD, and the simple bar was further clarified by showing eight percent. Not enough to survive another fight, that was for sure. My stamina became sixty-two percent in the green bar, and the blue mana bar displayed fourteen percent.

I had enough mana for one Firebolt, and maybe if I waited a few more minutes, I'd be able to survive a single punch, but that'd be it.

"Shit...shit...*shit*! Think, dude, think!" I muttered, scouring my brain for inspiration.

I felt around for options, and my hand grazed something blocky in my pocket and remembered my phone. Struck by a sudden thought, I pulled it out and checked it over. Yes, the screen was intact and very, very reflective.

Grinning at my reflection, I angled it and aimed the reflected sunlight across the room until it hit the nearby skeleton. Flinching back in surprise and pain, it covered its head and tried to scuttle away. Before it had the chance to get far, I hit it with a Firebolt in its crossed hands, blowing one off entirely and badly damaging the other. Rushing forward, I grabbed the outstretched arm and dragged it mercilessly into the light. A screech echoed from the inside the skull, the buzzing rising to a fever pitch for a brief second before its skull exploded into flaming shards.

Staggering back from the bone shrapnel that flew everywhere, I quickly dashed back into the safety of the light to catch my breath. The bone pile was shifting ominously. Grinning, I began to plan the next fight. I had to get the creature that was building itself now to either run away or give me the time to heal.

I didn't have any real chance in a straight-up fight, but these things weren't very bright, so maybe...

"Yeah, that'll work," I said aloud, pretending to ignore the writhing pile of undead remains. Aside from the night in the arena, I'd never been in so much personal danger in my life, nor felt so alive.

I could tell that the heap of remains was being drawn together quickly, building into a new creature by using all of the bones, as near as I could tell, but it'd take at least a few more minutes, and that would give me all the time I needed. I hoped, anyway. Taking a deep breath, I looked around the room and spotted the mace that one of the skeletons had been carrying, lying off to one side of the stairwell I'd exited earlier.

Before I could let my doubts build, I set off running across the room, scooping it up in my right hand and kicking off the wall nearby. I turned back to challenge the newly forming creature. As I closed the final few feet, a skull twisted to face me, rising out of the pile with a warning chittering.

Ignoring the danger and my low health, I cast the Firebolt that I'd just regained enough mana to afford again. The strike hit the skull just above the eye sockets, knocking it back as bones audibly cracked. I swung the mace hard across the bridge of the nose as it began to turn back, and I was rewarded with a sickening crunch of breaking bone. The pile sagged for a few precious seconds, and I grabbed the vertebrae connected to the skull, dragging it as fast as I could towards the light.

To avoid a swipe from a claw-tipped arm, I released my grip, dodged aside, and brought the mace down on its shoulder joint, breaking the bones again.

Aiming the upswing at its skull, I swore as the blow was deflected off a hastily raised limb. I grabbed the upper arms and dragged it another foot or so. Jumping back a second too late as another arm flashed out at me, a hot sting of pain tore down my cheek as bony fingertips scored three furrows in my skin.

My health bar dropped again, down to four percent. I was losing a fuckload of blood from multiple wounds, not to mention what felt like some seriously broken ribs and more. With my mana at three percent, I was out of my long-range options.

I swung hard, one blow after another, breaking as many bones in the heap as I could. I started shifting around the pile, careful not to inflict too much damage in any one area and force the parasite out into the open air. I had nothing besides the sunlight to fight it. My naginata was lying somewhere on the floor above, and I had nowhere near enough mana for another Firebolt.

Knowing I couldn't survive another hit, I dodged another clumsy swipe from the creature's fingers and smashed down once more as I staggered aside. I quickly knocked a second swinging limb aside and began kicking the body closer to the light.

As the seconds blurred into a dodging, desperate nightmare of mace swings, clawed fingers, and hissing chittering noise, I finally got the jumbled bones close enough that the leading edge touched the light. With a scream, it all lunged into motion. Bones cracked as they strained to drag it back from the one thing it seemed to truly fear.

As it began to rise to its feet, it forgot me in fear of its primal enemy, the sun. I took my last chance and lunged, striking the center of the flailing mass of bone, torn leather, and rotten flesh.

As it staggered, I dove into it, using all the force I could muster to drive my shoulder into it and shove it back into the light.

It shook and screamed, collapsing under the unforgiving rays of the sun. The bones being held together by the DarkSpore fell away, causing the inky mass to shrink as it tried to escape the cleansing light. As it dwindled, it kept trying to escape the light. But I waited with my mace, smashing bones and driving it back. After a handful of seconds that passed like hours, it finally exploded, once again peppering me with bone fragments, and finally I could check over the notifications.

Congratulations!

You have killed the following:

- 2x DarkSpore Wandering Guardian, level 3 for 50xp.
- 1x DarkSpore Parasite, level 3 for 25xp.
- 1x DarkSpore Devourer, level 5 for 100xp.
- 1x DarkSpore Melded Parasite, level 3 for 50xp.

Progress to level 5 stands at 1,985/2,700

I kicked the bones out of the light and collapsed down in their place.

Each time my mana was high enough, I cast Minor Healing. I rinsed and repeated until I was finally fully healed. It probably took just over an hour, but with the constant threat of something coming up the far stairwell to attack me when I had no mana, it seemed like days.

Finally, I was healed, and my mana was restoring, so I set to quickly looting the corpses. They had nothing that seemed to be of any real value. A green, mold-encrusted lump on one finger turned out to be a copper ring with a tiny red gem in it, but beyond that, all I found was a handful of copper coins in a rotted purse that I added to my pockets.

I immediately discarded all the weapons, since they were essentially useless, before setting off back up the tower. I'd had enough for one day. Gathering up my naginata as soon as I reached the next floor, I began to run, climbing the stairs as fast as I could. I walked when my stamina bottomed out, but only long enough for it to refill before running again.

By the time I reached the top level, I was exhausted, sore, and generally pissed off, as I knew I'd have to be careful going back down the stairs tomorrow. I'd have to find a way to take and hold a section of the tower. That way, I wouldn't have to clear the same ground each day.

I entered the chamber and sank to the floor, glad to be somewhere I could let my guard down again. In a bare few minutes, I was asleep.

CHAPTER SEVENTEEN

I woke up a few hours later. How long it had been, I had no real idea, but as I lay there in the darkness, I felt less exhausted and worn, so I figured at least six hours must have passed. I vaguely remembered West saying something about Tommy making a clock in his vision. Considering I had no clue what the local time was, when I'd tried it myself it'd not worked, so I called bullshit on that one.

I got to my feet and made a quick meal from my rations and some fresh fruits I'd found yesterday, then got down to business. First, I channeled all of my mana, save ten, to Jenae, then I got to stretching and exercising. An hour later, I was sweating, and my legs shook like they'd never hold my weight again.

I'd hammered the exercise routine I'd been given in training as best I could without any weights or equipment, concentrating mainly on sit-ups, sprints, and burpees. I'd checked my stats before I started, and after that hour, I'd raised my Endurance, Dexterity and my Strength by a point. Pleased with the rate of improvement, I resolved to continue every day, until I couldn't get any more gains, or…well, I grew too bored with it.

I needed to grow in every attribute, but some weren't as easily increased, like Luck, and my free points would be better spent there than anywhere else.

When I'd recovered, I gathered my gear together and started setting up the alchemy equipment. I knew the very basics of using the set; I'd had some training back on Earth, after all, and had learned chemistry at school, not to mention the hundreds of hours spent playing RPGs, but the skillbook seemed to provide the most information for me. It made links between certain items, such as junit berries and milk thistle being two common ingredients to make a cure poison potion, and that ginseng and milk thistle were used to cure diseases. I set to work, pausing only to drain my mana periodically to my new goddess.

Three hours later, I was exhausted. The grinding, boiling, and straining had taken forever, not to mention the distillation, but it was worth it. As I put the stopper in the last bottle and sat back, I used my Identify skill to determine what I had made.

Minor Cure-All Brew		Further Description *Yes/No*	
Details:		This brew will remove any low-level toxins from the body. Works against basic infections, poisons, venoms, and numbing agents.	
Rarity:	Magical:	Durability:	Potency:
Uncommon	No	100/100	1/10

I'd managed to make four of the small potions. It had taken ten sets of ingredients, and I was nearly out of a lot of them now, but I didn't mind collecting more. Even the times I'd failed had counted towards my experience, and I'd managed to level the minor cure poison recipe to level three, along with the minor cure disease recipe.

I'd even "made" a new recipe all of my own by combining the two into my new "minor cure-all brew." Between all of them, it had brought me sixty percent of the way to the next level in alchemy. It seemed that, for each aspect of the skill, such as making a cure poison potion, I gained a certain number of points.

The first ten levels of any given recipe would provide twenty points per attempt towards the next level. Levels eleven to twenty provided ten points.

At levels twenty-one to thirty, I received five points per attempt, and then from thirty onwards, I would gain one point per attempt. Each level of a recipe was also worth ten points in the overall scale of that skill, so leveling both of the recipes to level three had given me sixty points out of a hundred to reach the next level of alchemy. Each rank in the skill would come with small bonuses until I was making true wonders from simple ingredients and curing the illnesses of the gods with more complex things.

It seemed complicated, but considering the bonuses for the two skills I'd managed to raise to level two, they were a real target to aim for. So far, my leveled naginata skill had given me a boost of five percent to my speed, and my stealth skill was boosted by a further five percent by my cloak. I was especially excited to realize that reaching level twenty in staves would increase my naginata speed by one hundred percent!

It seemed weird, since I couldn't imagine what level forty could be like. A two hundred percent increase in speed would be insane, after all, but when I considered the fact that some of the deaths I'd suffered in the Dreams had come from beasts so fast I'd barely seen them, I'd need the skills to be able to fight creatures like that.

I began to ponder my current abilities, considering the rapid rate at which I was leveling so far. What would happen if I put every point for the next ten levels into Wisdom? My mana would jump to a regeneration rate of seven points per minute, or four hundred and twenty points an hour.

With Firebolt only costing ten points to cast, I'd be able to hammer any creatures like the ones I'd fought so far.

That begged the question about higher-level spells. Was it a case where the next spell up would cost twenty mana, or two hundred?

There was so much I didn't know, but I thought I might have discovered a really important fact: my physical stats would increase with exercise. Sure, it was boring, but if I increased them that way and dumped my points into my mental attributes, I could become something seriously dangerous, even a true spellsword or battlemage.

Forging myself into a warrior who was equally at home casting spells and fighting on the front lines sounded great to me. I had no friends or teammates here, so I had to become a one-man wrecking ball. The fastest way to do that was to make sure I leveled fast, rested little, and generally pushed myself to the limit. I'd find Tommy eventually, I knew I would, but it could take years. For now, I was on my own.

I set my mind back to work and drained my recovered mana again, then got on with my exercises for another hour before deciding that if the sun wasn't up yet, it wouldn't be far off, with a bit of luck. I checked my quest log and verified that I'd made a fair amount of progress toward making contact with Jenae. I had tithed 490 out of a thousand points in just a few hours. I resolved to have it done inside the next twenty-four hours, just to get it out of the way.

I gathered my gear, leaving the majority of the odds and ends in the room. I only equipped my weapons, my bag of holding, and some food and drink. I'd come back for the rest later, but I wanted to be as light as possible.

I had a tower to explore.

I opened the door to the room at the top of the staircase and stood waiting, half-expecting something to attack me immediately. When nothing came, I stepped through the doorway and moved to the right, bracing my back against the wall and sweeping my naginata from side to side as I looked around.

The floor was deserted. I couldn't even hear a single sound. Crossing the room to the huge windows, I started chipping at the gunk that covered one. After a minute of quiet cursing and grunting, I managed to get the point of a dagger under a section of the coating.

It came away with a loud crunch, faint cracks running out and spreading across the remaining coating, a small patch of early morning sky gleaming through the newly cleared opening. Setting back to it with a will, I spent another twenty minutes partially uncovering a window that soared higher than I stood and was easily twice as wide. It was still filthy, with bits of the coating stuck everywhere, but now when the sun rose properly, this room would be a death trap for the sporelings and their cousins.

I sheathed the dagger and stood listening for a brief second. Nothing seemed to be coming close, so I swept up my naginata from where I had leaned it against the wall and set off down the stairs, jogging as I went. Ten floors passed without incident, then ten more. I stopped to rest, always pausing as I walked out onto a new floor, making sure they were truly empty, but each time, I was the only thing there. I passed balcony gardens like the first, badly overgrown and crumbling stone everywhere.

The occasional footprints could be traced in the dirt and dust of millennia, but little else.

I began stopping to clean a window now and then, making sure I'd have some retreats if I needed them. As hours passed, and the thirtieth floor approached, I'd started to wonder if the SporeMother was, in fact, dead, or whether she had left. I'd seen nothing to indicate that she was still around, and if there had been anything else in the tower, where else would it be, if not hunting me? It'd be…yeah…they'd all be waiting for me as a trap. I just knew it.

As I rounded the final spiral of the staircase, it opened out onto a large floor, easily the biggest single floor I'd ever seen.

It was bigger than a cathedral hall, and in the center of the wall opposite was a doorway. It was huge and imposing and filled with the same crystal I'd found in the doorway of the first room that I'd hidden in upon my initial arrival. This had to be the Hall of Memories, the vault that held the spellbooks and the skill memories that Sintara had mentioned.

The floor was presumably circular, with a narrow crescent shape to the section before me, and the Hall of Memories as the vast majority of the rest of the floor.

The problem was, the SporeMother, or whoever was in charge here must have figured out I'd be heading here as well. There were a good dozen or more skeletons standing around between me and that doorway. Standing hidden in the doorway of the stairwell, I considered my options. I needed to get in that room. I couldn't just bypass it, and even if I wanted to, the opposite stairwell was clear across the room. I'd never manage to sneak past everything to reach it.

If I had to get into the room, I had to get past the skeletons to do so. That was a given. They'd never let me just run past, and judging by the motley collection of weapons they held, I couldn't just try to bulldoze my way through. I needed to narrow it down to just one or two at a time.

They weren't that hard to destroy, really. Their main advantage was the instinctive terror caused by facing a walking undead. I'd already fought several and had found that the actual bodies were easy to destroy. The real issue was the DarkSpore inside them.

Windows encircled the room, but they all had the same kind of crap covering them. Each would take time to open, and none would be easy, let alone with a dozen undead creatures trying to kill me.

Returning to the bottom of the stairs, I readied myself, naginata in my right hand, and my left ready to cast magic. I could cast a total of fifteen Firebolts before I was out of mana, but I'd regenerate enough for another Firebolt every five minutes.

Looking around the corner at the occupants of the hall, I counted eleven battered and decrepit skeletons in various states of decay. One creature that stood head and shoulders above the rest with better armor and a huge greatsword that it rested on the ground, tip-first, with its hands crossed on the pommel of the hilt. Finally, I spotted one last figure hunched over in the far corner, wrapped up in a long black robe with a staff in one hand.

It looked like a mage or caster to me, but as it was the first I'd seen, it could just as easily have been a particularly evil-looking janitor with the head snapped off his mop. I'd have to keep my eye on this one.

Taking a deep breath, I reviewed my options, then took one last look at the room. The various skeletons were scattered around the space, with the largest one standing directly in front of the doorway to the Hall of Memories. It was in better condition than the others, and obviously not as old. It appeared to be the remnants of a much more recently captured adventurer, with a long, red cloak obscuring its body beyond the dark bracers that covered its arms and dirty greaves on its legs. A tight-fitted metal helm sported short, ornamental wings flaring out behind completed its visible armor. The mage was still hunched over in the far corner, close to the stairs.

I suddenly had a flash of inspiration, recognizing that the mage and the giant adventurer were most likely my most dangerous foes. If I could take one of them out first, I'd have a much better chance of winning this fight. I doubted they'd stand still while I slaughtered their lesser companions, after all.

Sneaking back up the stairs, I climbed until I found one of the windows I'd uncovered. I slowly dug away at the frame until I could push an entire panel of glass out and sent it tumbling down into the forest below. I leaned out to examine the side of the tower, especially the level below me.

I could see plenty of handholds, as weathered and damaged as the tower was. While I couldn't see the windows that opened onto the Hall of Memories from where I was, I knew roughly where they were.

If I could either reach them from the outside and open them or climb past them to the next level down then sneak up the stairs to take the mage out first, that would greatly increase my chances of success in the upcoming battle.

I secured my naginata to my back, then looped my belt over my shoulder to make sure it was doubly safe.

Clambering out onto the window ledge, I looked up at the clouds that were slowly covering the sky to the east and knew I didn't have long. I'd always had an issue with heights like this, not being up, but...I'd loved rock climbing, right until I had to try and get down, and it became a game of searching for grips with my damn feet.

I decided to distract myself on my climb, so I put my earbuds in and put my music on for the first time in what seemed like ages, determined to get the damn solar cell on the outer case into the sun soon.

I turned it down low, so I'd still be able to hear anything around me but made sure it was loud enough to relax me as I climbed. I just knew I was going to end up with a fear of heights from this, and probably by association, a fear of bloody music. I flicked on a random playlist, letting the "Final Countdown" by Europe count me down to what was probably going to be a messy death.

I lowered myself gently until I found another handhold, then began to scale my way down the side of the tower, counting my breaths and moving my hands alternately with each breath. I didn't allow myself to stop or to rest. If I paused, it'd be harder by the second to continue, and fear was already fluttering around the edges of my mind.

After a few minutes of scaling down the wall, I spotted a window off to my left and veered toward it. Finding the window sealed tight, I paused for a few minutes, considering. I could force the window, but if I did, the creatures inside would know where I was. All it would take was one spell or blow from a weapon to knock me from the tower.

I decided to take the second option, and quickly clambered down further to the next floor, not letting myself second guess. I desperately wanted to smash the window and climb inside as fast as possible, no matter what was waiting for me. As I circled the tower again, I found I was in luck. There was a small, private balcony that extended out a few feet into the open air. I made it across the tower and dropped down onto it, collapsing against the wall and ignoring the closed door for a long moment as I got my hammering heart under control.

Eventually, after an insane amount of time, I managed to force open the door without too much noise. Putting my earbuds away, I quickly slipped inside, standing for a long moment as my eyes acclimated to the darkness. When I could see again, I blinked in surprise at finding myself inside a small, well-appointed room, which showed the signs of age, thick dust and all, but from the bed to the rugs and wall hangings, it spoke of privacy as well. The bed was placed against one wall, its covers piled up.

On one table were desiccated pots of what seemed to be paint, and a small wooden soldier stood half-painted beside them. This had been someone's home, I realized. I had no idea what had happened to them, which seemed more poignant because, unlike the rest of the rooms I'd seen so far, this wasn't trashed.

I left it as it was, feeling weird about intruding, and slowly flicked the latch as silently as possible, then cracked the door. A skeleton was patrolling the floor outside with its back to me. It moved slowly, one hesitant step after another, then a pause and a look around, then a few more steps. It was easily the most damaged creature I'd seen yet. One foot was missing, and each step looked unstable enough that it might topple over, never to rise again.

Between me and the undead guard were dozens of small planters and seats. Dozens of doors filled the outer edge of the floor, probably leading to more rooms like this one.

I quickly slipped out and hid near the largest planter, unslinging my naginata as I watched the skeleton walking its rounds. After half an hour, it meandered close enough for me to get a good look at it.

It really was much more decrepit than the others, dragging the base of its spear along the floor as it plodded along its circular route. I waited for the right opportunity as it came closer, knowing I couldn't afford any noise.

It finally drew level with me. Before it could spot me, I struck one fast hard blow to the back of its skull, sending it staggering. I darted past it and pulled open the door to the room I'd recently exited, causing it to shield its face from the faint sunlight.

I grabbed it and yanked it forward, dropping onto my back and bunching my legs as it fell on top of me. I straightened my legs out and pushed with all my might, causing it to hurdle over my prone body and out onto the open balcony. It barely had time to scream before it exploded into flames from the sunlight and tumbled away towards the forest far below.

I couldn't help but fucking grin at that, at how smooth and easy it'd been. I damn well hoped it was a sign of things to come, considering the fight I had next.

Sweeping my naginata back up, I quickly covered the distance to the opposite stairwell that led to the floor above and crouched, listening. I couldn't hear any movement, but I forced myself to wait cautiously. After a further few minutes to make sure, I began slowly creeping up the stairs. It took a lot longer to climb up, knowing that I needed to be as silent as possible. At first, I seemed to make more noise than walking normally, or at least I felt like I did.

As the minutes passed, I started to get the hang of it and finally began to move with a noticeably quieter gait. I didn't open the windows, as I needed to be as stealthy as possible, but I took note of how far apart they were spaced, in case I needed to smash them open in a hurry.

As I came around the final revolution of the tower and the edge of the stairwell doorway appeared, I stopped. Occasional sounds made their way to me from the room beyond as the undead shuffled and patrolled, seemingly independent of each other.

I lowered myself to be as unnoticeable as possible and crept forward. Another skeleton stood guard in front of the doorway, a spear in one hand and a buckler in the other.

It faced the stairs but luckily hadn't seen me yet. The mage behind it was facing the room beyond with its staff held upright. A gently glowing crystal topping the staff pulsed with an eerie light, clear to see now that I was so much closer.

"Soooo...yeah, that fucker's a mage, all right," I whispered to myself. "Couldn't be the janitor, could you? Oh no, had to have a fancy boomstick and all. *Motherfucker!*"

Jez Cajiao

Out of all the options available, the best was to go all out. No guts, no glory, and all that. There was a good chance of dying if I got bogged down by them all. I needed to take the mage out, and hopefully a couple of others, before retreating to either the little bedroom I'd entered or higher up the tower, depending on how the fight went. I crouched there, trying to work up the courage to get started or hoping a better plan would come to me, when my phone went off.

"Oh god, no…" I whimpered, as the music started to rise, echoing around the stairwell, even as I frantically slapped at the pocket, trying to get it out, and shut it up in time.

I'd set it months ago to remind me to leave in time to get to Jim's surprise birthday party. The alarm was going off because I hadn't bothered to turn the phone off after listening to the music. I glanced down at it in shock and then back up at the room before me; the damage had been done. I could run, and be chased, or…

I took off running up the stairs as fast as I could, the phone playing the song "Wir Lieben Dudelsack" by *Feuerschwanz* as a clarion call to battle. If I'd planned this, I'd have at least had a properly rousing '80s theme going, "Eye of the Tiger" or something. A small voice in my mind muttered in terror, criticizing my memory and music tastes equally.

As I cleared the stairwell and erupted into the room, the decrepit skeleton in front of the doorway braced itself, only to be smashed aside by my charging shoulder.

Its lightweight body did little to slow my mad rush as I deliberately impacted its shield full on, smacking the spearhead aside.

I barreled into the room. The mage had moved a few meters further in, and as it twisted around to face me, it lifted its right hand. A cold blue glow began to form as it croaked out something at me.

Groaning internally at my luck, I closed the last few feet. Its spell bloomed into a swiftly growing ice spray that billowed out from the outstretched hand. My body began to shiver, and my health bar dropped steadily as I finally reached close enough range and lashed out. Bringing my naginata down on its outstretched forearm, the bones cracked as the arm was knocked aside.

The spell suddenly ripped out to the side, giving me a second of respite as the arm guiding it pointed into its allies instead of me.

Before it could direct the spell back at me, I bellowed out my own, releasing the haft of my weapon with one hand to fire a Firebolt, blasting the rotten face glaring out at me from the depths of its black cowl before grabbing onto my weapon again. As it staggered back, I hit it with the naginata on the backswing, driving the metal-clad base into its stomach. Glass shattered somewhere beneath its robes.

I was about to hit it with another spell when I was body checked from the left, a decrepit skeleton piling into me and causing me to stagger a few feet before its teeth sank into the gap under my shitty pauldrons. Lashing up and across my chest with a gauntleted fist, I received a satisfying crunch as the blow connected.

The pain worsened as it ripped its teeth free and fell back. How the hell it had managed to find enough flesh around my armor to bite was beyond me, but I'd soon pay it back.

Spinning back around, I found the mage retreating, trying to get the room it needed to cast its spells while the rest of the room was in motion, closing on me from all directions. Most of them were between me and the opposite stairwell now, and a noise from behind suggested that the first skeleton was back on its feet. My options were rapidly disappearing as they flanked me.

Grinning at the mage, I put on a burst of speed and closed the distance between us. It finished its spell casting just as I hit it with another Firebolt, striking it in the right shoulder this time in the hope the blast would throw its aim off. The spell lashed out and filled the entire room in a howling blizzard of ice shrapnel. I was still in trouble. The undead were slowed by the ice and damaged by the shrapnel, but not to the level I was going to be. I had literally seconds left to escape this fight if I didn't want to die.

I was determined to take the mage with me, and I spun the naginata in a great overhead blow, hitting it in the crown of the skull and forcing it to its knees. A metal-plated skullcap came loose as its hood fell back, my arm ringing with the force of the blow.

I cast Firebolt with one hand while slashing out with the blunt end of my weapon, doing a continuous barrage of damage as my mana bar plummeted. Hitting the mage in the head with a Firebolt again for good measure, I was finally rewarded by a skull appearing in my Augmented Vision. I quickly twisted around, hammering the nearest window with a pair of blasts. As it blew open, the coating blasting apart and sending bits flying everywhere across the room, I switched my attention to the encroaching skeleton horde. As they flinched from the sunlight, I fired at the giant adventurer, only to have it deflect my Firebolt into one of its brethren with its sword and continue to advance on me.

I spun around again and kicked the skull free of the mage. The cloud of shimmering blackness roiled, only to be caught by the sunlight, which tore a high-pitched scream from it until it exploded.

I needed to get the fuck out of here, and fast. But fortunately, the door wasn't far, so I grabbed the remains of the mage in one hand, determined to loot the fucker, and tugged it toward the crystalline archway.

It was a pain in the ass, and I nearly dropped it, but if any of them would have anything that would make the next fight easier, it was this bony bastard.

I struggled to drag it with my right hand while still holding my naginata, my left hand blasting Firebolt after Firebolt to clear the way. I was almost to the doorway when the undead adventurer grabbed a spear from one of its lesser brethren and hurled it into my back.

It burst through my left side, low above my hip and under the cuirass's protection, tearing a scream from me as I grabbed at it instinctively. I twisted awkwardly to find the adventurer closing in again. The blizzard spell had continued after the mage's death for a few seconds as it wound down, but now it was gone. Without it to slow their movements, the undead were closing on me quickly.

Hissing in pain, I stared around, taking stock of the room and judging my chances quickly.

My right side was partially protected by a beam of sunlight from the damaged window, but the other windows were on the other side of the undead horde, where I couldn't reach them.

Not goddamn good!

I frantically backpedaled towards the doorway, screaming again as the spear jolted into the wall next to it and ripped my wound wider. Coughing up a mouthful of blood and spitting it out, I heard a whistling, bubbling sound to my breathing. The spear must have nicked the bottom of my lung.

Knowing I didn't have long to escape the oncoming group, I quickly emptied the last of my mana out on Firebolts. Managing to blow an arm off a skeleton that was getting too close, I completely took another's head off and gained a skull icon with a lucky hit. Finally, I hit the adventurer square in its chest, staggering it slightly. Its cloak had obscured the fact that it wore armor of a mottled green and brown. The flames from my spell licked across it before dissipating harmlessly.

The mana headache bloomed as I used the last of it. I spun to the doorway, which was filled with another solid piece of crystal like the Pearl chamber. I planted my left hand on it, bloody palm leaving a smear across the surface as I frantically willed it to open. A pulse of light flared out from my hand, and the crystal slowly dissolved into mist.

It had been much quicker the first time, but I couldn't waste time wondering what had changed. I grabbed the mage's robes again and staggered into the room, pushing my way through the evaporating crystal. A strange grittiness covered my skin as it dissipated, the chamber beyond flaring to life in an explosion of torchlight and welcome.

Dragging the skeleton mage in behind me, I was jerked from my feet to tumble to the floor as something pulled me back mid-stride, making me bite my tongue to keep from screaming. I twisted from my position on the floor, almost blacking out from the pain as the spear injured me further.

The undead adventurer had grasped the mage's leg and was pulling me back through the doorway as it swung its massive greatsword back up over its head one-handed. I gasped and tried to roll aside but couldn't, the spear trapping me in position.

"Close, close, close, close, close, CLOSE!" I wheezed out as I saw the blade descend, willing the door to close as the mage began to disappear back through the crystal.

With another flash of light, the doorway began to reform, the mage's body trapped with a leg half in and half out of the barrier, until it collapsed onto the floor by my side.

I could just make out the outline of the adventurer through the misty portal as it staggered back, the lower leg coming free in its grasp.

A scant half second later, the mist fully solidified, and the clang of a blade deflecting off it rang out.

I gasped in relief, about to collapse back and rest, until the pain reminded me that I couldn't. I levered myself to my feet and got the healing ring ready. I knew this was going to be close, as I could barely stand due to losing so much blood. The healing ring was my last chance, and I had to get rid of the weapon in my side first. I really didn't have any choice if I wanted to survive.

I grabbed the haft of the spear where it protruded from my gut, just behind the head. Before I had time to reconsider, I braced myself for the pain and yanked it through in two sharp jerks, flinging it aside as I fell to my knees. I managed to trigger the healing ring. As blackness flooded over my vision, I triggered it again before falling into blessed darkness, landing face-first into a small pool of my own blood.

CHAPTER EIGHTEEN

I regained consciousness slowly, my eyelids sticking together with gummy, coagulated blood. I let out a groan and tasted blood in my mouth. Pain ripped its teeth through me as though elated to still have me to torture. As I tried to sit up, notifications flashed across my vision. I brought them up, wincing at my depleted health bar.

Warning!

You have sustained serious internal injuries; this basic Ring of Healing is insufficient to repair more serious wounds. Further healing requires focused and repeated applications of magic or a more powerful item.

I dismissed the prompt and examined the seeping wound in my side. I'd managed to heal myself for one hundred points using both charges of the healing ring, but the damage had been severe enough that I'd still been bleeding out. My health had steadily dropped lower as I bled until it was at…sixteen out of one hundred and fifty. Thank God I'd woken up when I did!

Thankfully, my mana was full again, so I hastily forced out my healing spell, spamming it as soon as I could, over and over. I had to stop and wait for my mana to refill a bit before I could manage to fully heal all of it, but I considered that a small price to pay as my head thumped back down on the stone floor.

A short while later, I'd managed to heal all of the wounds, leaving only a bone-deep ache and an impressive new scar on my left side where the spear had caught me. I slowly forced myself to sit up and look around, pulling my helm off and setting it aside.

I scooted back to rest against the near wall as I examined the room. Dozens of bookcases stood against the far wall, with low, comfortable-looking couches, tables, and chairs spread around the middle of the floor. Covering the outer wall in between the bookcases and the occasional window were small holes. I hoped I knew what they held: the memory crystals, hundreds of them, glowing gently as they pulsed with all the colors of the rainbow.

I clambered to my feet, still weak from the injuries. My strength slowly started returning as I trudged around the room. The bookcases were full of books containing both skills and spells. But as I reached to pull one from the wall, a shimmering energy barrier flared to life, stopping my fingers a scant inch from touching them.

I pushed against it, feeling intensifying heat in response to the pressure, until I snatched my hand back with an oath, shaking my hand. I tried the memory crystals next. Finding the same barrier in place over them, I started to swear. My frustration rose as I turned away and started to search the rest of the room.

There was no point in building a room like this, one that recognized me and let me through its crystal door, just to refuse me the prize inside. There had to be some way to deactivate the shield, I just knew it!

I started at the door and worked my way around the room clockwise, slowly moving from wall to bookcase to wall. I inspected the windows, searching the corners and nooks to find a switch or hidden device.

Slowly, I grew aware of a faint blue light emanating from one of the tables. I approached the table quickly and found that what I'd dismissed as a shallow plant pot was instead another bowl, identical to the one at the top of the tower. The more I gazed at it, the brighter the light grew, until it was clearly visible, and a pair of notifications appeared.

Congratulations!

You have found a wisp manawell.
Mana required to reawaken the wisp: 0/400.

Congratulations!

You have discovered a Quest: A Place to Lay Your Head.

Wisps sworn fealty: 0/3
Locations cleared and secured: 0/5
SporeMother killed: 0/1
Guardians claimed: 0/10
Workers claimed: 0/10

Rewards: The Great Tower is yours to command. Surrounding area will become aware of your rightful ownership. Access to supplies and facilities. 100,000xp.

A quest! A proper quest! And for formal control of the tower, no less. Hell to the yes! However, I grimaced as I thought through the cost.

As depleted as my mana reserves were, I'd need nearly three and a half hours of channeling to reach four hundred and awaken the wisp. But at least I finally had a piece of the puzzle. I dragged the most comfortable chair I could find over next to the well and got my gear settled, sitting down and making myself comfortable.

Placing my hand on the lip of the pedestal, I felt a slow pull on my mana and watched as a small, shining droplet condensed in the middle of the bowl. I channeled mana into it until I reached ten percent, then reluctantly, I began to exercise instead.

As I staggered upright from burpees, catching my breath, I reflected that I could meditate and speed this process…but, dammit, I needed the increase to my stats more than the saved time.

After an hour, I repeated the process, draining my mana into the well and watching the droplet expand into a small puddle, then a pool.

As the hours passed, I lost myself in the monotonous task, pausing only when the notification showed that I had channeled 395 out of 400. I ran through another round of exercises and only collapsed into the chair again when my mana had fully regenerated. I didn't know what was going to happen, and I needed to be ready. While I waited for my breathing to slow, I checked my waiting notifications.

UnderVerse: Brightblade

Congratulations!

You have killed the following:

- 3x DarkSpore Wandering Guardian, level 3 for 75xp.
- 4x DarkSpore Parasite, level 3 for 100xp.
- 1x DarkSpore Ice Mage, level 5 for 100xp.

Progress to level 5 stands at 2,260/2,700

I'd gained a point in Dexterity, Strength and Endurance from the fighting and the exercises earlier, but now I was right on the verge of a point in Agility too. Man, I loved this system!

Name: Jax				
Class: Spellsword		Renown: Unknown		
Level: 4		Progress: 2,260/2,700		
Patron: Jenae, Goddess of Fire, Exploration, and Hidden Knowledge		Points to Distribute: 0 Meridian Points to Invest: 0		
Stat	Current points	Description	Effect	Progress to next level
Agility	15	Governs dodge and movement	+50% maximum movement speed and reflexes	93/100
Charisma	10	Governs likely success to charm, seduce, or threaten	Average success in interactions with other beings	37/100
Constitution	15	Governs health and health regeneration	150 health, regen 7.5 points per 600 seconds	68/100
Dexterity	16	Governs ability with weapons and crafting	+60% to weapon proficiency, +6% to chances of crafting success	11/100
Endurance	17	Governs stamina and stamina regeneration	170 stamina, regen 7 points per 30 seconds	14/100
Intelligence	15	Governs base mana and number of spells able to be learned	150 mana, spell capacity: 10 (8 + 2 from items)	29/100
Luck	12	Governs overall chance of bonuses	+20% chance of favorable outcome	33/100
Perception	13	Governs ranged damage and chance to spot traps or hidden items	+30% ranged damage, +3% chance to spot traps or hidden items	38/100
Strength	19	Governs damage with melee weapons and carrying capacity	+9 damage with melee weapons, +90% maximum carrying capacity	23/100
Wisdom	20 (15)	Governs mana regeneration and memory	+100% mana recovery, 2 points per minute, 100% more likely to remember things	66/100

Jez Cajiao

My experience was at 2260 out of 2700 points. Another few fights like the last one, and I'd hit level five! *Booyah, motherfucker.* I'd have loved it if I'd leveled, but I was moving in the right direction, at least. I took the time to eat and drink, then I channeled the last of the required mana into the pedestal.

The bowl had been gradually filling with a silver liquid that resembled mercury, but now that it'd reached the level required, the surface gently shifted, tiny eddies and forms moving beneath. I leaned closer, trying to make out the shapes, when it went suddenly still. Staring down into my reflection, I saw nothing at first, until I realized the face staring back at me now had silvery pale skin and light blue eyes instead of my own dark irises.

I blinked and leaned back as the face smiled at me, slowly drawing together and forming a tiny person who lifted free to stand on the surface of the liquid as though it was the most natural thing in the world.

"Greetings, Master. Have you the token?" a tiny voice emerged from the miniature version of myself.

"I...errrr..." I sputtered, surprising myself with my amazing linguistic abilities.

"Are you well?" the tiny figure asked, looking concerned.

"Ah...okay." I shook my head and gave myself a light smack to the cheek, starting again. "I'm Jax, and yeah, I'm your new master, I guess," I said, "What *are* you, though?"

"I'm a Wisp, Master Jax, one of three wisps that call this tower home. We are magical creatures who serve the needs of the Great Tower and its inhabitants. Do you wish to claim the tower as your own?"

"I'm killing the undead that infest it. That's about as far as I've gotten."

"Hmmm. I had hoped they would be gone by now. Never mind, Master. Were you sent to assume control by High Lord Falco? Do you have the token?"

"Yes! Shit, I'd forgotten about that. I've got his stone here somewhere," I said, searching through the pouch until I found it and held it out for the figure to examine.

"This sigil is acceptable, Master Jax. It shows his mana signature and was recently charged. In the absence of any other claimant, I accept you as master of the Great Tower and hereby allow you access to my Hall."

The tiny figure gestured around the room, and a hum arose, growing in pitch as the lights flared, until the room seemed to vibrate with it. All at once, it vanished, and the room returned to normal.

"Okay, what was that?" I asked, looking around in confusion.

"You have been acknowledged formally as master of this section of the Great Tower, Master Jax. You now have access to its treasures."

"Treasure! Okay, tell me about that," I said quickly, focusing on the tiny figure.

"The books and crystals around you are great treasures, my lord. Most can guide you in skills, techniques, and abilities that will aid you in your growth. There are over a hundred spellbooks, many in the master levels."

"Ah, knowledge is treasure, right?" I grunted, trying not to be disappointed. I had nowhere to spend treasure, even if I'd found it, but..."Ooookay. So, next question. Why do you look like a tiny version of me?"

"I am a Wisp, Master Jax, so I—"

"Please, for the love of god, just call me Jax. It's easier on both of us," I interrupted, rubbing my face with one hand.

"Very well, my…Jax. Thank you. I am a wisp, so I don't have a form in the same way you do. I am entirely composed of mana. I can, however, assume any form you wish. Should I change?"

"Yeah, it's kinda freaking me out, talking to a tiny version of myself. Look, just show yourself however you like, okay?" I said, shrugging in discomfort.

"May I link to your mind and find a pleasing form, Jax?" It reached out one tiny hand to me, and I leaned forward, allowing it to touch my forehead.

"Ah…I see. I can use this, and this…" I felt a slight tingle where its hand pressed. After a moment, it withdrew and shrank in upon itself, becoming molten silver again and shrinking down into the pool. After a few seconds, it began to reform, swelling up to create a figure barely six inches high, with two sets of wings sprouting from its back.

As it grew more and more defined, I watched in amazement. In under a minute, a miniature woman had grown from the liquid. She had wings that flicked and beat the air, lifting her from the pool's surface to hover in front of my eyes. I blinked as her features settled into a beautiful miniature woman with wings. She was also very noticeably naked.

I coughed, trying not to look at her obvious assets.

"So, why did you pick this form? And why the hell are you naked?!" I croaked out, fighting to keep my eyes locked on hers. *Don't stare at the tiny naked woman…don't stare at the tiny naked woman…don't…dammit!* I flicked my eyes back to her face, holding them there with an act of will that would have made a monk proud.

"Does this form not please you, Jax? It seemed the ideal mix from the images in your mind?"

My mind went blank when I started wondering what she'd seen. With the number of pornstars she could have become, I supposed I was damn glad she'd created a unique form, rather than mimicking one of them. After a couple of seconds, I shook myself out of it and focused my eyes again. The traitorous bastards had started to look…elsewhere…again.

"It"—*cough*—"it does please me, but perhaps you could put some clothes on?" I said, looking away awkwardly.

"Oh, of course, Jax. I thought you'd prefer this from the images…"

"Aaaand let's never talk about the images in my mind again either, okay?" I said, cutting her off sharply while trying not to think about getting a life-size version of a Wisp…*able to assume any form…ummm…NO!*

My gaze returned to her of its own volition, and I saw with mixed relief and disappointment that she was now clothed. It was a tiny sports outfit for some reason, admittedly, but at least she was decent.

"Okay, so do you have a name?" I asked, trying to get my wandering brain back on track.

"I have served in this capacity for centuries, Jax. Some have called me 'librarian,' while others have simply called me 'Wisp.' You may choose a name for me, if you wish?" She hovered there, smiling at me as I considered her words.

"So, you just accept whatever people call you? Don't you have a preference or a name you were given before you came here to help?" I asked. The thought of just writing her off as a nameless servant was somehow distressing to me.

I'd learned as many names of the citadel staff as I could, but it'd been impossible to learn them all.

Some, like the Nigerian, had never offered a name when I'd asked, barely speaking beyond a grunt most of the time. At first, I hadn't asked, out of determination not to humanize my captors, but by the end, we'd become close enough that it didn't matter. I'd really only known Xiao and West.

The maids who had come to me had talked, and we'd engaged in...strenuous horizontal jogging...together, but we'd never been closer than friends with benefits. They'd been one-night stands that went on for months, but without the emotional connection that would normally result. After Lou and Martin's betrayal, I'd shut myself off emotionally.

Whatever the reason, I found myself suddenly feeling very alone in this world, and I hated the idea of treating this wisp like a nameless, meaningless servant.

"I am happy to accept any name, Jax. The terms of my servitude enforce this." She smiled brittlely as she spoke, as though it was just one of those things.

"Servitude? What the hell! What's wrong with you all!" I exploded, throwing my arms up as I got to my feet, the tiny wisp buzzing away from me in surprise.

"I'm sorry, Jax! What's wrong?" she asked slowly.

"What's wrong? What's wrong?! Seriously? You're forced to serve? What terms?" I asked her angrily.

"I was brought to the Great Tower to serve its masters. I must always serve to the best of my ability until death. Any refusal will be punished through mana starvation or pain spells."

"That's slavery," I stated, furious. "How do I free you?"

"Free...me? I am a Wisp, Jax. I exist to serve," she replied after a few seconds, her voice hoarse.

"Why? What makes you destined to serve? Were you created for this? If so, it's a shitty deal!" I stormed.

"I...no, Jax. Wisps are born like any other creature, but we are highly prized. We are typically captured, then bound to a structure or individual. Our ability to use ambient mana is burned out of us to ensure we can never leave. Without a linked mana structure or pool, we will starve, then go into hibernation. If we are not awakened from it eventually, we die."

"Can I heal you somehow?" I asked. "Look, I know I need your help, but where I come from, we don't do this kinda thing. No slaves, not ever!" I ground out, pacing through the room in anger until noise from outside the room and a series of hard blows hit the crystal doorway. I stormed over to it and banged on the inside with a fist, shouting at the undead adventurer that I could see faintly through the doorway.

"And you can fuck off an' all, ya ugly bastard! I'll be out to fuck up your Tuesday soon enough!" I roared at it.

When I turned back to the wisp, she still floated there hesitantly, wings fluttering as she bobbed in the air.

"I...I am bound to the tower, Jax. Truthfully, I don't know of any way I could be freed, beyond a direct bonding. If I did try to just leave, I'd starve. I thank you for the thought, but...I am bound. It's okay; I came to terms with this long ago, and my masters have often been good..." She fluttered, wringing her hands together as she tried to make me feel better about her being a slave. A few minutes ago, she'd been a miniature version of me, and I'd felt nothing for her.

Now, she was a flying stunner who had told me she had been enslaved, and as quick as that, I needed to help her. *Man, I'm a simple creature...* I thought to myself.

"Okay, well, you might have accepted it, but I haven't. If I can find a way to heal you in these books or in my travels, I'll use it to free you, okay?" I asked, trying to give her, and myself, some hope.

"Thank you, Jax. That is good of you to say, but it's okay, as I say. I came to the conclusion long ago that nothing could be done. Now, you were about to name me?" she asked, a tentative smile making me want to make everything all right.

"Yeah, yeah, I guess I was," I said, sitting back down and shaking my head. "Well, what do you do normally? Tell me about yourself, please."

"I maintain the wards and spells of the tower and protect the Hall of Memories, aiding those who have the power to use this place to make wise choices on their path. I also act in concert with the other wisps who are bound here to protect the tower as much as we can."

"Shit, yeah, you did mention that; how many other wisps are there?"

"Two more. One at the top of the tower who maintains the physical structure, and one in the genesis chambers beneath the tower. That wisp creates and controls the golems and servitors."

"Okay, I found an empty mana pool or whatever it's called at the top of the tower earlier," I said, thinking out loud.

"A manawell, Jax. We store mana in them and feed from them."

"Why was it empty, then? Does someone have to fill it each time?" I asked curiously.

"No, they are usually fed from the tower's mana collectors, but those were shut down when the SporeMother took control. We were instructed by the Master at the time that we were not to allow the creature to feed from the tower, so we disabled the collectors and sank all the mana into the shield to drain the mana stores.

"When the Cataclysm struck, it was probably why we survived as well as we did. We had essentially overcharged the shields and structure to such a degree that we survived when so many others did not."

"Is the SporeMother still here?"

"I don't know, Jax. I can sense very little beyond this room, but there are possessed undead outside, so it is highly likely. No creature would give up a lair such as the tower without good cause."

"Great. Okay then, first things first. You need a name, I need to kill that motherfucker outside the door, and we need to reawaken the wisp at the top of the tower and see if they can aid us as well. We can do this," I said, taking a deep breath and inspecting the wisp floating in front of me.

I was seriously tempted to name her after a pornstar, but that would have been wrong. That being said, I wasn't asking her to change her appearance, either. Clothes and a name were a good compromise. "I name you 'Oracle,' as you know more than I do, and you are in charge of the knowledge of the tower," I pronounced, receiving a delighted smile in return.

"Thank you, Jax, I love it!"

"Okay, that's great! So, first things first. I need to kick these guys' asses. Any magic that will help me do that? I have two spell slots available."

"May I link with you, Jax? I will evaluate your current capacity and abilities." She flitted forward, hovering before me and lifting one tiny hand to my head as she waited for permission.

"Uh, Yeah, of course. Tell me what you can do," I said, inclining my head to her. I felt her tiny hand as she pressed it against my forehead, cool fingers gently caressing my skin as she closed her eyes and bowed her head.

Do you wish to allow the wisp, Oracle, access to your character sheet?

Yes/No

As the prompt appeared, I selected *yes* and dismissed it, looking between Oracle and the stacks of spellbooks behind her. After a short wait, she released my head and backed away, bowing her head before looking me in the eyes.

"Thank you for your trust, Jax. I have evaluated your abilities and the number of spells and the knowledge you have. Judging from your current repertoire, there are several spells I would recommend."

With that, she spun around and flew across the room, flitting from one bookcase to another, lightly tapping spellbooks and making them glow. I gathered them all together and laid them out on the table to sort through.

Airblade:
Creates a blade of air 5m long and razor-sharp. This will project from the tip of your weapon and activate with the next slashing attack, doing up to 15 damage to any targets in the targeted area. This spell has a casting cost of 25 mana.

Shocking Light:
Creates a burst of light at a targeted location. Burst lasts 2 seconds and has a 10% chance to inflict blindness on a target. This spell has a casting cost of 10 mana.

Wall of Light:
Creates a shield wall of solid light. This wall can absorb 100 damage before being dismissed and will last up to 30 seconds. Any enemies that come into contact with the wall will receive 10 damage per second until the wall is dismissed or the enemy ceases contact. This spell has a casting cost of 50 mana.

Lifebolt:
Creates a bolt of compressed healing energy. This can be used as either a ranged healing spell or an offensive spell against death creatures and will do 10 points of healing or damage to its target. This spell has a casting cost of 10 mana.

Flameburst:
An AOE (Area of Effect) spell that creates a rolling wall of flames outwards from the caster's body, knocking any enemies back. This wall will reach 10m and deal 5 damage to any targets caught in its way, with a 10% chance to inflict burning for another 5 points of damage for up to ten seconds. This spell has a casting cost of 25 mana.

There were several other spells, but I narrowed it down to these five and poured over them. I had two slots free and had to be careful with my choices.

Airblade was an easy one; slash sideways across the room and it'd do a decent amount of damage to everything, with the added advantage of a spell cast on my weapon that would release when I slashed, so I could cast it and let my mana regenerate before opening the door.

The light spell, on the other hand...well, it'd be useful, but not that great. It might burn them the way the sun did, or it might do nothing at all...I doubted they'd focus on it too much when they had a living, breathing target in sight.

The Wall of Light spell could be amazing, but it didn't specify how the wall worked. If it just created a barrier in front of me, I might as well not open the door, but if I could angle it across a room, that could make it a more manageable fight.

Lifebolt seemed decent, but it was another ranged spell, and I already had Firebolt, so that was probably a no-go. Finally, there was Flameburst. It didn't do a huge amount of damage, and I couldn't use it from just inside a door frame either. I didn't want to set fire to the library, after all, but with a knockback and a chance to set fire to the bastards, it was a good one.

I narrowed it down to Flameburst and Airblade for the first spell, and after a few minutes of further thought, I picked up Airblade. Immediately, the familiar prompt appeared.

You have found the Spellbook Airblade.

Do you wish to learn this spell? The Spellbook will be destroyed in the attempt.

Yes/No

I selected *yes* and began to read, flicking from one page to the next, speeding up as the symbols on the page glowed with increasing intensity, until the book collapsed to ash in my hands, and I fell back in my seat.

I blinked my eyes a few times, trying to dismiss the glowing symbols that seemed to be hovering in the air, burned into my retinas. As they faded, I found that the spell had been added to my repertoire. I grinned unconsciously, rubbing my eyes. I frigging *loved* magic.

"Jax..." Oracle called softly. I turned to regard her and saw a look of concern on her face as she alighted on the table. "I know you've probably been told, but still I have to warn you. You do need the spells and your magic to clear the tower, but using spellbooks always carries risks and results in only a cursory understanding of the spell. I recommend not using any more for at least a year as it can lead to permanent damage..."

I nodded as I sat forward, my mind still reeling from the strain of the arcane knowledge that I'd just absorbed, and I met her gaze as I tried to think. It felt like someone had just opened the top of my skull with a can opener and poured information in, and it was getting worse by the second, as more and more information seemed to be popping up and making itself known.

"Yeah..." I muttered, rubbing my eyes and shaking my head slightly at the fuzziness. "I can believe that. How frequently should I be using spellbooks? Is there a limit, like ten a month or something? My brain feels weird..."

"*Ten*? Jax, hasn't anyone warned you about this?" Oracle squeaked in alarm, taking a few quick steps forward and pressing her hand to my forehead again. I felt a soothing coolness spreading from her hand, and I sighed in relief, feeling my muscles relax as I recognized the feeling of her in my mind. I didn't care; the relief was worth it. "Jax, you used *nine* spellbooks? *Nine*?! *All* your spells came from books?!" she whispered in shock, pressing both hands to my head and forcing more of her strength into me.

"Feels...good," I muttered, relaxing more and feeling her tiny hands trying to hold my head up. Suddenly, I was falling, and everything went black.

CHAPTER NINETEEN

W hen I came to, I was laid out on the floor next to the chair I'd been sitting in, and Oracle was perched on my shoulder, watching me.

"Wha..." I managed to mumble before she slipped forward, shaking her finger at my eye as she leaned on my chin.

"You used NINE SPELLBOOKS! You're lucky you can speak. Mages have been left braindead from less...NINE! You are an idiot, a complete fool, Jax! Do you realize what you've done to yourself?"

I flinched back reflexively as the tiny form of Oracle continued to berate me. She took flight and hovered before me as I sat up shakily. I focused on taking a deep breath and trying to figure out what had happened. My health bar and mana bars were both lower than they had been before I lost consciousness, but I couldn't see what she was so worked up about. My head felt a little fuzzy, but...then the world suddenly seemed to tilt to one side.

"You've scarred your brain! Actually, *scarred* it! And it'd be worse if I hadn't been here! You could have erased your mind!"

"Whoa, seriously woman, stop!" I said as I straightened up. I gripped my head as the room spun, then staggered to the side before I tripped and fell to the floor again. This time, I stayed there, panting as I tried to figure out what was happening. Oracle buzzed back and forth over me as I scanned the room, panting rapidly as I began to panic.

"JAX!" Oracle shouted as she flew in close, hovering in front of my face and waving her hands in the air to get my attention. I focused on her, trying to calm my racing thoughts. I'd given myself brain damage! I'd fucked up so bad right now.

"Jax, stop! It's all right! Take a deep breath...there...now another," she said soothingly, hovering and lifting her arms with each inhale, lowering them with each exhale. "That's it. Just concentrate on me. In...and out. In...and out."

We continued for a few minutes as I forced myself not to think, focusing solely on her and my breathing while ignoring everything else.

"Okay, Jax I want you to sit up slowly. Don't stand, just sit up." I did as she asked, and the room spun slowly again.

It was like being really, really drunk, just before throwing up, but I hadn't drunk that much, had I? *Where am I?* My mind went blank for a second as I looked around, thinking I was in town somewhere, on a night out, maybe?

"JAX!" I flinched and returned my focus to the tiny flying woman, realizing that she'd been trying to get my attention for a while.

"Jax, I need you to help me do something. Can you do that?" she asked, and I nodded as she landed on the floor between my legs, she climbed up onto my folded knee and reached up with both hands to press lightly on my temples.

I frowned, trying to make sense of where I was and what was happening, as well as why she looked so familiar. Also, was she really small, or…

"Yeah," I muttered in response as I tried to figure out if she was real. Had someone given me something? I'd sworn off the drugs…hadn't I?

There was that one episode in Amsterdam; I'd ended up trying to swim in the canal when it was frozen over, and I was naked. I vaguely remembered the lads posting the videos on social media and swearing to myself "never again," but…

"Jax, this is important. I need you to concentrate, okay?" I focused on her again. She looked so familiar. She was really pretty, actually, and that body…

"Jax!" she shouted, making me jump again.

"Uh, yeah…sorry!" I muttered, trying to make sense of where I was. I started to look around the room again, and received a tiny, resounding slap for it.

"Look at me! You need to give me access. Just choose yes!" She slapped me again. "Focus, Jax! We don't have much time!" A series of words appeared in the air between us, golden letters flowing into a cursive script that said…something I couldn't make out. I closed one eye and squinted, making it slightly more legible.

…you choose to gi…cess t….internal…and mana?

Y…/No…

I blinked, trying to figure it out, when I heard a tiny voice shouting at me to accept it, calling me "Jax." That was my name, a name I'd chosen in a thousand battlefields and dungeon dives.

Only my friends and Tommy knew me as Jax…the voice must be a friend, then…I selected *yes* and felt a gentle presence surround me.

"It's all right, Jax," a voice said, warm and soothing. The world drifted away, like the sea receding when I had floated on a sun lounger at the beach in Crete, the tide coming and going, warm water lapping at me…The warmth of the sun caressed my face, and I relaxed, drifting off to sleep.

When I finally awoke, I found myself lying on the floor again, but my head was clearer. I blinked and sat up, a headache flaring as I moved too quickly. As it dampened back down, everything came flooding back to me. I'd given myself brain damage. I couldn't stand up, and I'd been somewhere else.

Memories filled my mind: games, my driving test, learning to parachute. Holidays, the taste of a minted kangaroo dish, sea salt and balsamic vinegar on chips, a cold beer with Tommy on the beach as we watched the sun setting, the warmth of a summer's evening in the air, the promise of a night out ahead of us…

All of it flashed through my mind in a flood of images, tastes, and even the coconut smell of the suntan lotion I'd used, mixed with aftershave and the tingle of lightly sunburned skin. All of it was as real as if it had just happened. I sat there, my mouth agape as I tried to process everything. As the memories began to settle, one sensation remained, a new one. A tingle at the back of my mind made me turn around, my eyes drawn inexorably toward a tiny pedestal with only the dregs of mana remaining in it, and Oracle, sitting on its edge, watching me as she slowly swung her legs back and forth, clearly nervous.

"Are you okay, Jax?" she asked. Her voice had changed. Gone were the piccolo fluting tunes, replaced instead with a woman's voice, strong but feminine. She drew her legs up and rose to her feet, shocking me.

She'd been six inches before; now, she was closer to twelve, almost double her previous size, and she *glowed*. There was no other way to describe it. There was no visible light emanating from her, but she seemed to shine with health and strength.

Her skin was flushed as though she'd gotten a tan and just finished a workout in the way that all exceedingly hot women did. She even *smelled* good…wait, I could smell her? Wasn't she just mana?

"What just happened?" I asked slowly, watching her. I could feel her. I knew precisely where she was. As I turned my back slowly, I could feel her location even as I looked around the room or closed my eyes.

"This is going to take some getting used to, I'm afraid, Jax," she said, smiling shyly. She waited patiently as I turned back to face her, her hands clasped behind her back. Her wings were folded down, almost brushing the floor with the tips, and she dug at the top of the pedestal with one toe self-consciously. "You see, I kind of *bonded* you."

"Bonded me?" I whispered. Clearing my throat, I coughed and then asked her again in a much stronger voice, "What do you mean, 'bonded?' What's that?"

Increasing anger and confusion were clear in my voice.

"You damaged your mind, Jax. Using spellbooks, skillbooks, and increasing your Intelligence and Wisdom so much in such a short time, you scarred your brain. Neurons were dying in the thousands as the scars grew worse.

"I didn't have any time to come up with a better plan, and when I tried to explain it, you…well, you didn't understand." She shivered as I got up, towering over her. She looked scared and embarrassed as she looked up at me.

"I had to do it! You were dying, or your mind was, at least. I…I've been alone so long, Jax. I didn't know what else to do, and you'd kept saying you wanted to free me…so I bonded you. Once we were bonded, I could access your mana pool and direct your healing. It was the only way. I didn't know you'd learned so much from using spellbooks, or I would never have let you use the book. I should have checked before I gave it to you; I'm so sorry."

She went on trying to explain how I'd been dying, how the excess knowledge I'd taken in had begun to override my memories, and that a human is only capable of learning a few new spells a year, usually learnt through painstakingly careful study. Even the strongest minds would be broken by excessive spellbook usage.

I let it wash over me, a barrage of noise, as I thought back to the Baron's actions, the way he had been very specific that I could only learn the lowest tiers of spells. I also remembered Xiao's warnings that I could learn from spellbooks, but that they were dangerous and could have side effects. One comment came back to mind straight away: "Any knowledge is useful…"

She'd even said I could fail to learn spells, but that it would be okay. Either she'd known that this was a possible side effect and had deliberately left it out, or the Baron had never bothered to tell her.

I remembered conversations we'd had, and now oblique comments that I'd dismissed before came back to me, suddenly making more sense.

…only the Baron's son could. And *A normal human can't just…*

West's shock as I told him the spells I'd learned. The way he'd looked at me askance, asking if I was all right, his comment to Xiao about the Pearl: *You'd be dead, and you know it…*

217

They'd all known, and they'd either thought I had also known, or—in the Baron's case—probably hadn't cared.

"Am I human?" I asked Oracle, my voice cutting across whatever she'd been saying.

"Sort of..." she said. I looked back at her sharply. "The Great Houses were all mostly human!" she defended quickly, holding her hands up to stop me. She patted the air placatingly as she went on. "They used a particular brand of magic, called Alteration, which allowed them to choose a trait or ability. Through some unknown method they would absorb genetic material into themselves."

"Why?" I asked leadenly. I wasn't human; I was some sort of science experiment.

"You have the dormant genes of a hundred or more species I can identify in you, Jax. Through them, you have the ability to improve on your previous limitations. You can adjust your body to accept the gifts of the other races, such as the wings of the T'ngu, allowing you the gift of flight, or the horns of the minotaur, giving you the strength of the great warriors of the Southern Plains."

"I'm a freak, a crossbreed!" I muttered, looking at my hands and feeling confused and uncomfortable. "I'm..."

"No, Jax! You are no freak. You are a different person from the humans you are used to, yes. I read your past as we bonded. I saw your memories, and I lived your life, if only for a second, so I know you now. I know what you are capable of, and what you can become.

"You are no ordinary human, it's true, *but you already knew this*. Your father came from this world; your mother is distantly descended from another transplanted noble. Your family is as different from the humans you surround yourself with as regular humans are from Neanderthals. A different species, but still one with the potential for good or ill.

"Jax, nothing has changed. You have always been this person, this being. It's not like humans are better than other species, and besides, you won't start eating babies suddenly!" That last bit was delivered with a scathing bite to it as I started to sink into doubt again. "Trust me, Jax, you're still you, and there's at least one other like you, don't forget."

"Tommy," I whispered aloud, memories of him flooding my mind: sharing toys, food, and our lives. Fighting back-to-back and running from the police. Tommy crying over a bird with a broken wing and breaking a grown man's leg when we'd seen him kicking a dog. A thousand memories flashed by, the rage and the compassion.

The happiness as he fell in love, the anger when she cheated on him, and the rage when we'd been crossed. The good and the bad. Oracle gave me space to think, and as the memories passed, somehow bright and fresh after all these years, I came to the conclusion she'd been pushing me towards.

I might be a freak, regardless of what she said, but I wasn't alone. I had a brother, and he was here somewhere.

I didn't care about anything else; I was going to find him. I sat up straighter and turned to Oracle, taking a deep breath and asked my last question.

"So, whadda ya mean, 'bonded'?" I said, half-afraid of the answer.

"Well, as I told you, I was bound to the tower, and still am, but…the only way to save you was to direct your own magic to heal you, and I didn't have the strength to do it alone. I bonded my soul to yours."

She went on hurriedly, her words tumbling over one another as she tried to get them out. "I wouldn't have done it otherwise, I promise…but you were dying. You'd torn a section of your brain and were bleeding heavily. The knowledge from the latest spellbook was trying to take up space you were already using. If it had been able to, you'd have lost memories, maybe more. I had to do it! I'm so sorry, Jax!"

She wrung her hands together, her cheeks flaming with embarrassment as she went on. "Wisps have healing abilities; it's one of the reasons we are hunted, or were. Our bond gives more than a management facility to a building. To a sentient, we can aid them, draw on their mana, and heal them faster…and, and…and you'd wanted to free me, you wanted me to be able to live my own life, and this…this is closer to that than I ever imagined I could be!

"I won't be a burden; I promise I won't! You won't regret this. People almost wiped us out in their desire to bond with us in the past. I'll be a good companion, I will!"

I sat down hard on the edge of a nearby seat as I tried to make sense of it all. I distractedly brought up the notifications flashing at the corner of my vision.

You have learned the spell Airblade.

This spell creates a blade of air 5m long and razor-sharp. This will project from the tip of your weapon and activate with the next slashing attack, doing up to 15 damage to any targets in the targeted area. Cost of 25 mana.

You have suffered catastrophic internal bleeding and are losing health at a rate of 10 per second.

You have accepted a soul bond with the wisp Oracle.
You receive an increase of 10% to your health regeneration and 1 point to your Charisma stat, losing 20 mana and 20 health to your new bonded companion.

**You have lost part of the knowledge gained by reading the Spellbook Airblade.
This spell is no longer usable.**

As I dismissed the last notification, I took my head in my hands and let out a deep breath. I'd almost erased my mind, then I'd lost the knowledge I'd gained, and somehow ended up bonded to Oracle.

She was nice enough, even though she was suddenly bigger for some reason, but I didn't really want to be sharing my frigging soul. There wasn't much to go around.

"Why are you suddenly bigger? And what does it mean that you're now bonded to me?" I asked.

"I'm bigger because I'm stronger. I…well, I take a portion of your mana and a portion of your health as a bonded familiar to form my physical body…but I'm pretty, aren't I? Isn't this what you like?" she asked, her face still red with embarrassment.

I'd definitely noticed the changes to her body. She was pretty and voluptuous as well. She'd obviously rifled through my mind again and found out *exactly* what my tastes were, as she'd made herself even hotter, if that was possible. She was still only twelve inches high, though, and I wasn't sure if I was glad she was so small or sad about it…when part of what she'd said rang a bell, and I pulled up my character sheet to confirm it.

Name: Jax				
Class: Spellsword		**Renown**: Unknown		
Level: 4		**Progress**: 2,260/2,700		
Patron: Jenae, Goddess of Fire and Exploration		**Points to Distribute**: 0 **Meridian Points to Invest**: 0		
Stat	**Current points**	**Description**	**Effect**	**Progress to next level**
Agility	15	Governs dodge and movement	+50% maximum movement speed and reflexes	95/100
Charisma	11	Governs likely success to charm, seduce, or threaten	+10% success in interactions with other beings	56/100
Constitution	15	Governs health and health regeneration	130 health, regen 8.25 points per 600 seconds, (+10% regen due to soul bond, -20 health due to soul bond)	69/100
Dexterity	16	Governs ability with weapons and crafting	+60% to weapon proficiency, +6% to the chances of crafting success	13/100
Endurance	17	Governs stamina and stamina regeneration	170 stamina, regen 7 points per 30 seconds	16/100
Intelligence	15	Governs base mana and number of spells able to be learned	130 mana, spell capacity: 10 (8 + 2 from items), (-20 mana due to soul bond)	61/100
Luck	12	Governs overall chance of bonuses	+20% chance of a favorable outcome	37/100
Perception	13	Governs ranged damage and chance to spot traps or hidden items	+30% ranged damage, +3% chance to spot traps or hidden items	41/100
Strength	19	Governs damage with melee weapons and carrying capacity	+9 damage with melee weapons, +90% maximum carrying capacity	25/100
Wisdom	20 (15)	Governs mana regeneration and memory	+100% mana recovery, 2 points per minute, 100% more likely to remember things	79/100

"Shit!" I cursed. I'd missed it before, but she was right. I'd lost twenty mana and twenty health to her! I'd gained a ten percent increase to my health regeneration as well, but the loss of that health and mana was really going to suck, as I'd have to basically replace those by using four of my points the next chance I got to level. Dammit.

I sorted through my gear, taking out some food and drink and seeing to life's necessities, including having a crap out of the window, which amused and horrified me in equal measure. Amused, because I had a vision of a bird flying past underneath and getting hit with instant karma from a thousand cars fresh from the car wash, and horrified by the fact that I had to explain what I was doing to a very curious Oracle, who wanted to watch.

I soon had myself cleaned up, thanks in part to the ability to create a spring of fresh, cold water literally anywhere by magic. It'd been a chilly, but *refreshing* experience, I had to admit, and made me realize what I had been missing all these years without a bidet.

I settled myself down with Oracle. As I ate, I got her to go through the details and drawbacks of having a bonded companion. I thought about it as logically as I could and came to the grudging conclusion by the end that I was lucky, really. After all, she could have just let me die.

From the positive side of things, I gained increased health regeneration, ten percent over and above my natural high regeneration. I essentially had a tiny healer with me at all times, unless I made her stay with the tower. She could travel with me as an advisor or stay behind and look after things as an overseer. I also had an extra set of eyes and ears, as well as more magical senses, so that was great.

On the other side, though, I automatically lost twenty health and mana to her and had a curious presence in the back of my mind at all times. Any healing she provided was from my mana pool, which could be awkward if I was trying to use all of it in a fight and she decided to use some for healing a minor injury, leaving me with an unexpected deficit.

We continued talking as I stripped off my armor, examining the damage done by the spear and the various other blows. I was surprised to find that the spear had been either insanely lucky, or unlucky, depending on the point of view.

It had somehow pierced between interlocking leather bands below the main cuirass of my armored chest plate, literally hitting the weakest place on my upper body armor, beyond the armpit. I really hoped that it had been dumb luck, as otherwise, there was going to be a shitty fight to come.

Oracle and I established some ground rules. Using healing spells on me without asking was never okay, unless I was under thirty percent health. However, when I asked her to, she needed to jump straight in.

We also spent time covering such important topics as not flying around to hover beneath me, staring in fascination while I was doing my business out of the window. I also found out that the glowing stones in the walls were, indeed, memory stones. They held selected memories of hundreds of people, stored ready for a master of the tower to use or bestow.

They worked like the skillbooks, but they held a lot more information. A single stone every year was the maximum I could use, while most humans would only be able to accept a few stones in their entire lifetime.

As far as I could tell, I'd been given all the knowledge in the world, but thanks to a combination of no useful explanation by those who guided me and my own choices, I couldn't use them.

Oracle was adamant that, from now on, I could learn one spell every few months if I chose to learn by spellbook, and only in very controlled and planned circumstances. She also made it very clear that I was only allowed another spell once she said I was ready. No skillbooks, no memory stones. Not until I'd had a proper chance to heal.

I eventually pulled two of the loungers together and curled up on them, dropping off to sleep in reasonable comfort for the first time in days. I was almost convinced that Oracle was going to be a blessing in disguise. Almost.

I woke up the next morning rather quickly, due to the feeling of a tiny hand prodding at my manhood.

"What the hell, Oracle!" I cried out, reflexively hunching myself up around my "morning glory."

"What is it?" she asked curiously, climbing onto my legs and trying to push my hands apart. "Do you want to mate? Is that why it's…"

"NO!" I half-screamed, my voice becoming an unmanly squeal as I pushed her off and straightened up. My mind raced as it shot from sleep to trying to calm myself down. Oracle was a strange creature. She'd basically scanned my mind for a "pleasing form" when we'd first met and decided an even more voluptuous version of a lads' mag model was the way to go.

It was great and all, but she combined that body with only a vague understanding of what sex was beyond "fun." Hell, at one point during conversation the previous night, she'd said she wanted to *try it*.

Her species didn't have it, but she'd taken great care in trying to explain all the adjustments she'd made to her body to ensure she could attempt it, even going so far as to dismiss her conjured clothes, asking if she'd formed things correctly. With all of that to contend with, it wasn't a surprise that a certain part of my anatomy had awoken first, as it often did. She'd noticed the…rise…and had decided to have a look. Thankfully, I'd been in a light sleep at that point and had awoken as soon as she'd touched me.

She was a combination of a sexual goddess and an inquisitive child, and she was twelve inches tall.

"Why can't I have a look at it? Don't you want to mate with me?" she asked, hovering in front of me with forlorn eyes.

"It's not that simple, Oracle! You're…well for a start, you're twelve inches tall. I'd kill you with it. I'd end up in court with a tag dangling from it with 'exhibit A, the murder weapon' on it, and I don't need that shit! Besides that, you're a child in a lot of ways, so no, you can't see it or play with it. Please, for the love of god, stop asking, okay?" I begged.

"I'm not a child, Jax. I've been a Wisp of this tower for centuries! And I can change my size!" she complained, trying to stamp one tiny foot while hovering in midair, which only served to cause her to wobble mid-flight.

"Yeah, and you were sexless and just took on a form. You act like a child, and think like one, so no. Besides, it's not physically possible, okay? Just leave it, please, Oracle. We need to concentrate; we're going to fight together for the first time today, remember!" And just that easily, she was distracted. I let loose a sigh of relief and took a long swig from my waterskin.

"Yes! We're gonna kick some undead butt today! We'll take back the tower! Then we'll wake up the other wisps and start getting things sorted out around here, find Torry, and have so much fun!"

"Torry?" I asked in confusion before it clicked. *Tommy!* "My brother, yeah? Tommy, not Torry."

"Oh, okay, him as well!" she called out cheerfully as she shot back across the room, spinning around the walls in the light of the glowing stones. I couldn't help but smile at her happiness and excitement. She alternated between concerned seriousness and childlike wonder and grace. She flew around me again, then zipped through the room back to the door that led out. She landed on the floor next to the body of the skeleton mage, and started kicking him in his remaining shin, shouting out, "Take that!"

"You!" I said, a grin spreading across my face as I rushed over to the corpse as well. "I'd forgotten all about you!" I quickly searched the mage from head to toe, finding a small pouch with a few gold coins, a plain copper ring, which went into the pouch with the coins, and a dagger that was rusted into its sheath. Its robes were the most valuable thing it owned.

Robes of the Ice Mage		Further Description *Yes/No*	
Details:		These robes give a 10% deduction to the mana cost of Water spells and an increase in power of 10% to any spell of that affinity.	
Rarity:	Magical:	Durability:	Charge:
Uncommon	Yes	54/100	N/A

They were good robes, still in decent condition. Giving that kind of boost and spell cost reduction would have me over the moon on a pair of greaves or a helmet, but with robes…I bundled them up and put them in my bag of holding.

Staff of Icebolt		Further Description *Yes/No*	
Details:		This staff gives an increase in power of 10% to any spell of Water affinity and can be used to cast Icebolt from its internal mana storage. Each casting requires 10 mana.	
Rarity:	Magical:	Durability:	Charge:
Uncommon	Yes	68/100	0/100

I liked the staff, but Sod's law that it was depleted. I'd have to look into charging it or whatever later. I also found a pouch in one pocket, the area around it still damp. Remembering the sound of breaking glass during the fight, I groaned and slowly opened the pouch to find it filled with the remains of maybe a dozen small vials. All but one of them was broken, the last intact one confirming my worst fears as I examined the blue liquid.

Tincture of Mana		Further Description *Yes/No*	
Details:		This mana potion will restore 40 mana immediately, followed by a further 1 mana per second for 60 seconds.	
Rarity:	Magical:	Durability:	Charge:
Uncommon	No	14/100	N/A

The remnants of at least eleven other potions, judging from the caps, were scattered in the pouch. I groaned again. Those could have been hugely useful, and one badly placed swing of my naginata had smashed the rest of them.

I swore under my breath as I thought about the uses I could have had for the mana potions. I could have been a Gatling gun of Firebolts! I could have stood a real chance against the undead, but now, I was practically back to square one. I emptied the glass fragments out in one corner and cleaned the pouch out the best I could before examining it.

Potion Pouch		Further Description *Yes/No*	
Details:		A simple pouch for potions, this will store up to twelve potions securely, depending on size.	
Rarity:	Magical:	Durability:	Charge:
Common	No	27/100	N/A

I attached it to my belt and cleared the corpse away from the entrance, then readied myself, checking over my weapons and picking up the naginata from where it had fallen when I had collapsed. I quickly checked its blade over, propping it in the crook of my arm as I reviewed my spell list. I'd planned on using Airblade to start the fight off, but clearly that wasn't going to happen.

The water and electricity combination that had worked out so well in the arena was pretty useless against the undead, as was Identify, as I had to kill them regardless. I'd use it if I had time, but the benefits during a fight were marginal at best.

Raising a weak skeleton would have been useful, but I was missing a leg and the skull from the only one I had access to. That left me with Cleansing Fire and Firebolt to depend on, so they'd have to do.

CHAPTER TWENTY

The big, undead adventurer waited on the other side of the door, occasionally swinging its sword at the crystal. Once it was dead, I figured I'd have an easier time killing the rest anyway, so I was happy to have it so closely available.

I took a deep breath, braced myself with the naginata, and commanded the door to open. The crystal dissipated into a gritty mist and retracted into the doorframe. I barely had a second to deflect the first blow of the adventurer's greatsword as it swung at me, sweeping it aside with my naginata to clang uselessly on the floor. I released the shaft with my left hand and cast Firebolt, hitting it square in the face. It staggered as it swiped at the flames.

The adventurer was bigger than me and heavily armored, reminding me of Wilhelm and the fight in the arena. I couldn't rely on pain to stop it, or stamina depletion, but it really didn't like fire.

It raised the greatsword again, swinging blindly for me as I leaped backwards. As soon as the blade passed me, I stabbed out, aiming for the creature's throat. Its left hand shot out, grabbing the blade, and deflected it into the doorframe.

I tried to pull it back, but its strength was a match for my own, and we staggered. Seeing no other option, I released the weapon, drawing a sword right-handed and parrying its next attack as I started to cast Cleansing Fire.

It threw my naginata aside and bulled its way forward, not giving me the time to close the door, and others were coming in from behind it. I jumped forward, burying the blade of my sword into its upper arm. The blow glanced off bone, desiccated flesh and muscle coming free as I staggered, when an undead left fist smashed into my face, throwing me back. I landed on the floor, something rolling under my leg. I grabbed at it, glad to find that it was the mage's staff, and brought it up to deflect the next blow.

My spell had failed under its fist, and I could barely concentrate from the mana backlash. I rolled to the side, dodging the next blow, and staggered upright, backing away again.

A sudden wash of healing energy flooded my body, driving the confusion back as Oracle shouted to me.

"The door, Jax! Close the door!"

I cursed and ordered the door to shut. Two other skeletons had managed to enter the room behind the adventurer, but the door thankfully stopped the third, leaving me to back away frantically as I tried to come up with a plan.

Swearing as I retreated across the room, I turned slightly to ensure I didn't get trapped against the wall. We traded blows, the adventurer's greatsword almost driving me to my knees with each impact, while my staff did little beyond slowing it.

The other two shambled forward, thankfully just following me as I kited them around the room.

If they'd tried to block me off, they'd have caught me without any great effort. *Be thankful for small mercies...* I told myself.

I cast Firebolt repeatedly until, after only four more bolts, the warning tingle of the mana headache began blooming. I was down to the dregs of my mana again, without enough left to cast another spell already!

The terror of my impending death rising, I tried to think of a plan, since I could no longer cast spells. I grasped the staff in both hands, bracing it across my body, and crouched, resolving that this creature wouldn't get to kill me without a damn good fight.

Deflecting a swing from the sword, I concentrated on hitting its legs as hard and fast as I could. My only advantages now were speed and the undead's lack of intelligence. With each strike on its legs, it stumbled, but the armor was negating the majority of the damage. Worse still, my hands were going numb with the reverberations, and if I kept this up, I'd lose before it did.

Taking a deep breath and ducking to avoid a swing that would have decapitated me had it landed, I hooked the staff behind its left knee, pulling its leg out of position, and smashed the other end of my staff into its face as hard as I could. The sudden blow combined with throwing it off-balance made it fall onto its back, and I took the opportunity to strike.

Stepping forward quickly, I stood on the wrist of the hand that held the sword and began raining blow after blow down onto its head, the helm bouncing with each impact. I glimpsed another opening and drove the butt of the staff into its throat, screaming as its left hand finally connected with my leg. Claw-tipped bones burrowed deep into my thigh, barely slowed by my thin leg armor as it tore deep into the thick muscle.

"Jax! Look out!" Oracle screamed as she flew across my vision. She intercepted a skeleton that had gotten closer than I had realized and distracted it as it swung its mace at her instead of me. The other one was closing steadily as well. I had no time, but this was my only chance to kill this thing!

"Keep them busy!" I shouted at her, ending the command with a scream of pain as the adventurer ripped its bony claw out of my leg, trailing bits of muscle and blood.

I collapsed on top of the undead, screaming in pain. Its left hand gripped my throat, claws digging deep into the skin and causing blood to flow. As it began to choke me, I felt it shift its weight to free its sword and try to bring it to bear.

In a last-ditch attempt to save my own life, I shoved harder with the staff, pushing the wooden length out the far side of its throat and scraping on the bones of the spine and the lip of its armor.

Even as I thought I was going to black out from the pressure on my throat, I used the staff like a lever and pulled down across its body as hard as I could. With a last yank, its head ripped free, the skull bouncing across the rugs to lie against the far wall.

Life seemed to leave the creature all at once, and I collapsed to my back as I ripped its claw free from my throat. I heaved in breath after breath, trying to calm my racing heart. Gritting my teeth, I tried to think through the pain, shifting my hands to my leg and almost screaming in agony.

I fumbled at my belt for the mana potion and gulped it down as fast as I could. I was surprised at its fresh, minty taste and felt the mana headache disappear as forty points of my mana were replaced instantly, along with the significant jump to my mana regeneration rate.

My mana bar took a jump, refilling until it stood at fifty-one, and I immediately began to cast Cleansing Fire. It took longer to cast than Firebolt, and if it didn't work, I was boned. But with two skeletons nearby and the adventurer's skull already enveloped in a cloud of DarkSpore, I had no time for another plan.

The ten seconds of cast time passed like an eternity. Watching Oracle as she flitted between the two undead to buy me time terrified me. All it would take was one hit, and she'd be killed, and the DarkSpore was inching towards me with every second that passed.

As my tongue tripped over the final few syllables, the parasitic cloud reached my leg. A thin tendril touched me, sinking through my armor like mist, and a sensation like red-hot needles burrowed into my flesh.

I managed the last word as a scream, forced out through my agony, but it was enough. The spell flared to life, my gestures having built the spell as I went. It flashed out into the protective circle, lines linking one to another as the flames licked out.

I writhed in anguish as the flames met the DarkSpore. It drove forward frantically, some level of sentience making it aware that only in me did it stand a chance of survival. As it burrowed deeper into my flesh, the cleansing flames rooted it out, burning the remnants of my leg armor away as it killed the DarkSpore.

I fell back, savoring the feel of the flames as they washed over my body. No longer fighting the parasite and burning me, they comforted me, and I felt impurities leaving my body. I gasped in relief as I tried to catch my breath. Immediately, my gaze scoured the room, searching for the other two skeletons, only to see them collapsing to the ground, covered in flames. Their bodies dropped like puppets with cut strings. The skulls flared with light as the flames scoured the last vestiges of DarkSpore from them before spreading out to fill the circle again.

I'd survived again, I realized. I lay on the floor, bleeding heavily from my leg as I panted and tried to master the pain.

"Jax! Jax, are you all right?" Oracle screamed, landing on my chest and looking into my eyes, her tiny hands gripping my beard as she stared at me.

"Aye."—Cough—"Aye, Oracle, I'm all right," I gasped out. She released me, flitting to land next to my leg and examining the wound, the torn muscles, the blood covering the ground, and the burned mess that had been my greaves and pants.

"This is bad, really bad!" she muttered to herself, pushing the flesh aside to look deeper even as I hissed in pain at her touch. "There's no infection, thanks to the flames, but we need to bind this until you can heal it! Quick, Jax, I need something to tie around it!" She started pulling at my bag of holding, and I fumbled inside it. The only thing I could find was the Robes of the Ice Mage, so they had to do.

I held my leg as tightly as I could, keeping pressure on the wound as she dragged my dagger across the robes, frantically sawing and stabbing until she had a small section free that I could wrap around my leg as a tourniquet. I groaned even as the limited healing from Cleansing Fire continued to chip away at the damage.

Thankfully, the mana potion I'd chugged was continuing to restore a point of mana every second. Before I could cast it myself, Oracle had begun casting my healing spell. As the golden light spread across my body, I watched it sink into my leg, the torn and bloody flesh regrown before my eyes. I collapsed back again, resting as my mana slowed to its regular rate of regeneration, and the flames surrounding me guttered out. After another minute, I had the energy to raise my right hand to Oracle.

"High-five, Oracle; you did amazing," I whispered. When nothing happened, I cracked an eye to find her staring at me in confusion. "Dammit. Okay, Oracle, when you do something particularly cool or impressive…"

I went on to explain the concept for her, culminating with a tiny hand slapping firmly into mine.

"That's it!" I grinned, sitting up and looking down at her, before following her gaze to find that, thanks to the combination of fire and a crazy goddamn giant skeleton, I was now more than slightly deficient in the pants area.

"Dammit!" I cursed. Oracle laughed as she flitted into the air and spiraled around me while I tried to cover myself, as certain parts of my anatomy tried to make a break for freedom.

I shuddered as I saw where the hair had been burned away, leaving me in no doubt just how close the flames had come to Mr. Happy.

Banishing that horrible thought from my mind, I pulled the remnants of the robe over my armor. I looked ridiculous, but at least it kept things from waving around through the new exit hole in my pants. I pulled the pants off and looked them over, finding little that could be done. I found some spare boxers and jeans in the bag of holding, but the leg armor that had covered me this far was beyond repair. I looked over at the rotten and burned body of the adventurer and took a deep breath.

On the one side…loot. That was awesome, and he had armor on already, double awesome. On the other side, he'd been rotting in it for years. The thought of putting on pants that someone else had died in, then continued to wear while walking around and falling apart was just…nasty. Beggars couldn't be choosers, though. I pulled up my notifications as I walked over to the adventurer's corpse.

Congratulations!

You have killed the following:

- 1x DarkSpore Adventurer, level 5 for 100xp.
- 3x DarkSpore Parasite of various levels for 75xp.
- 2x DarkSpore Wandering Guardian, level 3 for 50xp.

Progress to level 5 stands at 2,485/2,700

I was 215 points from my next level, but I was getting there! I searched the corpse, stripping it and piling the gear up next to me, before searching the other two corpses as well.

As I suspected, I found little of any worth on the two guardians, but the adventurer was a different story.

Greatsword of Durability		Further Description *Yes/No*	
Details:		This greatsword has a +2 durability enhancement engraved into the blade and will last longer without damage than the base metal would suggest. Melee damage 18+2.	
Rarity:	**Magical:**	**Durability:**	**Charge:**
Uncommon	Yes	86/100	N/A

Hunter's Cuirass		Further Description *Yes/No*	
Details:		This steel cuirass has been enchanted to lessen sounds made in the forest, allowing a skilled hunter to close on his prey. Stealth +10%, Armor 25.	
Rarity:	**Magical:**	**Durability:**	**Charge:**
Uncommon	Yes	44/100	N/A

Cloak		Further Description *Yes/No*	
Details:		A simple red cloak, worn and singed, with a house sigil in tatters upon it.	
Rarity:	**Magical:**	**Durability:**	**Charge:**
Common	No	27/100	N/A

Greaves of Swift Movement		Further Description *Yes/No*	
Details:		These hardened leather greaves have iron plates attached to the outside and are enchanted with a simple speed enhancing inscription. They will increase the wearer's speed by 5% and have an armor value of 15.	
Rarity:	**Magical:**	**Durability:**	**Charge:**
Uncommon	Yes	37/100	N/A

Bracers of Defense		Further Description *Yes/No*	
Details:		These metal bracers are attached to a hardened leather padding by an apprentice of leatherworking, giving +5 to the standard defense of +7 for this item. Armor 12.	
Rarity:	**Magical:**	**Durability:**	**Charge:**
Uncommon	No	52/100	N/A

Winged Helm		Further Description *Yes/No*	
Details:		This helmet has ornamental wings that extend from the sides but is badly damaged and corroded.	
Rarity:	**Magical:**	**Durability:**	**Charge:**
Common	No	7/100	N/A

I cleaned the previous owner out as best I could and pulled the Greaves of Swift Movement on over the remains of my jeans. They were a bit tight and stiff, but they were still an upgrade, as was the Hunter's Cuirass, which I replaced my original one with.

The bracers were an upgrade, but the hidden daggers in mine were still an awesome addition, so I stuck with the original ones. The helm was trash, as was the cloak, so I piled them up with the corpse of the mage in the corner of the room, adding the contents of the adventurer's purse to my own. That left me a total of six gold, three silver, and twenty-three copper pieces, as well as two garnets of average quality richer.

I felt a lot better, now that I was more heavily armored, and took the time to drink and rest before getting my gear together for hopefully the last time that day. I stuck the adventurer's skull back onto its corpse, then used my Raise Weak Skeleton on it, and a new Bob joined Oracle and me. I returned the greatsword to it and told it to stand at the door. ready to fight. I settled down with Oracle for a moment to recover my mana.

"I didn't say it before, but thank you," I said.

She turned from examining my minion and quirked an eyebrow at me with a quizzical smile. "What for?"

"For saving my life, for distracting the skeletons, or healing me—all of it. I…I'm not good with people, but I need you, and this fight really made that obvious, so thank you," I said, embarrassed that I hadn't thanked her right away.

"It's okay, Jax. We're bonded now, so we're a team!" She grinned at me happily, her tiny smile lighting up the room as she pirouetted round in midair. "Now, come on. We've got bad guys to fight, wisps to reawaken, and the whole world to explore!"

I grinned back at her, and as soon as my mana was full, I took up position behind Bob, commanding the door to open. As soon as it dissolved, he was off, piling into the few undead waiting near the door. He drove them back by sheer impetus, lashing out with his sword and smashing two into bone piles in quick succession.

While he worked, I hit one in the skull with a Firebolt, blasting it apart and causing the corpse to collapse as the controlling DarkSpore was destroyed. Since I had a few seconds of space, I quickly used my Identify spell on one of the nearest skeletons.

DarkSpore Possessed Decrepit Skeleton:

This creature was once a noble warrior of the Great Tower, until its corpse was discovered by the DarkSpore now inhabiting it. It has been turned into an undead slave to the SporeMother that puppets it.

Level: 4
Health: 50
Mana: 0

While the description told me little, it did explain why these were dying so easily as Bob smashed through another one. I quickly blasted it in the head with Firebolt, watching its skull explode with a satisfying scream, then headed past the majority of the fight toward the nearest window. One closed in behind me with a creak as I fumbled with the latch. But between my armor and my experience with these low-level undead, I was better off getting the window open.

I finally got the latch to snap off in my hand. That was not the way I had wanted to open it, but it was good enough. The light streaming in around me caused a scream and clatter from behind. As I whirled around, one of the undead, a shortsword in hand, reeled back from the light with a hand raised to its skull in defense.

Never one to pass up an opportunity, I swung my naginata hard, lashing through the legs and sending the walking corpse cartwheeling to the ground. I quickly stabbed it with the blade and used that to drag it into the light. Another tiny skull appeared in my vision as it died. Continuing on, I circled the room, opening three more windows before coming back around to give my minion some help.

With the undead mostly fixated on Bob, I got close quickly, but they were only minutes away from taking him down. A spear was stuck through his chest, his left arm was missing from the elbow down, and his jaw was gone entirely, courtesy of a mace strike.

I concentrated on taking as many out as possible with a sideways strike aimed to attempt to behead as many as possible at once. I severed two heads before my blade got stuck in a shoulder joint of the third. As I dragged the lucky recipient around, trying to free my weapon, I raised my foot, planted it on its hip, and kicked as hard as I could. The blow sent the skeleton reeling away into the sunlight and its doom.

I quickly scanned the space to ensure I wasn't getting snuck up on again. To my surprise, I found myself on the far side of a group of them.

They stood in a small cluster, trying to avoid the light and finding themselves unable to close on me without walking out into the deadly patches of sunlight. I took the time to catch my breath and investigated the room. Between the sunlight and the walls, the remaining undead were effectively hemmed in now on three sides. The only place they had left to retreat to was my sanctuary, dammit!

I cursed myself as I rushed around them, heading for the hall again. I had to kill them all without giving them time to retreat. If the SporeMother could change their orders, she might send them into the room, then I'd be well and truly screwed.

I cast Firebolt, taking another head off before realizing that the majority were still intent on dragging my minion down. With an internal grumble, I took the time to retreat inside again and let my mana recharge.

Watching the clouds of DarkSpore as they were released from their current vessels, I realized I didn't have a great deal of time after all.

They sparked and screamed as they frantically tried to possess another body, but the current inhabitants fought back.

As I watched, they began joining together again and melting into my minion, causing it to jerk and shake. Just in time, I realized what was happening and ordered it to grab the nearest undead and run into a large patch of overlapping sunlight created by two nearby windows.

It turned out to be more of a stagger and collapse than a run, but it worked better than I expected. A second undead latched onto it as it pushed past. My minion caught fire, writhing and screeching as the invading DarkSpore died, taking the other two decrepit undead and their DarkSpore with it.

As all three burned and fell apart, I turned back to the fight. There were only two left now, and I liked my odds. As the nearest closed on me, it brought up its sword and thrust one-handed at my stomach. The second was trailing a few meters behind it, wielding a mace again. I quickly deflected the sword swing with the tip of my naginata, sweeping it around after the parry to claim the creature's head.

Before the final skeleton could bring its mace to bear, I brought my weapon back up over my shoulder to unleash a devastating blow that smashed it apart from shoulder to groin.

Before the DarkSpore could escape, I quickly kicked, dragged, and punted the skulls and the rest of the corpses into the patches of sunlight. I was rewarded by new skull icons flaring in recognition of the joint deaths of the hosts and parasites.

I stood there for several minutes, catching my breath and surveying the devastation of the hall. Piles of bones were scattered everywhere near the light, while broken windows and smoldering shutters told the tale of my desperation to light the room. I'd escaped nearly uninjured this time; my mana bar was low but refilling. The worst damage I had taken was scratches and a few aches from swinging too hard.

I decided that tanking was definitely a job best left to others, and wherever possible, I was going to have a minion to do it. While I could hum the tune, to hell with trying to sing it. I'd always wanted to be some kind of ranger/rogue/mage mix. Getting to be all stealthy and stabby-stabby and great in the woods, then kicking ass with some spells sounded better to me than slogging through a battle on the front lines.

Looking through the logs, I discovered that I'd managed to rack up a serious amount of experience from that latest battle, as well as reaching my next level.

Congratulations!

You have killed the following:

- 9x DarkSpore Wandering Guardians of various levels for a total of 220xp.
- 9x DarkSpore of various levels for a total of 220xp.

A minion under your command has killed the following:

- 5x DarkSpore Wandering Guardians of various levels for a total of 110xp.
- 5x DarkSpore of various levels for a total of 110xp.

Total minion XP earned: 220xp.

As controller of this minion, you gain 25% of all experience earned.

Progress to level 5 stands at 2,980/2,700

Congratulations!

You have reached level 5!

You have 5 unspent Attribute points and 1 Meridian point available.

Progress to level 6 stands at 280/6,500

CHAPTER TWENTY-ONE

A fter the fight I'd got enough experience to level, and found out that for level five I gained a new meridian point. Being honest, I'd actually forgotten about the meridians in all the excitement since I'd gotten my pearl. I had found the vision boost thingy useful so far, but since it was a passive, I hadn't really thought about it. Now that I had another point, though, I brought up the list of options and considered them.

PRIMARY

Brain: 1/10 Spell Cost Reduction: -5% (Primary Bonus: 1 spell slot per point)
Head: Primary Node: Additional points invested will reduce mana cost by 5%.

SECONDARY

Eyes: 1/10 Vision Improvement (Secondary Bonus: +10% chance to notice important visual details)
Eyes: Important details will glow to your vision. This will level with the relevant skill.

Ears: 0/10 Hearing Improvement
Ears: Important sounds will become clearer with concentration. High levels will aid in translation.

Mouth: 0/10 Vocal Improvement
Mouth: Your voice will become 10% more likely to have a desired effect on a target, soothing, seducing, persuading as required.

Nose: 0/10 Tracking and Detection Improvement
Nose: Scents will be stronger, aiding in tracking.

Heart: 0/10 Health Increase
Heart: You will gain an additional ten points of health for each point invested in your Constitution.

Lungs: 0/10 Stamina Increase
Lungs: You will gain an additional ten points of Stamina for each point invested in your Endurance.

Stomach: 0/10 Sustenance Improvement
Stomach: You will gain the abilities to resist poisons by 5% and to gain sustenance from more sources.

Legs: 0/10 Speed Increase
Legs: You will gain a boost of 10% to your speed, as well as better stability over various terrain.

Arms: 0/10 Strength Increase
Arms: You will receive a boost of 25% to your carrying capacity and your damage output with melee weapons.

Hands: 0/10 Dexterity Increase
Hands: You will develop crafting abilities at a 10% increased rate, along with a greater chance to succeed in crafting complicated items.

It was going to be more difficult to decide than it had been last time, as I needed all of them. Heart would literally double my health; each point I earned or invested there in the future would be worth twenty points, rather than the usual ten. If the Head option had provided that increase with mana, I'd have taken it in a heartbeat.

Just comparing the differences if I invested all my points in one area was insane. I loved crafting; investing enough points into my hands would level my skills at a crazy rate, as well as almost guaranteeing success in making complicated items. I could make a damn fortune.

Legs would make me into a speed machine. As far as my voice, having the ability to convince people of practically anything? I could be a space wizard, go all "these aren't the droids you're looking for" and shit. *Plus, there were bound to be some ladies around soon…nope! Back on track!*

I thought about my options for a while, but eventually decided to invest my points in my Heart meridian. I wanted to use them in so many other places, but if I didn't live long enough to use them, then there was no point. Another five levels, and I would let myself pick something more fun.

I had five points to invest in my stats as well, and I needed to get the most out of each point. While I was tempted to add all five points into my Constitution, giving me another hundred health, I'd just doubled my health with the meridian point, so I moved on. Agility was a tempting one; it was one of the skills that leveled as I worked out, but gains were slower than my Strength and Endurance, and it'd make me a lot faster…

I decided to come back to that. Charisma, I bypassed without a second thought, but I considered Dexterity for a while. Five more points there would make me a better fighter, as well as make it easier to cast spells with all the snaky finger movements. Intelligence was always a good choice, even if I couldn't add any more spells for a while, since all five points would give me an extra fifty mana to play with.

Wisdom would take me from two points a minute to two-point-five, which would make an increase of thirty mana regenerated an hour. It didn't sound like much, when I could get fifty mana from my Intelligence for the same points, but in the long run, it would pay off more. Luck…well, Luck was just that. An increase of five points there would make me a lot luckier than I was, but I'd never know if it was down to skill or luck if something happened, and I couldn't rely on it.

Perception was a weird one as well, since five points would give me a fifty percent increase in ranged damage, as well as a five-percent increase in spotting hidden items. With the ten-percent chance I got from eyes as my secondary meridian, that added up to a respectable eighteen-percent chance, which was nearly a one-in-five chance of spotting things.

Added to all of this were the progressions to the next level I was making, simply by surviving. I was so close to leveling Dexterity and Agility naturally, I could practically taste it.

I went back and forth for at least an hour, sitting in the midst of the devastation I'd wrought on my enemies, before finally remembering I had a damage log. I pulled it up, and there was my answer.

When I'd used my Firebolt spell, I hadn't been doing ten points of damage like I'd thought I had. I'd been doing thirteen! My ranged skill was affecting the damage I did with my spells as well! I quickly decided to risk it for a biscuit, as the saying went, putting all five points into Perception, and confirmed it, feeling a burning in my eyes as the changes took place. As soon as I could see again, I brought my character sheet up and checked through it.

Name: Jax				
Class: Spellsword		Renown: Unknown		
Level: 5		Progress: 150/6,500		
Patron: Jenae, Goddess of Fire and Exploration		Points to Distribute: 0		
		Meridian Points to Invest: 0		
Stat	Current points	Description	Effect	Progress to next level
Agility	15	Governs dodge and movement	+50% maximum movement speed and reflexes	99/100
Charisma	11	Governs likely success to charm, seduce, or threaten	+10% success in interactions with other beings	59/100
Constitution	15	Governs health and health regeneration	280 health, regen 8.25 points per 600 seconds, (+10% regen due to soul bond, -20 health due to soul bond, each point invested worth 20 health)	79/100
Dexterity	16	Governs ability with weapons and crafting success	+60% to weapon proficiency, +6% to the chances of crafting success	98/100
Endurance	17	Governs stamina and stamina regeneration	170 stamina, regen 7 points per 30 seconds	28/100
Intelligence	15	Governs base mana and number of spells able to be learned	130 mana, spell capacity: 10 (8 + 2 from items), (-20 mana due to soul bond)	77/100
Luck	12	Governs overall chance of bonuses	+20% chance of favorable outcome	41/100
Perception	18	Governs ranged damage and chance to spot traps or hidden items	+80% ranged damage, +8% chance to spot traps or hidden items	47/100
Strength	19	Governs damage with melee weapons and carrying capacity	+9 damage with melee weapons, +90% maximum carrying capacity	54/100
Wisdom	20 (15)	Governs mana regeneration and memory	+100% mana recovery, 2 points per minute, 100% more likely to remember things	87/100

"Jax?" Oracle said, hesitation clear in her voice, distracting me from the details.

"Yeah, Oracle?" I answered, my attention still mostly on the screen before me.

"I know you said you want to find Tommy, but what are you going to do after that?"

"Well, I don't know. He's been here for five years, so he'll know what's going on. Maybe get a job, or something...why, what do you think we should do?" I said, my instinctive reaction to find a job sounding silly, now that I thought about it.

"Well, before I can advise you, Jax, I need to know your plans. We're in the wilderness. Before the Cataclysm, we were at the edge of the empire, one of the farthest-flung outposts at the very edge of the wilds. Your ancestors decreed that this tower be built in order to bring supplies and troops through the portals to begin conquering these lands.

"With the destruction of the local area, the tower barely survived. This tower could be your refuge; we could rebuild it and bring order to the surrounding lands, or you could abandon it and try to reach the empire or whatever has survived of it.

"I can sense that others have accessed the tower in the centuries I have slept, but I know not who or why. I know little of this world I find myself in, and much will be as new to me as it is to you. You must decide our path before I can advise on our next step.

"Will you act alone, or do you plan to recruit followers? Will you set out to conquer the empire and serve as its leader, or—as many of your ancestors have—will you leave it to find its own way and instead dedicate yourself to hunting evil and vanquishing it?

"Others in your position have chosen the path of domination instead, sacrificing all to become the most powerful in the land. Only you can choose, Jax. I will serve you in any way you command."

She stood there, barely a handful of inches tall, and laid my life out before me. I took a few minutes to think about what I wanted, really wanted, besides to find Tommy.

I had magic here, and I wasn't going to give that up. Just the little taste of power I'd found had me hungering for more. I wanted to stay in this world, for now at least, and I wanted to learn a fuck ton more magic. To do that, I needed somewhere safe to live, or a base to return to at least.

I also needed to find somewhere to buy better gear, as well as some beer and more boring supplies. If I was going to start my life over, I had already decided to take the opportunity to be a better man. I'd do my best to be one, anyway, remembering a favorite book from my childhood where a strong man was advised to tame the darkness inside all men by a hero's code.

I couldn't remember all of it, but something about "protecting the weak from the strong, and not stealing, lying, or cheating, as those were for lesser men." I was a realist. I'd never swear not to lie or cheat. Occasional thievery, well...it depended on the circumstances, and no way was I swearing off seduction.

I wanted to aim for a mix of the King in the North and the Cimmerian Barbarian, showing kindness to the weak and protecting them, doing right whenever I could, but also kicking ass when I needed to. Failing that, I would try not to kill too many people who didn't deserve it, and to hell with the rest of them.

"I don't know, Oracle, if I'm being honest with you," I said to her. "I'll be the best man that I can be, I'll find Tommy, then we will look at the world together and see where we want to fit in it. But…if I see injustice, or evil men and creatures preying on the weak, then I'll deal with it however I can. Beyond that, we will have to see. What do you think we should do?"

"We need to awaken the other wisps and clear out the SporeMother, yes?" she asked. I nodded, so she continued. "Once that is done, we can set out to search the nearby lands, find the nearest city or town, and go there to find news of Tommy. In the meantime, if we can bring the tower back online, it can begin repairing itself, building war golems, and preparing to support you."

"Whoa, Oracle, stop right there! What the hell is a war golem,' and why haven't you mentioned it before?"

"Well, Jax, the tower is normally manned by living soldiers of the empire, but this structure is over two miles high. The sheer numbers of servants, builders, and general staff needed are huge.

"The tower can maintain its overall structure through its magic, but specific constructions, such as tables, chairs, and glass, are built by craftsmen, and they, in turn, are supplied by golems. The tower was designed to maintain an army of various support creations, but over the millennia, they have failed, falling apart due to lack of mana."

"I thought you and the others purged the tower of mana when it fell to the SporeMother?"

"Yes, we did, Jax. That also removed the mana that would have maintained the constructs, unfortunately, so it hastened our end as well. My point in all of this, however, is that we also had war golems. These were specially constructed warriors, the guardians of the tower. They are designed to follow the master's commands and cannot act on their own. If we revived them, they could aid you in your battle with the SporeMother. They were built in the genesis chamber below the tower."

"Where the third wisp is; damn. Yeah, you mentioned it earlier, then I got distracted thinking about something else. There's too much I don't know!" I took a deep breath and stretched. "Okay, let's think about this logically. We need to repair and reclaim the Tower. It's too valuable, and potentially too powerful to leave in this state. I have you, so I now need to reawaken the wisp at the top of the tower, then the genesis chamber wisp. From there, I can *hopefully* get some help to deal with the SporeMother, right?" I asked, looking up at Oracle.

"That is correct, Jax. The SporeMother is likely to be in one of the subterranean levels, as far from the light as she can get. Reclaiming the genesis chambers will likely cause her to come after you with everything she has, if she's not emerging already. We can only hope she's in one of the deeper rooms, rather than the genesis chamber itself. If we reawaken the wisp at the top of the tower first, it will be able to tell us more about what is happening inside its walls."

"How come that wisp can, but you can't?" I asked curiously.

"That wisp is the tower's controller. Where I spent my time cataloging and protecting the magic of the tower, it spent its time subsumed into the tower. That wisp had very little personality left, being only an extension of the tower. It was able to respond to commands and queries, but it became rare for it to think for itself."

"Didn't it have a name? Even amongst yourselves?" I asked.

"Not really. We each have a magical signature, if you will, to identify ourselves to each other, but it relies on senses you don't have. To describe its identity to you

237

would be like explaining the taste of yellow. I'm sorry, I just don't know how to. I'm not trying to be offensive…" She wrung her hands together as she floated before me. I just shrugged and went on, dismissing the issue of names entirely.

"Okay, so we awaken it, take control of the tower, and it can help us, right?"

"Yes, Jax."

"And you say it can control the tower, tell what's going on within its walls and such, yeah?"

"Well, yes?"

"Can it alter the tower at will?" I asked, a plan coming to mind.

"It can; however, it is a slow process, taking many hours for small changes and days or weeks for larger ones. Growing the tower took many years."

"Well, it's miles high, so I expect it took a fuck ton of power to build. I just want some small changes…"

"Such as?"

"Not fully sure yet, but if it's possible, it'll make the fight a hell of a lot easier. Let's get our gear and head for the top of the tower. Do you need me to do anything to allow you to come with me, or do you want to stay here?"

"I'll come with you, Jax! I've got some of your mana to sustain me. I'm…uh…sorry about that…" I waved her apology aside and gathered up my gear. Sealing the Hall of Memories behind me, just in case, I set to searching the corpses to find the strongest of those that remained after Bob's valiant dash into the sunlight. It took a few minutes to put one body together that was mostly intact, taking the legs from one and an arm and head from another. As I finished, Oracle spoke up again.

"Jax, why are you doing that?"

"The skeleton? I need another minion, Oracle; it can take some hits for me, distract my enemies, and make it easier for me to win a fight. Why?" I asked distractedly as I looked over the corpse I'd sort of constructed.

"Yes, I understand that bit, but why are you making it the same way it was?"

I looked at her then back at the corpse at my feet. "I don't think I follow; what do you mean?"

"You can control a skeletal minion. It doesn't have to be human, or more to the point, human-shaped." Oracle looked at me sideways.

It could have been human or an elf, or something. I hadn't thought about it, just assuming it was a human, so when I put it back together, it needed to be the same. She had a point. I'd already found that I could substitute skulls or reattach them. The force that animated the skeleton didn't seem to care what it had been before. It made my enemies work for me, and the bones stayed together despite some of them having no flesh or muscles to connect them…*fuck! Facepalm moment!*

"You're saying I can change the shape of the corpse and give it more arms or legs, aren't you?" I asked her, chagrined.

"Yes. Jax, it's your magic and will that matter, not the form." She looked at me with one perfect eyebrow raised, as though she'd just caught me licking the windows and asking why they didn't taste of strawberries.

I stood for a while, studying the piles of bleached bones and desiccated flesh before grabbing some more parts and building a new skeletal minion.

"For now, the bonds that join the bones together will be as weak as normal, but when you have healed enough, there are books on necromancy in my hall. With that knowledge, you will be able to meld bones, strengthen them, or even add abilities to them. High-level necromancers can even bring forth new life to possess the forms they create, if this is your passion."

"'Passion' is not the word I'd choose, Oracle, definitely not passion. But yeah, it seems useful. How is necromancy looked upon here?" I asked as I worked away.

"It is simply another school of magic. Some dislike it, but most people aren't concerned, as there are good and evil people in all aspects of life. Necromancers are often given certain rules in a city or town, such as leaving the dead to rest and only using corpses obtained from official channels, such as criminals or those without families to mourn them. Necromancers also allow communion with the dead, so while the use of corpses may be unpopular, the ability to commune with the deceased is highly prized and respected."

"I bet it is. Hope they're better than the charlatans back home," I muttered, pulling the last bits together. I took a deep breath and cast Raise Weak Skeleton on the bones I'd laid out on the floor. It took almost double the mana, but as the corpse rose to its feet, I got notifications immediately, as well as a much more robust minion.

Congratulations!

You have gained a level in Raise Weak Skeletal Minion. More information will be displayed when your skill reaches level 10. Increase this or other Death spells nine more times to reach level 2 in Death Magic.

Congratulations!

You have raised your spell Raise Weak Skeletal Minion to level 5. Once this spell reaches level 10, you may choose its first evolution...

I dismissed the prompts as soon as I'd read them and grinned at my new tank as he towered over me. I'd used the adventurer's corpse again. Despite its blackened state, it was still the biggest of them, but now it was the base of the creature. The new minion stood on four legs like a centaur with an upper body composed of heavier, interlocking ribcages to make it as sturdy as possible.

It had four arms in two sets, upper and lower, with the lower pair holding maces, the upper holding swords. It walked unsteadily at first but slowly grew more stable. I ordered it to spar with me after giving it very specific orders not to harm me. I had visions of it slaughtering me because of a mis-phrased order, but the commands worked well.

At first, it was slow and unwieldy, the weapons missed more than they connected, and the feet became entangled, causing it to trip more than once. After an hour, it seemed much surer of its capabilities. I ordered it to lead the way, and we set off for the upper reaches of the tower with Oracle flying alongside me.

It took most of the rest of the afternoon to reach the top. We paused each time we entered a new floor, just in case, before we reached the garden level. I was also constantly funneling half my mana to Jenae as it filled. I'd decided not to let it drop below half while I was exploring, instead using the chance to work on my total. I ordered a halt, both because I was out of breath and needed a break, and because I wanted more alchemy ingredients, food, and water.

I scoured the garden outside, but with the sun growing low on the horizon, I decided to cheat slightly, casting Weak Lightning Bolt at the pool. As soon as the spell had dissipated, I sent my new Bob into the water to get me a fish, which I gutted and cleaned before packing it away, and ran around picking what ingredients I could. We resumed our run, level after level flashing past, until at last we approached the pinnacle of the tower.

As we passed the final bend, the top floor came into view, and Oracle landed on my shoulder, one hand resting on the top of my head as she guided me.

"The wisp who controlled the tower is in deep hibernation, Jax. I can sense him, but only faintly. He may take badly to the state of his home."

"Really? Believe me, I'm not exactly fucking ecstatic about it either." I groaned as we slowed to a walk.

Crossing the floor towards the pedestal, I ordered Bob to take up position at the door to the stairs and warn me if anything came.

With aching thighs and heavy breaths, I climbed the last few steps to the throne, which stood before the great windows. My workouts were clearly working, triggering a notification to flash away merrily. I grinned and dismissed it as soon as I read it. Yup, definitely working, but damn, it was a pain in the ass to have to run up and down the stairs constantly.

Congratulations!

Through hard work and perseverance, you have increased your Agility by 1 point.

Continue to train and learn to increase this further.

I slumped into the throne, wincing as my ass hit hard stone, before examining the wisp manawell that stood by my side. Now that I knew what I was looking at, a prompt appeared instantaneously.

Congratulations!

You have found a wisp manawell.

Mana required to reawaken this wisp: 10/400.

I took a deep breath and started to channel my mana into it, draining myself down to ten percent before sitting back to let my mana recover. I had planned to exercise through the regeneration period again, but after that run up the stairs, I dismissed the idea as madness. Instead, I went into the side room and sorted through my gear, bundling up my bedroll to make the throne a bit more comfortable, as well as getting some food out.

I enjoyed the meal, washing down some strong, nutty cheese, heavily seeded bread, and dried meat with fresh water I summoned, deciding I'd save the fish for tea.

As soon as my mana had refilled fully, I drained it into the well again, then carried all my gear back into the adjacent room and set up a sleeping area before setting off to wander around the floor again. I needed something to do while my mana refilled, and I was bored of exercising.

On a whim, I grabbed my weapons and ordered Bob to move out. The floor directly below me held several locked doors. I had a lockpicking kit in my gear, so it was time to make the most of it. I explained my plan to Oracle, getting an excited squeak, so we headed down a floor. Bob clattered across the hall to stand at the top of the far set of stairs on lookout as I investigated the floor properly.

I'd barely glanced at it last time I'd come through, and besides trying the doors and finding them locked, I'd never really looked at them twice. The floor had four rooms, with two on either side of the corridor, and no apparent names or signs on them. Apparently, everyone was just supposed to know whose rooms they were.

I picked the first door on my right, crouching down to examine the lock and test the handle again, just in case. Nope, definitely locked.

I pulled out my lockpicking kit, spreading the roll on the floor and sorting through the contents.

There were a few training locks, a dozen different picks of various shapes and sizes, and another half-dozen levers. I picked up the simplest practice lock. I'd played around with it before, but I had never really tried beyond fiddling.

It was encased in clear plastic, letting me see the tumblers as I slipped the pick in. I found I could easily lift a single tumbler up and out of the way, but moving onto another, I'd often shift the lock minutely, causing the one I'd just moved to drop back into place. After a few minutes, I closed my eyes and concentrated on doing it by feel, slowly lifting first one, then another, then the third into place.

With the pick holding the third up, I slipped the lever in and slowly twisted...*yes*! The bolt came loose, and I couldn't help but grin at the freed lock in my hands. My notifications window started flashing, and I pulled it up, knowing what I'd see.

Congratulations!

You have reached level 1 in a new skill: Lockpicking!

No locked room, chest, or chastity belt is safe from you now!

I paused for a second, considering the chastity belt comment, then shrugged and got on with the next practice lock. After an hour of fiddling around, I'd managed to level the skill up to level two and had opened three of the four training locks. I was ready to try the real thing. I slowly slid the pick into the lock, eyes closed, and felt for the tumblers.

At first, I couldn't feel anything, but just as I was about to give up, I found one. I carefully slid it up and moved on. Finding the second took longer, until I realized it was at a right angle to the first. The third and fourth followed the same pattern, until...*chunk*!

With an oath, I sat back, looking at the snapped remains of the pick in my hand. The damn lock had shot out a bar that had snapped my pick!

My swearing tirade was interrupted by Oracle as I tried to find another pick the same shape and size as the first.

"Jax, why are you doing that?" she asked.

"I want to get in here, and I don't have a key!" I snapped at her, then grimaced and took a deep breath. "I'm sorry. I shouldn't have shouted. The damn thing just broke my pick, is all."

"It's okay," she said, landing next to me and peering at the lock. She'd been flying around looking at things while I'd been practicing, but now she was looking the picks over a second time, as though understanding their use at last. "You've been using them to try and open the door?"

"Yeah, no key, after all."

"When you have the entire tower sworn to you, you will be able to open any door with a command, but for now, why not use your magic?"

"Magic? I don't have a spell for this," I said, looking at her askance.

"Not specifically for this, but you have Identify, and that gives you information on things like the lock, plus you have high Perception. You should be able to adjust the spell."

"'Adjust it,' how?" I asked, curiosity flaring as I sat back.

"The same way you changed your Firebolt spell. You channeled mana into it, past what was needed, and changed it into an explosive detonation, right?"

"Well, yeah, but—"

"Why do you think you could only do that with that one spell?"

"Well, I don't want the door to explode, so—"

"No, Jax, I mean why only change one spell! You learned Airblade. Most of it was lost, I know, but if we link together and use Identify, combined with some of the bits you remember from Airblade, we should be able to create a mixture of the two!"

"Finally, another spell? Let's get to it!" I said, grinning, before I started to frown, remembering how Xiao had hated the idea of me experimenting. "I thought you said I couldn't learn another spell yet?"

"You can't learn another externally sourced spell, but there's nothing stopping you from creating a new spell based on your knowledge. It's already yours, after all. You would have to form it, control the mana in it, and name it, but once you've done that, it would become a new spell of your own. That's how all spells were created in the first place. Do you want to try?"

"Hell yes!" I said, and we got started. Oracle insisted on sitting on my knee, with my head bowed so that she could put her hands on either temple. This left my face tilted at an angle, with my eyes positioned directly over her more than generous cleavage. Awkward.

I spent the first few minutes trying not to look, until I realized that this was deliberate on her part. Trying to get a—*ahem*—rise out of me. It was working, too. I could see the darker tinge of one small areola peeking out from...*nope, no, no, no, no, Jax!*

I closed my eyes, forcing myself to feel for my mana and ignore the...interesting view. It took a few minutes, but it was helped by the feeling of amusement I could sense coming from Oracle. The little minx knew *exactly* what she'd been doing.

"Okay, feel the mana coming from your core, flowing around your body and all around you. Concentrate on the feeling of the air, and try to remember the way the mana and air interacted when you learned the spell." She spoke to me as I worked through it, but her words conjured images and memories as her mind meshed with my own.

"Think about how Identify reaches out, the way it integrates with its target before coming back to you and giving you knowledge..." As the minutes became hours, we slowly worked through the steps, feeling the weave of mana fall apart time and again, until at last, we were left with a stable construct.

UnderVerse: Brightblade

Congratulations!

You have consciously created your first personal spell, Manatouch!

Manatouch:

Creates a finger of mana-infused air that can be used to interact with your target at will. Cost of 5 mana per second.

"Woot!" I crowed, chucking my hands up and grinning at Oracle. "We did it!"

"We did it!" Oracle cried out, leaping into the air and doing a series of barrel rolls and loops, looking very much like a pornographic version of Tinkerbell on acid.

I immediately started using the Manatouch spell on the lock, feeling around inside and building up a far more accurate mental image of the interior. I tried to pick the lock with the spell, but after a few attempts, I gave up and used the pick in conjunction with it.

Between the two, the lock soon gave way, and I began opening the door.

Congratulations!

You have reached level 4 in your skill, Lockpicking!

No locked room, chest, or chastity belt is safe from you now!

"This is awesome!" I crowed as the door slowly swung inwards, the darkness of the room beyond hardly hindering my DarkVision-enhanced eyes. The room within was surprisingly large. As I climbed to my feet, ignoring the aches and pains from crouching on cold stone for so long, I looked around in stunned amazement.

The room covered nearly a quarter of this floor, if I guessed right, and had huge, floor-to-ceiling windows on one side, with a small balcony and a pile of rusted remains outside, suggesting a table and chairs had once stood there. The room had a huge bed against one wall, a chest of drawers and wardrobe, and a writing desk complete with ink and quill and a sheaf of papers.

Against the opposite wall to the bed, next to the writing desk, stood a chest. An honest-to-goodness treasure-chest-looking thing, even if it was cliché. All the furniture, bar the chest, was sagging, half-collapsed, and disintegrating in one way or another. A thousand years of decay had really done a number on it all. The inkwell was unsurprisingly dry, the quills felt like they'd snap at a touch, and the paper...well it pretty much collapsed into dust as soon as I touched it.

I went to the chest, sweeping the dust from the floor and sat before it, spreading my picks out and using Manatouch again.

This time, I felt something else besides the lock, and after careful examination, I backed away and moved to the side. There was a tiny needle embedded in the metal of the lock. I could feel something *wrong* about it, and as I concentrated, information began to build up.

Trapped Chest		Further Description *Yes/No*	
Details:		This chest has been enhanced with a magical spell and a trapped lock. It is unknown what will happen if the trap is triggered: an explosion that blows up the room, an alarm, a horrific smell that offends your friends and colleagues? Only one way to find out...	
Rarity:	Magical:	Durability:	Charge:
Rare	Yes	48/100	1/1

"What do you think, Oracle?" I asked her, and she flew down, landing lightly on the ground to peer into the lock.

I half-reached out to pull her back, then reminded myself she was literally made of mana, making her incorporeal at will. She was probably at far less risk than I was.

"I don't know, Jax, maybe try to pick it from a distance?" she suggested, backing away.

I thought about it, then moved in closer instead. I'd learned the skill Trap Making earlier, after all. It was probably the only reason I knew the needle was there, so I spent some time looking the rest of the chest over. After another hour, I was convinced I knew how the chest had been trapped.

A simple hook had been attached to the tumbler, so as soon as the lock turned, it would release the needle. If you had a hand directly in front of the lock, you were in trouble, but if not, there would be no real issue. That left whatever magic I could sense about it. After spamming Identify and backing away to the other side of the room by the door, I started using Manatouch again. I'd learned all I could from passive observation, so it was likely best to get on with it.

The first step was unhooking the needle from the trigger. That took three tries, but eventually, it came loose, and I breathed a sigh of relief. Next was the magical field I could feel around it. I used my spell to feel around the edges, slowly finding areas where the spell seemed to sink into the chest, and others where it reached out, waiting.

Hours passed as I slowly examined it from every angle, until I finally found what I was looking for. There was a small section of the chest on the rear, near the ground, that linked to the spell. I took a deep breath and, using my new spell, I pressed it. A loud click resounded around the room, and the magical field vanished, sucked inside the chest. A new notification began blinking. I opened it, discovering that I'd been automatically muting others while I worked.

Congratulations!

You have reached level 1 in a new skill: Magical Lockpicking!

No locked room, chest, or chastity belt is safe from you now!

(This is a subskill of Lockpicking and has increased your overall skill in Lockpicking by 1.)

Congratulations!

You have reached level 3 in your skill: Trap Making!
Try not to catch yourself in these diabolical creations. Now that would be
embarrassing!

Congratulations!

You have managed to salvage a magical trap!
Do you wish to take (Paralysis Trap)?

Yes/No

There wasn't a decision to be made at all as I picked up the trap. I examined the small crystal filled with orange and green colors swirling idly, then slipped it into a pocket and started examining the inside of the chest. I found two potions, a length of cloth, three rolled-up scrolls, and a pair of small pouches. As I tipped the first pouch out onto my hand, a collection of rough-cut rubies, sapphires, and a single large jade tumbled into view.

The first few were all around the size of my fingernail, while the jade was a rough rectangle, an inch across and three inches long. I slid them back into the pouch and pocketed it. Checking the second, I expected to find coins, but instead found something else. I dipped my hand in and pulled it out, looking in confusion at the sparking white handful of sand I held.

Firax Dust		Further Description *Yes/No*	
Details:		This dust is used in many magical crafting recipes. A few grains scattered across a creation will increase the magical potential and lower the chance of enchantments failing.	
Rarity:	**Magical:**	**Durability:**	**Charge:**
Rare	Yes	N/A	1/1

I grinned and pocketed the dust. I didn't know what I'd do with it, but at least it boded well for crafting. Finally, I examined the two potions.

Mana Boost Potion		Further Description *Yes/No*	
Details:		This potion boosts the manapool of the imbiber by 25% and mana regeneration by 2 points per second for 300 seconds.	
Rarity:	**Magical:**	**Durability:**	**Potency**
Rare	Yes	87/100	2/10

Silverbright		Further Description *Yes/No*	
Details:		This mixture of ingredients holds no known alchemical properties identifiable at your level, but it glows with a faint, comforting light...	
Rarity:	**Magical:**	**Durability:**	**Potency**
Unique	Yes	99/100	10/10

The mana boost potion would come in handy, but I had no idea what the other one was. The fact that it had been kept in a locked and trapped chest suggested it was valuable, at least, and its rarity was unique. I shrugged, pocketing them both and pulled up the scrolls.

Scroll of Summon Arcane Eagle		Further Description *Yes/No*	
Details:		This scroll will summon an Arcane Eagle construct. This air affinity spirit will last 600 seconds and share all it sees with its summoner.	
Rarity:	**Magical:**	**Durability:**	**Charge:**
Rare	Yes	84/100	1/1

Scroll of Greater Mapping		Further Description *Yes/No*	
Details:		This scroll will create a map of an area as far as the beholder can see, marking places of interest. The greater the distance and number of locations, the less information will be given. This information can be added to an existing map.	
Rarity:	**Magical:**	**Durability:**	**Charge:**
Rare	Yes	87/100	1/1

Scroll of Soul Trap		Further Description *Yes/No*	
Details:		This scroll will allow the caster to cast Soul Trap on their target, provided an appropriate gem is available. The target's soul will be trapped for use at a later time.	
Rarity	**Magical**	**Durability**	**Charge:**
Rare	Yes	73/100	1/1

All three scrolls sounded good. I could use the arcane eagle to find out what was going on in the lands around the tower, and the map scroll would explain a lot of the terrain. The soul trap, I'd use on the SporeMother, given the chance, and see how it liked being enslaved for a change.

By the point that I finished looking over the items, I was utterly exhausted. I checked the one door that led off the unlocked room, finding a small bathroom, as I'd suspected. Once the tower was reclaimed, I'd probably move into this room, but for now, I gathered my gear and headed back up to the top floor to rest for the night. I locked myself in, leaving Bob to guard the door as Oracle buzzed around to examine the room, and I slept like the dead.

CHAPTER TWENTY-TWO

The next morning, I bolted awake as Oracle knocked my naginata over with a resounding clatter. I tried to leap to my feet but they were caught in the sleeping bag, and I fell over. My sleep-addled brain flushed with adrenaline, and I caught Bob staring at me. I summoned a Firebolt before I had time to think about it, and only Oracle's panicked shout stopped me from hitting him in the face with it.

"Jax! Sorry! I'm so sorry! I didn't mean to!" She flitted across the room to hide behind Bob, landing on his back and peeking around his arm as I tried to figure out what was going on. I took a deep breath and relaxed, recovering the mana and allowing the Firebolt to disappear.

"Damn, Oracle, I nearly shit myself!" I grunted as I heaved myself to my feet, untangling myself, before snorting in relieved laughter at the state of me. I quickly summoned a spring to refill the canteens and wash my face and as I finished, I reflected on how commonplace magic had become to me, to use it without a thought.

God, I loved this world.

"I'm sorry, Jax! I won't do it again, I promise!" The note in her voice finally got through my sleep-fogged mind, and I straightened up.

"It's all right, Oracle, seriously. Calm down," I said, looking at her in confusion. There was real fear in her eyes. "Are you okay?"

"Are you mad at me?" she asked in a small voice, still half-hidden behind Bob.

"Oracle, come here, please," I said firmly, holding one hand out, palm up. She flew across the room and alighted on my hand hesitantly.

I could feel her tiny feet trembling.

"Stop," I said. "Oracle, it's all right; you just woke me up. It was a shock, that's all. What's wrong?"

"You aren't mad at me?" she whispered, looking up at me through her long hair.

"Hell no. I was shocked, that's all, like I said. Why are you so scared?"

"Are you going to break the bond?" she asked sadly, her voice barely audible. She looked down at her feet, wrapping her arms around herself, and her wings dipped low.

"What? No, why the hell would I do that? I didn't even know it could be broken. No, I'm not breaking it…unless you want me to?" I asked, hesitation entering my voice as a thought occurred to me. *Maybe she wanted to be free?*

"No! I…I just, I'm not good with humans, Jax. You're all so strange, and I made you jump, I woke you up again, and you seemed so angry…"

"I woke up from a deep sleep, that's all. I was surprised. Seriously, Oracle, you are literally the only friend I have in this world besides Tommy, and I have no idea where he is, or if he's even still alive. I need you," I said gently as she tucked her hair back behind one ear and looked up at me with a small smile. Her wings lifted and began to twitch as she spoke.

"Really?" She sounded so hopeful, it made my heart ache for her. *Poor little bugger.* I couldn't imagine her life, captured, forcibly bonded to a fucking tower and the ability to do magic, as a creature of magic, burned out. She'd been forced to go to sleep, not knowing if she'd ever wake up, and she'd basically been a glorified librarian program for the residents.

"Really," I said, "Now, come on. I'm awake, so why don't we go wake a wisp up?" She clapped her hands together and took off, pirouetting as she flew up over my head and spiraled around me.

"Yes! And then we'll have two friends! And Bob! Don't forget about Bob!" she called out, flying across the room and landing on his head. Patting him, she faced me sternly. "Bob shall be my trusty steed, carrying me wherever I need to go!"

She looked so ridiculously proud of herself as she sat there, I had to smile at her. She was a mix of childlike and adult curiosity that I found endearing, even if I was only going to admit it to myself.

I gathered my gear and went to the door, sending Bob first as Oracle flew over to hover behind me. We entered the main room and swept it carefully, making sure nothing had come up. The door to the stairwell was still only slightly ajar, as I'd left it the night before. Bob was dispatched to guard it, and I resumed draining my mana to the wisp well. Eating, drinking, and doing my best at cleaning the windows served to pass the time while I waited for my mana to regenerate.

Heeding Oracle's warning about the possible anger of the wisp, I waited until it stood at three hundred and ninety of four hundred and stopped, waiting for my mana to fully regenerate before giving up the last ten. As the mana disappeared into it, I sat forward on the throne, staring with fascination at the manawell.

This transformation was slower, the mana seeming to ebb and flow sluggishly. A whirlpool started to spin in the center of the well until a small figure formed, lifting slowly to stand on the liquid mana. It was humanoid, barely six inches tall, broad of chest, with small, stout legs, and a craggy face that lacked definition. As its eyes opened, it searched around the room before coming back to me, and it looked pissed.

"You awoke me?" it asked in a monotone voice.

"Oh yeah, I've got a token somewhere," I said, starting to rummage through my bag until Oracle stopped me. She flew forward to land on my knee and spoke up quickly.

"He is the new Master of the Great Tower, and I vouch for him," she said proudly, crossing her arms and smiling at the creature before her.

"Vouch for him, *and* bonded to him, I see. Traitor," the tiny form said in a flat, hard voice as it glared at Oracle, then turned from her with an abruptness that made my anger start to heat.

"Traitor? I saved his life! He is our rightful master!" she spat out, taking a step forward, her hands flashing to her hips as she leaned over the small figure.

"You bonded him. Traitor to the tower, you are no longer impartial. You no longer hold it first. Master will hear of this."

"He *is* the Master, you stone-brained fool! You are required to accept his authority. I am a recognized tower wisp, and I am bonded both to him and to the tower. I declare him to be the master, proven and faithful, and I cannot lie."

"He is…the master? Master told me to sleep, to protect the tower. Keep the tower standing. It stands."

"Uh, okay," I said, once again proving why I was in charge with my amazing grasp of things and mind-blowing articulation. As they both turned to me, I cleared my throat and started again. "I mean, yes. I'm the new Master of the Tower. Falco gave me his token and told me to take control of the tower as my own. I saved Oracle, and I reawakened you. I am the master."

The small creature stared at me for a while before finally grunting and turning away, looking around the room instead.

"The sporelings…I see you've not cleaned them out. Or the undead. You cannot be the true master of the tower while a hostile force holds sections of it." He paused for a moment, then said grudgingly, "I accept you as master, though you must clear the tower, grounds, and facilities of enemies before full access will be granted."

"Okay, question: how do I 'clear and secure' an area of the tower?" I asked the pair of wisps who still stood glaring at each other.

"You must kill any enemies inside the area, then secure it against further invaders, obviously," the miserable little one stated coldly.

"He is the rightful ma—"

"That's enough!" I cut them both off as they started to argue. "I'm the master here, yes?" I said, receiving grudging acknowledgement from the new wisp and enthusiastic smiles and nods from Oracle.

"Right, then. Let's get this sorted, and then you can answer my questions properly. If I ask a question, I expect an honest and accurate answer from you. Feel free to elaborate on anything you think I need to know, and I'll thank you for it.

"Keep acting like an asshole, and I'll do everything in my power to make your life hell. Up to and including breaking your bond with the tower, if I need to. Understand?" I said, my voice calm and cold, both wisps stared at me in horror.

"Jax, to break his bond to the tower…he'd die, and the tower—"

"It'd what, collapse?" I said, receiving a hesitant nod from her. "That's fine. I'll be clear about this," I said, leaning forward so I was closer to their level. "Either you help me, and we can be friends and work together, or you serve me, and do as you're told, or you die. If I destroy the tower as well, I'll be pissed, but I'll get over it. I don't give a shit about you right now, so choose quickly."

"Jax…"

"Quiet, Oracle. I want to hear from the little miserable fucker," I said, cutting her off with an upraised finger.

"I…will serve," it responded, "I acknowledged you as master already." It ground the words out resentfully.

"And I remember that, but you will either be a willing part of the team, or I can't trust you, and I won't turn my back to you. Why are you being so pissy?"

"Pissy?" it asked me in confusion.

"Miserable, grumpy, acting like an asshole," I said. It stared at me before finally erupting and gesturing around the room wildly.

"Look at it! My beautiful tower: it barely stands! Creatures infest it, more than half of it doesn't respond to my touch, and they've covered it in…waste."

"Waste?" I asked Oracle.

"The black stuff on the windows. It's bodily waste from the sporelings, Jax," she explained.

"And I've been digging at it? Trying to clean the damn windows with my hands?!" I cried out, looking at my hands and then at the windows. "Oh, hell no!" I summoned the water from my magical spring with one hand, then quickly summoned a Firebolt.

Holding the Firebolt in the spring as it flowed, I managed to create hot water that quickly heated to boiling and I began to scrub my hands clean in earnest.

"You have tried to clean the windows?" the little wisp asked cautiously.

"He did; whenever he has had the time, he has picked at them, breaking the waste away with his bare hands." She sounded so proud. I groaned and redid the spells, scrubbing my hands again.

"Hmmm. You *were* trying to help the tower, then. Very well. You may be unaware, master, that the tower has the facilities to construct servitors. They will enable me to repair the tower and its grounds over time.

"For now, however, if we can restore the mana collectors, I will be able to begin repairs on the tower myself. I require direct orders from the new master, as the last orders of the old master were to prevent the mana collectors from charging the tower."

"Why?" I asked, "Why did he tell you to do that?"

"To prevent the SporeMother from feeding off the mana. She would have become far more powerful, spending centuries feeding off the refined mana of the tower."

"Right. You did mention that before." I grunted, thinking. "Can the SporeMother access the mana collectors if we do this now? What's changed?"

"She would need to take this location to feed properly," the wisp said, and Oracle nodded in agreement.

"And you can stop her from taking this?" I asked.

"We had no warning before, or I could have then. I can repurpose stone to close stairwells or doorways. It will take several hours, but once they are done, this section will be secure."

I didn't miss the phrasing. "Secure" was exactly what I needed; not just for the quest, but to make sure I didn't have to clear the tower repeatedly, searching it each time I changed floors to keep from being ambushed.

"Okay, can you close off the tower from the Hall of Memories down? Make sure we have that floor safe, and from there up?"

"I can, but it will take several hours, and I will need to activate the collectors to have enough mana for it. The SporeMother will also respond by attempting to take the tower. Maybe start at this level and clear down over time?" it suggested.

I couldn't help but notice the sudden shift to deference. Now that it believed I was interested in saving the tower, its surly attitude had changed to one of interest.

I thought about it, but ultimately decided it would be better to have a safe point lower down. Once it was clear and safe, I could start to sort out the rest of the upper floors; plus, the Hall of Memories would be safe for times when I could use it.

"No, I want you to seal the upper floors of the tower, starting at one level below the Hall of Memories. That way, we've got plenty of the tower to ourselves," I said decisively.

"Yes, Master," the wisp said, dipping its hands into the well below and closing its eyes. It knelt for several seconds before looking back up at me and speaking again.

"I have begun to grow a wall across the stairwell, but it is using my mana reserve. May I reactivate the mana collectors?"

I cursed myself for a fool. How many times did I need to be asked?

"Yes, sorry. Reactivate the mana collectors and seal off the lower half of the tower. Begin cleaning and repairing as you can."

It returned to its position, kneeling in the rapidly reducing well as thin tendrils of glistening mana wove out from the pedestal, crossing the floor in the blink of an eye and racing up the walls. As they reached the ceiling, they began to branch out again, first in ones and twos, then in dozens, and finally hundreds of filaments as they formed a pattern overhead.

I watched as it moved, one color glowing brighter, then another, until entire sections seemed to shift and grow bright with a golden light. The room shook faintly, and dust fell in rivulets. A grinding noise began outside, and I rushed to the window, looking out of the small cleared sections as I tried to make out what was happening. Several levels below me, long stone spikes were sliding out of recessed areas. As they moved, birds screeched and took wing, circling the tower as their ancestral roosts changed. The spikes continued, becoming pillars as they lengthened, until a crown seemed to ring the top of the tower.

From each of the pillars' tips, a single, faint light began to bloom. At first, it seemed tiny, barely visible against the greater light of the rising sun, but as the seconds passed, it intensified. Each light became a tiny vortex, sucking in the ambient mana of the world around it.

The tower pulsed again, this time with energy, as mana flowed back into it. Stone long starved of mana drank it in greedily and began to change.

Where I stood, the weathered, pitted stone smoothed, the crumbling edges reforming and taking on the luster of marble. The damage under my feet slowly began to fix itself as I spun around.

Small crystals set in the walls, which I had not noticed before, began to glow, softly at first, but quickly bringing the room to brilliance. A chandelier hung from the ceiling in the center, holding a single huge crystal that began to pulse and glow with an inner fire.

"It is begun, my master." A voice came from behind me, one I didn't recognize. I spun around again, facing the small wisp that had knelt in the manawell. It had changed, becoming more defined, less craggy, and more polished. It had also grown slightly, reaching Oracle's shoulder now, and it spoke with a rich timbre that made the air vibrate faintly.

I looked at him, consciously deciding to see the wisp as male.

"It's beautiful. Do you have a name, wisp?" I said, returning to the throne and shifting the bedroll to a more comfortable position.

"I do not, master. Our last master simply referred to me as Tower." His voice showed no concern either way, but there was a hint of curiosity as he replied.

"Well, then, you need a name! Do you have a preference?" I asked him with a grin, watching as he turned to Oracle.

"You have a name now, and this change in form. Why?" he asked her.

"Jax, our master, asked me to assume a distinct form, so I accessed his memories and chose this one. He granted me a name, and swore to provide me with freedom, if possible."

251

"Freedom?!" he asked, twisting to look at me, "You would free us?"

"Yeah. Look, I'll be clear on this. Where I come from, slavery isn't allowed. Even if it was, I don't care. Those that practice slavery are scum and need to die. It's kinda that simple. Even if you were still being an asshole with me, I'd free you, given the chance. It's the right thing to do." I shrugged, feeling slightly embarrassed as the pair of wisps stared at me.

"You permitted a memory scan?" he continued, looking from me to Oracle and back.

"Yeah, why?" I asked.

"It is rare that one such as you would permit a lesser creature to touch your mind, let alone read your memories. I ask permission to do the same. I will swear wholehearted allegiance to you, provided I find the truth in your mind." The small wisp looked at me, hesitation and fear radiating from him, but hope was there as well. I looked to Oracle, and she nodded.

"Okay, just…any images you find there of ladies with no clothes—" I started to say before Oracle interrupted me.

"He has a lot of memories of naked females, both his own memories and pictures of them, but he doesn't like to talk about them.

"I picked this form from mixing some of them. Do you like it?" she explained to him, completely unconcerned as she tugged at one corner of her outfit and it dissolved into mist, her exceedingly voluptuous figure bouncing free. I froze, my eyes locked onto her nakedness as my brain seemed to short circuit. Oracle, of course, showed no hint of modesty as she looked from the other wisp to me, lightly bouncing on the balls of her feet.

"He says he doesn't want me to show my form off like this, but his heart rate just went through the roof and his—"

"Gah! Stop, Oracle!" I managed to get out, frantically trying to force my eyes not to return to her body as I locked them on her face.

"But you like to look!" she cried out, bouncing again. "You know you do, and I like you looking. Please, Jax, just enjoy looking at me!" She spun around to face the other wisp, her more pronounced areas almost throwing her off balance from sheer force of inertia.

"You should take a form like this, too! Then we can have different colors! He likes different colors!"

"NO!" I shouted, then I took a deep breath and repeated myself more calmly. "No. *Please*, don't take a form like that. Yes, you can look at my memories if you need to, but for the love of God, don't choose a form like Oracle has. I have enough trouble as it is."

I shook my head and leaned forward to put my face within reach of the small wisp as he looked from Oracle to me and back again. I closed my eyes, seeing a rush of images, memories, scents, and sounds filling my mind as soon as I felt a cool hand being pressed against my head.

In a minute, it was over, and I sat back, my head swimming as I tried to make sense of all I'd seen.

The small wisp before me began to change, growing taller, becoming a slim humanoid, and wearing a cloak that reached the ground and a helmet that covered his face. His entire figure appeared to be formed from a single piece of silver, reflecting everything perfectly and covering the wisp underneath. I was unsure, as the change finished, if I was pleased or disappointed. He had not become a hot, naked woman. I decided to go with relief and moved on.

"Nice; it suits you," I said, looking at him as he inspected his hands. As his arms lifted from the cloak, it was clear that he wore armor underneath. Tiny, scaled, silvery material covered his body, and his hands were encased in gloves.

"Thank you, master. It feels...right. I still require a name, however," he said, tilting his head to look at me.

"I...well, you run the tower for me, so how about Seneschal?" I asked him, receiving a satisfied nod in return. He lowered himself to one knee in a single fluid motion, his head bowed as he began to speak.

"I, Seneschal, swear my loyalty to you, master. I will aid you and serve you, until death releases me or the All-Mother wipes me from the land." I had no idea what to say, so I went for the memories I had of these things from books and TV.

"I, Jax, accept your oath of fealty, and will protect and raise you up as I would my own. I will not break faith with you, so long as you do not break faith with me," I said, the words seeming foolish and badly phrased as I spoke them. But he seemed pleased, rising to his feet and looking to me.

As he spoke, I received a prompt, and the room seemed to flare with a faint light in response.

Congratulations!

You have made progress on your Quest: A Place to Lay Your Head.

Wisps sworn fealty: 2/3
Locations cleared and secured: 0/5
SporeMother killed: 0/1
Guardians claimed: 0/10
Workers claimed: 0/10

Rewards: The Great Tower is yours to command. Surrounding area will become aware of your rightful ownership. Access to supplies and facilities. 100,000xp.

"Thank you, master. I have managed to extend my senses toward the lower floors of the tower now. The furthest depths are closed to me, but I have found dozens of undead and other creatures of the night moving about. They have just entered my furthest range and are working their way up as fast as they can. They are coming here, and something comes with them. Something dark; it is absorbing the mana I am attempting to use to sense the tower effortlessly..."

"Fuck," I groaned, pushing myself to my feet and grabbing my naginata. I checked my armor and set off running for the stairs, Bob opening the door wide and beginning to race downwards in response to my mental command.

"Thanks for the warning; now get that passageway sealed!" I yelled over my shoulder as I ran out of the door.

I sprinted as fast as I could, hoping to reach the halfway point of the tower before they did. I might be able to hold them there until it finished sealing. I hoped.

"We can do it, Jax! Try to keep up!" Oracle yelled as she whipped past me, her tiny wings blurring, and her naked ass disappearing around the bend, leaving only her laughter in the air as I yelled back at her. "Put some goddamn clothes on, for fuck's sake!"

Despite my best efforts, I found myself idly wondering about the air resistance that chest must cause.

CHAPTER TWENTY-THREE

W e spiraled round and round as we hurtled down the tower, doors flashing by on either side as we sprinted past. I slowed after half a dozen floors, the combination of exhaustion and dizziness slowing me down as I realized I'd be useless fighting like this.

"Oracle!" I called out as I slowed to a walk, catching my breath. After several seconds, she reappeared from the gloom below.

"Jax! This is no time for a rest! Come on!" She spun around and started to dart off when I called out again.

"Dammit, woman, stop!"

She halted, looking at me in confusion. "But the enemy…"

"They'll be there when we get there, or here, or wherever. It's us they want, after all! It's no use sprinting at them and then dropping dead from exhaustion. Just rest for a minute, then we can go again, okay?" I wheezed out, drawing deep breaths like a blacksmith's bellows.

"Oh, okay. I'll get Bob to carry me, then. Good point!" she said, starting off again.

"Oracle! Wait, dammit." I groaned, jogging after her. After a few minutes, I found her, not because she'd waited, but because I'd ordered Bob to return to me, and she was riding on his head.

"You should make one of these for yourself, Jax! Bob is such a good minion!" she gushed, patting his skull as he ignored her.

"Oracle!" I gasped out, nearly on my knees as I rested against the wall.

"What is it?" she asked in concern. "You really need to learn to pace yourself, you know; you're going to be no good in this fight if you don't rest!"

She sat perched atop Bob's head, waggling a finger at me in reproach. I wheezed out a breath and focused on my feet as I tried to recover. She'd put some clothes on, but she'd picked from my memories again, and the outfit she wore was…less than suitable for battle. A corset, knee-high boots, and…I shook my head, forcing myself to look away. The knowledge that she had to have found this somewhere in my mind was not making it any easier to ignore. I just shook my head in resignation. I'd have to discuss it with her later.

She continued to insist that I needed to look after myself more and took off, flipping upside down to look me in the eye…until she started to strip out of the corset to try to make herself more comfortable.

"So, was there something you wanted?" she asked innocently, and I realized both that I'd been staring and that it had been deliberate on her part.

"Dammit, Oracle!" I grunted, forcing myself to my feet and directing Bob to set off back down the tower. She laughed at me, a throaty sound that made my blood boil as I tried to banish thoughts from my mind. "Yes, I needed something! Seneschal can sense the undead and the rest of our enemies. Can you contact him and find out where they are?" I asked hopefully as she caught up to Bob and settled down to fix a suspender that had mysteriously come loose.

"Of course, but we're in the tower. It's an extension of him, so you can just ask him directly, you know?" she said, grinning as she caught me looking again. *Dammit...get ahold of yourself, Jax...and not like that!*

"Seneschal?" I said aloud, receiving something that registered as a tickle on my brain almost in response. A notification began to flash, and I brought it up.

Your Oathsworn companion Seneschal wishes to speak to you.

Do you wish to allow contact?

Yes/No

I selected *yes* and felt a presence join me, as though he were following directly behind me as I ran, and Seneschal's voice filled my mind.

"Yes, Lord Jax?"
"The enemy; where are they?"
"They are spread out across multiple floors. The most advanced are five floors below you, and the greater presence is currently twenty-seven floors below the Hall of Memories."
"Is it the SporeMother?"
"Unknown. It is a creature of power, however. If it is not the SporeMother, then it is likely a very powerful servant. It is surrounded by other undead and is considerably more powerful than the guardians that fill the rest of the tower. It covers the area in a pervading darkness as it passes through."
"Well, that's just fucking peachy, isn't it!"
"Master Jax?"
"Sorry, Seneschal, just an idle thought. How far is it to the Hall of Memories? And you don't have to call me lord or master. Just Jax is fine."
"Thank you, Jax. It is nine floors from your current position to the Hall of Memories."
"How the hell did they get to five floors below me already?! They've passed it and they're still coming! Is the barrier nearly done?"
"No, Jax, these closer minions were only a few floors below the Hall when we reactivated the mana collectors. The SporeMother must have felt it and sent all her minions immediately. The barrier is currently twenty percent complete and growing."
"Shit! Is there anything you can do to slow them?"
"Like what?"
"Ah...the windows! Can you either clean some of them between the main group and the barrier, or break them, or something?"
...
...
"Seneschal?"

"I can break the glass by flexing the window frames that hold the panels in place, but this is against all I exist to do. It will take time and mana. I can do only one window at a time."

"Do it for the main group, then. Stop them wherever you can, hold them while we get to the barrier, and I'll reinforce it as best I can"

"Good luck, Jax."

"Thanks, mate."

I dismissed the mental communication with a thought, too winded and worried as I ran to think more on it as I passed floors and sprinted down stairwells. From up ahead, I heard the clash of weapons and felt my mana dip as Oracle cast some magic.

I took a deep breath and forced myself on, staggering around the corner and barging onto the next floor to find Oracle buzzing around as high as she could go. A spear flashed out and barely missed her just as a pair of skeletons tried to trap her in the corner. Bob was battling with three others and was slowly being beaten back.

Since the first pair had their backs to me, I sprinted to strike them from behind. I wasn't having anyone attack Oracle. Not just because she was crazy, or because I liked looking at her half-naked ass as she flew around (and I also knew damn well I shouldn't be looking at all, regardless of her teasing). She was my friend, and anyone fucking with her was going to regret it.

I plowed into the pair from behind, stabbing out with the blade of my naginata at the one on the right. Grunting, I leaped at the one on the left, throwing a flying kick that would have made my instructors wince at how awkward it looked. What mattered was the speed and momentum, however.

As I planted my foot in the small of its back, I shoved off as hard as I could, transferring that inertia to the skeleton and sending its much-lighter body flying into a wall. The one on the right had taken my naginata in the back, and the weapon was lodged in its spine. I wrenched it from its feet as I jumped back, clinging to my weapon.

I landed awkwardly and staggered, but the skeleton was facedown, trying to push itself back upright.

I lunged forward, slapping my left hand down on its skull as I finished summoning the Firebolt. It burst into life in the middle of my enemy's skull, and the DarkSpore shuddered. The skeleton collapsed into a pile of bones as the force animating it died. I straightened up, yanking the naginata free, and spun to find the skeleton I'd kicked crawling across the floor toward me, one of its legs missing.

"The window!" I shouted to Oracle. She spun, flashing across the floor to the window I'd indicated, as I ran and punted the skull from the crawling skeleton, field goal style. As it hurtled past the three skeletons fighting Bob, one turned to see what was happening. It got a mace to the back of the head from Bob as a reward for its lack of attention. As it went down, the one on the far side leaped onto Bob's back, driving its own sword into his ribcage, and the remaining one smashed downwards onto his front right leg with a hammer.

Bone gave way with a crunch as I tackled the skeleton with a hammer and drove it to the floor, both our weapons flying away. We rolled about, my opponent's lack of weight offset by the fact it had claws and teeth, while my punches glanced off bones and ancient armor. It lunged forward, its teeth snapping shut a scant millimeter from the tip of my nose as I tried to get its arms locked down.

I reared back automatically. The rotten teeth snapped and bit at the air as I tried to get control of the possessed creature scratching and tearing at my armor. Oracle fought with the window, beating on it with her tiny fists, until my mana bar dipped again as she screamed.

A flash of fire burst out from her hands, impacting the window and smashing the glass and crap out into open air. The sunlight streamed in, hitting Bob squarely, but he ignored it. The creature clinging on his back, on the other hand, screamed and shook, trying to escape. Bob twisted around under Oracle's direction, grabbing the one on the floor and the one on his back and shoving both through the window.

The glass smashed out farther as both corpses tumbled away, spinning and screeching toward the ground as the light of the sun burned the corruption of the DarkSpore away. Bob clattered over to me, grabbing the thing I was fighting, yanking it upright from behind, and chucking it out of the window.

I collapsed back, panting, trying to catch my breath as Bob rounded up the rest of the remains. It threw the DarkSpore-infested skulls out of the window, followed by the rest of the bodies, under Oracle's gleefully shouted orders.

I rolled to my feet after a second and swept up my naginata, ordering Bob to take the lead again. Oracle landed on my shoulder, patting me on the top of the head as I followed Bob down the staircase once more.

"You"—*cough*—"know that would have been easier, if you'd"—*cough*—"waited for me, right?" I wheezed out as I jogged down the stairs. I really needed to invest in Endurance next. Damn, I needed it. I didn't care if it would level on its own; I *really* needed more stamina. Even as I considered it, I knew I'd want to put the points into something else instead, but *Perception?!* What had I been thinking?

I staggered out onto the next level, running forward more on sheer stubbornness than anything else.

As I began to descend the next set of stairs, a message flashed up that indicated Seneschal wanted to talk to me. I accepted it and continued on, slowing as I tried to control my breathing.

"It is done. I destroyed a window that had stood there since the tower was formed. It was stained glass, showing the battle between Orgus and the Draken; it took six craftsmen a ye—"

"Oh boo-fuckin-hoo, Seneschal! Seriously, dude, I'm battling for my life and sprinting down the goddamn miles high tower here. If I needed air to talk to you, I couldn't; I'm that fucking exhausted. I don't give a shit about a window! We can have it repaired, if we live!"

...

...

"The main group of undead has stopped, with several of the weaker ones destroyed. They are attempting to get around it now.

"Good, that's great. Damn, I'm unfit. Look...I'm sorry, Seneschal, I'm an ass at times. It's great that you've done that, and I'm sorry you had to break the window. But seriously, if we don't win this, we're fucked anyway, okay?"

"As you say, Jax. There are six more undead spread out across the next two floors, and I sense something nearby, but it is so faint, I can't be sure..."

"Okay, thanks, man."

I broke the connection again and concentrated on staggering on. Oracle had flitted away to rejoin Bob, and I stopped in the middle of the floor and bent over, gasping for air. I didn't know what it was at first—an itch between my shoulder blades, maybe—but I started looking around as I panted. This floor was seemingly empty. A low, domed ceiling was supported by circular, fluted columns, with several windows. The floor was covered in a pattern, but it was too dull to make anything out, even with my enhanced vision. There were alcoves set into the walls on either side, filled with seats and great bookshelves, that were thickly coated in the dust of millennia.

I thought I'd seen movement off to one side, and spun to follow it, my naginata held warningly in my right hand, my left summoning flames at a thought. Something felt very wrong, and the shadows were deeper than I'd thought at first. *Shadows? My ability should...*

Before I had time to finish the thought, there was a flash of movement to my left, then nothing. As I tried to decide if I was getting paranoid with the sudden darkness, or there really was something in here, a terrible pain spiked through my back as something ripped into me, cutting a shallow gash from the back of my right hip up to my shoulder. My armor parted like butter.

I screamed in pain and dove away from whatever had hit me. Rolling across the floor, I turned to face my attacker, only to see nothing but empty air. Whatever it was had sliced me open like it was gutting a fish then disappeared without making a sound. I wasn't sure if the movement I'd seen earlier was the thing moving into position or if it was a distraction, but staying here would be a death sentence.

I ran straight to the nearest wall and slammed my back to it, ignoring the flare of pain from the impact of the stone against my torn flesh. I started scanning the room frantically, my eyes darting from one patch of shadow to another. My breathing rasped in my ears as I tried to look in all directions at once.

I forced myself to calm down after a few seconds and think. Whatever had attacked me had to have come from somewhere, and something hard had cut into me, so it had to have a physical form. It wasn't invisible, or I wouldn't have seen the movement that distracted me earlier. Whatever it was had some power over darkness, maybe?

I contorted my fingers into the gestures for a spell, shouting as my left hand shot out fast as a thought as I made the connection. A Firebolt blasted out of my hand and into the recessed ceiling directly *above* me. With a scream, something was blown free, landing heavily with a bone-crushing impact a few meters from me as I scrambled along the wall away from it.

I kept my naginata in my right hand and sent another Firebolt into the ceiling, illuminating another two creatures clambering towards me across the ribbed supports.

They were small creatures with six limbs. Four of the legs ended in some kind of suckers, a pair of claw tipped hands clacked at the ends of the upper arms, and the upper body seemed all teeth and hatred.

Their bodies were narrow, more like fat worms, but the upper half was guaranteed to give me nightmares if I didn't kill them all. They had huge mouths that were filled with jagged, rotting and blackened teeth, and I could find no eyes. The fact they clearly knew where I was without eyes was freaking me out even more...plus, the one on the right had blood smeared across its claws, which I'd seen in the split second of light.

Oh, I was having that bastard.

Blasting upwards with another Firebolt in the general direction of the blood-smeared creature, I stepped forward and swung the blunt end of my naginata down into the head of the stunned one that was trying to rise. As it smashed into the floor again, letting out a squeal of pain, I blasted it with a Firebolt at point-blank range, and a small skull icon appeared.

Grinning as I turned from the corpse, I cast another Firebolt, this time at the nearest window. The shutters were blown apart, and the light streamed in. Screams and frantic scuttling sounded overhead as the creatures fled the light. I glanced at the one I'd killed and realized that light was shining directly on it, but it wasn't exploding or anything. Confused, I moved close to the window and put my back to the wall. I kept watching the room and picked out the darkest corner of the ceiling.

There were three more of the creatures there, huddled away from the light. Now that I had a few seconds to examine them, I decided I liked them even less. I had no idea how these things survived, but they looked to be ambush predators: creatures that fed on blood but died easily enough. Judging from the corpse laid in the light, they also weren't possessed. Either they were something that supported the SporeMother, or something it permitted to live. I'd soon fix that either way.

I quickly brought up the Identify spell and cast it at one of them.

Scenttal

This creature is well known for its vicious stealth attacks, creating a magical cloud of darkness around itself as it hunts. They are highly prized as a source of alchemical ingredients but have given many a brave adventurer a final surprise.

Level: 7
Health: 40
Mana: 30

Congratulations!

You have killed a level 7 Scenttal for a total of 70xp.

Whatever the hell a scenttal was, it didn't have the DarkSpore identifier, so that was something at least. I leaned my naginata against the wall where I could grab it easily and grinned up at the small evil-looking creatures.

"My turn, you little bastards!" I grunted up at them, holding both hands out and casting one Firebolt after another. The spells flew from alternating hands to hammer into the creatures as they tried to hide. First one, then another, and finally, the third fell from the ceiling and curled up on the floor. They reminded me of spiders in the way their limbs seized up in death, the skull notifications cheering me up to no end. The last thing any world needed was more creatures that looked and acted like spiders.

I checked my mana, only to see it drop as Oracle cast another spell somewhere below me. I swore, sweeping up the naginata and setting off running again. I'd barely begun to recover my stamina, but as I staggered down the stairs, it plummeted again, settling as a faint green glimmer at the bottom of the bar as I finally exited onto the floor below.

Two of the windows were blown open, and the sunlight glaring in had trapped four undead in the middle of the room, with two trapped at the top of the stairs at the opposite end. Each time they stepped forward into the light, they would scream and jump back, their bones becoming more and more blackened.

Bob stood calmly near me, with Oracle sitting on his head, proud as punch about the way she'd managed to trap them on this floor.

As soon as I arrived, all six shifted to stare at me, and the glowing red in the pits of their eyes flared as they stared. They'd obviously had a change of orders, since they ignored my companions, staring at me with obvious hatred and hunger.

I stepped back out of sight and sank to the floor, panting as I tried to recover. My mana sat at twenty-three, and I needed fifty to cast Cleansing Flames. It looked like I was in for another stand-up fight, as I couldn't afford the time it would take to recover that much mana.

I pulled myself to my feet and called Oracle to me, telling her to stay back and be ready with the heals.

"Okay, motherfuckers, let's do this," I whispered and sent Bob racing forward. In true rugby style, as he closed on the enemy, he lowered himself and plowed into them. He lifted two clear off the ground and knocked the other two aside as he ran at the window. I'd told him to get them through the window however he could, and he did it by sheer power.

As he slammed into the far wall, he shoved the first one's head through the open window and pinned the second to the wall in a patch of sunlight by its throat as it stabbed and beat at him with a dagger. They died within seconds of each other, flames erupting from both as they fell apart, and skull symbols flared to life in my vision.

While Bob was busy immolating those two, I'd followed him in his run, stabbing another one through the chest, before abandoning the weapon and grabbing a fourth by its ankles. It had lost its weapon, and I used my enhanced strength to lift it from the ground as I started to spin. As it struggled against my grasp, I accelerated my spin before letting go and sending it flying with a clatter of bones down the corridor into the pair that stood waiting at the end.

I staggered, dizzy from spinning around, and went back to the last corpse to retrieve my naginata from where it protruded from its chest. I used the leverage to drive it into a patch of sunlight, holding it there while it shrieked and twisted in a desperate bid for escape. After another second, it was over, the DarkSpore exorcised from its host by the cleansing rays of the sun.

I let the remnants collapse to the floor as I extracted my weapon, kicking the ribcage free and turning to Bob.

He picked up his weapons and backed up, at my direction, to stand ready nearby. Oracle fluttered overhead as we prepared ourselves for the next leg of the fight. I stepped forward, moving into the light and angling my naginata blade until it reflected the sunlight straight at the undead. As soon as it hit them, they started scrambling back, trying to hide, and Bob struck.

He lunged forward with his spears, punching deep into their ribcages through rotten armor as his swords struck out at limbs. I swept the reflected light across their faces constantly, making them flinch and cower back while Bob dismantled them.

In a handful of seconds, both skeletons were stuck on his spears, literally disarmed. I took one spear, and he took the other, as we dragged them forward into the light. They joined the growing bone pile, and we set off again, with me staggering slightly and wheezing, while Bob powered on, the bastard.

The last revolution of stairs passed in a blur as we raced to reach Seneschal's growing barrier, but at last, it was there before us. I almost collapsed in relief and outright exhaustion. The distance from the top of the tower to this point was only a mile down the outside, but with the constant spirals, it was easily triple that, if not considerably more. Adding to that the strain of running in full armor and fighting...I was lucky I was still alive.

I staggered over to inspect the barrier, leaning on Bob for support. It was stone, or appeared to be, and grew out of the wall on either side of the doorframe to this level, hanging from seemingly solid stone hinges.

It looked like Seneschal was creating heavy overlapping stone doors that would swing together and drop into a recessed line on the floor, becoming almost impossible to lift and open from the far side. I watched them grow, struck by the realization that this must be what continental drift looked like. The rock on either side of the doorway wasn't visibly growing, but if I held something close to it, the shift became clear.

It was expanding a millimeter at a time, but constantly growing. I gave it a rough distance of around three feet left to grow until the two sides were complete. As the minutes passed, I finally managed to catch my breath and recover some more mana. As I was about to check my levels, Seneschal reached out to me again.

"The creature has escaped the trap we set, using its lesser minions as shields. I can sense their bodies still. They are twelve floors below you now and should reach you soon. The barrier will close the stairwell off in thirty-six minutes; you have to hold them until then."
"How many are there?"
"Unknown. At best estimate, forty, but this does not include the creature that leads them."
"Forty?!"
"There may be more or less. I judge it on the basis of weight crossing the floors in areas I can sense. Whatever leads them is blocking me from using my more advanced senses."
"Forty, seriously? We can't fight that many!"
"You have no choice, Jax, unless you wish to give up and die?"
"Well...yeah, right. Thanks for the fucking pep talk! Love you, too!"

I cut the connection, feeling the sense of his presence recede as I took a deep breath, my heart hammering like crazy. I checked my mana. I had enough for one use of Cleansing Fire, but I'd need more than that...I had to come up with something.

The only windows on this floor were behind me and wouldn't help. I glanced around frantically as I tried to plan. If only I had another couple mana potions! With those to refill my mana, I could afford to hammer out some spells to keep them back, but I didn't have any. The recipes I knew didn't work for the ingredients I had...I had only a few minutes, but maybe?

I pulled out the alchemy equipment, setting it to the side on the floor, and frantically laid out the ingredients. I searched my memory, bringing up the recipe for the minor mana potion.

Minor Mana Restoration Potion

- Labian leaves

- Manaberries

- Clear water

First, boil the water to remove all impurities. Grind the Manaberries into a thick paste and add to the boiling water. Stir three times and remove from heat. Leave to cool to room temperature. While the mixture cools, strip the interior from the Labian leaves and grind into a paste. Add a little of the mixture to the ground leaves as you work. When the paste has reached a thick consistency, smear it on the remaining sections of the leaves and boil for seven minutes before passing through a sieve and cooling. Bottle when completely cool.

I didn't have any manaberries, or labian leaves. *Fuck! Okay, okay, be cool…*

I hurriedly searched through the ingredients I did have before shrugging and pulling out a water canteen. I started picking ingredients at random, grinding them with the mortar and pestle and adding a little water before putting them in a vial. I'd make only the weakest versions of a potion by doing this, but it was all I had time to do.

I could hear the enemy approaching, so I ordered Bob to guard the barrier with his spears. He'd have to hold the line for now.

I had seventy-seven mana left, with the time it'd taken me to make the potions up, and Identify would cost me ten points per turn, so I had to hope I'd managed to make something useful. I could either chug them now, one after the other, and hope for the best and try to save the mana, or I could identify all of them, maybe wasting it, but definitely not poisoning myself. I swore and picked five out of the seven mixtures I'd made and cast on each. *Luck, don't fail me now…*

Failed Potion		Further Description *Yes/No*	
Details:		This mixture of ingredients holds no known alchemical properties	
Rarity:	**Magical:**	**Durability:**	**Charge:**
Trash	No	100/100	N/A

Failed Potion		Further Description *Yes/No*	
Details:		This mixture of ingredients holds no known alchemical properties	
Rarity:	**Magical:**	**Durability:**	**Charge:**
Trash	No	100/100	N/A

263

Weak Poison of Confusion		Further Description *Yes/No*	
Details:		This poison causes the debuff "confused" to afflict its victim, causing slowed reactions, confusion, an inability to cast spells and discern friend from foe for up to 30 seconds.	
Rarity:	**Magical:**	**Durability:**	**Charge:**
Common	No	100/100	N/A

Minor Stamina Boost Potion		Further Description Yes/No	
Details:		This potion boosts the user's stamina pool by 5% and regeneration by 2 points per minute for 5 minutes.	
Rarity:	**Magical:**	**Durability:**	**Charge:**
Uncommon	Yes	100/100	N/A

Unknown Potion		Further Description *Yes/No*	
Details:		This mixture of ingredients holds no known alchemical properties, yet you get the feeling it is a potion…or is it a poison?	
Rarity:	**Magical:**	**Durability:**	**Charge:**
?????	????	100/100	N/A

I didn't wait. I chugged the stamina boost potion in one gulp, quickly followed by the mana boost potion I'd found upstairs. Coolness spread through me, and I observed an immediate jump in my mana regeneration, with a much smaller jump in my stamina. I took a deep breath in relief. It wasn't all I'd been hoping for, but just maybe it'd keep me alive.

"Jax! They're here!" Oracle cried out, just as I finished downing them. I cursed, leaving everything strewn across the floor, and set off running to take my place alongside Bob. The pair of us stood before the doors, his spears lowered and my naginata ready.

The stairwell was narrow here, and with both of us standing side by side, there was little room, but I hoped it was our best chance.

"Oracle, can you cast Cleansing Fire?" I asked.

"Yes, Jax. Since we're bonded, I have access to all your spells."

"Okay, good. Be ready with it and let me know as soon as we have enough mana again to cast it. Beyond that, don't cast anything unless I tell you, okay?"

"But…but without mana, I can't help."

"Seriously, Oracle, if I need this spell, it will be better if you can cast that than a few Firebolts. Just stay back and wait for my signal, okay?"

"Yes, Jax," she said dejectedly, backing away from the front line. I heard her muttering under her breath as she went. "One Firebolt wouldn't make any difference, and he knows it's what I do best! He's just no fun…"

I shook my head at the daftness of the wisp, grinning to myself in spite of the danger. I could now hear what had alerted Oracle. A faint rattle from below had risen and was climbing steadily. What had started out as a clicking and rumbling had become the grating of bones, clattering, metal clashing, and an occasional roar of creatures as they ascended the final spiral of stairs to our position.

Bob and I positioned ourselves in the stairwell, which was wide enough for us both, where we stood on the far side of the barrier. I spun my naginata end over end, building momentum. Bob crouched, setting himself to receive the charge. The first to come into sight were a trio of skeletons, their bones clattering together as they ran. One with an axe came slightly ahead of its two compatriots, both armed with sword and shield.

I lunged forward, using the fast-moving weapon to slash the axe wielder's head from its body before spinning around low and sweeping the legs out from under the following two with the butt of my weapon.

I stepped back as Bob moved forward, stabbing down with swords and spears, smashing the skulls open to release the DarkSpore. As they started to rise, the inky blots of darkness buzzed in fury and hatred.

Before they could fully form, the next wave charged into the clouds, coating their lower legs and feet like they'd run through oil.

The next pair was another skeleton, clattering away, and what looked like a rogue type, heavily wrapped in the remnants of black leather. Jagged, torn, rotten flesh protruded through tears in the clothes; however the original owner of the body had died, it'd been hard.

As the skeleton moved toward me, the rogue leapt into the air, twisting itself around to kick Bob in the face and driving him back as the oily mess of the DarkSpore transferred willingly from its boots onto Bob's skull. The rogue pushed off, leaping back as Bob staggered under the kick, but before it landed fully, his spears were flashing out to pierce the rogue's armor.

Both spears punched clean through, their tips flashing in the low light of the stairwell. Meanwhile, I was deflecting a thrust from a rusty sword. I knocked it aside, grunting in pain as the skeleton's bony fingers scored burning lines across my face.

I released my weapon with my right hand and grabbed the skeleton by the throat, yanking it forward into a headbutt by reflex. It hurt me more than it could possibly have hurt a skeleton, but as I shoved it back, it lost its footing and tumbled down the stairs, one outstretched arm sweeping a scenttal from the wall where it was sneaking toward me. I brought my naginata around, stabbing out to catch another of the little bastards as I saw it racing up.

The scream of pain and sight of one leg going flying as the rest of the creature tumbled to the ground gave me a sense of satisfaction that was short-lived, but welcome, nonetheless. I even took the time to punt the little shit down the stairwell.

More and more creatures were coming, a mixture of skeletons, a handful of scenttal, and two bigger undead that reminded me of the adventurer I'd fought before. All of these rushed up the staircase, while Bob repeatedly stabbed into the rogue he had trapped on his spears. As he gradually dismembered it, the transferred DarkSpore seeped deeper into his bones, attempting to possess my creation.

Other DarkSpore spread free from the bodies we'd dismantled so far, and the hallway grew tighter and darker. I threw my thoughts to Seneschal, hoping he'd be able to hear me.

"How long until the barrier is ready?"
"Three minutes. It is almost complete, but I sense something big approaching."

I struck out, parrying a sword thrust, and backed up another stair. The sheer press of the undead was forcing us both back, step-by-step. I concentrated on demolishing as many of the undead as I could as Bob threw the ragged remains of the rogue back into the oncoming enemies.

He stabbed out with both spears and his swords, cutting and slashing to slow the onrushing tide as I backed further away, a rotting corpse leapt at me, only to be caught on my naginata as I twisted it sideways and slammed the fucker into the wall, bones snapping.

A flash of pain made me cry out in both surprise and agony as a claw opened the back of my neck. The blow caught the base of my helmet, tugging it out of place and across my eyes, blinding me. I grabbed it with one hand, trying to straighten it as I lashed out blindly, before giving up and hurling my helmet down the hallway.

I dodged a mace as it swung inches from my head, then a face out of a nightmare lunged at me.

It was heavily rotted, flesh falling from it even as its jaws opened wide to tear at me. Fangs unfolded as it lunged and tried to take my entire head into its mouth.

I cried out, flinging myself backwards as the jaws slammed shut before me with a click of teeth. Losing my footing, I fell back on the top few steps, landing hard on my back and staring in horror at the creature that was attacking me. I'd thought it was a regular skeleton, until it opened its abnormally wide mouth, but now that I looked properly, I recognized a creature of legend I'd always disliked, a naga.

It was a man above the waist, a dagger held in one hand, but below the waist, it was a snake. Thick bands of cartilage and bone enabled it to move with an uncanny speed and grace, even as decomposed as this one was.

It gathered itself as I braced my naginata across my chest, leaping the distance between us to pin me down. One hand grabbed the shaft of my weapon, while the other hand drew back and stabbed downwards with the dagger.

The blade skittered and screeched across my armored chest, lodging into my shoulder and cutting deep into the muscles of my arm. My pauldron seemed to guide the dagger to a vulnerable spot and catch it there, rather than protecting me. I screamed in pain and cried out to Oracle.

"Now! Cast it now!"

Instead of responding to me, Oracle flashed forward, her hands and lips twisting as she began to cast. I returned my attention to the naga, releasing my weapon and grabbing onto it. I tried to throw it back, only to feel its tail wrapping around me and tightening, binding itself to me as it lunged again and again.

It dove forward, its embedded dagger abandoned in favor of its clawed hands and fangs. The battle dissolved into a frantic wrestling match as I tried to dodge them all, grabbing its wrists in my hands as best I could.

I ordered Bob to push the rest back from the doors as far as he could. I sensed him surging forward, laying into all those near him and momentarily forcing them back, even as the DarkSpore began to take control of him.

The naga's fangs flashed forward again, and I threw myself to the side, screaming as I felt one puncture my ear, tearing flesh and cartilage free from my head in a spray of blood. At last, I managed to plant one foot firmly on the floor. I flipped us over, slamming the naga onto its back and releasing its wrist.

My right hand surged up, ignoring the claw-tipped hand that now flashed towards my face. As I forced my fingers through the rotten flesh of its throat, the remnants of flesh fell apart like slow-cooked meat as my fingers burrowed deeper…until I found the solidity of its spine.

I yanked my head aside, trying to avoid the trio of claws as they drove into my face, cutting into my cheek, muscles in my jaw twanging from being cut as they ripped deeper.

Feeling the bone underneath my fingers, I grasped it and heaved with all my strength. First one and two, then dozens of strands of flesh and desiccated sinew snapped. I tore the spine free, watching its head come loose as the body began to lose all control. Its digging fingers suddenly spasmed and went limp. I tore the head free with one almighty jerk, roaring in pain and triumph, and hurled it into the stairwell.

The fingers ripped from my face in a spurt of blood and ribbons of flesh as I fell backwards. Meanwhile, something huge battered Bob aside. He smashed into the wall, mobbed by lesser undead attempting to butcher him while the creature lumbered closer.

It filled the stairwell, rubbing against the walls on either side, having to force its way up, but still casually crushing a scenttal under one foot as the thing failed to move fast enough to dodge.

It was the SporeMother.

My heart seized up in my throat. It was fucking *huge*, easily eight feet across and twenty high. The tip of its head brushed the top of the low ceiling, and it seemed to be made of smoke and nightmares. Its skin was black and green, with pale, mottled patches that revealed pulsing veins. It somehow seemed to disappear into the shadows as though the darkness protected it.

It hunched down, bringing its long, triangular, prow-shaped head closer as it forced its way partially onto the floor and from the stairwell. Dozens of eyes, laid out in a V shape, ran from one side of the skull to the other. Some focused on me, others peered around the room, and still more showed the pale milky hue of blindness. Its mouth slowly opened in a smile, displaying broken teeth, blackened with age, that were as long as my fingers. A blood-red tongue flashed across them, and I felt a mind that radiated with age and evil reach out and touch my own.

"What is this…a tasty morsel? You have cost me slaves, little fleshling! You will pay for that, but the power filling my nest; oh yes, this is sweet, indeed…"

I tried to move, pushing myself backwards, but one massive, taloned limb slammed down onto my stomach, driving the air from me. A finger to either side of my chest held me in place as the middle one tapped slowly on my armor.

"Ah, ah! No, you don't get to creep away now, my pet. You are mine!"

The talon that had been tapping on my chest stopped. Pressing the tip into the center of my breastplate, she slowly began to push, piercing her way into the metal.

With a loud noise, the metal began to deform under the pressure, buckling inwards. I groaned, grabbing onto the claw and trying to force it back. I might as well have tried to lift the tower itself.

A second arm lashed out suddenly, idly backhanding Oracle as she neared the end of the spell, breaking the spellform before it was completed and hurling her across the room to smash into one wall. The little wisp slumped to the ground, dazed.

The claw finally pierced my armor, the tip digging into my flesh, and a rib broke under the force. I screamed in pain as it began to cut down across my chest diagonally from under my left nipple toward my belly button. She laughed as she scooped me up, raising me from the floor to dangle in her grip as she stared into my eyes. Her tongue slowly slipped out to lap blood from my cheek before disappearing back into her maw.

"Tasty! We've not fed in soooo long, barely a morsel here and there. But you, sweet, sweet meat, with blood so red and full of potential, you will make a perfect host for a new brood!"

As she spoke, she emerged further from the stairwell. Fully half of her body was now inside the room, and my agonized eyes saw her for what she was. A monstrous spider's body, bulbous and multi-legged, carried a thick insectile torso, topped with a blunt, wedge-shaped head.

Her dozens of eyes arced back in a row above the mouth, climbing a frill reminiscent of a triceratops, complete with sharply tipped bones protruding all around the edge. Two smaller arms extended from the torso, one gripping me and the other clamped onto the edge of the doorway to steady herself as she slowly pushed herself further through.

Burned patches remained where the sun had managed to touch her on her way up to this floor. I observed the creature's hatred of the light in the way she glared at the open windows further down the hall before focusing on my chest.

"What's this? Something hidden...what is it?"

I felt the full horror of such an ancient evil focusing on me entirely. This thing had killed thousands, had been alive before Columbus had sailed the seas of my world, and men far better than me had fallen to her. That thought sparked a flare of anger, and I glared into her eyes, making her pause as she lowered her head, getting closer to my face.

"Well, little fleshling? Nothing to say, no pleas for mercy?"

I opened my mouth, feeling it sag on one side from the injuries I'd taken already, and I spat blood out before speaking up. "Beg you? Fuck, no. Ya can suck it, ya big jobbie!"

"...Jobbie?"

"Shit! You're a giant turd, floating in life's toilet!" I wheezed at her, moaning in pain as she squeezed me harder. The finger under my chin pushed into my throat as I fought for breath.

"It tries to anger us. Many have tried. Death will be slow for you, mortal, but first...what do you hide?

She dug deeper, the tip of her claw flicking and peeling the front of my armor aside, another smaller pair of arms that hung below the larger ones reaching out and pulling at the metal. The bigger claw cut deeper, through the remains of my armor, my padded undergarments and tearing fresh lines in my flesh, until...

Her claw impacted the edge of the Baron's rune, the one he'd carved into my flesh and filled with unholy energy. She sensed it just as her claw impacted it, and then it was too late as the energy broke containment.

The rune seemed to explode, ripping energy from my chest to punish any that dared interfere with its master's design. A lightning bolt, or so it seemed, hit the SporeMother.

"IT BURNS!"

Her claw disintegrated as the energy lashed out, hammering into her body and knocking her back onto the ground, stunned.

I lay on the floor for a handful of seconds, trying to make sense of what had just happened as the backlash of energy coursed through my already weakened body. Thankfully, whatever the Baron had done was obviously intended to punish whoever broke the spell, not me.

The second effect of breaking the rune was that *he* was released, and he came crashing back into my mind with the force of a freight train, scattering my barely coherent thoughts.

KILLITKILLITKILLITTrespasserItShouldBeDeadShouldAllBeDeadKillI TKILLITKILLIT

As the voice filled my head, I reached into my bag. My only thought was to find something to help heal me, though I'd no idea what I'd find.

As I fumbled, the voice hammered into my reeling brain again, more aware than it had been in the past.

There!IsItTrueItIsHeHasItUseItUseItUseIt!

My half-formed call into my bag for something to heal me was overruled by the far louder call of the voice as it saw something it wanted, and something filled my hand. I pulled it free and stared at the faint, silvery light radiating out from my fingers in confusion.

Silverbright...SoLongItsBeenSoLongSinceWeSawHer...use it! Use it now, you fool!

The voice became more coherent, seeming to speak clearly for the first time. The madness that usually filled it was lessening somehow, and I saw a prompt flash up. My usual desire for the prompts to stay out of the way was overruled by someone else.

???? wishes to share memories with you.

Will you accept a mind link from ????

Yes/No

I blinked in confusion as the words swam in and out of clarity. It overrode me, selecting before I could refuse, the middle of a battle no place for this shit. I fought to make sense of it all as the memories began. Oracle wasn't the one making contact this time.

It was another mind, much older, and much more broken than I could have ever realized.

A stream of memories flooded my mind, most flashing past too fast to understand. I sensed they were being directed, the mind that was linked to mine focusing tighter, until the perspective changed to cave high in the mountains. A trio of huge figures towered around us while our servants and guard huddled in the lower halls. Their magic was barely enough to keep them safe, even as my own deflected the atmosphere to make it comfortable without effort.

We knelt before her. Our oldest friend lay dying; the birth had strained her beyond measure, coming so close after the battle with the Valspar. She had barely the strength to reach the mountain. Others of her race had flown as swiftly as they could, but all had arrived too late. We, to our eternal shame, hadn't even heard the call. The soldier responsible for monitoring the beacon had taken word to his liege lord first, and Sanguis had waited until we'd awoken the next morning.

There would be consequences for this, we silently vowed, as tears ran down our face and soaked our beard.

She lay there, her breathing labored and coming in short pants. Bloody foam covered her mighty lips, as yellowed teeth like greatswords slowly slid out of view and vanished. We remembered Her as she had been when we had first bonded, strength beyond compare, beaten only by her majesty. Impetuosity of youth had filled us both as we swore to always be there for one another.

And we'd failed her...She was dying because we'd slept the sleep of a drunkard and missed her call for aid.

Others had been dispatched to erase the stain of the Valspar from the land in retribution, but that wouldn't help Shustic 'Amon, Ruler of Dragon's Reach, soul-bonded to the Emperor, and new mother to a brace of three eggs. Eggs that could be the future of her race would now grow up without the love of a mother, if they survived at all, as premature as they were.

The memory changed, following conversations between our self and the towering figures of the other dragons. Accusations, anger, and recriminations were thrown back and forth.

The knowledge that if we were any other mortal, we would have ended as a meal, rather than forcing them to kneel in supplication or to flee our rage.

More memories flashed, and Shustic spoke, charging all of us to protect her children, to raise them and protect them. She could barely speak, and still, she tried to soothe our heartbreak at her passing. The barriers between our minds dissolved in our shared despair.

We felt as though we'd never be able to cry another tear, our eyes scratchy from hours upon hours of flowing. Even now, she thought of others.

We wept, barely able to choke out our words as we stroked her cheek. We swore upon our soul that we'd protect them, raise them as she would have, and gift them a better world to fly in.

We imbued our vow with all of the mana we had, sensing the changes that came from such a vow, and we glimpsed her final smile.

Hours more passed as she slept, waking intermittently as her once-legendary strength slowly declined. Toward the end, she awoke briefly and struggled to speak before reaching out with a tentative mind link to us all. She gave gifts to us, sharing knowledge to be returned to her children when they were old enough. To us, she gave one more gift, and it was one that had never been given to a mortal before.

She gave of her body. The Great Dragons usually ate their dead, growing far stronger from the terrifyingly mana-rich bodies, and they hunted any other creature that dared to do so, with a rage that rivaled the gods. She gave us three vials of her heart's blood and her right foreleg, scales that could reflect lava, bones stronger than diamond and all.

When she breathed her last, we accepted her gifts and departed from the mountain, leaving Tuthic'Amon, her mate, to guard the eggs. We swore that an entire legion would be dispatched to the mountain to serve and protect the dragons while we brought peace to the surrounding lands.

The memory ended then, as we used our magic to transport our followers and our self back to the empire, our storage heavy with her gifts, and our heart heavier.

My brain kicked back into gear, soul-shredding grief filling me as I looked down at the vial I held, filled with her heart's blood. A sound drew my attention to the SporeMother as it shifted in the corner, still recovering from the surprise attack of the rune…and I was livid!

This creature, this descendant of the Valspar, dared to exist?! It dared to live, let alone trespass in one of *my* creations?!

I could feel Him now, his thoughts resonating with my own. Our anger reinforced one another, feeding it, building it even as we forced ourselves to our feet.

Our mana and body were weak, our spells pathetic as we remembered destroying entire continents with a single powerful creation, but for this? To erase this creature from existence, all we needed was already here.

I reached out, my Manatouch spell grasping my naginata and catapulting it across the room to slam into my right hand. With a thought, it popped the cork from the bottle, and I poured it onto the blade.

I flooded what was left of my mana into the Silverbright as it seeped into the metal of my weapon. A steady, strong glow emanated from it as the weapon began to change.

The SporeMother lifted from the ground, glaring at me in anger.

CHAPTER TWENTY-FOUR

S atisfaction radiated from Oracle, mixed with concern at the changes she sensed in me. She'd taken advantage of the distraction, though. Whatever we had become after He and I shared our memories, it had resulted in a drop in mana needed to cast, as well as the time needed, and she'd managed to get off the Cleansing Fire spell at last.

The flames radiated out from her, as she was closest to the creature, filling the surrounding area and burning into the SporeMother even as they began to heal me. The ancient nightmare tried to back away, only to find she had partially wedged herself in the doorway when she had come for me.

"C'mere, bitch!" I wheezed out, hefting my naginata in one hand, and gesturing with my weakened left hand. "C'mere, and let me fuck you right up…"

I was close to death from my injuries, and my mana was too low to cast anything useful. I didn't expect to live, so I resolved to sell my life dearly. She slammed her right arm down, and I fell to one knee and braced the naginata across my chest, taking the full force of her attack on its haft.

Her hand closed around the gently glowing weapon, and the tiny amount of mana I had remaining was sucked from me, filling it. She screamed, and my eardrums vibrated with the violence of her pain.

The naginata flared to life; runes that had never existed before glowed brightly against the night, and they *burned* into her. Her hand blackened, closing in reflex as it had, she couldn't open it fast enough. Light ate its way into her. Her skin lost the nightmarish, smoke-like texture as she became fully solid, no longer able to phase in and out of reality. The veins leading from her blackened hand filled with light, slowly seeping up her arm as her fingers charred and fell off.

Her other hand flashed out, smashing me from my feet to crumple into the far wall. My naginata clattered away across the floor, and the light cut off. The SporeMother was badly injured, and her eyes blazed in anger and bloodlust, even as she ignored the devastation that the Cleansing Fire spell was inflicting on her.

I rolled to all fours, coughing blood onto the floor, and grabbed my hidden daggers from the sheaths in both bracers as I forced myself to my feet.

One way or another, only one of us was walking away from this fight. I felt His approval with that thought. I bled heavily, the Cleansing Fire's healing aspect the only thing keeping me from death already.

"Come on, bitch," I ground out weakly, spitting a glob of blood onto the floor and gesturing with my blades to the SporeMother. "Daddy's got something for ya!"

With that, I drove myself forward, ducking under a swing from the near-useless club limb of her right arm and leaped, bracing on one of her lower legs and kicking off, jumping up and slamming both daggers into her face.

My left dagger, held by my weak and injured left arm, skittered across the skin, cutting but not carving deeply enough before my grip gave out, and it fell. However, my right blade struck true, digging into one of her bulbous eyes.

I held onto the dagger as the creature whipped its head back and screamed in pain, yanking me from side to side as I ripped through nearby eyes, dangling by one arm before being slammed into the wall.

I slumped to the floor, spotting the dirk hanging from the SporeMother's face as she hunched down again, trying to get free of the doorway. She'd obviously decided enough was enough and was pulling back. As she tried to retreat, Bob, or what remained of him, jumped onto her back. His single working arm drove a sword deep into her body and caused her to scream in pain again. I grinned at the summoned minion's moxie and forced myself to my feet, wheezing.

My chest felt like a vice had gripped it, but I stumbled forward. Bob continued stabbing her as the flames of Cleansing Fire scoured the DarkSpore from him and further injured the SporeMother. I looked around for a weapon, finding my naginata off to one side. I lunged forward, sweeping up the weapon before staggering to my feet.

I braced the weapon as best I could. Blood dripped from numerous wounds, my chest partially crushed and my armor all that seemed to be holding me together. My face was a mess of torn flesh and exposed teeth and bone. I knew there was only one thing I could say at this point.

"LEEEEROY JEEEENNNNKINS!" I hissed out. A liquid burbling noise accompanied my cry as blood started to fill one lung, and I half-ran, half-staggered forward.

I kicked off a step and jumped, putting all my strength into my last push, and stabbed with the naginata. Its razor-sharp blade pierced the SporeMother's chest and sank deep. She collapsed backwards, her attention focused on Bob. As her face swiveled around to see me, her multiple eyes widened in pain and terror.

The blade of my naginata was half-buried in her chest as a silvery white light bloomed forth, filling the stairwell and banishing all shadows. Her legs spasmed, collapsing under her, and we fell backwards. A claw tip pierced my right thigh, and bones broke as her body rolled over me. We clattered down the stairwell, round and round, until I lost consciousness.

My final thought as the darkness took me was that the bitch hadn't known who she was fucking with.

I drifted for some time, no clue how long, buffeted by pain and encroaching white light, numbness filling me, and cold. There was muttered madness from the voice and confused images of the dragons filling my mind, until She was there.

A great silver dragon, huge and imposing, bigger than the largest jets I'd ever seen, and projecting…warmth and…amusement?

"YOU DID WELL, LITTLE ONE." Her voice was…kind? I felt warm as she leaned in closer and breathed over me, a sudden tingling and burning sensation building and flowing through me as flesh that was dying was forced back to life.

"AMON IS WEAK AND LOST. HE DOES NOT, OR *CANNOT* RESPOND TO ME, AND SO I CHARGE YOU TO PROTECT AND GUIDE HIM UNTIL HE IS READY TO REJOIN ME."

I mumbled something, not understanding, staring up at her, knowing that this, this dragon, was long dead, but had still saved me somehow. I blinked, and the darkness rolled in again, the last sight I had of her, the glow of eyes I could have stood inside.

It was Oracle's voice that I heard first as I drifted in the darkness. A whispering sound slowly built, until I recognized it as conversation, even if it was a one-sided one.

"No, Bob, slower!"

"..."

"I know you've only got one arm! Do I look blind? Just free that clasp!"

"..."

"Pull it free, that's it!"

"..."

Then I felt something, a sudden wrenching pain. As weak as I was, I felt something come free. My chest felt like a weight was lifted as the breastplate was removed. I gasped and coughed, blood spraying from my mouth and pain roaring through me as I came fully awake.

"It's okay, Jax! We've got it. Just try to relax!"

A healing spell enveloped me again, and I winced as my chest was rearranged by the magic. After a second, something popped, and my bones began to shift. I screamed, finally able to get enough air to make a sound loud enough to echo through…wherever I was, before passing out again.

The next time I awoke, I was more lucid, with a gently glowing Oracle resting on my chest and peering into my eyes. As soon as I focused on her, she smiled and straightened up, wiping her eyes as though brushing aside tears and visibly relaxing.

"Jax, do you know where you are? Are you okay? We nearly lost you!" she whispered, leaning forward to stroke my face with one tiny hand.

I frowned, trying to recognize where I was. Long, thin columns rose all around me, and the room was dark, but light shone down from a stairwell to my right, and there were piles of bones everywhere. It seemed to take a few seconds, but as I focused on one of the columns nearest me, it resolved. In the way a picture can be a young woman or an old witch, depending on perspective, I watched the column become a long, chitinous leg, curled up in death. My eyes widening, I stared around, discovering that they were surrounding me, and my mind kicked into high gear. I rolled over and kicked myself free, lunging to my feet as Oracle flew aside with a squawk of annoyed protest.

I'd been laid out on the underside of the SporeMother, her curled legs forming a loose cage around me. I found Bob standing to one side, watching me, and Oracle flew over to sit on his skull as I looked around the room in shock. I was alive, Oracle and even Bob had survived, and the SporeMother was dead!

"How…what?" I muttered, my hands going to my chest, then my face and arm in turn. All were healed, and my mana bar was slowly refilling, even as notifications flashed for my attention.

"We did it, Jax! We killed the SporeMother!" Oracle crowed, leaping to her feet and starting to dance on Bob's head, swaying, sultry movements that were interspersed with poses straight out of 'Saturday Night Fever'.

I dropped my gaze from her to Bob, who was standing impassively with a dagger jutting out between some ribs. A sword stuck out from his lower chest, held in place by bones that had trapped it. Dozens of cracks covered the bones that were mostly whole, while other sections of him…well, almost an entire third of his mass was missing.

If he'd been alive to start with, he'd never have stood a chance. As it was, he stood there unconcernedly, watching me and waiting for another command. Scanning the rest of the room, I discovered that it was as I'd expected. My quick glance was enough to pick out bones freed of the taint of the DarkSpore. I looked back to Oracle, and she grinned at me.

"That's right, Jax! We killed them! The Cleansing Fire stripped the corruption from all the lesser creatures, and whatever you did to the SporeMother, you killed her, too! I used Bob to get your armor off and to straighten you out as best I could, then I healed you! Aren't you proud of me?"

I shook my head in confusion, before catching myself and speaking up as a hurt expression appeared on her face.

"I mean, yes, of course I am!" I assured her, before breaking off and coughing before going on. "Sorry, Oracle; it's just a bit of a shock, you know? I…I don't remember much of it. It all happened so fast, and that potion, the Silverbright…it was *Her* blood," I whispered, memories flooding back to me as I searched my mind for Him. He was back from wherever He'd been locked away, but whatever He'd done to support me had left Him exhausted.

"Who's 'she'? And that magic, Jax! Whatever it was, it was *awesome!*"

I grinned tiredly back at her, then looked down at the SporeMother's corpse, which had shriveled up in death much like a spider would. My flashing notifications finally filled my mind's eye as I let them expand.

Congratulations!

Through hard work and perseverance, you have gained points to the following stats, continue to train and learn to raise them further.

Agility +1
Dexterity +1

I smiled as I saw that the battle had raised my Agility and Dexterity again, more points in those stats were always nice. The next prompts were all experience and kill prompts, so I dismissed them in favor of the kill prompt from the SporeMother.

Congratulations!

You have killed a level ?? SporeMother for a total of 12,600xp.
Progress to level 6 stands at 14,350/6,500

Congratulations!

You have reached level 6.
You have 5 unspent Attribute points and 0 unspent Meridian points.
Progress to level 7 stands at 7,850/14,000

You have achieved progress in your Quest: A Place to Lay Your Head

Wisps sworn fealty: 2/3
Locations cleared and secured: 2/5
SporeMother killed: 1/1
Guardians claimed: 0/10
Workers claimed: 0/10

Rewards: The Great Tower is yours to command. The surrounding area will become aware of your rightful ownership. Access to supplies and facilities. 100,000xp.

I blinked, dismissing my notifications, and brought up my stats page. I called out to Oracle as I read the text.

"Hey, Oracle, you said I couldn't use any more skillbooks or spellbooks for a while. How soon could I learn another one? I know it hasn't been long, but I've leveled again, so come on, give me good news!"

She flitted over to me, sitting on my shoulder and putting one hand flat against my temple.

"Good try, Jax. It's been two days since I said that. Seriously. You can learn another spell in about four weeks' time, by your calendar, and that's only if you get plenty of rest and some very specific healing. A skill memory, well…not yet. I'm sorry, but it will probably cause you permanent damage if you try, and the majority of the knowledge would be lost."

"Damn. I could have done with some memories from a damn alchemist, that's for sure," I muttered, going back to my stats.

"Well, there's nothing to stop you from experimenting and learning on your own, then hopefully, you can add the skill memories over the top later. That way, you might even retain more than a normal aspirant would!"

"Meh, I'd still rather have it now," I muttered, looking at my details. My Charisma and Luck were by far my lowest stats, and I had five spare points to use, but where to put them. I could use them to boost my mana pool, or mana regeneration; I could make myself faster or stronger. It really came down to my build, in the end. I could be a jack of all trades, or a glass cannon dealing tremendous damage but unable to take it.

I liked the idea of the glass cannon build. The power I could get eventually by doing that was amazing, but despite having Bob, and despite planning to let him take the lead in fights, I still found myself in the middle of it. I needed to stick to what I'd planned before by putting my points into areas I couldn't develop as easily on my own and exercising for the rest. I took a deep breath, and dumped all five points into Luck, boosting it from twelve to seventeen. While I checked over the details one last time, the world around me seemed to shake slightly in response to my choices, but thankfully no pain this time.

Name: Jax				
Class: Spellsword			**Renown**: Unknown	
Level: 6			**Progress**: 7,850/14,000	
Patron: Jenae, Goddess of Fire and Exploration			**Points to Distribute**: 0 **Meridian Points to Invest**: 0	
Stat	**Current points**	**Description**	**Effect**	**Progress to next level**
Agility	17	Governs dodge and movement	+70% maximum movement speed and reflexes	17/100
Charisma	11	Governs likely success to charm, seduce, or threaten	+10% success in interactions with other beings	64/100
Constitution	15	Governs health and health regeneration	280 health, regen 8.25 points per 600 seconds, (+10% regen due to soul bond, -20 health due to soul bond, each point invested now worth 20 health)	92/100
Dexterity	17	Governs ability with weapons and crafting success	+70% to weapon proficiency, +7% to the chances of crafting success	23/100
Endurance	17	Governs stamina and stamina regeneration	170 stamina, regen 7 points per 30 seconds	38/100
Intelligence	15	Governs base mana and number of spells able to be learned	130 mana, spell capacity: 10 (8 + 2 from items), (-20 mana due to soul bond)	86/100
Luck	17	Governs overall chance of bonuses	+70% chance of a favorable outcome	45/100
Perception	18	Governs ranged damage and chance to spot traps or hidden items	+80% ranged damage, +8% chance to spot traps or hidden items	50/100
Strength	19	Governs damage with melee weapons and carrying capacity	+9 damage with melee weapons, +90% maximum carrying capacity	65/100
Wisdom	20 (15)	Governs mana regeneration and memory	+100% mana recovery, 2 points per minute, 100% more likely to remember things	98/100

I grimaced; putting the points into something that I'd never be sure was working was always going to suck. I shrugged and reverted to my habit whenever I encountered an issue I couldn't fix with my fists: I forgot about it and moved on. I searched the SporeMother first, Oracle healing me again and again until I was back to full health, but I found no wealth or usable gear. There was, however, a large selection of potion ingredients that I packed away carefully.

You have found:

- SporeMother Eyes x19
- SporeMother Venom Gland x6
- SporeMother Kidney x2
- SporeMother Liver x1
- SporeMother Essence Core x1
- SporeMother Brain x1.

I had no idea what an essence core was, but figured it'd probably come in handy somewhere along the line. Looking poor Bob over, I could tell he really needed an upgrade. The poor bugger was barely able to stand upright. I laced my fingers together and cracked them, shaking my hands out and grinning at him, seeing that my mana had nearly refilled again already, the time taken to gut that fucker having been longer than I thought.

"Upgrade time, Bob!"

I ordered Bob to stand in the middle of the room, surrounded by the bones and remains of the fight, casting Raise Weak Skeletal Minion on him.

I channeled my mana continuously as I rebuilt him. Bones lifted on waves of magic as I picked them out from around the room, old fleshy connections falling apart, new ones forged by my will alone.

When I finished, Bob stood straight again, once more on two legs, but far stronger, thicker legs than before. He was at least twice as broad as he had been, humanoid in shape, but built for war. His four arms and two legs were made of multiple overlapping bones, his torso enhanced with layers upon layers of ribs, and his skull had been replaced with that of the naga, giving him a fearsome bite.

I'd considered using the SporeMother's head, but that was still a bit too raw for me, and I needed to be able to relax with Bob around. Plus, it was far too big for his body right now. In addition to his four arms, two upper and two lower, he now had two of the SporeMother's shorter spiked legs attached to his back as flexible chitinous spears, ready to stab out. I had also given him a tail, made up of dozens of spinal columns fused together and tipped with a scenttal's bladed arm.

He looked fucking terrifying, and I loved it. As soon as I finished my creative experimentation, which took nearly all of my mana again, I received another series of prompts.

Congratulations!

You have raised your spell Raise Weak Skeleton to level 5...6...8.

Once this spell reaches level 10, you may choose its first evolution.

Your creation Bob has survived long enough to earn an upgrade!

UnderVerse: Brightblade

Choose from the following options:

Level 1 Upgrades:

Augmented Defense
Strengthen your creation's physical form to increase its resistance to damage by 10%.

Magical Resistance
Grant your creation increased resistance to arcane effects and damage by 10%.

Skeletal Minion
Grant your creation a basic level of sentience, enabling it to carry out simple tasks without direct supervision.

I didn't even pause. As soon as I read the options, I chose the Skeletal Minion perk and confirmed it.

Bob could always be a little harder to kill; it was a rabbit hole to disappear down, and while arcane resistance would be great, to have him able to act and react on his own? That was awesome.

I decided to test his upgrade by telling him to collect all the loot together on one side of the room for me while I went back up the stairs with Oracle to check on the barrier we'd been building.

"Seneschal, you able to hear me, buddy?"
"I can hear you, Jax."
"Can you sense anything else in the tower, now that bitch is dead?"
"I cannot sense anything else in the tower itself—"
"Booyah!"
"—but I can only extend my senses to the seventh level. The final manawell must be claimed by you to allow me full access to the tower's lower and subterranean floors."
"Crap...so there could be anything left down there still. Another SporeMother, or who knows what!"
"Unlikely. A creature such as the SporeMother would not permit a rival to survive near its nest. There may be other slave species nearby that have escaped detection until now, such as scenttal burrows, but beyond that, the area appears clear at this time."
"Crap! Okay. The barrier, it's ready now, right?"
"Yes, Jax, it can be sealed at any time."
"Well, keep it ready just in case. I'll look it over and collect my gear then check over the loot Bob has found. Once I've done that, it's time for food and rest, then setting off for the last wisp."

I disconnected from Seneschal, the sense of his mind fading as Oracle flew silently alongside me. We hurried up the stairs, spiraling around and around. I stepped over loose bones and the occasional bit of leather or detritus that had fallen from the undead as we went.

279

Finally, we reached the pair of freshly grown stone slabs that sat to either side of the doorway leading to the Hall of Memories. Looking them over, I could see how they would move, sliding almost effortlessly into place, then dropping down into grooves cut into the walls and floor.

Forming an overlapping plate, they would fully cover the passage before a final growth of stone would seal them in place against any attempts to move them. It would be as easy to rip the stones out of the ceiling or wall with bare hands as it would be to move this barrier once it was in place.

I grinned and returned down the stairs to Bob, pleased to find that he'd piled everything up that was noteworthy. He was waiting patiently and hefting a pair of swords, one in either upper hand, while the lower ones held daggers. Damn, he looked lethal now.

I checked over the gear, disappointed that most of it was junk. My breastplate was beyond repair, so I replaced it with the one I'd been wearing on my arrival. I also found a dozen silver coins, three copper, and a silver ring set aside for me.

Beyond that was some armor that had most of the previous inhabitant still rotted to the inside, or weapons that were frankly crap, covered in rust and chipped so badly they'd likely shatter with one good blow.

Last of all, I collected the dirks I'd used, sheathing them in their hidden slots and scooping up my naginata. As I lifted the weapon, something caught my eye. In addition to the usual brilliant gleam of steel, the blade seemed…different.

I found my water skin and used it to wash the blade clean, but the steel blade was altered somehow. Rather than the dull gleam I had come to expect, it now had the brilliant shine of silver. As I turned the blade this way and that, a pattern moved, almost like a sluggish liquid, but it remained bound within the form the blade had always held.

I tried spinning it then working through some experimental jabs and blows before bringing it in close to examine it again. The silverbright potion I'd used had somehow altered the weapon. It was still solid—banging it with a fist proved that—but the metal itself seemed to slowly shift as though contained within an invisible mold.

"Hey, Oracle!" I called out, holding my weapon out to her as she flew over. "What do you think of this?" I watched as she alighted on the haft and looked into the blade as though mesmerized.

"It…it's beautiful!" she said, gently touching it with one outstretched hand. When she was sure it was solid, she tried pressing on it and hitting it herself. "What happened to it?"

"Well, I was kinda hoping you knew!" I muttered, checking my mana. I nearly had enough. As soon as it had replenished to ten points, I cast Identify and began to grin.

Naginata		Further Description *Yes/No*	
Damage:		24-40 +6	
Details:		This two-handed weapon was built from a combination of modern Earth techniques and traditional Japanese skills, creating a weapon that is truly deadly in the hands of a skilled user. *Enhanced: This weapon has been enhanced through its contact with Silverbright and has absorbed some of the souls of its victims. Current capacity: 6/100* **Bonus ability granted**: *Please select from the options.*	
Rarity:	**Magical:**	**Durability:**	**Charge:**
Unique	Yes	87/100	N/A

"Okay, so what; the potion turned it into a vampire weapon?" I asked Oracle. "No! It evolved it! It's made it into an evolving weapon, somehow? Everything you kill with it should make it stronger, and the first creature you fed it was an ancient SporeMother! A creature that had killed thousands in her time!"

"Okay, so the 'soul' of that thing, for want of a better word, filled six slots in the naginata, and it now does six more damage than it did before. Everything I kill with it is going to increase the damage I do with it? That's awesome! If I get it to a hundred, even killing weak-ass things, I'll be unstoppable! And there's a bonus ability…" I concentrated on the bonus option, and it expanded before me, offering three choices:

Bonus Weapon Ability	Effect	Level
Health Bonus	Increase your base health by X, where X is the amount of soul slots filled.	1
Magical Infusion	Casting your spells through this weapon will infuse it with that spell for the duration of channeling and cause X damage, where X is equal to the damage done by the cast spell.	1
Pain	Cause additional phantom pain from strikes with this weapon, distracting your enemies and making it harder to cast spells.	1

"Okay, that's just confusing," I muttered. "So, if I chose the health bonus, since the weapon has six soul slots filled, I'd get a boost of six to my health? That's crap!"

"Jax, it's an evolving weapon. This is at level one; if you select one of these traits, then get enough soul energy to level it again, it might double, or more! Imagine if you leveled it to ten, to gain ten times the soul energy stored. Get it to a hundred, and you'd have an extra thousand health!"

"Or, more importantly, I could do a fuck-ton of magical damage. If we'd had this earlier, the SporeMother wouldn't have stood a chance. Or, if I'd infused my naginata with fire, I could have killed DarkSpore with ease. Holy shit! Wait, this could be seriously overpowered. Not that I'm complaining, you understand, but if I can do this, surely other people could as well?"

"Whatever that silverbright is, it isn't listed in any of the books I know. I'd never heard of it before. But you can't waste the capacity on weak enemies; imagine the difference if you used it only on stronger enemies! Oh, wow!"

She suddenly gasped, grabbing her cheeks and staring at me with wide eyes. Her voice dropped to a mere whisper. "Do you know what this means?"

"Wait, what did you just think of?" I asked, grinning at her.

"Armor!" she squealed. "Imagine what you could do if you made armor like this! Stealth gear that could make you truly invisible! Or heavy armor that would be invulnerable! What could stop you? You could find Tommy; you could kill anyone that tried to stop you! You could become a god!"

She trailed off into a whisper again, hands covering her mouth as she stared at me. I frowned at her, my mind caught up in the possibilities. I'd be lying if I said that didn't make the pickle tingle; the thought of being a god, maybe going back to Earth and gutting the Baron and his kind...but no. I could imagine the kind of path I'd end up going down if I set out with the aim of becoming a god.

"When power becomes all-important, the ends justify the means." I whispered to myself. I didn't know where I'd heard that, or if I'd just bastardized a quote, but it was true, nonetheless.

I remembered snatches of the memories of Her that I'd been given and resolved not to spread the knowledge of Her gifts. Even as I felt my heart ache in memory of Her death, I also realized that the Oath we had sworn had transferred to me. Looking back, I wasn't even sad about it. She deserved it, and more, even if I'd never really known her.

I'd come here for Tommy, and to help the people I'd spent my life Dreaming about. Power without a good reason was pointless, but growing stronger to protect them? That, I could do.

I pondered the choices again. Health would be a huge help, especially considering how close I'd come to death so far. And pain...well, it would be useful as a distraction, but it felt wrong.

No, the best choice for me was Magical Infusion, upgrading my weapon into a magical one. I selected it and grinned as the entire length of my naginata flashed with silvery light.

You have chosen Magical Infusion as your weapon evolution.

CHAPTER TWENTY-FIVE

W e ate a little food and drank some water, checked over our weapons, and made sure my armor was as ready as it could be, then descended deeper into the tower. As we went lower, I found that the tower spread out considerably, going from dozens of meters across to hundreds. Either the Baron or Sintara had told me the base was over half a mile across.

The mind boggled at that, half a fucking mile across? I tried to work it out, my mind fumbling at the barely remembered edges of lessons from ages ago, before giving up. Either way, a half-mile-wide base had to have a truly insane number of rooms.

The occasional level with a garden was badly overgrown, and most of the rooms we passed had been destroyed. Here and there, I found piles of rubble, and Oracle dipped to them now and then, resting a hand on them regretfully.

"What are they?" I asked as she mumbled a benediction, before lifting back into the air to land on my shoulder.

"The remains of the tower's war golems," she whispered sadly. "I only had a little contact with them, but several were imbued with the memories of great legionnaires, becoming Eternal Guardians of the Empire…or they should have been."

"What happened to them?"

"The SporeMother," she said. "It came out of the forest with no warning. I wasn't involved in the defense, but I remember the panic. We had nowhere near the guards we should have had, the local legion having been sent away, and only the tower's basic guards and golems here.

"The SporeMother brought hundreds with her, huge trolls and shir, bak'shi, and even prometheans…she must have been preparing since the tower was first germinated. The outer wall was breached, and the lower levels taken in only a few hours while the prometheans attacked from the air, picking off the mages.

"We still thought we'd win, even as more and more of the mages fell. We had the tower, after all. Then the gods went silent. Holy spells failed, and in the confusion of battle, the tide turned. Terna, second Paladin of Sint, was leading the fight, and when her spells all failed at once…" Oracle shook her head. "I wasn't involved, ordered to maintain the magical shielding and to keep out of the way of my betters, but I remember her cries."

She hung her head, leaning in to rest against my cheek. I reached up, settling a hand on her and trying to comfort her, awkwardly, while inside I seethed over her acceptance of her "betters."

That shit boiled my piss.

"I take it that it was bad?"

"Her god had abandoned her, abandoned the world, as near as we knew. Your memories of the discussion with the Baron Sanguis means I know more of what happened now, but..."

"But then nobody did." I grunted. "The Baron said they assassinated the priests and so on, making the gods weaker, so while this Terna was fighting, all her friends were being murdered all over the realm. Then her god vanished..."

"She froze in fear, screaming out to Lord Sint, and the SporeMother killed her. It turned the tide. I remember that; the DarkSpore-possessed creatures were being held back by her power, and without it..." She shook her head sadly and gestured around at the devastation.

"When we knew the battle was lost, we were ordered to purge the tower's mana collectors then shut the tower down. All the stored mana was fed into the shields, then, hours later, the Cataclysm struck, and the world went mad. Seas boiled, islands rose and fell, mountains crumbled..."

I walked along, occasionally stumbling over piles of rock and collapsed sections of ornate scrollwork as she talked about the end of her world and being forced into slumber while everything she knew fell apart.

It was heartbreaking as she spoke of hearing people screaming for help, banging on the crystal doorway to her hall, demanding entry, pleading for help. She'd done as she was commanded, holding it sealed despite the inhabitants' pleas, while she sat in her manawell, weeping.

"Eventually, it went quiet, the creatures stopped trying to get in, and we were forgotten. I went to sleep, feeling the others winking out and the tower growing dead around me. I obeyed and went to sleep, never expecting to wake," she whispered.

I gently stroked her back, the warmth of her tiny face pressed to my cheek. Oracle fell silent as we moved on, the hours passing as we descended.

The floors we passed were empty, confirmed by Seneschal, as well as by my own "mark 2-enhanced" eyeballs. Soon there were hundreds of small rooms, or dozens of large or even huge ones on every floor. Many walls and doors had collapsed, with piles of rubble marking more sites of both magical and mundane battles.

Random piles of ruined equipment were scattered everywhere, and Oracle went back to describing in hushed whispers the battles that had been fought by the few defenders against the SporeMother's forces.

I'd been insanely lucky, not only to defeat her at all, but also to face her as I did, as years of decreasing meals and old age had atrophied her forces and abilities. I'd fought the equivalent of a ninety-eight-year-old grandmother, as opposed to the creature in her prime. And I'd still only survived by a combination of blind luck and sheer bloody-mindedness.

If I had not become bored of feeding the manawell and had attempted to loot the top floor, I would have died. Blind luck, greed, and my own low boredom threshold had saved me.

"Oracle, what level were the defenders here? On average, I mean?" I asked quietly, looking at the devastation surrounding me.

"I think the common soldiers were about level twenty, officers and the mages maybe thirty, and the Tower Magus would have been at least forty-five, from what I remember. He was always despairing about reaching level fifty; I remember that much. Why?"

Level forty-five. I couldn't even imagine the power he must have had. I was so outclassed, it wasn't even funny. I'd faced low-level creatures in here, purely because the higher levels had died or atrophied centuries ago. The SporeMother herself had kept everything away that might have moved in, but now? For all I knew, there were goblin hunting parties or orcs investigating downstairs, All in their twenties and above. *Shit, shit, shit!*

"We need to get the defenses up and working here, Oracle, and fast!" I muttered, speeding up and heading for the next level.

"What? Oh, yeah, okay!" she said, a big smile on her face as she forgot about the old residents of the tower, their deaths surrounding us even as we picked up speed.

As the size of the floors increased toward the lower levels, so did the height. Rather than the occasional cathedral-like ceiling, those had become the norm. Oracle was constantly pointing out sections that had been barracks and crafting sections, food halls, and areas for dancing. I passed through them all in a daze, feeling small and insignificant.

Someone had created this tower from *magic*. They'd made a dance hall for the common people and soldiers that made the Sistine Chapel look, well, cheap and half-assed. The walls were covered in murals that were, in turn, covered in ash and the detritus of centuries. Yet, knowing that they were there, covering walls that had to in turn cover literally hundreds of miles? It was mind-blowing.

As I walked, I noticed the complete lack of so much as a rat, and Oracle pointed out that the SporeMother and the sporelings would have eaten them. All that survived inside were occasional insects. I cursed as one bit my neck, slapping my hand on it and looking at the bloody mark it'd left behind. Little bastard had been the size of my pinkie nail. I grimaced and flicked bits of its corpse away to land on mushrooms that climbed out of a crack in the stones. A tiny rivulet of water flowed down one wall and across the floor to disappear into another crack. I frowned and reached out to Seneschal with my mind.

"Seneschal?"
"Yes, Jax?"
"What condition is the tower in? Can you see all of it yet?"
"I have extended my senses to the first subterranean floor now. I sense no living or undead, but there are...bodies...and the tower is in extremely poor condition. Even with the mana collectors finally drawing in significant quantities, it will be a long time before I can fully repair and rebuild the tower."
"Roughly how long?"
"At this rate, just under two years to fully rebuild the tower."
"Okay. How long to make it structurally safe? Because I gotta tell you, I'm not liking seeing streams running through the lower floors and collapsed walls, considering all the weight that's above me right now..."
"Structurally safe is my priority right now. I estimate three months to seal the walls and repair the majority of dangerous leaks."
"What about security? Making the doors, things like that?"
"Depends on the door, really. Sorry, Jax, but there are over seven thousand doors currently broken or damaged. Windows are missing, and the lower floors

are entirely overgrown and will need to be cleared before they can be repaired. It becomes a question of safety versus infrastructure.

"If we get the golem facilities online, they would speed up repairs and clearing out areas. Plus, they would function as a security force. However, in the time they would need to be repaired, I could repair thirty percent of the most dangerous structural damage.

"Add to that, the golems themselves would require parts and mana upkeep. Can we afford to wait for the damage to be repaired? The risk is very real that we could repair the golem facilities, only to have the roof collapse on top of it before it produces a single unit, wasting a month of our mana production..."

"Damn, I was hoping it wouldn't be that bad."

"It's worse. If you hadn't awakened me when you did, the tower would be unlikely to survive another decade. Even now, a particularly bad storm could end us."

"Feck."

"Indeed. Now, if you don't mind..."

I felt Seneschal disappear after a few seconds, and I grunted, shaking my head. The tower was on its last legs; I was even luckier than I'd thought to have survived so far.

I began to hear birdsong again, and as I reached the next level, a large pile of debris was stacked over what I assumed was a low balcony.

I clambered over it, pulling stones out and chucking them aside. My need for fresh air and sunshine made me less cautious than I should have been. But with Bob's help, directed by his mounted wisp no less, we soon cleared away enough ground that I could push and wriggle through until I stood outside.

The light was diffused by thousands of leaves overhead. The trees that I'd seen from above were true giants, each hundreds of feet tall. The floor where I stood was maybe two floors above the ground level, but still rested under the tree canopy. I took it all in, reveling in the vibrant life. Colorful birds flitted from tree to tree, and, while few other life forms were on display, with the SporeMother's death, more would soon return to the nearby forest.

I walked across grass and clambered over tree roots, amazed at the life on this side of the wall. Inside, there were occasional piles of mushrooms and bare roots, but all was dark and silent. Out here, the forest exploded with life. I loved it.

I sat down on a moss-covered boulder by a tinkling stream, watching flies flit across the water as birds dove to eat them. Apples and other fruit hung from the trees. Some I recognized from the gardens above, others from home, and still there were many I'd never seen before.

"Jax, are you okay?" Oracle asked, landing next to me and gently reaching out to touch my cheek. It was only then I realized that tears covered my cheeks. I laughed and ignored my tears in unashamed joy.

"Okay? Oracle, this is beautiful! I've never seen anything like it!" I gestured out with one hand. The stream ran out from where I sat to fall over the edge of the balcony. I felt the mist of the water landing behind me, pouring down from floors above to continually replenish the stream winding away through the undergrowth of the forest floor far below. Occasionally, I watched animals, always in the distance. There, a dozen deer ran through a section of the collapsed outer wall, a solitary great cat pursuing them. Here, something that looked suspiciously like an oversized squirrel stared at me from across the clearing.

I was enraptured and sat for long minutes, the horrors of the last few months finally slipping away. Everything I'd done to get here, the fights, the arena, the pain, all of it was worth this moment of perfect peace, centering me in this terrible, wonderful realm.

I sat there for a while, enjoying the scents and feel of the forest all around me. The ground outside the tower was covered in moss and small plants. Collapsed buildings and a tumbled down outer wall were all consumed by the forest. I'd never seen the wilderness so…wild. It looked beautiful, yet also sad. This had been an outpost of a great civilization, but now, it was buried in the forest, abandoned by all save an evil creature that had killed and tortured so many.

Eventually I got up, my thoughts taking a darker turn as I reflected on the SporeMother and the many victims she must have fed on.

Oracle had left me to myself, but as I climbed back inside, she flitted through the hole we'd made and into the tower proper.

We let Bob lead the way now, passing down long corridors, over collapsed walls, and through rooms seemingly without end. Without the clear path left by the SporeMother in her mad rush toward me earlier, we'd have been hopelessly lost. Entire sections that should, according to Oracle, have been the best path were instead buried, forcing us to use secondary stairwells and even servants' sections.

Even the moss and fungus had withered where she had walked, leaving a trodden path of death and destruction across the lower floors.

Eventually, we found a hole in the main floor, the path leading straight to it then dropping down into the subterranean levels. The three of us stood staring into the darkness below. We'd long since moved from any rooms with even a hint of outdoor light, but here, the darkness seemed oppressive, and the smell…there was no doubt this led to the creature's lair.

I hunted through the bag, finding what I needed in my survival kit. Chemical lights. I'd either not needed them or had not had time to get them until now, but damn I was glad I still had them.

Pulling two chemical lights out, I snapped them both and threw them in, one after the other, counting how long it took until they hit the ground. When they both hit only seconds later, less than a bare second apart, I stared at the tiny area illuminated below. It was easily a dozen feet down, and the floor was covered in bones and debris.

I swallowed hard and, before I could think about it, I had Bob grab onto me, lowering me down by my legs face-first into the pit for a quick look around. As near as I could see, it was a corridor below.

I fired off a Firebolt each way, the spell finding a collapsed wall blocking the tunnel to my right, while it widened out at the end of the tunnel to my left. The spell I'd fired in that direction vanished into the gloom, with even my magical sight only able to pierce the darkness so far.

I grabbed onto a section of stone that jutted out from one side and had Bob let go, swinging myself around and dropping the last few feet to the ground with a grunt. Bob, of course, just jumped down, landing next to me with a clatter of bones, while Oracle buzzed around us.

We crept along the corridor, or at least I did. After a few minutes, I started to feel really stupid, as I couldn't hear anything besides the constant grate and clatter of Bob's bones, so I gave up and started walking normally, deciding to trust in Seneschal's senses. He had contacted me just before we had reached this point, saying he couldn't sense anything living or moving in the area at all. If there was life or undeath, it would have to be deeper in, where the final wisp well was located.

The tunnel opened out into a cavern at the end, where several floors had collapsed, creating a giant room. I threw the chemical lights in deeper, relying on their meager light to augment my DarkVision. Piles of rubble had been pushed aside to form rings and concentric circles, centered on a tall structure in the middle of the cavern that stood maybe twenty feet high.

"That's it!" Oracle whispered into my ear. "That's the golem genesis chamber, or at least that's one of them. The others were spread out around this floor, but they're all gone."

"Is it functional?" I asked quietly.

"How would I know from here?" she replied, sounding cross. "Honestly, Jax, you can see what I can see; can you tell from here?"

"Well, I thought you'd know more, that's all. Or maybe you would be using some senses of magic or something. Oh, forget it. Let's go," I muttered, setting off down the side of the cavern. Bob clattered after me while Oracle floated overhead.

"Look, Jax, I'm sorry, it's just...this place was my home. I saw such wonderful things done here.

"It was filled with hope for the future, pride in all that the empire was and could be, and now...I'm just having a hard time looking around and making this match with what it used to be," Oracle said quietly after a minute.

"It's okay, Oracle. Really, it is. It's...well, it's hard to see something you love messed up like this. And for you, with the tower literally being a part of you? I can't imagine," I replied, shaking my head as I looked around. "You can talk to me about it, if you want?"

"Maybe another time, Jax, but thank you," she whispered back, landing on one shoulder to give me a peck on the cheek before taking off again.

We crossed the floor in a matter of minutes, moving cautiously from one pile of rubble to another. I wrinkled my nose in disgust as we neared the center. There were piles of bones, shattered and splintered, with obvious gnaw marks, and a floor that reminded me of a seedy bar where I used to drink in Newcastle.

You stuck to the floor as you walked, wiping your feet on the way *out* of Planet Earth. I tried not to think about the centuries of accumulated crap that I was walking over, and it was...sticking...to me. The smell was horrific, but as we approached the genesis chamber, an opening appeared on the far side facing away from us. As we circled it, we stopped in horror and disgust.

There were dozens of bodies hanging inside, bloated and rotting. Some were obviously alive recently, the freshest ones maybe only a few weeks dead. The nearest was the corpse of a man, hung from his arms and encased in some kind of semi-solid mesh that held him upright. His distended stomach was slowly writhing.

Other corpses hung the same way, some old, some young, but similarly full. Something was alive in there, something that moved and grew, feeding slowly on the hosts as they rotted and putrefied.

I threw up. Not a little bit, either—it was a spectacular projectile vomit, spattering across the floor to my right as I turned away from the vileness. When the SporeMother had been threatening to make me into an incubator for more of her young, this is what she'd been planning. If the fight upstairs had gone even a little differently, I'd be here now, screaming. Fuck.

"What do we do?" Oracle asked quietly.

"Burn it," I forced out, between heaves. "We burn it all. Make sure that *fucking* thing doesn't spread itself any further!"

CHAPTER TWENTY-SIX

O racle flew directly over the corpses and began to cast. I turned away, getting myself under control, and tried to look anywhere else as she cast Cleansing Fire. Screaming rose immediately from the corpses. They were torn apart as immature sporelings forced their way out, trying to escape.

They perished in seconds, and I turned back to be sure none survived, stamping down hard on one as it tried to drag itself out of the flames. Tiny bones crunched underfoot and...fluids...spurted out. I'd be burning these shoes, given the chance, or at least cleaning them really, really well later.

"Ummm, Jax?" Oracle called to me half an hour later and multiple castings down. She hovered off to one side where a cleared area held a series of stones piled haphazardly.

"Yeah, Oracle?" I asked wearily, slowly walking over to join her. "God, that was nasty!"

"Do you know what these are?" she asked hesitantly, pointing at the stones. Most were dull, square, and maybe an inch on each side, but here and there were some that glimmered with a trace of mana.

"Yeah...from your hall, they look like..." I started to say, remembering the niches in the walls.

"Memory stones," Oracle whispered. "They're memory stones. Like the ones I have in the Hall of Memories, but these are smaller. They're often called HeartStones. Usually, lovers give them to each other to share memories if they have to part."

"Someone loved that thing?" I asked, disgusted.

"No, Jax," Oracle replied, her voice flat. "Someone was sending memories to it, though, and judging from the pile of blank stones over there, they'd been getting replies." I followed her gesture to see a small package. The top had been ripped open, and dirty paper was strewn about. Inside were half a dozen HeartStones, the remains of a larger collection, judging from the space in the package.

"Why the hell would you do that?" I asked. "What would you want to talk to a creature like this for?"

"It's a way to guarantee it doesn't kill you, and if you send someone you don't mind losing, I suppose the risk is worth it," she replied.

"Yeah, I can see why it's safer than meeting it face-to-face, but still, why bother? And how would you convince it to start using the stones, or explain how to in the first place?"

"I don't know. The majority are dead. When the mana is used up, the memory is gone, but there are a couple left with traces. Maybe try one?"

"I thought you said using things like that could fuck with my mind?" I said, looking at her askance. "Does that mean—"

"Skill memory or spellbooks *would*, Jax. They can contain months or years of knowledge. This couldn't hold more than a few minutes, at most. You're safe, and it's the only way we can find out what happened here," she said, shaking her head in resignation.

"Honestly, Jax, you're like a child. You can't have the shiny books and memories upstairs, so stop thinking about them. I'll tell you when you've healed enough. Until then, just trust that everything I'm doing is for you."

I glanced at her guiltily. Yeah, I'd been thinking about it, I had to admit, even if it was just to myself. Fuck it.

I picked up the topmost stone and rotated it in my hands. The flickering flames from the Cleansing Fire spell dying out behind me were reflected in its smooth surfaces.

"So, how—"

"Close your eyes and channel a spark of mana into it." She cut me off with a long-suffering sigh. One minute, she was finding any excuse to strip naked and tease me, and the next, she was treating me like an idiot child.

Acting all superior was a new one for her, but as irritating as it was, I followed her advice as she landed on my shoulder and pressed one hand to my temple.

When I opened my eyes, I was sitting with one leg crossed over the other in a comfortable armchair. A nighttime city sprawled out before me, with rain lashing the window an arm's reach ahead of me, while velvet curtains surrounded it. Thick carpets cushioned our feet as we looked out at torches that flickered in the darkness. The occasional flash of lightning illuminated the night-drenched streets as people ran here and there. My hand lifted, holding a brandy snifter, and it swirled the alcohol around leisurely as I spoke on, dismissing the unimportant scurrying of the scum below.

"...delivery was short, and we both know it. Our agreement was for bodies. I provide you with healthy live ones, and you do the same for me. I gave you sixteen to feed on and impregnate, but I got fourteen sporelings in return. If the next delivery is short, there will be no more coming. You agreed not to try to grow your nest, and I agreed to give you the bodies you needed to survive and recover.

"I will send one more shipment, and with it, I'll be sending some of my men by airship. You will *not* harm them, and you'll let them examine the tower. If they find things I can use, then maybe I will send you more of the fresh bodies you continue to demand. If you harm my men, I will send nothing else. Fifty cycles of the daystar from when you receive this message, they will..."

The memory cut off there, and I was suddenly back in my body, blinking in confusion while Oracle hissed angrily and took off, buzzing around in agitation.

"What was that?" I asked, trying to sort the memory out in my mind. It sounded like they were making deals. Some rich guy I didn't get to see was actually making a deal with the SporeMother, and...he'd been buying her offspring?!

"Some idiot; no, some shit-sucking scumbag, was selling her people to feed on!" Oracle snarled at me. "I'd read about how greedy some creatures were, but to give people to that thing? Why, Jax, WHY?!"

"I...I've no idea, Oracle," I said, watching my companion flitting from one pile of debris to another until she suddenly paused then landed abruptly. Choking off a sob and covering her face with her hands, she turned away from something on the floor.

I rushed over and found some splinters of bone, cloth, and a few bits of twine. Then I looked closer. The cloth had a pattern of dancing flowers along the hem, and it was tiny. A stone resting next to the cloth resolved into a section of a skull. A small child. It must have been too small to have been any use to the SporeMother. It'd been eaten instead, the skull cracked open and teeth marks scoring the few intact sections of bone.

Some fucker had sold people to this creature, *children*! She had eaten the bairns and impregnated the adults, leaving them to be eaten alive as the brood inside them grew. Even as the hosts died and rotted, still their corpses were fed upon.

White-hot rage consumed me. Kneeling before this unknown child, I swore I'd make this right and avenge the poor little thing. I screamed, straightening up, my rage flowing out of me as I channeled my mana into my voice subconsciously, needing an outlet. The air around me vibrated, causing dust and debris to cascade from the walls and ceiling. The ground was blown clear as a great burst of air flew out in all directions, with me as its center.

When my mana was spent, I collapsed to the floor, gasping, with tears flooding my cheeks. I wept for this unknown child and for the other bones I could see strewn about the room, the dust now blasted free of them. There were hundreds of splintered bones, bits and pieces laid everywhere.

"Why?" I asked Oracle numbly. "Why were there so few sporelings, and such weak ones we faced? Where were the *rest*? I thought she was half-starved, but this? She had food, she had bodies...I even fought a few when I first arrived, but they were tiny compared to that thing."

"It must have been nearly dead, Jax. Someone must have found it and started to feed it, letting it grow stronger, but taking its young and any guards it made. It must have been hiding the ones you first fought, trying to build up its strength, maybe by using corpses that were old and useless, ones that'd never be missed."

"Seriously, Oracle, why do that? Why would anyone want these creatures?" I asked in despair, looking at the bones around me. "What would have to be wrong with you to think that feeding this thing was acceptable?"

"I don't know. But if they could tame the sporelings, they could eventually make an enslaved SporeMother...then use it to create an army," she whispered, looking horrified. "Imagine the army you could create, if you didn't care about the people you sacrificed to it. You could use DarkSpore to raise the dead from the graveyards; every defender you killed would be another slave you could raise to replace your own losses. It'd be the Armies of the Night all over again!"

"The what?" I asked leadenly.

"The Armies of the Night!" she snapped at me distractedly, still lost in the horror of her vision. "It's the name given to the Necromancer Wars, when a group of vampyr necromancers began raising armies. They flooded the Amir Basin with the dead.

"The breadbasket of the empire became a graveyard that remained contaminated with the dead even hundreds of years later. It took direct intervention from the gods; Jenae Herself strode the battlefield to finish it. Even then, millions died in the war and the famine that followed."

"What the hell is wrong with these people! All they had to do was let the damn thing die. Why wouldn't they do that?! And as for feeding it, trying to tame its bloody kids? Seriously, what the fuck?"

I paced back and forth, waving my hands as I ranted about the madness of the rich, thinking they could control something like this. After a few minutes, Oracle interrupted me.

"It's here, Jax!" she called out, gesturing at a pile of fecal matter and bone fragments.

"...what is?" I asked, cut off mid-rant by her declaration.

"The last wisp pedestal; it's buried in there somewhere. I can feel it!"

"Well, I'm not fucking digging through that, I'll tell you that right now! Bob! Get your bony arse in there and do some good!" I snarled, gesturing at the pile. I was furious, not with Oracle or Bob, but with everything. No matter where I was, people were the same. Fucking idiots! Back home, it was nukes and bioweapons. Here, it was...well...bioweapons, I guessed, and magic.

At least this place wouldn't have global warming. *I hoped.*

"Hey, Oracle, you ever hear of pollution, or global warming?" I asked suddenly and got a frown in return.

"Pollution, like the bodies of the dead in the Amir Basin? Those broke down into the ground so completely, they're probably still trying to cleanse the land of disease. Is that what you mean?"

"Nope!" I said, a little of the depression lifting from my soul. "Don't you worry about it!"

"Seneschal, you there, buddy?"

"Yes, Jax, I am here. Now what?"

"Just curious; can you sense all of the tower now?"

"Most of it. I can sense some of the room you're in. Once you have freed and activated the wisp pedestal there, I will be able to see all of it. Why?"

"Looks like the SporeMother was working with someone else. She was selling her sporelings and getting fresh bodies to breed in. I guess the ones I fought upstairs were all she could hide away. So...somewhere out there is a crazy motherfucker with a load of sporelings he's trying to tame. We need the golems, mate. Sorry."

"..."

"Go on, use your words..."

"Why would anyone try to deal with a SporeMother? They're an ancient scourge of all life, evil beyond measure and...and why?"

"Yeah, that's pretty much my take on it, too. Some shitbiscuit out there is batshit crazy, and they're going to be sending more people here soon to trade for sporelings we don't have and to search the tower for loot. Something tells me they won't take it well when they find out we killed their project."

"How long do we have?"

"No idea. The bit of the message I saw said fifty days, but I have no idea if it's been here a day or a month or what. We need to get things moving, and fast. No time for playing it safe. Oracle says there's a golem genesis chamber here; can you reach it?"

"No, that is not my skill set, either. You need to awaken the wisp pedestal for that area. It used to manage the golems and will be far better suited to using it."

"Shit. Okay. Bob is digging the pedestal out now, but it will take me hours to route enough mana to it to reawaken it. Can you speed it up?"

"The mana pathways aren't regrown that far down yet. I was concentrating on higher levels, as you ordered."

"Shit, sh...okay. Start work on the entire tower. Get the most vital repairs done as fast as you can. I'm going to concentrate on the golem section. Once I've got it up and running, then we can start working out our next step. You just...you just fix shit, okay?"

"Yes, Jax. I'll keep doing what you keep interrupting me from doing. Is that what you're saying?"

"Smartass."

I shook my head and considered Oracle as she floated over the debris pile that Bob was powering through. "Seneschal's a real asshole, you know that?" I muttered.

"Probably why you two get on so well, Jax!" she replied tiredly.

"Ha! Thanks for that. Love you, too. So, can we move the pedestal from here?" I asked.

"You...you *love* me?"

I twisted around at the stunned tone in her voice and replayed the conversation in my mind. Damn.

"Ah, no. Sorry, Oracle, it's just a turn of phrase, you see..."

"You don't love me?!" she wailed, the burgeoning smile dropping from her face and a look of horror and heartbreak replacing it.

"No! I mean, yes, I do, I mean...oh, for fuck's sake!" I took my head in my hands and stopped for a long second, drawing a deep breath before looking at Oracle again. "You see, I care ab—oh, you little shit!"

I cut myself off, realizing I was being played. The edges of a grin tugged at her lips as she tried to keep a straight face.

"Goddamn wisps and your fucked-up sense of humor!" I muttered as she burst into silvery peals of laughter.

"Oh...oh, I'm sorry, Jax! I couldn't help it! Bahahaha! Oh, your face!"

"I'll get you for that!" I promised, a smile tugging at the edge of my lips as well, despite everything, until a sudden waft of heavier stench hit me. Bob had pulled the last pile of rubbish clear of the wisp pedestal, revealing a filthy basin that reeked of crap.

"Oh god," I muttered, backing away from it and covering my mouth with one hand. "I think when it couldn't get rid of it, it decided to use it as a toilet..."

"What do we do? Any wisp you summoned here would be...well, they wouldn't be inclined to help you, I'll put it that way."

I checked my mana over and grinned. "That's okay, Oracle, watch this!" I said, casting Summon Water directly next to the pedestal. As soon as it appeared, I switched to Firebolt, but, as before, I held it in my hand, using the flames to superheat the water and creating a boiling fountain that washed across the pedestal. With a thought, Bob was burrowing his hands into the mess, pulling chunks free and throwing them aside. Within a few minutes, it was clear and reasonably clean, making me realize just how bad the rest of the room was. The water had brought a wave a fresh air with it for some reason, and without that...God, it stank!

I channeled my remaining mana into the pedestal then told the other two to turn around; we were getting out of there. I'd recover my mana outside, and we could come back down each time I was filled and ready. I just couldn't stay in that filth any longer. Oracle was flying out of the room almost before I'd finished explaining my plan, and Bob followed along dutifully.

It took the better part of an hour to get outside, but when I did, I felt relief immediately. I staggered across to a low, fallen wall covered in moss and sat. Oracle landed next to me and stretched out on her back, her long wings folding up gently. I sent Bob off to jump into the stream nearby, ordering him to get clean. Although I knew it was my imagination, he seemed eager to do it.

I just sat back and thought about the madness of trying to tame a SporeMother. *I mean, seriously, what kind of a mind would come up with that?* I was thinking about all the things that could go wrong, when I noticed Oracle calling my name.

"Jax...Jax!" I blinked and focused on her, realizing I'd been staring at her, but seeing another world of horror and possibilities instead. Now that I was paying attention, I discovered that she'd changed her clothes again, and I'd completely missed it.

"What's wrong?" I asked, looking around the clearing.

"What's wrong? WHAT'S WRONG?" she snarled at me. "I got naked and changed my clothes right here, Jax. I did it so you could watch, and you didn't even notice! I was *naked*, Jax! NAKED!"

"I...uh...sorry, Oracle, I was kinda thinking about..."

"You weren't supposed to be thinking about anything! You were supposed to see me naked and be totally distracted by that! It was supposed to make you happy! I made this body to please you! Did I get it wrong?" The clothes she was wearing, a small green tunic and pants, vanished into mist, leaving an irate naked wisp hovering before me, one hand pointed at my face.

"Is this wrong, Jax? Is my body ugly? Is that it?!" she growled.

"Stop! Please, Oracle, just stop for a minute, okay?" I managed to get out, sounding strangled.

"But why?!" she cried out, flying up to hover in front of my face, her nakedness filling my vision. "Why don't you want me, Jax? I remember the residents mating. It looked like so much fun, and in your memories, you love it! Why won't you mate with me?!"

"Because you're like twelve inches tall, and you're my friend!" I said all in a rush. "Look at yourself, Oracle, and look at the size of me. I'd kill you with it, for a start! It's not physically possible, never mind the whole master-and-servant thing that we've got going on. It would be wrong!"

"My size?" She looked at herself, then at me, before her mouth became a perfect O of understanding. "You're worried about my size? I'll grow, Jax. You're so silly! Of course, I couldn't mate with you properly in this form! Watch!"

She took a deep breath and closed her eyes, a tiny furrow appearing in her brow as she concentrated. Suddenly, she blazed with light. I had to look away, the light was so bright, but when I looked back, she stood before me, wings and all, stark naked and almost as tall as I was.

"Wha—I mean, how—" I gasped out, deep in shock.

"You didn't realize, did you?" she asked quietly, a low purr in her voice causing my pants to bulge as Mr. Happy made his presence known. She looked down and smiled in appreciation before returning her gaze to my eyes.

"You really thought I was stuck at that size, and that I was just teasing you?" she asked.

I couldn't figure out how to get my words working again, as something about her had short circuited my brain, so my response was more a gurgle than the agreement I tried to get out. She understood, though.

"Jax, I'm a Wisp. I can assume any form I want to and be any size I desire; it just takes mana."

A glance at my mana bar showed that it was two-thirds empty again, rather than steadily refilling as it had been. She gently took my cheek in her hand and smiled at me. "Jax, you saved me. I was dying in hibernation, my friends all either dead already or dying the same as I was.

"You gave me life, a purpose, and you let me bond to you. I'll get to explore the world by your side, seeing things I only ever read about before. Through our bond, I get to access your mana and have a physical body whenever I want one. I've watched the inhabitants of my tower for years before the long sleep. I saw them doing many things to each other. *For* each other. I want to try them all. Please, Jax, do you really not want to…"

"JAX! Incoming!"

"Wha—"

"Get your head out of her and get ready! You have enemies incoming!"

I barely noticed Oracle's growl as my fuzzy brain tried to get back into the world of fight and flight, rather than naked women that could fly and shapeshift. I stared around in confusion, searching for my weapon until I spotted where it had fallen off to one side of the low wall we'd been sitting on. I grabbed it and set my stance.

Bob clambered out of the stream to my right and clattered across to take up his position at my side. My attention, however, was diverted by Oracle's perfect bare ass as she flew up into the air ahead of me, screaming out at something I couldn't see yet.

"YOU DARE! You interrupted us; I WAS GONNA GET LAID! *I'LL KILL YOU!"*

She slammed both wrists together and screamed as a large, black, horned cat leapt into sight, landing atop one of the collapsed walls. As quickly as it appeared, Oracle finished her casting. A bolt of lightning flashed out, thick as my wrist. The white-hot energy slammed into the cat, smashing it from its perch to fall convulsing to the ground.

I used the last of my mana and cast Identify.

Vatin Hunting Cat – Insane

This creature is well known as an ambush predator, spoken of in whispers as the cause of death of many travelers. It is said that for every Vatin you see, three more are hidden. This creature has been driven insane by the death of its mistress and will hunt and kill anything it can.

Level: 8
Health: 18/130
Mana: 70

Hidden…I heard a faint sound behind me and spun around, my naginata flashing out by reflex, only to slam into the side of another vatin. My blade cut into its right foreleg and nearly severed it as the massive cat crashed into me, its weight sending us both toppling to the ground.

I brought the naginata up just in time to brace the handle across its throat. I worked frantically to keep its teeth at bay while its claws screeched across my armor and ripped at my legs. I screamed, managing to firmly plant one foot and flip us over, slamming the vatin onto its back.

It twisted, its typical cat reflexes giving it the leverage to get out from under me. It limped back, hissing its rage. I swung the naginata around, keeping the point between us as I staggered to my feet. Blood ran down my legs from the cuts and scrapes its claws had left.

Before it could attack again, though, Bob smashed into it. Swords stabbed, daggers drove deep, and the claw-tipped legs lashed down from above, repeatedly puncturing the cat until it collapsed, dead. My mana was low since Oracle had used a huge amount of it on the supercharged version of my lightning bolt. She had apparently finished her vatin off with a Firebolt to the face.

I spotted two more sprinting across the clearing at me, their roars making me back up instinctively. I couldn't face these; they'd slaughter me! They were the kings of the jungle. They…*what*…?

Fear effect resisted. Paralysis effect resisted due to high Luck stat.

Those cheating bastard cats! My rage flared to life as I realized the damn things had some fear-based ability that had nearly gotten to me. I raised my naginata and caught one cat mid-leap, impaling it through the chest and killing it instantly. The weight of it sent me onto my back again, but as the second cat went for me, I didn't waste any time. I didn't have time to get up, so I stayed down, drawing my dirks from both wrist bracers and stabbed out as I lunged. One plunged into its mouth, and the other stabbed deep into its chest as I hunted around for its heart.

It bit down on my wrist, one tooth punching all the way through to erupt out the other side before the pain of my dirk slicing its throat open made it release me reflexively.

Something gave, and my right-hand dirk slid deeper, free of the thick, corded chest muscle that had caught it. The sudden fluttering on the end of the blade let me know I'd found my target. One quick twist and slice, and then, because I was pissed, a handful more stabs as I roared into its face. Then it was all over, blood gushing from its mouth to cover my hand as it died.

I shoved it off and rolled to my feet. Pain radiating from my wounds let me know that I'd need to heal up soon, but I wasn't in any immediate danger. I looked over to find Bob finishing off the last cat in sight as Oracle flew toward me.

She had returned to her normal size, although she was still naked. She quickly observed my face and wounds, and with a sigh, called clothes into being. Tight jeans and a low-cut top appeared, but the outfit was still better than the ones she usually chose.

"What happened?" I asked her.

"I guess maybe they were being used as guardians or something by the SporeMother." She shrugged. "I don't know for sure, Jax, but you saw the same thing I did when you used your spell on them. They were driven insane by the SporeMother's death. If it had other creatures like them around..."

"Great. One more reason to get the golems up and running, I guess. Come on, back inside for now. Let's get a move on."

As I turned to walk back, I told Bob to grab two of the corpses and drag them inside. I'd look them over once we were settled and I'd gotten some more work done on the manawell.

It took us a while to get back to the main cavern, but once we were there, I didn't waste any time. I summoned a second spring of water and heated it up to wash over the manawell again. It took me three castings before it looked properly clean, but by the time it was done, I didn't think the wisp would throw up as soon as it was summoned.

We spent the next few hours working on the surrounding area, as disgusting as it was, clearing away compacted shit and the remains of hundreds of years of meals and byproducts. The tedious, smelly job was interspersed by me funneling as much mana as I could into the manawell. It went a lot quicker, thanks to Bob, who never tired or got bored of it, while Oracle kept me company—dressed, thankfully.

I sat at one point, thinking about Oracle as she sat atop Bob, watching him and chattering away as he dug and tore at the compacted, well, crap.

She was sexy as all hell. Fuck, there was no way she could be hotter. She'd literally scoured my brain looking for the things I found most attractive, and she was fun. Yeah, at times she was childish, innocent and more, but...but she was also mature in other ways. She'd spent millennia watching people and living her own life presumably before she was captured.

She acted like she was sex-starved, but really, she was just curious and didn't understand what she was asking for. I wasn't any better though, alternating between desperate to jump her, now I knew she was capable of growing enough to "do the deed" and determined it'd be wrong to do so.

First of all, she was innocent, in this way at least, and secondly, we were *bonded*. We had a whole master-and-servant thing going on that freaked me the hell out when I thought about it. Hell, I'd run from any kind of responsibility my entire life. Fights and dying, yeah, fine. Having someone actually *need* me? That terrified me, and now if I fucked up, it'd kill her as well.

Even forgetting about that, as she flipped herself around, blurring past me in a streak of smiles and insane sex appeal, what if I *did* have sex with her? I mean, yeah, I was all alone out here, besides her and Bob, I could send Bob away for a bit, and…okay, maybe tell Seneschal and whoever this wisp would be to look away or something.

But if I did? What then? What if she became all possessive? Or worse, what if she shrugged and decided she wanted to try other things out? I mean, that was what she was interested in. What if I got attached to her in that way, and she started fucking around, like Lou had done? We were bonded; it wasn't like I could just tell her to fuck off and stab her boyfriend.

I shook my head, forcibly banishing the thoughts. I'd have to think about it all more soon. But for now, Oracle was a friend, and as much as I liked looking at her, that was all she could be.

I got back to work, gritting my teeth as Bob and I dragged shit away, forcing myself not to look too closely at the bones that were laid here and there. I took the time to rest when I needed to, trekking out of the black pit that the genesis chamber had become. But as soon as my mana was fully replenished, I'd head back again.

When we finally reached the magic four-hundred mark, the liquid silver mana began to swirl and bubble in the now-familiar way. I settled down with a sigh of relief.

Oracle flew down, landing on the edge of the well and dipped a hand into the glowing pool. Closing her eyes, she communicated her knowledge and experiences far faster than I could have with words.

When she finally moved back, reaching out her hands to me to be lifted onto my shoulder, the pool had quieted. When it moved again, after a long minute, it drew together to form itself into a short, muscular humanoid.

This wisp chose a form that was almost as broad as it was tall, a stocky creation with thickly muscled arms and legs, a bald head, and a beard that plaited itself as I watched. It slowly absorbed all the liquid before stomping to the edge of the well and staring up at me, its body now covered in what looked like thick leather.

"You're a dwarf!" I said without thinking.

"Aye, laddie, a dwarf I be. It be the form most o' my interactions were with, ye mind?" He looked up at me questioningly, a deep frown beginning to furrow his brows as he waited for an answer.

"Ah! No, no; just a bit surprised. I'm not really—"

"From around here! Aye, Oracle told me. She shared her memories of you, and all that's happened since she was awoken. Includin' the state o' ma genesis chamber!" He looked around, spitting in disgust. "This needs ta change! I'll be reachin' out to Seneschal now. He be needin' ma permission ta join with this section of the tower, and I be needin' his mana! Once I've got that, I'll be startin' ta rebuild me glorious machines!" He clapped his hands together and grinned up at me, before looking around the room. "So! I need a lot o' mana, a damn lot o' resources, especially marble, crystal, iron an' silver. An' seems I need a name! That's your job ta sort, laddie!"

"Okay, what are dwarf names like, then?" I asked, a grin on my face. I didn't like the idea of needing a lot of resources, but I'd always loved the dwarves of popular culture. To find them talking and acting as gruff as the Scots I'd grown up with cheered me immensely.

"What kinda question is that?" He huffed, fixing me with a severe look. "Dwarves have names like normal folk, ya speciesist shit!"

"Whoa, ya little bastard, calm down, or it'll be 'Grumpy' I call ya from now on!" I snapped back, then grinned when the edge of his mouth quirked up. "All right, you got me," I said, shaking my head in resignation.

"Bahahaha!" he roared, pointing a stubby finger at me. "I got ya good!"

"Aye, you did, you little bastard," I admitted. "Don't think I'll let this slide, though. I'll get you. Don't know where or when, but I'll get you!"

"In yer dreams, laddie! Now, a name, then we need ta discuss plans, see what we're gonna do first."

"Yeah, we do. Can Seneschal show himself down here? Think we need to all be together to talk this one out," I said.

"Nope, too far for him!" the dwarf said, smacking his chest proudly. "Need ta be stronger than that bugger ta manifest so far from his well!"

"We could all manifest in the Hall of the Eternal, Jax?" Oracle offered, gesturing upwards. "Now that the mana collectors are working, and Seneschal is feeding mana into the tower, there would be enough for each us to appear there."

"Where's that?" I asked cautiously, already fearing the answer.

"At the top of the tower," she replied brightly, a big smile on her face.

"No," I said, shaking my head.

"But..."

"NO," I said firmly. "I'm not climbing the entire goddamn tower just for a conference. Fuck that."

"Another option, laddie. Want ta hear it?" the dwarf said.

"Yeah, all right. If we have no other choice, I know I can communicate with him at this distance, but it feels like we need a better way to talk than that."

"Aye. Well, me genesis chambers are a bit fucked here. I either need ta repair 'em entirely before I can start rebuildin', or we could make a few basic golems and have 'em move me manawell upstairs to a more secure area, followed by the single functional chamber. Then we can work on repairin' and rebuildin' this whole cavern ta be me home again!" He looked at me hopefully as I frowned in thought.

"Yeah, that sounds like a plan, but how long is it gonna take? And what do we need to do to build those first couple of golems?"

He grinned at me and pointed to the far corner of the room urgently. "Ye see that corner? Where all the rubble be?" I nodded, and he carried on quickly. "Well, all ye need ta do is clear it! There be a storeroom beyond it! Enough gear in there ta build at least a couple o' golems!"

"That seems simple enough...what aren't you telling me?" I asked, peering into the gloom. I could make out some debris, but...

"It be the emergency store, sealed away just in case, that be all," he said nonchalantly.

"And..."

"Well, it be a wee bit...buried...and it be...a bit heavy. That be all, nowt ye canna deal with, I'm sure. Go on there, laddie!"

I wandered over to the corner he'd indicated, summoning Bob, and we investigated the mess. It was a rockslide the size of a house, with no sign of any storeroom, or door, or even a damn wall!

"Are you kidding me?" I called out to the damn dwarf. "This isn't feckin' rubble, it's a damn collapsed mountain!"

"Ah, quit ya whinin'! A real man, or even a wee dwarf bairn, woulda cleared it by now!" he called back at me. I could hear the grin in his voice. "And dinna be forgettin' I need ta be named! In fact, mebbe I'll pick ma own name…"

He trailed off, and I could hear the occasional laugh or muttered comment from him as Bob and I set to work. I instructed Bob to collect the animal corpses, and I cast Raise Weak Skeletal Minion, using the vatin corpses to augment him further. As the flesh and bits melted away, his legs, arms, and trunk all received heavier bones.

As I continued adding, shifting the smaller bones aside and replacing them with greater ones, he grew. When I was finished, Bob stood a good foot taller than before, and he hulked. There was no better way to describe him.

The general outline was the same, but where his arms had been one or two bones before, now they were each composed of three at least, all adding together to give him greater strength and reach. I brought up my notifications as soon as I was done, delighted to find what I'd been hoping for.

Congratulations!

You have raised your spell Raise Weak Skeleton to level 10.

You may now choose your first evolution of this spell.

Congratulations!

You have raised your spell Raise Weak Skeleton to its first evolution.

You must now pick a path to follow.

Will you augment your own abilities to SUMMONER, or will you concentrate on your minion and pick the path of the REANIMATOR?

Choose carefully, as this choice cannot be undone.

Summoner:
As you have grown more familiar with your spell, you have seen the warp and loss of mana caused by issues with the spell formation. Perhaps you could improve upon this? Your Raise Weak Skeletal Minion will evolve to Skeletal Summoning, doubling the minions you can control!

Reanimator:
As you grow in familiarity with the dead, you sense differences in the corpses around you. Perhaps some bones hold more potential than others? Your Raise Weak Skeletal Minion will evolve to Skeletal Reanimator, granting a 10% increase in physical attributes and a chance to develop magical talents and increase the level of sentience your minion enjoys.

I stopped and contemplated the potential that these spells opened up for me. If I could double the number of minions I summoned with every ten additional levels of skill, that'd be two, then four, then eight, then sixteen, then thirty-two, then sixty-four, then one hundred and twenty-eight…at level one hundred, I could summon one thousand and twenty-four minions. That was if it only increased by double with each level. What if it went higher, or if there were items that could increase my power? Hell, I could command armies of the undead!

I fantasized about that for a second before shaking myself. I was using the spell because it was useful now, not because I was some Lord of the Dead type. I quickly switched my attention to the second path. Reanimator could be good. I wouldn't get a second minion, but if I continued to level Bob and spent time on improving him, I could make him into an absolute beast. Plus, it came with the chance for him to gain powers? Hell yes! I selected Reanimator and moved onto the next prompt.

You have chosen Reanimator for your first evolution.

Your minion, Bob, has been granted an additional 10% to his stats, increasing his damage dealt, his damage resistance, and his sentience. No magical capabilities exist in his current form. Perhaps adding more unusual resources to him will improve this?

In addition to the evolution of your spell, you have gained two new abilities:

Clairvoyance:
You have gained the ability to speak to the recently deceased. Costs 10 mana to cast, plus 1 mana per second active.

Bonemeld:

Through experimentation, you have developed the ability to create new creatures from the bones of the dead. It is now possible for you to meld bones together using this skill, greatly strengthening your creations! Costs 5 mana per second active.

I already had a few plans for Bob's next form, as I suspected I'd need to have something a bit more lethal when fighting outdoors. For the time being, though, I was happy with him. While I'd been playing with my options, Bob had been working away at the pile. Despite the extra power he had, he could only do so much alone. I set my thoughts aside and began digging with him.

CHAPTER TWENTY-SEVEN

I took the better part of a day to clear enough rubble to be able to find the chamber hidden beyond. It would have taken twice that, if not for the recently upgraded Bob being the machine that he was.

Oracle had flown upstairs and kept an eye out, while Bob and I worked, moving multiple tons of stone and dirt until we finally uncovered the top of a doorway.

Barely an hour later, we slowly broke it open to find a partially collapsed storeroom. Most of the room was buried in the rubble, but on the wall to my right, three shelves still stood, the supports half-hanging from the wall, and stacks of a grey metal piled beneath it.

Each shelf held a single large ruby the size of my fist. Coating it on all sides were bands of silver and bronze. As I picked one up, it began to glow with a weak inner light.

Golem Core		Further Description *Yes*/No	
Details:		This magical artifact forms the core of a multi-use Golem.	
Rarity:	Magical:	Durability:	Charge:
Rare	Yes	99/100	4/100

I hefted it in one hand, feeling a slight tug as it drew mana from me to replenish itself. Inside the ruby, the light began to grow stronger.

Slowly spiraling and spinning, the glow flashed with increasing brightness until, at a charge of ten out of one hundred, it seemed to vibrate like a car engine starting. The light changed from a weak flicker to a steady pulse.

I grinned and ordered Bob to grab the remaining two cores from the shelf and as much of the metal on the floor as possible. As he stooped to obey, I set off walking back to the manawell. When I reached it, the damn dwarf was lying in the basin on his back, eyes closed, floating in what seemed his own personal, if small, pool! I coughed and glared down at him, disgruntled at my own dusty, dirty, and exhausted condition. He merrily waved up at me, floating in comfort.

"Maybe I should name you Gollum or something," I muttered, thinking about how the little bastard had me doing all the work, when he grinned wider and shook his head.

"It be all right, laddie. I saw ye were busy, an' I dinna want to distract ye, so I named meself. I liked yer legends; Oracle be tellin' me about yer memories o' them. So now I be Hephaestus, creator of weapons!"

I frowned and was about to wind him up when Oracle flew across the room and piped up from behind me.

"That's wonderful! Welcome to the family, Hephaestus!" I spun around, and she smiled at me shyly. "You don't mind me coming back down, now do you? Seneschal has managed to extend his reach to cover the entire tower now, so you don't need me out there anymore, right?"

I took a deep breath and shook my head, turning back to the grinning dwarf. I was going to have to get him back soon, or he'd become unbearable. I just knew it.

"Anyway, I see you've a core! And Boney over there has some iron for me. Between those and some stone, we can be makin' a basic golem! Enough to get us started at least!"

"Wait," I said, holding up one hand. "I don't like how this is going. I'll listen to your advice, and I don't mind you naming yourself. I'm totally fine with all of that, Hephaestus, but I want to hear the options before we start."

"Ach! Aye, o' course. Sorry, master. I tend ta get a wee bit carried away, is all," he said, shifting to standing atop the manawell again.

"Call me Jax. That's fine, but I want to hear the options, all right? And can Seneschal hear us? I know he can't appear here, not yet, but can he hear—"

"I can hear you, Jax. Thank you for including me."

"Ah, that's great. Welcome to the party, Seneschal," I said, getting myself comfortable on a pile of rubble. "Okay. Options, people, let's hear them," I said, clapping my hands together. Oracle and Hephaestus looked at each other, then the dwarf shrugged and started talking.

"Well, Jax, it be simple. There be only one genesis chamber intact, and it be a bit o' a mess as well, needin' a class-two repair and renovation. Using that, I can make us a basic golem or servitor, difference between them be that a golem be for more heavy work, like diggin', buildin', an' fightin'.

"And a servitor be more delicate, better at makin' things, cookin', that kinda thing. Golems be split into two castes, construction and war, while servitors be split into servant and crafter. They both have seven ranks, going from basic ta simple, complex, advanced, greater, lord, an' king. As a rule o' thumb, the lower the level, the dumber they be.

"A 'basic' golem has t' be controlled by meself constantly. A simple one can be given the commands and sent away. Complex can be given a set of things ta do and ways ta respond and will report back for orders if it can't solve an issue. Each level adds abilities, until you reach 'king.' A crafter king can create things the like of which you canna imagine.

"Only been one, as far as I know, and he…well, he created things like the flying islands, the Prax, and the Great Portal. Same for a king o' war, except not only could he fight like nothin' else, he could assume command of all other golems. Took a lot o' battles to destroy the only one of those that was ever built. All the empire and the kingdoms agreed to never build another." He looked at me, waiting as I digested the information, until I finally spoke.

"So, we have three cores. We desperately need to repair things, but we also need to clear away and collect resources. If we can only build 'basic' level, I guess that means we need what, two construction golems and one servant-class servitor?" I asked, looking from him to Oracle, and then concentrating and throwing Seneschal a comment as well.

"Feel free to say if you disagree, mate!"
"I do not disagree."
Hephaestus grinned at me. "Aye, laddie; if you've got three cores, that be a blessin'. Time was, we had thousands of 'em here. Even between looters and damage, we've probably still got a few dozen lyin' around. All we gotta do is uncover 'em! There be other storerooms on the first level below ground, but they're buried for now. We can have one golem clearin' away the rubble in here and gatherin' resources; what do you want the other two doin'?"

"I think we need to move the working genesis chamber to somewhere more secure, once it's made the three units. Then the servitor can work on repairing it, while the other golem works on sealing up the ground floor. In the meantime, let's see if we can make this place a bit more defensible."

"Aye, laddie, that works. I can have the servitor move my manawell, make it bigger, and maybe have it construct a creation table when we get time." Seeing my confused look, he carried on. "A creation table shows the state of a bonded area; in this case, the tower and whatever outbuildings happens to surround it. It can give information on whatever you want to see, including any notes you want to add to it. It be like a map, but one that you can command the tower and its capabilities from. There be one at the top o' the tower, but I dinna think ye want ta be climbin' that far, eh?"

I shuddered at the thought of climbing the tower every time I wanted to look things over.

"Can one of the golems bring that one down? And why is it at the top, anyway? I mean. Seriously, people, why the hell does everyone have to climb the entire goddamn tower every time? It takes all day!" I said, exasperation staining my voice.

"It can be, or at least there's no reason it can't be moved. Also, not everyone would need to. Only the leaders of the tower were permitted in the higher levels, and they would each be taught a teleport spell as part of their induction," Oracle said cheerily as I growled at the ridiculousness of it all.

"Well how about teaching me a spell like that?" I asked hopefully.

"Well, it requires considerably more mana than you have access to, and it's only valid for places you've already been, so…"

"How much mana?"

"I think, given your level of skill and abilities…" Oracle frowned as she concentrated, before smiling sunnily and dropping the bombshell. "Just over a thousand mana."

"Feck."

"It's not that bad, Jax; it's only one hundred points into Intelligence, not including class skills and bonuses."

"Double feck," I said, turning back to Hephaestus. "Okay, then. How long will it take to build them?"

"Well, the servitor will take about three hours, normally, but with the state the chamber be in now, I figure about seven. Then it can be workin' on the chamber while the golems be built. They'll be takin' about ten hours each, state my poor chamber be in," Hephaestus said, shaking his head in sorrow.

"Great. Well, get building, I guess, but start with a golem, then the servitor, then the second golem. As soon as the first golem is built, get it up to the top of the tower and bring the creation table down. We can set it up on few levels up once I've sorted out where we're going to base ourselves from now on. Then we can set it to clearing the ground floor and reinforcing the entrances. I want it sealed up enough that we can at least sleep safely while I decide on the next move."

"Aye, my lord, and congratulations. You do be on your way to full control of the tower now."

You have achieved progress in your Quest: A Place to Lay Your Head.

Wisps sworn fealty: 3/3
Locations cleared and secured: 3/5
SporeMother killed: 1/1
Guardians claimed: 0/10
Workers claimed: 0/10

Rewards: The Great Tower is yours to command. Surrounding area will become aware of your rightful ownership. Access to supplies and facilities. 100,000xp.

I grinned at them as I dismissed the prompt. I had a hell of a lot to do if I wanted to make this place safe to live in, and that was only the first step. I needed to find Tommy. He could be anywhere, but knowing him, he'd stick out like a sore thumb. All I had to do was get this place ticking along, then I could get out to look for him.

"Hey, Hephaestus," I said, a sudden thought coming to mind. "Do you have any golem designs that can fly?"

"Several, laddie, but none that can be built right now. We'd need more cores, more resources, and ta level the genesis chamber up ta 'advanced level for true flight. Why?"

"I want to scout the area surrounding the tower," I said, unable to hide my disappointment.

"Ach, we can do that easily enough. I thought you meant really *fly*! We could build a basic scout, nowt more than a glider, and we'd have ta get its core back ta the tower ta see what it saw, but we could build one sharp enough. We'd need, let's see…" Hephaestus flicked up a screen in the air and started drawing, discarding designs and improving on others. After a few minutes, he flipped it around so I could see it and grinned up at me. "Well, what do ye think?"

I stared at the design in amazement. It was a giant eyeball hanging down from a long wing, much in the same way the body of a microlight hung below its canopy. Dozens of small wings extended from the main one, slowly moving in different directions as the image shifted.

"It'd no be capable o' real flight, ye understand, but chuck it from the top o' the tower, and it'd glide for at least a day. Then we just collect it an' bring it back. We can then update the maps from whatever it sees."

"It's brilliant, Heph, but what about the collecting? How do we find it?"

"Heph, is it? Humph! Well, it do be a mouthful, I suppose, but no callin' me that around company! Anyway, we tell it to land somewhere we can find it, o' course! Send your minion out to wait at that location, and it can bring it back while we all do the real work."

"What would we need to make it?"

"That's where it becomes a wee bit trickier. We need a golem core, a damn ton of wood—about twenty boards should do it, give or take with damage, and then we'd have ta cut the core free when it was recovered—something ta protect the core and keep the eye safe, so maybe ten ingots o' iron. Yeah, that should be enough," Heph said, nodding to himself in satisfaction.

"Okay, where the hell will I find another core?" I asked. "I know we can get wood when the golem starts clearing the first floor, so that's no issue, and the iron we found should be enough, right?"

"Hmm, well, it'll be enough fer one, but that'd be all that we have left. We need ta get the rest o' the storeroom cleared and get this whole room sorted out. There be more buried here than just that, after all. Anyway, another core, ye say? There will be some in the tower, probably dozens still intact, but where is anyone's guess. I'd bet the safest place ta find them be where the old golems were.

"Might take a while ta find an intact core, but there were dozens of war golems destroyed on the first floor, dozens higher up where they made their last stand. Ye might be able ta salvage some gear from them?" Heph shrugged. "Beyond that, yer guess is as good as mine, laddie. I'd bet looters have had bits away, and the SporeMother will have drained any cores it could find, so maybe search this room, too?"

"I'll leave this room to the golem, and I'll start on the ground level," I decided, summoning Bob and setting off with a casual wave to Heph as we left. He was already absorbed in building the first golem, with bits of materials floating upright and spiraling into the chamber at his command.

We jogged up until we exited out into what I was coming to think of as the atrium, a huge room that took the majority of the front of the ground floor. There were obvious windows that had been buried and broken, and piles of debris blocking as much of the light as possible. The narrow exits were heavily overgrown, and I realized I had no clue where to start.

"Uhh, Seneschal, little help here, buddy?"

"Of course, Jax. To your left, there is a concentration of high-grade metals and resources. I believe this to be a golem corpse. I will make each deposit more identifiable for you momentarily."

"Thanks, Seneschal!"

I broke the connection and turned my attention to the area he'd indicated. In one corner, there was a noticeable mound covered in overgrown moss, fungus, and the black tar-like crap the sporelings had left everywhere.

I shrugged and dispatched Bob to the pile, letting him tear into it. After a few minutes of examining the rest of the room, I started to notice certain areas giving off a faint glow, similar to the way my enhanced vision worked.

"Hey, Sen—"

"Yes, Jax, that is my work."

"Coolio, thanks again, buddy!"

I dismissed the connection to Seneschal and turned to Oracle. "Your connection with me…are you still connected to the tower and the others, too?" I asked, an idea coming to mind.

"Yes, of course. What are you thinking?"

"I have a minimap in my HUD, can you populate it with data from Seneschal? Such as showing the golem corpse locations for now and we can get rid of it later?"

I caught the look on her face and took a deep breath. This was going to take some time to explain, I just knew it.

In the end, it didn't take as long as I'd expected, and after an hour of experimentation, The minimap in the top right of my vision showed glowing dots where golems were located. It faded into the background unless I concentrated on it, so it wasn't as distracting as I'd feared.

With the map in place and Bob clearing the last of the debris away, I moved over and helped him out, using my combination spell again to create boiling hot water. I washed the pile down until it was clean enough that I thought I could handle it without vomiting. As I finished, I noticed Bob staring at me with what I could only assume was reproach. He was covered in literal crap, mud, and fungus, and here I was refusing to touch the pile he'd uncovered until it was cleaner.

"Sorry, Bob," I said, turning the same combination of spells on him, leaving him cleaner and seemingly, even if only in my mind, happier.

Once I was finished playing cleaner, I turned to inspect the pile of rubble. Sometimes the chunks were solid stone, while others were marbled with what my Identify spell recognized as metal alloys: copper, tin, steel, a few I didn't recognize and even a few trace amounts of gold and silver. Eventually, I found the core, or what I assumed were remnants of it. The bronze and silver bands were shattered, and the ruby had cracked like glass.

Destroyed Golem Core		Further Description *Yes/No*	
Details:		This magical artifact forms the core of a multi-use golem but is damaged beyond repair.	
Rarity:	Magical:	Durability:	Charge:
Rare	Yes	0/100	0/100

After using my spell to be sure, I chucked the core aside onto the pile of rubble and useless bits we'd uncovered. There was a significant load of useful ores in it, but I had no way to remove them at the moment, so they'd have to wait until later. Bob and I moved onto the next pile indicated and began to work. The two of us working together uncovered it much more quickly.

Again, the core was shattered, but we also found more piles of metal and gem-infused stone, so we went on. For the rest of the day, we worked with Oracle standing guard over the nearest entrance, despite Seneschal's reassurances that we were safe. We cleared three more individual corpses, and finally sorted through a pile of nearly a dozen corpses out in the open area beyond the tower, despite needing to almost dig them free, thanks to the grass, vines, and worse.

I stood over the intact head of a golem, the first I'd seen, and examined the features. It seemed to be asleep, a carving of a handsome male face, surrounded by waves of alabaster hair. As I looked at the head, I realized the hair was laid as though it had solidified after death. The head lay on its side, eyes closed in death or sleep, with debris piled around it. The hair had been crushed on one side, where the weight of the head had compressed it against a piece of a leg.

For long seconds, I looked at the serene face, wondering about the last sight those eyes had seen, when Oracle flew over to me, shaking me out of my daze.

"You found one!" she shouted, spinning around me before landing lightly by the head and stroking its face. "Sleep well, honored fallen," she whispered, gently kissing its cheek.

"Wait, what?" I asked, confused as I watched Oracle.

"A core! I did tell you that war golems have the cores in their heads, didn't I? It's intact, I can feel it!"

"A war golem? No, you didn't tell me that," I said quietly, crouching next to the head where it lay half-hidden in the dirt. I carefully swept the soil free, lifting the head with a grunt.

Balthazar Core		Further Description *Yes/No*	
Details:		This is the intact head and core of the golem warrior Balthazar, Legion Knight of the Second Circle and thrice-honored duelist. His memories were transferred into the golem core upon his death at his request, so that he may continue to serve the empire.	
Rarity:	Magical:	Durability:	Charge:
Unique	Yes	87/100	0/100

I read the details before looking back at the head that I held in my hands.

"He transferred his memories into the core. Does that mean what I think it does?" I asked quietly.

"He was a soldier of the empire, a high-ranking one. I remember him, a little. War golems are generally simple constructions, but the higher level they are, the stronger they are, and the more capacity they have for memories and abilities. I thought him lost, but all this time, he was sleeping. Balthazar was the leader of the tower's war golems, and was a highly intelligent, capable warrior."

"Can we restore him?" I asked, looking at the body parts nearby. It was easy to pick out the parts that had come from him. Where others were constructed from limestone or granite and a little base metal, some tin and iron, his body was as different as night and day. His primary material had been white marble interwoven with faint traceries of gold. I tried my Identify spell on the metal that had coated sections of him but got nothing. Whatever he had been, it was a far cry from the others.

"It's probably possible to restore him; well, I think it is, but he was a golem lord. We'd need to fully rebuild the genesis chambers to their old state and have a lot of materials ready. But it's probably possible," Oracle said, sounding unsure.

"Well, he gave his life for the empire; twice already, in fact. I think he deserves us trying at least, don't you?" I asked her.

Surprisingly, it was Bob that responded first, moving forward and reaching out with one clawed hand to pat the marble head in my hands.

It was awkward and nearly drove the head through my hands and onto the floor, but when I looked up at him, staring into the red light that glowed out from the depths of his eye sockets, I couldn't help but smile.

"Looks like Bob agrees," Oracle said softly, landing on my shoulder and smiling up at the giant skeleton. He straightened up, returning to clearing the ground and uncovering bits of corpses, but every once in a while, he looked over as though considering.

"Yeah, I think that's the first sign of life from him, isn't it?" I whispered as we watched my minion work.

"There have been a few others, nothing I could be sure of, but yeah, that's definitely him being, well, him, I guess."

I grinned at her and we went back to work. I tried talking to Bob, as did Oracle, but either he wasn't ready to talk or couldn't yet. It took the rest of the day to clear the section we were working on. When we finally hauled it all to the third floor, the location I'd picked as our new base, we were all exhausted. I took an inventory of the parts I'd managed to free that Heph said were usable. He'd estimated the amount of materials we could get from the rest, once we had access to a smelter, anyway.

Golem Cores:

- 1x Balthazar Core
- 2x Golem Core

Materials:

- Copper ingots x42
- Gold ingots x3
- Iron ingots x17
- Lead ingots x4
- Orichalcum ingots x11
- Starsteel ingots x23
- Silver ingots x16
- Tin ingots x12

All told, it was easily enough to build dozens of golems. We only had two cores, so that was the limit for now, so I settled on building two construction-class golems.

Heph informed me that it would take a few days to finish construction of the golems, move the genesis chamber, and get everything built. So, I settled in for a sleep, confident in Bob and the wisps' abilities to watch over me.

I'd wanted to set up the scout to cover the immediate area at least, but after the time I'd spent reviewing the state of the tower, I just couldn't justify it.

Besides, I still had the Scroll of the Eagle, which I could use to get a good view of the area. It'd be gone once I did, but at least then I could control it.

"Hey, Oracle," I said, a thought coming to me unbidden. "That essence core thingy I got from the SporeMother, can we use that in place of a golem core? Is that what it's for?"

"No! No, no, no, Jax. An essence core is what it sounds like; it's the compressed essence of the creature. I know some of the nobles of the empire made a game of collecting them for some reason, but hell no. Why would you want to put something like that in a body of stone? All you'd have done is created a stronger version of the SporeMother, with no brain to guide it. It'd be horrible!"

"Ah, righto. I get it, leave the core alone." I shuddered at the thought and packed it away again before going to sleep. *Every day is a damn school day*, I thought to myself.

CHAPTER TWENTY-EIGHT

When I finally awoke the next morning, the golem that had been sent to retrieve the creation table from the top of the tower was approaching, its heavy footfalls echoing in the silent halls. Looking around the room I'd appropriated, I decided to clear the room fully before settling on a location for everything.

The room was square, a single large chamber with two doors, including the entrance. I had designated the second smaller room that led off it as the storeroom and had set Bob to clearing it before moving all our golem materials inside. He'd managed that fairly quickly, and either with Oracle's direction or his own burgeoning awareness, he'd decided to continue working. He was currently about a third of the way across the main room, stripping out the variety of plant life, fungus, soil, and general assortment of hundreds of years of accumulated debris.

I quickly got myself sorted, a drink and a mouthful of hard jerky to keep me going while I joined in to help clear the room. Once the golem had set the table down, I directed it to dig in. In short order, the room was, if not livable again, at least not the absolute shit tip it'd been before.

I'd take that as a win. While we'd been busy, the servant class servitor had been completed. Before long, it arrived in our new base of operations. I sent the golem back downstairs to begin clearing out and reinforcing the entrance, making it as safe as possible, while I directed the servitor to strip the crap from the great windows on one side of the room.

"Heph, can you hear me?"
"Aye, Jax, I be here."
"How's the golem construction coming?"
"It be acceptable, although the additional golems ye requested will require some repairs be made ta the genesis chamber first. Ah'd bet six hours 'til the second construction-class golem be completed, then two hours ta move the chamber ta yer location. Three hours ta reassemble and carry out the most basic repairs and we can begin construction o' the second batch.

"The servitor class can continue with the repairs while the chamber works, so I estimate the third construction-class golem will be ready to be deployed around midday tomorrow."

"Coolio, and while the chamber is working, the second golem can be used to excavate and clear the genesis cavern out?"

"Genesis cavern? I like it, aye. The second construction-class unit will return there and begin clearing and repairing ma home...wait...Seneschal is cutting in."

"Go on, Seneschal, what's up?"

"I have detected a disturbance on the twenty-sixth floor. Hephaestus confirms that he feels it as well. It began four minutes ago but appears to be spreading to the entire floor. Inside the area of effect, all our senses are dulled. It appears that there has been no change, but we cannot be sure. As this is also the tower garrison's upper armory, it seems suspicious, so I'd recommend checking it out. In addition, it was the logical place for a last stand for the tower's defenders, so there may be more intact cores available there."

"What the fuck! Wait a minute, what damn armory? Nobody told me about this!"

"It was inaccessible to you until we took the lower floors of the tower, so I didn't see any reason to mention it." Oracle spoke up.

"So there's an armory on the twenty-sixth floor? How many others are there?" I asked, thinking it was a strange place to locate it.

"There were two others. The one on the ground floor is buried. The roof has collapsed in that section, and, well...it's not stable. I think we need to avoid it until the area is rebuilt. The other one is at the entrance to the labyrinth, but it looks fairly overgrown."

"Okay, hold the fuck up. First of all, *tell me these things*. Don't just make the decision that I don't need to know, okay? Secondly, what labyrinth?!" I asked in stunned disbelief.

"It's standard for each one of the Great Towers to be constructed with a training labyrinth. Ours had a small watch post set outside the entrance, complete with an armory and medical center. It seems fairly self-evident. Why?"

"So, there's a place pretty close that's teeming with monsters and creatures and traps and shit, and you didn't think this was important news to mention?"

"Ah! No, Jax, you don't understand. The SporeMother would never have permitted other creatures this close to her nest. As soon as she cleared out the remaining defenders of the tower, she would have turned to the labyrinth. The entrance looked like it had collapsed ages ago, so I didn't think it was important when we were outside earlier—"

"What, so it'll have just collapsed, and that's it? End of story?" I said, growing more and more annoyed. It felt like every time I sneezed, there was something new going on, and my advisors were keeping it from me.

"Probably. Look, the entrance has collapsed. The buildings that were on either side of it were destroyed at some point shortly after the SporeMother first broke into the grounds. When I asked Seneschal to look it over, it didn't look like it'd been disturbed in hundreds of years. I didn't want to get your hopes up, that's all. I'm sorry," Oracle said, her voice close to tears.

Sap that I was, my anger dissipated like smoke in the wind.

"Okay, but come on, guys. I'm supposed to be the boss here! Tell me this shit, okay? If I'm doing something wrong or missing something, I need to know!"

"Such as askin' questions and no' investigatin' something weird going on in the remainin' easily accessible armory?"

As soon as Heph interjected, I cursed and grabbed my weapon, directing Bob off up the stairs ahead of me as we set off running.

Allowing myself to be distracted so easily and basically doing a Dr. Evil monologue about being "the big cheese" was *not* the way to have a good, long, and productive life, I reflected. Jumping over a small pile of rubble, I ran along behind Bob as he pounded up the stairs.

It took what felt like hours, but probably wasn't more than forty minutes to reach the twenty-fifth level. Bob was waiting for me, as I'd ordered him, with Oracle settled atop his skull. Once I staggered onto the floor, wheezing, I collapsed to one knee and tried to stop my heart from exploding from sheer overwork.

I'd literally run miles in full armor with weapons up more than twenty-five flights of stairs. My old trainers in Black Sheep would have been proud of me. Although, knowing them, Lee would have probably beaten Bob here and been doing push ups until I arrived. Crazy bastard. The thought was fleeting, but I found myself strangely missing the days when I trained there, and I felt slightly better about things.

I forced myself to my feet and cautiously began to walk across the hallway toward the far stairwell. This floor was one of the "room" layouts made up of a dozen small rooms on either side of the corridor, with small balconies and benches set out at regular intervals. I concentrated on moving as carefully as I could, casting a spell I'd hardly used since arriving, Chameleon.

My skin darkened, the oily substance flowing over me as I began sneaking up the stairs. Unlike most of the spells I had, this one was a silent cast, and the change it made in a darkened corridor was considerable. I crept up the stairs until my mana reached the two thirds mark, then I crouched, waiting for my mana to refill. Each time it finished, I set off again, sneaking higher and higher until I got a notification.

Congratulations!

You have increased your Sneak skill by one point.

Continue practicing to increase this most useful skill.

I stopped instantly. In the games I'd played, getting a marker like this meant active improvement. *That* meant someone was close enough to see me, but I was preventing it somehow. Oracle had swapped from Bob's skull to sitting on my shoulder, while Bob waited at the bottom of the stairs. His sneak skills were slightly worse than mine, which is to say he clattered like a shitting dog wearing a necklace of tambourines.

I moved against the nearest wall and crouched, letting my timer expire. When nothing happened, I slowly recast it, and inched up further.

I still couldn't see anything, but wind from an open window was blowing down the stairs, and it carried some really weird sounds. They were muffled by distance and the shape of the tower, but it still sounded somewhat like arguing voices, as well as an engine humming.

It wasn't as loud as a car close by, but judging from my rough position in the stairwell, I had at least a hundred meters to go before I reached the next floor. For it to be that loud from such a distance…

SLAM! I grunted in pain and shock as something hit me forcefully in the back, throwing me to my knees and driving my face into the wall.

I felt as much as heard the crunch of my nose breaking...again. Cold, sharp metal grated against a rib as Oracle dashed from my shoulder, disappearing up into the darkness of the vaulted stairwell.

"Stay down, thief!" A voice whispered in my ear. I coughed blood and convulsed against the wall. The bastard had stabbed me in the back!

I growled and twisted my fingers into the needed forms, and with a few words muttered under my breath, I cast Weak Lightning Bolt. I couldn't see my attacker, but I didn't need to. I'd spared the time to tell Oracle to heal me through our link, then grabbed blindly behind me, flooding the body I felt with the magic.

As we both collapsed spasming on the stairs, we twitched apart and slid down. I felt the dagger ripped from my back, then the glorious feeling of healing magic flooding my body. A few feet away, a dark blur rolled down the stairs. As the lightning faded, the dark shape flowed to one side, trying to disappear again. Whoever they were, they were much better at stealth than I was!

A clattering noise below told me Bob was on his way, and I grinned. All I had to do was hold this asshole here for a few minutes, and I'd have backup. In the meantime, Oracle was keeping as high as she could, and I was trying to look everywhere and nowhere. I blinked and realized the blur was gone, and I heard a chuckle from the other side of the stairwell. I spun around reflexively, looking to see where he was and how he'd gotten around me, when pain seared through me as a knife cut deep into my left leg, bypassing my armor.

I cried out and tried to turn around, only to have the leg give out as I collapsed to the ground. I grabbed at the knife with my left hand, drawing a sword with my right and lashing out aimlessly in circles as I tried to drive my attacker back.

"Really, boy? Is that the best you can do? I expected more from someone that dared trespass in my lord's Great Tower!" The voice came from my right. I looked in that direction again before I could stop myself. My eyes widened at the last second as I realized I'd felt this trick before. I rolled to the right, bouncing down first one, then another, and finally a half dozen steps.

Metal hit stone behind me, and low laughter filled the stairwell.

"Well done. You dodged my dagger and probably caused yourself more damage in the act!"

I growled, biting my lip to prevent a moan from escaping, then gasped in relief as Oracle's next healing spell took hold. I rolled to my feet, drawing my second sword with my left hand. Setting myself with my back against one wall, I tried to spot any telltale sign of movement.

"Well, speak up, boy. Last chance to do so; your little pet can't heal you all day!" The voice came from my left, higher up the stairwell again, and this time I was ready.

I crouched low, both swords flashing out in upwards overlapping arcs and spiraling over my head. The left blade flashed through the air unobstructed, but the right snagged on something. An indrawn breath and a hiss of pain followed resistance against my blade. The tension released, as if someone were jumping away.

I remembered the arena, fighting against that bastard rogue. Although those tactics might work, the third fight had gone better. I grinned to myself as I dropped my left sword, summoning a fountain of clear water off to one side. I made sure to cause the water to splash down on steps higher up than the ones I stood on.

Oracle repeated the spell three more times until a veritable small flood of water flowed down the stairs. All I needed to do was distract him long enough, and I was going to fry him in the water with my lightning spell. *Let's see you hide from that, asshole!*

A small dagger sprouted from my left shoulder with a blossoming pain, ending my spell casting with that hand just as Bob came bounding into sight further down the stairwell. I swore as laughter echoed behind me.

"What, you think one of her servants would dare attack me? Watch and learn!" The darkness a few steps further down the stairs suddenly seemed to flow apart, and a man appeared, wrapped in dark leathers. A hood covered his face, and daggers protruded from sheaths all over his body. The only sign of me fighting so desperately for my life was a short tear in his cloak and a thin line of blood dripping from his side.

He held out a small stone in his left hand, and it emitted a weak, red light which quickly grew stronger, illuminating the stairwell around us.

"I am Lucius, and I serve High Lord Barabarattas, your mistress's master! You will detain this thief for me and carry him up to our ship. Once I'm done questioning him, your mistress can have what's left, per the agreement." He spoke with confidence, obviously used to commanding the dead and diseased things that resided in the tower.

What he didn't consider was whether Bob was one of those, until it was too late. Shame for him, really, as he received a terrible shock when Bob lashed out with the mace he held in his upper right hand and crushed his opponent's skull with a sickening, meaty crunch.

The freshly made corpse stood for half a second, as though unable to understand why his orders hadn't been obeyed, before his bones seemed to liquify, and he collapsed to the floor.

I let out a gasp of relief and slipped down to join him on the floor as Oracle stopped casting her fountain spells and used the last of the mana to heal me fully.

I lay back on the stairs for a couple of seconds to catch my breath before forcing myself to my feet. I clapped one hand on Bob's bony shoulder and looked at him in the glowing red flare that served as an eye.

"Thanks, man," I said simply. "I don't want to know if I would have won without you intervening. Thank you. You, too, Oracle; thank you both."

She flitted down out of the darkness and sat on my shoulder, leaning in and giving me a hug that I assumed was meant to be reassuring. In actuality, it probably could have killed me, given her impressive chest and the fact that she was perched on my shoulder. She'd somehow shifted her size again, growing to nearly two feet.

I resisted the instinctual urge to bury my face deeper in the cleavage that was threatening to cut off my air and held my breath until she moved back.

"You scared me there, Jax!" she scolded, stroking my hair. *Mixed messages all the damn day,* I thought.

"Scared me too, Oracle. That fucker was terrifying," I said, bringing up a new notification.

Congratulations!

You have killed a level 19 Rogue for a total of 290xp.

Progress to level 7 stands at 8,140/14,000

Your Minion receives additional experience.

"A fucking rogue. Damn, I hate fighting those sneaky shits," I muttered to myself as I stretched. I was fully healed; I could see my health was full and everything, but I still *felt* wrong. It was most likely the disconnect between the knowledge that I should still be injured and the reality of healing magic. I shrugged; I'd get over it.

I took a deep breath and hunted around quickly, gathering up my weapons and resolving to come back and loot the corpse later. I could still hear the sounds from the level above, and the thought of more of these cocksuckers had me on edge.

I gave my mana a few more minutes to refill, then started sneaking again. As soon as the doorway from the stairs onto the main floor appeared, I cast Chameleon and gave a little sigh in relief when I didn't get any warnings about my sneak level increasing. I decided that was because there was nobody around, not at all that they were watching me and about to stab me. Definitely not that...

I'd ordered Bob to come up behind me very slowly, like one-step-at-a-time slowly, to minimize the noise. Now that I was there, though, something else was making a hell of a racket.

It was a mixture of sounds: clattering metal, muffled shouts, and occasional banging, filled in by a deep underlying *thrummm*, like an engine whirring away.

I made my way onto the floor, seeing what I'd ignored in my earlier haste to reach the lower floors. This entire floor was split in two. One side held the stairwells with a large balcony with an area I'd taken for a scoured clean garden, and a huge number of collapsed rooms and rubble piles cutting off the view to the other side.

Upon closer inspection, the rubble was mostly made up of destroyed golems, bits of corpses, and what looked like a collapsed wall from a large room I assumed was the old armory.

I took all of it in with a single glance, now that I knew what I was looking at from digging through the piles of golems downstairs.

The thing that really caught my eye was in the space I'd taken for a garden, but now I recognized it as an outdoor marshalling yard. It was a ship, an honest-to-god ship-looking thing that hovered a few feet off the ground!

It had a broad hull, a long gangplank lowered to the ground, and four large cylinders attached to the sides of the ship. Each cylinder was pulsing with a blue light that flared from pale to deep indigo and back again.

As the light cycled to the paler end of the spectrum, the ship would slowly sink, then, as the color deepened, it would rise again, giving an impression of bobbing in the wind, as though at sea. With each rise and fall, the wood creaked, the sails that were furled above the deck and to either side flapped and rattled, and the clatter of people walking up the gangplank increased.

I stared in shock, the ship distracting me from realizing what they were doing at first.

A dozen or more figures of different races and species were stomping up and down, carrying weapons and armor! There were piles of both set off to one side, and as one group loaded up from them, I heard the stomp and jingle of heavily laden boots coming from behind!

Bob darted back out of sight on the stairwell before I could order him, Oracle riding his skull as she often did. I took a few quick steps to the side and dove behind some rubble. I lay on my back, as still as possible, well aware that the rubble was barely high enough to hide me from an inquisitive toddler, never mind anyone looking properly.

As a Chameleon spell rippled into place, I allowed a very quiet sigh of relief. Glancing to the stairwell, I saw Oracle watching me. She'd cast it before I could, bless her! I quickly told her and Bob to stay hidden and wait, and she melted back into the shadows.

The sounds came closer; the jingle of chainmail, clinking of armor plates, and clatter of metal on metal, until figures walked past. I shifted slowly, moving as carefully as I could to get an unobstructed view. Then my blood ran cold.

A huge figure stopped with its back to me, clad in heavy armor, a spear in one hand and a large triangular heater shield strapped to his back. Before him, a line staggered past, headed towards the marshalling yard. The men, women, and children who stumbled and limped under pounds of equipment were of many species: human, dwarves, and some kind of cat person.

But what really stood out were the god damn chains.

They were chained together by their necks, a tight collar linked to the chains leading from one to another. Every single one of them looked half-dead from starvation, struggling under what had to be dozens, if not hundreds of pounds of equipment. Piles of swords, armfuls of axes, and mounds of rotted leather and metal armor weighed down people who looked like they should be starring in a famine aid commercial. The fact that the figure with his back to me seemed utterly unconcerned that his slaves carried weapons told me volumes as well.

These people were broken, mentally more than physically. The burden of resignation hunched their shoulders, and defeat haunted their eyes.

"Please, sir," A weak voice whispered as a dirty, blonde elven girl who looked to be six or seven turned to the figure as the line moved past. "Please...some water...a rest. I beg—"

With a growl, the figure lifted one steel-gauntleted fist and backhanded her, knocking her from her feet with a cry of pain.

As she fell, others connected to her on either side were jerked from their feet. The line came to a halt, equipment falling everywhere as a shout came from deeper into the hall.

"Esold! Ye gods be damned, fool! Ye damage the merchandise, and who'll replace it? We barely got enough crew to keep my damn ship afloat! The SporeMother'll be pissed!"

"It'll keep its mouth shut, or Lord Barabarattas'll gut it! And you'll keep your mouth shut, worm, or I'll shut it for you!" He raised one booted heel and kicked the small girl in the face as she tried to rise.

Blood sprayed from her mouth as she fell onto the floor again, crying out as she cut herself on the pile of daggers she'd been carrying.

My blood flashed from ice cold to boiling with rage, and I was on my feet, closing the dozen feet from behind the armored figure before he knew I was there.

I lifted my naginata in both hands and drove it forward, avoiding the shield, and piercing the thinner chainmail covering his lower back. It ripped into his kidneys before exiting through the front, trapping itself in the twisted steel.

I hissed through gritted teeth, "Surprise, motherfucker!" before lifting and throwing aside the skewered man, then drawing both my swords.

There were three more armored figures. One was short, and wore cheap, older armor, but was backing away. I focused on the other two who spun at the sound of their comrade screaming in shock and pain. I took three quick steps and leaped across two fallen slaves to land before the man I judged to be the greatest threat. Clad all in red, he was human with a shaved head and a beard that reached mid-chest. He was heavily muscled and dressed in an armored robe, of all things.

His chest was covered in interlocking leather sections that separated out like a Roman legionnaire's kilt from his waist. His arms were covered in bracers and blue, woad-like tattoos, as was his face. He was the first to react, both hands raising and electricity flashing between his fingers as he pointed them at me. I landed and rushed forward, stabbing out with both swords as he released his spells. The strike catapulted me away in a flash of light and searing pain.

I was sent flying backward, my feet catching on a pile of rubble and flipping me over to come crashing into the wall upside down, braced between two particularly large stones.

I jerked and shuddered as the last of the spell ran through me, then slumped down and almost wedged myself on my head. I had to twist and kick off the wall, but by the time I landed on my back on the floor, a second pair of lightning spells slammed into me, causing tremendous pain and dropping my health bar to half.

When my eyes cleared, I was pulled half-upright. With a click, a smaller figure locked a thick collar of metal around my neck. He was now recognizable as a dwarf wearing armor a size too big for him.

"Sorry 'bout this lad...ye should have stayed hidden there. I'd no' have said owt," he whispered as he just barely inclined his head toward my previous hiding place.

I grimaced as I reached up to grab the collar, feeling it send a warning shock through my body as I touched it. I tore my hand away and reached for my daggers, only to have my hands freeze an inch from the hilts.

"Ye canna touch owt ye think of as a weapon, laddie. 'Tis the collar's magic. Try, and ye'll only hurt yerself," the dwarf said, looking ashamed as he avoided my eyes. I tried to punch him, and again, found that I couldn't. This time, a flare of pain ran down my body from the collar as a reward.

"Get him upright, Oren! I want a look at my new slave. And you, Toka! What do you think I pay you for? Get my face sorted then get Esold healed!"

I was pulled to my feet and saw I'd managed to land a hit on the mage, but it was only a thin cut from his jawline up to his cheek on the left side, barely deeper than a scratch. The last figure scurried across to the tall mage, gesturing at the man I took to be Esold. He was writhing on the floor with my naginata driven through him.

The new figure spoke up with a clear, sibilant lisp. "Shall I heal him first, master? He's—"

"I said, heal me, witch!" The mage backhanded the one he called Toka hard across the face, driving him to his knees to spit blood onto the floor. I looked down at the kneeling figure in shock, then recoiled instinctively.

Toka wore a collection of leather-studded straps and little else. I assumed it was human, but lines of scars covered every exposed inch of flesh, and the straps were barely big enough for decency. When it looked at me, it grinned and licked the blood from the split lip it had been given, shuddering in pleasure and winking at me.

"You'll be fun to train…oh yes…you will!" it whispered. The standing mage grabbed it by its lank, greasy hair and pulled it to its feet.

"Now heal me!" the mage bellowed at Toka.

"I'm sorry, lad," I heard the dwarf whisper by my side as he started relieving me of the daggers he could see.

"Jax! Can you hear me? Are you okay?"

Oracle! In the shock of everything, I'd forgotten that I'd ordered her and Bob to stay hidden!

"Yeah, Oracle. I'm here, and I'm all right. Fuckers stunned me and put a collar on me, though. Can't touch my weapons! I'm gonna need you to do something about that."

"A slave collar? A black metal ring with a lot of symbols carved into it?"

"Can't see it, as I'm wearing it, but it was black, yeah."

"I should be able to block its magic. Just give me a minute…"

I walked beside the dwarf until I stood a few feet from the mage, and looked him in the eyes, ignoring everyone else. Mana flowed through my body, pulsing in and out of the channels in my neck and hesitantly touching the collar before moving more confidently. The collar seemed to give a little shudder then lay still against my skin, inert. God, I loved having Oracle with me at times.

Toka finished healing the mage and stepped aside to head toward Esold, who lay writhing on the floor in a pool of blood.

"What are you grinning at, fool?" the mage said, frowning at me as Oracle spoke up again.

"I can block it for a few minutes, but that's all. It will drain our mana pool quickly; I'm sorry!"

"Don't be sorry, Oracle. That will be all we need. Once the fighting starts, though, get Bob up here and make sure no more of the ones outside come to ruin the party!"

"Well, slave?!" the mage shouted, backhanding me across the mouth.

I shook my head slightly and spat to one side, eyeing the dwarf who stood at my side while holding my weapons.

"If you know what's good for you, you'll stand aside while I sort this tosser out," I said, then turned from his shocked face to look at the wide eyes of the mage as he began to sputter in rage, lifting both hands.

My left hand flipped the toggle on that side of my belt free, sending it flying out to the side as the razor wire unraveled. My right hand pulled the toggle on the other side, and I flicked it upwards.

Both loops unfurled, wrapping around the mage's throat three times before he managed to grab at it. His fingers came away bloody as he gagged.

The spell he'd been summoning died as soon as his fingers abandoned their gestures, and he found himself unable to speak. He tried to twist away from it, reaching for something in a pouch. But I increased the pressure, and he froze, blood seeping down from his new necklace as I spoke.

"Ah, ah! Let's not do anything we might regret, eh?"

My left hand grabbed one of the hidden throwing blades in my bracers, and I turned. Toka was bending over Esold, oblivious to the change in our relative positions and reveling in the obvious pain the warrior was suffering. I threw the blade with a slight grunt of effort, watching it sink into the creature's back below the neck, leaving Toka to collapse, twitching to the floor with a cry of pain and surprise.

I turned back, checking on the mage to make sure he was behaving himself, before turning to the dwarf. He looked worn out, old before his time, with a salt-and-pepper beard, ill-fitting armor, and light spots on his hands where rings were missing. The armor was clearly missing decorative touches; it appeared as though they'd been pried off, leaving just the bare metal behind.

"I take it you don't want to fight me?" I asked him. His eyes widened, and he shook his head. "Good. In that case, put my weapons down, and go sit over there out of the way. You and I'll have words later."

I gestured with a flick of my chin to a pile of rubble off to one side where the slaves were all huddled. He ran to them, dumping my weapons as he went. Then he froze as Bob came thundering out of the stairwell and galloped across the open floor toward the doorway out onto the marshalling yard area.

"No!" he screamed, gesturing wildly and grabbing at a mace nearby. "Get away…leave them alone!"

With that, he set off running after Bob, screaming wildly at the people outside to run. They'd already paused in loading, and most had retreated to the ship, but when they saw Bob, one of them screamed out in panic and spun around, leading a sudden rush of people up the gangplank.

"Spore creatures!"

"Run for it!"

"Get aloft!"

These things and more were screamed as the sailors fled, with a sudden increase in power from the ship's engines as the steady hum grew to a roar.

I felt a change in the razor wire and looked back in time to see that it was unraveling itself, the far end floating in the air as the mage took advantage of my distraction.

I growled and kicked out, Sparta style, catching him in the chest as I pulled on the wire. But it was too late, and the wire came loose.

One hand he pressed to his own throat, trying to staunch the flow of blood, while the other lifted towards me. The familiar blue lightning spell I'd already encountered began to build up as he fell back.

I dove to my left, hitting the ground and rolling, coming to a halt behind a stone pillar that took the brunt of the spell fired at me. My muscles locked up as pain flared, but it only lasted a second. I was back on my feet, one hand tugging free and throwing my hidden blade from my other bracer as I moved to Esold. He was barely alive now, his guts torn open by my earlier attack. He continued bleeding heavily as I ripped my naginata free from him and spun around.

321

I searched for the mage. He'd pulled a potion from his belt rather than start another attack and was hurriedly biting the cork as my flying blade bounced off the wall by his head. I'd missed, but the flinch as he spat out the cork made it clear he realized how close he'd come to being hit.

I ran at him, and he threw up a barrier of sparking light, hunching behind it as he gulped the potion down. I slammed my weapon into his glowing shield. It flared, but I was the one who fell back. Electricity flowed up my arms from my weapon and shaved off even more from my health pool, leaving my arms feeling numb.

"Use your weapon, Jax! Cast through it!"

I heard Oracle in my mind, and a flood of images and knowledge accompanied her sending. How to channel into a weapon, rather than around it, how to funnel it to the point I wanted, and how to counteract lightning. It was simple really. Just match it—lightning shield, meet lightning bolt…

I grinned at the sneering mage as he crouched in perceived safety. Slamming the butt of my naginata down on the floor between us and locking my hands together with it held tightly between them, I summoned the "feeling" of the spell, the desire. I spoke the words, forcing the mana down my arms and into my weapon as I twisted my fingers into the accompanying gestures. I set no limits on the mana to take, flooding all I had into the weapon, which sent my mana bar plummeting even faster than Oracle had been using it up.

The length of the weapon flashed to light, carvings and lines appearing from nowhere as it took on the spell, making the air around me crackle and hum.

With a scream of effort, I flipped the naginata over, changing my grip until it was suspended over my head, point-down. I lunged, driving it with all my strength into the barrier. The mage's sneering expression turned to one of shock as I pierced his barrier with surprising ease. A cascade of sparks rained out as my blade punched through, sliding almost effortlessly into his chest and out his back, neatly bisecting his heart as his barrier collapsed. The collar around my neck gave a twitch before settling again.

I ripped my weapon back from the dead mage. Something hissed as the blade came free, and I twisted around. Bob had pinned the dwarf to the wall with one hand while the ship took off. I took two quick steps and threw my weapon with all my might, watching as it hurtled through the air to slam into the left hindmost engine of the ship before ricocheting off to bounce across the floor. The engine exploded, making the ship list to one side, losing altitude and exposing a second ship on its far side, which was trying to get enough power to lift off as well.

The first ship twisted to the side before its captain could compensate for the change in power and smashed into the second, tearing both of the second ship's engines on one side free with a scream of tortured metal.

The first, larger ship flared its engines again and unfurled its sails, dipping as it fell off the end of the yard before catching itself and limping up into the air. The massive vessel headed away to the south as fast as it could go.

The second ship twisted in the air, half its engines gone, sails and rigging torn from one side, and it began a dive off the end. The crew were screaming, fighting against the engines as they powered the dive faster. As it disappeared, it began to tip over, rolling and spiraling to the ground.

"NOOOOOOOO!" the dwarf screamed, slapping ineffectually at Bob as he was held in place. I collapsed to one knee as the combined pains of the mana drain headache and slave collar reasserted themselves.

I grunted in pain and forced myself to my feet. The slaves huddled off to one side, staying as far away as possible in one big bunch. Toka and Esold had collapsed together, steadily bleeding out.

"Keep him there, Bob. Oracle, come see what you can do with this collar, please," I whispered, closing my eyes against the brightness of the sun as the migraine started to get worse. I sat down roughly on the floor and covered my eyes with one hand, trusting my companions to warn me if anything happened.

"Jax? Can you hear me?"

I recognized the feeling of the contact and responded to it wearily.

"Yeah, Seneschal, I can hear you...what's up?"

"I've managed to lock down whatever is blocking my senses. It's coming from the balcony floor. Something out there is causing it, and I expect the ship that just crashed into my already-damaged courtyard is your work?"

"Ha, yeah that's us, trashing the place as usual. Sorry, mate. How bad is it? I'll get to whatever is causing this as soon as I can."

"The damage is minor. More a heavy landing than a crash, I suppose but only just. Still, more debris for our golems to clear."

"Any survivors?"

"I am unsure of the original complement of the ship, but there are at least a dozen creatures moving around on it currently. They seem concerned about the golem I have watching them."

"Ha! I bet they are! Keep an eye on them, and I'll take care of those fuckers as soon as I can. Does it look like they can take off again?"

"Definitely not. The keel has snapped in half, and while the impact was slower than I worried it would be, it was still considerable. Many repairs will be needed."

"Great news. Okay, as I said, keep an eye on them, but get the golem back to work. I doubt they'll be coming inside, given any choice. Bob and I will be down once I've asked some questions of the survivors."

"As you wish."

I felt Oracle's fingers at work on the collar, tugging and pushing sections, but after a minute, she huffed and gave up.

"I'm sorry, Jax. I think we need a key. One of them must have one, surely?"

"We can check," I said, before automatically adding, "and don't call me Shirley."

"What? But—"

"Dammit!" I groaned, knowing I'd just given Oracle a new line of questions that would come back to haunt me. "It's not important, okay, Oracle? Just a bad joke."

"But—"

"Please, just leave it," I groaned, forcing myself to my feet and hobbling over to the pair of assholes bleeding out on the floor.

Esold was unconscious now, and probably very close to death, while Toka lay unnaturally still, the hilt of my throwing knife still jutting from between its shoulders. It moved its head slightly as the sound of my approach, wincing in pain before licking its lips and grinning up at me.

I grimaced upon seeing that its teeth had been filed to points. The androgynous features flicked between terror and excitement as it lay there paralyzed and watched me approach.

I knelt down next to it, looking it in the eyes and trying to ignore the frenzied sobbing and shouts from the dwarf as he struggled with Bob, who held him effortlessly.

"So, want to explain why I should spare you?" I asked Toka as I looked into its eyes.

"I…I'll serve you. I'll serve you well, yes, serve you in any way you like! Just heal me and use me, master! I'll give satisfaction…oh yes, I will!" The voice changed as it spoke, at times wheedling, then excited, then pleading.

I looked away from the excitement in its eyes and focused on the outfit it wore. Strange strips of leather wound together, and large studs and spines pinned it all over, piercing outwards and inwards with equal measure. Something about the leather looked wrong, and I frowned, summoning Bob and his prisoner with a thought. Once Bob was standing over me, I called out to the dwarf without looking up, a horrible suspicion filling my mind.

"Tell me about this one, and about the outfit…it…wears."

"Ye bastard! Ah tried to help ya! I wanted to free ya! You're one o' *them!* A creature of the dark! Ye killed ma men, destroyed ma ship! Ma family! Oh, gods, ma poor family! They're all gonna starve, all because of ye!" He sobbed as he spoke, consumed with horror and pain.

"Don't be such a fucking idiot. Look at Bob, he's not DarkSpore." I snapped at him. "The second ship crashed below, but there are survivors, and there'll be a better chance of them surviving if you answer my *goddamned questions*! Now…tell me about this fucking creature!"

Silence reigned for a few seconds, then the dwarf spoke up quietly, his breathing ragged. "They're alive? Ye promise? Wait. No, I canna believe the word of a creature like ye."

"Bob, take him outside and let him look over the edge, then come back in here with him. Make it quick," I said, deciding to grant Esold a quick death in mercy. I drew a dagger from Toka's belt and stabbed the warrior through the throat, which generated a death notification.

Congratulations!

You have killed a level 27 Dark Paladin for a total of 420xp.

Progress to level 7 stands at 8,560/14,000

I pulled the dagger free, noticing the serrated edge and hooked tip dragging out a gobbet of flesh as I did. This wasn't a weapon meant to kill cleanly; this thing was a fucking torturer's delight. I looked down at Toka. Excitement and fear were etched deep on its face, and I wanted to be sick.

The more I saw of this *creature,* the more bile rose as my first reaction. I verified that it would live a few minutes more at least, and I turned to find where Oracle had gotten to. She had flitted across to the mage's corpse and was busily rifling through his pockets, throwing things aside as she went and muttering about the crap she was finding.

I left her to it and made my way over slowly to the huddled slaves, seeing the way they'd all drawn in to form a protective circle around the little elven girl as she crouched behind the remains of a section of wall, sobbing.

"I...I'll not let you hurt her! You can't! Just...you leave us alone, okay? Or else!" A young boy said, straightening up as far as his chains would allow and tried to step between us. I focused on him, my heart aching.

He must have been nearly ten, scrawny and barely decent, covered in rags with weeping, open sores where the chains had rubbed his skin raw. Short, dark hair looked like it'd been cut as close to the skin as possible with a dagger, and healed scars on his scalp showed it had not been the first time. He glared up at me, blue eyes puffy with tears and nose streaming with snot.

"Shit, kid, calm down," I whispered as I looked him over. The group that had huddled behind him slowly moved around, a couple of adults coming to stand with him between me and the girl. I shook my head and called over my shoulder to Oracle.

"You found that key yet?"

"No! The shit this guy had in his pockets!! I swear; what use is there for a dried human ear?! I...wait! I think this is it!"

Oracle was up and flying toward me in an instant, landing quickly on my shoulder and shifting the collar around until she found a specific spot. She pressed a small triangular metal part to the collar. My legs weakened as a wave of dizziness flooded through me. I grabbed at the wall nearest to me as my head spun, until I felt hands holding me upright.

When my vision cleared, I looked into the face of a catman...person...whatever. He stood as tall as I was, even with his back half bowed from years of working with a collar on. Thick lines creased his face, and his fur was streaked with grey. His clothes were as bad as the rest of them, but he at least met my gaze as he helped me to stand.

"You are not like them, yes?" he said, a faint thrumming noise underlying his words. "You will help us?"

I straightened up, and he let go, retreating a few steps, but stood with his hand's half-outstretched as though ready to catch me, should I fall. I shook my head again to clear it of at least some of the dizziness and looked him in the eyes.

"No, I'm nothing like those dicks," I said, reaching up and tugging my collar free as Oracle finished whatever she'd been doing. The thing hinged open easily now, and my mana began flowing again, refilling at its usual rate. "Let me see the girl," I said, and the cat dude turned, gesturing to the others to step aside. All moved, save the boy, who stayed where he was, little fists raised as though to fight anyone he had to.

"Step aside, Caron...you do no good here. Either he will help us, or we will all die. There is nothing left to lose." With that, the cat reached out and forcibly drew the boy aside, gently but firmly holding his arms close to his chest. I stepped around the wall and crouched down until I was level with the girl.

She cowered away from me, turning her face to the stone, stifled sobs wracking her tiny frame. Her meager woolens were stained with fresh blood and worse.

"Oracle, I'm going to need your help here. I can heal her body, and the others, but I'm going to need you to help heal her mind and soul."
"We will help, Jax. We live to serve the tower's residents, after all."
"Residents...yeah, I guess they are now. Fuck knows they've obviously got nowhere better to be! Seneschal, I need places for them to sleep sorted out, somewhere safe, with water and food, I guess. Heph, get the golems built as fast as possible."

I sensed agreement from all three wisps, then they were gone, save Oracle. She settled to the ground next to me, passing me a mana potion she'd likely found in the mage's pockets. I downed it quickly, licking my lips unconsciously at the fresh, minty taste.

She reached one small hand out to the girl and stroked her hair back from her face, exposing the remains of an ear. Someone had taken a knife to it long ago in an attempt to disguise the distinguishing pointed elven upper half. It'd been done badly, and the wound had healed looking like she'd lost a fight with a hedge trimmer.

"I need you to keep your eyes closed for me; can you do that?" I whispered, gathering the healing spell in my mind. I had more than enough mana to heal a handful of the group, provided I could take a few minutes between castings, but I didn't hesitate in altering the spell as I reached out to her with it, feeling Oracle's knowledge guiding me.

With her help forming the mana threads into forms that hovered in the air, I slowly shifted them to surround her, before allowing them to slide down into her damaged body. As each level overlaid the last, a complex matrix of spell forms began to build up. At its base was the same simple healing spell I'd used dozens of times, but each layer was repeated time and time again, each with a slight variant.

A touch of earth here to strengthen and straighten her bones, a pinch of fire and water there to replace the lost blood, air and dark mixed just so. Each section of magic slowly built, until the last dregs of my mana bottomed out, and I'd done all I could. I released it with a long exhalation, crumpling backwards to sit on my ass on the floor.

The spell activated, lifting her from her feet and suspending her several inches above the ground. She arced her back and took in a deep, whistling breath, opening her eyes in shock. Light flowed around her, into her, and buoyed her up. The spell form was visible to all as it wove in and out, gently forcing her crooked limbs straight, then fixing them. Her eyes were wide in wonder as her feet finally touched the ground, all traces of injury gone from her body. The only evidence remained in her battered, bloody clothes and deep in her eyes, reflecting the shock of new health.

"Kayt!" the boy, Caron, shouted, breaking free from the cat dude's grip and running to her.

He took her in his arms protectively as he checked her over, then dragged her back away from me, glaring at me with distrust clear on his little face while I was distracted with a new pop-up.

Congratulations!

New spell learned: Focused Heal-All
This apprentice-grade spell includes over a dozen separate weaves designed to heal specific injuries, and can be customized to focus on specific areas, or can be empowered with higher levels of mana to supercharge the target's normal healing abilities.
Cost: 25 mana – unlimited
Duration: 5 seconds - unlimited

"You…ah…you planning on doing that for all of us?" the cat asked, scratching one ear awkwardly as I met his gaze. "I know it took a lot out of you, but…"

I couldn't help but give a weak chuckle as I lay back on the floor, stretching my back out and taking a deep breath.

"Aye, well, we can talk about it. I'll not leave anyone hurt that I can help, that's for sure," I said.

"You mean that?" The voice came from a woman who hadn't spoken yet. She looked grim, hardly an ounce of fat on her anywhere, dressed in rags and with great bags under her eyes.

Her body was covered in angry, red welts, long lines crisscrossing her body that made me think she'd pissed off someone who liked a whip.

"Yeah. Yeah, I do," I said. "What about you? What about all of you; what are you wanting from me?"

"From you? Depends. What are you offering? And what's it gonna cost me?" she replied, folding her arms across her chest and frowning at me.

"Lydia! For the love of the gods, woman, shut up! He's already fought to free us from their clutches and healed Kayt! If you turn him against us, so help me!" the catman interrupted us, lifting a finger to her in warning before turning back to me.

"You ask what we want from you? What you've already given, *my Lord*: protection, healing, and if you have any to spare, maybe a little food? We're slaves, all of us. We want a fresh start, somewhere to live and raise our children! We know why we were brought here. We're to be fed to that thing that claims the tower. Now we're trapped here. What do we want? We want freedom! Get us out of the tower, and any of us that survive will bend the knee. We'll serve you, my Lord!"

"I'm no Lord," I muttered, even as the group of slaves started speaking up, agreeing with the cat.

"You might not have been, but if you save us? We'll serve you as sworn men and women. Nations have started with less. Give us your protection, and you'll be our lord," he said quietly, putting one hand on my shoulder and staring into my eyes. "I don't know much, but I know a good man when I see one. We need your help. Will you take us?"

I snorted in disagreement as I returned his look.

"I'm not a good man. Hell, I'm spending most of my time just trying *not* to be a bad one!" I said, shaking my head. I closed my eyes and thought for a second, hearing the voices all around me peter off into silence as they waited.

Jez Cajiao

You have been offered a Quest: Who Will You Be?

The slaves sent as tribute by Lord Barabarattas have offered to swear loyalty to you, provided you escort them to a safe location and swear to protect them.

Rewards: 27 villagers of varying loyalty and confirmation of your noble title

Will you accept?

Yes/No

I took a deep breath as I read the notification that floated before me. Varying loyalty? Wow, what a way to sell it...

"Ah, fuck it," I muttered, mentally hitting *yes* and accepting the quest. After all, I was halfway there.

I'd already killed the creatures of the tower. All I had to do was seal it back up so that random creatures couldn't get in, and at least there'd be people who could make dinner and help out. I opened my eyes to find that everyone had a strange look on their faces as they read something that only they could see.

I realized that they had all received prompts at the same time I'd accepted the quest, and they were reading them now. After a second, the cat looked at me and grinned nervously before bowing deeply.

"Thank you, lord! I see we're already classed as slaves of the Great Tower. I had hoped that, as we will be swearing to you—"

"Oh, fuck that!" I growled out. "You're all free. I'm having naught to do with slavery! If someone can find that damn key again, you can use it to free yourselves."

"And Toka?" he asked, gesturing across to the still form of the androgynous healer that I'd almost killed.

"That's...a different matter. Something's wrong there, care to tell me about...it?" I said, drawing a tired breath, getting back to my feet and trying to ignore the mana migraine. These damn things were getting too common now, and I resolved to try to see if I could get through a day without one and get a real night's sleep. Probably optimistic, but a man could dream.

"Toka is a...Toka is a murdering fucking animal that tortured and abused anything and everything it could. It used to be a human, caught by the slavers and tortured until all it understood was pain and pleasure. They gelded it, staff and stones removed, then healed the wounds over, experimented on it, broke it again and again.

"It kept getting fixed and broken until it was remade as this thing. Loyal to whoever gives it enough pain, gifted as a healer, but sick in the head. All I know is that it's been free to come and go for years, and it spends its time trawling the slave pens. It goes out of its way to find the most innocent and abuse them, breaking them until they're like it. Now the Lord Barabarattas has a dozen of them at his beck and call, torturing anyone he decides deserves it. I'd say kill it, and slowly, for the things I've seen, but the gods know it's not entirely its fault that it is what it is."

"Well, I..."

"Give it to me," a voice growled from the slaves, and we both looked over to see who'd spoken. A tall, stick-thin elven man drew nearer, looking down at Toka and back to me. "Please, lord, I'll swear any oath you want; just give me that sick fuck. I'll make sure it suffers!"

"And why—" I started to ask, but he cut me off.

"Look at it! Just look at it! The outfit it wears, it's made *from* my people! My *wife* is part of it, for all I know! Just give it to me. Let me kill it for you, if you won't do it yourself. That thing deserves to suffer!"

I spun again, taking the few steps to cross the floor to where the bleeding creature sprawled and leaned in close to look at the "leather" outfit it wore. There were several different colors woven in together, which I had already noticed, but then I saw it.

On one wider section it wore over a shoulder, the material had a brand burned into it, the same brand many of the other slaves wore, except it was folded, following the twists of the braiding. My anger must have shown on my face as even Toka looked scared suddenly, the enjoyment it'd been showing gone in an instant.

"Is it true?" I asked in a low whisper. "Are you *wearing* the skin of people you've murdered? Tortured?"

Toka swallowed hard and looked up at me, licking its lips as if unsure what to say.

"Ye...ye were tellin' the truth, laddie!" the dwarf interrupted as Bob brought him back across to where I crouched. "I need yer help! They be my lads, crashed down there. Mebbe ah can fix ma ship, mebbe no, but ah can save ma lads! Help me, laddie. Help me to save 'em, an' ah'll be your man fer life! Ah swear it!"

I looked up at him, fury and disgust in my eyes as I growled. "What makes you think I want your help? You were with this creature! And those fuckers that are over there!" I gestured at the dead men, then at the piles of weapons.

"You're fucking thieves, stealing from me, and you want my help? Give me one good reason why I shouldn't help you get to your men right now, using the fucking fastest route!" I pointed to the edge of the balcony. The dwarf's eyes widened in fear again.

"Wait!" came a whisper from my right, and I turned my head. The young elven girl was on her feet, pushing her way through the crowd that seemed to have formed around me. "I...he helped us, Lord. He helped to keep us alive. After Lord Barabarattas's men took over his ship, they made him come here. But he still slipped us food and water when he could, even after Toka was given permission to hurt him if he did it again. He helped us."

"Did you?" I snarled at him. "Did you help them, or were you a coward who went along with things, keeping your mouth shut and looking after your own?!"

"Ah'm both," he whispered, eyes downcast. "Ah'm a coward, an' ah helped them when ah could. Ah tried to keep me ship afloat, feed me family, an' pay the lord's thrice-damned taxes so they'd no' take me ship away. Ah helped them when ah could, just like when ah tried to ignore ye hidin' there, but ye got stuck in an' started fightin', and ah had to do what they said. Please, lord, help me. Ah'll do owt you want."

"Is this Toka as bad as they say?" I growled, trying to stifle the anger flooding me, and the dwarf grimaced, spitting on the floor before nodding abruptly.

"Aye, and worse! Toka be a wretched thing. It delights in torture, skinnin' its victims an' makin' outfits from 'em. You only seen this one; it's got dozens! Some are made up o' all kiddies' skin. I saw what it were wearin' a few days back, before we set off. Kiddie couldn't'a bin more'n two…and it—"

I cut him off with a raised hand and yanked my blade out of Toka's neck, loosing a spurt of blood and a groan from the creature. I stood up and lifted it, heaving it upright and ordering Bob to take it outside. I gestured to the elf that had begged to kill it, and I had him and the others follow me.

Toka was bleeding out, and couldn't have more than a few seconds left, so I cast healing on it, and then again, using almost all the mana that had regenerated and making my mood worse as my headache began to pound again.

"I'll serve you! I'll pleasure you! Anything you want, master; thank you!" Toka whispered, trying to get its feet under it as Bob dragged it over to the edge of the marshalling yard at my direction. I checked down below and judged that the ship was far enough off to one side that it was safe, then told Bob to let the wretched thing go, leaving it standing unsteadily on its own feet.

Toka tottered at the edge of the platform, looking over the side at my gesture. "What? What do you want me to do, master?" it whispered. "You want me to go to them? Teach them their place? Make them fear you, love you like I do? I can do that for you, that and more!" It was practically salivating as it watched the wounded so many stories below.

"This is *my* tower. If you want to stay here, you follow my rules," I called aloud, turning around to address everyone else. "They're really fucking simple, for now at least. Rule one, don't be a dick. Rule two, fuck with me, and you'll regret it. Rule three, while you're here, you're family, so fucking act like it. Protect each other. No stealing, no abuse. We all work, and we all get to relax! Rule four, everyone gets a fresh start, but don't abuse it."

I gestured to Toka with one hand, pointing at its clothes.

"Toka here, though, is literally *wearing* evidence of the fact it is a sick fucker that's been torturing people, then making their corpses into clothes. That's a fucking lightyear too far."

"I've been bad, I know. Punish me, master, pun—" Before it could finish its sentence, I took three quick steps and spun, ducking low and lashing out with my right foot in a sweeping spin kick with all of my force.

Toka cried out in shock as its feet shot out from underneath, its face falling forward into my perfectly timed uppercut that hit it full force. My enhanced Strength worked in conjunction with my other stat increases to send Toka cartwheeling off the side of the platform with a scream of terror, blood and teeth spraying as it went.

CHAPTER TWENTY-NINE

I took a deep breath and enjoyed the silence. Even speaking to that creature had left me feeling dirty somehow. Now it was off my tower, and I felt a lot better for it, even if I did miss the perfect chance to...*ah, fuck it.* I straightened and took a quick step up to the edge and leaned over.

"Hadoken!" I screamed after Toka as it fell downwards, instantly feeling like the universe had been put to rights. I turned back to the shocked onlookers and clapped the elf who had asked for permission to kill Toka on the shoulder.

"Sorry, friend, but it's my place to dispense justice. If you'd done it, it would have been revenge," I said, making eye contact. "I understand why you wanted to do it, but it wouldn't bring her back."

I turned to look at the rest of the group, finding the dwarf Oren standing in the middle. Several of the slaves had their collars off and surrounded him, but none showed any hostility toward him. If that wasn't proof, then I had no idea what would have been. I forcibly made myself release the anger I was holding toward him and gestured for him to walk forward.

"Okay. Oren, right?" I asked him, receiving a nod in affirmation. "I'll help you and your men, but you're going to have to help me with them. They don't know me, and as far as I know, they're all assholes."

"Nay, laddie! They're good lads, ah swear it! Most 'o 'em ha' bin wi' me fer years!" He wrung his hands together unconsciously.

I looked him over again, noting the armor with its missing sections. I straightened up and gestured toward the stairwell down, walking back inside to look around at the mess. "Okay then, Oren, it's that way to the ground. On the way, you can tell me your story."

"Ah will, lord, an' thanks! Errr, b'fore we go, though...ah...we still might have a wee problem." He looked at me, then the rest of the group, hesitantly rubbing his hands together in discomfort.

"Out with it," I said, trying to keep my face calm.

"Well, laddie, it be like this...we're not a party o' two airships...we be a party o' three." He paused, waiting for the feared explosion of rage from me.

Instead, I set off running to the balcony and looked up into the clear sky, searching all around and trying to spot the second and third ships. When I couldn't see anything, I turned back to him as he came running out behind me, huffing to a halt and holding up his hands to calm me down.

"There *were* three of us, laddie. Two transports, me an' Decin. We were hired ta help transport troops and mebbie cargo to and from somewhere top secret. No details, just a pouch o' gold and a wink. Ah could'na refuse; ah were almost outta manastones fer ma ship. Anyway, few days before we be due to leave, one o' the big ships made it back from patrol, mebbe a hun'red feet long, forty across the beam. She's a big, six-engine thing, hardly needs her sails at all, proper shark o' the skies. The lord was'ne expectin' her back for weeks, but she were damaged."

"They decided she'd last long enough for this delivery and put a team aboard ta do the most urgent fixes en-route. Thing is, she landed a few days back, told us ta go ahead, that her captain had 'some business' in a village we passed. She were supposed ta catch up. If Decin thinks I be dead, and everyone else as well, he'll be looking for 'em, wantin' ta bring 'em back for some payback."

"And what are the chances of him finding them? Wait, first, what are the chances of them getting there? They were pretty banged up."

"Ah did'na see them crash, laddie. Might ha' gotten far enough away ta feel safe and land fer repairs. Might be all right, might be on fire somewhere; I just dunno!"

"Okay. Right, give me some space, all of you…just…go be somewhere else for a bit, okay?" I sighed, picking a glowing stone up off the floor. "Oren, this mean anything to you?"

"Aye, it be te keep us hid from tha creature. One-use thingy apparently," he started. I grunted, throwing it off the side of the tower, then gesturing to them to bugger off as I walked over to the edge of the stone balcony and sat down. My feet dangled over the edge as I ordered Bob to keep everyone away from me for now. I searched through my pockets and bags until I found it, sitting there as calm as could be, waiting until I needed it. The scroll of Summon Arcane Eagle.

Scroll of Summon Arcane Eagle		Further Description *Yes/No*	
Details:		This scroll will summon an Arcane Eagle construct. This air affinity spirit will last 600 seconds and share all it sees with its summoner.	
Rarity:	Magical:	Durability:	Charge:
Rare	Yes	87/100	1/1

I pulled it out and looked it over. It was maybe six inches long and had been rolled up tight. A wax seal secured it, with the spell details embossed in the wax. I looked it over for a few seconds more, noting the signs of age in it before breaking the wax seal with one thumb and unrolling it.

Do you wish to activate Scroll of Summon Arcane Eagle at this time?

Be aware; as the seal has been broken, this scroll will begin to deteriorate at a rate of one point of durability per three minutes.

Yes/No

I mentally selected *yes*, of course, and the spidery, handwritten letters that made up the page burst into blue flames, quickly consuming the parchment until I held a handful of cool fire. The flames roiled in my hands, weaving in and out and picking up speed until they formed a ball, which then grew to an egg.

As the seconds passed, the egg grew bigger and solidified, becoming heavier and more tangible. All at once, something inside shook the egg, and cracks appeared across the surface. As the cracks grew, it was obvious something was breaking free, something that was quickly too big to have been inside the tiny shell, yet I'd seen its birth mere seconds ago. It was an eagle, an eagle that grew even as I looked into its eyes.

The bird was made from blue fire that seemed solid, until it shifted slightly, and I could see through it.

It finally stopped growing, reaching its full size with a wingspan of easily six feet. Even then, it still seemed to weigh almost nothing and appeared from second to second to be a hologram then solid.

I sensed a faint drawing sensation begin, one that grew stronger by the second, until I made eye contact with it. The next second, I was perched on my own hands, staring at my own body holding me. *Okay, this isn't freaky as fuck or anything, at all...*

I took a deep breath and thought about what I wanted to find: the airship that had escaped the tower and the final, larger airship that was on its way inbound now. With that thought, the eagle dove from my hands, wings folded tight, and plunged towards the ground.

A dozen feet down, it flared its wings wide and began spiraling, quickly finding a thermal and beginning to ascend. It passed the floors that had taken me hours to climb in mere seconds. Its speed was amazing, as was the lack of any kind of stamina restriction. It beat its powerful wings, building speed even as it passed the apex of the tower and continued to climb, then spiraled outward in ever-increasing circles.

It took less than three minutes in total, from the spell beginning until the second ship was spotted. Decin had headed straight south from the tower, then turned to the west, skirting the edge of a valley before landing maybe ten miles away on the shore of a lake to make repairs. Once I'd found it, the eagle headed straight for the clearing, showing me the damage to the ship that had escaped.

It looked severe from here, but the crew was working quickly, some tearing out sections of the deck and replacing them, as others worked to frantically install replacement rigging and sails.

Reassured that at least they weren't attacking me, I sent the eagle searching again, spiraling higher and higher. After another minute, it finally spotted the third ship as it lumbered along. It was heading in from the coast, for some reason, a good thirty or forty miles to the east of the crashed airship.

I knew there was no way I could reach the ship with the few minutes of flight remaining to the eagle construct, so I set it to search the area around the tower for anything of interest.

I returned to my own body with a start a short while later, when the spell expired.

I took a deep breath and looked down at my hands as I waited for the vertigo to subside from my eyesight changing. I almost felt blind in comparison to losing the eagle's vision, but after a few seconds, it normalized, and I felt good enough to get up and walk back into the gloom of the tower. I checked the popups I'd received, dismissing the death notifications for Toka and the mage and blinked in surprise:

Congratulations!

You have made progress on your Quest: A Place to Lay Your Head.

Wisps sworn fealty: 3/3
Locations cleared and secured: 4/5
SporeMother killed: 1/1
Guardians claimed: 0/10
Workers claimed: 0/10

Rewards: The Great Tower is yours to command. Surrounding area will become aware of your rightful ownership. Access to supplies and facilities. 100,000xp.

Clearly, taking control of the armory on this floor had counted towards the target, which was a bonus, considering I'd not even bothered to enter it yet. I guessed as people sworn to me had entered, then it'd added it to my list. The next notification was even more surprising.

Congratulations!

You have found seven (7) notable locations within eleven (11) miles of your current location.

Your map has been updated.

Will you explore your surroundings to uncover secrets of the ages, lost to memory and time?

Yes/No…

I automatically accepted the quest, then closed the screen down, coming to a halt while standing over Oren, who shot to his feet quickly.

"Did ye find 'em? Is Decin alive?" he asked, concern etched deep into his face.

"Yeah, I found them. They're a couple miles from here, landed at the edge of a lake. No idea who's on board, but there was a fat bastard of a dwarf shouting at people when I saw them," I said, remembering the image of the short figure stomping up and down the deck, berating everyone as he went. "I think he was wearing purple?"

"Ha! Aye, that be Decin. Found those robes in a scrap pile and fell in love; bin wearin' 'em ever since! Tells everyone he fought off a lich, and they were his prize! Now, what about the others? An' can we talk on the way? Go help me lads?" He held his hands out to the sides and went on, pleading. "Please, lord, those lads ha' bin me crew fer years. They be family, good lads stuck out here while tryin' te help me outta ma debt…"

"Yeah, we can. Two minutes, though," I said to him, holding up a hand in supplication.

"Oracle, time for a quick test, I think. Stay out of sight and watch over our new residents while I take Bob down to meet Oren's friends."

"Okay, Jax, but be careful!"

I turned to the cat and grinned at him a bit self-consciously, realizing I'd been neglecting my abilities in the heat of the moment. I cast Identify and scanned the details that popped up.

UnderVerse: Brightblade

Cai'Amanth a-Ull

Member of the Felinoid race, sub race: Panthera.

"You're casting at me?" Cai'Amanth a-Ull asked, seeing my unsubtle gestures directed toward him and putting two and two together.

"Ah…yeah, sorry. Just trying to get a handle on who you all are?" I responded, a little embarrassed.

"A handle?"

"I mean, I'm trying to learn about you." I replied, swearing internally about colloquialisms.

"Ah! Here, I can share, since as a slave, you accept that privacy is no longer a concern," he said coolly. With that, he made a few quick gestures, and I received a prompt asking if I wanted to see his character sheet. I clicked *yes*, and a new screen flashed up before my eyes.

Name: Cai'Amanth a-Ull				
Title: ?		Renown: ?		
Level: 12		Progress: ?		
Patron:?		Points to Distribute: ?		
Stat	Current points	Description	Effect	Progress to next level
Agility	8	Governs dodge and movement.	-20% maximum movement speed and reflexes	?
Charisma	12	Governs likely success to charm, seduce, or threaten	+20% success in interactions with other beings	?
Constitution	4	Governs health and health regeneration	40 health, regen 1 point per 600 seconds	?
Dexterity	20	Governs ability with weapons and crafting	+100% to weapon proficiency, +10% to the chances of crafting success	?
Endurance	7	Governs stamina and stamina regeneration	70 stamina, regen 1 point per 30 seconds	?
Intelligence	13	Governs base mana and number of spells able to be learned	130 mana, spell capacity: ?	?
Luck	10	Governs overall chance of bonuses	Average chance for a favorable outcome	?
Perception	20	Governs ranged damage and chance to spot traps or hidden items	+100% ranged damage, +10% chance to spot traps or hidden items	?
Strength	13	Governs damage with melee weapons and carrying capacity	+3 damage with melee weapons, +30% maximum carrying capacity	?
Wisdom	14	Governs mana regeneration and memory	+40% mana recovery, 1.4 points per minute, 40% more likely to remember things	?

"It is common to ask before you use magic on another, but I understand, with the way we have met, why you would cast that aside," he said, making it very clear he didn't appreciate it.

"Right, sorry." I took a deep breath and looked over his sheet again, seeing his abnormally high Dexterity and Perception, while his other stats trailed way behind.

"Can I ask about your build? Look, I'm just gonna say it; I'm from a long way away, and I really don't know much about your customs and what's considered good or bad manners here. If you're in any doubt whether I meant to offend you, I really didn't.

"Easy rule of thumb with me is I'm not very good at subtle. If I do or say something that upsets you, I didn't intend to. When I want to upset people or let you know I'm angry, you won't be in *any* doubt, believe me. Until then, just assume I'm a bit of a rude and unobservant ass."

"Very well, I shall bear that in mind. As to my...build...yes, ask away."

"You're really heavy on the Dexterity and Perception, and light on the rest?"

"Yes...ah. Okay, first time meeting one of my kind? I am of the line of Panthera. We gain a single point to Dexterity and Perception with each level, plus two to assign as we wish. You are human? You receive three points to assign however you wish, yes?"

I frowned and looked over my details to be sure. I always received five points, not three, but decided to keep that quiet. I'd embarrassed myself enough already, and going from conquering hero to village idiot in one conversation was a record I didn't want to earn.

"Okay, that's great, then. Thanks, uh, Carama...math..."

"Cai, Cai'Amanth a-Ull is my full name, but Cai is acceptable. You are..." He bared his teeth in what I took to be a small smile.

I grinned back. "Sorry for butchering your name there. Cai, it is. I'm Jax. Just Jax is fine," I said and reached out without thinking. He saw the gesture and reached for my wrist instead of my hand, leading to some awkwardness as I tried to grip his palm. I took a deep breath and showed him a handshake. "This is how we do it where I'm from; how do you do it here?"

"Ha! Like this!" He disengaged from my hand and gripped my wrist instead. I grinned again and nodded.

"Right, okay, I'll remember that. I need to take Oren down to the ground level and kill anything that gets in our way. Do me a favor, okay? Loot the corpses of these dicks and put everything aside for me to look over. Also, get everyone together and start moving the weapons back into the armory where you found them.

"For now, though, just get everyone free of the chains and find somewhere to rest. You'll find a garden level three floors further down. It's probably best to recover there. There will be fruits and water at least."

"Of course, but the creatures that call the tower home? The monster?" he asked, looking concernedly at the darkened stairwell and Bob.

"Yeah, Bob there"—I gestured to my companion, and he waved an arm absently in response—"he's my minion, so don't worry about him. As for the monster that used to live here? The SporeMother? It's dead, don't worry. I just need to sweep for any last surprises now."

"We were to be given in tribute to something. If it was a SporeMother..." Cai shook his head as several of the slaves around us began to cry and mutter. "How long has it been dead...Jax? Whatever killed it may come back."

"Oh, sorry. Yeah, *I* killed it, couple of days back, so don't worry about that! Sorry, everyone! I should have said!" I called out, holding both hands up as I looked around. "My bad."

The former slaves surrounding me jerked back at my words, shock obvious on their faces. Most of them took a step back, moving quickly away from me. I turned back to Cai and raised an eyebrow in question.

"You killed it?" he asked cautiously.

"Yeah, why?"

"The SporeMother. You actually fought one?" he asked again, slowly moving back from me while trying to hide it. I frowned and looked around at them all, suddenly realizing the one commonality in the way they were all moving. They were all backing steadily into the brightest lit patches of the ground they could find.

"You don't believe me, do you?" I said, then shook my head in annoyance, striding quickly back into the full sunlight, as though I'd not just been standing out here with them all.

"Seriously, people! I'm not infected, I'm not possessed, and yes, I killed the damn thing, okay? Look at Bob; I used two of its legs to give him extra stabby spears when I rebuilt him."

There was a long pause as everyone looked at Bob, who, with a little mental prodding, turned a full circle, flexing the SporeMother's legs in demonstration.

"How? Forgive us, Lord Jax, but killing such a creature usually takes teams of highly trained adventurers, or entire legion squads? Unless you have a team hidden elsewhere?"

"Oh, for...no, okay? I'm just a lucky fucker that's good at killing things, that's all," I said in exasperation. "Now I'm starting to lose my patience, and you're all wasting time. Loot the bodies, get the weapons back in the armory, and go down three levels. You'll find a large, open outdoor space. There's food and water; go chill out and if you really want to be sure, the SporeMother's body is a dozen or so floors up, it's really hard to miss."

With that, I set off at a light jog across the floor and down the first set of stairs. Bob clattered along behind me, with Oren huffing and puffing as he brought up the rear.

"So come on, then. This third ship, it's about thirty, maybe forty miles to the east, and headed straight for us. Decin has landed for a moment, but how long he'll stay grounded, I don't know. What are the chances they'll see each other?" I asked, calling to Oren over the sounds of jingling metal and Bob's clattering bones.

"They'll probably be usin' the beacon. It were attached to ma hull. Same with Decin's ship. They were to make sure we did'na try and sneak off wi' anything. Like we'd ha' tried it wi' those fuckers aboard!"

"Why head for us, then? Why not head for the other ship's beacon?"

"They were movin'. Ah was supposed to stay, while they looted owt they could from the 'secret site' and fucked off again.

"They'll prob'ly be assumin' Decin's ship left and are headin' back, but they'll no get to us here now before sunset tomorrow, the damage she'd taken was mostly ta her drives, makin' her slow as crap.

"Ah bet they'll be heavin' to and settin' down somewhere. They'll no want te try landin' in the dark, just in case..."

"Okay, that seems sensible," I said, taking a moment to tell Seneschal to keep a look out as best he could, and asking Heph to come up with something to help him.

"Let's pick up the pace a little and get this sorted, then I need to make some plans for the defense of my tower!"

We sped up, much to the horror of Oren, who began huffing like a bellows as we passed floor after floor.

It took considerably longer with Oren running than it would have with just Bob and myself. The trek highlighted just how unfit he was, despite the desire to push on, especially after he collapsed barely halfway and began to bounce down the remaining stairs.

Bob grabbed him as he rolled past and hefted him easily. Finally free of the little dwarf's attempts to keep up, we picked up speed, and a short while later we came out on the ground, pushing through low-hanging branches to emerge into the dappled shade of the forest floor.

The first thing I saw was the crashed ship, a couple hundred feet off to my left. It was small, by the standards of the ships I knew from Earth, more a large pleasure boat than a real ship. It measured maybe twenty feet wide by sixty feet long. The hull had broken on a collapsed section of wall when it had crash-landed, and the hole in its side revealed that it had two levels below decks, with the remains of a wheelhouse protected by a platform that came off what could only have been the captain's cabin above.

The rest of the upper deck was taken up by broken masts covered in torn sails, various piles of scrap that had likely once had functions, and a series of cages. Most had been rendered into scrap by the impact, but one had pinned a crew member underneath it, and four of the crew were trying to free him. The rest were armed and facing out, watching for any movement or tending to the wounds of two injured people.

All in all, there looked to be ten crew on the ship left alive. Two bodies covered by a tarp off to one side proved the landing hadn't just been hard on the ship, and nobody looked to have gotten off scot-free, judging from the groans and blood. Oren struggled and squirmed as he and Bob emerged behind me, causing cries of shock and anger to rise from his crew.

"Oh, for...Bob, drop him!" I said, wincing as I realized I'd just given them their worst nightmare: a huge undead with their captain as its prisoner.

"At last, ya stupid bag o' bones!" he cried as he righted himself and scurried away from us, rushing towards the group, who immediately raised weapons to forestall him.

"Don't come any closer!" one called, stepping forward from the group and pointing a wicked-looking axe at him. "We know how to deal with your sort!"

"Ya wee fool!" Oren cried at him in annoyance, gesturing at himself. "Do ye no recognize me? 'Cause I recognize ye, Barrett! Ye always wanted to be captain; well, ye can wait a wee bit longer, ye damn eejit!" The crew seemed confused as Oren went on quickly. "Those damn fools were beatin' their slaves again, so Lord Jax—him that's standin' behind me—he kilt them *all*. He's freed the slaves, and near as ah can tell, he's kilt every other damn thing that was in the tower an' all! Last damn thin ya be need doin' is pointin' a weapon at him, right!"

"Bollocks!" shouted one of the crew hunching down behind his shield even further.

"Aye, ah got a great big pair o' them laddie, unlike ye! I recognize yer voice, Smit, so pipe down or get back ta pipin' off the crew! Yer fuck-all use, besides that!" Oren snapped back at the shouter, making him sputter in outrage as the rest of the crew grinned and seemed to relax slightly.

"How do we know you're still Oren? How do we know you're not enslaved?" said Barrett, gesturing to the rest of the crew to settle down.

Oren quickly looked around and spotted a patch of sunlit earth a dozen feet to one side. He dashed over to it and stood straight and (almost) tall in the warm light.

"Ye see? Would one o' them be standin' here?" Some of the crew relaxed, while others began shouting questions and suggestions for tests. Most of which seemed ridiculous to my mind, so I spoke up as I walked forward.

"Oren, you can stay out here and talk to your crew. Get them settled, and they can either stay here or sod off, for all I care. Come find me on the third floor when you're sorted out." Then I spoke to the crew, raising my voice. "Do any of you know who Toka is?" The looks of anger and disgust that I received gave me a clear answer. "Okay, did any of you see him recently?"

"Aye, that piece of shit came screaming down about half an hour ago; made a big hole over that way, why?" Barrett gestured off to one side and frowned at me.

"Because I want to make damn sure the fucker's dead," I responded, striding off in the direction he had indicated. It didn't take long to spot him, since I had a good idea where to look.

It seemed he'd hit a portion of the ground with a room dug below, as a combination of his impact and the eons that had passed had weakened it enough that he smashed a hole through the overgrown courtyard and into the room below.

I found a good amount of blood covering the stones surrounding the impact site and could just make out something pale in the darkness.

I knelt down, getting Bob to hold my ankles, and lowered my upper body down for a better look inside the exposed room. At first all I could see was darkness, but as my eyes adjusted and my DarkVision activated, I began to chuckle.

Toka had been useful after all, it seemed. His impact had given me a way into one of the blocked-off storerooms that Heph had told me about. While there weren't any golem cores that I could see from here, there were refined ingots, hundreds of them.

I'd found a way to bring the tower back to life! His corpse was crumpled in a pile of collapsed masonry. Blood pooled all around him and was spattered across the walls and contents of the room. Judging from the sheer amount and the exposed bone and viscera, he'd died very quickly.

"Heph! You there, you grumpy bastard?"

"Grumpy! Ah'll have ye know, ah'm the soul o' cheerful!"

"You will be soon, aye. I just found a way into one of the storerooms! It's full of refined metals, and blood, but hey!"

"Blood? Who cares about blood! Get me some o' that metal, an' ah'll make ye more golems!"

"That's the plan, Heph! How are the repairs going?"

"As well as can be expected, why?"

"I'm thinking you build, say, two normal construction golems as fast as you can, and then we build ten servitors? Have them get to work on getting the genesis chamber up to scratch as soon as possible? How's that sound?"

"Sounds good, but what about cores, laddie? Ah canna do nowt wi'out them!"

"There was a big battle on the armory floor at some point. When I was up there earlier, I spotted dozens of golem bodies straight away. There have got to be some intact when we get there and do a proper search, surely?"

"Get searchin' then, laddie! Ah assume ye mean the two construction class are ta look for more cores? And that they be the two we already planned ta build, not two more?"

"Aye, they are."

"Well, ah'll get back ta work then! Ah'll have a golem go and strip that storeroom you found when ah have one free. One more point now, though, laddie. The table's up an' runnin' now, so mebbe ye should make interfacin' wi' it a priority, aye?"

With that, the sense of Heph's presence faded, and I clambered back out of the hole and got to my feet, heading back over to the entrance to the tower. I waved absently at Oren as I passed him, deep in thought about my next step. As near as I could tell, most of the jobs I could do to help were scouting and searching the tower, looking for cores, and getting the former slaves organized, potentially getting the more loyal ones to search as well.

The bigger jobs would require golems and lots of them. My first priority was to get to the creation table and see what Heph was hinting at. Then I had to see what I could find out about the tower's newest residents, find them somewhere safe to stay, and sort out some food. Hopefully, Oren could convince the crew to join me as well, then I could at least raid their ship for supplies?

I began to jog without consciously thinking about it, returning into the cool darkness of the tower and heading up to the section that I'd started thinking of as the command center. It took a handful of minutes to reach, and Oracle had checked in with me on the way.

It seemed the former slaves had taken my request and warning to heart and were behaving themselves. They'd stripped the corpses of anything of interest and set it all aside for me and had begun busily returning everything to the armory. A few had retained weapons as well, but they were from the armory, and Oracle assured me they were low-grade and low in value. I decided to let them keep them, if it made them feel better about things.

As I came out of the stairwell onto the floor we were using, I slowed to a stop in shock. The servitor-class golem had clearly been working its ass off while I'd been busy. Not only was one of the huge windows clear, it'd been repaired! The rest of the room was similarly spotless, and the golem was now in the hallway, working on the door!

I strolled past it, admiring its work, and found that the damn thing had even repaired a chair for me, placing it by the creation table. Instinctively, I compared it to the throne I'd seen accompanying the table when it was upstairs, but I really had no cause to complain here. Not sitting on the ground was a vast improvement.

I settled myself in, sending Bob to take up station by the door and watch out for threats, and reached out to the creation table. The surface sparked to life as soon as my fingers touched it.

Do you wish to take ownership of this Creation Table?

***Warning:* this item is linked to the Great Tower of Dravith. Taking ownership of this item will alert the Lord of this Tower.**

Yes/No

I selected *yes*, of course, figuring that, if it made me aware I'd claimed the table, it didn't matter. But the next prompt made me groan as I realized I'd been neglecting other quests…again.

Congratulations!

You have taken Ownership of the Tower of Dravith's Creation Table!

You now have additional options in your interface.

Do you wish to declare this Tower as a religious center?

Bonuses may be awarded by your god or goddess for claiming territory in His or Her name.

Yes/No

I left the notification and brought up the religion one that I'd started what seemed like ages ago. The required tithe was at nine hundred and two of one thousand mana donated, and I took a deep breath. This needed to be done first. I concentrated and allocated the mana necessary, watching the numbers tick over until it read one thousand of one thousand.

CHAPTER THIRTY

I sat back, looking around the room, and…nada. Nothing happened. I'd been kinda hoping for some trumpets, a big flash of light, and the Goddess appearing in it, or even some big old gong going off, like in the movies, but…

"Eternal? Is it truly you?"

I jumped. The voice that resounded in my ears was…weird. It carried a sense of warmth, hope, and curiosity, but mostly, it was full of exhaustion. As though the speaker was dead tired and ready to give in.

"I…ahh, hello?" I whispered aloud, then coughed and tried again, this time in a stronger voice. "Hello?"

"No. Not my Eternal, but you feel like…why do you feel so much like him, and who are you? A supplicant? It's been so long…" The voice trailed off, as though too tired to go on, before coming back stronger. *"You…you're the one who prayed to me."*

"Uh…yeah. Yeah, I suppose I did. You're Jenae?" I asked, feeling a bit weird about talking to her so casually.

"Jenae…yes…that was my name…" She trailed off into silence again, and my misgivings grew. I'd tied myself to a goddess who wasn't even sure of her name.

"My name? I know my name, mortal. Try sleeping for centuries and see how you feel when you wake up!"

The voice was stronger as anger filled it, resounding through my mind and driving me to my knees as the pain of her displeasure made itself known. I had time to realize that she could read my mind, and that was about it, as she went on.

"I was banished, cut off from my faithful. I had to watch as they died in their hundreds and thousands! I've been asleep for centuries as the UnderVerse went on without divine guidance. My temples were destroyed, my name stripped from the land, and you whine about me being confused?!"

My head throbbed with the echoing voice, a burning pain filling my mind and radiating down my arms and legs, sending me to the floor in spasms as my muscles twitched uncontrollably.

I screamed in pain, trying to roll into a ball, desperate for the agony to end, only to flinch as it vanished as quickly as it had appeared, Jenae spoke again, although her voice was quieter, kinder, and regretful.

"I am sorry, mortal. I did not intend to harm you. It has been so long, and so much has gone wrong. I lashed out without thinking about it. Please forgive me and let us speak."

A warmth flooded through me, faint but steady, making my muscles relax as a notification popped up before me.

Congratulations!

You have received a blessing from the Goddess Jenae:

Hearthfire's Comfort:

Your body relaxes. Minor ills and aches are swept away by the warmth of the hearth. You receive +1 to Intelligence and +1 to Charisma for the next two hours.

I blinked, then dismissed the notification, my body forgetting the pain I'd felt even as my mind tried to hold onto it, holding it up as a reason not to trust Jenae.

"I understand the impulse, little one, but you chose to pledge to me, taking me as your Patron Goddess. Perhaps we should try to start again; after all, there must have been a reason you chose me?"

"Okay, that's gonna get really old, really fast!" I said, forcing myself to climb back into my chair and take a deep breath. "Reading my mind is going to freak me the fuck out all the time. Do you have to do it?"

"Your mind is an open book to me, it's true, but only the surface thoughts. I still don't know who you are, or why you feel like my Eternal."

As soon as she said she didn't know who I was, I thought about my name reflexively, a condensed version of my life flashing before my eyes, then my suspicions about the voice in my mind, prompting a response from her.

"Ah! Hello, Jax. You've had an interesting path to reach me, it's true. And it's true, then? Amon was murdered by those he loved most?"

"Gah!" I cried out, grabbing my head as she spoke. "Fuck's sake! Stop with the mind reading shit! Seriously! And who the hell is Amon?"

"Amon was the Eternal Emperor, bond-mate to Shustic, the Silver Maiden of the North and—"

"Fuck! Seriously, just stop!" I swore, clutching at my head as I looked around, I drew a deep breath and started again. "Right, yes. I'm Jax, okay? And Amon, he's well…I think it's him, and he's sort of here," I said, having put two and two together.

As I named him aloud, I felt the voice stir in the back of my mind, before a stream of consciousness flowed across my mind, a meaningless mélange of words, concepts, pictures, and memories that left me staggering at the enormity of it. It was as if someone had condensed a movie into half a second and sprayed it across my brain.

I sat back, numb, trying to make sense of everything, when Jenae spoke again. Her voice was contemplative as it filled my mind, but it sounded gentler, too.

"I…see. Jax, Amon does exist still, but in a far reduced capacity. You have had interactions with him, I see, but as fragmented and pain-filled as his mind is, I don't blame you for ignoring him.

He's shared as much as he was capable of his history with me, and it will take some time for me to come to terms with this. For now, please accept that I have returned to the realm. Yes, I am weakened, far weakened from what I was and will be again, but I can help you. I suggest a trade; will you listen?"

"Yeah. What do you want, and what are you offering?" I whispered, trying to wrap my mind around the confirmation that I had an emperor from an earlier time living in my head, and a mad one at that.

"I'm offering knowledge, Jax. I can give you advice and suggestions, and in return, you will help bring us back, my siblings and I, and return balance to the land. With me as your patron and personal goddess, of course!" she added that last bit quickly, as though wanting to make sure I understood I was hers, and not to go playing with anyone else.

"I will grant you quests, assist you to grow, and give you advice you can't get from anyone else. For example, you know that there's a flying warship approaching. It's two days out from landing here."

"It is at the very limit of my reach at the moment, but I can tell you a way for you to grow strong enough to survive their attack. It won't be a safe long-term strategy, but it'll give you the chance to survive to have those problems later, so what do you say?"

I wasn't sure what to do. I needed information, but also…I wasn't religious. I'd been thinking of the patron like I had approached things many times so far, like a damn game. This was my feckin life now, and did I really want to tie myself to a goddess? Or any divinity, really. I didn't care about who they were. They could be a goddamn toaster, for all I cared. I would, however, totally judge them if they were ginger. Even an enlightened arse like me had standards.

"As I say, Jax, this doesn't have to be a normal religious relationship. I'm weakened and have slept for centuries, while you are new to this realm entirely. We could instead work together, as friends or allies at least. You agree to help me, and I'll help you. Maybe in time, we will grow to trust one another more, but until then? You help me to recover and dedicate any shrines you come across to me, and I'll assist you with knowledge and quests as we go?"

The more I thought about it, the fewer downsides I could find. I needed help, and so did she.

"Okay, hell with it, I'm in," I said, sensing her relief tinged with amusement.

"Excellent. I'll offer a simple deal first, then. I'm your patron, and you've already proven that you can both think for yourself and survive in this realm. I need mana to be able to grow and return to my rightful place, so would you like a quest?"

"Go on," I said, settling back into the chair.

"You have claimed the Great Tower as your own. If you were to name it as a center of my religion, then I would be able to join with it. Rather than needing you to sacrifice your mana to me, I could absorb, say, twenty percent of the mana the collectors have access to? In return, I'll assist your wisps in repairing the tower, and grant you access to designs of my own creation."

"What do you mean, designs?" I asked cautiously. Twenty percent was a *lot* of mana, after all, and I needed it.

"Well, I am the Goddess of Hidden Knowledge and Fire, so as an example, when you come to build a smithy, I can grant you access to upgrade blueprints, such as a Lava Foundry. You will gain access to blueprints and upgrades in direct response to the amount of mana I receive from you, and the Marks of Favor I grant you for completing my quests."

A tiny spark ignited in the air before me, burning the air like parchment and spreading out until it was a meter square. Inside, instead of nothing or burning ashes, there was a constellation of stars radiating outwards from a central point, each connected to others. The first and most central star glowed red, flames licking at it. The words "Chosen of Jenae" appeared above it. A notification pinged for my attention, and I flicked it open.

Congratulations!

You have received a new Title: Chosen of Jenae.

This Title grants you access to Jenae's Constellation of Secrets.

I looked back into the void, observing the lines that led off like spokes in a wheel to six more dead stars, starting at the top, their names could just barely be made out. Enhanced Construction, Magical Research, Crafting, Governance, Personal Enhancement, and Exploration. Each of these stars had lines leading off from them to others, but I couldn't make out any other details.

"So, I guess I give you mana and do quests, and you let me pick from this tree?" I said slowly, my eyes flicking from one section to another. "What do these sections do?"

"The starscape is very simple, yet oh, so complicated at the same time. Take Enhanced Construction as an example; once you've unlocked this school, there are three sections to invest in within it: Magical, Mundane, and Warfare. Magical deals with increasing the magical aspects of your buildings, such as the way this tower repairs itself. If you want to increase its capability by five, ten, or even fifty percent, this is the area of knowledge for you. Mundane deals with non-magical buildings, but that doesn't make them any less important."

"Want to build a logging camp with percentage increases to productivity? This might seem minor, but believe me, it can be a huge advantage over your opponents."

"Lastly, Warfare involves magical ballistae and walls that reflect their damage tenfold upon the attackers; all are secrets I hold. The tree is synergistic with the lessons you have learned, so the more you know, the more complimentary secrets will be opened to you. I can tell you many things, Jax, but I need mana to survive. Aid me, my Chosen, and I will aid you in return."

"And the others?" I asked, my mind whirling with the potential this skill tree opened for me.

"Magical Research deals with changes to spells and teaches you more about the nature of magic itself. Crafting is as obvious as you can imagine, from blueprints for weapons and recipes for potions, to the myriad tiny secrets that separate the bumbling amateur from the master craftsman.

Governance deals with leadership, breaking down into three areas again, Self, Realm, and Opposition. Self deals with your abilities, teaching you and increasing your ability to lead, to persuade, and to identify your weaknesses. Realm gives bonuses to productivity, morale, and everything your people do, while Opposition deals with everything from spying to assassination, to making friends and allies.

Personal Enhancement is all about you, ways to enhance yourself magically and naturally, and improving everything from your weapon handling skills to how you speak. The mind is your greatest weapon, Jax; I recommend you do not neglect it. Finally, we have Exploration. This realm is ancient, yet never fully explored. There are secrets awaiting you that you cannot imagine!

"Some are from the past, creations that slumber beneath the shroud of ages, while others are entirely new and fresh to behold. Studying Exploration will allow you to find things long thought to be myth and legend."

"And the cost?" I asked.

"There is always a cost, that is true; but for now, we truly need each other. I will allow you access to the first ring for ten thousand mana and five Marks of Favor.

"Each level of secrets within the sections will cost more than the last, but how much depends on your knowledge and that of your followers. The second ring will cost fifty thousand mana and twenty-five Marks, the third two hundred and fifty thousand mana, and one hundred and twenty-five Marks. I'm sure you can see the pattern by now."

"Yeah, five times more expensive each time, and I have to give you twenty percent of the tower's mana? Hmmm, I don't know; seems kinda steep. We both know the tower is going to pull in a huge amount of mana when it's repaired, after all," I said, bluffing as I went.

"Maybe I could, you know, go to six percent of the mana, provided you work to help Seneschal to fix things faster. After all, if the tower collapses, you'll get nothing..."

"Nineteen percent!"

"Seven."

"Fifteen."

"Nine."

"I'll tell you what, Jax. I'll accept fifteen, but I'll make sure the tower's capacity grows by more than that in the first week, so it's practically free to you..."

I could sense the pleasure in her voice as we bartered, as well as the hunger.

"Twelve, and you agree to work with Seneschal to increase it by as much as possible."

"Fourteen, but I'll throw in a free hint to you on how to further increase the capacity yourself, past what I will cost you."

"Fuck it. Tell me how we survive the week as well, and it's a deal. I've not forgotten about the assholes incoming," I said, well aware that if we didn't win the upcoming fight, this deal didn't matter.

"Ha, deal!" I felt the tower shudder slightly as a pulse spread out from the top, flowing down and into the ground as the mana collectors had tiny realignments made.

"Jax? What did you just do?!"

"Oh...hi, Seneschal. Sorry, buddy, should have said before; my bad. I just struck a deal with Jenae, Goddess of Fire and Knowledge. She's now our patron goddess and will be taking fourteen percent of the mana we take in. She's agreed to help us to improve the efficiency...has it worked?"

"Yes. I'm sorry, I just wasn't expecting the touch of a goddess, that's all. The mana collectors are drawing in mana at a six percent increase in efficiency, and the repairs I need to make to them have been marked up to increase their

speed. All in all, it will come to an increase in mana collection of twenty-three percent. Even with Her tithe, this will greatly increase our growth."

"Funky! Keep me informed if anything changes, okay?"

"Of course."

I separated from the strange wisp's mind and looked back at the starscape that still hovered before me. As I watched, I sensed Jenae's amusement. In rapid succession, the stars for Magical Research, Enhanced Construction, and Governance pulsed once, twice, then a third time, before the starscape vanished.

"That's all the hint you get. Now for the second part of our bargain, there is a way to survive the incoming ship, but it won't be easy..."

She went on to explain the plan, and while I agreed it stood a good chance of working, it was going to be a pain in the ass to pull off, not to mention the chance of drawing a target on my back for the world to see. *Not that I had much friggin' choice!*

"Hey, Jenae, what happened to the quest you offered?" I asked aloud, suddenly remembering what she'd said. After all, a quest was a quest...

"Dammit...so much for divine infallibility."

I had a mental image of a goddess facepalming, and it was worth it.

You have been offered a Quest!

Establish a Holy Site for Jenae, Goddess of Fire, Hidden Knowledge, and Exploration!

Dedicate a Site of Power to your goddess, gaining her favor and more:

Rewards: 1000xp, 1 Mark of Favor, and Access to the Constellation of Secrets

Do you accept?

Yes/No

You have accepted the Quest: Establish a Holy Site for Jenae Goddess of Fire, Hidden Knowledge, and Exploration!

"So, how do I do this, then?"

"Simply will it into being when in contact with the control interface for the tower."

I reached out, putting my hand on the table and watching as a ripple of light spread across it, now that I'd formally claimed it as my own.

The table was crescent-shaped, and my chair sat at the fullest part, with the horns sweeping out on either side to come together across from me. Seneschal's manawell had sat there, and he'd be pissed that he wasn't connected to this anymore, considering how little he seemed to like change.

"There's one more thing we need to discuss before I return to my rest, Jax."

"Okay, uh, my Goddessness?" I replied, thinking I should be a bit more respectful, but coming out like a dick, as always.

"Ha! Don't even try to pretend respect at the minute, Jax. You don't feel it, I know. Give it time, and remember what I am. Okay, there is no 'nice' way to put this, so I'll make it simple. You're broken."

"Love you too," I retorted automatically.

"Ha. I'm not being offensive, Jax. Your body is different—that's not necessarily a bad thing, but you have a great many issues in your genetic makeup. The end result of this is that you're leveling far slower than you should be."

"Really? I thought I was leveling pretty quick?"

"Think about it, Jax. Most people don't go around fighting the creatures of the night, so yeah, fighting them has leveled you quickly. The issue is that it's not leveling you quick enough. A farmer who fought something like the SporeMother would have jumped ten levels."

"Okay, can we fix it?"

"Yes and no. I can't fix it for you. I can recommend a way to fix it in the future, though, and give you a boost of experience with your quest to tide you over. That's the best I can do until I accumulate more power."

"How do I fix it?" I asked cautiously.

"You need to give some of the spellbooks and memories to someone, create a healer, a highly dedicated one, and at their tenth level, they will have access to a specialization called 'reconstructor.' It's a rarely chosen class, but it will enable them to heal your issues, as well as heal the scarring in your brain."

"I'll be able to learn more spells?" I asked excitedly.

"You could. You could learn two spells from a spellbook, then give it time to heal, maybe another in a few months…or…"

"Or?"

"You could learn a profession." Jenae paused then, letting me think about the possibilities, before going on. *"I'm tired, Jax. I'm going to rest now. I'll be in touch soon. Think on what I've told you."*

With that, the sense of her presence disappeared, and I sat back, thinking. If I'd not used all the spellbooks I had, maybe I'd have leveled faster already? I knew that the higher the level, the more experience I needed.

So, while it'd not really been apparent now to me, I guessed it would have been as I started to really climb the levels. I shook my head and dismissed it; I needed to get on with things here and now, not worry over the future.

The table had a lip around it that stood a few inches higher than the rest of the surface and maybe provided an edge that was three inches deep. As I watched, the rest of the table slowly began to fill with liquid mana, like quicksilver.

It took less than a minute, then a familiar form began to grow, flowing upright from the pooling liquid until Seneschal stood before me, looking around at the room in disappointment. Where I saw the improvements from the dilapidated state in which I'd first seen it, he saw how far it'd fallen from the past.

"Humph. Well, it will have to do, I suppose. I'll need my well to be moved down here as soon as possible, though. While I can survive linked in this way, it is…unsatisfying."

"Yeah, well, we'll put it on the list, buddy. Might be a while though. So how do I use this thing, then?"

"Simply think, and it will obey, Jax."

"Well, that's really unhelpful, mate. I'm thinking of a decent glass of rum and a naughty lady, and I know I'm not getting either! How'd—"

"Jax? Did you call?" Oracle's voice echoed in from the hallway, and I had a sneaking suspicion she was damn well listening at the door or something, waiting for the perfect time to join in. She flew into the room a few seconds later, smiling innocently as she landed on the opposite side of the table to Seneschal.

She immediately dipped a toe into the liquid and grinned at me as her clothing melted away before reforming into a bikini. The kind that highlighted rather than hid. The kind she could have only gotten from the depths of my mind...*dammit!*

"I..." It came out higher pitched than I'd would have liked, as my groin short-circuited my brain. I *knew* she didn't have to strip off to change. I damn well *knew* it, and she knew that I knew!

I shook my head, in lieu of slapping some sense into myself, before speaking up again. This time, it came out a bit more like my normal voice, thankfully. "Didn't...ah, didn't I ask you to watch over the new people?"

She grinned at me mischievously. I had to close my eyes to pray for strength; one of these days, once my hands were actually on her, I'd end up throttling her or worse, if she kept teasing me like this.

When I opened my eyes, she'd grown again, and was now almost the same size as me. She was sitting on the side of the table, perfect legs hanging down and kicking idly as she raised an eyebrow at me. *Another one that could read my mind...!*

"You asked me to stay and keep an eye on them while they stripped the corpses and cleaned up. That's done now, so I asked Heph to monitor them, and he said it was fine. I think he's been lonely, and he likes watching people."

"I...you know what, it's fine. Good job that you're here. We've got a lot to do," I said, shaking my head free of the thoughts I was having. "So, Seneschal, try again, mate."

"Hmmm. Think of the tower, Jax," he said, and I did, my hand resting lightly on the edge of the table.

The silvery liquid shimmered before flowing together and rising. It built rapidly, becoming trees and bushes, walls and overgrown courtyards.

It grew, faster and faster, the viewpoint spiraling constantly as the trees and ground level grew smaller. In under a minute, the entire tower stood there before me, rendered in exquisite detail, down to the wrecked ship that lay before it.

I blinked and smiled as text began to flow into existence, golden words, with reds, greens, and yellow layers rendering as the tower's status appeared in an easily digested way for the first time.

The tower slowly rotated, and sections were highlighted, starting from the underground portions. There were dozens of rooms and entire floors I'd still not seen, which were all buried. These sections were all marked as red, as was the majority of the lower tower and all of its rooms, barring the one I sat in, several empty chambers, and the storeroom I'd discovered.

The outer walls of the tower were marked as yellow and showed various numbers, from a lowly three percent up to forty-five. The higher I went, the better it looked, as these sections had escaped the ravages of battle, and had instead succumbed to the inevitable destruction of time instead. The outer walls of the tower itself were even green in places, ranging from several deep red sections at the base, where it looked like the tower was open to the elements and the floor had collapsed through.

Other areas, like the Hall of Memories, were green and almost eighty percent intact. I focused more closely on the tower and thought of the armory near my last fight. The diagram expanded, rebuilding until it showed the entire floor in brilliant detail.

I could see the outlines of weapon piles, collapsed walls, and frames that must have once held armor or other sundries. I could even make out the still forms of the bodies I'd left behind, and I wondered idly about the equipment they had left.

More importantly, I looked over the opening to the floor and the restrictions on movement that I could impose.

I grinned, seeing a few easy solutions to make it as hard as possible for the invaders to get anywhere, provided I could entice them to an area like this, damaged heavily enough that they wouldn't look too closely, but provided plenty of cover. First things first, though, I needed to lure them to land somewhere high enough that I could restrict their movements and keep them from surrounding me. Besides, I had some new allies, or at least, I hoped I did.

I concentrated and thought "dedicate as a place of worship" at the tower interface, and it responded with a prompt.

Do you wish to dedicate the Great Tower of Dravith as a Holy Site?

If so, please confirm your selection and confirm the deity this site will belong to.

I saw a list begin to blur into being. I thought "Jenae" at the interface, ignoring the list. I really didn't have time to fuck about with it all.

You have selected Jenae, Goddess of Fire, Exploration, and Hidden Knowledge.

Is this correct?

Yes/No

I selected *yes*, and the tower shook slightly, dust falling from the walls and ceiling as subtle changes occurred. The visible stone took on a slight luster, and the tower seemed to warm perceptibly as Jenae's presence became stronger.

"Oh, that's better!" I heard her voice in my mind, and the tower interface showed a drop in the mana available for repairs as she took her tithe. I realized I'd probably been hosed on the deal, as she began to hungrily accept the mana, but I also realized that having a goddess on my side was likely to be seriously helpful, so I'd take the deal, regardless.

The tower structure gently spun over the table as I examined it, but just as I was about to dismiss it, I realized I'd been missing something. All around the base of the tower were black rectangles filled with symbols I couldn't make out. I only noticed them because, as the tower rotated, one came into view that pulsed faintly golden, followed by a second that shone steadily.

My attention jumped straight to the solidly glowing section, and it expanded to show the doorway of the Hall of Memories. The perspective changed, and I zoomed toward the door, which opened smoothly to reveal two smaller doors inside. I chose the one on the right first, which housed shelves filled with magical books. The books organized easily when I thought of "healing spells" or "Fire."

I practically began salivating and forced myself to not go any deeper, backing up mentally and opening the second door. I found myself in a room filled with hundreds of glowing orbs.

Each pulsed with their own internal light and gave off impressions as I looked at them. One drew my attention and quickly filled my mind with the scent of fresh baked bread, memories of building my own bakery, and the bonuses and buffs I could create with the right ingredients and equipment.

I blinked, backing away, and the memories faded. Peering into another, I remembered the joy of glassblowing, shaping sand and a simple handful of colors to become a kingfisher perched exquisitely on the edge of a branch, and the pleasure I felt as customers sang my praises.

Backing away again mentally, I realized that these were the skill memories, and Oracle's earlier comment about treasure was right. This one room held gifts that could turn my people from the sad collection of ex-slaves and sailors that they were into a true community. One that could bring beauty to the tower, as well as life.

I backed all the way out of the image room and focused on the irregularly pulsing section, receiving a warning when I tried to look at it.

Beware!

This interface is currently severely damaged. All construction, management, and upgrade facilities are unavailable until the genesis chamber has been repaired to basic functionality.

"Seneschal, is this for the golems?" I asked quietly, reading the warning over again.

"Yes, it is the main interface for the genesis chamber. Once repaired, it will give you options for upgrades, building queues, and customization, including alterations to the basic golem designs. Upgrades will give further options for higher capacity golems."

"Cool. Okay, it's clearly buggered right now. What about the rest?" I asked, drawing my attention back until I could see all of the tiles slowly rotating around the base of the tower.

There were dozens of them, but they were all dead, except for one more I hadn't noticed before.

Beware!

This interface is currently severely damaged. All construction, management, and upgrade facilities are unavailable until the labyrinth has been repaired to basic functionality.

"These are the interface tiles for facilities or systems that are currently damaged or destroyed. Much as the genesis chamber will give options, these other sections will do the same. At this point, however, you have no access."

"Well, what do we have?" I asked, trying to make out the symbols on some of the dead tiles.

"Nothing beyond these three heavily damaged tiles. The rooms that they once represented are so badly damaged that they are no more. The foundry and smithy are both little more than tumbled down walls and rusted metal scraps, I'm afraid. To bring life back to these tiles, you will need to construct new buildings or facilities."

"Well, that's a bit depressing, mate, but we can do it, I suppose. The rest of the servitors should be getting built soon. Once they've repaired the genesis chamber, they can start on the rest of the tower."

"Of course. Perhaps the time to plan the next steps and the growth of the tower facilities would be after we have secured the land?"

"Smartarse," I muttered, as I released the table and stood up. Gathering my naginata and gear, I gestured towards the door and began walking.

"Come on, then, Oracle. Let's go see if Oren has gotten things sorted out and give him the bad news!"

"What bad news?" she asked, hopping down from the table to walk by my side.

"The bad news about his ship. I think I'm going to need it!" I said, looking at her out of the corner of my eye. "Also, you might want to either put some more clothes on, or go back to your normal size, 'cause you're kinda distracting like that…in fact, do both, please!" I said, trying to get my head back in the game. She idly evaporated her clothes, creating more on the spot.

She'd opted for jeans that were so tight, they looked like they'd been painted on, and a barely decent crop top, while her hair became a lustrous blonde and blew about in its own breeze.

She shrank down to her normal size as I'd requested, but also landed on my right shoulder, and that was still kinda distracting.

"You know, the ship, it's…well, it's not in very good shape," she said as I started to jog down to the entrance floor.

"Aye, a more accurate description would be 'fubar.' 'Fucked up beyond all recognition,'" I replied. "But that's fine, because we only need some of it."

"Heph, you there, buddy?"

"Aye, laddie. Where else would ah be?"

"Good point. How are we coming along with the golems? And how strong are they?"

"They be plenty strong, and not much has changed. It still be another eight hours until the third construction-class golem be finished. The other two are workin' away merrily, and the servitor is workin' on the repairs. Why?"

I proceeded to fill Heph in on my plan, overriding his objections as he raised them. He was right that infrastructure was important, but if we were all dead, it was no comfort that the floors were clean and the gear fixed up.

By the time I'd gotten Heph on board with my plan and explained it to Oracle and Seneschal for good measure, I was jogging the last few feet to the previously overgrown doorway leading out of the tower.

The golem stationed there had done well, clearing away most of the debris and using it to shore up the walls where it could. It had blocked all other ways into the tower on that floor with fallen masonry. One large entryway remained, which had a huge stone door growing to seal it. *God, I love magic.*

I emerged into the late afternoon dappled shade of the forest floor, reveling in the hum of insects and call of the birds as I slowed to a fast walk. I made my way across the moss- and grass-covered courtyard toward the crashed ship.

Oren stood next to the ship, looking in one of the broken sections while a bearded, dark-skinned short human stood next to him. As I approached, I recognized the man as the one Oren had called Barrett and listened to them as they gestured at the ship.

"...and she's pretty buggered up, captain. I'm sorry, but she is. We'd need a full shipyard to get her fixed up before winter, and I don't see one of them around, do you? Just look at the keel. We'd need to replace it entirely, out here, without proper tools and with just these idiots to do the work?"

"They do no' be too stupid; ah'd have kicked them overboard long since otherwise!" Oren retorted. He gestured at the huge trees around them. "Look at the wood, though. One o' those be more than enough. That be all we need, and she only need hold together fer a week. Ah bet we could make it ta Shint'hamek. They do know me there, they'd mebbie help..."

"Or they might have thrown in with that prick, Barabarattas, and there might be a price on our heads by now."

"Ach, he wouldna ken we swore to Lord Jax; no yet, anyway," Oren said, waving his hands in dismissal.

"You swore to him, captain. We didn't, and for all we know...ah." He went silent at seeing me out of the corner of his eye and swallowed hard. "Lord Jax."

Oren spun around and met my eyes, shifting his attention to the two golems that were heading out of the tower and stomping across the ground to the remains of his ship.

"Golems, wait! Aye, that's the ticket! Jax...I mean *Lord* Jax, fergive me! Those golems, could we no borrow them fer a few days? Ah could get ma ship fixed, an' mebbie we could all get oot o' here afore that warship arrives." Oren grinned, then started gesturing at his ship in an effort to convince me.

"Ha, no, I don't see that working out for us all, Oren. But we'll get back to the ship and the golems in a minute. First of all, call your crew out for me, please. I need to see them." Oren looked concerned but shouted and whistled. In less than a minute, the remaining crew were appearing from all over the ship, jumping and climbing down until they stood a few feet away, nervously eying me.

Counting Oren, there were eleven of them, two of whom looked decidedly worse for wear. One had his arm in a sling and a long cut down the side of his face. The other was carried by two of his friends, his left leg wrapped in blood-stained bandages.

The crew was composed of six humans, one catman of some kind, a big guy that looked like an Ewok the size of a grizzly bear, and two other dwarves. All of them wore clothes that looked like they'd been handed down from a charity shop's reject basket, and it was evident that they were all only a few meals away from starving.

The image of the cool steampunk airship crew I'd had in my head was totally buggered. These guys looked like they'd all fallen on hard times so often and were so used to it, it had become the norm for them.

I took a deep breath and looked to Oracle, getting a nod in return as she rested her hand on my temple in preparation.

"Look, I'm crap at speeches, so I'll make it short," I said, seeing a few of the crew look at Oren and back.

"I'm in charge of the tower behind me. I'm also the guy that killed the SporeMother and the rest of the assholes that you brought to trespass. I freed the slaves upstairs, too. I don't give two shits who you are right now.

"Oren has sworn to me, and he said you're a bunch of dicks, but you're good dicks, so I'll extend the offer to you that I made to the others. You can swear to me and take up residence in the tower. I'll feed you and heal you, and I'll do my best to look after you all. In return, you do as you're told, don't fuck around, no stealing, no abuse. That's the first option."

I then gestured to the south and the deep forests. "Option two is far simpler. The city you came from is a couple hundred miles or so in that direction, and you can tell me to get fucked and start walking. You don't get to stay here if I can't trust you, and without an oath, no chance I'm going to do that. Choose quickly."

Silence filled the clearing as they looked at each other and then to Oren and back to me.

"Well, laddie, yer right aboot one thing…ye really do be crap at speeches!" Oren chuckled, finally getting a nervous laugh from his crew. He stepped forward to stand between me and his crew and turned to face them.

"Look, lads. We were dyin' back there, an' ye all know it. We could'na feed our families, never mind pay tha bills and keep tha ship fueled. We be offered a choice here: a fresh start, or a walk home. If we make it back, then what? No ship, no work, no gold, silver, or coppers, and we'll starve sharpish.

"At least fer now, our families can divide up tha gold we got paid upfront. They'll be good fer a few weeks. Only chance we got is ta start again here." He turned to me and went on. "Ye offered us a home. Do oor families be included in tha'?"

"Aye, you can bring your families. Same rules: everyone that can work does, and no dicks," I said, nodding. "No idea how you'll get them here for now, though. We've got plenty to sort out first."

"That be good enough fer me. Right then, laddies. Time to make a choice!" He walked over to stand in front of me and went down on one knee, right hand to his chest. Slowly at first, they followed. Barrett walked over to join Oren, then the pair of dwarves, the monstrous Ewok lookalike, then the rest of the crew all moved as one, as though afraid to be last.

"I swear te serve Lord Jax, ta be faithful to him, and ta no be a dick!" Oren said, with the others repeating along behind him. I swore to protect them, to look after them and to help them where I could, and I received a new notification.

Congratulations!

Your fledgling village has received eleven (11) more members of varying loyalties.

There was the loyalty bit again. I found that a bit concerning, but I didn't have time to worry about it now. I gestured for them to rise and, with Oracle's help, cast the new Focused Heal-All on both of the wounded men. It was still astonishing, seeing their bodies repair themselves, wounds disappearing in seconds as they drew in sharp breaths in shock.

The crew all looked stunned, but I didn't give them time to respond. I gestured to the golems, sending them towards the remnants of the ship.

"Okay, guys, I hope that reassures you about the choice you just made, because I know you're not going to like this part. I need your ship."

The golems began to attack the ship, cutting the rear ten feet free and breaking the rest up. Oren began to cry out in distress.

"No! Ma ship, ma beau'iful baby!"

"Sorry, Oren, but we need it. Don't worry, though. If everything works out, you'll come out of this ahead yet. What we need to do is…"

CHAPTER THIRTY-ONE

I t took us almost all of the remaining time we had to prepare for the ship's arrival, and to hide the remnants of what was left of Oren's ship in the lower floor of the tower. The golems' first—and arguably longest—job was transporting the rear of his ship, after breaking it free, up to the armory floor. I gathered my thirty-eight new villagers and spoke to them. Eleven of them took me up on my offer of a life in my new military, sick as they were of having their lives decided for them by stronger beings. *Besides me, I guess…*

The remainder, I promised to gift with skill memories if they earned them, on the condition that until the threat had passed, they would serve the tower as workers, cooking, cleaning, and repairing whatever they could.

I armed my new military with a mixture of weapons from the armory and the gear that I'd won from the team that had led them here. I'd taken my pick of the loot first, of course.

Cuirass of Night's Embrace			Further Description *Yes/No*	
Details:			This chest armor is made of vertical strips of blackened high steel laid over toughened leather. It gives a bonus of +5 to stealth. All attacks made when undetected will do extra damage.	
Rarity:	Magical:		Durability:	Charge:
Rare	Yes		82/100	N/A

Greaves of Night's Embrace			Further Description *Yes/No*	
Details:			These greaves are made of vertical strips of blackened high steel laid over toughened leather. They give a bonus of +2 to stealth.	
Rarity:	Magical:		Durability:	Charge:
Rare	Yes		82/100	N/A

Pauldrons of Night's Embrace			Further Description *Yes/No*	
Details:			These pauldrons are made of vertical strips of blackened high steel laid over toughened leather. They give a bonus of +2 to stealth.	
Rarity:	Magical:		Durability:	Charge:
Rare	Yes		82/100	N/A

Boots of Night's Embrace		Further Description *Yes/No*		
Details:		These boots are made of vertical strips of blackened high steel laid over toughened leather. They give a bonus of +3 to stealth and reduce the sound of footsteps made when wearing them.		
Rarity:	Magical:	Durability:		Charge:
Rare	Yes	82/100		12/100

Dagger of Ripping		Further Description *Yes/No*		
Details:		This dagger is enchanted to tear a wound wider than normal, ensuring the target bleeds heavily.		
Rarity:	Magical:	Durability:		Charge:
Rare	Yes	81/100		57/100

Ring of Pain		Further Description *Yes/No*		
Details:		This ring is enchanted to inflict 20% more pain on damage done by weapons held in this hand.		
Rarity:	Magical:	Durability:		Charge:
Rare	Yes	67/100		11/100

I'd shared out the rest of the gear, including my own normal armor, trusting instead to the Night's Embrace set. I was wearing four items from the set, but the rogue hadn't had any other pieces. The hood he had been wearing when Bob smashed his skull in with his mace…well, it really needed cleaning before I was going to consider wearing it, and it wasn't part of the set, thankfully. The gloves he'd been wearing were just standard gauntlets, nothing special, so I resolved to keep my eyes open for the rest of the set, especially as I got a notification pop up when I had equipped them.

Congratulations!

You have discovered four parts of the Night's Embrace set.

For assembling four out of six set pieces, you have an increase of 6% to all Stealth-based abilities, and 12% to all attack damage done when hidden. Find more set items to increase the bonus given.

I'd retained my original belt, gauntlets, and bracers, and had added the Dagger of Ripping to my belt, as well as equipping the Ring of Pain. Once everything was in place, and the last of my new subjects were sworn in to obey the orders and needs of the tower, second only to my own. I led my new team of soldiers down to the ground level and out to the collapsed labyrinth. It took an hour of poking around to confirm parts of it still existed, but the majority was a ruin, with nothing of value beyond the interface.

Congratulations!

You have discovered the Labyrinth Interface.

Do you wish to assume control of this Interface? Adding it to your existing structures will provide additional options once it is brought up to operational standards.

Yes/No

I chose yes, there was no way I wasn't going to do that, and I grunted as power seemed to gather inside me, before, shuddering through my bones. The world seemed to shimmer and shake, thanks massively to Jenae's adjustment of the experience awarded by the quest.

Congratulations!

You have made progress on your Quest: A Place to Lay Your Head.

Wisps sworn fealty: 3/3
Locations cleared and secured: 5/5
SporeMother killed: 1/1
Guardians claimed: 11/10
Workers claimed: 27/10

Rewards: The Great Tower is yours to command. Surrounding area will become aware of your rightful ownership. Access to supplies and facilities. 450,000xp.

Congratulations!

You have completed a Quest: A Place to Lay Your Head!

WARNING:

Hostile beings are approaching this location. Full ownership cannot be conferred until all hostiles are removed. Declaration of ownership suspended until this condition is met.

The world seemed to take a deep breath, and all was silent as power rushed through me. Four hundred and fifty thousand experience was mine, all in one go. The world just went right on changing for me as I reached level thirteen straight from level six. I also gained another meridian point to invest and a whopping total of forty attribute points, five for each of the seven levels I'd jumped, then a five bonus points for hitting level ten!

I knew it was all part of the plan that Jenae and I had come up with, but damn! It felt amazing, and as Xiao had said, I was faced with a choice in my notifications.

Class Evolution Recommendations

Common:

Enchanter: You've discovered how to infuse your spells into an object. Perhaps you'd like to do so permanently? Choosing this as your first class evolution will grant you a one-off bonus of five points to Intelligence and five points to Dexterity.

Slayer: As your current life choices testify, you're a natural monster hunter. Perhaps this would be a sensible class for you? Choosing this as your first class evolution will grant you a one-off bonus of five points to Constitution and five points to Perception.

Magister: You have shown aptitude for becoming a mage that is at home on the battlefield. Perhaps you'd like to focus on your magic? Choosing this as your first class evolution will grant you a one-off bonus of five points to Intelligence and five points to Wisdom.

Rare:

Harvester: You've got the gift for hunting creatures. Perhaps you want to profit from this in a more tangible way? Choosing this as your first class evolution will grant you a one-off bonus of five points to Dexterity and five points to Perception.

Spell Warden: Perhaps your fights would go better with more careful planning and use of defensive spells? Or any at all? Choosing this as your first class evolution will grant you a one-off bonus of five points to Constitution and five points to Wisdom.

Templar: This is a rare class, not often offered. You will be able to call down Holy Wrath with one hand and wield cold steel to smite your enemies with the other. Choosing this as your first class evolution will grant you a one-off bonus of five points to Endurance and five points to Wisdom.

Unique:

Tomb Raider: You seem to have a knack for surviving in monster-infested remnants of an earlier civilization. Perhaps it is destiny? Choosing this as your first class evolution will grant you a one-off bonus of five points to Constitution and five points to Perception.

Justicar: You yearn to dedicate your life to protecting the innocent and punishing the guilty. Choosing this as your first class evolution will grant you a one-off bonus of five points to Perception and five points to Wisdom.

Lord: You have become ruler of a place of power, and leader of your people, but can you make it last? Choosing this as your first class evolution will grant you a one-off bonus of five points to Luck and five points to Perception.

Jez Cajiao

Name: Jax	
Class: Spellsword	**Renown:** Unknown
Level: 13	**Progress:** 101,930/120,000
Patron: Jenae, Goddess of Fire and Exploration	**Points to Distribute:** 40
	Meridian Points to Invest: 1

Stat	Current points	Description	Effect	Progress to next level
Agility	17	Governs dodge and movement.	+70% maximum movement speed and reflexes	89/100
Charisma	11	Governs likely success to charm, seduce, or threaten	+10% success in interactions with other beings	74/100
Constitution	16	Governs health and health regeneration	300 health, regen 9.9 points per 600 seconds, (+10% regen due to soul bond, -20 health due to soul bond, each point invested now worth 20 health)	10/100
Dexterity	17	Governs ability with weapons and crafting success	+70% to weapon proficiency, +7% to the chances of crafting success	33/100
Endurance	18	Governs stamina and stamina regeneration	180 stamina, regen 8 points per 30 seconds	27/100
Intelligence	15	Governs base mana and number of spells able to be learned	130 mana, spell capacity: 10 (8 + 2 from items), (-20 mana due to soul bond)	92/100
Luck	17	Governs overall chance of bonuses	+70% chance of a favorable outcome	68/100
Perception	18	Governs ranged damage and chance to spot traps or hidden items	+80% ranged damage, +8% chance to spot traps or hidden items	72/100
Strength	19	Governs damage with melee weapons and carrying capacity	+9 damage with melee weapons, +90% maximum carrying capacity	87/100
Wisdom	21 (16)	Governs mana regeneration and memory	+110% mana recovery, 2.1 points per minute, 110% more likely to remember things	34/100

I pulled up my character sheet and looked it over. In the course of the last two days, I'd also managed to raise my Constitution, Wisdom, and Endurance, as well as my progress to my next earned increase in all of my attributes. Based on my current stats, I honestly had no idea where to allocate all the points. Well, that wasn't entirely true, actually. I wanted to put them *everywhere*!

I wanted to select the class evolution to boost flagging areas like my Charisma, but I didn't want to waste it. I could also see the benefits of both spreading the points out evenly on one hand, and min-maxing on the other.

After all, I'd always wanted to "bullet-time," and putting a straight forty points into my Agility would probably allow that! Or I could go all Hulk smash, if I dumped them into Strength, or...

I could go on for hours. Oracle and Jenae were surprisingly little help. Despite their opinions on everything else, they just told me to trust myself and allocate as I wanted. *I just know they're going to tell me I've done it wrong later.*

I thought about the fights I'd had since arriving, and how I'd basically survived by the skin of my teeth through a combination of sheer stubbornness and luck. I took a deep breath and selected my evolved class to be justicar, getting a bonus of five points to Perception and Wisdom. I then decided to play to my strengths, as my fighting style was both melee and magic-based, so I put ten points into Constitution.

God knew I'd been lucky to survive at all, so far. A further ten points went into Intelligence, giving my mana a serious boost from one hundred and thirty mana to two hundred and thirty. Thanks to losing twenty to Oracle, it also meant when I healed up, I'd be able to learn more spells. *At least when Oracle lets me, anyway.*

For the remaining twenty points, I still had the dilemma of deciding to min-max or spread them out. My fighting style was heavy on the melee, but I could increase those stats from practice and training.

My more esoteric attributes, like Intelligence and Wisdom, I really couldn't. Alternatively, if I died fighting these assholes, it really wasn't going to matter if I had the mana regeneration of a king.

I took a deep breath and chose what I really didn't want to, but I felt it was my only real option, after talking to Jenae. I had to be fast; I had to be able to appear and disappear. I had to whittle their numbers down, as these guys were soldiers. They'd slaughter me in a stand-up fight. I put all twenty points into Agility, cursing myself as I did. I hated those stabby-stabby bastard rogues, but damn if it wasn't what was needed now!

I now had a total of five hundred and twenty health, two hundred and thirty mana, and moved like a snake on a hot griddle. I bit my tongue, tasting blood as the pain of the changes ripped through me. Muscle fibers and nerves altered at a molecular level to rebuild me as a faster, leaner, and far deadlier opponent.

There was one change I had left to make before they arrived, and this was one I was either going to love or hate. Jenae had told me the truth of the essence cores and how the nobles had used them. They weren't trophies; they were weapons. They were the secret to the Augmentations the Baron had referenced. Using them granted a portion of the power of the creature, but they were irrevocably part of you from then on.

The SporeMother essence core would grant me some of her powers, but they'd take a terrible toll as well. Jenae explained that they needed to be balanced carefully, lest I become a worse monster than the Baron.

For an ability that required stamina, a second essence core was needed to provide that kind of boost, or the core would feed on me. Do something that took too much mana, and I'd be brain dead; too much stamina, and my heart would stop. It was all about balance, and the thing was, I didn't have a second meridian point available, or a second essence core. I had one choice, really: risk it for a biscuit.

I pulled the core out of my bag and examined it. It was the size of my thumbnail, round and hard like a marble, and it shone with an unhealthy internal light that shifted from green to grey, even becoming weirdly black at times, sucking all color from everything it touched.

I held it in my right hand and stared into its depths. I concentrated, focusing on the meridian point I had available. At first, nothing happened, but then I felt it. A stirring in my hand, then pain as the Pearl's tiny filaments in every part of my body slowly shifted. Blood swelled in my hand as tiny sections of my skin were sliced free, the filaments exposing themselves to air and reaching out to touch the SporeMother essence core. When they connected, the core flashed brightly, and a new notification appeared in my mind.

You have found a SporeMother Essence Core.

You have the capacity to absorb this Core, gaining the following abilities:

Child of the Night: You can alter your body, becoming incorporeal at will. All items you are in contact with and wish to include will also gain this effect.

Cost: 10 health per second when in darkness, 200 health per second in direct sunlight.

Nightmare: You can inflict Fear on a target at will.

Cost: 5 health per second for a 5% increase, builds with time. Once fear effect has risen to 100%, target can be commanded. Depends on target's will and is canceled by direct sunlight.

This Essence Core can be located in one of the following Nodes for the corresponding bonus:

Head: (*Alongside Primary Node*): Increase in Stealth abilities of 10%, anger increase of 25%.

Eyes: (*Alongside Secondary Node*): Increase in vision in darkness of 20 ft, decrease in vision in sunlight of 90% of normal vision

Ears: No bonus, 20% decrease in range of sounds detected

Nose: Bloodsense will activate at will, allowing you to track living prey. You will be filled with an intense hunger for flesh.

Mouth: You can use Voice of Fear on targets, feeding on their fear of the dark and what lurks within it. Dead meat will no longer satisfy your hunger.

Heart: You will gain additional health in proportion with that of any target that you drain of lifeblood.

Lungs: Your stamina will increase when in darkness, but decrease in light.

Stomach: Living flesh will increase your stamina by 10% per meal you eat for up to six hours. This counter will be reset with each living meal you eat.

Legs: You will gain a boost of 10% to your speed in darkness. Speed in daylight will be decreased by 20%.

Feet: You will be more silent when moving in darkness, but easier to detect in direct sunlight.

Arms: You gain a 20% increase in Strength, but a 40% decrease in limb speed.

Hands: You will gain chitinous tips to your fingers, able to shred flesh far easier. These claws cannot be retracted and are permanent.

I looked over the abilities and their costs. I'd basically lose at least as much as I gained in darkness when I was in direct sunlight, if not worse, but goddamn it, I needed any advantage I could get! When Jenae explained this side of it, she stated that humans are essentially creatures of balance. She advised that all I needed was to absorb the core of a creature with an affinity to daylight to even things out in the future.

Thankfully, with my increase in speed from my Agility attribute dump, I could afford to give up the twenty percent loss I'd have after selecting my legs as the node location, and the ten percent increase in speed in darkness would help as well.

With that done, I asked Seneschal to order my new security force to gather at the armory. I could talk to them before dispatching them to the two defensive positions we'd chosen, so I headed there myself, Bob and Oracle accompanying me.

It took a little over an hour for us to reach the armory, and it was nearly two hours later when the last member of the security team staggered in, collapsing in exhaustion onto the floor. I stood up from the pile of rubble where I'd been snoozing and wandered over to stand over him as he gasped and wheezed for breath.

"You know, pushing yourself this hard isn't healthy, Oren," I said, observing the purple of his cheeks and the unhealthy blue tinge to his lips. Before I could say anything else, Oracle hit him with a healing spell, making his color return to normal, and he sagged back in relief.

It took him a long moment to get his breath back fully, during which Barrett and several other members of his crew tried to get him upright. All were met with an explosion of dwarvish swearing and, in Barrett's case, an ill-aimed punch.

Barrett laughed and dodged easily. While he'd appeared thin as a rail when I'd met him earlier, it quickly became apparent that it wasn't down to a lack of strength. If anything, the crew of Oren's ship had muscle to spare. What they didn't have was any fat on them.

Two of the former slaves were hunters who had fallen on hard times, and between them, they'd managed to knock up a few snares and traps as examples that would hopefully soon be providing us all a little meat with our meals.

The supplies that we could use from the ship were dwindling, and I'd been told that winter was fast approaching, so we were hoping the military airship would have plenty of provisions. If not, we might starve before the winter was out, with so many mouths to feed.

I shook my head, dismissing the thoughts, and clapped Barrett on the shoulder, grinning at him.

We got along well. Oren was his captain, and probably always would be, but the dwarf was a crap fighter and had no idea about tactics.

Barrett, on the other hand, was a great fighter, and the rest of his former crew looked to him as much as they did Oren. The giant Ewok guy had turned out to be an engineer, rather than a fighter, which was a shame, as a hit from him would have done serious damage. But he was also a pacifist, ginger, and a vegetarian, so he had enough going wrong in his life without adding to it by putting a spear in his hands.

I'd enlisted Oren as titular leader of Squad One, with Barrett as his second. They had conscripted both the sibling dwarves from the ship crew, each over thirty, despite the lack of beards. Trin was the eldest, and she was also undoubtedly the stronger of the two. Rikka had shown himself to be skilled with a crossbow that had survived the crash, and both of them were fierce in their desire to fight for their new home.

I nodded to both as they each caught my eye, Trin prodding Oren none too gently with one thick boot until he got to his feet. The last member of their little team was a human from the group of slaves.

Short and darker skinned, with black hair that had been cut into a mohawk, Jian was a real spitfire of a man. He'd asked which team was more likely to see heavy fighting and had chosen that one to join. That earned him a few points from me in the balls department, even if he lost more in the brains. He had picked two shortswords that he seemed barely able to lift. As I looked over the team, I had to admit to myself that they were the best I had.

The members of Squad Two sat off to the left, talking quietly, ignoring the more boisterous ribbing that Squad One gave their leader.

The second team was made up entirely of former slaves, and I suspected that they'd be the better fighters once they'd recovered. For now, though they had little armor and rusty weapons, and two days of admittedly better (but still not good) food wasn't enough to make them into all they could be. They were led by Lydia, the woman that'd been the most outspoken and aggressive of the slaves when I'd shown up.

She was tall, as rail-thin as the rest of them, and had an almost permanent scowl painted across her face. However, I'd also seen her watching over the kids, making sure they had all they needed and sharing her food with them. I'd healed them all, even those who had insisted they were fine. As a result, they were at least recovering from the physical damage.

The mental damage would take longer, but I hoped that gutting some of the people that had enslaved them would help towards that.

Teaming up with Lydia was the tall elven man who had wanted to kill Toka. His name was Makin, and he'd been a farmer before, but he could swing an axe. Driven by his festering hatred, he'd been quick to sign up to fight. He concerned me, but I needed all the help I could get.

A dwarf, An'na, had also joined her. His name kinda freaked me out, as he spoke with the deepest voice I'd ever heard. Unfortunately, I couldn't help imagining him in a dress, singing along to a Disney song, and I hadn't been able to explain why I was grinning when he'd asked me.

An'na fought with a pair of maces, and when I watched him practicing, I didn't mind admitting he scared the shit out of me.

The damn things seemed to blur in his hands, and he laughed the entire time, and I mean laughed. The. Entire. Time. He was clearly batshit crazy, but I was going to take whatever I could get.

Last were two humans, Arrin and Rol. Arrin was determined to learn magic, and I'd given him a Firebolt spellbook. The man had fallen to his knees crying and had taken to the spell like a duck to water. Rol...well, Rol was kinda crap at everything, as near as I could tell. He meant well; he really did. He was always the first to volunteer, happy to help, and all that, but whatever he touched seemed to go wrong. I'd eventually given him a spear and told him to stab the bad guys with the pointy end, but that was about all I felt he could manage.

Oracle and I had debated giving out more spellbooks and even a few of the precious skill memories, but in the end, we'd decided not to. We were going to rely on surprise as much as possible, and between Bob, Oracle, and myself, we were going to do the lion's share of the fighting. The two squads had spent a lot of the intervening time building choke points on the stairs, starting three floors above and below where we planned to draw the enemies in. All they had to do was keep them bottled up and not die.

I'd decided I'd give out more books and memories to people once they proved themselves. At this point, it'd be a killer if I gave someone an irreplaceable set of memories, then they died ten minutes later. Yeah, it was cold, but shit happened and all too often.

I gathered the two squads together with a whistle and looked them both over in the light of the afternoon sun.

We were standing just inside the main hall, with the rear of Oren's ship poking out onto the marshalling yard, as though it had crashed into the tower. We'd deliberately left a lot of space for them to land their ship safely, making it as attractive a location as possible, even going so far as to pile loot up outside as though it was being sorted.

I'd gotten a group of volunteers to stand around, looking busy while wearing their slave collars again. The collars were unpowered and unlocked, but it was impossible to tell that from a distance.

"Okay, guys—fuck, everyone, I mean, sorry," I said, making the crappiest possible start to a rousing speech in history. "We've got a chance to protect our home here, and we're going to take it. All you have to do is get to your defenses, use the weapons you've got, and not die, okay? We'll take care of as much as we can."

There was silence for a few seconds until Barrett strode forward to stand beside me, turning to address both teams with a sigh.

"We all now know he's no speech-maker, for sure. Right, people! You've got two choices, and you've made them already, so suck it up! You joined the Great Tower Military, you all swore to serve Lord Jax, and this is the first time you can prove what you are and why he should give a shit if you want to bring your families here!

"He saved us, he damn well nearly died for us, and what's anyone else ever done for you? Your old lord sold you to a fucking SporeMother! Your new one killed it and set you free! Who else is ever going to stand up and face something like that for the likes of us?

"Kill those asshats that are coming, and we can go get our families and bring them somewhere safe. He's even given Arrin a damn spellbook! Now he's offering more, and all we've got to do is kill the men who are coming to kill us and literally not die. That's it! Survive, people, and I bet that fucking ship is loaded with booze!"

That got a round of weak smiles from them, and I clapped Barrett on the shoulder before sending them to their positions to get ready. I'd never led people before. The thought of standing up and giving a speech had made me panic as a kid, and I was asking these people to die for me. No, I was *ordering* them to die for me. I resolved to put some more points into goddamn Charisma as soon as possible.

As the two teams filed out of the hall, Oracle rode out of the stairwell on Bob's head and gave me a merry little wave.

Bob lumbered over to the ropes we'd strung under the marshalling yard, then slowly lowered himself and Oracle over the side, hiding as well as he could. We needed the soldiers to land here, but we also really needed them to not escape once we had them. Bob and Oracle were in charge of boarding and securing the ship, preferably with as little damage as possible.

My job was much simpler, and yet so much more complicated. I needed to get them to land, and thanks to my snazzy new armor, I hoped I had that in the bag. After that, I just needed to convince them to follow me inside…then kill them all. I walked back and forth for half an hour before Seneschal got in touch. His message was simple.

"Jax, they're here."

I didn't answer him. I just walked out into the open air, squeezing past the rear of Oren's ship to emerge onto the balcony. The ship wasn't hard to spot, maybe five miles out and coming straight at us. As it got closer, I could make out more details. The ship looked exactly as Oren had described it, a damn shark of the skies.

It had sails that looked like fins extended to the left and right, with a high rear sail. Cannons were rolled out on the decks. On either side, engines flared, and easily two dozen soldiers stood armed and ready on the deck. In the middle of the ship were two large cages, each filled with slaves. Behind them in the center of the raised rear deck, stood five people.

They appeared to be the captain, the navigator—due to the giant wheel he maneuvered—and three others, two in heavy armor, and one in bright white robes that reflected the sunlight. I assumed these were the elites of the ship, a mage and two melee types.

The captain lifted something that reflected the sun, and I grimaced. A spyglass. The fecker was looking at me and examining the landing area. I waved at them and pointed at the space, then turned and began to walk back inside, as though uninterested in them.

"Kick me," whispered a voice from my left, and I looked over at Cai. He'd volunteered for the "slaves" group to make it look more natural.

"What?" I asked him, confused.

"Kick me! They all think we're less than shit. Show that you're one of them, quick!"

I paused for a heartbeat, then gritted my teeth and shoved him hard against the side of the ship, gesturing at the weapons scattered around him. I gesticulated wildly, then hauled him over to the side of the balcony as though I was going to throw him off.

"Break free and run inside, quick!" I said, and he did.

I grabbed a spare throwing knife and drew back as if to throw it, before sheathing it and running after him. The remaining slaves all quickly moved out of sight as well, their part in the deception complete.

Behind us, the ship came in for a landing. I grinned, calling my thanks after Cai as he led his people to the nearest stairwell. He waved and called back.

"Good luck!"

With that, it began: the final fight for the Great Tower of Dravith.

Agamemnon's Wrath

Torin 'Ek Thun, captain of the cruiser *Agamemnon's Wrath*, narrowed the distance to the Great Tower of Dravith with a sigh of irritation.

It'd taken all his considerable skill as one of the premier airship captains in the fleet to get *just* enough damage to be able to retreat for repairs from the border skirmish with Narkolt. It had looked serious, but it hadn't been enough to actually put him at risk. He'd recognized it for the boon it was immediately and had pulled back to their home city of Himnel, and what did he find on arrival?

Not the welcome deserving of a brave airship captain who'd been risking his life for the glory of Himnel. Oh, no. All he got was a gaggle of scruffy, dirty, smelly engineers on his ship, and an order to protect the city lord's emissary!

It was intolerable. Little more than peasants had been walking about his ship with impunity when they departed! He'd soon taught them manners, but even now, they interrupted his sleep at all hours, banging and clattering, as if they couldn't carry out their repairs and upgrades without making noise.

They were doing it just to spite him, Torin decided. It was the only reasonable answer. He'd make an example of another one of them today. Give one of them as a gift to the advance team to include with the slaves being bartered to whoever ruled here.

A whimper from behind him broke him out of his contemplation, and he glanced over his shoulder at the young man chained to the back post of the deck. Blood seeping from the numerous crisscrossing whip marks on his back and buttocks was washed away by the light drizzle. The precipitation made his decks slippery, even as they shone with reflected light from the swinging, bouncing lanterns.

The boy had been the first he had broken, initially by whip. He'd started beating the lad in front of the captives of that pathetic little village, then again in his cabin. It had almost made this diversion worthy of his time, and it truly would be, once he received his pay and sold his bounty from this trip.

The smells and cries of the captives contaminated the deck of his once-pristine ship, but he'd had to leave the battle without the chance to capture any slaves, and commissions like his were expensive.

He had to recoup the cost somehow. Especially after the pathetic tribute they'd offered him when he landed.

No, the young men and women of the village, some older, but still pretty ones, and even a local reeve, the lowliest and most pathetic rank of bought nobility that existed. Well, he'd be sold as well, along with a few more skilled older villagers he would capture on his way back. It'd allow him to turn a nice profit on the trip. It was his due.

He and his men risked their lives to protect the land, even simple fly-speck villages like theirs, so why shouldn't they take an occasional tax for their bravery?

He'd even allowed a few of the crew to enjoy the captives. Some of them had refused, and one had even spoken out against him. There were always dissenters, and the rest of the crew had learned their place when the first was "set free" to walk the clouds.

Now the crew were clearly separated out, dissenters below decks scrubbing and helping the engineers, while the rest flew his ship and reveled in their places.

"How long until we land?" asked the mage, Reyt, gliding over to stand beside Torin. His gleaming white robes marked him out as a light magus in service to Issa, the God of Light in Dark Places, and a member of the Pantheon of the Dark. His escort stomped along behind him. Their heavy armor gleamed in the rain, with the symbol of the Light glimmering from its home, etched into the center of each breastplate.

"Well, Jory? You heard the magus's question; how long?" Torin barked at his helmsman.

"Mebbe half an hour, m'lord," Jory replied, tugging his cap and half bowing in respect to them both before turning back to the wheel. "We need to circle the tower, see if we can spot a better landing site. Looks like Oren has gone in too fast and too hard. He'll have a devil of a time getting out of the tower, by the look of things!"

"No, land there," the magus stated coldly, gesturing at the open marshalling yard as it rapidly approached.

"But m'lord, we don't know if there's damage to the tower. It might not hold—" His words were broken off as one of the guards stepped forward and his heavy gauntlets backhanded the helmsman across the mouth, making him stagger and spit blood.

The entire ship lurched to one side before Jory managed to right it, and he ducked his head in fear of a second blow.

"The magus gave you an order, worm. Do it!" the soldier snarled, stomping back to his place behind his master.

There were several tense seconds during which Jory and Torin waited to see if anything else would be said before the helmsman shifted their course and began to approach the designated landing site.

"Now, Reyt, perhaps your men could refrain from beating the helmsman when he has the helm? Perhaps allow me to summon another to take his place first," Torin said offhandedly to the magus, who nodded curtly.

"Of course, captain, my apologies. My man simply wanted to make sure your order was obeyed immediately. After all, you did say last night that we were to land and complete this with all possible haste? And did we not just see Lucius directing us to land there?

"I assure you, my lord captain, Lucius would not show himself so blatantly unless the area was already secure," Reyt replied with an oily smile as he blatantly ignored the veiled suggestion that his man had done anything wrong.

***

369

"We…we will be landed in mebbe ten minutes, then, m'lord," Jory quavered around an already swelling lip. Blood dripped from his chin onto his tunic, his old hands shaking where he gripped the wheel and prayed to survive another trip. *Just get home one more time, you old fool, then jump ship; better to starve in the city than* this, Jory thought to himself.

As the marshalling yard grew closer, the crew began rushing from position to position, frantically pulling lines, hauling in the sails, and making ready.

Reyt ordered his soldiers to prepare to deploy, all two dozen or so of them forming up in an approximation of attention. *It was as close as they could manage, the mercenary scum that they* are, thought Jory, blinking tears away as he concentrated on landing the huge ship. The engines flared as he pulled levers and caressed the activation runes for the landing gear with hands that shook and ached.

Joints swollen with age and rheumatism were made almost young again as he felt the power of the ship responding to his will.

At last, the ship settled down on the designated landing area lightly, with barely a bump to show she was no longer free to soar the skies. Instead, her engines powered down as she became bound by gravity again.

Jory sighed as he caressed the last symbols, sending the engines into standby. He knew he'd miss this; it'd been his life for so long, but with captains like Torin…*I'd rather* starve, he confirmed to himself, a weight lifting from his shoulders as the decision was made.

"Why are the engines still drawing mana?" Torin snapped at him, and Jory squeezed his eyes shut before responding.

"Well, lord captain, if the dock gives way, and the engines are dead, it'd take long minutes to re-fire them. But from standby, it only takes seconds. Plus, the cost in mana is small, so I thought—"

"Well, it's costing *me*, not you! Turn them off. You heard the magus; this area is secure!" With that, the captain stomped off down the deck and headed towards his cabin as the magus and his men went to join their soldiers.

Jory stood there for long seconds, knowing it was a mistake, but eventually, he gave in to the orders.

With a wince, he powered the engines down fully, allowing the ship's true weight to settle on its landing struts. There were a few groans from the metal and a crunching sound of stone settling, then nothing, and he let out a breath.

Madness to power down the engines fully. Utter madness. But he was only a helmsman, and after Gimil had spoken out and been thrown from the ship.…Worse, he could end up like the poor sods in the cages. *No, better to starve. Just get through and get back to the city. You can lose yourself there,* he reaffirmed to himself.

CHAPTER THIRTY-TWO

I grinned to myself as the ship settled behind the remnants of Oren's ship. One hurdle down. Time to move back further before they spotted me.

The gangplank slammed down, and men and women streamed off, all human. As I watched through my concealed gap, at least one conversation with Oren was confirmed: these assholes were seriously against the "lesser races," as Oren had said they called other species.

The soldiers ran and stumbled down the wooden causeway, making it shift and bounce under their feet. As they reached the ground, they split off to either side, forming up into a sloppy honor guard for the man I'd seen on the raised deck. He strode down, white robes flapping in the constant breeze at this altitude. His two heavy soldiers flanked him.

The captain spoke to the white-robed man for several minutes before joining him. It appeared that the rest of the crew had been instructed to wait aboard the ship. The soldiers began to file across the marshalling yard and into the tower, edging around the rear of Oren's ship to enter one at a time. While they were busy making their way in, a flash of movement darted around the rear of the ship, and I grinned. Oracle was off and heading to the first engine.

Oren had spent hours going over the design of these ships, explaining where the weak and strong points were, how the engines came already assembled, and that only engineers from the Airships Guild could make changes to them.

In their rush to maintain their monopoly over this technology, however, they'd made a grave error. They'd put a dead man's switch on each one. If the engine housing was opened, the script powering it would die, taking hours to recalibrate, if it could be made to work again at all. Warships therefore carried spare engines, and most ran on at least fifty percent more engines than they needed to stay aloft, in case of damage.

What nobody seemed to have considered, though, presumably because the tech was so new, was what happened if someone simply opened up *all* the engine housings.

Oren had pointed out that there were engineers aboard the ship currently, having been forced aboard to do some repairs and upgrades.

Oracle landed on one of them and gave me a wave before disappearing. "Come on, girl, you can do it!" I muttered to myself, glancing back and forth between the ship's engines and the soldiers who slowly made their way inside the tower. They obviously couldn't see properly in the dark, so they bunched up around the entrance, making it harder for others to get in as they passed the choke point.

They only needed to go another dozen feet, and they'd be able to see the truth of the ship: it was only the rear section, made to look like it'd landed and somehow slid into the tower too deeply by accident.

It wasn't a great disguise, and any real examination would show it up easily enough, but the thing people forgot was that they were assholes.

Assholes never looked too closely; they always just saw what they expected to see and plodded on. All I had to do was hope they were all assholes.

I needed that ship grounded. If it took off and decided to stand back and pound us, there was little I could do. I had to wait until Oracle had incapacitated their engines.

Maybe thirty seconds passed, and two more men had clambered inside, when I felt Oracle reach out to me.

"Jax!"

"Yeah, Oracle? Give me good news, baby!"

"Done! The first engine is dead, and I'm moving onto the second. Should be quicker now that I know what I'm looking for!"

"Brilliant! Okay, let me know when you've got four of them down, and then we can start!"

"Going as fast as I can!"

The sense of her in my mind dissipated and I crept forward. I'd deliberately had the golems pile up the debris on this floor in strange patterns. Some areas were higher on one side than the other.

One small wall had a hole that led straight down to the next floor on its far side, but the hole was big enough that anyone trying to cross over would have to really jump to clear it. Other sections provided cover for me as I moved closer and closer, catching the nervous whispers of the men as they gathered together.

I'd also had Oren and a couple of his more skilled men help me in making traps, including a little more tinkering with the needle trap I'd recovered from the trapped chest. That particular one was set into a mound of rubble at the top, right in front of Oren's ship.

I planned for the soldiers to find the trap one way or another and hopefully decide that it was best not to climb over the rubble.

As a last surprise, I'd made some sections of the floor into deep indentations and filled them with water. One of the puddles was covering the area they were standing in now, and I could hear the splashes as they moved, the clatter of weapons and whispering and throat clearing of nervous people.

After another minute or so, I got a heads up from Oracle as I slid into place behind a low mound of stone.

"That's three, Jax! One more to go!"

Then she was gone again, someone swearing at the soldiers to move, followed by a clang as someone hit a metal helm with a gauntleted fist. The elites were forcing their way in and making the soldiers spread out more.

"Lucius!" a voice called out, and one of the heavily armed soldiers clanked into view, a bright light growing behind him as the mage moved inside as well. "Where are you, you bloody fool!" the same voice bellowed.

"Come on, Oracle!"

"I'm trying! They kinda don't want people playing with these things, okay? I've never seen so many clips and chains!"

"Sounds like one of my ex's bedrooms…"

"What?"

"Dammit. Forget I said anything. Just get it open!"

"It's...almost...there! It's open! The fourth engine is powering down now. What did you mean about—"

"No time! See if you can get any other engines they have left down! Make sure they can't lift off!"

I took a deep breath and started to whisper the incantation I needed, my hands moving in a pattern as the spell began to form. The light caused by its creation was thankfully blanketed by the bright white glare of the light mage's staff as he strode in.

"Spread out! Find the crew and bring that goddamn rogue Lucius to me!" he snarled at the soldiers as they huddled together, practically blind inside the tower. They slowly started to spread out, splashing through the standing water as they headed deeper into the small maze I had created. The walls were only six or seven feet tall at the highest, though most were only two or three feet. The piles of debris blocked their vision of each other as they began the search.

"Engine five is down, and Bob is climbing up the rear of the ship now. He's ready to start whenever you are!"

"Keep him in place. When I need him, I'll really fuckin' need him!"

I compressed my hands tighter and tighter, feeling the spell resist as I pushed more and more mana into it, until it felt like the spellform was bucking and thrashing in my grasp. I slowly curled my lower fingers in tight, standing up and flicking both sets of upper fingers forward and creating an opening in the compression.

The spell burst free, flashing across the intervening distance to hammer into the nearest heavy soldier. I'd wanted to get the mage, but, thanks to Murphy's law, he was on the far side.

The heavy soldier was staring in shock at the roughly cut edge of Oren's ship, his brain working to make sense of it, when my lightning bolt slammed into him from behind. He was smashed into the frame with enough force to make his armor ring like a bell. His screams came out more like a high-pitched whine as his muscles and teeth locked in place.

More importantly though, as the spell flowed through him, it was conducted down his armor and into the standing water to spread out to all of those standing around him.

The mage disappeared as a barrier flared to life. All but a tiny fraction of the spell I'd cast was deflected, but even that small amount that was carried through the standing water to him was enough to momentarily freeze him in place with pain and shock.

The second heavy soldier had just stepped from the water and received a much less powerful impact, but it was still enough to make him grunt in pain.

Lesser soldiers still in the water thrashed around and collapsed as the spell worked its way through them.

It was all over in fewer than five heartbeats, but the change to the room was immense. The first heavy soldier had collapsed to the floor in a heap of metal, small wisps of smoke rising from him. Of the dozen soldiers who were inside the hall already, five were killed outright. Two were so heavily injured, they were effectively out of the fight as well. That left seven, in various states, that rushed back to the mage and formed up in a protective ring around him.

The second heavy soldier was already thundering toward me, as the mage behind him stepped out of the pool and began to cast.

"Check on Rolk!" the heavy soldier shouted over his shoulder as he came closer. I took a deep breath and swept up my weapon before activating Child of the Night. As soon as it activated, I felt the pain of my health being drained. But as the world around me seemed to slow down, I grinned. My body had become as smoke, and as I flowed back into the shadows, I disappeared from the soldiers' sight.

The heavy stumbled to a halt, his large kite shield sagging slightly as his eyes opened wide. His sword point flicked nervously from side to side as he tried to spot me.

I moved about a dozen feet to the left and six backwards, flowing to a halt behind a low wall to become solid flesh and blood again. As soon as I became fully corporeal, a wave of nausea washed through me, making me stumble and grit my teeth. A debuff flashing up in my vision informed me that I was suffering from using a darkness-aligned spell next to a consecrated light mage.

Warning!

Attempting to use a Darkness-related ability inside the Area of Effect (AOE) of Light's Chosen will do significant damage to the user unless your Darkness alignment is higher than the caster's Light alignment.

I blinked and tried again to keep my breakfast down, before I checked my health bar. It had taken me maybe six seconds to shift to the area where I now crouched. I had figured that I should have lost sixty, maybe seventy of my four hundred and eighty total.

I hadn't. I'd lost over two hundred!

My greatest advantages in this fight were always going to be the facts that I could flit back and forth and heal myself whenever I wanted. I was going to be the stealthy, backstabbing type of mofo, despite my hatred of that kind of thing, because it meant I'd win easily, but now? Dammit. I didn't want to have to fight fair!

I quickly cast a healing spell on myself, feeling my health start to inch its way back up, even as a voice shouted out from ahead.

"Over there! To the right, he's hiding behind there!" I swore under my breath as I realized that the mage must have sensed me using magic, and he jumped even higher up my "fuck up his Tuesday" list.

I swallowed hard, the nausea still making my stomach roil as I moved as fast as I could, keeping my head down. I managed three steps before something bright white smashed through the wall where I'd been crouching.

It looked like a baseball, but it had moved so fast, it left a solid bar of an afterimage before it exploded and sent me flying end over end to splash down headfirst in a puddle.

As I landed, my internal monologue spoke up from the back of my mind and informed me calmly that it had moved the mage all the way to the top of the list and added "Burn him to death and piss on the ashes."

I was blinking and trying to figure out what had just happened when I saw my health slowly lowering further. I quickly discovered a white tendril that had latched onto my leg and begun to suck the very life out of me.

I reacted instinctively. I'd spent hours upon hours practicing channeling into my naginata. As flames illuminated its length, I slashed down, cutting the tendril loose and rolling to my feet before letting the channeled spell die. I was left with less than half of my health and a third of my mana. Between the low walls I'd made all those plans for, I caught a glimpse of the mage casting healing spells on the few soldiers I'd thought were out of the fight, but not dead.

"Okay, Seneschal, plans A through Y are fucked. Tell Oren to get his arse in here with his men. It's gonna get messy!"

"Yes, Jax. I will pass your message on."

All the sneaky plans I'd made, all the fallbacks and ways to slowly bleed the group, all of it left my mind in an instant. I spat blood on the floor and set off running at them. The mage was backing away toward the choke point to get back onto the marshalling yard, screaming for more troops while the soldiers already inside were preparing to hunt me down.

I needed that fucker dead. The rest of the soldiers were neither here nor there in the grand scheme of things. I could fight them head on or use magic or whatever, but the mage was the real threat.

The soldiers were spreading out, searching in twos and threes through the gloomy interior to try to find me while I dove behind one of my rubble walls and began to creep forward. The mage might be able to sense magic, but he clearly couldn't see any better than his men, and the light he'd brought on his staff only illuminated so far.

Their first trap loss was to the tripwire one of Oren's men had made. The man stumbled, falling full-length into a puddle with a great splash. He made a sound of annoyance that soon changed to a short, quickly cut-off scream as a nearby wall fell onto him.

Blocks too heavy for anything other than a golem to move made short work of the soldier, and his friends backed away in horror. Another man stumbled in the darkness, screaming as he frantically tried to stop himself on the sides of the hole that dropped through to the next floor.

"No, no, noooo!" he managed to get out before he fell through. The sides had been deliberately smoothed to prevent any grip. He fell about fifty feet or so, landing on a stone floor below in full armor with a fatal crash. The final trap victim was a woman who'd tried to climb to the top of the rubble to get a better view, triggering the trap needle. I couldn't see any details from where I hid. I just heard a scream and a thud as she fell, then silence as the paralysis trap drowned her in the few inches of water she'd fallen into.

It was now or never. I'd managed to cut them down quite a bit from the soldiers, the two elites, and the mage. I was left to contend with just the mage, one elite, and four soldiers. I couldn't risk losing the advantage of momentum.

I ran as fast as I could, my newly overpowered Agility coming to the fore as I splashed through the puddles and leaped over small walls. As I barreled toward them, I felt Oracle channeling. I recognized the spell she was working on as she hurried to me, entering through a small hole Seneschal had made yesterday in the wall for her.

I covered the last few feet to emerge into the light cast from the mage's staff, the soldiers crying out in warning. Several more were wriggling through the gap to help their fellows and quickly formed up in a second row. The first few hesitated for a second before stepping forward. Their rank was made up of two swordsmen in the middle, each of whom had a small shield. Two men with spears flanked them on the outside.

Behind them, the others were pushing in, their drawn weapons causing the mage to shout in fury as he tried to get past them and back outside.

The heavy soldier was stolidly backing away, making sure he kept between his charge and me.

As the first men closed the distance, I jumped to my left. Planting my foot firmly, I kicked off, lashing down with my naginata. I transformed the spear to my right into a thin quarterstaff as I sliced the metal point away. The severed spearhead flashed in the dim light as it was flung into the darkness. I landed and spun, sweeping the blade low and arcing back up. The motion pushed aside the shield of the swordsman from the right.

The point of my naginata flicked out, barely kissing the inside of his throat, but as it came away, I was rewarded with a gurgle. Bright arterial blood sprayed forth as his hands flew to his neck in panic.

I moved into the middle of the pack, my naginata flowing around, up, and down, sweeping from one side to the other in a veritable dance of death.

I batted aside the remaining sword and spear until I could land another blow, this time slicing deep into the leg of a man on the left, his scream of pain barely registering with me as I frantically tried to keep up with all of them.

I could feel sweat pouring down my back. My hands grew clammy, and a droplet flew from the tip of my nose as I tried to remember forms I'd practiced with West and the others in training sessions that felt like years ago. The only thing keeping me alive was the twenty points I'd dumped into my Agility.

The naginata seemed to spin and move almost of its own volition as I tried to watch everywhere, until a blade got through. A sword glanced off my left bracer, pushing my hand slightly out of alignment. Then another bounced off my right greave, stabbing down too quickly. Neither one did any real damage, but as another and another hit me, forcing me back step by step, I felt myself losing control.

More men were joining the fight, the second rank pushing forward to join the first even as I felled another of them.

The swordsman barely had time to hit the ground before he was enveloped in white light. As I lost sight of him behind the advancing troops, I realized that the bastard mage had stopped fleeing. He was healing the men I was fighting!

I stabbed out frantically, overextending in my desire to make sure of the hit, and was rewarded with a stab to my left leg that went through the armor, cutting deep into the flesh and muscles before bouncing off the bone. I groaned in pain and half-hopped, half-fell back, waving my weapon threateningly.

It had worked, though; they'd all stayed clustered up around the choke point, and just when it felt like I couldn't keep going any longer, Oracle's spell flared to life. Cleansing Fire roared out, centered on me as it flooded the group of soldiers with flames that immediately began burning into them.

The momentary distraction alone allowed me to step back, and I felt the flames climb up my legs. The healing aspect of the spell was almost as welcome as the damage it was doing to the soldiers as small wounds began to seal themselves up. My health slowly climbed while the soldiers fought amongst themselves to back away. Most importantly, my leg no longer felt like it wasn't going to hold my weight.

I resolved not to give them a second chance and lunged forward, stabbing the blade of my naginata up to pierce one man under his chin. The crunch as it broke through his jaw and speared his brain let me know that the mage wasn't going to be getting this guy back on his feet.

I waded in amongst them, striking for all I was worth. Weapons shone in what little reflected light there was.

Pain flared along my side as a lucky hit got between the plates of my armor, scoring across the top of my hip. The world devolved into a mess of pain, flashing weapons, screams, and blood, until finally I was standing there alone.

Cleansing Fire had dissipated, and still I stood, clinging onto my naginata as I heaved in exerted breaths and waited for my mana to refill.

All around me were the bodies of dead and dying soldiers, but the mage and his guard had escaped. As I tried to catch my breath, I stared at the small choke point. Climbing out there to attack him was going to suck, I just knew it.

A new sound finally registered over my thundering heartbeat, and I glanced to my left, watching the stairwell as Oren and his men ran around the corner. They slowed down, having as much difficulty seeing in the dark as the soldiers had. To their benefit, they'd helped me in here for days, so they soon picked their way across to where I leaned against my weapon. Oren was the first to speak.

"So, laddie, wha' happened ta drawin' 'em ta us? And stealthily killin' 'em all? You're a wee bit crap at battle plans. Ya know this, aye?"

I just snorted at him and breathed out a sigh of relief as Oracle hit me with a heal. I straightened up and faced the team. Oren, Barrett, Trin, Rikka, and Jian stood around me, weapons at the ready. They nearly shit themselves as I tried to come up with a sneaky way to get outside without us all being murdered in the first few seconds, when, wonder of wonders, it stomped into view.

The golem, the next one that had been due to be finished! I'd forgotten about it in the heat of battle and everything else. I'd just told Heph to get it finished and send it to me when it was done!

It took less than a minute to give the thing its orders, then it was off, smashing up the remnants of the ship until there was no choke point left. Instead, Oren and his team were all shielded behind a mobile wall that was carried by the golem. Bob was in place, sending a mental acknowledgement as he clung to the outside of the captain's quarters just out of sight of the crew.

All that was left was me and the one thing I had in abundance: my raging stupidity.

CHAPTER THIRTY-THREE

I ran as fast as my limited stamina and wounds would allow. Healing myself as I went, I dashed up the stairs to the next level. As I hurried to gain the next floor, I explained my plan to Seneschal, then attached the length of rope that Cai had brought me to a nearby boulder.

"So, this rope is definitely long enough, right?"

"No. I told you it was all we had on hand, and you'd probably survive the fall…it's not long enough at all."

"Oh, fuck my life!"

I cursed over and over as I studied the window he'd directed me to. It was small and still blackened by sporeling crap, but it happened to be the best one for positioning. It also was slowly becoming more and more unsteady as Seneschal removed the stone around it. If it fell outward, there was my last sneaky trick, wasted.

I took a last breath and checked on Oracle. She'd stayed with Oren and was helping to heal them as the team distracted the remaining guards on the ship. Oren and company had marched out behind the golem and the huge hunk of the ship it carried as a shield. Rikka was firing crossbow bolts at the crew, who were firing back with bows and arrows while the mage was using light-based spells, so they were basically at a standoff.

The other crew members on the ship were frantically trying to get its engines back online, or its cannons to bear, and neither was having any kind of success. Every so often, the mage would nail someone with that explosive ball spell he had, then Oracle would heal everyone, or Rikka would hit one of the crew, and the mage would do healing.

They were locked into an unsteady tie for now, but I'd called in reinforcements in the shape of the second squad, and they were nearly in place. In the time it had taken me to get to this floor, secure the rope, and finish healing myself, they'd gotten close to the entrance as well.

"They're here, Jax!"

"Go, go, go!"

As soon as Arrin began slinging Firebolts, I started moving, the end of the rope in one hand and a very urgent need to use the toilet filling my mind. I clambered up onto the ledge and began prying at the window, digging my fingers in around the edges until it gave.

I yanked it back and dropped it on the floor inside the tower, making a loud crash and tinkle of breaking glass. Seneschal probably disapproved intensely.

Then I looped the rope around me, and using a belay technique, my belt, a bit of metal handily bent by a golem, and a sheer excess of balls, I stepped out to fast walk down the side of the building. Seneschal was right as well, I saw. I was directly over the airship, facing down.

I slowly let the rope out in my left hand, trying frantically not to slip or let out too much, but equally not able to go too slow at the risk of falling off or dangling, rather than practically jogging as I was.

I'd seen it years before on "Universal Soldier," then again on some mental Japanese TV show, and much to my relief and utter amazement, it worked.

As I got closer, I summoned a Firebolt, charging it up continually until it was blazing in my hand. Then, just as the mage finally sensed something was wrong and looked up, I hurled it at him.

It slammed into the ground where the bastard had stood only a second before, exploding and sending him and his guard flying. The remainder of the two squads broke cover and started sprinting to the ship. They grabbed whatever handholds they could find and started climbing, while I started sprinting and releasing far more of the rope than was safe. I reached the end of it all too soon and pushed off hard, leaping out and just barely making it to the deck of the ship.

I landed heavily, clattering across the deck as I bounced and rolled. Trying to absorb the shock of my impact, I almost knocked myself out as I heard my naginata clang and bounce away into an open hatch.

The deck shook as the heavy soldier neared. I rolled to my back and launched myself to my feet, arcing my back like a ninja warrior, flipping like an Olympic gymnast and landing like a braindead seal with one foot in the open hatch.

I screamed and fell sideways just in time to avoid being hit in the face by the remaining elite soldier's mace.

As I clanged, banged, and swore my way down the steep ladder, I had a split second in which my thoughts were clear. I wondered if the heroes of the stories I always loved reading had ever had this shit happen to them, or if this was a mixture of reality and the fact that several gods clearly hated me.

Then I slammed into the floor face-first and lay there for a second, stunned. I coughed, my nose pulsing in agony, and I realized I'd broken the damn thing again. I'd lost track of how many times this year I'd had it broken. *At this rate, it's never going to heal* right, a stray thought informed me. *Okay, a better helm, put that fucker on the list.*

I grunted and braced my hands in the push up position as I started to get up, only to fall back down, screaming with pain, as the elite's mace slammed into my outstretched right hand before clattering off into the well-lit hallway.

The bastard had thrown it from above me, and it felt like I had a glove full of broken glass, rather than a hand. I got back up and backed away, glaring at him as he clambered down the remaining rungs of the ladder.

"Bob, need you now, buddy. Get the captain, and anyone who doesn't surrender, kill them!"

A faint acknowledgement returned from him as he finally started moving, then a scream and the tinkle of breaking glass came from somewhere overhead. I used the last of my mana to heal my hand as best I could, hoping Oracle didn't need the mana for someone else, and backed down the corridor.

The heavily armored figure was clearly having problems in the narrow hallway, considering he couldn't face me fully without scraping his armor against the walls and slowing down. He hunched down behind his shield, angling himself carefully and shouted something.

Did he just say shield bash? I wondered a split second before he flashed across the intervening distance and smashed his shield into my chest, sending me flying backwards into a closed door.

Or into a formerly closed door, as my body battered it open, deforming my armor and cracking ribs from the force of the blow.

I bounced across the floor of a room that I recognized as the ship's hold, or one of them at least. Several startled people hastily flattened themselves against the walls and tried to stay as far back from me as possible. I forced myself to my feet and focused on the elite as he hunched over to get through the small doorway.

He straightened and drew his sword, clanging it against his shield as he started to circle me. I drew a sword in my right hand and a dagger in my left before snarling at him, using the pain to clear my head.

"I don't have time for this shit!" I spat out, darting forward, slashing and stabbing, only to have every strike deflected effortlessly. We circled each other, and he didn't even bother to counterattack, content to let me wear myself out against his shield.

"Never fought a shieldbearer, have you, boy?" the elite mocked me, his voice deep and gravelly. I wanted the fight over with, but the bastard was much more skilled than I was. Every attack, every feint, he could clearly read and was steadily wearing down my stamina bar.

After another minute of this, I could barely move, staggering backwards even as cries of pain and battle continued from above. This asshat was keeping me from my people, and they could be dying, dammit!

I had a recollection of fighting in the arena, and I grinned as I checked my mana bar. It sat at twenty-two points—two whole points higher than I needed!

I threw my sword at his head, making him duck behind his shield reflexively. As soon as he couldn't see, I cast Summon Water between his legs. The small magical fountain erupted, making him cry out in surprise as it soaked him, pouring into his armor and flowing across the floor under him. He backed away, then looked at me in annoyance.

"Really, boy? Is washing my balls the best you can do?" he said, stomping forward again, his boots splashing in the last of the water.

I grinned back at him, backing away and holding up my right hand. The crackling lightning filled my palm just as he started to move out of the puddle.

His eyes widened in understanding through the slit of his helm.

I released it, sending it flashing across the intervening few feet. It hit hard, flooding his body with lightning then streaking back and forth inside his wet armor. The tiny bolt shocked him repeatedly as he screamed and thrashed over and over.

He collapsed to his knees, twitching and shuddering. His sword fell from senseless fingers, and only the fact that his shield was strapped to his arm kept it in place.

"No, asshole, I just don't have time to jerk around with you right now," I whispered. He blinked, the shock wearing off just in time to feel me lift his chin in my right hand. He stared up at me, eyes unfocused and stunned, until I stabbed with the dagger. I didn't dare give him the time to recover, his warm blood spraying across me as I cut his throat.

It wasn't an honorable kill, and it must have looked terrible to the people huddled in the darkness, but I couldn't afford to think like that.

I had people to save.

I quickly searched him, finding what I'd hoped to find in a pouch on his belt: two healing potions! I downed one and put the other in my storage. Gathering my sword and dagger, I headed across the hold to the nearest ladder, rushing to join the fight again.

I glanced at the sailors as I passed them. They held hands out to their sides to show they were unarmed, so I ignored them. I knew what I had to do: kill that bastard mage and capture or kill the captain. I could only hope Bob was doing well!

I dragged myself up the ladder, cursing under my breath all the way. I was getting stronger. Damn, I was getting much fitter and stronger than I'd ever been in my life, but still, climbing even stairs in full armor was painful. Climbing ladders introduced issues involving chafing that I resolved to avoid for the rest of my life.

The twenty or so rungs to the upper deck felt far too long to climb, but once I reached the top and pushed open the hatch a little, I had to grit my teeth in anger. I'd made it to the hatch just in time to see the mage blast poor batshit little An'na from their feet. They'd been running straight at the mage, then were sent flying through the air to disappear off the side of the ship, their body trailing smoke.

I could only hope there was something between them and the ground, preferably the marshalling yard, but with all the turning around, I just couldn't be sure.

I heaved the hatch up, pulling myself out and drawing the dagger and sword before the bang from the hatch's impact had finished ringing in the air. A handful of battles were going on across the deck.

Lydia was rolling around on the floor with a man on top of her, both fighting to plunge a single dagger into the other. Oren was facing off against a human with a broadsword, deflecting the clumsy chops to the sides of an old, battered shield and lashing out with an axe in response, crunching it into the chainmail he wore. The golem lay on the floor, one leg entirely missing and the other damaged, but it was still crawling forward stoically.

Arrin was ducking and diving behind barrels and the cannons, occasionally firing a Firebolt back at someone above me. As I turned to follow the trajectory, the mage's hand emerged from the raised deck above. A flash of light streaked across the air to end in an explosion of wood splinters that made Arrin cry out in pain.

I was having that bastard.

Before the thought had finished echoing in my brain, I was running to my left, kicking off the wall of the hull to boost me as I practically flew up the stairs. I jumped two steps at a time while I tried to come up with a plan to get close enough.

I breached the top of the stairs, finding two men trying to kill Bob. The captain was dead at his feet, as were two others, but Bob was in a bad way.

The mage stood in the center of the upper deck, firing spells first one way, then the other, trying to kill Arrin and my men while also aiding the soldiers that were fighting Bob. He didn't look so pristine in his white robes now. Blood splattered them, and the left side of his face was blackened, the eye a milky white and hair singed away.

I grinned as I ran, pleased with the damage to his face as he spun to confront me. Looked like Arrin had scored a good hit!

His one remaining eye opened in shock then blazed in anger as he recognized me, realizing perhaps for the first time that I wasn't Lucius, and that all of this was down to that mistake he'd made on his approach to the tower.

He snapped off a small, arcing flare of light at me, too fast to dodge. I moaned as it hit my breastplate, splashing like a water balloon. Instantly, the liquid burned as noxious fumes assaulted me, making me cough and squint to see through suddenly watering eyes.

You have been hit with Acid Splash!

You will take one point of damage per second until the acid is purged from your body or it has run its course.

96 seconds remaining...

He'd been about to cast the spell at Bob, but had changed the target at the last second, slowing me instead. My health bar turned a sickly green, but it didn't stop me from lashing out with my sword in an attempt to take his head.

He dove backward, the railing of the upper deck stopping him as I swung again. He dodged to his right and my sword dug in, getting caught on some ornamental wooden frieze. However, my Dagger of Ripping combined with the Ring of Pain's pain amplification made him stagger, blood spraying from his shoulder where I'd managed to catch him.

He grabbed a small stick from his belt with his right hand, snapping it cleanly in half. I was close enough to feel the runic device activate, and a shield flared into being between us as he moved to the side and started backing away.

I gritted my teeth, releasing the sword, and tore at the latches on my armor. The pressure and the burning relented as the armor clattered to the ground. I'd have washed the acid, or whatever it was, off, but I needed my mana to finish this.

Something was on fire nearby, the smoke flowing through the barrier to wrap around the mage. As I made multiple attempts to lash out, my dagger just bounced off, causing the mage to grin at me evilly. He pulled out a mana potion and began trying to work the cork free. I had only seconds, judging by his struggle with his wounded arm. If he managed to get spells back in action against me, I was screwed.

I had one chance left, but it wasn't a good one.

I cast healing on myself, glad to see my life bar creeping up again. I was at nearly three hundred now and climbing steadily, but I needed all that and more.

My last thought as I backed up a few steps to start running forward as fast as I could was, *I really hope "light drizzle" doesn't count as direct sunlight...*

I activated the ability I'd gained from the SporeMother. Child of the Night caused me to seemingly bloom into an explosion of darkness. I deactivated it a split second later, screaming as I passed through his barrier, as both the effects of his consecrated light magic and the semi-direct sunlight did a number on me.

The world spun, and I lost control of my stomach as nausea the likes of which I'd never experienced ripped through me—and I'd had bad Indian takeout and the norovirus all in one go.

I became fully solid as I crashed into the mage, taking us both to the ground. The impact knocked the mana potion free of his hand as I managed to gain enough control of my wildly spinning brain to stab out with the dagger. We landed hard, with him below, and I closed my eyes against the spinning world lashing out again and again, while my stomach and bowels cramped and released.

It seemed to last forever, but when I could get control of my mind enough to focus, I felt Oracle's cool hand on my brow. I was laid out on the deck, heart hammering in my chest. My mana, stamina, and health bars were all flashing red. Even as they slowly refilled, I realized I didn't even have double digits in any of them...I was a mess!

The stink of vomit and my own bowels assailed my nose as Oracle spoke softly to me.

"It's okay, Jax. You did it! He's dead! Just drink this. Please, Jax, drink the potion, and I'll make it all okay again." She was on the verge of tears.

I opened my mouth, feeling something being poured in. I gulped it down, only to have another potion replacing the first, and Oracle told me to swallow that as well. I did, blinking in relief as I saw my health and mana bars start refilling at an increased rate. Someone shouted something from the lower deck, and she spun around. A furious tone I'd only heard once before, when the vatin interrupted us, filled her voice.

"Stay down there! I told you before, he needs to recover! Bob, if they come up here..."

I heard the clattering sound of Bob dragging his half-broken form to the stairs. A raw, low growl came from him that made the hackles on my neck rise in instinctive fear.

Then she was back, stroking my face and telling me there was nothing to be concerned about.

Using our shared mana pool, warm water, and healing spells alternating, she cleaned me down while I remained lying on my back.

My health and other bars were climbing rapidly, but I'd come too close to death too many times in a short period of time, and I stayed put. My mind was still reeling in shock over the side effects of that last ability.

Notifications blinked rapidly, seemingly desperate for my attention, but until Oracle cast her final spell, I just didn't want to move.

When it was done, and the upper deck was washed clean, the blood and bodily wastes flushed out to drain away down the side of the ship, I slowly sat upright. Drawing a deep breath, I shivered from the water drenching my body.

I was clean now thankfully, but damn, I was cold.

"I didn't think you'd want them to see you like that, Jax," Oracle whispered to me. "They wouldn't leave you. The crew of the ship are all dead or captured, and Oren handed out all the health potions he could find. Everyone who survived is in as good a condition as possible, but they won't go anywhere. They want to see you. They want their lord."

"I'm no lord, Oracle. I...how many? How many did we lose?" I asked, my voice hoarse as I studied my sopping armor.

"An'na, Rol, and Makin died. The others are alive and will be okay. I sent a golem to the Hall of Memories to get the spellbook for Lay on Hands, and it should be back soon. It's a book we've got two of, and it's just a basic healing spell. Is that okay?"

"Three of them...three people died because I wasn't good enough, Oracle. They died because I failed to plan properly, to be as strong as I could be.

"They're dead, and you want to know if giving a healing spell out is okay? Damn, you can give one to everyone, as far as I care! If I'd thought about healing, about support rather than killing, those three might still be alive!" The last words came out as a half shout, immediately followed by a warning growl from Bob. The top of Oren's head peeked over the stairs, and I spoke up quickly as Bob moved to intercept him.

"Bob! It's okay, man; stand down," I said, giving him a wave.

Bob looked over at me before lowering his arms and backing up to let Oren onto the upper deck, who was swiftly followed by Cai. They headed straight to me, Cai reaching out a hand. I took it, letting him assist me to my feet.

"Nae, laddie! Ah heard whut ye said. You think tha deaths be on yer head? Nae. They be free now; they fought fer their freedom and won! Dinna ye be takin' that away from them!" Oren said. Cai spoke up, nodding in agreement.

"He's right, lord. They volunteered to fight, to defend our new home. Even though we've had only a few days here, they were altogether better than years lived as a slave. They died free. You don't know what that means until you are classed as property, less valuable than a chair or table."

"I…all I can say is that I'm still sorry. They died to defend us. I'll do my best to make their sacrifice worth it," I said, tears wetting my cheeks. I'd barely known them, but they'd died for me. For my decisions.

An'na came back to me in that instant, a memory of them standing holding the twin maces, slowly trying to do the figure of eight move I'd shown them, a grin splitting their face from ear to ear.

Rol, tripping on a spear he was carrying and jumping back to his feet, shamefaced but laughing along as Arrin poked fun at his friend.

Last of all, Makin, with the tiny figure I'd seen him clutching when he thought nobody could see, a carving made of wood he'd created somewhere over the few days he'd lived free. He'd kept it hidden from others, but he'd kissed it and spoken to it quietly.

I stepped to the front of the raised deck and looked down at the people gathered below me. The ship's crew that had surrendered, including the old helmsman, sat off to the left, ankles crossed, hands on their heads. To the right were piled bodies of the slain, our own three laid on the tower marshalling ground, well clear of the attackers' bodies. And there, in the middle, stood my own people, not just the ones that had fought, but the others as well, all lending a hand to help.

"All I can say to you all is that I'm sorry," I said, my voice breaking. I coughed and pressed on. "I'm sorry our friends died; no, I'm sorry our *family* has lost members. They fought for us. They fought for all of us, and now they are gone, sleeping the long sleep and dreaming, while we think of them.

"We will not forget them, nor forget the bravery of you all. I saw you, Arrin. I watched you drawing the mage's spells, running and diving, throwing your Firebolt back at him. I saw you saving your family, and I'll never forget that.

"I saw you, Oren, charging into the oncoming fire. I saw you use your shield to protect Rikka; you risked yourself without a thought. I saw you, Lydia…" I went on, picking out bits of the fight I'd not even realized I'd seen, the details coming to me easily.

I praised them all, each and every one of them, and their grieving backs straightened, tears flowing unashamedly. I praised those who hadn't fought in the battle, but had built traps, or fed their brothers, sisters, and kin. I found something for everyone, but I praised the dead most of all.

"I'm proud of you, all of you," I said at the end, receiving smiles and nods, embarrassed glances, and half-salutes as I made eye contact with them all one-by-one, before turning to Oracle and Bob. Oren and Cai had long since joined the others below.

"Thank you, both of you. Oracle, you're my friend, my soul-bonded companion, and my compass, and you, Bob? You're my friend as well. You've got my back, and I know I can rely on you, always. I had no fear in asking you to get the captain and his lackeys. I knew you'd do it, if anyone could. Thank you again, both of you."

I stepped forward, Oracle flying into my arms and cuddling into my neck as I gave Bob an awkward one-armed hug. He looked down at me for a long moment before jerkily wrapping his left arms around me and squeezing until my ribs creaked.

"Okay, Bob!" Oracle gasped, disentangling herself from us. "That's enough!"

Bob released me and returned to standing by my side, watching the crowd. But as I looked into his glowing eyes, I swear I felt something more. He was definitely becoming...more.

I turned to my notifications, bringing them up and flicking off the ones that dealt with the fight, experience earned, and other minor details, until I found the one I was looking for:

Congratulations!

All invading creatures that could contest your Right of Ownership to the Great Tower of Dravith have been slain or captured!

Do you wish to assume full ownership of the Great Tower of Dravith?

Yes/No

"Ah, Jax...maybe..." Oracle warned, but it was too late. I'd already mentally flexed that muscle and clicked *yes*.

Attention, Citizens of the Territory of Dravith!
The Great Tower of Dravith has been claimed by a worthy aspirant of ancient and noble bloodlines!
All Titles, Deeds, and Laws in the Territory of Dravith are hereby held for review, and can be revoked, altered, annulled, or approved.

All Hail High Lord Jax of Dravith!

I paused for a second, reading the prompt that had sprung up, overriding my choice to gleam in the center of my vision.

Where other prompts were hazy and elegant, this held all the subtlety of a sandpaper condom. It turned the edges gold with a solid black plaque in the middle. The words gleamed like rubies and shone until the reader had fully read the prompt. Only then would it move, adjust, or dissipate.

I had visions of people riding on horseback, or flying the airships, or hell, having sexytime, and that had popped up. Then the second prompt appeared. Like the first, this one overrode my desires and just appeared.

This time, it took the shape of a roll of parchment, sealed with a glowing sigil. I felt it pulse and somehow knew it had come to me directly, as something only I could read. I looked at it, acknowledging its presence, and it unrolled. Its message was simple.

To the pretender "High Lord of Dravith"...

I am High Lord Barabarattas, Lord of the City of Himnel and true Lord of Dravith!

I am already crushing the fool Rewn that dared to raise his head from the City of Narkolt. He has airships and armies, what do you bring to the field?

It matters not; I have already laid claim to the Tower of Dravith, sending troops to secure it. When they arrive, you would do well to surrender, or you will feel the tender mercies of my pet, Toka, all the way back to Himnel.

I give you one chance. Surrender now, renounce all claim to MY property, and I may make your death swift!

You have one hour to comply; else I declare a state of War exists between us...

Barabarattas

I read the scroll repeatedly, hints and half-seen images slipping into place in my mind. I grimaced, and the scroll pulsed in my vision.

Do you wish to send a reply to: Barabarattas of Himnel?

Yes/No

I selected *yes* and gasped as two hundred health and mana was sucked out of me without warning.

"Goddamn it! I need a wiki!" I groaned, taking a deep breath and straightening up before returning my attention to the scroll before me.

I knew my tower's condition, and the extent of my troops, *all eight of them*...but I still knew what I had to do.

To the asshole "Lord of Himnel"...

I am Jax, High Lord of the Great Tower of Dravith, and I know who you are. I've read the memory stones in the tower, I've seen the creatures that populated this relic, and I've faced the creature you were feeding.

Send your troops. Send your airships and your armies. I'll slaughter them as easily as I killed the SporeMother!

I'll offer you a chance in return, Lord Skidmark of Shitstain.

Surrender, or run...run and hide, and pray I never find you!

UnderVerse: Brightblade

For the sake of the child whose remains I found, I make this Oath:

I will make you pay for their deaths; I will kill any who dare to keep you from me. I will rip off your fucking head and shit down your neck!

I reject your offer of an hour. I hereby declare war on YOU, Lord Fucknugget of Himnel!

I'm coming for you.

Jax

P.S. Wear something nice. I'm going to make our first date memorable!!

!

The scroll curled back up and vanished, and I stared daggers at the space in front of me. It lasted barely a minute before a final prompt arrived, again overriding my settings. This one took the form of a flag. Standing tall before me, it unfurled to the right as though blown by a stiff breeze, every word on the flag easily legible.

War!

War has been declared and acknowledged between the Great Tower of Dravith and Himnel, Prior disputed Capital of the Territory of Dravith.

Civil wars are always messy. Consider well the side you choose. Your life and more could rest on the roll of the dice.

"Wow, Jax, you really know how to win friends," Oren said. Expressions of fear and surprise crossed the faces of the people standing around.

"That asshole sent you here. He was feeding the SporeMother, and I can only guess what he's done to the rest of the population. If this is how he treats his own citizens, he deserves what's coming to him," I growled. My anger, which had been simmering since finding the remains of the little girl, now fully blistered to life where they could all see it.

"Oh, don't get us wrong, Lord Jax, we're with you," said Barrett. "It's just that normally the conversations that lords have like that are…more polite and kept private. You must have blasted that out to everyone in the land!"

I frowned and looked at Oracle, who winked and blew me a kiss.

"You did that?" I asked her.

"I figured we could do with everyone knowing what was happening. And besides, there's nothing in there for you to be ashamed of. If anything, I think you might get a few more followers for this. Did I do wrong?"

"Hell no," I said to her, grinning back as I imagined the asshat's face when he realized everyone had read that response.

"Okay, people, let's get a move on! As of now, we're at war!"

387

EPILOGUE

Thomas woke with a start. The door to the dungeon banged open, and the thud of armored boots stomping down the corridor reverberated in his tiny cell. He tried to burrow deeper into the rotten straw pallet that was his only comfort.

"Up, worms!" a voice screamed, accompanied by a clatter of the jailors club being dragged across the bars of the cages as he passed. Thomas jumped to his feet, frantically trying to ignore the pain of his sores and his infected leg. He staggered, but managed to right himself in time, pushing himself against the rear wall and facing away from the doorway with a strangled half-sob of terror.

"Please, please, please don't let them," he whispered to any god that might be listening, tears carving new paths in the dirt that coated his cheeks.

"You're all in for a treat! Your great and merciful Lord Barabarattas has decided to show you mercy! Not that *any* of you deserve it!" a new voice bellowed, the echoes of the dungeon making it hard to understand. "The great city of Himnel is at war, and with war comes the chance for advancement! Even to scum like you!"

The voice dropped but was close enough that Thomas could still make out what was being said.

"Get them cleaned and dressed. Their past as mercenaries makes them useful here, even if they are just fodder for the walls. Once they're clean, take them to the wagons outside. They're to be taken to the Dark Legion camp. Once they're in the camp, they're no longer our problem. Let that prick Edvard break or make what he can of them."

With that declaration came the clatter of several people marching back the way they had come, and the jailor screamed out at the prisoners again.

"You scum! You worms! You don't deserve this chance! You've all earned your places here. You deserve to rot here 'til you die, but I won't give you up that easily. Oh, no! You belong to me, rabbits! I'll be taking you to your training, and I'll be bringing you back here when you fail! You're scum, and you could never, ever be good enough to lick the boots of a real soldier!"

The jailor strode up and down as his men grabbed Thomas and the rest of the prisoners, dragging them out to stand in the hallway. Chains bound their wrists and throats, ensuring that those few with the strength of muscle or the ability to cast were kept under control.

As the jailor passed Thomas, he twisted around and lashed out with his club, breaking a rib and making Thomas cough blood. He half-fell into the man behind him before being roughly dragged upright. The gleam of hatred in the jailor's eyes as he leaned in close was clear, as were his foul breath and borderline insanity.

"But *you*, boy? Oh, we've got special plans for you. We'll make sure you fail, then me and the boys will get what we was promised! You took our lad from us, got him kilt.

"Well, we know the truth! Don't care what you say! *You* got him kilt, so we're gonna return the favor, but not before we cut off your hands and feet and take those pretty eyes! We'll send them to him, burn them at the temple! Next life, only way you get to do anything is if HE decides it! Eternity paying off your debt!"

Thomas screwed up his eyes, forcing himself to gaze at the floor as the jailor got another hit in before moving on. He'd learned since they'd caught him that fighting back, speaking, flinching, any response at all, just made things worse. He had to just take it, and eventually they'd get bored and leave him alone. Today was different.

Today, he stood his first chance of surviving the shit-pot his life had become, and he was going to make the most of it. Trapped down in the dungeon, a magical field blocked all access to his abilities, preventing him from sleeping, even healing properly. Hell, even his notifications were blocked, not that he wanted to know how many bones were still broken.

No, he'd do whatever he had to. He'd train; he'd kill whoever needed killing. He didn't care anymore. The past didn't matter. The future didn't matter. All that mattered was survival.

If all he had to do to survive was help Himnel conquer someplace? Hell yes. He'd do that with bells on.

THE END OF BOOK ONE

SPOREMOTHER

UnderVerse Omnibus Two

20th September 2022
(Combining books 3&4 of the UnderVerse)

The city of Himnel is a cesspit of slavery, violence, and back-stabbing, in the midst of a full on industrial revolution, barely kept on the rails by drugs and magic. Jax has found himself in the middle of it.

Jax has made enemies on all sides, but he's found allies as well. They're the kind that you can stand with your back against, even if some of them might help themselves to your wallet when you do.

Robbing the city blind might seem like a tall order, but he doesn't care about the odds, and when all you've got is a hammer, everything looks like a nail.

Add to that, the Sunken City is out there, infested, overrun and crumbling, but it's also full of loot, and Jax damn well needs to get his act together, so once he's robbed the city, why not stop off there for a little 'recreational looting'?

If it's not claimed, it's available, after all…

Get ready for the second Omnibus of the UnderVerse, and the Rise of the Titan!

UnderVerse Omnibus Three

8th November 2022
(Combining books 5&6 of the UnderVerse)

Jax might not have started the war, but he'll damn well finish it. But can he and his allies make it through unscathed?

When Jax entered the UnderVerse, it was with the plan of finding his brother, holing up somewhere and maybe, just maybe, trying to take over the world. He's making progress in all of those goals, but maybe not in the ways he wanted.

The God of Death has personally intervened to send his Dark Legion against Jax and his people, with the aim of grinding the upstart Empire usurper into dust. Jax has refugees by the hundreds, Legionnaires of the Empire by the score and best of all, a team that are cheering as he spits in the God of Death's eye.

The sun is setting though, with new enemies appearing and hidden forces being revealed.

The War of the Gods is growing, and when the sun rises again, it'll be in a changed Realm…

Finish the journey of UnderVerse Season One with Omnibus 3!

UNDERVERSE 7

6th December 2022

The war between Jax and Nimon is on hold, the borders established, and a form of peace should be descending on the Imperial Territory of Dravith…

But life rarely goes as Jax hopes.

New and old enemies are on the horizon, the land itself is disturbed, and worst of all, the Gods are not all he believed they are…

The Dark Tide Rises…

REVIEWS

Hey! Well, I hope you enjoyed the book? If so, please, please remember to leave a review, its massively important, as not only does it let others know about the book, it also tells Amazon that the book is worth promoting, and makes it more likely that more people will see it.

That in turn will hopefully keep me able to keep writing full time, while listening to crazy German bands screaming in my ears, and frankly, I kinda really like that!

If you want to spread the good word, that'd be amazing, and if you know of anyone that might be interested in stocking my books, I'm happy to reach out and send them samples, but honestly, if you enjoy my madness, that's massive for me. Thank you.

Facebook and Social Media

If you want to reach out, chat or shoot the shit, you can always find me on either my author page here:

www.facebook.com/JezCajiaoAuthor

<u>*OR*</u>

We've recently set up a new Facebook group to spread the word about cool LitRPG books. It's dedicated to two very simple rules, 1; lets spread the word about new and old brilliant LitRPG books, and 2: Don't be a Dick!

They sound like really simple rules, but you'd be amazed…
Come join us!

https://www.facebook.com/groups/litrpglegion

I'm also on Discord here: **https://discord.gg/u5JYHscCEH**

Or I'm reaching out on other forms of social media atm, I'm just spread a little thin that's all!

You're most likely to find me on Discord, but please, don't be offended when I don't approve friend requests on my personal Facebook pages. I did originally, and several people abused that, sending messages to my family and being generally unpleasant, hence, the *Author* page.
I hope you understand.

PATREON!

Okay then, now for those of you that don't know about Patreon, its essentially a way to support your favorite nutcases, you can sign up for a day or a month or a year, and you get various benefits for it, ranging from my heartfelt thanks, to advance access to the books, to signed books, naming characters and more.

At the time of me writing this, the advanced Patreon readers are getting a sneak peek at Age of Steel, and are voting on the next batch of Character Art as well, so yeah, you get plenty for the support!

There's three wonderful supporters out there that I have to thank personally as well; ASeaInStorm, Leighton, and Nicholas Kauffman, you utter legends you. Thank you all and as promised, the characters are in the works.

www.patreon.com/Jezcajiao

RECOMMENDATIONS

I'm often asked for personal recommendations, so if this book has whetted your appetite for more LitRPG, please have a look at the following, these are brilliant series by brilliant authors!

Ascend Online by Luke Chmilenko

The Land by Aleron Kong

Challengers Call by Nathan A Thompson

SoulShip also by Nathan

Endless Online by M H Johnson

Silver Fox and the Western Hero, also by M H Johnson

The Good Guys/Bad Guys by Eric Ugland

Condition: Evolution by Kevin Sinclair

Space Seasons by Dawn Chapman

The Wayward Bard by Lars M

LITRPG!

To learn more about LitRPG, talk to other authors including myself, and to just have an awesome time, please join the LitRPG Group

www.facebook.com/groups/LitRPGGroup

FACEBOOK

There's also a few really active Facebook groups I'd recommend you join, as you'll get to hear about great new books, new releases and interact with all your (new) favorite authors! (I may also be there, skulking at the back and enjoying the memes…)

www.facebook.com/groups/LitRPGsociety/

www.facebook.com/groups/LitRPG.books/

www.facebook.com/groups/LitRPGforum/

www.facebook.com/groups/gamelitsociety/

Printed in the USA
CPSIA information can be obtained
at www.ICGtesting.com
LVHW010204250324
775416LV00016B/239